A Dharmic Social History of India

A Dharmic Social History of India

Aravindan Neelakandan

ink | OCCAM

ISBN: 978-93-92209-79-6

First published in India 2025
This edition published 2025

BluOne Ink Pvt. Ltd
A-76, 2nd Floor, Sector 136, Noida
Uttar Pradesh 201301
www.bluone.ink
publisher@bluone.ink

Printed and bound in India at Nutech Print Services - India

To Amma for all those stories from *Periya Purāṇam* and *Śrī Mahā Bhakta Vijayam*.
To Appa for the Amar Chitra Katha books.

Contents

Foreword

In my view, Hindu Dharma has two facets. First, the spirit of universal welfare filled in Vedic Mantras, the Ramayana, the Upanishads, the Gita, the Bhagavata Purana, and regional spiritual works like those of Nammalvar or Tukaram. Second, the impulsive urge to safeguard conventional practices without compromise or change, whether they have Shastric approval.

Though the latter is also important, ill-treatment in the name of caste, which belongs to the peripheral and crude part of the latter, has to be discarded. A few groups attempt to preserve some outdated practices that are irrelevant today and rather harmful. Unfortunately, the mainstream media propagates caste-based ill-treatment as the core of Hinduism.

Marginalized class ill-treatment is an ugly human instinct found throughout medieval history worldwide. Swami Vivekananda views it as less prevalent in India than in Europe. Using this as a hypothesis, Dr P.V. Kane, a great scholar, provides extensive data analysis in his voluminous work *History of Dharma Shastra* and substantiates this view. Though this data analysis cannot justify the downtrodden ill-treatment, it is consoling that it was less prevalent in India even in the medieval era, filled with downtrodden-castigation in major parts of the world. We need to think about why this was so.

All our traditions agree that if Smriti (scriptures other than the Vedas) contradicts Shruti (Vedas) in some contexts, Shruti's stance is authentic. We Hindus need to validate Dharma with Shruti.

The corpus of Vedic Mantras is the core of Hindu Dharma. Almost all traditions within the Hindu fold accept it.

If we examine whether caste-based ill-treatment exists in the Vedic Mantras, the answer is a resounding NO.

The Rig Veda's consideration of Shudra as the feet of the cosmic Being is interpreted as Shudra's ill-treatment. Dr B.V. Ambedkar wonders how this small passage of the Rig Vedic text is odd and completely different from the style of the entire corpus of the Vedic Mantras that stand for unity (*Who were the Shudras?* 14, Bombay: Thacker & Co., 1947).

To me, this does not seem odd or inconsistent with the style of Vedic Mantras. First, the Veda never considers any limb of the human body as inferior. Second, in several other contexts in the Vedic Mantras, feet symbolize the foundation (e.g., *Rig Veda*, 10.87.10). This means that Shudra is the foundation of human society. This is not a derogatory statement against Shudra. A Sannyasin or any spiritual person is called Shri Charana or Shri Pada or Adigal (in Tamil), which means feet. This is not to insult the Sannyasin but to honour him with sacredness and veneration.

Shri Rudram, considered the heart of the *Yajur Veda*, says, 'Salutations to the carpenters and the chariot-makers! Salutations to potters, bird keepers and foresters!' The Veda salutes all of them, seeing the Divine in them. These mantras become a part of everyday recitation in almost all Hindu priests. Many Hindu pontiffs like Shankaracharyas chant this mantra in their daily Puja.

Shri Aravindan, in his extensive historical analysis, has shown how birth-based discrimination and social stratification have existed worldwide and why this is not exclusive to Hindu society.

Some of the propositions he makes in this book are penetrating, noteworthy, poignant, and convincing. The most piercing postulation is about how the post-Buddhist era experienced radical caste-based ill-treatment and discrimination compared to the pre-Buddhist period. This is bound to ruffle feathers, and rightfully so.

His pan-India examples from the Bhakti movement, which uplifted the downtrodden, are remarkable and immense. In our contemporary world, Shri Krishnapremi Swamigal elevated many downtrodden spiritually and materially through the path of bhakti. Jumping out from the book are pearls of wisdom such as this one: 'Our Dharmic value systems should follow the footprints of Bhakti saints like the calf following the hoof marks of the mother cow. They are not the exceptions. They are the Sanātana Dharma in action.'

Hundreds of stories show how the Hindu God always stands for the downtrodden when there is a conflict between the privileged and the downtrodden. These saints may belong to various denominations, eras, and regions. But the unity that links them in diversity is the 'spirit of universal welfare'. Strikingly, most of these saints mentioned in this book rely on Vedic values and glorify the Vedas showing that they are of Sanatana Dharma. Sample references are given towards the foreword's end.

Instead of seeking corrective measures from Buddhism or any other religion, it is always safe to follow the course of the saints abundantly available within Sanatana Dharma, who stood for the upliftment of the downtrodden. To my knowledge (which is very limited), this is the first book to shed light on the casteist ideas in the Buddhist context.

Sri Aravindan's comparison of socio-spiritual thoughts between Sri Aurobindo and Dr Ambedkar stands out because it is insightful and noteworthy and should open doors for further analysis of historically inspirational figures. 'Both Sri Aurobindo and Dr Ambedkar derived the cardinal principles of "liberty, fraternity and equality" from Indic and not Western sources' is a premise hard to challenge.

I differ from Shri Aravindan in a few ideas. For instance, regarding his understanding of the chronology of Hindu scriptures and his views on Kanchi Maha Swamigal. I am surprised that he did not discuss in this book the services rendered by Shri Jayendra Saraswati Swamigal to the poorer classes. His Shankara hospitals conduct rural medical camps and Shankara schools help in educating the poor. Swamigal encouraged Thiruvilakku Pujas in many rural areas among the poor. He offered free cymbals to many poor people who got involved in bhajans. He built a shrine for the great sage Nandanar, who belonged to the downtrodden.

In the well-known 1982 riots of the Kanyakumari district (Mandaikadu Kalavaram), Swamigal went directly to the riots-affected villages in which mostly economically poor Hindu households were destroyed and made sure they were given assistance to regain their livelihoods. Similarly, even before and also in the aftermath of Meenakshipuram conversions, Swamigal performed yeomen services to the poor and marginalized sections of Hindu society. His service to the tribals of Northeast India is equally significant. Kamakoti Vidya Bharati School of the Northeast contributed greatly to the education of the poor. Assam's Balaji Mandir encourages the rich culture of tribal communities in northeastern states like Arunachal Pradesh. When Punjab was suffering from female infanticide, Swamigal offered Rs 600,000 to 60 families with more than two girl children to discourage female infanticide.

Aside from such observations, I sincerely appreciate his efforts to highlight the dharmic emancipatory services rendered by Hindu saints and leaders, regardless of their denominations and faiths.

We are, as a nation and civilization, at a critical juncture. Many biased and malicious-intentioned works, both in academic institutions and media, blame Hindu Dharma for the social exclusion of marginalized communities and their sufferings. This confuses thinking and righteous-minded Hindu youths as to what is the real nature of Hindu dharma with respect to the question of social inequalities and social liberation. For such perplexed Hindu youths, this book is ambrosia. To the thinking and conscientious Hindu youths, this book brings awareness about the matchless contribution of Hindu saints in uplifting the downtrodden and shows this as the path to be continued in the future.

If we do not follow this path, we will certainly perish. If we follow this path, then Sanatana Dharma can show the world how to attain maximum welfare for all people, from material to spiritual welfare.

Sample References on Reverence to Vedas in Saints across Denominations, Languages, and Communities

Shaivites take the Vedas as a great guidance. For example, Tirumoolar says, 'There is no Dharma which is not dealt in the Vedas. All advisable Dharmas are told in the Vedas. Giving up the debate, the wise got liberated by chanting the Vedas that are rich in content.'[1] Thirunavukkarasar, a great Shaiva Vellalar, talks about his reciting of the *Rig Veda* while doing Shiva-Puja. He connects Shiva with *Sama Veda*, and in that context, he talks about Chandogya specifically, a branch of *Sama Veda*.[2] Chekkizhar[3] describes Shaivam as the branch of the Vedic culture and describes the purpose of Jnana Sambandhar's birth as the growth of the Vedic culture.

Vaishnava saints follow the Vedas. Nammalvar, a Vaishnava Vellalar, says that the Lord is expounded in the luminous Veda.

He says that he pays salutations to God through those who chant the Vedas.[4] Pillai Lokacharyar and Alagiya Manavalap Perumal, who strongly discard the caste-ill treatment in Shri Vaishnava tradition, glorify the Vedas in the very beginning of their works 'Shri Vachana Bhushanam' and 'Acharya Hrudayam'.[5]

Purandara dasa, in his famous song 'Mareyabeda manave neenu', says, 'Veda Shastra Odhi Nodi' (recite the Vedas and see. Meditate the lotus feet of the Lord with delight, who can be obtained by the Vedas).[6] Kanaka dasa describes the Divine as Veda-Gochara (obtained or perceived through the Vedas).[7]

Guru Nanak says in Guru Granth Sahib that Gurumukh contains the contemplations found in the Vedas (932). Gurumukh remembers and thinks of Shastra and Vedas (942). The way darkness is dispelled by a lamp; the same way the reading of the Vedas destroys all the sins afflicting the intellect (791). Ravi Das says in Guru Granth Sahib, 'The Vedas bear witness to the Lord' (710).

Jnaneshwar, in his commentary on the Gita, says that his path of reciting the name of the Divine is Vedic.[8] Tukaram says that his devotional service to the Lord is the Vedic path.[9] Molla, a Lingayat poet of the so-called lower class (15th century), glorifies the Veda as eternal.[10]

The mentors of Krishna Chaitanya's Gaudiya tradition had a great reverence for the Vedas. For example, Krishnadasa Kaviraya, the disciple of Chaitanya's disciple, in his *Chaitanya Charitamruta*, taken as an authentic text in this tradition, says while talking about God's human incarnation, 'although the supreme Godhead is transcendental to all Vedic injunctions, he strictly followed the Vedic rituals'.[11] This passage is about Shri Virabhadra, who is considered to be God's incarnation in the Chaitanya tradition.

The saints of all traditions give more importance to inner realization than the bookish knowledge of the Vedas. Guru Arjun

Dev says in Guru Granth Sahib, 'The wise contemplate on the Vedas and then preach them in different ways; the inquisitive hear them by various ways and means' (1355). Guru Nanak Dev says, 'The Holy Saints preach the teachings of the Vedas, but the unfortunate fools who are deficient of their essence do not understand them' (717). Ramananda says in Guru Granth Sahib, 'I have searched through all the Vedas and the Puranas. I would go there, only if the Lord were not here' (1195).

The right way of understanding is that they consider the direct realization greater than the greatest bookish knowledge of the Vedas. But when it comes to scriptures, their reverence for the Vedas is undoubtedly unmatched. This style can be seen in the Vedas themselves (e.g., *Rig Veda*, 1.164.39). Swami Vivekananda considers this to be a unique feature of the Vedas.

Sri Rama Jeyam

Dr R. Rangan
Srimad Valmiki Ashrama WEBOLIM
Ragihalli Village
Bengaluru
June 2024

Preface

The study of the history of Hindu society and its dharma has always been dominated by one narrative. The dharma narrative is as follows:

For millennia, Brahminism, functioning as both a social force and a religious ideology, has exerted enduring all-permeating influence over Hindu society in all its walks of life. This was punctuated by significant but fleeting interludes of reform attempts by rebellious movements, often in the form of religious movements.

Brahminism itself was not native to the land. The Brahmins, primarily speakers of Indo-European languages and known as Aryans, rode into India from the steppes on horseback. This was a predominantly male-led invasion-cum-migration. They came upon the Indus Valley Civilization (IVC), a Bronze Age society far more advanced than their own. The encounters between these two cultures, both violent and peaceful, led to a synthesis. Despite fundamental differences between Harappan or IVC religion and Indo-European religious beliefs, the 'Aryan' people incorporated the popular IVC religion into their own Vedic cult. Thus was born the Brahmanical religion what we know now as Hinduism.

At the heart of this Brahmanical religion is Cätur Varṇa, a societal division categorizing human beings into four fundamentally different groups, forming a hierarchical structure as dictated by the *Puruṣa Sūkta* of *Rig Veda*. The dominant Indo-Europeans positioned themselves at the apex of this pyramid, relegating the indigenous populations to its base or even beyond. This system bestowed privileges upon the Brahmins, the priestly caste at the top while imposing disadvantages on the Śūdras, the labourer caste. This system stands as perhaps the world's oldest documented instance of birth-based discrimination. This socio-spiritual apartheid is unique to the Hindu religion and Hindu society.

However, there came a time when heterodox religions such as Buddhism arose, offering egalitarian alternatives. Buddha himself challenged Cātur Varṇa and Brahmanical exploitation. Buddhism became India's dominant religion, nurtured by great ancient Indian emperors like Ashoka and Kanishka. Yet Buddhism was eventually overthrown by a resurgent Brahmanism, which cleverly used another rebel movement called Bhakti against these religions. The advent of British rule brought about the democratization of education, dealing a fatal blow to Brahmanism. English education introduced enlightenment values into Hindu society and gave rise to social reformers. The voices of those marginalized and oppressed for millennia under Brahmanical rule began to resonate louder.

The narrative above can be called the 'standard model' of Hindu social history.

This book challenges this 'standard model'.

Birth-based social stratification has existed in most of the pre-modern societies throughout the world. There are secular factors that trigger the evolution and sustenance of such systems. Social exclusion and social aristocracy also exist in many cultures. Further, in pre-modern societies, religious theologies and codes played a role in preserving the social status quo. In fact, even certain modern governments have further solidified the social divisions and profited from the modern regimentation of these systems. So, the depiction of caste and untouchability as uniquely Indian socio-religious phenomena is more of a prejudiced distortion than an empirical reality.

With Indian exceptionalism discarded, what is actually needed is a Hindu anthropological view to study Indian societal evolution and the structural as well as functional dimensions of Hindu society. The discourse surrounding Varṇa and Jāthi is often framed within either Western paradigms or those that have become static over time. There is a pressing need for a novel framework that is not only responsive to contemporary challenges and societal shifts but also accurately reflects societal observations. This framework should not only be able to explain the social and historical reality but also transform the society and discard the vestiges of colonial influence as well as the malignant manifestations of social stagnation. Interestingly, even among those who identify as traditionalists, the pervasive influence of colonial perspectives on their worldviews and values is evident. The current foundations of social science, even among those who oppose colonialism, are steeply inclined towards a colonial bias. This book addresses the necessity and groundwork for the evolution of a social science discipline that aligns with Hindu principles, which could aptly be termed 'Hindu Social Science'. This proposed discipline would offer a fresh perspective, free from colonial bias, and provide a dynamic approach to understanding society.

The intricate relationship between the Vedic and Harappan civilizations remains a fervently debated topic in academic circles. The once-dominant model of Aryan Invasion theory, with blonde-haired nomads driving their horse-pulled chariots, has lost much of its credibility but has not been entirely disproven. It remains a possibility, with its probability space shrinking. This leaves the question unanswered whether these two civilizations were separate entities or interrelated facets of a single entity. The language spoken by the Harappans is another point of contention, with theories spanning from the illiterate Harappan hypothesis to the proto-Dravidian language theory. The concept of race, specifically the Aryan race, has been largely abandoned in contemporary discourse. Despite all these, the prevailing narrative in social science textbooks posits that the complex caste-Jāthi-Varṇa system was introduced and enforced by the Aryans/Indo-Europeans/ Brahmins. The dichotomy between the Harappan and Vedic civilizations plays a pivotal role in this narrative. With respect to the mystery of the origin Jāthi-Varṇa, a multidisciplinary approach combining archaeology, linguistics, molecular genetics of ancient populations, and anthropology offers a more nuanced and intricate depiction of social evolution than what is suggested by simplistic notions of Aryan invasion/ migration or out-of-India theories. The book delves into this aspect in a detailed manner.

The prevailing narrative, found in both history and social science discourse, as well as in a significant portion of Indian political ideologies, asserts that the Vedic religion instituted a birth-based social hierarchy predicated on physical or racial features. This system, allegedly rooted in racial or ethnic discrimination, was purportedly imposed by the Brahmins and Kshatriyas and sanctified by the Vedic religion. This schema, perpetuated mainly by colonial studies of Indian culture during British rule, has continued almost unquestioned by post-independence Indian scholars influenced by colonial perspectives.

The alternative view presented here posits that the Vedic society itself should not be identified with the values that Vedic dharma stressed. While the Vedas do reflect the social reality of their time, this book argues that the values enshrined in the Vedic texts actively challenged the social exclusion and inequality present in that social reality. Central to this dynamic is the presence of multiple narratives/frameworks on the origin of a social system within the Vedic texts. The aim is to offer a new viewpoint on Vedic society, advocating for a more nuanced understanding beyond the conventional narrative of social hierarchy and discrimination. It is an impassioned plea for re-evaluating our understanding of Vedic society, urging us to look beyond simplistic narratives and delve deeper into the rich tapestry of Vedic texts to uncover a society far more complex and inclusive than commonly depicted.

This book raises what may be considered a controversial question: Does Buddha and His Dhamma pose a revolutionary challenge to Vedic Dharma, or does it merely represent a natural offshoot firmly anchored within the Hindu social cosmos? The narrative has often been framed in a way that emphasizes egalitarian excerpts from Buddhist sources while selectively showcasing pro-hierarchical passages from Vedic/Brahmanic sources, thereby creating a dichotomy of the liberating Buddha dhamma versus the oppressive Vedic dharma. To dissect this dichotomy, the book examines one of the foundational spiritual texts of Hinduism, the Bhagavad Gītā, to broaden the hermeneutical space. It puts forward a counter-intuitive argument that the overemphasis on universal non-injury to all life forms (*ahiṃsā*) and a rigid moral code has inadvertently led to the defilement of certain trades, thereby creating the social space of untouchability. In contrast, it contends that the Vedic Yajña's conceptualization of society functioned to eliminate occupation-based stigma, which was often inherited through birth. This impassioned yet academic discourse invites readers to critically examine these religious philosophies and their social ramifications.

Bhakti, rooted in the Vedic tradition, is fundamentally anchored in the archetype of Yajña. This spiritual practice has been and continues to be, a conduit for self-realization and transcendence within Hindu civilization. Often ignited by an individual's pursuit of enlightenment, the Bhakti movement naturally catalyses societal liberation. This phenomenon is evident in the Saivaite and Vaishnavaite Bhakti movements during ancient India's classical era. It has persisted through the Islamic period and remains relevant in both the colonial and post-colonial eras. Bhakti forms the spiritual foundation of India's social democracy, offering a non-violent, often entirely peaceful, route to mass liberation. It circumvents divisive, binary conflicts by cultivating an atmosphere free from animosity. Throughout history, it has repeatedly facilitated the decentralization of ecclesiastical authority, thereby promoting a more egalitarian society. Thus, Bhakti embodies a spiritual practice that nurtures individual growth and fosters societal progress.

This book explores the rich and diverse spiritual-social movements, especially in South India, moving well into the modern and post-colonial periods. It sheds light on how the Yajña-Bhakti framework, which combines ritual sacrifice and devotional love, has inspired various spiritual personalities to profoundly transform society. Some of these leaders are well-known, while others are obscure but have exerted equally significant influence in their local contexts. Together, they have all played a part in fostering a more just and harmonious society, guided by the spiritual vision of unity and diversity that is the essence of Hinduism. However, this journey has been far from straightforward; instead, it has been fraught with challenges and obstacles. Hindu spirituality has faced many obstacles and threats from colonial oppression, social conflicts, rigid traditionalism, global competition, and distorted political and academic narratives. Nevertheless, it has displayed remarkable resilience and creativity in surmounting these challenges and offering solutions for a more peaceful and just society and world.

This book extends a sincere, humble and heartfelt invitation to every concerned Hindu as well as academics and social activists, requesting each one of them to draw wisdom and experience from these Hindu spiritual traditions and to apply them to the current social issues that we face. It is high time we realize that a caste injustice anywhere is a threat to Hindu existence everywhere because all birth-based discriminations are not only Adharmic but also Asuric.

The book requests every Indian scholar—whatever their creed, caste, gender, region or language—to realize that the Hindu model of social emancipation is the most harmony-oriented and the least conflict-oriented and yet uncompromising in bringing social justice by emphasizing spiritual equality in society. That way, this model is a blessing unto the entire humanity. Thus, it becomes imperative for every Indian to be a blessing to all humanity by becoming an instrument of the Hindu model of social emancipation.

Any greatness you may see in the book belongs to Dharma and the Mahatmas of this sacred land. All deficiencies you find are entirely my own.

Acknowledgements

In 2021, I was visiting Rishihood University for a lecture series. There, Sri Raghava Krishna, then with the varsity, asked me if I would be interested in a programme Dr Vikram Sampath was pursuing. I answered in the affirmative. Later, Dr Sampath asked me if I would be interested in a year-long scholarship from the Motwani Jadeja Family Foundation for a book on history that I would like to write about. It has been churning inside me for so long that a rooted narrative of Indian social history is needed. So, I sent a synopsis. Dr Sampath at once accepted it. And I started working on the project. So, I express my heartfelt gratitude to the Motwani Jadeja Family Foundation, Dr Vikram Sampath, and Sri Raghava Krishna. But for them, the book will not exist.

As a child, my mother used to tell stories from *Periya Purāṇam* and *Śrī Mahā Bhakta Vijayam* while feeding me. My father used to provide me with a perennial supply of *Amar Chitra Katha* issues, which brought in the lives of saints and sages from all parts of India. Then, in my teenage going to Rashtriya Swayamsevak Sangh (RSS) Shakas, I learned their 'Ekatmata Stotra'—a long litany of all great sons and daughters of Bharat from every geo-cultural zone. My parents are no more. I have moved away from the RSS. But the invaluable gift of true Sanātana dharma I obtained were the seeds from which this book has flowered.

Writing this book has been quite a *sadhana* for me. It has been a journey through the heights and depths of human consciousness, with each setback presenting an opportunity for greater evolution. For me as an individual, apart from being a challenging intellectual exercise, it has been a transformative existential pilgrimage, evoking a range of emotions that included anger and sadness, disgust, frustration and depression and finally, elation, inspiration, hope and fulfilment. The inhumane treatment meted out to our own kith and kin, our own civilizational family members, the insensitive arrogance displayed by certain so-called authorities of dharma, and the ongoing suffering of marginalized sections of Hindu society within a framework that preaches the highest vision and ideals of spiritual equanimity have all stirred feelings of rage and shame within me. Overcoming these emotions required strong family support. I am ever thankful to my wife, Fontia Daniel Neelakandan, my son, Shukoh Neelakandan, and my daughters, Shubruh and Shuptah.

Here, I should express my gratitude to Sri Ma Venkatesan, a scholar and extraordinary and honourable chairperson of the National Commission of Safai Karamchari workers. He opened my eyes to the spiritual dimensions of the marginalized sections of society that are often neglected, either by intention or ignorance.

Swarajya is more than a magazine. It is a movement. And for me, it is an extended family. *Swarajya* has given me extraordinary flexibility and, more importantly, an understanding that only a family support system can provide. I am ever thankful to Amar Govindarajan, Prasanna Viswanathan, Arush Tandon, and, of course, the entire *Swarajya* family. BluOne has been a blessing for a writer of my kind. Ever patient, ever professional and ever friendly, they are, as I always consider, a writer's dream Publishing House come true.

Writer Sri Jataayu, who is more than a friend and a great scholar of Tamil and Sanskrit, spent two days intensively reviewing the draft and suggesting changes. His review is also the most exhaustive, detailed, and in-depth review of my previous book, *Hindutva*.

I gave the draft to Dr R. Rangan, a true Vedic scholar, the founder of Valmiki Ashram and, in my humble opinion, the most authoritative scholar of the Ramayana I have had the fortune to meet. I requested him to provide a foreword. The book can become controversial and may not be to the liking of traditional and radicalists. Yet Dr Ranganji agreed without hesitation and went through the entire draft and provided a foreword that is objective, critical, and Dharmic in spirit. Words cannot express my gratitude to him.

Finally, dear reader, this book is incomplete without you. But it is written not only for you. It is for your posterity. A time will come when one day your inquisitive child will come to you and ask with righteous indignation if dharma is nothing but caste discrimination. At that time, if this book has helped at least one parent answer that question in a dharmic way, my pranams to that parent. The book has then accomplished its mission.

CHAPTER 1

Indian Exceptionalism of Birth-based Stratification: Genuine and the Constructed

The *Jāthi* (traditional endogamous communities associated with an occupation) and Varṇa (the container matrix of the four major occupational social archetypal spaces) systems in India are considered unique to the country by a dominant section of radical opponents of the systems who view them as the root of major human suffering in India. This pertains to the genuinely concerned people as well as activists and academics. This also includes vested interests who are on the anti-Jāthi bandwagon simply because of their hatred for Hinduism or because it is a smart career choice. On the other hand, some traditionalists consider the Jāthi and Varṇa systems as almost the same and uphold them as the panacea for all the problems and deem that the present problems are because the traditional systems have not been properly followed and not because of the systems themselves. This includes genuinely concerned people who practice no ill will towards any section of society and who desire the welfare of all. According to a growing section of this school, the misunderstanding and distortions in the system are because of colonialism. It also includes caste supremacists who have hatred for the marginalized sections of Indian society.

What is common to both the radical anti-Jāthi annihilationist and pro-Jāthi traditionalists is that both view the birth-based system of 'graded inequality' (as Dr Ambedkar put it) as unique to and even central to Indian culture and spirituality. This chapter examines this claim of Indian exceptionalism.

In 2017, Ramachandra Guha, an eminent historian of the modern history of India, gave the London School of Economics India Summit 2017 lecture. There, he made the following remark:

> The French anthropologist Louis Dumont famously described Indians (and Hindus in particular) as 'Homo Hierarchicus'. The characterization was not unfair. For the caste system is the most sophisticated, as well as the most diabolical, system of social exclusion and discrimination ever invented by humans.[1]

On 4 August 2020, Oprah Winfrey made a tweet. It has 27,000 likes and nearly 10,000 retweets as of writing this line. The tweet is an appreciative recommendation of the book *Caste: The Origins of Our Discontents* by Isabel Wilkerson.[2] The book, which became a *New York Times* bestseller, views both Nazi racism and racism in the United States as variants of a more sustained system of 'caste' in India.

> Throughout human history, three caste systems have stood out. The tragically accelerated, chilling, and officially vanquished caste system of Nazi Germany. The lingering, millennia-long caste system of India. And the shape-shifting, unspoken, race-based caste pyramid in the United States. Each version relied on stigmatizing those deemed inferior to justify the dehumanization necessary to keep the lowest-ranked people at the bottom and to rationalize the protocols of enforcement. A caste system endures because it is often justified as divine will, originating from sacred text or the presumed laws of nature, reinforced throughout the culture and passed down through the generations.[3]

As the book reaches its crescendo, an 'upper-caste' Hindu informer is brought in, and Wilkerson describes in detail how he found the evil of caste coming out of the sacred thread he was wearing:

> The Brahmin came to know and to admire the few Dalits who crossed his path in his work, who had pushed through the walls of caste to become educated, professional.... These were the people whose very sight and touch was said to be polluting, and yet here he was sitting across from them, sharing and learning from them.... He shared this realization with a Dalit he had come to know and told him of a decision he had made. 'I have ripped off my sacred thread,' he told the Dalit, a professional man. 'It was a poisonous snake around my neck, and its toxic venom was getting inside of me.'... And so he had discovered. 'There was a stench coming from my body,' he said. 'I have located the corpse inside my mind. I have given it a decent burial. And now my journey can begin.'[4]

What unites Louis Dumont, Ramachandra Guha, and Isabel Wilkerson is an axiomatic stand that Indian society is fundamentally based on social stratification derived from its sacred texts. These sacred texts, created by the 'upper-caste' Hindus, have kept the caste system imposed on Hindu society for millennia, making it the most sustained apartheid system in the world. Both German Nazism and American racism are variants of this more sustained evil. At the root of this evil is Hinduism.

This is the essentialist exceptionalism with which the Hindu religion is charged. At the heart of this essentialist exceptionalism is the Purusha Sukta—a hymn in the tenth Mandala of *Rig Veda*—the sacred text of Hindus.

But how correct is this view?

It is true that many Hindu social reformers but not all, during the colonial period also thought along the same lines as they genuinely fought the ill effects of social stagnation. Yet facts say that birth-based social stratification, social aristocracy, and social exclusion with claims of divine sanction have existed in almost all pre-modern societies.

Social Stratification in Other Pre-modern and Quasi-modern Societies

Historian Kathy Stuart points out that in pre-modern Europe, 'throughout the Holy Roman Empire, dishonourable tradesmen suffered various forms of social, economic, legal, and political discrimination on a graduated scale of dishonour at the hands of "honourable" guild artisans and in "honourable" society at large':

> Executioners and skinners might be pelted with stones by onlookers, they might be refused access to taverns, excluded from public baths, or denied an honourable burial. Dishonour was transmitted through heredity, often over several generations. The polluting quality of dishonour is one of its defining characteristics. By coming into casual contact with dishonourable people or by violating certain ritualized codes of conduct, honourable citizens could themselves become dishonourable.[5]

The hardships of castes of peasants and serfs were seen as arising out of varied degrees of distributions of sin through hereditary. The Biblical myths of Noah's son Ham and the sin of primordial fratricide of Cain were both used to give theological justification for the hardships of these hereditary peasants and serfs. Their hardship was somehow for their spiritual benefit. Yale Historian Prof. Paul H. Freedman, who specializes in the medieval peasantry, cites the *Elucidarium*, a theological compendium written around 1100 CE by Honorius Augustodunensis, in his book *Images of the Medieval Peasant*, how theology correlated physical work as a means to purify the sinful or cursed nature of those deemed to work with their sweat:

> Discussing the various estates, the master in this dialogue states that most rustics will be saved because they live simply and feed the people of God by their sweat.... Yet in Honorius's work some penitential attributes of work remain, notably in his acceptance of the common opinion that servi are descended from Noah's cursed son Ham. Labor does confer spiritual benefit but is presented as the activity of a morally tainted population. Its undoubted merits are set alongside an accumulated spiritual deficit.[6]

He further says that the peasants and serfs were atoning through their labour for their sinful nature.

> According to Brother Ludovicus, rustic labor, on which all depend, pleases God. Ill-usage at the hands of their lords makes the peasants all the more God's chosen children, a favorable condition not fully realized since they persist in laziness and iniquity. Were it not for their thievery, dishonesty, and perjury, peasants would be saints.[7]

Before the Hamitic myth was associated with specific races and ethnicities by colonial scholars of Christendom, it was considered applicable to their own society with indifference to (or irrespective of) race.

> Western medieval writers thus showed a tendency to mix theories of origins, but not just at random. A rough correspondence was established between cursed biblical figures and the taxonomy of outcasts.... Cain functioned as the originator of the monstrous races and *also of peasants*, whether free or unfree. Ham had two medieval roles: as the father of a number of peoples, including black Africans, and as the ancestor of European serfs. If Cain

> was an archetype of the peasant regardless of status, Ham was the progenitor of the unfree of whatever race.[8]

With colonialism and the development of the colossal transatlantic slave trade, we see a remarkable change in the use of the Ham myth. Rather than representing the European serfs and peasants, now it becomes totally centred on non-European and non-white people. And this was not limited to Christendom.

This birth-based social stratification or 'caste' can be seen in pre-modern Islamic societies as well. There are the well-known Ashraf–Ajlab divisions, which are hereditary. Despite the propaganda of equality, even in the 20th century, there are Islamic societies where, 'marriages between sayyid women and non-sayyid men were publicly denounced'. Islamic societies have historically enforced birth-based social stratification with religious sanction.

> Firstly, sayyids preserved their line of descent by upholding the Islamic principle of kafā'a (equality between marriage partners). This meant that a female descendant of the Prophet, namely a *sharifa*, was barred from marrying anyone other than sayyid. The sayyid lineage was incompatible with any but its own. In practice, a man was allowed to marry outside of a sayyid clan when no spouse of equivalent descent was available, but this dispensation did not apply to women.[9]

During the beginning of the colonial era with the Ottoman Empire still existing, Islamist politics actually promoted the superiority of Sayyids as part of their propagation of Islam:

> Sayyids began to restore this prestige as they initiated the turn to Istanbul and played an important role in the rise of the corresponding Muslim political culture. In some instances, they saw themselves as the bearers of a civilising mission over native Muslims because of their esteemed genealogy.

> The Ottoman Consul in Batavia extolled the noble descent of sayyids in order to encourage them to take the lead in donating to his causes; he thereby further affirmed the centrality of genealogical distinction.[10]

In Yemen, birth-based social stratification and social exclusions are quite common. Here is a description of 'lowly' groups who can only marry among themselves:

> These are 'people of the suq' (market) i.e., townspeople who engage in a number of disvalued occupations which have different names in different parts of Yemen. Regardless of name, their low positions in the local hierarchies remain failrly (sic) constant. The important thing in Yemeni eyes is that they have no honourable descent.... Occupations included in this category are the butchers (Jazzara); the barbers (Muzayyen) who perform such roles as circumcision, the potters, weavers; bath attendants (Hammami), Gisham (vegetable growers and peddlers), Khadem (servants) and the semi-nomadic public criers (Dawshan). The inferior groups generally can marry among themselves, but not outside this low-status group of occupations. They lack the pedigree and values of tribesman and historically their functions have been to provide services for the Sayyids, Qadis and Qabilis.[11]

The caste system, or mostly birth-based social stratification, was not limited to isolated Islamist and pre-modern and late-medieval Christendom. Consider the following actual incident.

John Flower, an American scholar, and his wife were visiting an Asian country and attending a festival in a rural village. During their visit, a seventeen-year-old girl from the village acted as their guide for the day. At the end of the day, the couple decided to visit the village animal husbandry bureau. The official welcomed them and offered chairs to sit on. However, when the couple asked the girl to sit on one of the chairs, the official forcefully lifted her and made her stand. The officer then continued to talk as if nothing had happened. Later, when the couple asked the girl about the incident, she simply mumbled, 'We lower castes always run into this kind of incident'.

At this point, if the reader is asked to guess the location of this event, the answer would most probably be India. And Hinduism would be held responsible for this humiliating incident. However, the incident happened in the small city of Ya'an in the Western Sichuan province of China in 1992. A girl named Yao Suhai muttered to Flower and his wife, 'We peasants (nongmin) always run into that kind of thing'. The incident was recorded in 1992 in Flower's field notes and published in 2001 in an academic publication.[12]

State-Sanctioned Social Stratification in Modern Maoist China

Traditional Chinese society had its own social discrimination like any other pre-modern society. The system called *hukou* (*huji*) allowed the authorities to assign a person's place, role and resources available to him or her at birth. The system was inherently biased against the 'peasants' or, in traditional Indian terminology, the 'Shudras'.

It severely restricted peasants' access to quality education, medical services, and a decent lifestyle. But like most traditional systems encountering modernity, it underwent changes for the better in pre-Mao China, and like most traditional hierarchies, it was flexible. One would have expected Mao Zedong, the Marxist revolutionary, to abolish the hukou system lock stock and barrel. But despite all lip service to socialism and equality and ruthless experiments in Stalinist style, Mao made hukou even more rigid but profitable to the state machinery and party bureau elite. In other words, 'The socialist system, while eliminating market-based class distinctions, created a caste system where one's status was determined at birth.'[13]

As industrialization and modernization began, there was an influx of peasants from villages to urban areas. Leaders of Mao's Communist Party detested this. Despite the explicit and exhibited hatred for tradition that Maoists showed, the party leaders did not hesitate to quote the admonition of traditional Chinese scholar Guo Tinglin, 'When the masses dwell in the villages, order prevails; when the masses flock to the cities, disorder prevails.'[14] Initially, the system was based on where a person was residing. *From 1959 onwards, the system became birth based and the residency status became inheritable.* The anti-peasant masterstroke of the Maoist regime was that the inheritance was not patrilineal but matrilineal.

Historian Prof. Glen Peterson explains:

> By assigning *hukou* status through the maternal parent, the opportunity for upwardly mobile fathers to bequeath urban hukou status to their offspring was eliminated.... Hukou controls were the state's primary mechanism for allocating and denying access to a wide range of state-supplied goods and services: schooling, food, housing, employment, consumer products, and other benefits. Following the great famine of 1959-61, moreover, China's leaders came to regard a peasantry bound legally and permanently to thc land as the most effective means of guaranteeing the country's precarious food supply.[15]

Thus, in China, one has a system that is birth based, with little possibility of any upward mobility. Further, it is this system that predominantly determines the allocation of resources and services – from food to health, quality of the education given, to the type of employment one gets. It was only in 1998 that hukou inheritance was made possible also 'by the biological or adoptive father's hukou'.

The way this birth-based division changed literacy in China is quite revealing. In India, the Maoist-Marxist narrative accuses Manu and Hinduism of denying education to the masses, which was quite untrue, as had been definitively shown by the much familiar work of Gandhian historian Dharampal. Actually, it was Maoism that denied quality education based on birth in the case of, not a pre-modern but Maoist and modern, China. Peterson writes:

> After 1949, these traditional stimuli to literacy were either eliminated or driven underground. Literate specialists were denounced and forced to renounce their former 'feudal' occupations.... The hukou system made urban state schools – which were always remote from villagers – effectively out of the reach of most production team children.

According to him, there were only three ways a child under peasant hukou could get an education:

> One was to join the Communist Party, a second was to join the army, and a third was to gain entry to the state school system. Of the three, entrance to state schools appears to have been the most rare. Literacy and education were means of advancement under the collective system but only within the closed corporate confines of the production team or brigade.[16]

This apartheid in education stems from another deeper historical fact. In the traditional pre-Maoist hukou system, social exclusion was directed towards those considered living on the fringe or socially undesirables. So, social exclusion never enveloped the entire masses thoroughly. However, in China's case, the system design was changed and implemented to exclude the masses. Dr Fei-Ling Wang, a Professor at Sam Nunn School of International Affairs, who, as late as 2005, had to depend inevitably on 'anonymous interviews' from China for his book, *Organizing through Division and Exclusion: China's Hukou System,* on the hukou system, points out:

> China's imperial hukou system functioned as a quasi-institutional exclusion. In addition to the location-determined population immobility, there always lingered an inherited hukou categorization of various noble clans, ordinary people (mainly peasants), and various low-class clans (slaves, floaters, untouchables such as paupers or prostitutes). In the last two dynasties (Ming and Qing), the legally equal ordinary people were categorized into four inherited hukou types: military, peasants, merchants, and handicraft workers. They had the same legal status but frequently different and adjustable treatment regarding tax burden and the right to participate in the imperial examinations, as well as the right to move. Several categories of low-class clans were further excluded.... Unlike the current PRC hukou system, however, the imperial hukou system formally excluded not the majority of the population but mainly the socially undesirable minority or fringe groups.[17]

While in India, knowledge has been sought across all strata of society for liberation and seeking of truth, in China, it has been for becoming 'an official'—a surprising resonance with Thomas Babington Macaulay's 'education for creating clerks'. Only in the Chinese case, it was even worse. Anthropologists Sulamith Potter and Jack Potter (whom Peterson also quotes) explain this situation in their detailed study of Chinese society under Maoism:

> As a result, from the point of view of social control, Maoist Zengbu was a kind of bureaucratic feudalism, with party cadres closely controlling peasants who had been structurally immobilized in their teams. Peasants were separated from urban residents by legal restrictions creating a caste-like barrier against both geographical and social mobility that was virtually impenetrable. *If one was born a peasant, one remained*

> *a peasant for life and was not free to leave one's team.* The structural similarities between Maoist bureaucratic serfdom and the classical forms of European feudal serfdom are clear. The Maoist peasant was fixed as firmly in his team as the serfs of feudal Europe were fixed on the manor. By fixing peasants on the land, and having the team control their labor, the Maoist state created a set of serf-like conditions more classically 'feudal' than the pre-Liberation society, in which peasants controlled their own labor, and could leave their villages.[18] (emphasis added)

What we have in China is not a historically (and hence naturally) evolved system of social hierarchy and exclusion as in India. In India, such a social evolution also creates a scenario in which the forces of social emancipation also play a strong role in deciding the evolution with currents, flows, and counter currents. What we have in China is an imposed system of largely birth-determined discrimination. And it is imposed by a totalitarian State with no space for reformist or emancipatory forces. This is designed with the singular aim of strengthening the State ruthlessly while benefiting largely the elite and their posterity.

A study of literature and media reports on this system shows a curious phenomenon.

Looking at the comparative studies of India and China, like the ones made in the 1980s, one finds that India's caste system has always been pointed out as a defining character, while hukou is seldom mentioned. For example, there is a paper comparing 'Chinese and Indian education systems' by Robert Arnove in *Comparative Education Review* (August 1984). The paper mentions caste twenty-eight times in the Indian context, but hukou is not mentioned at all. Though the paper touches upon the cadre/non-cadre divide and even points to the better educational infrastructure of urban China, it does not point out the hukou system, which was a birth-based serf system. In 2008, Pallavi Aiyar, who worked as China bureau chief for *The Hindu,* published a book on China. She too never touched upon the hukou system as if it were almost invisible and insignificant.

Nevertheless, the existence of hukou is well-known within informed circles that study and/or observe China, and it is surprisingly well-documented. Still, hukou remains the enigmatic dragon in the room, never discussed except for a handful of reports in the media. Unlike the studies on caste and 'Brahminism', which have become major 'cottage industry' for every 'South Asian' department in the West, there is no flourishing 'cottage industry' studying the hukou system. This is despite the fact that studies show that the hukou system adversely affects human potential, very similar to any unjust system of social stratification.

In India, society at large, reformers and the state have been fighting against caste discrimination, while in China, the state has designed and imposed the system. According to Prof. Fei-ling Wang, hukou is a system that 'serves as the basis for a nationally uniform institutional exclusion with a scope, rigidity, effectiveness, and resilience rarely seen elsewhere'.[19]

Naturally, such a discriminatory social stratification imposed by the totalitarian elite with all the tools of the State also results in all sorts of exploitation. For example, hukou plays an important role in the sexual abuse of migrant women workers. Writes social psychologist Eileen Yuk-ha Tsang:

> Each of the sex workers I interviewed unanimously hates the hukou system, because if they get sick in the city they must return to their hometown for treatment or pay extra for local care. These women are denied access to public services, basic welfare, health care, and affordable public housing in urban China. Migrant women are marginalized and face a high rate of labour abuse, a culture of widespread prejudicial attitudes towards them, and socio-economic disparities between urban and rural communities. In the particular context of the

> 45 women I interviewed who were dagongmei, their prospects were pointedly bleak. Additionally, their labour conditions included daily experiences of flagrant sexual harassment, exhausting working conditions, and labour violations. Many of the women affirmed that prostitution actually seemed a step up from working in the factory.[20]

Despite all these, why is the West not waging a war of conscience against the hukou system even though the United States today looks increasingly hostile to China? The answer may lie in the economic benefits the West may obtain from China because of the cheap labour that the hukou system provides.

In his book on Chinese capitalism, veteran journalist-author Dexter Roberts, who reported on economics and business from Beijing for two decades, points out how central hukou is to the success of present China:

> By ensuring that migrants remained an underclass in the cities, the *hukou* also guaranteed that there would be no end to China's pliable, low-cost labor force; with little recourse, legal or otherwise, most migrants accepted, albeit unhappily, the meager wages and poor working conditions. That in turn was to underpin the rapid GDP growth China experienced over the last several decades. As Chan wrote, the policy is perhaps China's best-kept secret behind its unprecedented economic growth. And so a policy that sacrificed the living standards of rural workers to ensure cheap raw materials for industry and food for elite urbanites, once central for industrialization, now had a new role: ensuring that China had the labor force necessary for the current era. Excessively long work hours and harried workers under the yoke of the hukou would support the rise of China's export-oriented economy.[21]

In the end, Mao created a state machinery that imposed serfdom, providing cheap labour for Western capitalism. Perhaps that may be the reason why the Western media is largely silent about the system and definitely does not essentialize China with hukou, though the Maoist Reich fits such essentializing far more deservedly better than the Hindu society, which is fighting the ill effects of caste system through democracy.

Now the question arises: why is it that dominant forces from academia and media still do not follow such scientific principles to study caste problems in society, and why do they still try to essentialize Hindu society and religion with 'caste' and untouchability?

Secular Reason for Social Stratification beyond Cultural Specifics

Social stratification and exclusion based on birth are not unique to Indian culture or society. Western social sciences have also recognized this phenomenon. In 1974, St Martin's Press published *Anthropology through Science Fiction*, an innovative anthropology teaching tool that featured science fiction stories by various authors. These stories explained social science concepts and anthropological observations. One of the stories, 'Strikebreaker' by Isaac Asimov, provided a concise explanation for the origin of caste societies with defiled occupations and social exclusion. Asimov argued that caste structures become more rigid and social exclusion extreme in societies with resource scarcity and limited mobility.[22] This is a secular and scientific insight that explains why pre-modern societies universally evolved caste structures and social exclusion. It also demonstrates how Western societies and those with new resources, such as petroleum, have made caste irrelevant and apparently invisible.

Hindu Exceptionalism: The Colonial versus the Authentic

While it is true that social stratification and social exclusions were common in most pre-modern societies, India experienced two factors that created a strange, complex phenomenon: one was its colonization and the second was its status as a non-Abrahamic civilization with diverse spiritual traditions.

European administrators in the colonies and the evangelists (sometimes significantly and crucially, both these circles intersected), who were part of the colonial enterprise, created a framework based on a strange mixture of enlightenment values and Protestant values to view Indian social conditions. They essentialized Indian religion with Indian social conditions, particularly its negative aspects. With colonialism increasingly draining the resources of India, the 17th and early 18th centuries saw increased social stagnation. The ill effects of social stagnation, in turn, were used to further define the entire Indian civilization and spirituality. Dr Barton Scott, a cultural historian studying early nineteenth- and 20th-centuries South Asia points out that how the early 19th-century British representation of Hinduism was that it was 'a ruse concocted by sacerdotal elites to dupe and debase the gullible masses' and adds significantly that this representation said more about Britain than India:

> Protestant missionaries transposed well-worn anti-Catholic polemics onto the subcontinent's unfamiliar religious terrain. Christianity was no stranger to the ideal of absolute obedience to religious authority.[23]

Hindu dharma has been equated with birth-based stratification. This was primarily due to the colonial scholars, administrators, and educators referring to it as 'Brahminism'. By Brahminism, often the colonial Indology and post-colonial social studies, as well as Indian media, mean the ideology that was used to justify and maintain the four-fold Varṇa system and Jāthi system. Although these two terms, Varṇa and Jāthi, are used as synonyms, they are not. This justification, in turn, was associated with concepts of ritual and body-based purity and impurity.

So, in this view, Brahminism also comes to mean justification of untouchability. According to colonial historiography, Brahminism worked through the collusion of Brahmins, considered hereditary priests, and Kshatriyas, the ruler class. In this view, all the spiritual and philosophical richness of Hindu dharma was considered sophistry with no innate value, invented by the dominant classes—Brahmins and Kshatriyas—to support their socially vested interests.

For example, here is what Prof. Jayantanuja Bandyopadhyaya (1933–2009), one of the chief pioneering architects of India's international policy, wrote about Purusha Sukta and *Advaita*:

> The mythology of the *Purusha Sukta* was fabricated by the ruling class with a view to attributing a divine origin to this iniquitous social order, especially to sanctify and perpetuate the sub-human socio-economic status of the Shudra class that produced all the surplus value. But with the rapid swelling of the ranks of the Shudras and the sharpening of class contradictions, the crude mythology of the Purusha Sukta proved to be an inadequate ideological instrument in the hands of the ruling class for the pacification of the masses of deprived and exploited working people. The ruling class found it necessary to refine the mythology of the Purusha Sukta into the metaphysics of Advaita and the social philosophy of renunciation as an integral element of it. The 1000-headed, 1000-eyed, 1000-armed and 1000-footed Purusha was transmuted into the omnipresent, omniscient and omnipotent Brahma as the supreme ruler of the universe and human society. The development of Advaita philosophy represented a transition from the mythology of primordial Purusha to the metaphysics of Brahma in response to the developing class contradictions of Vedic society. But the ideological objective and political strategy of the ruling class was the same in the Purusha Sukta and Advaita philosophy.[24]

Popular worship, on the other hand, was viewed as the invention of priestcraft, mainly Brahmins, to keep the masses in subjugation.

Buddhism and Jainism were the early movements that protested against the Brahminical system, much like the Protestant movement. Buddha was reinvented as a pioneer in ancient India as the way Martin Luther was in Europe. Instead of Catholic priests and Jews, Brahmins were substituted. Anthropologist Anya Bernstein has highlighted this fact:

> Buddhology or Buddhist studies originated as an offshoot of Indology, Sinology, philology, and archaeology in the early nineteenth century and, similarly to earlier forms of Orientalism, was inextricably linked to imperialist ideologies and the colonial context.... In certain strands of European Buddhology based on Indological scholarship, Buddhism—which had effectively disappeared from India by the time of the British rule—was safely considered a rational religion, often opposed to 'idolatrous' Hinduism, with Buddha often portrayed as 'an Indian version of Martin Luther,' a social and progressive reformer struggling to cleanse the corrupted religion of ritualism and superstition.[25]

The Bhakti movement, too, is characterized as a protest movement against the 'Brahminical' system. Vinay Lal, a Professor of History and Asian American Studies at UCLA characterizes the Bhakti movement as 'revolt within' in the book *Introducing Hinduism*. [Fun fact: the illustrator Borin Van Loon in the book has confused Swami Dayanananda Saraswati (1930–2015) of Arsha Vidya with Dayananada Saraswati, the founder of Arya Samaj (1824–1883); so much for historical accuracy!]:

> If Buddhism and Jainism were revolts from outside, the Bhakti poets initiated a revolt from within. Most of the bhaktas were lower-caste; some were women. Both had been denied access to the Vedas; neither were seen as fit to receive spiritual instruction. Dadu was a cotton carder, Kabir a weaver (julaha); Namadev was a tailor, Raidas a chamar (leather worker and scavenger).[26]

So, in this entrenched narrative, Hinduism as Brahminism is the historical villain of India.

Today, the deep impact of this establishment historiography is such that even the discourse of decolonizing primarily accepts birth-based social structure as the basis of Hindu dharma. On the other hand, the reformist discourse views Hinduism as flawed and needing correction through reforms, implicitly accepting the colonial view of Buddhist and Bhakti movements as 'reformist'.

The truth, when one goes through the primary sources of Hindu dharma, is quite different. The primary sources of Hindu dharma are not merely text based. They contain a vast variety of materials—from oral traditions to local rituals.

As we explore the vast array of materials spanning over 5000 years of Hindu history and tradition, we discover that the unique social values of Hindu dharma are not based on a birth-based social system but rather on a constant striving for human emancipation through a diverse range of spiritual traditions. Naturally, this has had the consequence in the social dimension of questioning both social stratification and social exclusion.

In fact, it can be said that no other religious/spiritual tradition has consistently questioned the social status quo through its spiritual values as Hindu dharma has done. In the West, social stratification became irrelevant when colonialism brought in the vast inflow of capital and a huge expansion of land and natural resources. For example, Australia, which was completely colonized and owned by the West, was nine times larger than India. Additionally, till 1833, the Transatlantic slave trade and the slave trade in Caribbean islands created a lot of wealth for the West. Later, this was replaced by indentured labour, particularly from India. Historian Rozina Visram writes:

> After African slavery was legally ended in 1833, 'indentured' labourers were recruited from India to work on plantations in

> Mauritius, Guyana, Trinidad, and Jamaica. This was slavery in a new guise: many laboured under conditions no less degrading than slavery. Thereafter wherever need arose, Indian labour was employed. Indians worked in the plantations and mines in Ceylon, Malaya, Burma, South Africa and Fiji. Indian labour provided the manpower to build the East African Railway. Indian sailors worked in the British merchant navy. Indian soldiers not only helped to maintain the British Raj in India, but were used as cannon fodder overseas in colonial wars of conquest to extend its frontiers.[27]

But all these rendered the native birth-based social stratifications of European civilization less relevant and more invisible. In other words, the apparent egalitarianism seen today in the West has come at a great cost to entire humanity in terms of extreme misery and suffering. It has been obtained by the West as only a transactional exchange in human suffering. The consequences of this transfer of human misery continue well into the present centuries. Consequence of this quasi-slave indentured humanity uprooted and planted in alien lands by colonialism, can be seen in the Indian populations living in African countries and on the Fiji islands.

Is it possible to create a model for social emancipation for all humanity without such a transactional transfer of human misery to another section of humanity? If one is to forge such a model, it should have a historical legacy as well as to it being a working model. It does not need to be perfect, but it should have roots in history with a significant amount of success. It should have brought emancipation to quite a large number of human beings over a considerable period of time. It should be scientific and humanistic. It should be the least violent and replicable. Though emerging and evolving in one culture, it should have universal principles for replication, adaptation, and updating.

The Indian Varṇa–Jāthi caste question has been studied either as a problem or as a misunderstood system. But what has been overlooked is the way Indian culture addressed social stratification based on its own core values and its view of human nature as well as socio-ecological relations. Identifying those core values and systemic processes that have been integral to human welfare in historical time provides us with the foundations for a better way of dealing with the problems our species have in their social organization. In the following chapters, we will explore these values and processes in detail.

CHAPTER 2

Need for a Hindu Social Science and a Fresh View of Varṇa and Jāthi

The criticisms and endorsements of Varṇa and Jāthi typically come from either Western or stagnant frameworks. However, what we really need is a fresh framework that is at once open to modern challenges and changes, consistent with the observations of the society, equipped with explanatory and transformational capacity for the society, and free from colonial perspective. Unfortunately, even those who consider themselves traditionalists often have a deep colonial perspective, which is deeply ingrained in their worldview and values. Furthermore, the present basis and framework of social science are heavily influenced by colonial biases, even among those who are opposed to colonialism. This chapter aims to highlight the need and basis for developing a social science called the Hindu Social Science, which can address these issues and provide a better framework for understanding society.

Haldane-Goel Diagnosis

John Burdon Sanderson Haldane (1892–1964), the British-Indian scientist, was an evolutionary biologist, physiologist, biochemist, statistician, and polymath. He was one of the architects of modern evolutionary theory. In 1917, Haldane came to India. Barely twenty-five, his views were typically that of a

British colonial military man. His observations of Hindu society were negative to the extreme. He wrote, 'The key to India was snobbery. The Hindu caste system is the greatest glorification of snobbery that the world has ever known.'[1] He compared Hinduism unfavourably with Islam:

> Hindus are born, not made. And Islam is a religion of universal brotherhood, whilst Hinduism perpetrates a complex hierarchy of classes. Further, I am sufficiently prudish to find the human sexual organs unsuitable as religious symbols.[2]

But as time went on, the inner world of Haldane began to evolve. In the decades to come, Haldane gained recognition as a scientist, being one of the chief architects of the synthesis between genetics and evolution. Additionally, he was a gifted popular science writer. His popular science articles were highly knowledgeable, taking the core science to the lay public. This required a deep understanding of both scientific concepts and society. Naturally, Haldane's views shifted from those of the typical British upper class to a more socialist one, eventually leading him to become a Marxist. His observations of society became increasingly multidimensional. In 1942, he became a card-holding member of the Communist Party of Great Britain (CPGB) and the scientific face of the party.

Then came the notorious Lysenko crisis.

Under Stalin's patronage, Trofim Lysenko (1898–1976), a plant breeder, castigated genetics as a bourgeois science. Ideological commissars agreed in chorus. Information started leaking to the outside world that the geneticists were being persecuted in Stalin's USSR. Geneticists were arrested, asked to recant or jailed, tortured, and executed. Haldane was torn between his commitment to party and science. Within party circles, he argued against what was happening in the USSR to the geneticists. Outside, including in an infamous BBC debate, he half-heartedly tried to justify what was happening in the USSR.

This included the death of Nikolai Vailov, personally known to Haldane. Haldane was misled into thinking that Vavilov had been released and died while working in the Arctic. He even stated so in a BBC debate and went to the extent of calling the brilliant scientist Vavilov a 'plant breeder'. However, the party was not pleased with his half-hearted defence. Finally, he had to sever ties with the party and denounce the USSR. By that time, the Soviet Union had gone to the extent of characterizing genetics as bourgeois science and even denied the existence of genes. Teaching genetics was henceforth banned.

In 1948, Haldane quit the party.

One should not underestimate the power Marxism, in particular, and left-wing worldview, in general, had on a large number of scientists of that time. Haldane was no exception. However, among most of the pro-Marxist scientists, Haldane alone was ready to openly denounce the stance of the USSR. In a detailed study of this painfully fascinating phase in the history of genetics, Prof. Diane B. Paul concludes thus:

> Most of the party's scientific members ultimately left it but, surprisingly, not over the Lysenko issue. ... As far as I have been able to determine, Haldane alone broke with the party over Lysenkoism, choosing his scientific over his political loyalties.[3]

With the aggravation of the Cold War, Haldane became increasingly uncomfortable with living in England. He could not emigrate to Stalin's USSR either. During this time, he was also reading Hindu philosophical traditions and observing Hindu society. As a result, not only did his views on Hinduism and Hindu society change slowly, but he also started to see the importance of a Hindu framework of looking at society.

This framework had been completely ignored by the colonial and Marxist frameworks and foundations of social sciences.

In 1954, he was still convinced of the ultimate triumph of Marxism, but he would not underestimate the 'flexibility' of Hindu dharma. Still categorizing *Advaita* as 'absolute idealism' as opposed to scientific materialism though, he considered the latter to be true:

> If I state my opinion to the officiating Brahmin that Sarasvati has no real existence, he will probably reply, 'Of course not, nor have you or I, all three of us are illusory forms.' We can then proceed to discuss the nature of illusion. The fact that such an opinion is not only common but even orthodox implies that Hinduism will offer a different kind of resistance to humanism from the other great religions. It may, of course, go down before a frontal attack by Marxism, but it is so plastic and undogmatic that I believe that it may incorporate a great deal of humanism without succumbing.[4]

In 1958, he wrote a book, *A Passage to India,* in which he adhered to an assimilationist model of the caste system. He drew a parallel between the relationship between Spaniards and native Americans and the relationship between Brahmins and Scheduled Castes communities and tribes. Although it was still not correct, it was an improvcment over his earlier observation that the caste system was the 'world's most snobbish system' during the earlier part of his scientific career:

> A person born into one of the Hindu castes had a series of duties and rights. One born outside them had fewer duties and also fewer rights. He was maltreated, but he was not persecuted in order to make him become a Hindu. In fact, the descendants of such people gradually became Hindus, while preserving a good deal of their primitive religions, and found themselves within the Hindu system as members of castes so low as often to be

> untouchable by Hindus of high caste. This may have involved as much human suffering, or more, as the methods adopted by the Spaniards in Mexico or Peru, where the conquered people were violently persecuted, but their descendants are now under little disadvantage compared with those of their conquerors, but it meant that the practice of killing a man for his opinions was foreign to Hinduism.[5]

Then, when observing the events at a college founded by a Maharajah in India, he made the following observation:

> I reflected that at Oxford the College servants did not dine at the High Table. Nor do the tenants of the College estates, who provide it with money rather than services. Nor did the servants at Man-lion College. Had they done so at Oxford, they and the Fellows would have been equally embarrassed. True, the Fellows would not have had to take a formal bath after such an event. But until recently the Fellows of English colleges were the victims of an even more serious superstition about untouchability, enunciated by St Paul, namely that 'It is good for a man not to touch a woman'. Even now, married fellows must '*per noctate*', that is to say, pass a certain number of nights per term in college without contact with their wives. The Indian government has made it a crime to exclude 'untouchable' men and women from streets or temples. The British government regards bequests to religious foundations whose members must treat women as untouchable as charitable bequests. I regard the Indian government as more progressive, in this respect, than the British.[6]

In the given statement, Haldane made a thought-provoking observation about comparing not the old institutions of India with contemporary institutions of the West but comparing the transformational processes happening in India with the socially stagnant practices that might still exist in the West. What Haldane demonstrated in the above paragraph is that it is important to avoid the cardinal fallacy found in the worldviews and conceptions of many social activists and academics of humanities. This fallacy was described by Hindu thinker Sita Ram Goel:

> An intellectual inclination to compare Hindu ideals and institutions from the past not with their contemporaneous ideals and institutions in the West but with what the West has achieved in its recent history—the 19th and the 20th Centuries.[7]

Thus, in Haldane's work, we see a clear propensity to move beyond the strong colonial prejudices and view Indian culture in an evolutionary context while making comparative observations. But the most significant part of his observations of Indian systems of knowledge and their application to the social sciences came when he gave the Huxley Memorial Lecture. This lecture, held in remembrance of the great evolutionist and comrade of Charles Darwin, Thomas Huxley, was delivered by Haldane in 1956 at the Royal Society in Piccadilly on 29 November 1956. After pointing out that anthropologists also need to investigate animal cultures, he suggested that most anthropologists lack the necessary tools to study different human cultures without prejudices. He proposed an alternative approach:

> In my classification of human cultural features I shall use a Hindu classification rather than a modern European or American one for the following reason. Modern cultural anthropology is a by-product of colonialism. It consists of accounts given by persons almost all of European origin of the behaviour of members of other cultural groups over which they exerted dominance, largely through the greater efficiency of their weapons. Colonialism lasted for about four centuries, and is now drawing to a close. Hindu anthropology is similarly a by-product of the caste system, which is now also drawing to a close, but

> which lasted for over two thousand years. Soviet anthropology is a by-product of yet a third system. We do not know how long it will last, but it is not yet forty years old, and some of its tenets are taken over from Morgan's study of the Iroquois, which was a by-product of colonialism. I shall therefore employ a terminology of respectable antiquity, in the form given to it by my friend Professor Nirmal Kumar Bose in his *Cultural Anthropology*.[8]

This passage assumes importance for many reasons. Foremost, it initially ties what he calls Hindu anthropology to caste and then asserts that the caste system will eventually come to an end. However, there are aspects of Hindu anthropology that are more important than the caste system, which is merely a birth-based social stratification. It is these core aspects that have allowed Indian society not only to survive through millennia but also to generate constant cultural innovations and evolution. So, what is this core aspect of Indian civilization? Haldane investigates this through the work of Prof. Nirmal Kumar Bose (1901–72), a renowned Indian anthropologist of his time. In Bose's work *Cultural Anthropology* (1929), he identifies certain principles that are universal, i.e., across the diversity of cultural specifics. These principles can be found not only in human civilizations but also primarily in non-human animal cultures.

Haldane presented an almost faithful reproduction of the above scheme in his lecture while pointing out that this is not the only anthropological framework Hindu dharma has:

> According to the Hindu classics, human desires can be classified according as they are concerned with *artha*, economic needs, *kāma*, reproductive needs, and *moksha*, the need for emancipation from these other needs. Perhaps there is also a *dharma* concerned with beauty, *sundara*. A culture is characterized by various dharmas which satisfy these needs to a greater or less extent. Each *dharma* acts through five agencies, *vastu* or material object, *kriya* or

habitual action, *samhati* or social grouping, *vicharamulaka tattwa*, namely 'knowledge based on experience and subject to criticism', and *viswasamulaka tattwa* or knowledge based on faith. These interact with the *svadharma* of each individual, which, to some extent, corresponds with our notion of genotype.[9]

The critical point here is that Haldane extended this classification to all human cultures irrespective of their variations:

> Anthropologists study all five of these agencies, and it is clear that the differences between them in different cultures are due mainly to differences of tradition, rather than of biological heredity. A human being brought up in one culture can adopt the traditions of another, though with some difficulty.

Then he went on to suggest that this might apply even to animals:

> Do social animals transmit vastu (material objects) from one generation to another? Most certainly. The most striking example is the transmission by females (queens) of the agricultural ant genus Atta of pieces of the fungus Rhozites which they cultivate.... Do animals use material objects for communication? They do so both to communicate with other members of their species, and with themselves in the future, as men use writing for both purposes.... The kriya or habitual action is quite often learned. Kuo's (1938) experiments showed that cats would not generally kill mice or rats unless taught to do so by their parents.... Some member of an animal species may invent a new kriya, and it can spread, apparently by imitation. A few years ago a Stevin or Watt among great tits (Parus major) invented the practice of opening milk bottles left on human doorstep.... On the other hand it is more doubtful that samhati, or social organization, is traditional in animals. Vertebrates have to learn their functions in the society into which they are born.... It would perhaps be rash to build too large a theoretical superstructure on this foundation. The question of a traditional tattwa, or knowledge, in animals is difficult, because we can only infer knowledge

> from habitual actions.... We do not know whether some kinds of infantile learning in vertebrates are as difficultly effaceable as moral and religious notions learned from the mother are in some human beings. But this seems to be so in insects.... It is not known whether human societies can exist without traditional *viswasamulaka tattwa*. They can certainly exist with very different and mutually contradictory ones, and the 'knowledge' acquired in this way need not include supernatural elements.... Returning once more to Bose's classification, a few animals, such as bower birds, show sundaradharma, behaviour satisfying aesthetic need.... Have animals a mokshadharma? So far as I know this question has not been asked. It is too seldom asked concerning human cultures.... I think it conceivable that some higher animals can perform moksha-dharma in their post-reproductive period, but there is no evidence for its cultural transmission.[10]

It is necessary to quote this lengthy passage because Haldane shows the remarkable value of Hindu anthropology in studying other human and non-human cultures. What is even more important is that Haldane did not take the Jāthi-Varṇa taxonomy as universal or applicable in a universal manner, even transcending species barriers. Instead, he used an improvised framework of *Purusharthas* and showed that it could be used to create a foundation and a framework that could transcend even the species barriers, making it possible to study culture and society in its form and process.

As mentioned earlier, Haldane's Hindu anthropological perspective was shaped by *Cultural Anthropology* by Dr Nirmal Kumar Bose, who was a distinguished academic with a strong commitment to activism. Bose was actively involved in both the freedom movement and *Harijan* upliftment, initiated by Mahatma Gandhi. Gandhi had launched this movement to bring social justice to the highly discriminated against socially excluded communities, which were the Scheduled Communities.

Bose worked for their economic upliftment through the cottage industry and adult literacy programme. He also participated in the Civil Disobedience Movement (*Salt Satyagraha*) and the Quit India Movement. He was arrested on both occasions. During his time in prison, he was categorized as a 'C' class prisoner, which meant he was subjected to poor prison conditions. Usually, political prisoners used to be categorized in the 'A' category. However, he never complained and used this opportunity to study society. It was only in 1934 that he met Gandhi for the first time during Gandhi's visit to Wardha Sevagram. Here, Gandhi used to conduct a rigorous routine of spiritual practices even as he planned his strategies against the British. Bose travelled with Gandhi during his visit to Noakhali in East Bengal (now Bangladesh), where pogrom against Hindus was being concealed by both Muslim League and British government. Bose thus combined both academic rigour and rootedness in Indian sociocultural reality.

The framework that Bose brings out for studying the cotre dimensions of *any* society from the Hindu worldview is as below:

> We may start with a classification of human desires. These can be roughly divided into three groups, viz., those connected with *Artha* or economic needs, *Kāma* or sexual desires and *Moksha* or the desire for spiritual freedom. What we customarily do, or are trained to do, in order to satisfy the above impulses can be called *Āchara* or institutionalized behaviour, which forms the core of social culture. Social culture itself may be called *āchara* if we remember that it acts in four phases, namely *Vastu* or material object, *Kriya* or habitual action, *Samhati* or social organization and *Tattwa* or abstract ideas, which may mainly consist of personal beliefs and opinions (*viswāsa-mūlaka*) or of a consistent body of knowledge obtained through the application of logical methods (*vichāra-mūlaka*).[11]

Prof. Bose further points out how these principles can help us understand the structural and functional dimensions of society and individuals at both macro and micro levels. As an example, he suggests that this framework can be used to explain the Vaishnava movement, which was significant during the proto-renaissance phase of Bengal and continues to exert its influence today:

> The central object in *Vaishnavism* is however the deliverance of the individual from the bondage of life, so that the trait can easily be placed under moksha of the present scheme. It is therefore a trait belonging to the third category of our scheme and operating through all the four possible phases of expression. But among the four, *tattwa* probably predominates over the rest.

He applied the same framework to understand the functional unit of family and states this:

> The family life of man is intended to satisfy partly his sexual and partly his economic needs. It centres round a home, common objects of property, and certain conventional beliefs regarding the relationship between members of the family. We can, therefore, look upon the family as something which satisfies the desires of *artha* and *kāma*, while it operates through the three phases of *vastu*, *samhati* and *tattwa*.[12]

The anthropologist acknowledged that this 'two-dimensional classification' to studying human cultures may look 'clumsy'; however, it is important because 'it emphasizes the connection of culture with basic human needs and desires' and 'also indirectly helps to emphasize the basic unity which underlies all cultural phenomena'.[13]

It is unfortunate that Indian academics have not followed this lead given by Haldane. Instead, he was sidelined and criticized for having 'Brahminical bias', which was not the case. Haldane had studied both colonial Western and Marxist anthropologies before arriving at the concept of Hindu anthropology. He had removed the caste question from the Hindu social model as it was not considered central to it. He showed that Hindu anthropology can be a viable model without Jāthi and Varṇa.

In fact, Bose had studied the impact of Jāthi–Varṇa on what he considered the process of absorption of tribal communities into Hindu society. Like most academics of his time, he believed in the Aryan invasion/migration theory. According to him, the Aryan/Brahmanical culture spread through the interiors of India, defeating and assimilating the tribal populations:

> In the Rig Veda there is proof that the Aryans were surrounded on all sides by hostile tribes who were variously designated as Dasas or Dasyus.... But in the age of the Mahabharata the term Dasyu lost its specific significance and was applied in general to such tribes as the Kirata, Yavana, Gandhara, China, Savara, Barbara, Pulinda, Raniatha and Kamboja.... Thus, between the end of the Rigvedic period and that of the Mahabharata many non-Aryan tribes had gradually become absorbed in Brahmanical society.... The lower class in Brahmanical society was formed by the Sudra. Conquered and subsequently assimilated tribes were usually assigned the status of the Sudra in society.... A mixed feeling of avoidance as well as of tolerance was thus exercised towards the Sudra. It had important social and economic consequences, and...the structure of society and the economic organization which grew up in ancient India, as well as a particular philosophical attitude which was current here, were all the outcome of this basic ambivalent attitude towards a conquered and subjugated people.[14]

It is important to remember that during Bose's time, the Aryan theory was the dominant paradigm in social sciences. As a result, Bose was influenced by it and derived his sociology from this colonial construct. This colonialism-derived strand could be seen in many academics of the period, and it was rarely challenged. However, Indian seers such as Śwāmi Vivekānanda, Śrī Aurobindo, and Dr Ambedkar challenged this framework.

Unfortunately, their works were not given much attention by the academics. Śwāmi Vivekānanda was perceived as a spiritual, patriotic monk; Dr Ambedkar was seen as the leader of the Scheduled Caste communities and not much in sync with the freedom movement spearheaded by Gandhi; and Śrī Aurobindo was once a radical revolutionary who had turned into a mystic seer. So, their words on Aryan theory were not taken seriously.

The influence of Mahatma Gandhi enabled Bose to view the social reality from an Indic perspective. Hence, he could never discount the spiritual element in the interaction of different communities through historical times. This model made Jāthi-Varṇa, though a historically important process in the society formation of Hindus, not essential for the Hindu worldview. When contrasting the way the Hindu system and the Soviet system managed the ethnic-cultural-communal differences, Bose pointed out:

> Whereas the social scientist in the Soviet Union looks upon tribal religions and social cultures as so many unwanted survivals from the past, the Brahmin believed in the permanent necessity of many forms of cultures fitted to different stages of mental development. Thus he was like a pantheist in social idealism. But whether this catholicity sprang from a genuine sense of human love or whether the priestly class fashioned it and struck to it in order to prevent the 'low' castes from rising high in social scale we cannot say accurately at this distance of time. *The chances are that both the motives operated in the society at the same time. Some idealists like Sankara or in more recent times, like Ramakrishna Paramahamsa seemed to have desired the progress of all castes in mental development, while others surely wanted to keep them in their old place in order to preserve their aristocratic distinction.*[15] (emphasis added)

He later elaborated on this aspect of Hindu integration of differences:

> One of the central ideas which thus ruled was that each culture is built round one core idea; and as no culture sees Truth in its wholeness – i.e. every community sees Truth only in fragment – the religion of a community should not be interfered with as long as its members allow the same right of freedom to others also to follow their own. There was, however, a unifying factor, and this consisted of no more than the social practices prescribed by Brahminical priesthood, which sat *very lightly* on the multiplicity of practices prevalent among the constituent elements of Hindu society. This idea of about the multiplicity of fractional views of Truth was a dominant element in Hindu religious thought.[16]

Even in the rigidity of caste (Jāthi), Bose identified *Saṃnyāsa* as an important emancipation pathway that allowed the complete self-actualization of the individual.

> The *Hitopadesha* says that the individual has to be sacrificed for the family, the family for the village, the village for the country, but the whole world itself has to be sacrificed for the sake of the soul. Definite arrangements were therefore made in India for releasing the individual from all forms of social obligation if he so desired, and actually stood in need of it. The price demanded of the individual was indeed heavy. He had to surrender all the benefits normally derived from the collective life; he had to live upon the minimum clothes, have no roof over his head, and to be constantly on the move. He was to become God's beggar. And in order to enter into the *Sannyasa* order, the individual had to perform the last rite of *shraddha* for his own soul. The Sannyasi was put beyond the normal operation of social laws. He was no longer obliged to maintain the sacred fire, which is the householder's first duty. Thus although, Hindu society suppressed the individual under normal conditions, yet the restriction took a volunteer character as he could escape from its rigours through the backdoor of the institution of *Sannyasa*. We may imagine that this safety valve was to some extent, for the stabilization of the Hindu order of the society.[17]

Nirmal Kumar Bose's work, as highlighted by Haldane, reveals two aspects of Hindu anthropology: one is core, and the other is temporal. The temporal refers to social stratification, while the core aspect is the spiritual understanding of diversity. This core aspect has always influenced and course-corrected the temporal aspect. Understanding this process in Indian history can help us create a dynamic decentralized framework to harmonize the cultural, religious, and ethnic differences globally. It can also help us improve the Jāthi–Varṇa system by removing the negativities of social stagnation that have accumulated because of various historical and inherent factors.

This non-essentiality and non-centrality of Jāthi-Varṇa to the Indian concept of society, its evolutionary dynamics and values, by J.B.S. Haldane, has been independently shown by Madav Sadashiv Golwalkar (1906-1973), the second all India leader of the Rashtriya Swayamsevak Sangh. When asked if the revival of Hindu dharma would also mean the revival of *Varna Vyavasta*, Golwalkar answered in the negative. The following is the question and the answer he gave:

> Q: Is it (*Varna Vyavasta*) not a must for Hindu Society?
> A: It is not an *avasta* or a condition of society. It is only a *Vyavasta*, a system. You may keep it or reject it according as it serves the purpose or not.[18]

Taking as a whole the work of Nirmal Kumar Bose, one can consider creating a healthy framework for studying Hindu society and the processes that run through it, historically and geographically, culturally and psychologically.

In the anthropological realm of Bose, there are dominant three strands. The first one is the Aryan-non-Aryan racial theory, which views history through the interaction between Aryans and non-Aryans, and the Aryanization of the tribals. The second strand is the concept of priestcraft, which is the result of the dominant discourse of Protestant components of colonial social sciences. The third and the most unique strand is the Hindu element, which is mediated by Gandhian influence. It emphasizes the unity-multiplicity harmony and the institution of Saṃnyāsa. Bose believed that even as the production system and the economic relations emanating from them move irreversibly in society, two critical components from ancient India should be at the heart of even the modern and emerging society:

> The democracy of cultures and their federation under one system as in the case of Hinduism and secondly the safety valve of Sannyasa, through which the individual could seek his/her way out when the authoritarian character of the social structure proved oppressive for him/her personally. Society and state even gave a person a respected place if one surrendered the economic advantages accruing from social conformity.[19]

Despite the mainstream academic emphasis on the so-called Sanskritization process alone, the supposed inequalities that were artificially mapped over the process were given more importance. This process was seen as the Hinduizing of the tribals, who were then supposedly relegated to the bottom rungs of the Hindu society, mostly providing cheap labour to the other sections of the Hindu society. However, the exploitation of tribals as cheap labour was a phenomenon that emerged with the colonial British Raj and not with traditional Hindu society. In fact, the tribals had more autonomy and egalitarian relations with non-forest-dwelling communities. The Aryan-non-Aryan binary and the so-called absorption of tribal communities later developed into 'Sanskritization' by the famous sociologist M.N. Srinivas. Soon, in the dominant discourses developed in India's premier social science institutions, 'Sanskritization' was considered an unwanted process that led to the 'Hinduisation' of tribal and 'subaltern' communities who, in turn, were categorized as ‘non-Brahminical’. This fed into the second component of priest-craft. Almost all works subsequently focussed on this aspect.

As against this, the very Indic components, the unique defining features of Hindu anthropology envisioned by J.B.S. Haldane, of Bose’s anthropology, namely Purusharthas, unity in diversity, or democratic harmonization of diversity and the role of the agency of Saṃnyāsa have not been studied in either historical or social context. The upcoming chapters are attempts to do this long overdue development of Bose’s framework for social science.

CHAPTER 3

Harappan 'Caste' Mystery

The relationship between the Vedic and Harappan civilizations continues to be a subject of intense debate. The once widely accepted Aryan invasion/migration theory is highly contested. It is still unclear whether these two civilizations were distinct entities or complementary aspects of one another. The language of the Harappans is another contentious issue, with theories ranging from the illiterate Harappan hypothesis to the proto-Dravidian language theory. The concept of race, particularly the Aryan race, has also been largely abandoned. However, the prevailing narrative in social science is that the caste-Jāthi-Varṇa complex was introduced and enforced by the Aryans/Indo-Europeans/Brahmins. The dichotomy between the Harappan and Vedic civilizations plays a crucial role in this narrative. Today, a combination of archaeology, linguistics, molecular genetics of ancient populations, and anthropology paints a more nuanced and complex picture of social evolution than what is suggested by simplistic notions of Aryan invasion/migration or out-of-India theories.

To truly grasp how Indian society and its cultural dynamics have evolved, it is crucial to understand its complexity. This chapter, along with Chapter 4, aims to unravel the Indus Valley Civilization social system and examine how its sociocultural elements have transformed or continued into contemporary Hindu social life.

Bronze Age Totalitarian Empire or Egalitarian State?

Encompassing a vast region of South Asia, from the western mountains to the eastern plains, a civilization of astonishing diversity and richness flourished along the Indus river system and its branches. This civilization had no kings, palaces, or glory but one that built its cities with precision and order, traded with distant lands, and worshipped unknown gods. A civilization that left behind no monuments of conquest, no temples or idols, no legends or epics. A civilization that vanished from history, leaving only its mysterious script and its enigmatic seals.

They were the Harappans, the people of the Indus Valley Civilization, and they baffled the modern world. How did they manage to live without rulers, wars, or art? How did they create such a complex and harmonious society? And why did they disappear without a trace? These were the questions that haunted the British archaeologists who excavated their ruins in the 20th century. Sir Mortimer Wheeler (1890-1976) and Stuart Piggott (1910-1996), who had studied other Bronze Age civilizations in the West, could only see the Harappan culture as a puzzle and a frustrating mystery. They imagined it as a totalitarian state ruled by a priestly elite devoid of any creativity or individuality. Wheeler wrote in his book *Harappa 1946: The Defences and Cemetery R37*:

> Documentary and archaeological evidence has familiarized us with the general structure of society in Egypt and the Middle East during the third millennium BC.... It would be but natural to find that this similarity of supply and opportunity combined with a roughly analogous equipment, produced in India, is a social organization not altogether unlike those of the contemporary west.[1]

Then he drew imaginary parallels with other such civilizations:

> In Sumer, the wealth and discipline of the city-state were vested win the chief-deity, i.e. in the priesthood or a priest-king.... Thus in the temple of Baü at Lagash were twenty-one bakers with twenty-seven female slaves twenty-five brewers with six slaves, female wool preparers, spinners and weavers, a male smith and other artisans and officials. Similarly, a cloth-factory employing ninety-eight women and sixty-three children was situated within the enclosure of the temple of the Moon God Nannar at Ur and came within the administration of the city and the temple.... In essence the picture is one of a rigid and highly-evolved bureaucratic machine, capable of organizing and distributing surplus wealth and defending it, but little conducive to the political liberty of the individual. To this picture Harappa, amplified by Mohenjo-daro, begins to assume a significantly similar outline.... It can no longer be doubted that, whatever the source of their authority – and a dominant religious element may fairly be assumed – the lords of Harappa administered their city in a fashion not remote from that of the priest-kind or governors of Sumer and Akkad. In other words, the social structure of Harappa conformed in principle with that of other riverine civilizations of the day.[2]

What was expressed by Mortimer Wheeler in his reports was taken to the educated public at large by Stuart Piggott. Piggott's widely read works presented the Harappan civilization as a totalitarian and oppressive regime. In his influential book *Prehistoric India to 1000 BC* on ancient India, he portrayed Harappan culture with scorn and contempt:

> [T]he Harappa sites and objects ... lack not only the barbaric spontaneity of the older and more primitive cultures, but even the cheery *nouveau riche* vulgarity of Early Dynastic Sumer ... and display instead a dead level of bourgeois mediocrity in almost every branch of the visual arts and crafts. The dead hand of conservatism in design, rather than in technique, lies heavy on all the Harappa products. Complex technical processes were known, well understood, and admirably organized for

> production, but the output suffered from standardization and an almost puritanical utilitarianism. Working within such narrow limits of traditional forms, fossilized over the centuries into a rigid, inescapable mental prison, the artist or craftsman could have found little outlet save in developing technical virtuosity.[3]

From artefacts, he moves to the entire excavated cities themselves:

> The secrecy of those blank brick walls, the unadorned architecture of even the citadel buildings, the monotonous regularity of the streets, the stifling weight of dead tradition all combine to make the Harappa civilization one of the least attractive phases of ancient Oriental history. One can grudgingly admire the outcome of its ruthless authoritarian regime rather as one admires the civil engineering of the Roman army in the Provinces, but with as little real enthusiasm. I can only say that there is something in the Harappa civilization that I find repellent.[4]

These totalitarian ruling elite, the so-called priest-kings, controlled both the social and the cultural lives of the people. Even while admitting that it was 'dangerous to make deductions from the evidence with any confidence', Piggott was very sure that

> in its remarkable conservatism and scrupulous preservation of even the details of everyday life intact for centuries, the texture of the Harappa civilization has a strongly theocratic tinge, and surely implies a social system wherein the unchanging traditions of the temple were of more account than the ambitions of an individual ruler or the secular instability of the court, and in which the form of land tenure was dictated by the priestly hierarchy.[5]

In 1953, Mortimer Wheeler authored the volume on the Indus Civilization as part of the famous *Cambridge History of India*. Here, he looked into the religion of the Harappan civilization and concluded that it contained an assortment with an assumed hierarchy as he perceived it in India today. He wrote:

> Moreover, a religion such as we may expect to encounter amongst the Harappans is more likely than not to be a loosely knit complex of accumulated beliefs and observances, elaborately if implicitly graded, in which the lower grades may in fact have a greater hold upon the popular mentality than the higher. That is so in India today, where the crudest animism and demonism still underlie the semi-philosophical and ethical concepts of the educated few; where the symbols of the higher thought are the awesome physical realities of the peasantry. Something of this duality or multiplicity would appear to have been present already to the Harappan society of the third millennium, as it was still present to the more evolved societies of the classical world. In particular, the numerous terracotta figurines of an almost nude female, which have been supposed to represent a Mother Goddess, have no clear counterpart in the seals or major sculptures and may more easily be related to a household cult than to a state religion.[6]

Villainy of Priestcraft

In the above passages, whether they are from Piggott or Wheeler, one could see that Harappan culture was shown as being controlled by a priestly king class that governed with authority derived from a religious belief system and enforcing a totalitarian society with a strangled and stifled cultural life. Even more central to our discussion is how Wheeler, a colonial scholar, contrasted the 'State religion' of the Harappans with the local religion of the people. He then compared this to the modern Indian religious situation, as some colonial and evangelical scholars saw. This passage is similar to what Bishop Robert Caldwell said about the 'Brahmin' religion and the older 'demonolatry'. His statement, made a hundred years before Wheeler's, shows how colonial and evangelical views influenced anthropology and history. In his lecture on Thirunelveli missions, Caldwell said in 1856:

> Human nature when left to itself is bad enough, but it becomes still worse when the devil, in the shape of a bad religion, gets the management of it, and when God's gifts are placed at the devil's disposal. I may here remark, that it is the peculiar policy of the Brahmans to render all the religious systems of India subservient to their purpose by making friends of them all. Brahmanism repudiates exclusiveness; it incorporates all creeds, assimilates all, consecrates all. People are permitted to entertain any opinions they please, and to practise any ceremonies they please, provided only that the supremacy of the Vedas and of the Brahmans is acknowledged. When that acknowledgment has been duly made, the new heterodoxy becomes another new authoritative orthodoxy, especially revealed by the Supreme Being himself for the enlightenment and salvation of the particular class of people amongst whom it has become popular. Thus Brahmanism yields and conquers; and hence, though the demon worship of Tinnevelly is as far as possible repugnant to the genius of orthodox Hinduism, and was not only independent of it in origin, but, as I believe, long anterior to it, yet even it has received a place in the cunningly-devised mosaic of the Brahmans, and the devils have got themselves regarded as abnormal developments of the gods.[7]

This characterization is based on two elements: the projection of the Soviet totalitarian state, which was a Western fear, onto Harappan society, and the Protestant aversion to priestcraft. Wheeler seems to be obsessed with pointing out how women were kept in temples and how children and slaves served the priesthood in other Bronze Age cultures. Unfortunately, these colonial frameworks became the basis for interpreting theo-diversity as either a priestly strategy or a conspiracy. Later, this would be linked to the caste system in India in a peculiar way. In free India, a Soviet-style socialist state, adored by Jawahar

Lal Nehru and almost universally accepted as the best form of government with few exceptions, became an ideal. This gave a new twist to the perspective on Harappan civilization, which was seen as a non-Aryan utopia without social stratification like the Varṇa system. In this narrative, the Aryan invaders brought the Varṇa system and conquered the Harappans, who were proto-Dravidian and spoke an ancient form of Tamil. This idea fuelled Tamil identity politics and anti-Hindu ideology. The Harappans were portrayed as egalitarian and civilized, while the Indo-Europeans were violent, savage, and oppressive. They imposed a system of ethnic discrimination, where they claimed the positions of kings, priests, and traders and reduced the original inhabitants to servile or outcaste status. This was the origin of the Varṇa-caste system. Vedic religion also justified and reinforced this system, which centred on priest-mediated sacrifices. These sacrifices maintained birth-based discrimination, which was seen as a form of karma. Vedic religion was thus an early and perhaps the oldest form of apartheid.

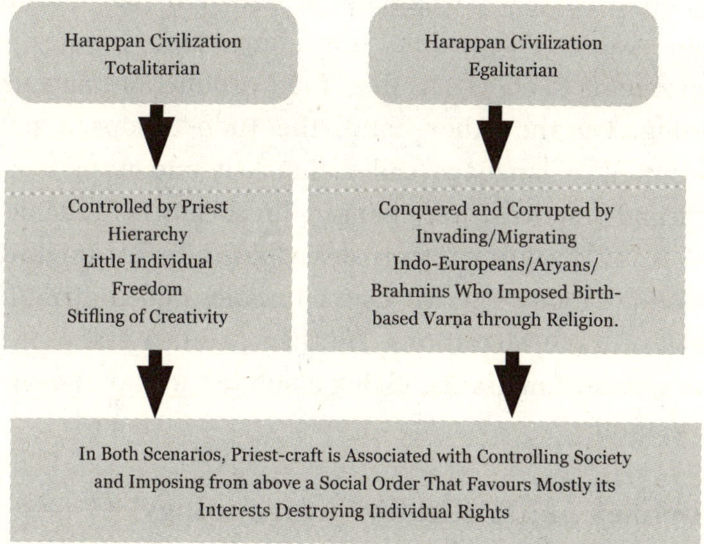

Figure 1 Making pagan priestcraft the villain is a major theme in colonial as well as post-colonial narrative

To this day, this format is dominant in the thinking of anthropologists and sociologists who study Indian society, culture, and religion. The following passage is from an article by Tony Joseph on genetics and the 'Aryan migration debate' that appeared in *The Hindu* in 2017:

> The Out of Africa immigrants, the pioneering, fearless explorers who discovered this land originally and settled in it and whose lineages still form the bedrock of our population; those who arrived later with a package of farming techniques and built the Indus Valley civilization whose cultural ideas and practices perhaps enrich much of our traditions today; those who arrived from East Asia, probably bringing with them the practice of rice cultivation and all that goes with it; those who came later with a language called Sanskrit and its associated beliefs and practices and reshaped our society in fundamental ways; and those who came even later for trade or for conquest and chose to stay, all have mingled and contributed to this civilization we call Indian. We are all migrants.[8]

The above passage suggests that the non-Indo-European people were responsible for important civilizational achievements such as farming, food production, and urban planning. On the other hand, the Indo-European people contributed 'a language called Sanskrit and its associated beliefs and practices' that 'changed our society in fundamental ways'. Tony Joseph not only describes different migrations but also attributes specific characteristics and contributions to each of these migrations. He then paints a grand picture of the waves of migrants, giving a subtle racial dimension to such mapping.

Comeback of a 'Catholic Anthropology'

This can be linked to what one can call 'Catholic Anthropology' from Germany.[9]

In 1902, Wilhelm Schmidt (1868-1954), a Catholic cleric and scholar, attended a lecture by a German Indologist, Leopold von Schroeder (1851-1920). Schroeder was an anti-evolutionist convinced by the ideas of Andrew Lang (1844-1912), a Scottish poet, novelist, and literary critic. The lecture's core idea was based on Lang's speculations that there was a higher primitive monotheism—a belief in a higher single God. Schroeder-Lang also held that ancient humanity had three cultural-religious-linguistic circles. They were the 'totemic cultural circle' of mostly hunters, which consisted of animism, totemism, and ancestral worship as its religious practices, 'higher hunters' 'agrarian-matriarchal' circle, which consisted of a mixture of monotheism and polytheism and the 'Central Asian herding culture'. Schroeder-Lang considered the last as patriarchal, a belief in a single creating god, and, importantly, this cultural circle domesticated horses and performed horse sacrifice.

Schmidt was inspired by this lecture and collaborated with another Catholic scholar, Wilhelm Koppers, to develop a theory of ancient races. He presented this theory in 1936 as an alternative to the Nazi ideology, even though it was also based on race. According to Schmidt, there were three 'cultural circles' worldwide. The first was the 'agrarian-matriarchal' circle, which included Indochina, China, the Indus culture, Mesopotamia, Africa, and Europe. This circle was neither rational nor irrational in its cerebral culture. The second circle was the 'totemic cultural circle of the higher hunters', which consisted of the Dravidians and the Aboriginals. This circle was 'irrational' in its traits. The third was the 'Central Asian herding culture', which he believed was the closest to the 'original culture's family culture and religion'. This circle was patriarchal and primitive monotheistic. Schmidt was the Catholic Church's expert on anthropology. He strongly disagreed with the Nazi historiography, which he thought glorified the pagan culture. However, he shared the

Nazi's anti-Semitism. Schmidt viewed Nazism as modernist, and he wanted Europe to return to a Church-dominated 'medieval type of society with stable hierarchies and integrating corporations'. His anthropology was a way to promote this worldview. This vision of a medieval-type Catholic society was also supported by the 'Austro-Fascist regimes', which had the backing of Pope Pius XI and Benito Mussolini.

In Schmidt-Koppers' thesis suggests that the Indo-Germans emerged from the steppes as both livestock breeders and warriors. They started a world-conquering mission, which also was to bring order and stability to the civilizations around the world. To achieve this, they rode on horse-drawn battle chariots from the steppes. Later on, they were joined by the 'Hamito-Semitic' peoples, who were also great conquerors of humanity. However, as they conquered other people, they underwent a transformation. This is the crucial part of Schmidt-Koppers' speculative thesis. Historian of religion and linguistics Stefan Arvidsson explains this particular turn thus:

> These people (Indo-Germans) were, according to Schmidt, 'born rulers,' and typically enough belonged to an especially strong racial type:... The totemic and agrarian-matriarchal cultural circles had already melted together at an early stage and formed city-states, with trade and crafts.... It became the civilizing task of the Indo-Germans and the Semites,..., to create hierarchies that could integrate the city-states.... For Schmidt, it was obvious that social 'order' and hierarchies were civilizing steps forward, but he also claimed that the Indo-Germanic ruling class had become arrogant and proud. When the Indo-Germans had lived on the steppes, they had humbly worshipped the creator god as the heavenly father, but when they now ruled over foreign peoples, they began to see themselves as equals of the gods.... Schmidt continues that we can see what Indo-Germanic arrogance can lead to in South Asia, where the Brahmans 'who claim to represent the Aryan racial purity' uphold a caste system

> that is completely destroying India. The Brahmanic religion shows that the ruling castes have created 'a heavenly elevation where one no longer walks on earth and where every similarity with the people as a whole has been lost'.[10]

Let us revisit the 2019 narrative presented by Tony Joseph. He provides a racial interpretation of the emergence of endogamy and suggests that the mixing of communities came to a halt in ancient India. According to Joseph, the ancient texts indicate 'shifting attitudes towards the mixing of the races'. He also claims that the 'Aryans' brought many things with them, such as Sanskrit, beliefs, rituals, and a patriarchal social structure. He says that these things 'reshaped our society in fundamental ways'. This is a polite way of saying that the 'Aryans' introduced the caste system and placed themselves at the top of the hierarchy. The deep similarity between Tony Joseph's narrative and the speculative Catholic racial anthropology of Fr. Schmidt that he developed in the 1930s cannot be considered entirely coincidental.

Approximating Reality with Ancestral DNA

The mysteries of the past are intriguing, especially when, as in the case of the Harappan civilization, they date back more than 5000 years. How did people live, think, and interact in those ancient times? How did they shape the society we see today? Many theories have been proposed over the years, but some are based on Biblical myths and/or colonial biases. One of these theories is the Aryan invasion/migration and subsequent dominant cultural replacement theory. However, many modern studies that use scientific methods and evidence have challenged and refuted this theory. These studies, which include genetic analysis, linguistic modelling, and archaeological excavations, demonstrate that there was no mass migration or invasion of

Aryans into India. Instead, the Harappan civilization declined due to environmental and political factors. The studies also show that there was continuity and interaction between the Harappan and other cultures and all of them contributed to the diversity and richness of Indian society. Therefore, it is important that we focus on the facts and not the myths as we try to understand our past. Both the Harappan civilization and the Vedic age are part of our heritage, and we can learn a lot from them. By using scientific tools and methods, we can get closer to the truth and appreciate the complexity and beauty of our history.

In 2018, popular media published several articles highlighting the research in molecular anthropology in relation to the people of ancient India. The interest in this new research was sparked by the new advancements in ancient DNA (aDNA) recovery and analysis. Most of these papers were based on the Steppe hypothesis, which suggests that the migration and invasion of Indo-European speakers' occurred between 1700 and 1500 BCE.

The same year, a study was published by Dr Ajai K. Pathak of Estonian Biocentre, Institute of Genomics, University of Tartu and an international team. The paper titled 'The Genetic Ancestry of Modern Indus Valley Populations from Northwest India' is a genome-wide study of four Northwest Indian ethnic groups: the Ror, Gujjar, Jat, and Kamboj, all associated with the geographic region of Indus Valley. The paper compares their genetic data with that of ancient and modern populations from South Asia and West Eurasia, revealing a complex genetic interaction and diversity. The paper's holistic approach made it the best paper at the 2018 International Conference on Human Genetics and Genomics.

This paper examines how 'several historic and prehistoric population movements between South Asia and West Eurasia' influenced the genetic diversity of four Northwest Indian populations. The study utilized 'new genome-wide genotype data for 45 modern individuals'.[11] According to Dr Pathank, the Ror community from Kurukshetra is 'genetically more akin to populations living west of India' than the other groups. The study also suggests that 'a sort of genetic continuity between populations living west of the Indus Valley and east of the Indus Valley suggesting a higher mobility during prehistorical time in the Indus Valley region'. The research was assisted by Anurag Kadian, an IITian, who was interested in tracing the ancestral origin of the Ror population. All the samples were collected from individuals living within 100 km to 400 km of Kurukshetra.

The study reveals that modern Indus populations are very diverse genetically. This diversity may have originated during the ancient Indus era, as archaeological evidence suggests that the 'Harappan culture must have integrated diverse regional and tribal features'. The study also compares ancient DNA worldwide and finds that the Ror and Jat communities are closer 'to extant and ancient populations that lived west of India'. However, these two communities also share some genetic affinity with 'Central Asians and Bronze Age Steppe groups' and 'higher affinity with Anatolian Neolithic than Iranian Neolithic.' Dr Pathak, the lead author of the study, suggests that the Ror and Jat communities could be a key population 'very close to a root population that spread the Ancestral North Indian (ANI) component in South Asia due to high inward and outward mobility of the Indus people probably for trade'. The study supports the idea that the original population was not replaced by an invasion or a large-scale migration from the Steppes.

In 2018, Prof. Vasant Shinde, a renowned archaeologist, and a team of Korean scientists explored a 'cemetery district' at a Harappan site in Rakhigarhi, Haryana. Later, Shinde and an international team also extracted genomic data from the remains of a female individual (named I6113) who lived in the Harappan civilization. Their study revealed some surprising aspects regarding her ancestry:

> A significant finding of this paper is that I6113 is best modelled as a mixture of two ancestral components: one related to ancient Iranians and the other to Southeast Asian hunter-gatherers. Interestingly, this ancestry profile of I6113 is shown to be very similar to that of 11 ancient individuals from Turkmenistan and eastern Iran, buried in sites with cultural connections to the Indus Valley Civilization (IVC).... Perhaps the more striking result,..., is that the ancient Iranian component of the IVC derives from a lineage that is ancestral to ancient Iranian hunter-gatherers, herders, and farmers. This suggests that movement of farmers from farther west did not drive agricultural innovation in South Asia or, at least, left little genetic trace. The second key finding of the study is the lack of steppe-related ancestry in the IVC individual.[12]

The paper explains further:

> This result in consort with the absence of Anatolian and Iranian farmer components in I6113 supports the notion that Indo-European languages arrived from Eastern Europe via Central Asia sometime after 2000 BCE, rather than from Anatolia via Iran with the arrival of farming (Anatolian hypothesis).

In other words, this is a typical 'Aryan' or Indo-European Steppe invasion/migration hypothesis with the time scale neatly fitted within after-2000 BCE coming of Indo-European languages. However, archaeologist Jonathan Mark Kenoyer was not entirely satisfied by this explanation. Cautioning against such generalizations based on the study of DNA from a single person, he pointed out that the Harappan sites were cosmopolitan centres of their age, and hence 'one person's genetic makeup might not match the rest of the population'. He also emphasized that 'burial was a less common way of dealing with the dead than cremation'. So 'whatever we do have from cemeteries is not representative of the ancient populations of the Indus cities, but only of one part of one community living in these cities.'[13]

In 2019, sometime before the publication of the Rakhigarhi paper, another paper was published in *Science* by a team of as many as 92 scientists from various international institutions. The authors of this paper analysed the ancient DNA of 523 people who lived in Central Asia and northern South Asia over the past 8,000 years. Their findings suggest that the people who brought the Steppe ancestry to modern South Asians were mostly men. Additionally, they found that the Steppe ancestry was more common in certain groups, such as Brahmins and Bhumihars than others. These findings support the idea that the Indo-European languages spoken in South Asia came from the Steppe.[14]

Three years later, Kenoyer reinforced his opinion on Rakhigarhi a-DNA analysis and wrote:

> The one fragmentary DNA recently recovered at Rakhigarhi provides some hope that more DNA will eventually be recovered as new techniques for recovery are developed. However we must remember that only a very small segment of Indus society practised the burial of the dead. Most of the ancient Indus dead would have been treated in other ways, such as cremation, water burial or exposure in the forests. Since we will never be able to recover DNA from most of the people who lived in these cities, we need to understand from the outset that we may never sort out the diversity of people living in these early urban centres from DNA studied alone.[15]

Parallel to and complimenting such studies, it is also important to consider linguistic studies. As linguistic models of ancient languages became more refined and robust, they shed light on the problem of their formation and spread. The studies have revealed complexities that defy simplistic notions of invasions, migrations, and replacements.

A More Complex Picture from Linguistic Studies

A study published in *Nature* in 2003 investigated the origin and spread of Indo-European languages. The study analysed 'a matrix of 87 languages with 2,449 lexical items' and concluded that these languages 'expanded with the spread of agriculture from Anatolia around 8,000–9,500 years Before Present (BP)'. The study compared two dominant hypotheses: the Steppe hypothesis, which proposes that Indo-European languages spread by horse-riding pastoralists, and the Anatolia hypothesis, which suggests that Indo-European languages diffused by farming. The study found more support for the Anatolia hypothesis.

At the same time, the study did not rule out the Steppe expansion hypothesis, also known as the Kurgan expansion, completely. It is the well-known theory that traces the origin and spread of the Indo-European languages and cultures to the nomadic pastoralists who lived in the Eurasian steppes. These people, often (wrongly) called Aryans, are believed to have migrated or invaded different regions of Europe and Asia with their horses and chariots. This theory is familiar to many Indians, who have a complex and contested history with the concept of Aryan invasion. So when the study also stated the following, it kept the windows open for possible linguistic validation of Aryan invasion in future detailed studies:

> The consensus tree also shows evidence of a period of rapid divergence giving rise to the Italic, Celtic, Balto-Slavic and perhaps Indo-Iranian families that is intriguingly close to the time suggested for a possible Kurgan expansion.[16]

Then another paper published in 2015 used 'a phylogenetic analysis in which ancestry constraints permit a more accurate inference of rates of change' to support the steppe hypothesis suggesting that 'the Indo-European languages originated in the Pontic-Caspian steppe and spread through migration and cultural diffusion.' However, the paper had a questionable assumption as it dated Vedic Sanskrit to 1500-1000 BCE or 3250 BP.[17] The same year, another paper in *Nature* concluded a 'massive migration from the steppe' as 'the source of Indo-European languages in Europe.'[18] Of course, this was in the context of Europe. But this had clear implications for Indo-European languages coming to India in a similar manner.

Meanwhile, in 2018, another paper published in *Royal Society Open Science*, based on 'a Bayesian phylogenetic study of the Dravidian language family' calculated 'a median root age for the Dravidian language family' as around 4,000–4,500 years BP' while not excluding 'the possibility that the root of the Dravidian language family is 6,000 or 6,500 years old'.[19] This is important because the possibility of the non-deciphered Indus script being a proto-Dravidian has been conflated in the political discourse of India as the Tamil language itself.

In 2023, Paul Heggarty and his team published a groundbreaking paper in *Science*. The paper caused a significant stir in the academia studying the origin and spread of Indo-European languages. The team of researchers used a more rigorous approach to study the subject, applying Bayesian phylogenetic methods to a large dataset of core vocabulary from 161 Indo-European languages. The study results suggest a new, earlier chronology for the origin of these languages. They also propose a hybrid hypothesis that combines insights from linguistics and genetics.[20] (All subsequent quotes are from this paper.)

The Steppe Hypothesis suggests that about 3,500 years ago, Indo-European languages were introduced to the Indian region through horse-based pastoral expansion, which is currently referred to as the 'Aryan' invasion theory. It is believed that Indo-Iranic separated from Indo-European around 4,300 years ago (approximately 2300 BCE). Furthermore, the Indo-Iranic branch has been linked to the Balto-Slavic branch of Indo-European, which is a key aspect of the Steppe Hypothesis.

The paper constructs the timeline for the major branching out of the Indo-European languages:

> Our analysis indicates that the Indo-European family began with a series of major branching events in relatively quick succession. From ~8120 yr BP (6740 to 9610 yr BP) to 6140 yr BP (4540 to 7880 yr BP), Indo-European had split into seven branches, long before 'steppe' ancestry spread into Europe and the Altai. These seven include the Anatolian, Greco-Armenian, and Indo-Iranic branches, for which aDNA shows little or no genetic influx from the steppe at ~5300 to 4900 yr BP—that is, at time depths early enough to match our estimated split times.

It explains the incompatibility of the Steppe hypothesis with the available data:

> Recent aDNA data from Central and South Asia have sought to trace movements of people into Western and South Asia by migrations southward from the steppe. However, for the period 4300–3700 yr BP, samples from the Bactria-Margiana Archaeological Complex (BMAC) do not yet attest to any such southward migration. Steppe ancestry is not found until ~3500 yr BP, in the Gandhara Grave Culture in northern Pakistan, and only at limited proportions. The interpretation that this ancestry can be identified with the first Indo-Iranic dispersal into South Asia is not straightforwardly compatible with our earlier date for the separation of Indo-Iranic from the rest of Indo-European (~6980 yr BP).

Crucially, linking Indo-Iranic to the Balto-Slavic branching from Indo-European, which is, as already pointed out, a vital component of the Steppe hypothesis, is also shown as unsupported by data:

> In particular, in (steppe) hypothesis, Indo-Iranic, the major eastern branch of Indo-European, was one of the last two main branches to emerge, out of a final major clade with Balto-Slavic. Our results contradict this in both chronology and tree topology. Indo-Iranic branches off early, ~6980 yr BP (5650 to 8400 yr BP), and support for a common clade with Balto-Slavic is minimal....

The 2023 paper also looked into a possibility previously excluded in the 2019 paper on the ancient genomic data of Harappan individuals:

> Previous interpretations of aDNA from one individual from the Indus Periphery sought to exclude a direct eastward route on the basis of the degree and timing of Anatolian admixture, but these have been superseded by methodological and analytical refinements, which no longer exclude this scenario entirely. More parsimonious geographically, at least, would be a route for Indo-Iranic directly eastward out of a South Caucasus homeland through the Iranian Plateau, south of the Caspian.

Combined, these studies increasingly suggest that the Harappan civilization was not a monolith. It was a more complex and diverse society with multiple sources of ancestry and multiple languages. Despite the apparent gradual collapse around 1900 BCE, its genetic and linguistic heritage has continued to persist in South Asia and was later renewed with strong continuity.

The history of the Harappan civilization and its subsequent transformation is a complex and fascinating one. Researchers have long sought to fit new data into the *Yamnaya*/Steppe expansion hypothesis, which suggests that Indo-European languages were brought to the region by horse-riding invaders around 1500-1200 BCE. This theory has been set against the backdrop of the demise of the Harappan civilization, with some even suggesting that it was the cause of its downfall. However, as more data emerges and more rigorous scientific methodologies are applied, this simplistic model fails to hold up. Indian historians and archaeologists have often questioned this scenario, advocating for a civilizational continuity and highlighting the continuities and similarities between the Harappan and the present-day Indian civilizations. They propose a gradual transition rather than a sudden apocalyptic demise and even question the use of the term 'Aryan' as an ethnic label.

What emerges is a picture of a multilingual, non-monocultural Harappan civilization, one that embodies the spirit of unity in diversity that has been present in this land since ancient times. As the line from *Atharva Veda* states, '*Janam bibharti bahudha vivachasam nanadharmanam Prthivi yathaukasam*' (People of different ethnicities, languages and religious traditions-the earth supports them all).[21] Historian Vasudev Agrawala, in his study of ancient Indian folk traditions, quotes the above Atharva Vedic verse to emphasize this diversity with almost a mystical unity as the basis of India's unique continuity:

> The diversity of the peoples inhabiting the various parts of the country (*yathaukasam bahudha janam*), the variety of their dialects (*vivachasam*), and the multiplicity of their cults (*nanadharmanam*)—these were the three significant features of our racial life in the past as they are with us even today. But these distinctions did not operate to divide the children of the soil whose devotion to the Mother Earth served as an overall.[22]

The above passage made in the context of Vedic India's diversity also seems to describe Harappan society with its ethnic diversity, linguistic diversity, and theo-diversity. And yet, the civilization forged a unity in that diversity. In this sense, in a more fundamental way than any other, the Harappan civilization was indeed Vedic, a vibrant tapestry of diverse cultures woven together in harmony or Vedic civilization was truly Harappan. And in today's Indian culture, there is an unbroken continuity.

A Holistic Perspective from Mainly Indian Anthropologists

For a long time, the prevailing view in academia and popular culture has been that Indian culture and religion were shaped by a sophisticated and fair Harappan society that was later conquered and oppressed by invading or migrating 'Aryans'. This narrative also asserts that the Aryans imposed a class system based on birth, which relegated the indigenous populations to subservient positions.

However, a more nuanced and realistic scenario is emerging that portrays the Harappan civilization as a complex, diverse, and integral part of the Vedic culture. Rather than being confrontational and two distinct entities, the relationship between the two, if at all they were that, was harmonious, representing the diversity and the unity within the same cultural matrix. This understanding brings fresh insights into the evolution and nature of the future social dynamics in India. This new perspective based more solidly on empirical evidence and free from colonial and ideological prejudices, challenges the simplistic narrative of a monolithic cultural-religious-linguistic-political entity being destroyed by outsiders. It offers a richer, more nuanced view of India's past.

Harappan Social Structure and Formation of Classical Hindu Society

The Harappan civilization had unique characteristics, such as impressive urban planning and standardized weights and measures. These characteristics raise intriguing questions about its society. How did the Harappans achieve social cohesion? Was there a sacrifice of creativity in favour of uniformity? Or was it a society that balanced totalitarian control with egalitarian principles? What kind of empire was it? Did it colonize neighbouring regions? Was it an empire at all? These questions have been the subject of much debate among scholars since the discovery of the Indus Valley Civilization. However, they are primarily discussed in frameworks of colonial and/or Marxist theories.

One of the earliest scholars to propose a caste-like structure in Harappan civilization was the pioneering Indian social scientist Irawati Karve (1905-1970). She inferred this structure from the archaeological data available:

> In India each caste at present has a separate living area. This was the case in ancient India also if one takes into account the oldest records which describe cities and villages.... In the excavations of Harappa a whole street was found with stone mortars, where cereals, perhaps rice, were either husked or pounded into flour. The Western archaeologists have called it the slave quarters or places of government enterprise where slaved pounded cereals. That scores of 'mortars' were found in one 'street' is a fact. The rest is conjecture. I venture to give an alternative conjecture. Probably it was a street lived in by a caste-like group, who specialized in pounding rice.[23]

One should remember here that most Indian social scientists, with very few exceptions, considered the Aryan invasion and the non-Vedic nature of Harappan civilization as almost foundational truths of India's civilizational history. However, what is important here is that Irawati Karve saw caste as not a system brought by outside invaders but as an indigenous evolution. This in itself was defying the dominant academic view then. She went on to differentiate between the Varṇa and Jāthi, with the previous as an Aryan social system and the latter as Harappan or indigenous. She pointed out that there was no record in Sanskrit literature that suggests 'caste was "created" by race-conscious Brahmins'.[24]

The next insightful critique of Western theories of Harappan culture came from Prof. S.C. Malik. As an anthropologist studying ancient Indian society and its evolution, Prof. Malik proposed a theory of deep continuity. He suggested that the salient features of the Harappan civilization persisted from the pre-Harappan period through to what is known as the post-Harappan period. This perspective offers a fresh lens to view the Harappan civilization, challenging Western notions and opening up new avenues for understanding this enigmatic society. Compared to Irawati Karve, he also had access to more archaeological data and as early as 1968, he made a scientifically rigorous criticism of Gordon Childe's 'surplus' doctrine and the Western understanding of imagining Harappan civilization as an 'empire':

> [T]he anthropologists have implicitly accepted the surplus theory that was specially developed by Childe, following Marx, in his 'Urban Revolution' and other works. The argument developed by Childe was that social stratification (class-specialization) and the increase in population had become possible only because of the increased quantity of abundant food 'surplus' which had enabled the release of greater leisure time.... To confine evolutionary processes of such magnitude and fundamental morphological significance to the appearance of superabundant food supplies is to fly in the face of the most central of all evolutionary doctrines: the superiority of reproductive potential over productive ability.[25]

Dr Malik considers the food production activities as being based on small-scale irrigation technology, which was not labour intensive. This subsistence food production in Harappan was naturally diverse. It was not a monoculture of wheat alone:

> This broad-based subsistence base must not only have ensured protection against natural calamities, but it must also have been essential for the long-term cultural growth and sustenance of Harappan society. Nevertheless, such subsistence on a diversity of food resources also requires redistributive institutions which, in turn, must have enhanced the growth of some form of a centralized 'authority' that we know is reflected in the archaeological evidence of granaries, citadel, etc.... However, in view of the subsistence-economic base noted above, Harappan society had very little chance to establish itself like the 'city-states' of its contemporaneous West Asian society.[26]

Still, there is a challenge at hand of identifying the 'agency' that provided the 'authority'. Proceeding from the fact that 'Harappan society had very little chance to establish itself like the "city-states" of its contemporaneous West Asian society' and yet it had an authority that could not have been coercive, Malik looks for 'the possible socio-cultural institutional means by which integration was achieved, and especially the motivating forces which must have enabled this non-coercing "authority" to effectively act upon the individual members of this society'.[27] He considers 'specialization, redistribution, and the related centralization of authority which can integrate still more complex societies' as the nature of such agency which fits 'in most appropriately with the known archaeological evidence of Harappan society'.[28] Quoting anthropologist Elman Service (1915-96) from his study on 'primitive social organization' Malik concludes the following about the 'central agency' of Harappan civilization:

> In short, Harappan society was most probably integrated and 'stabilized by strict rules of hereditary succession and sanctioned by mythology, custom, values and so on, then to the extent that these are strong and consistent so is the authority strong and consistent.'... Thus, the central 'agency' of Harappan society

> must have served many different functions, such as the social, political and economic ones, in addition to the religious one.[29]

He identified the following three elements from Harappan social organization well into the current indigenous sociocultural life of current India:

> This is the genealogical means of the perpetuation of caste status by birth. Associated with the above characteristic institution is.... This characteristic, as we have noted, must also logically have been present in Harappan society. Another characteristic, which is also of considerable significance in Indian society, is the importance which is given to the memorization process, specially in descent reckoning, ritual prayers, etc., which are all learnt by oral repetition.... For instance, it was not until the second half of the 14th century AD that the Rg Vedic hymns were properly edited, written down and commented in South India. The text had till then been memorized syllable by syllable, but not generally committed to writing. The oral means of imparting education is one of the chief means of learning even today, specially in the indigenous educational school system, and it is this process that has maintained and preserved India's traditional civilization. Once again, it is this characteristic of the Indian Style which may also be seen in Harappan society because we know about the unchanging script which had generally remained the same for many hundreds of years.[30]

It is important to note that Dr Malik, who is primarily an anthropologist, interpreted the available archaeological data through the lens of his domain. During that time, the prevailing archaeological paradigm suggested that Indo-European migration or invasion succeeded the Harappan civilization. As a result, Dr Malik proposed that the 'Aryans' adapted or borrowed their social system from the Harappans. However, what is central to Dr Malik's thesis and relevant to the current study is the notion that the Jāthi-like structure originated in

Harappan society. This notion has since been validated by further studies of Harappan archaeology.

Almost two decades after Malik proposed his thesis, archaeologist Jonathan Mark Kenoyer in his study of the possible socio-economic structures that could have been present in Harappan civilization, he pointed out:

> The archaeological representations of hierarchical segregation and ritual purity have not yet been systematically studied in early historical sites, but these studies are beginning at Vijayanagara, a medieval site in Karnataka.... I do not intend to suggest that the organization of Indus cities was as rigid as those of Early Historical or Medieval South Asia. However, if a concept of hierarchical stratification based on ritual purity was present in the Indus social order it is likely that it would be represented in much the same manner as it is represented in later societies in South Asia; segregation of living areas, private water sources, drainage and waste disposal and distinct sets of ceramics, specifically those connected with cooking, food preparation and food serving. If we look at the Indus settlements, all of the basic data sets are present.[31]

Epigraphist Iravatham Mahadevan (1930-2018), who studied the Harappan seals, also suggested what he considered as a strong indication of social stratification, which could have been hereditary with symbolic religious reinforcement. However, this was not in the sense of the castes we understand them today. He contends that they were flexible and connected. In the Harappan tablets, the terminal 'Jar' signs are the most frequent, which Mahadevan connects with three important functional categories. In 1982, Mahadevan proposed that the 'bearer' group of signs are ideograms that probably indicate the occupations and social status of the persons whose names these signs are found affixed to. 'the related signs ("bearer", "jar", and "lance" signs) are all treated as substantives and suffixed elements in name-formation.'[32] These Harappan functional categories were officers with priestly duties, officers with military duties, farmers-tillers-tenants, servant-attendants or lower functionaries. The categories correspond with the 'Varṇa' system (Figure 2).

IRAVATHAM MAHADEVAN'S

INDUS SCRIPT

"DICTIONARY"

Sign/ Sequence	Pictorial value	Ideographic meaning	Comments
	Jar	Priest	The most frequent and almost always terminal sign of the Indus script is read as a jar and connected to the legend of 'jar-born' sages and the symbolism of the jar connected to priestly ritual in Indian tradition.
	Lance	Warrior	Also a terminal sign, pr suffix associated with names or titles on seals like the 'jar' sign above.
	Man	Servant, attendant or lower functionary	Simple pictogram, frequently shown with 'jar' (lower order of priestly functionary?) but never with 'lance' sign.
	Bearer	Officer or functionary	Also appears to be a suffixed element, interpreted as officer because of later Indian traditions referring to senior officers of the king referred to as 'yoke bearers.'
	Jar + Bearer	Officer or functionary with priestly duties	Clearly combination of two signs, could be related to later Indian traditions combining the two motifs.
	Lance + Bearer	Officer or functionary with military duties	Also combination, perhaps designating officer with military duties.
	Harrow	Farmer, tiller, tenant	Also characteristically a terminal sign, sometimes in conjunction with 'jar,' 'lance,' or 'bearer' signs, suggesting combination of categories or serving under them.

Figure 2 The possibly hereditary office bearers in Harappan society as per Dr Iravatham Mahadevan. Figure courtesy Harappa.com

Mahadevan also suggested a continuity:

> The native tradition of India was largely one of janapadas, before the Mauryan Empire, before even the 6th century BC. Before that time, north India was divided into a large

> number of republics, janapadas; both Mahavira and Buddha belonged to republican clans. It is quite possible that the Harappan states were earlier examples of janapadas. I know I am speculating, but one has to explain the absence of royal graves and royal paraphernalia. It could be they had elders, they had ganas, they had republican, a crude republican form of government, they had priestly oligarchies and the chief went by rotation. All these things are not impossible, and for the keys to these one must look at the surviving institutions. The republican *janapada* tradition could be an important element in judging the absence of royal paraphernalia in the Harappan polity.[33]

Archaeologist and historian Madhukar Keshav Dhavalikar (1930–2018) builds upon the framework of Karve. While Karve believed that Jāthi was Harappan and Varṇa Aryan, Dhavalikar proposed the possibility of the Varṇa system itself being pre-Vedic. Even though the 'fourfold division of society in the hierarchical order and caste system' was 'ultimately blamed on Vedic Aryans', it was 'quite possible that some sort of fourfold division of the society, something approximating the latter day Varṇa system was in vogue in Harappan society'. So for him, 'it may not, therefore, be far-fetched that the fourfold division existed in the Harappan society'.[34]

Another important anthropologist who shares this view is Prof. Lamberg-Karlovsky. Indologist Edwin Bryant explains this 'provocative' thesis in the following words, which is worth quoting in full:

> [Lamberg-Karlovsky] draws attention to the astounding degree of cultural homogeneity in the vast area of the Indus Valley Civilization, juxtaposed with the lack of any evidence for a centralized political structure. Not only is there a uniformity of culture, but the physical layout of the community is replicated irrespective of whether it is the 5-acre site of

> Allahdino or the 150 acre site of Mohenjo-Daro. Lamberg-Karlovsky believes this 'enigma' can be adequately explained by supposing that only an exceptional social organization such as the caste system can account for this. He finds a variety of archaeological evidence to support this. The residential units at Indus sites, for example, were much larger than other contemporaneous sites, suggesting a stronger sense of kin identities or groupings. He notes that competition in a class-structured society results in a much wider variety of styles and methods of production, whereas in a caste system, much more uniformity is to be expected, as is evidenced by the artifacts unearthed in the Indus Valley sites. Caste organization would also explain the social stability of such a massive culture in the absence of a centralized state or chieftainship. Finally, the concern with purity in a caste system is amply evidenced in the archaeological record by the unparalleled attention and concern given to the control of and access to water and sanitation; at Mohenjo Daro, there is an average of one well for every three houses. Lamberg-Karlovsky (forthcoming) notes that, 'if valid, such a hypothesis would impose a radical rethinking of the current consensus of the allegedly Indo-European origins of the organizational patterns characteristic of traditional Indian society.'[35]

Regardless of whether the Indo-European versus Harappan divide is accepted as a stark dichotomy or questioned due to the increasing research and discoveries that blur these boundaries, the argument for the Jāthi-Varṇa system being an indigenous evolution rather than an imposition by outsiders gains strength. This explanation is more compelling in light of archaeological data. Beyond the Jāthi groups and Varṇa system, which likely originated from the Harappan civilization or their prototypes, there is another significant dimension to Indian socio-cultural-economic life. This aspect, too, may have its roots firmly planted in the Harappan era.

CHAPTER 4

Harappan Yajña and Vedic Agni: Roots of a Social System

Had Harappan society been characterized only by hierarchical authority, solely based on ritual power and heredity in a pyramidal manner, as often the Varṇa system is characterized, then it would have shown the power and splendour of the upper sections of the society in sharp contrast to the deprived sections. Archaeological data does not suggest such a gulf dividing the society. For a society to function for millennia, there should have been a system of reciprocal redistribution. What was it? Can we identify it? Did it vanish with the Harappan society, or can we find its existence even in modern times with considerable changes and yet retaining some archaic memory? Will discovering such a system in the past also change how we look at how Indian society is organized today? This chapter tries to answer these questions.

'*Jajmānī*'—Inequality versus Redistribution; Ritual Pollution versus Inclusion

For long, archaeologists researching Harappan civilization have attempted to reconstitute the social mechanism that characterized and ensured the civilization's sustainably for over three millennia without much power or violence. Archaeologist Jonathan Kenoyer suggested a mechanism of reciprocity being present similar to the '*Jajmāni* system', which has continued in most Hindu villages even in modern times. According to him, it was 'hereditary relationships of reciprocal exchange'.[1] Kenoyer based his system on the anthropological authority of Gerald Berreman (1930–2013), a leftist who protested against the Vietnam War but was nevertheless Euro-centric in his approach. Quoting Berreman's famous paper 'The evolutionary status of caste in peasant India, social anthropology of peasantry' on the evolution of caste system in India, Kenoyer writes:

> The structure of *Jajmāni* relations has been likened to the 'estate' relations which developed in the feudal system in Europe and Berreman suggests that it is the mechanism whereby inequality was organized and sustained 'at the watershed between kin-based, unstratified, pre-state institutions of inequality and class-based, stratified state-organized institutions of inequality'.[2]

Berreman also used the classical 'Aryan' invasion scenario in his 1983 paper,

> Indo-Aryans placed themselves and those they could not dispossess of their land in the elite castes—those in the three 'twice-born' varnas at the top of the hierarchy—appropriating to themselves the land and labour of those they dispossessed. The latter, in turn, had little choice but to assume their assigned, economically enforced, and ritually endorsed social roles and statuses, to perform their assigned tasks, and to contribute the *corvee* (beggar) labour, clientship [*Jajmāni*], rents, and taxes imposed upon them in the peasant economy of the emerging state.[3]

As one can see, Berreman's thesis almost acquires a tone of racial conspiracy. Modern scholarship has rejected such scenarios. As seen in the Chapter 3 of this book, the fourfold system itself could have emerged in its protoform much earlier than the time conjectured for the arrival of the mythical 'Aryans'.

Vilification of Jajmāni System

So, is the 'Jajmāni' system only a hereditary hierarchical system of inequality? Or is it more a redistributive system than a hierarchical one? What was its core concern? Was it ritual pollution or a process of inclusion? Archaeologist Jane McIntosh, who researched the contacts between the Indus Valley and Mesopotamian civilizations in her book *The Ancient Indus Valley: New Perspectives* considers both Jāthi and Jajmāni systems as complementary and simultaneously existing in Harappan society.

> Allied to the social structure dictated by caste is a redistributive mechanism known as the *Jajmāni* system. In this system, all members of the community have reciprocal obligations to provide the products of their labours and certain services to others with whom they have a formalized relationship that to some extent resembles kinship. Payment for these goods and services is made in kind and fixed by tradition. The payments take place at regulated intervals and often in the context of religious festivals or other special occasions. Underlying the system is the notion of ritual purity: Some activities are pure, others not, and the caste hierarchy, based on degrees of ritual purity, is reflected in the division of labour. Ritually pure individuals require the services of impure individuals to perform tasks that would pollute them. Crosscutting this system, which operates at the level of the community, is a wider network that links all members of a particular caste (Jāthi), wherever they live.... Something akin to these two systems may have underpinned the organization of the Harappan state. Local officials and local priests, supplied by the official distribution system, may have provided goods that people required for social, economic, and ritual purposes, in exchange for subsistence products and various types of labour such as craft activities or public building works. Kinship ties could also have resulted in the movement of goods and the supply of foodstuffs between town and country through the medium of pastoral members of the extended family during their seasonal

> movements, and a tithe of these could have been extracted by the state upon their entering or leaving the town or city.[4]

Here, apart from the emphasis on redistribution, Jane McIntosh also emphasizes ritual purity. Thus, in the works of Kenoyer and McIntosh, one finds that words of negative connotation, 'ritual impurity' and 'inequality', mostly define the Jajmāni system. This is understandable given that the most defining work on the Jajmāni system, which has shaped all subsequent studies, was written by William Henricks Wiser (1890-1961), a missionary turned sociologist. This work, published in 1936, remains the basic text most social scientists follow when discussing the Jajmāni system. Though the book is exhaustive and academic, at the same time, it also contains prejudices. Wiser's discussion of the religious philosophy underlying the Jajmāni system is based on 'the Laws of Manu'.

> The Hindu *Jajmāni* system has philosophical and religious sanction in the Laws of *Manu* which have served as guide for the Hindu social and economic organization for almost 2000 years.[5]

Then, on the authority of social scientist Radhakamal Mukerjee, who, in another context, contrasts the mostly 'Dravidian' 'tribal' social organization with that of 'Aryan invaders', Wiser concludes that 'the Hindu Jajmāni System in its purest form was a corruption of the ancient system of 'the custom of communal ownership' directed by the *panchayat*.'[6] He also emphasizes the inherent inequality of the system:

> The individual who profits most from the system is the Brahman.... The one who profits least is the low caste menial.... Equality was not the aim of those who devised the Hindu *Jajmāni* System. 'If Aryans and non-Aryans inter-change their occupations and conduct (the one taking that of the other, there

> is) equality (between them)' (Buhler, *The Sacred Laws of the Aryas*, p. 231. Vol, II, Sacred Books of the East).... And 'finally this system gives rise to what psychologists recognize as "slave-mentality", a mentality that is, reflected in the 'hath jhorke' method of approach, and the deferential attitude, shown by servile castes in the presence of their more favoured *jajmans*'. It leads to a fatalistic conception of life which feeds on superstition and is easily influenced by those who are unscrupulous enough to exploit their ignorance.[7]

Wiser provided colonial descriptions to support his argument on the advantages of the Brahmin and the disadvantages of the 'low caste'. To illustrate the Brahmin profiting from the Jajmāni system, he cited an anecdote by Henry Sumner Maine. It featured a Brahmin who rejected the concept of equality and claimed that 'according to the clear teaching of his religion, a Brahmin was entitled to twenty times as much happiness as anybody else'. Maine believed that 'Indian Aryans had been enfeebled by their intermarriage with India's indigenous population' and he supported 'the old order of the Aryan world'. While in the West, the Aryan institutions of civilization evolved, in India, because of their 'intermarriage with primitive indigenes', this progress was arrested and social institutions were 'in a far earlier stage of growth' unlike their Euro-Aryan counterparts. According to Tony Ballantyne, a cultural historian specializing in the British Empire, 'Maine had depicted India as a stagnant and timeless society, an enduring trope of western representations of India, and communicated this vision to thousands of young men entering the Indian Civil Service.'[8]

To explain the conditions of what Wiser called 'the low caste menial', he referred to William Adam (1796-1891), a Baptist missionary from Britain who journeyed to India. Adam's interactions with the Hindu social reformer-philosopher Raja Rammohun Roy (1772-1833) led him to renounce Trinitarian

Christianity in favour of the Unitarian faith. He also became an abolitionist. Despite these progressive views, Adam harboured a strong prejudice against what he termed the 'idolatry' of Hindus. In 1840, Adam published *The Law and Custom of Slavery in British India*, where he asserted that Hindu law regarded 'the slave as the property of his master, familiarly speaking of this species of property in association with cattle, under the contemptuous designation of bipeds and quadrupeds'.[9]

This statement was influenced by the authoritative work of mathematician and early Indologist Henry Colebrook (1765-1837). It is worth noting that the term 'slaves' referred to individuals who were not necessarily associated with the Jajmāni system. These individuals were often war captives or household attendants. Adam's rigid interpretation of Hindu Dharma Sastras, which are diverse and open to multiple interpretations, was skewed by his view of the *Adscripti Glebae* system. This system bound labourers to land that could be sold along with them, essentially making them a part of the land. All these factors call to question the accuracy of Wiser's injunction regarding slavery from 19th-century English translations of ancient texts in describing the conditions of the 'low castes' in a 1930s North Indian village's Jajmāni system questionable. Nonetheless, it highlights the fact that colonial biases have influenced the principal study of the Jajmāni system.

Despite the oft-repeated negativities of the Jajmāni system, such as the apparent limiting of human mobility and perpetuating hierarchical inequality, it primarily serves as a mechanism for redistribution. The essence of the Jajmāni system lies more in its role as a redistributive mechanism than in its function of enforcing hierarchy. Within a society where ritual purity and hierarchy are instruments of control and regulation, the Jajmāni system emerges as a conduit for the redistribution of not only material resources but also ritual power.

Case for Revaluating Jajmāni System through a Gandhian Framework

Today, with a handful of post-colonial academics delving into the raw data with a rejuvenated perspective, the antiquated perceptions of Indian peasants and the so-called lower castes leading a life of mere subsistence and servitude in pre-colonial Indian hamlets get contested. Historian Prasannan Parthasarathi, in his 1998 work *Rethinking Wages and Competitiveness in Eighteenth-century Britain and South India*, comparing the real earnings of South Indian peasants and their British counterparts in the 18th century, questions the stereotype of Indian farmers as impoverished slave-like labourers. According to his research, South Indian peasants in the 18th century had higher earnings and more financial security than their British counterparts. This was mainly because of the higher productivity of land in South India, which allowed weavers and other artisans to maintain better diets than the average Europeans. More importantly, these farm workers experienced lower unemployment rates due to their superior contractual rights and greater economic power. Interestingly, even agricultural labourers from the so-called outcastes in South India had higher real earnings than English farm labourers.[10] Therefore, far from a fatalistic system, Jajmāni, while being a system with inequality in it, was a far better redistributive system than other contemporary systems. It was also perhaps the longest-surviving system that has existed, with much less violence than other systems.

The word Jajmāni or *Yejmāni* (known in South India) is derived from *Yajña*. The relation between Yajña and Jajmāni systems has not been discussed much. In 1988, German Indologist Bernhard Kölver (1938-2001) expressed surprise at how Yajña metaphor of high philosophy similar to that of the Bhagavat Gitā could permeate villages across India.

> The etymology of *jajmān* leaves no room for speculation: it is derived from *yajamāna-*, the old ritual term denoting the person the priests performed a sacrifice (*yajña-*) for. And indeed there is a patent functional analogy between the *jajmān* and the *yajamāna-*: just as the latter receives priestly services, and pays for them, so does the former receive and pay for the multiple services he needs in his day-to-day existence. But how was it possible for the work of artisans, down to low castes, to be encompassed by a purely priestly term? One could well imagine the Brahmin to have reacted violently when seeing the washerman's services thus being put on a par with his own.... There are, of course, the *Bhagavadgitā* injunctions in praise of disinterested work, of the kind appropriate to one's caste: these at times expressly teach one was to take one's work (*karman-*) as a sacrifice (*yajña-*) (BhG 3.9; 4.23; 4.32 etc.). No doubt this brings us to the very verbal root of the word jalman is derived from, and does so in a context sufficiently similar. Still, one feels it would have taken somebody of Gandhi's stature and bent of mind to impart currencyand wide acceptance to a notion so clearly grounded in contemporary ethics, and to get it transferred to secular contexts like the relation between a patron and the various specialists working for him. If a process like this ever did take place, it has left no trace.[11]

Kölver touched on a core problem that has always puzzled Western anthropologists studying India and Westernized Indians studying Indian society through a colonial lens, even in their post-colonial studies.

Gandhi's Focus on Yajña

Definitely, the Jajmāni system, as it existed in the villages, had negative features. From medieval invasions to colonial impoverishment to the evolution of entrenched vested interests in the village community, all could have contributed to it. However, these negative aspects were not the only defining features of the system. Nor was it conceived with a negative intention of sustaining inequality. Six years before Wiser, Mahatma Gandhi, then incarcerated in the Yeravda Central Prison, had highlighted the Yajña spirit of the Jajmāni system without naming it in a series of letters to Satyagraha Ashram in 1930. He used a few examples of strong real-life characters to explain its positive aspects.

> Yajña means an act directed to the welfare of others, done without desiring any return for it, whether of a temporal or spiritual nature. 'Act' here must be taken in its widest sense, and includes thought and word, as well as deed.... A merchant, who operates in the sacrificial spirit, will have crores passing through his hands, but he will, if he follows the law, use his abilities for service. He will therefore not cheat or speculate, will lead a simple life, will not injure a living soul and will lose millions rather than harm anybody. Let no one run away with the idea that this type of merchant exists only in my imagination.... All of us know of a philanthropic tailor in Wadhwan. I know of one such barber. Every one of us knows such a weaver. And if we go deeply into the matter, we shall come across men in every walk of life, who lead dedicated lives. No doubt these sacrificers obtain their livelihood by their work. But livelihood is not their objective, but only a by-product of their vocation. Motilal was a tailor at first, and continued as tailor afterwards. But his spirit was changed, and his work was transmuted into worship. He began to think about the welfare of others, and his life became artistic in the real sense of the term. A life of sacrifice is the pinnacle of art, and is full of true joy. Yajña is not Yajña if one feels it to be burdensome or annoying. Self-indulgence leads to destruction, and renunciation to immorality.[12]

Mahatma Gandhi was able to rightly identify the spirit of Yajña, which he discerned in individuals of different rural vocations.

While the British anthropologist could see only inequality and fatalism, Gandhi saw a means of self-emancipation. With all its faults, the system has worked to minimize inequality and maximize the redistribution of resources and human productivity.

Yajña, or the Vedic fire ritual, forms an archetypal basis for Indian civilization. It is not just about offering material things to various deities, but it is also the co-creation of the Universe as a continued process. Yajña is a ritual re-enactment of manifestation, sustenance, withdrawal, and restarting of the cycle. The process of manifesting the One into various names and forms and then sublimating all the names and forms until the One remains is enacted in Yajña. It is also performed to propitiate gods who draw their sustenance from the Yajña. According to Indologist Stella Kramrisch, 'the sacred order of the cosmos is enacted on the site of the sacrifice in the rhythm of rites and hymns' and 'are analogous to the rhythms that pervade the cosmos'.[13] Yajña became a very central sacred process to Vedic civilization. The cosmic creation process by Prajāpati got itself embodied not just in the Yajña but also in the activities related to Yajña, and they also became part of the Yajña.

Kramrisch explains:

> The myth and rites of *Prajāpati* in his relation to time were recorded in the *Śatapatha Brāhmana*. The human being as the sacrificer was implicated in the renewal of time by building up the fire altar, the terrestrial homology of the cycle of the year and of *Prajāpati*. By his participation in the piling up of the fire altar, by rites of architecture, the sacrificer recreated the body of *Prajāpati*, who had fallen down in sheer exhaustion after having spent himself into creation. By architectural rites, man participated in the reconstruction of *Prajāpati* and, at the same time, effected his own regeneration.... Creating, *Prajāpati* had dispersed himself into the manifold universe. The breath of life left him, and the gods abandoned him; he asked *Agni*,

> the Fire, to restore him (*ŚB*. 6.1.2.12-13). Hence the gods built up *Prajāpati* and gave him the shape of the fire altar (*ŚB*.6.1.214-18). Brick by brick they built him up in the fullness of a year, the time in which nature renews and spends itself. The building of the altar was a paradigmatic rite in which Prajāpati was recomposed symbolically by the piling up of a structure. As the gods had done first, so man, the sacrificer, was to build up the fire altar as the counterpart of *Prajāpati* (*ŚB*.11.1.8.3). By doing this sacred work, the sacrificer consecrated himself magically, for he meted out the proportions of the altar according to his own measure. The fire altar thus became a work of identification, a homology by sacred, architectural rites, of man and the Creator. Reassembling the fallen, exhausted, dispersed *Prajāpati* by sacred knowledge and sacred work, the sacrificer restored the Creator to pristine totality, to last as long as time lasts in its cycles, of which the year is the unit.[14]

The detailed passage above explains how mythology and ritual work create a space for interpretation that can be applied to all physical work. It highlights the sacralising nature of Yajña, which requires various groups of workers to come together to perform a process. It is possible that Yajña existed in one form or another before it was explained in the *Śatapatha Brāhmana*.

Case for Yajña Value System in Harappan Civilization

Was Yajña present in some form in Harappan civilization? Harappan fire altars has been a topic of debate for quite some time. In his report on the Kalibangan, a Harappan site from Rajasthan, B.B. Lal, an Indian writer and archaeologist (1921–2022), first reported the presence of fire altars used for community rituals and in private houses.[15] Many archaeologists have questioned the interpretation of the structures as fire altars. Even insinuations of ideological vested interest were thrown. Nevertheless, Lal's interpretation of these structures as fire altars has been vindicated to a considerable extent. Archaeologist Shereen Ratnagar, whose work has focused on the Indus Valley civilization, in her work on the political organization of Indus Valley, has this to say about the discovery made by Lal:

> The fire altars consist of a clay lined pit about 75 ´ 55 cm, bearing an upright clay column in the centre, the depression being full of ash, charcoal and terracotta cakes. Thus Lal suggests that fire and water ritual as well as animal sacrifices were conducted in the southern area.... Lal's argument for the ritual and ceremonial function of the southern half of the Kalibangan Citadel is forceful and convincing. It is supported by the location of the Great Bath in the Citadel of Mohenja-daro, and by a curious architectural feature flanking the west wall of the Harappa Citadel.[16]

Since then, in many Harappan sites, fire altars have been discovered. McIntosh writes:

> While water seems to have had a religious significance throughout the Harappan realms, ritual installations involving fire are at present known only from the southern parts, along the Saraswati and in Gujarat. These fire altars were first uncovered at Kalibangan, where one of the platforms in the southern part of the citadel had a row of seven oblong clay-lined pits containing charcoal, ash, and terra-cotta cakes; such cakes were used in kilns to retain heat and perhaps had a similar function in these fire pits. In each pit there was also a cylindrical or faceted clay stele, perhaps representing the lingam (sacred phallus)*. A paved bathing platform and a brick-lined well were associated with these pits. On another platform, a single fire altar was found alongside a rectangular brick-lined pit containing antlers and cattle bones, presumably from animal sacrifices. The use of these pits for making burnt offerings therefore seems a reasonable supposition. There was also a mound with other fire altars to the east of the town. Many of the houses in Kalibangan's lower town are reported to have had a room containing a fire altar, set aside as a domestic shrine. Many Indian houses today

> likewise have their own shrine, where incense is burned and food and flowers are offered to the gods.[17]

Here, a small explanation is in order. Dr McIntosh connects Lingam with the stele of the fire altar and calls it a sacred phallus. One of the earliest debunkers of purely phallic symbolism of Lingam was Swami Vivekananda (1863-1902). In 1900, at the Paris Congress of the History of World Religions, countering German Indologist Gustav Oppert, Śwāmi Vivekānanda associated the emergence of the Lingam concept with the Yupa-Stamba of Yajña. *Udbodhan,* the bulletin of Sri Ramakrishna Mission, had this to report:

> The Swami said that the worship of the Shiva-Linga originated from the famous hymn in the Atharva-Veda Samhitâ sung in praise of the *Yupa-Stambha*, the sacrificial post. In that hymn a description is found of the beginningless and endless *Stambha* or *Skambha*, and it is shown that the said Skambha is put in place of the eternal Brahman. As afterwards the Yajna (sacrificial) fire, its smoke, ashes, and flames, the Soma plant, and the ox that used to carry on its back the wood for the Vedic sacrifice gave place to the conceptions of the brightness of Shiva's body, his tawny matted-hair, his blue throat, and the riding on the bull of the Shiva, and so on – just so, the *YupaSkambha* gave place in time to the *Shiva-Linga,* and was deified to the high Devahood of Shri Shankara. In the *Atharva-Veda Samhita*, the sacrificial cakes are also extolled along with the attributes of the *Brahman.*[18]

Indus Valley civilization was discovered only after more than two decades of the Samadhi of Śwāmi Vivekānanda. Śwāmi Vivekānanda had not only made the association of Yupa-Stambha with Lingam but also pointed out a few more aspects—all of which would, in one way or another, be connected with Harappan religious life.

So, there is a strong case for the very physical Yajña as a significant part of the religious life of Harappan society. However, it is unclear whether the practice of Yajña was accompanied by a social philosophy or if it was a manifestation of a deeper and more ancient worldview that promoted harmony within Harappan society.

In 2002, anthropologist Gregory Possehl (1941-2011) suggested that Indus Valley civilization was 'more corporate than exclusionary' and its peoples 'formed more of a heterarchy than they were a hierarchy.'[19]

Anthropologist Piotr A. Eltsov, in his thesis ('From Harappa to Hastinapura: A Study'), which focusses 'on the continuity of Harappan elements into the later historical culture of India', argues that the same kind of institutions were present in both. He suggests that the emergence of agricultural society was followed by the rise of social systems that sustained Harappan civilization and then the gradual decline of Harappan civilization and its eventual reorganization. Eltsov proposes that this sequence may have been preserved in the Puranic memory, particularly through the concept of Yuga. This Puranic narrative evolved during the early phase of the historical period, separating the Harappan civilization by more than 2,000 years. Yet Eltsov puts forth a strong case for the Puranic Yuga narrative incorporating the historical experiences of Harappan civilizational experience. Based on the narratives of *Vayu Purana* and *Brahmanda Purana*, he considered the formation of this unique Indian civilizational foundation of Hindu society thus:

> The sociocultural ethos of ancient India is formed before the formation of the Harappan Civilization. Like the Treta Yuga, which begins with the transition to agriculture, the ethos of the ancient Indian Civilization is shaped during the Neolithic and Chalcolithic Periods. Rooted in the rural life style, it can be defined by four traits found in the historical narratives of the

Sanskrit Puranas and representing the perspective of historical agents. Modified in the language of contemporary social science, these four traits can be presented as follows:

1. Agricultural economy and predominantly rural lifestyle;
2. A set of orally transmitted sacred and legal codes;
3. An idiosyncratic semi-hierarchical, semi-heterarchical social system based on a set of beliefs and ideological norms rather than on access to the means of production;
4. And a set of ritual and sacrificial practices[20]

Here, we look into the last two features. According to Eltsov, the empirical indication is that 'during the initial stages of urbanization, the social systems of the Harappan and Ganges civilizations shared a similar set of quintessential traits', and to 'pinpoint' these traits, he 'modified' the *varṇāśrama* system and sees it as 'the idiosyncratic, semi-hierarchical and semi-heterarchical social system which is based on as set of beliefs and norms rather than on the access to the means of production'.[21]

He calls this 'idiosyncratic' and 'uniquely South Asian' and 'the foundation of this system was ideational rather than economic'. While refraining from using the terms 'caste' and 'varṇāśrama', he states,

> The subtext or the theoretical premise of using the terms 'caste' or *varṇāśrama* nevertheless deserves attention. Without doubt, the disclosed similarities between the Harappan and Ganges urbanizations – in particular, the role that fortifications played in the solidification of authority and in the formation of territorially bound identities–are indicative of the similar social structures.[22]

With respect to the trait of 'ritual and sacrificial practices', he sees them as

> a set of sacrificial and ritual practices that begin to form possibly prior to the emergence of the Harappan Civilization and continue

> to be shaped and modified throughout the third, second and first millennia BC. There is no need to reiterate the argument of those scholars who believe that the archaeology of the Harappan Civilization provides evidence for the existence of religious practices reminiscent and possibly prototypical of those, exercised in the Vedic and Mauryan India. A variety of shared iconographic motifs, the linga and yoni stones, fire altars and the importance of water have been cited as symbols of religious continuities between the Harappan Civilization and early historical India since the time of John Marshall. Anyone working on the Harappan material today would probably agree that at least some of the traits characteristic of early historical India are indeed present in the Harappan archaeology.[23]

He concludes,

> In summary, I believe the two models of the Indian Civilization extracted above from the Sanskrit Puranas include *Yajña* for good reasons: certain ritual norms are likely to have been developing since the Neolithic or Chalcolithic Periods. The Wasserluxus and prototypal iconography could be the expressions of this development, yet the ideology, ethnicity, religion and language of the people who practices these norms could be very different.[24]

His thesis of the social structure continuing irrespective of whether or not various human groups came inside or went out of India in the past provides a realistic picture of the experience of the social system in India.

This suggests the ability of Yajña to become a substrate-independent archetypal basis of Indian society in its core functional dimension. It has a dynamic hermeneutic space to accommodate future social developments. At its highest conceptual level, Vedic *Yajña* is the recreation of a cosmic process of maintenance of *Ṛta*. And Ṛta also manifests in human society and interactions. Here also, Ṛta should be maintained.

Participating in *Yajña* should accomplish that, making it a tangential proof of what it accomplishes in the transcendental realm. It does that directly by making the entire society with various social groups participate. Religious studies scholar Prof. Pankaj Jain takes the concept from cultural anthropologist Victor Turner (1920-1983) who said that that 'ritual activity, existing as if outside the structures of society, existing in a subjunctive mode of play and pretend, is neither here nor there but is liminal' and applies it to Yajña and concluded that 'the people engaged in grand *Śrauta* rituals may have enjoyed their liminal state during the performance by intermixing of different social groups for several days (and weeks in longer version). This intermixing beyond any social barriers may have, in turn, resulted in sociopolitical coherence in Vedic society'.[25]

Apart from bringing together the different social groups, the Darshana behind Yajña also created the space to transform all activities into the variants of Yajña. The *Yajña Vedi,* a carefully constructed brick altar platform, becomes the basis for the Vastu Purusha Mandala, which is fundamental for construction plans in India. Therefore, construction itself becomes a Yajña and those involved in it become Brahmins performing this Yajña. Similarly, in agriculture, the field itself becomes Prithvi Mandala, a variant of Vastu Purusha Mandala, which, in turn, is the Vedi. Thus, agriculture becomes Yajña. Fine arts, dance, drama, and all other activities become Yajña. This means that a dancer, a carpenter, a farmer, a merchant, a barber, a washerman, a potter, and all other professions can be the Brahmin performers of their Yajña*, and those who utilize their skills and knowledge become yajamāna*. This Yajña archetype behind every vocation has the potential to make all works sacred, and none defiled. This also means that social exclusion and social aristocracy can be challenged by such a value system whenever social stagnation leads them to inhuman proportions.

CHAPTER 5

Revisiting Vedic Society, Its Values, and Vision

The prevailing narrative, both in historical and social science discourse and in a significant portion of the Indian political ideologies, posits that the Vedic religion instituted a birth-based social hierarchy predicated on physical or racial features. This system, purportedly rooted in racial or ethnic discrimination, was allegedly imposed by the Brahmins and Kshatriyas and sanctified by the Vedic religion. Colonial studies of Indian culture largely perpetuated this schema during British rule, and post-independence Indian scholarship, influenced by colonial perspectives, has continued to accept it without much questioning. This chapter seeks to challenge this dominant narrative and argues that the Vedic society was distinct from the values that Vedic Dharma stressed. While the Vedas do reflect the social reality of their time, this chapter posits that the values enshrined in the Vedic texts actively challenged social exclusion and inequality. Central to this dynamic is the presence of multiple frameworks on the origin of a social system within the Vedic texts. In essence, this chapter aims to provide a fresh perspective on the Vedic society, arguing for a more nuanced understanding that goes beyond the conventional narrative of social hierarchy and discrimination.

Vedic Racism and 'Spiritual Fascism'

Consider the following passage:

> Varna generally refers to the appearance of something (its form and colour), and we find the term used with significance in the Rig Veda to differentiate the Vedic Indians, who called themselves 'noble ones' (āryas), from the other peoples they encountered (chiefly the Harappans to begin with).... Not only do they look different (e.g. RV 5.29.10 probably refers to 'noseless' (anāsa), i.e. snub-nosed Dasyus) but they speak and worship differently (e.g. RV 7.6.3, 7.21.5), and therefore unacceptably. Thus it appears that in the beginning var a was a term which had racial, indeed racist, connotations. It heralded a Hindu preoccupation with social and religious hierarchisation based on natural attributes.[1]

The passage was not written by Max Müller in 1853 but by Prof. Julius Lipner of the University of Cambridge in 1994. This is just one of the many examples of how Jāthi-Varnā got a racial interpretation and turned into the foundational basis of Indian society in all disciplines ranging from anthropometry and anthropology to sociology and the study of folklores. However, with the advancement of modern science and archaeology, the concept of race has been categorically disproven, and the thesis has taken a more nuanced form. As recent as 2018, eminent historian Romila Thapar wrote,

> The earliest mention of varna in the Rigveda, is the two-fold *Arya* and *Dasa varna*. The authors of the text see themselves as *Aryas* and see those that differ from them as the Dasas, as the 'Other'—the ones to be excluded from the identity of the *Arya*. The *Dasas* were equal or more in number to the *Aryas*. The term *Arya* is not used in a racial sense but marks a linguistic and cultural differentiation. They are the Aryan-speaking people,

> who are respected for their distinctive culture, all of which allows them to presume superiority over the *Dasas*.[2]

But just a few paragraphs later, we find her very tactfully slipping in the racial aspects of the thesis in a very subtle manner:

> The concept of *varna* has its own history. The literal meaning is colour, or in some senses, cover. It is also used to describe the colours of the day and the night. It could well be symbolic of two moieties where colour is a symbolic separator. Its meaning as colour drew on the reference to the *Dasa* as being *tvacam-krishnam* (dark-skinned). Interestingly the medieval commentator, *Sayana*, does not suggest skin colour, but maintains that it refers to the skin of a demon named *Krishna*. Some physical differences are mentioned but are the subject of scholarly debate. Does 'anas' mean 'without a nose' i.e., snub-nosed, or does it mean 'without a mouth,' i.e., speaking another language.[3]

The basic framework that operated from Max Müller in the mid-19th century to Romila Thapar in the 21st century, is that there was some kind of distinction between two groups, Arya and Dasa/Dasyu. This distinction was either racial or religious and one group discriminated against the other, and Vedas sanctified this discrimination. Coupled with this is the notion of *Puruṣa Sūkta* being the theo-ideological basis of discrimination. Western scholars and Westernized scholars have an obsession with relating social discrimination seen today with *Puruṣa Sūkta*. They combine the Aryan invasion/migration theories with the four categories mentioned in *Puruṣa Sūkta,* and the narrative created is impressive. One such is presented in the book *The Hindus an Alternate History* (2009) by Indologist Wendy Doniger. Though marketed with the line 'an alternate history', it was very much the same colonial racial view of Hindu society that was presented in the book. She wrote:

> The four classes of society come from the appropriate parts of the body of the dismembered Primeval Man. His mouth became the priest (the Brahmin, master of sacred speech); all Vedic priests are Brahmins, though not all Brahmins are priests. His arms were the Raja (the Kshatriya, the Strong Arm, the class of warriors, policemen, and kings); his thighs, the commoner (the Vaishya, the fertile producer, the common people, the third estate, who produce the food for the first two and themselves): and his feet-the lowest and dirtiest part of the body-the servants (Shudras), the outside class within society that defines the other classes.... The fourth social class may have consisted of the people new to the early Vedic system, perhaps the people already in India when the Vedic people entered, the *Dasas*, from a system already in place in India, or simply the sorts of people who were always outside the system. The final combination often functioned not as a quartet but, reverting to the pattern of Arya and Dasa, as a dualism: all of us (in the first three classes, the twice born) versus all of them (in the fourth class, the non-us, the Others).[4]

According to Wendy Doniger, it became the foundational myth of the Brahmin class. This notion of *Puruṣa Sūkta* that it was 'Aryan' and it relegated the non-Aryan Dasas to the lowest sections of the society became a strong polemical weapon of hatred in the hands of ideologues. One such is Kancha Ilaiah. A political theorist who retired as the director of the Centre for Study of Social Exclusion and Inclusive Policy (CSSEIP) at Maulana Azad National Urdu University, Hyderabad, he has written numerous books. He starts by labelling what he calls 'Brahmanism', 'the mother of all parasitic cultures':

> Parasitic needs that are not controlled by labour may become a source of anti-social behaviour. The mother of all parasitic cultures is the culture of Brahmanism. Among the reptiles and insects, parasites look for a strong support base among the

> birds and animals. All parasites perfect the art of deceptivity and construct a permanent support base for themselves. Among humans, the Brahmanic forces constructed parasitism as knowledge, and the mechanism to work out the parasitic processes as culture.[5]

From culture, he moves to psychology. 'Brahmans', because of the unique social environment they developed, also had an 'underdeveloped animal instinct':

> The process of hunting and grazing among animals take place with the individual enterprises of animals, within their broad social collectivity. But Brahmans did not allow any individual enterprise in their own social collectivity. They carried the underdeveloped animal instinct of penguins and sheep into human beings. And that instinct is being sustained by regenerating the same instinct in members of their group from childhood onwards.[6]

The author transitions from psychological categorization to genetic determinism, asserting that 'the Brahmanic childhood formation thus has both genetic and social characteristics of non-transformability.'[7] This narrative of disdain is meticulously constructed, starting from societal aspects (parasitic processes as culture), moving to psychological categorization (underdeveloped animal instinct), and culminating in biological determinism (genetic...non-transformability). The language employed, ranging from 'mother of all parasitic cultures' to 'underdeveloped animal instinct...in members of their group from childhood onwards', bears a striking resemblance to the vitriolic literature disseminated by *Der Stürmer* in Nazi Germany prior to the Holocaust. What exacerbates the situation is that these excerpts are sourced from a book published by the esteemed academic publisher Sage.

The term 'Brahminism' is often portrayed as an entity deserving of such loathing. To achieve this, *Rig Veda*'s *Puruṣa Sūkta* is employed effectively. The author describes 'the essence of Brahmanic life' as being 'against human freedom' and 'structured in spiritual fascism'. According to him, this spiritual fascism can be traced back to 'the first book of the Brahmans—the Rigveda' and is specifically found 'in a section called the *Puruṣa Sūkta* .'

> In other words, it says: the Purush called Brahma created the Brahmans from his mouth, the Kshatriyas from his shoulders, the Vaishyas from his thighs and the Shudras from his feet. This is the theory of the creation of the four varnas. It was in this theory of varna that Hinduism constructed a theory of natural inequality of human beings. This is where spiritual fascism originated.[8]

The preceding exploration illustrates how scholarly interpretations, when intertwined with a particular group of contemporary political ideologies, can surreptitiously morph into a form of not-much-concealed racism, masquerading as social justice. Nevertheless, the examination of such political discourse is not within the purview of this book. The objective here is to uphold an academic perspective, offering a well-rounded and historical comprehension of the place of *Puruṣa Sūkta* within Hindu Dharma.

Dissection of *Puruṣa Sūkta* by Dr Ambedkar

One of the most scholarly and stringent criticisms of *Puruṣa Sūkta* comes from Dr Bhimarao Ramji Ambedkar (1891-1956). In his *Who Were the Shudras*? (1946), he presented perhaps the first holistic socio-historic approach to the hymn. The first thing he pointed out is it is a hymn of cosmogony—not only of the natural universe but also of the social realm:

> The *Purusha Sukta* is a theory of the origin of the Universe. In other words, it is a cosmogony. No nation which has reached an advanced degree of thought has failed to develop some sort of cosmogony.... Cosmogonies have never been more than matters of academic interest and have served no other purpose than to satisfy the curiosity of the student and to help amuse children. This may be true of some parts of the *Purusha Sukta*. But it certainly cannot be true of the whole of it. That is because all verses of the *Purusha Sukta* are not of the same importance and do not have the same significance. Verses 11 and 12 fall in one category and the rest of the verses fall in another category. Verses other than 11 and 12 may be regarded as of academic interest. Nobody relies upon them. No Hindu even remembers them. But it is quite different with regard to verses 11 and 12.... Verses 11 and 12 of the *Purusha Sukta* are, therefore, not a mere cosmogony. They contain a divine injunction prescribing a particular form of the Constitution of society. The Constitution of society prescribed by the *Purusha Sukta* is known as *Chaturvarnya*.[9]

Ambedkar argues that in creating the four classes, *Puruṣa Sūkta* 'stands in complete contrast...with the other parts of the *Rig Veda*'.[10] He also points out that *Puruṣa Sūkta* is not the only account of cosmogony in *Rig Veda*. In the other accounts of cosmogony in the *Rig Veda,* these four classes are not mentioned, despite this social stratification existing at the time of the composition of those cosmogonies. Even concerning the origin of humanity (which Ambedkar calls in this context Indo-Aryans), he points out that the *Rig Veda* contains 'a secular theory'. He notes that *Purusha* is not the only stock simile. In fact, he gives various instances of different types of Brahmins engaged in different works in a sacrifice coming from different parts of the Divine as given in *Hari Vamsa* and points out that here, even thighs are included, but feet are avoided.

Dr Ambedkar puts forward two fundamental theories. One is that there was in Vedic culture (whom he calls Aryan) a strand that did not believe in the divine nature of *Cätur-Varṇa* but saw it as only of secular origin. Second, originally, there were only three Varnas. In support of the former theory, he cites *Vishnu Purāṇa*. According to *Vishnu Purāṇa*, the Cätur-Varṇa system was created by Śaunaka. According to commentator Ratnagarbha, this means his sons became the four Varnas.[11] Dr Ambedkar contrasts this with *Puruṣa Sūkta*:

> (1) One is sacerdotal in colour and character, the other is secular; (2) One refers to a human being Manu as the progenitor, the other refers to God Brahma or Prajapati as the originator ; (8) One is historical in its drift, the other is supernatural ; (4) One speaks of the deluge, the other is completely silent about it ; (5) One aims at explaining the four Varnas, the other aims at explaining the origin of society only.[12]

With respect to his second theory, he quoted the *Śatapatha Brāhmaṇam* (11.1.4.11) and the *Taittirīya Brāhmaṇam* (III.12.9.2), which speaks only of three Varṇas. So Ambedkar concluded

> It consists of an inference from the Rig Veda and two statements from two Brahmanas which in point of authority are co-equal with the Vedas. For both are Shruti both say in definite and precise terms that there were only three Varnas. Both agree that the Shudras did not form a separate and a distinct Vama, much less the fourth Varna. There cannot, therefore, be better evidence in support of my contention that there were originally only three Varnas and that the Shudras were only a part of the second Varna.[13]

In the book, Dr Ambedkar also rejected the formulation of the term 'anāsa' as referring to snub-nosed characterizing another race:

> The term Anasa occurs in Rig Veda V.29.10. What does the word mean? There are two interpretations.... Sayanacharya reads it as an-asa while Prof Max Muller reads it as a-nasa. As read by Prof. Max Muller, it means 'without nose.' Question is: which of the two readings is the correct one? There is no reason to hold that Sayana's reading is wrong. On the other hand there is everything to suggest that it is right. In the first place, it does not make non-sense of the word. Secondly, as there is no other place where the Dasyus are described as noseless, there is no reason why the word should be read in such a manner as to give it an altogether new sense. It is only fair to read it as a synonym of Mridhravak. There is therefore no evidence in support of the conclusion that the Dasyus belonged to a different race.[14]

Here, one should remember that Dr Ambedkar was one of the earliest scholars outside a small group of Vedic scholars to dispute the racial characterization of the term. He did so as early as 1946. Usually the scholars, even those who were historians, had accepted as received wisdom what Max Müller has suggested. But it was highly speculative. Yet it played a decisive role in shaping the colonial ethnography and its effects are felt even today. In 1997, Prof. Thomas Trautmann, an anthropologist from the University of Michigan, wrote extensively about how the entire misreading of Vedas happened, fifty-one years after Ambedkar wrote the book:

> This first effort to find direct evidence of the physical features of the Indian aborigines in the Sanskrit text dating from the time of the Big Bang that brought Indian civilization into existence boiled down to a matter of noses. Max Muller himself later abandoned his own interpretation of the word sipra, so that the evidence as to noses was reduced to a single words (anasa) in a single passage (RV 5.29.10).... But Risley, for quite different reasons, put noses right at the center of his ethnology of India.... In identifying the populations that fall between the extremes it tracks the gradations of the caste system, as Risley says in

> what has become an epigram: 'The social position of a caste varies inversely as its nasal index'.... Risley's conclusion is that 'community of race, and not, as has frequently been argued, community of function, is the real determining principle, the true causa causans, of the caste system' (1891:260).... Race, then, is the true origin of caste and the fictional idiom of its continuing differentiation of units. For Risley, caste is race, in origin and by metaphorical extension.[15]

Despite the matter being resolved, one can observe that a distinguished post-colonial historian like Prof. Romila Thapar subtly reignites the issue, seemingly with the intention of sparking a debate rooted in race. Dr Ambedkar was an angry man. His anger was righteous. Reading a racial conflict would have helped him in terms of socio-political rhetoric. Yet, in his pursuit of truth, he preferred to stand by what he, through his own analysis, arrived at as empirical truth.

According to the theory of Dr Ambedkar, the Vedic society originally contained only three Varṇas known as classes. The Śūdras, who were originally Kṣatriyas of the solar race and the descendants of Vedic king Sudās, had a continuous feud with the Brahmins. In this 'the Brahmins were subjected to many tyrannies and indignities'. As a retaliation, the Brahmins refused to invest the Śūdras with the sacred thread, which led to their social degradation. Once this social space called Śūdras was created for the Kṣatriyas who fell out with the Brahmins, into that space were absorbed the non-Vedic communities as Vedic civilization started spreading.[16] So, to Dr Ambedkar, *Puruṣa Sūkta* was a political revenge within the same Vedic civilization. It was enshrined and became the bane of Hindu society because of its unquestionable acceptance.

Through his analysis, Dr Ambedkar, who had his justifiable anger against Brahmins and the Hindu religion, was able to dismantle several colonial myths. Additionally, he also paved the way for a more comprehensive and holistic analysis of Vedic literature. He demonstrated that the Vedic literature and subsequent Puranic literature have multiple cosmogonies and multiple narratives with respect to the formation of society and even the four Varṇas that are non-offensive and non-hierarchical. His strongest criticism, or as he calls it 'the riddle', was why the Hindu society and lawmakers should adhere and give centrality only to the *Puruṣa Sūkta* , a hymn which, according to Ambedkar, was born out of political malice towards a group of one's people and interpolated into the body of Vedic literature, as the framework to understand the society and for perpetuating ritualistic inequalities.

Prof. Arvind Sharma Highlights Upanishadic Alternative

In an important paper on *Bṛhadāraṇyaka Upaniṣad* and modernity[17], Prof. Arvind Sharma, the Birks Professor of Comparative Religion at McGill University, points out that the alternate 'account of the origin of the four Varnas, which is quite different from the one in (*Puruṣa Sūkta*) and which also like the *Puruṣa Sūkta*, with its interest also historical and etiological, has gone relatively unnoticed'. Historically, the tenth *Mandala* of *Rig Veda* is considered quite later and even here *Puruṣa Sūkta* is considered a still later addition. This would bring it to the time period of 1000 BCE. On the other hand, *Bṛhadāraṇyaka Upaniṣad* is a pre-Buddhist *Upanishad,* which is mostly dated around 800 BCE.

The *Bṛhadāraṇyaka Upaniṣad* explains the formation process of Varṇas in the fourth chapter of its first book, in the verses from 11 to 15. Here, initially, there were only Brahmins. Desiring more completion, they created the Kṣatriyas and then again, the Vaiśyas, still not fully completed, created the Sudras. Then, after the creation of Śūdras, one of the most vital principles of Hindu social life, both secular and sacred, was created: 'He was not yet developed. He created still better form – Dharma. Therefore there is nothing higher than the Dharma. So a weak man controls a strong man by Dharma, just as if by a king.'[18]

The passage ends by saying that 'therefore people desire a place among Gods in Agni and men in Brahman, for by these two forms (per-eminently) Brahma appeared.' This account makes it clear that through dharma, the power structures are not fortified but instead challenged. It asserts that even a common man without any power should be able to challenge these power structures and yet stand protected by dharma 'like a king.'

Prof. Sharma points out that the account in *Puruṣa Sūkta* is more like an established creation—a divinely willed order. As against this, *Bṛhadāraṇyaka Upaniṣad* suggests an evolution. In fact, the very same sequence is also given in *Śatapatha Brāhmaṇa.19*. Prof. Sharma calls this the 'primal egalitarianism' and that of *Puruṣa Sūkta* the 'primal hierarchicalism'. The problem with the *Śatapatha Brāhmaṇa* account, despite it being the same as the one found in *Bṛhadāraṇyaka Upaniṣad,* is that it tries to create a compromise between these two notions, ultimately leading to the justification of inequality. In contrast, this *Bṛhadāraṇyaka Upaniṣad* completely jettisons the *Puruṣa Sūkta* account and makes the 'primal egalitarian' narrative stand alone.

Further, in *Śatapatha Brāhmaṇa*, conflicting versions show ambiguous approaches to the status of Sudras. In one place, it implies that all the four Varṇas, including the Śūdras have the right to partake in *Soma*.[20] In another, it forbids Śūdras from obtaining milk for sacrifice. In Vedic literature itself, we find evidence for Vedic learning to be open for all, as seen in *Yajur Veda*: 'This blessed word of the Veda which I have proclaimed to the public,—to the Brāhmaṇa, to the Kṣatriya, to the *Śūdra*, and the Vaiśya, to the noble and the servant, to the relative and to the non-relative, may make me a favourite of the gods, the reward givers.'[21]

That brings us to the crucial question. What are the values that Vedic literature insists upon? Is it social discrimination and exclusion or social inclusion and a voice against social exclusion? From what has been observed, it is evident that there are verses in the literature that discriminate against the Śūdra. However, they alone cannot be considered as defining characteristics of Vedic literature, let alone its core spirit.

Sarasvatī Comes to the Rescue[22]

On the banks of River Sarasvatī at least four thousand years ago, a scene unfolds as described in *Aitareya Brāhmaṇa*. The rishis were conducting a sacrificial session on the banks of the river and Kavaṣa, the son of Iluṣa (Kavaṣa Ailuṣa), was among them. However, the assembled rishis found his presence disturbing and even disgusting. They said among themselves, 'How should the son of a slave girl, a gamester, who is no Brahmin (*dāsāyaḥ putraḥ kitavo brāhmaṇaḥ*), remain among us and become initiated into all sacrificial rites?' They decide to throw him away. They drove him away into a desert and said that there he would be struck by thirst and would not be able to drink the water of River Sarasvatī (*atrainam pipāsā hantu saraswatyā udakam mā pād iti*). Thus humiliated in mind and left in the desert, afflicted with thirst, in that moment of utter agony, Kavaṣa Ailuṣa becomes a *Kavi*. He who was humiliated as *dāsāyaḥ putraḥ* and as *abrāhmaṇaḥ* became verily a *Mantra Draṣṭā*.

> *Prá devatrá bráhmane gatúr etu apó ácha mánaso ná práyukti*
>
> Translations: The way to the festive speech should go 'god-wards', to the waters, as upon its [own] incentive of the spirit (Laurie L Patton)[23]
>
> Let the path of the Word lead to the godheads, towards the Waters by the working of the Mind. (Sri Aurobindo)[24]

These fifteen verses called the Aponaptrīya (child of the waters) are placed in the tenth *Mandala* of *Rig Veda,* as its thirtieth section. These verses describe how the sacred waters of River Sarasvatī went to him. The waters surrounded him and embraced him (*enam kavaṣam parisasâra*), making the place itself became known as *parisâra*. Now, the rishis who had expelled Kavaṣa Ailuṣa witnessed all these and returned to him. The fifteen verses became an important part of the Vedic Yajña.

The episode of Kavaṣa Ailuṣa holds a special place in the heart of India's cultural heritage. It intertwines the sacred and the mundane, where the life-giving waters of ceremony mirror the celestial waters above us, which when they descend, through agriculture, sustain the individual and the society. This narrative is more than just a memory from the past; it is a powerful statement against social exclusion and marginalization.

It gives voice to those who, like Kavaṣa Ailuṣa, were considered outcasts, known only by their mother's name. The fact that his hymns found their place in the revered tenth *Mandala*, alongside the *Puruṣa Sūkta*, challenges the conventional understanding of what shaped historical Hindu spirituality and society. Prof. Arvind Sharma suggests that *Puruṣa Sūkta* may not be the sole or even the central influence in the Hindu spiritual realm. Combining this with Dr Ambedkar's thesis that *Puruṣa Sūkta* was more political than spiritual and Sharma's idea that Vedic literature presents a more evolutionary social universe rooted in 'primal egalitarianism', we gain a broader perspective. This perspective enables us to understand better the movements towards social emancipation in Hindu society throughout history. It paints a picture of a society continually striving for equality and inclusivity, echoing the sentiments expressed in Kavaṣa Ailuṣa's hymns.

Sarasvatī indeed dispels our ignorance.

CHAPTER 6

Lutheran Buddha and Buddhist Jerusalem

This chapter delves into the colonial re-construction of the image of Buddha. This colonial project was unintentional but had inherent Euro-centric biases, resulting in the creation of a Buddha of ancient India that was more Christological and Lutheran in nature. This reconstructed image was seamlessly integrated into narratives propagated by activists and ideologues during both the colonial and the post-colonial periods in India.

However, this colonial re-construction of history has a darker side, a negative and vitriolic portrayal of Hindu Dharma. Buddhism, as shaped by colonial constructs, positions Hindus as an ignorant populace subjugated by a detestable priesthood. Regrettably, this perspective on Hinduism and Buddhism has been accepted without much scrutiny by Hindus themselves, particularly those who are influential, educated, and belong to the elite class. Buddhism is projected as a beacon of social emancipation, a reform movement against Hinduism and the caste system that evolved into an ethically superior religion fundamentally opposed to Hinduism. Bodh Gayā emerged as a symbol of Buddhist 'othering' of Hinduism, painting it not merely as inferior but as a malevolent other.

This narrative has had profound implications, resulting in significant human tragedies across the expansive Indian subcontinent referred to as South Asia. The chapter delves into these consequences, shedding light on the complex interplay between religion, colonialism, and societal perceptions.

Bhagavān Buddha: Colonial Re-Emergence[1]

In 1831, German orientalist Karl Friedrich Neumann (1793–1870) published a translation of a traditional Chinese Buddhist book. In the preface, he wrote, 'Buddhism is the Lutheranism of the Hindoo church; and the Brahmans were not less cruel than the priesthood of the Catholic church; the reformers of the East were extirpated by fire and sword, like the reformers in the West.'[2]

It was a religion that was like Hinduism in its 'outworks' but 'without that most cruel and abominable invention of the human mind – the infamous system of castes'. This was one of the many early projections of Buddhism into the West. French orientalist-translator Eugène Burnouf (1801-1852) proposed that there was a pure Buddhism that 'originated at some indefinable period and was re-established by the ministry of Gotama Buddha'.[3] In the fervour of the 19th-century colonial mindset and the Western oriental discourse, Buddha's image was passionately sculpted as a Luther-like figure against an oppressive Hindu religion. This portrayal of Buddha in the likeness of Martin Luther achieved two significant objectives in the colonial narrative:

1) It portrayed Protestant reactionaryism as a Buddhist movement, which was embraced by Europe. In contrast, Hindus were perceived to have succumbed to Brahmanism by rejecting this Buddhist reformation.
2) The term 'Brahmanism', coined by colonialists, was envisioned as a corrupt and oppressive religious framework akin to the corrupt medieval Catholic Church. The Brahmins, seen as the agents of Brahmanism, were reimagined as manipulative practitioners of priestcraft, exploiting their positions for personal gain and keeping the masses in ignorance.

The more Buddha is portrayed as a Lutheran figure, the more Hinduism is depicted as an oppressive religion.

John Whitchurch Bennett (1790–1853), a British military officer who briefly served as a magistrate in colonial Sri Lanka, wrote a book in 1843 on the natural resources of the island. Even in such an account, Buddhism was depicted positively as suited to Western sensibilities: 'The religion of Buddha is so extremely inoffensive, the offerings presented by its followers, which consist only of odoriferous flowers, so pure, and the doctrines it inculcates are altogether so humane.'

Proportionately, Hinduism gets demonized. The book calls the Hindu priests 'devil priests'. The 'inoffensive' worship and 'humane' doctrines of Buddhism get 'contrasted with the obscene and sanguinary rites of that of Brahma, which was more to be lamented than otherwise.' Then the book gives a part of a lengthy poem written by one Captain Anderson of 19th infantry:

> The Hindoo's foul idolatry,
> Whose ponderous pyramidal pile,
> What strange disgusting rites defile!
> Where crafty Brahmins guard those shrines
> On which no lively sunbeam shines,
> Where never strangers' searching eyes
> Can pierce their horrid mysteries,
> And where in many a dark recess
> Forms that no language can express,
> Vile beastly idols grin around,
> And grisly monstrous gods abound!
> May never such a horrid creed,
> To Buddha's simple faith succeed.[4]

Then, in 1854, three years before the great Indian uprising, Willian Knighton, who was 'formerly secretary to the Ceylon branch of Royal Asiatic Society' published his two-volume *Forest*

Life in Ceylon' in which he had this to say about how Siddhartha became the Buddha:

> Judging from all that I have read of him, and heard of him from others, who have read more, I should be inclined to give the following explanation of the enigma. He saw Brahmanism in active operation around him, and of all creeds, Brahmanism is the most foul and soul-polluting. The frenzied widow, shrieking on the funeral pile of her husband under the scorching influence of the flames, whilst the ministers of hell around, exhort her to endure, thrust her back if she attempts to escape, and command her to keep her thoughts fixed on heaven; the devotees crackling beneath the wheels of Juggernaut's car, their dying groans drowned in the horrid music of the Brahmans; these, and of rites as bad as these, there is no lack in Hindooism – these destroy the body, but the teaching and example of the diabolical Brahmans, destroy the soul. Sensuality and cruelty go hand in hand in their creed, the one not more refined, though varied in phase and nature, than the other. Gotama saw all this, and a thousand times more than a European public could be told, or would believe.... Cruelty, and the shedding of blood, were the characteristic features of Brahmanism, benevolence, and tenderness for life, were the leading dogmas of Gotama.[5]

Prof. Philip C. Almond, in his work on how British colonialism discovered and constructed the image of Buddha, points out:

> Alexander Cunningham in 1854 looked upon the Buddha as 'a great social reformer who dared to preach the perfect equality of all mankind, and the consequent abolition of caste, in spite of the menaces of the most powerful and arrogant priesthood in the world'.... Linus Brockett in 1861, William Sargant in 1864, The Intellectual Observer in 1867, Otto Kistner in 1869, and Richard Armstrong in 1870, all saw Buddhism as a protest against a despotic, tyrannical, oppressive, and corrupt Brahmanical priesthood, and the institution of caste that it supported.[6]

It should be remembered that Alexander Cunningham was the first director general of the Archaeological Survey of India. He held a very low opinion of Indian art and expressed contempt for the 'inanities and bestial obscenities' of Hindu temples. According to him, the Indian art of sculpture was derived from the Greeks and during the Buddhist Mauryan period, with the Greek and half-Greek rule of Indo-Scythians, India had 'the art of sculpture, or certainly of good sculpture' and 'retained its superiority' and 'it deteriorated more and more the further it receded from the Greek age, until its degradation culminated in the wooden inanities and bestial obscenities of the Brahmanical temples'.[7] He visited Gaya in 1801 and popularized the idea of Brahmins desecrating the spiritually and aesthetically superior originally Buddhist sites by converting them into Hindu shrines, particularly with 'Lingams'. This would ultimately reach genocidal proportions, which will be seen later. Max Müller also deserves a special mention as he wrote a review of a publication of the life and travels of Chinese Buddhist monk 'Hiouen-thsang' by one Stanislas Julien in the *Times* (April 1857). Later, with additional material, this was published as a book, *Buddhism and Buddhist Pilgrims: A Review*. In the article, he formulated his favourite thesis of a guided evolution of religions in which Vedas occupied an infantile stage:

> Children cannot think the thoughts of men, and the poets of the Veda could not speak the language of Aristotle.... Names were stammered forth in anxious haste, and no single name could fully express what lay hidden in the human mind and wanted expression, the idea of an absolute, and perfect, and supreme, and immortal Essence. Thus a countless host of so-called gods was called into being, and for a time seemed to satisfy the wants of a thoughtless multitude.[8]

As against this, Buddha and his religion functioned as a 'reaction against' and catalysts for the later evolution of 'Brahmanism'. Buddha was universally open to all sections of society.

> Buddhism, as a religion and as a political fact, was a reaction against Brahmanism, though it retained much of that more primitive form of faith and worship. Buddhism, in its historical growth, presupposes Brahmanism, and however hostile the mutual relation of these two religions may have been at different periods of Indian history, it can be shown, without much difficulty, that the latter was but a natural consequence of the former.[9]

Buddha was open to all, irrespective of caste, economic status, and/or intelligence:

> What was original and new in Buddha was his changing a philosophical system into a practical doctrine; his taking the wisdom of the few, and coining as much of it as he thought genuine for the benefit of the many; his breaking with the traditional formalities of the past, and proclaiming for the first time, in spite of castes and creeds, the equality of the rich and the poor, the foolish and the wise, the twice-born' and the outcast.... A Brahman was born, nay, twice-born. He could not be made. Not even the lowest caste, that of the Sûdras, would open its ranks to a stranger. Here lay the secret of Buddha's success. He addressed himself to castes and outcasts.[10]

Max Müller, however, distinguished between the superficial notion of Buddha being 'atheistic' against Vedic deities and a deeper philosophical 'atheism' of Buddha, which was more related to Sāṃkhya Darshana:

> This doctrine of salvation has been called pure Atheism and Nihilism, and it no doubt was liable to both charges in its metaphysical character, and in that form in which we chiefly

> know it. It was Atheistic, not because it denied the existence of such gods as Indra and Brahma. Buddha did not even condescend to deny their existence. But it was Atheistic, like the Sânkhya philosophy, which admitted but one subjective Self, and considered creation as an illusion of that Self, imaging itself for a while in the mirror of nature. As there was no reality in creation, there could be no real Creator.[11]

In the West, this comparison was only critically and cautiously made by Christian theologians because of what they perceived as the atheistic tendencies of Buddhist teachings. But it was different for evangelicals working in India. Müller himself would observe in 1869 that Catholic and Protestant missionaries vied with each other in their praises of the Buddha.[12]

This colonial image of Buddha later fed into two important streams, both having some very significant similarities. One is the anti-Brahmin movement and the other is the Singhalese resurgence.

Buddhist 'Jerusalem's' Colonial Crusaders versus the Polluting Hindu 'Others'

As mentioned above, in 1801, Alexander Cunningham visited Bodh Gayā. He had nothing but contempt for what he considered a 'Brahmanical' religion, i.e., Hinduism. In 1879, a poetry book was published in England, which would soon become a major hit not only in Britain but also in most parts of Asia. *The Light of Asia* or *The Great Renunciation (Mahâbhinishkramana)* was written by Sir Edwin Arnold (1832-1904). The book-length poem was built on the 'positive Christological depictions of Buddha that had emerged among the second and third generations of missionaries in Ceylon and Bengal'. The poem was translated into many languages, including Bengali (1885), Marathi (1894), Tamil (1898) and Telugu (1902). Kavimani Desiga Vinayakam Pillai, a poet well known for his very popular poems for children, did a very lyrical translation of the poem in 1941. An excerpt from it became, for a considerable period of time, a part of Tamil language primers for children. It was also translated into Japanese and Thai. Prof. Nile Green, a historian of South Asian religions at UCLA, suggests that while it would be 'difficult to statistically verify', Arnold's *Light of Asia* was probably the most widely translated work on Buddhism into Asian languages during the late 19th and the better part of the 20th century.[13]

In 1886, Edwin Arnold visited Bodh Gayā and wrote a series of articles about his visit in the *London Daily Telegraph*. Even as he was thrilled to be 'the spot, most dear and divine, and precious beyond every other place', which would become 'the Mecca, the Jerusalem, of a million Oriental congregation', he 'was grieved to see Mahratta peasants performing 'Shraddh' in such a place and thousands of precious ancient relics of carved stone inscribed with Sanskrit lying in piles around.'[14] Was Edwin Arnold only motivated by his Buddhist devotion? After visiting Gaya, he wrote to Sir Arthur Gordon, who was the administrator of the colonial Government of Ceylon: 'I am venturing to suggest to you a government act which would be historically just, which would win for you the love and gratitude of all your Buddhist populations and would reflect enduring honour upon your administration.'[15]

Gayā, the most sacred place of the Buddhists world over, was 'occupied by a College of Sivite priests who worship Mahadeva there and deface the shrine with emblems and rituals foreign to its nature'. As the land belonged to the colonial Government of India, he suggested that 'there would be little difficulty after proper and friendly negotiation in procuring the departure of the Mahant with his Priest and the transfer of the temple and its grounds to the guardianship of Buddhist monks from Ceylon'.[16] The fascination for Western Indology constructed Buddhism, colonial administrative interest and eliciting the personal glory of colonial administrator converge here, creating an imagery of 'Buddhist Jerusalem' being liberated by enlightened colonialists from the clutches of idol-worshipping heathens in their own land. This is despite the fact that both the colonial administration and later the Prince of Siam (current Thailand) had expressed their appreciation of Mahant's cooperation with the restoration and conservation efforts at the Museum and the devotion with which the site was maintained, respectively.[17] There was also a very effective narrative being sown here, which gave the Hindus the power to make the '*mlecchas*' in their own land by the sheer power of academic control of the discourse of history. Scholar of comparative religions Jacob Kinnard brings out this aspect of the 'pro-Buddhist/anti-Hindu dichotomy' created by the Orientalists:

> Furthermore, because Bodhgayā represented the fount of Buddhism, what the second-century author Aśvaghoa referred to as 'the navel of the world', and what Arnold celebrated as the Buddhist Mecca and Jerusalem, the presence of the Hindu Other was all the more offensive.... Thus the Śaivas who effectively owned the temple, and the Vaishnavas who came there to worship, were portrayed by the non-Indian scholars who opined on the matter as outsiders—*mlecchas*—in their own country, polluting the birthplace of Buddhism.[18]

Into this arena entered Henry Steel Olcott (1832–1907), an American military officer turned co-founder of the Theosophical Movement along with Helena Blavatsky. After being spurned by Swami Dayananda Saraswati of Ārya Samāj because of the Theosophical preponderance towards occultism, the couple converted to Theravada Buddhism after arriving in Ceylon in 1880. That was a time when Sri Lankan indigenous traditions, including Buddhism and Hinduism, were facing the onslaught of state-aided proselytizing war against indigenous spiritual traditions. In fact, Sri Lankan Buddhists and Hindus were required by the colonial State to register their marriages in a Church to be considered legitimate. With a missionary zeal, Olcott founded no less than 460 Buddhist schools in the island nation. Though he sided with Buddhism in the war of colonial proselytizing against Buddhism, Olcott was deeply a 'Victorian American'. As Joseph Cheah, specializing in theology and philosophy, points out, his Buddhist conversion did not necessitate 'a wholesale break or complete disavowal from his Victorian cultural background of equating rituals and cultural practices of Asian Buddhism with superstitions'.[19] Traditional Buddhism began to be supplanted by a colonial-discourse-constructed textbook Buddhism.

Anagārika Dharmapāla (1864-1933), originally named Don David Hewavitharana, was born when Buddhists were required to adopt Christian names and convert to Christianity to solemnize their weddings. This practice continued until 1884 when Olcott intervened and put a stop to it. Hewavitharana received a Methodist Christian education, but it was through Olcott that he discovered Buddhism. Becoming a kind of born-again-Buddhist, this zealous and intelligent young man joined Olcott's mission. Don David Hewavitharana emerged as Anagārika Dharmapāla, a champion of Buddhism. In 1886, he resigned from his government service and joined the Theosophical Society as the General Secretary of its Buddhist Section and Assistant Secretary of the Buddhist Defense Committee.

The year 1891 turned out to be a crucial year in the life of Dharmapāla. In January of that year, he visited Bodh Gayā with Olcott. There he stayed till March. He later wrote that he made a vow to 'liberate' Bodh Gayā, even though the Hindu Mahant who possessed the temple did not obstruct the Buddhists. In fact, Dharmapāla himself observed that Mahant was 'a genial man of liberal disposition'. In October that year, Olcott and Dharmapala were at Calcutta, and the latter gave his first English lecture, titled 'Kinship between Hinduism and Buddhism'. Afterwards, they travelled to Japan, where Dharmapāla suffered from rheumatic fever and, while recuperating, read Edwin Arnold's *Light of Asia* which created in him an epiphany. In 1892, he founded the *Maha Bodhi* journal and by 1893 he had become so famous that he went to the World Parliament of Religions in the United States. On the way, he landed in London as the guest of Sir Edwin Arnold. It is speculated that this meeting triggered Dharmapala's latent aversion to Hindu-misia into full-blown hatred.

After returning to India, Dharmapāla became quite aggressive in the reclamation of Bodh Gayā and getting the Mahant out. He even started making remarks that almost every Hindu temple could be claimed as Buddhist:

> As for the images of Hindu gods and goddesses there is hardly a figure which the Hindus could identify as belonging to them exclusively. The image of Vishnu and Brahma and other gods are of Buddhist origin, for the sculptured images have on each of their foreheads a *basso relievo* figure of the Buddha. In the Ellora and other caves wherein the images of Vishnu, Indra etc., are found this characteristic basso relievo figure of Buddha is invariably found carved on their foreheads.... Priest-craft has been busy in converting purely Buddhist statues into the Puranic Hindu pantheon.[20]

So now, not only Bodh Gayā but even Ellora could be claimed as Buddhist.

In April 1894, Dharmapāla wrote to the British Government to evict the Mahant and transfer the temple to the Buddhists. The reply he received from the Lieutenant-Governor of Bengal conveyed to him that there was 'perfect freedom of worship for all Buddhists at Bodh Gayā and that any well-grounded complaint that difficulties were imposed would meet with ready attention and redress at the hands of the Bengal Government.'[21] The following January, Dharmapāla and others removed the tilaks and other vestments from a statue of Buddha in the shrine, offering worship to it as Buddha. The Mahant did not object to this. On the morning of 25 February 1895, Anagarika entered the Maha Bodhi temple and placed a Japanese Buddhist statue in the shrine, leading to a court case at Calcutta High Court. Olcott cooperated with Dharmapāla in this and obtained him 'excellent legal representation'. The Calcutta High Court gave its judgment on 22 August 1895. The court observed that the Buddhist nature of the temple had never been questioned by the Mahant, nor had he or his subordinates ever obstructed or disturbed Buddhist worshippers:

> It may be conceded that the Mahabodhi temple, which is very ancient and very sacred to Buddhists, was a Buddhist temple; that, although it has been in the possession of Hindu Mahants, it has never been converted into a Hindu temple in the sense that the Hindu idols have been enshrined or orthodox Hindu worship carried on there, and that Buddhist pilgrims have had free access and full liberty to worship in it. It does not appear that any hindrance was ever offered to them or that any complaints were ever made by them, and, before the occurrence in question, there is no instance of any disturbance between the Buddhist worshippers and the Hindu Mahants or their subordinates, in regard to their respective rights.[22]

In 1904, Dharmapāla had a disagreement with Olcott and campaigned to remove the term 'Theosophical' from the Theosophical Buddhist Society of Ceylon. Despite this disagreement, when he founded Sinhala Bauddhaya in 1906, he was leveraging the infrastructural and ideational strength that Olcott had created.[23]

This also marked the beginning of the Buddhist-Singhalese nationalism as a religion-fuelled movement. Dharmapāla succeeded in transforming 'the pluralist indigenous tradition of his new-found faith into an ethnocentric myth which proclaimed Sinhalese racial superiority' and this was 'imbued with the Aryan mythologies of superior and inferior races so prevalent at the turn of the century and latent in Theosophy'.[24] As a result, a martial Buddhist identity was formed that moved from offering resistance to colonial proselytization to demeaning the non-Buddhist 'other'.

Dharmapāla seemed to alternate between mellowing down, appealing to the Hindu-Buddhist common family fraternity, while at the same time, asserting not only the superiority of Buddhism but also the viciousness of caste-ridden Hindu religion under Brahmins. The *Maha-Bodhi* journal appealed to the Khilafat spirit of the Indian National Congress with a watered-down veiled threat:

> What Mecca is to Mohamedans, what Jerusalem is to the Christians and Jews, the Maha-Bodhi Temple at Buddha Gaya is to the Buddhists. Therefore with a view to restore the lost religious treasure of the Buddhists it is highly appropriate and advisable that steps should be taken to give to the Buddhists what is due to their religion. Just as the question of Khalifat and the Muslim holy place is likely to awaken the true national religious sentiments of our Musulman brethren the question of Maha Bodhi Temple is of no less significance and religious importance to Buddhists.

In 1923, Dharmapāla spoke about the unity of Hinduism and Buddhism, but it seems like this was only a temporary strategy to use Indian nationalist feelings for the cause of Bodh Gayā. He expressed this sentiment most strongly during his address at the 7th annual session of the Hindu Mahāsabha held at Benares in 1923. The session was presided over by Pandit Madan Mohan Malaviya. In his address, Dharmapāla said:

> The Buddhists held Benares as sacred and everlasting 'Achala-chaitya'. Buddha preached his doctrine of love in Benares. It was believed that Maitreya would soon be born in Benares.... 400 millions of people were worshipping Buddha. They were all Hindus, (cheers). Some might call them un- Aryans ('no', 'no',) but Buddhists crossed the seas, taking Hindu civilisation with them to Japan and China and made them Aryans. He said, 'I am an Aryan. My forefathers came from Bengal.' The Japanese called themselves Aryans. The speaker was anxious to unite Buddhists? and Hindus, the two great families together, ('hear, hear.').[25]

Although Hindu Sanghaṭanists (proponents of Hindu socio-organisational consolidation) were willing to compromise with Dharmapāla, the orthodox sections of Hindu society stood their ground. However, the Hindu Mahāsabha continued with its pan-Hindu agenda, which encompassed Buddhists and other India-born religions in its Hindu identity. During the 16th session of Hindu Mahāsabha, Buddhist monk Ottama Bhikku was elected as its President. By 1935, Hindu Mahāsabha declared that it 'stood up for the Buddhist cause' with respect to the Bodh Gayā issue.[26]

Even as Hindu advocates of pan-Hindu unity in Hindu Mahāsabha were making such conciliatory efforts, the very same year Dharmapāla made his plea for pan-Hindu unity from the Hindu Mahāsabha platform. However, his *Maha Bodhi* journal published articles and speeches that vilified Hinduism through the stereotyping of Brahmins. Barrister S.C. Mookherjee, who was the Vice President of the Maha Bodhi Society, had this to say in his paper read at the first Buddhist convention:

> The decadence which spread in India throughout the Post-Buddhistic period in the Hindu principalities which came into existence gave rise to another culture—the Brahmanic culture which drove out Buddhistic culture from the land.

> This Brahmanic culture triumphed in India because of the Mussulman conquest.... But considering India's own home troubles exemplified now in the Brahmin and non-Brahmin question dominated by the disruptive Islamic and Christian forces and India's troubles abroad exemplified in the fact that Indians now the products of purely Hindu culture are looked down upon throughout Europe, America, South Africa and Australia and Japan, should not Indians throw off their narrow Brahmanic culture and adopt the broader Buddhistic culture? Brahmanic culture is essentially conservative to say the least of its defects. It abhors proselytising whereas Buddhistic culture is world-wide in its catholicity.[27]

One can see the anxiety in Mukherjee's speech to gain respectability in the eyes of the colonial masters. Only a month after Dharmapāla's speech at the Hindu Mahāsabha convention, *Maha Bodhi* published an article that praised Mrs Mary Mikahala Foster of Honolulu (1844–1930), the first convert from Hawaai to Buddhism, for her philanthropic contributions. However, in the same article, published in *Maha Bodhi* she launched a ballistic attack on Hinduism.

Exalting Buddhism, the article constructs a religious history where Vedic religion is priestcraft while Judaic religion is replete with immoral prophets. A Hindu gets converted to a 'Semitic' religion and becomes a cow-eater. Brahmin tyranny is the reason for that. Then the article places the negative features of colonial government itself at the doorsteps of Hinduism. The British, when they read the translations of 'Brahmin law-givers', became like them. Brahmanism corrupted the British to become exploiters from the original benign empire builders they were!

> The only religion that teaches a purifying morality is that which was proclaimed by the Blessed One. The religion of the Vedas was only for the high born, the low born was not allowed to listen to the Vedic mantras. The sacrifice of innocent animals was part

> of the early Vedic religion. The Brahmans who belong to the *agnihotri* class were very fond of beef. The early Brahmans ate beef and drank wine and went after other women.... The religion of the Semitic races that had their birth in Arabia were for the nomadic barbarian. The older religion made God a beef eating, wine drinking personality, whose command was to kill them that did not accept the ordinances enunciated by his prophets. The prophets were of the immoral type.... Buddhism teaches mercy, compassion, and love to animals as well as human beings, while Muhammadanism Saivism and Christianity, preach a contrary doctrine. They destroy the characteristic of mercy from the heart of the adult and the child.... To the arrogant haughty brahman the human being who belongs to a lower caste is a repulsive creature.... A more bigoted, conceited class of people does not exist than the priestly class of Brahmans, Love they have not; they will follow the code of some ancient antiquated law giver who laid down cruel laws to keep the power in the hands of the Brahmanical hierarchy. The code of laws promulgated by the Brahmanical law givers have been translated into English by Oriental scholars and published by the Secretary of State for India under the editorship of Max Muller. These laws have become now the inheritance of the British bureaucrat, who after studying them think like the Brahman, and begins to hate the dark complexioned races in all lands. The haughty spirit now being shown by the British was entirely unknown in the early days of the establishment of British power in India.[28]

The passage, though unattributed, appears to have been written by none other than Anagarika Dharmapāla himself. The bundling of 'Muhammadanism Saivism and Christianity' together is a telling sign. While Christianity was actively proselytizing in Sri Lanka, poaching into Buddhist and non-Christian populations, with covet and open colonial State support, definitely Hindu Saivaite and mostly Sri Lankan Muslim populations were not engaging in conversion at that time. Yet this bundling shows the Sri Lankan 'other' of Buddhism, a tell-tale sign that Anagarika wrote it. The passage provides the distilled essence of the 'othering' that neo-Buddhist doctrine held.

In independent India, the first prime minister Pandit Jawaharlal Nehru had a mindset that inherited the Western Indological constructs of positively rational and ethically superior Buddhism and unhistorical, superstitious, priest-craft-ridden Hinduism. Nehru's fascination for Buddha derived from Edwin Arnold, even at a very young age. He found Asiatic traditional Buddhism wanting when compared to the West-constructed image of Buddhism, which he took as authentic:

> When I visited countries where Buddhism is still a living and dominant faith, I went to see the temples and the monasteries and met monks and laymen, and tried to make out what Buddhism had done to the people.... There was much I did not like. The rational ethical doctrine had become overlaid with so much verbiage, so much ceremonial, canon law, so much, in spite of the Buddha, metaphysical doctrine and even magic. Despite Buddha's warning, they had deified him, and his huge images, in the temples and elsewhere, looked down upon me and I wondered what he would have thought Many of the monks were ignorant persons, rather conceited and demanding obeisance, if not to themselves then to their vestments.... But I saw much also that I liked. There was an atmosphere of peaceful study and contemplation in some of the monasteries and the schools attached to them. There was a look of peace and calm on the faces of many of the monks, a dignity, a gentleness, an air of detachment and freedom from the cares of the world.[29]

He even unconsciously looked down upon non-Buddhist Hindu art while having a fascination for the image of Buddha:

> I know nothing about art, eastern or western, and am not competent to say anything about it.... The Buddha statue at Anuradhapura in Ceylon moved me greatly and a picture of it has been my companion for many years. On the other hand

> some famous temples in South India, heavy with carving and detail, disturb me and fill me with unease.[30]

This Nehruvian fascination for Buddhism had a subtle pro-Theravādin bias to it. This also helped in the exclusive Buddhist brand building of Bodh Gayā by the Government of India itself. Yet the presence of Mahant as the owner and the Hindu worship could not be done away with. In 1949, the state of Bihar passed 'the Bodh Gaya Temple Act (1949)' in which the temple complex management was brought under a committee comprising four Hindus and four Buddhists, with the chairman being the ninth member who had to be a Hindu. In 2013, the Bihar government changed this and made a provision that the chairman could be of any religion.

Here are some significant historical facts. Bodh Gayā was a sacred place even before the arrival of Buddha. Robert DeCaroli, a historian of early Buddhism, shows an interesting continuity in the Buddhist narrative and the pre-Buddhist 'Brahamanical' traditions. He states:

> Although Bodh Gayā is well recognized as an important Buddhist site, it is worth considering this importance in relation to Gayā's role as a Hindu sacred center. In recent centuries an estimated 80,000 Hindus have travelled every year to Gayā, located a few miles from the Buddhist sacred center at Bodh Gayā, in order to perform the śrāddha rites intended to grant emancipation to dead ancestors.... More specifically, the 'special sanctity' of the site attracted 'Sakyamuni to the outskirts of Gaya where he engaged in meditation that resulted in the attainment of Buddhahood.'[31]

He draws a connection between the story of Sujāta offering food to Buddha, as told in the earliest biographies of Buddha, and the śrāddha ritual. Meanwhile, another scholar of the Buddhist tradition, Matthew Sayers, while questioning the pre-Buddhist śrāddha at Gaya, nevertheless points out that its sanctity predates Buddha's arrival or perhaps caused Buddha's arrival there:

> [T]he analysis of (Buddhist) literary references suggests that Gaya was in the time of the Buddha a sacred place of some significance, probably due to its ritual association with purificatory baths. This also suggests that the Buddha may have been attracted to Gaya because of its general sanctity and its reputation as a place frequented by ascetics. The Mahāvagga also supports this argument by highlighting the presence of fire-worshipping ascetics, the Kaśyapa brothers, who lived in this region.[32]

Chinese Buddhist pilgrim Faxian (Fa-Hien) visited India in the early 5th century CE and referred to the Gayā territory as *Brahmayoni,* which today is the name of a mount.[33] Gupta emperor Samudra Gupta, a ruler from the Vedic tradition, allowed the Sri Lankan ruler to build the Bodh Gayā Buddhist temple.[34] Xuanzang or Hiuen Tsang, a 6th-century Buddhist pilgrim from China, mentioned in his pro-Buddhist pilgrim chronicles that a small temple at Gaya built by Ashoka was later enlarged by a Brahmin 'who was not a believer in the law of Buddha, and sacrificed to Mahesvara'. This Brahmana had a brother. The elder one built the Vihara and the younger one built the tank.[35] Thus, Gayā was a centre of pilgrimage from pre-Buddhist times and throughout the classical post-Buddhist times Hindus visited the place for a longer period than Buddhists, but Buddhism contributed significantly to increase the sanctity of Gayā.

The site was attacked during the Islamic invasion. The number of monks living there had dwindled because of repeated Islamic invasions. Archaeologist Abdul Quddoos Ansari, in his *Archaeological Remains of Bodhgaya*, now made famous by Belgian Indologist Koenraad Elst, has this to say about the Brahmins' role during these tumultuous times:

> The iconoclastic fury of Islam must have [had] a terrible effect on the shrines of the Gaya region, and particularly on Buddhism, with the result that a time came when, there being no Buddhists to look after their own shrines and worship at Bodh Gaya, the Brahmins had to do their work even by going [outside] their jurisdiction.[36]

Perhaps the last time the Hindus saved Bodh Gayā was when Mahant stood up against Dharmapāla's transgression in 1895. As historian Prof. Sarao points out, had Dharmapāla met with no resistance from Mahant, he would have taken complete control of the temple complex. He would have forbidden not only non-Buddhist Hindus but also non-Theravadin Buddhists from entering the Bodhi complex.[37]

Overall, the Bodh Gayā confrontation became the symbol of this inferiorized othering of Hinduism. The 'anti-Hindu/ pro-Buddhist dichotomy' was more a creation through 'the opinions of a select group of mostly British Orientalists who were engaged in a prolonged and diffused anti-Hindu polemic'. Since then, whenever it has been manifesting, as through Dharmapāla's confrontation in 1895, 'at the center of this discourse is not, in fact, the axis mundi of Bodhgayā, but rather a vilified Hindu other'.[38]

This would resurface time and again in post-colonial South Asia in both India and Sri Lanka, with violent potential and disastrous consequences. In India, this would make it possible for the neo-Buddhist Ambedkaraite movement to take on a serious hate campaign against Hinduism. Just as how British Orientalism made the pro-Buddhist/anti-Hindu dichotomy an effective tool in making 'outsiders' out of Hindus in their own land. Similarly, the 'Dalit discourse' during the Ayodhya movement of Hindus started a movement to reclaim Bodh Gayā. They demanded an all-member Buddhist committee. Activists of the movement beat up the Brahmin priests of the complex and wanted all Hindu symbols removed. In the larger political discourse, every atrocity, every violence, every conflict related to caste would be blamed on Brahmanical Hinduism. Increasingly, Buddhism started getting mapped to a separate ethnic identity (the so-called non-Aryan) and a separate religious identity in which a very Protestant-like constructed Buddhism is pitted against the perceived and real negativities of age-old Hindu society with which Hindu Dharma gets essentialized. Academicians like Romila Thapar supply covet academic justification to openly hateful and even historically absurd toxic ideologies like the ones spread by Kancha Ilaiah.

Bodh Gayā can thus be considered one of the main fountainheads of the genesis of the modern deep schism between Buddhist Hindu identities with particularly far-reaching consequences for the Tamil (mainly Hindu) minority in the island nation of Sri Lanka. A reinvented Buddhist identity, shaped through colonial Indological frameworks, served as its religious fulcrum in the Singhalese racial political revival. This was inevitably accompanied by an anti-Hindu sentiment, which became a significant, albeit not exclusive, catalyst for what would become in post-colonial Sri Lanka, a protracted civil war. The conflict was characterized by numerous anti-Tamil pogroms, military aggression and abuse against Tamil civilians, and suicide bombings orchestrated by the Liberation Tigers of Tamil Eelam (LTTE) targeting Singhalese civilians and leaders. The conflict further escalated with the assassination of a former Indian Prime Minister on Indian soil by an LTTE suicide bomber, the recruitment of child soldiers by the LTTE, and their use of Tamil civilians as human shields. The Singhalese army's actions included aerial bombing of civilian targets, including designated safe zones, systematic sexual violence, and the execution of not only surrendered Tamil fighters but also civilians. The conflict culminated in the infamous Mullaivaikal Holocaust of 2009, which resulted in the massacre of over

30,000 Tamils, predominantly Hindus. This event underscores the devastating human cost of this conflict.

Anti-Brahmin movements in India (particularly Tamil Nadu and Andhra) under the ideologues like E.V. Ramasamy ('Periyar' for Dravidianists) and Kancha Ilaiah do show the potential to move towards such a violent elimination of Brahmins or whoever deemed 'Aryan', with a doublespeak of 'eradicating Sanatana Dharma.' In both discourses, Hinduism is depicted as appropriating Buddhism and destroying Buddhism.

How true is this image of Buddha as a social emancipator that colonial Indology created? That shall be seen in the next chapter.

CHAPTER 7

Bhagavān Buddha, His Dhammā, and Its Impact

In this chapter, we shift our focus from the previous discussions and delve into the profound teachings of Buddha. Our exploration centres on Buddha's perspective, if any, on 'Cätur-Varṇyaṁ', a term denoting a four-tiered social hierarchy based on birth, believed to be deeply rooted in Indian society. Buddha, the founder of the path to enlightenment, challenged the Brahmins' perceived monopoly and denounced animal sacrifices. He reinterpreted the Vedic Yajñá, diminishing its significance as a social process model. As Buddhism transformed into an institutionalized religion with royal support, it profoundly influenced the Indian social structure. It planted the seeds for viewing occupations as either noble or defiled, inadvertently hastening the institutionalization of untouchability. This influence extended beyond India into Myanmar (then Burma), Sri Lanka, and Japan. However, colonial interpretations often associated Jāthi and Varṇā solely with Hinduism and viewed Buddha as a Christological or Lutheran figure. This led to these significant developments often being overlooked in conventional views of Indian history.

Varṇā-Jāthi and Buddhist Worldview

Even during the colonial Indological phase of the reconstruction of the image of Buddha as a rationalist and social reformer of a Lutheran type of Christological figure, there were scholarly dissenting voices. They questioned whether Buddha really rebelled against the existing social conditions. Was he against the Chātur-Varṇa or the principle of the four-fold division of the society? One of the earliest and most significant challenges to this Western Indological characterization of Buddha came from Thomas William Rhys Davids (1843–1922), a British Buddhologist who was one of the most scholarly authorities on Buddhism of that time. Despite working within the framework of the 'Aryan race' and the usual Victorian prejudices against 'Brahmanism' as priestcraft, Davids still found the anti-caste-rebel image of Buddha problematic. This was because, in his view, the caste had not yet solidified during Buddha's time:

> There was no caste in India, in those days, in the sense in which that word is now used. There were social grades, technically called Colours, the boundary lines of which were not always or strictly observed. There where restrictions as to intermarriage, and as to eating together, just as there were then everywhere throughout the world among peoples in a similar stage of culture. Certain trades, especially among the most despised occupations (such as scavengers, leather workers, and butchers), tended to become, a few of them had already become, hereditary.... The elements, the foundations, of the caste system were there; but the system itself did not, as yet, exist.[1]

Certainly, Buddha could not have opposed something that had not yet come into existence. Many contemporary Buddhist scholars concur that despite His universal compassion, a significant and splendid aspect of human spiritual history, Buddha was not a rebel or a social reformer. Also, it is now widely accepted among these scholars that Buddha was neither a rebel nor a reformer of the so-called 'Brahmanical religion', as Vedic dharma gets labelled. However, in academic narratives, media, and political discourse, any perceived criticism of 'Brahmanism' is often interpreted as advocating social equality.

The polemical criticism of Brahmins found in Buddhist sacred texts is frequently conflated with the rejection of the Chātur-Varṇa idealism. Even those who have dismissed the Lutheran or Christological model of Buddha continue to uphold the colonial stereotype of 'Vedic Dharma = Brahmanism = Puruṣha Sūkta-world-view'. As a result, Buddhism's ethical superiority over 'Brahmanism' is often asserted in academic narratives, media, and political discourse.

What this dominant form of historiography fails to recognize is that the idea of certain birth-based occupations being considered defiled while others are regarded as superior in the general social and secular society can be traced back to early Buddhist literature. In *Vinaya Piṭaka*, a Pāli text, the author explains how monks should conduct themselves and mentions that they should not be discriminated against based on their birth. He divides birth into two types: upper and lower:

> Birth means: there are two (kinds of) birth: low birth and high birth. Low birth means: birth as (a member of) a despised class, birth as a bamboo-plaiter, birth as a hunter, birth as a cartwright, birth as a refuse-scavenger-this means low birth. High birth means: birth as a noble, birth as a Brahmin-this means high birth.[2]

It can be argued that this only reflects the Brahmanical society around and that as Sangha demands that one should not insult the other on account of birth, in principle, Buddhism is against such discrimination. But what this shows is that *Sangha,* or by becoming renounced, one comes out of the social system, and in enlightenment there is no discrimination. Yet in society, Buddhism and Buddha did not care about discrimination, except when the Brahmin strawman of their argument stressed his birth-based superiority. This can be further substantiated by two data: One is the way Buddhist texts present the choice of family. Even in non-Indian texts, the superiority of the caste of Buddha is stressed.

Thus, in *Lalitavistara Sūtra*, one finds that caste distinctions do not exist in the higher realm where all Divine Bodhisattvas are gathered. However, when the Blessed One comes to earth, his choice is based on both the purity of the caste bloodline and the notion of higher varṇa. In front of the assembled Bodhisattvas and Devas of the highest realm, the Blessed One states that 'sixty-four qualities appertain to the family ... in which the next-coming Bodhisattva would make his appearance'. Of these sixty-four qualities, the very third is that the family should be of a high caste, i.e., either Brähmanā or Kṣatriya. Additionally, the sixty-second criterion is that it should be free of 'caste defects'. The Burmese version of the text explains that the caste of the people and that of merchants appeared too low, and much wanting in respectability, and, moreover, no Buddha had ever come out therefrom.... He therefore fixed his choice upon the caste of princes, as most becoming his future high calling.[3]

The text on the birth of the Blessed One reveals another important defining paradoxical aspect. *Tushita* is the higher realm, the abode of joy. It was here, when all the Bodhisattvas and Devas were assembled, that Bodhisattva Śvetaketu declared his intention of being born as Siddhartha to become Buddha. This Tushita is described *Sarvairekajáti-pratiboddhah* or a place where all distinctions of Jāthi cease to exist. In other words, the Jāthi system and its hierarchies do not exist in higher realms of existence, but when on earth, they are important and have to be accepted. This is similar to the Buddhist equivalent of the *Pāramārthika* (higher true reality) and *Vyavahārika* (conventional reality) duality in Vedantic systems. Particularly when used to justify social stratification despite acceptance of the presence of the same spiritual essence in all.

Even in the famous *Ambuṭṭha Sutta,* where Buddha humbles a Brahmin, he does so at two levels. One is at the absolute level, which is 'the attainment of unexcelled knowledge-and-conduct'. At this level, all the birth-based distinctions and hierarchies are eliminated. Then there is the other level of worldly affairs. In this, Buddha recognizes the superiority of *Khattiyas* (Kṣatriyas) over all others.

To prove the inferiority of Brahmins relative to the Kṣatriyas, Buddha used the flexible attitude shown by the Brahmins with respect to marriages between Brāhmanās and Kṣatriyas. To Buddha, this was the proof of their inferiority. According to Buddha, Kṣatriyas treat a child born out of such wedlock as inferior to them. And for Buddha, this rigidity was a sign of their superiority:

> Then the Lord said: Suppose a Khattiya youth were to wed a Brahmin maiden, and there was a son of the union. Would that son of a Khattiya youth and a Brahmin maiden receive a seat and water from the Brahmins? '...Would they allow him to eat at funeral-rites, at rice-offerings, at sacrifices or as a guest?' '... Would they teach him mantras or not?'[4]

When asked whether a child born out of a Kṣatriya male and a Brāhmanā female should be considered a Brāhmanā, the Brāhmanā answers affirmatively. So the Brāhmanās honour as their own a child born out of a Kṣatriya male and a Brāhmanā female. But would the Kṣatriya honour such an offspring? The Buddhist text makes the Brāhmanā answer in the negative for this, and Buddha asks why—a rhetorical question. And the Brahmin is made to answer: 'Because, Reverend Gotama, he is not well-born on his mother's side.'

Now Buddha reverses the situation. What about the offspring from the union of a Brāhmanā male and a Kṣatriya female? Still, the Brāhmanās would not deny any of the ritual honours and right to mantras of such a child. But the Kṣatriyas would not consider such a child as their own. Buddha rhetorically asks again why this is so, and the Brähmanā is asked to respond: 'Because, Reverend Gotama, he is not well-born on his father's side.'

Then Buddha points out how even an excommunicated Kṣatriya is socially considered superior to a Brähmanā while an excommunicated Brähmanā falls below a Kṣatriya. Buddha says, 'So even if a Khattiya has suffered extreme humiliation, he is superior and the Brahmins inferior.'

Buddha quotes a verse he attributes to 'Brahmā Sanakumāra': 'The Khattiya's best among those who value clan; He with knowledge and conduct is best of gods and men.'

Then Buddha Himself endorses the statement, repeating it and adding, 'This verse was rightly sung, not wrongly, rightly spoken, not wrongly, connected with profit, not unconnected.'

At the same time, for those of any *Vaṇṇa* (Varṇā) among the four, *Parinirvana* is assured if they follow the Buddhist principles, all four Vaṇṇa can join the Sanghā. Again, this is a stand already present in Vedic literature. *Sukla Yajur Veda* declares that the auspicious word should be announced to all irrespective of Varṇā and even clan/ethnic affiliations: 'That I to all the people may address this salutary speech, To priest and nobleman, Şûdra and Arya, to one of our own kin and to the stranger.'[5]

Quoting this Vedic verse Swami Vivekananda forcefully rejected any form of birth-based restrictions on Vedic learning:

> Thus says the Shukla Yajur Veda (XXVI. 2). Can you show any authority from this Veda of ours that everyone has not the right to it? The Purânas, no doubt, say that a certain caste has the right to such and such a recension of the Vedas, or a certain caste has no right to study them, or that this portion of the Vedas is for the Satya Yuga and that portion is for the Kali Yuga.

> But, mark you, the Veda does not say so; it is only your Puranas that do so. But can the servant dictate to the master? The Smritis, Puranas, Tantras – all these are acceptable only so far as they agree with the Vedas; and wherever they are contradictory, they are to be rejected as unreliable. But nowadays we have put the Puranas on even a higher pedestal than the Vedas! The study of the Vedas has almost disappeared from Bengal. How I wish that day will soon come when in every home the Veda will be worshipped together with Shâlagrâma, the household Deity, when the young, the old, and the women will inaugurate the worship of the Veda![6]

Also, as mentioned earlier, Kavaṣa Ailūṣa, a non-Brahmin and the son of a maid who was despised as a gambler, became a *Mantra Dṛṣṭā*.[7] *Chāndogya Upaniṣad* speaks of Raikva, an enlightened cart-puller imparting wisdom to King Jānaśruti.[8] Therefore, this idea is not entirely new, but rather in line with Indic spirituality.

The second is the fact that Buddha Himself explains to the monks how the birth of inferior Jāthis innately impairs a person to be inert and unmotivated:

> And who, monks, is the person that longs not?
>
> In this connexion, monks, suppose a certain man is born into a low family, the family of a scavenger or a hunter or a basket-weaver or a wheelwright1 or a sweeper,2 or in the family of some wretched man hard put to it to find a meal or earn a living, where food and clothes are hard, to get. Moreover he is ill-favoured, ugly, dwarfish, sickly, purblind, crooked, lame, or paralysed, with never a bite or sup, nor any clothes, vehicle, bed, dwelling or lights, no perfumes or flower-garlands.[9]

Then Buddha goes on to extend this classification to the monks. He provides a three-fold classification of humanity based on the innate nature and then attributes this nature to be the reason for a person to be born in 'a low family' into which are bundled quite a lot of hereditary occupational groups. These three modes of innate nature that Buddha describes (these three persons are seen to exist in the world. What three? He who longs not, he who longs, and he who has done with longings) maps to Tamasic, Rajasic, and Sattva. Then this tri-nature provides justification in the Buddhist Universe for not just the four-fold system of society but even the so-called 'defiled trades'. The equanimity that Buddha provides is only through renunciation of the society and joining the Sanghā—the Buddhist order. But as we will see, even that would not be a practical reality.

For the first time in India's sociocultural history, the terms *Hīna Jāthi* (low jāthi) and *Ukkāṭa Jāthi* (higher jāthi) clearly surface in Buddhist literature as in *Vinaya Piṭaka*. Historian Uma Chakravarti portrays the following as the social world-view of Buddhism:

> The linear order of castes of the Brahmanical texts, where the four vannas are ranked one below the other, were reduced to two strata by the Buddhists in one passage of the *Majjhima Nikāya* where King Pasendadi asks the Buddha whether there could be any distinction between the four Vaṇṇas. The Buddha answers by saying that among the four Vaṇṇas, the *khattiyas* and *brāhmanas* are pointed to as chief (settho) in the manner in which they are addressed, saluted and served. The *vessa* and *sudda* are opposed to the khattiya and brāhmana here in an implicit relationship of high and low. However, the khattiya and brahmana appear to stand in a relationship of equality between themselves.... A basic opposition between high and low appears in the context of *jāti*, kula, kamma (karma-work) and sippa (craft): thus there are high jātis and low *jātis*; high kulas and low kulas; high kamma and low kamma; and high sippas and low *sippas*. The conception of high and low is quite explicit in the classification of *Jāti* and *kula*.[10]

The *Majjhima Nikāya* cited by Chakravarti highlights an important facet of pre-Buddhist 'Brahmanical' statecraft. It reveals that the penal system prevalent then did not differentiate punishments based on the Varṇas. Buddha employs this fact to argue against the special status of any of the Varṇas:

> What do you think, great king? Suppose a Brahmin...a merchant...a worker were to break into houses...or seduce another's wife, and if your men arrested him and produced him, saying: 'Sire, this is the culprit; command what punishment for him you wish, how would you treat him?'
>
> 'We would have him executed, Master Kaccāna, or we would have him fined, or we would have him exiled, of we would do with him as he deserved. Why is that? Because he has lost his former status of a brahmin...a merchant...a worker, and is simply reckoned as a robber.'[11]

Chakravarti argues that 'the Buddhists were reflecting an existing conception of high and low prevalent in the region where Buddhism was located'.[12] The historical reality is different. Historian Prof. Vivekanand Jha, an expert in the history of social exclusion, has pointed out that in the case of both Buddhism and Jainism, 'the emphasis... laid on non-violence evidently coloured their attitude and perception towards many of these castes'.[13]

That Buddhism implemented the high-low binary in the case of Jāthi, Kula, and Varna in a sustained way is evident in early-modern and modern Buddhist societies. However, despite this fact, most academic studies, both Indologists and Buddhologists, have missed the overall picture. Chakravarti provides a detailed listing of the 'high' and the 'low' binary:

> A long passage in the *Vinaya* texts represent *Jāti*, *nāma*, *gotta*, *kamma* and *sippa* as being of two kinds: *ukkaṭṭa* (high) and *hina* (low). While *nāma* and *gotta* refer to individuals, *jāti*, *kamma*, and *sippa* refer to groups.... Thus *ukkaṭṭa jāti* is defined as *khattiya* and *brāhmaṇa*, while *hina jāti* is defined as *chaṇḍala*, *veṇa*, *nesāda*, *ratthakāra* and *pukkusā*. The

> later categories are conventionally translated as low casteman, bamboo worker or basket maker, hunter, cartwright and flower sweeper or scavenger by Buddhist scholars.... In one reference the high *kulas* of *khattiya, brāhmaṇa* and *gahapati* are associated with while and low *kulas* of *chaṇḍala, veṇa, nesāda, ratthakāra* and *pukkusā* with black. Further the high kulas or the unit of *khattiya,brāhmaṇa* and *gahapati* are invariably associated with attributes which are evaluated as high such as wealth, eminence and learning. In contrast the *chaṇḍala, veṇa, nesāda, ratthakāra* and *pukkusā* are described as low and it is stated that fools will be born into such kulas in their next life.... The division of *kamma* (work) and *sippa* (craft) into low and high in the *Pacittiya* passage of the *Vinaya Piṭaka*... throws some light on the Buddhist view of stratification. Low *kamma* is defined as *koṭṭhaka kammam* (work of storeroom keeper), and *puppachaḍaka kammam* (work of a flower sweeper), or 'what is disdained, disregarded, scorned, treated with contempt and despised in these districts'.[14]

The two categories considered as *hina kamma* can be seen here, which are *koṭṭhaka kammam* (work of a storeroom keeper) and *puppachaḍaka kammam* (work of a flower sweeper). The low status of 'flower sweeper of scavenger' is repeated again and again. This has a strong socio-historical correlation. She also points out that Buddha stated that it does not matter for a Muni whether he was born in a mean clan, as it is irrelevant to a Muni. So she speculates that Buddhist texts only reflected the social divisions that existed in the milieu, and these divisions were irrelevant as conceptual or empirical categories in Sanghā.[15] However, as stated earlier, Buddha himself categorized births in certain jāthis as inferior. That an enlightened seer (Muni) should be respected irrespective of his status in the society or his origin, is very much part of the Vedic values and not unique to Buddhism.

Pagoda Slaves: Buddha to Myanmar

In Buddhist Myanmar, from classical times to the early modern era, untouchability was practised against castes of people categorized as '*hpaya kyun*' or Pagoda slaves. Historically, those captured in war and raids, along with other outcaste groups, were made into slaves by the Buddhist kings as it was common practice in the then contemporary societies. However, there is a difference. While in many societies, outcast groups are associated with perceived pollution and unclean works such as butchers, grave diggers, and executioners, in Burma 'the lowest status outcast groups were hpaya kyun or "pagoda slaves", who were responsible for the repair and upkeep of pagodas and other sacred Buddhist sites, places that are venerated by Burmese Buddhists and are the centre of the country's religious and spiritual life. The Buddhist system of Pagoda slaves traced its origin to the account.[16]

One of the colonial period accounts of the system describes the system vividly:

> The first king who made his prisoners of war pagoda slaves was *Du-la-ka-ma*, King of Ceylon. He conquered the city of *Chakim* and brought the rebels to his country, where, after cursing them, he offered them to the *Ta-de-daw* pagoda as slaves. Naw ral-ta-ya, the famous King of *Paghn* (the Holy City of Burma), who reigned about the time of King Canute, conquered the King of Tha- tone, from which country he brought the prisoners back to Paghn; he then cursed them, and offered them as slaves to the Thw-ye-gon Pagoda in his own city. Kyan-yil-tha, also King of Paghn a little later, about the time of William the Conqueror, after he became king, revenged himself upon his wife's relations by cursing them and offering them as pagoda slaves; this he did because they had called him a pagoda slave in the days when he was poor![17]

And so on. It gives a long list of political rivals, making the families of their rivals Pagoda slaves. However, the system traces itself to Buddha Himself. The text *Mahāvihārin Vinaya* considered the oldest text on monastic code, narrates the following incident, when 'King of Magadha, Seniya Bimbisara' requested the Blessed One that he would supply servants for the commune of Buddhist monks. After initial hesitation, Buddha consented:

> The king asked venerable Pilindavaccha 'Reverend, does the Noble One need an attendant for a monastery (ārārmka)?' The venerable Pilindavaccha answered: 'Great King, the Blessed One has not allowed an attendant for a monastery.' The king then requested: 'Then indeed, Reverend, when you have asked the Blessed One about this you should inform me'. The Venerable Pilindavaccha agreed saying 'Yes, Great King.'... The Venerable Pilindavaccha sent a messenger then to the Blessed One to say: 'Reverend, the King of Magadha, Seniya Bimbisara, wishes to give an attendant for a monastery. How, Reverend, should it now be done?' When the Blessed One had given a talk on Dhamma on that occasion, he addressed the monks: 'I allow, monks, a monastery attendant.'[18]

However, subsequently, the king forgot about his offer. When he remembered, he asked his minister how many days had gone without fulfilling his promise:

> The minister then counted up the nights and said to Bimbisara: 'Lord, it has been five hundred nights.' 'Therefore indeed, sir, you must give five hundred monastery attendants to the Noble One', said the king. The minister assented to the king saying 'Yes, Lord,' and gave five hundred monastery attendants to the Venerable Pilindavaccha. A separate village was settled. They called it a 'Village of Monastery Attendants (ārāmika-gāmā)'.[19]

According to Buddhologist Gregory Schopen, though 'abruptly' introduced the term '*ārāmika*' seems to require that it 'be taken in its technical and specifically Buddhist sense of a-for the moment- forced labourer attached to or owned by an individual monk or monastic community'.[20] The Buddhist texts further elaborate the institutionalization of the slavery system in the monastery context:

> When they had built their bondmen's quarters they went to the vihara and worked. The monks explained to them the work.... Because they performed the proper tasks the designation 'proper bondman', 'proper bondman' came into being. Because they took care of the ārāma of the Community the designation 'proper slave', 'proper slave' came into being.[21]

Buddha made it clear to the supervisors of the slaves that there should be no food and clothes if the slaves did not work. When the monks refused food and clothes to the sick slaves, Buddha said they could be given food and clothes. As a result, an entire settlement of bondmen or slaves was established by the monastery, which was supplied by the royal power. It is easy to see how the system evolved. The kings supplied slaves to Buddhist monasteries and even individual monks. These slaves were required to live in settlements, which consisted of war captives, slaves caught through raids, and rebelling communities. Kings changed. In Buddhist lands, monasteries continued and were centres of power. The slaves were responsible for maintaining gardens, flower garlands, and flower scavenging, among other tasks. The communities that performed these tasks were already categorized as Hina-Jāthis. Naturally, the Pagoda slave communities became untouchables strictly through the values of the Buddhist social worldview. While the initial Pagoda slaves may have been given by the king, their descendants became untouchable communities. Even as recently as the late 19th and early 20th century, 'no king has had the power of liberating them, and should a Burman marry one, even unknowingly, he and any children he might have by a previous marriage would become also pagoda slaves'.[22] British rule finally outlawed 'Pagoda slavery', but prejudices and discrimination still continued. For colonial proselytizers, this was justification for the destruction of Buddhism itself: 'Under British rule this form of slavery has nominally ceased to exist. But no law of a civilized government could restore the pagoda-slave or his descendants to equal social standing with their neighbours. They are outcasts still, and outcasts they will remain, until Buddhism is no more.'[23]

One can see the same prejudiced attitude of hatred colonial and colonialism-influenced 'reformers' show with respect to Hinduism and caste. Social inferiorizing, as well as social exclusion of communities, are found in Buddhist societies both in South Asia and in other Asian countries. This should be seen more as a complex interaction of Buddhist worldviews, values, and social evolution of the localized settings. Similar trends in social evolution were present in pre- and early modern Christendom. Hence this is in no way peculiar to Buddhist societies. But the problem arises here because of the constant portrayal of Buddhism as an egalitarian movement and essentializing non-Buddhist Hinduism as almost nothing but 'Brahminical' superiority. Here we look into some more instances of social inferiorizing and exclusion as present in Buddhist societies.

Apart from Pagoda slaves, there were other socially excluded communities that also reflected the Buddhist worldview. These were *Thubayansa* (grave-diggers), *Don* (fishermen), *Hari* (sweepers), *Hara* (washermen and barbers), *Keba* (hereditary beggars), and also 'hunters, butchers, actors, intoxicating drinks sellers, and midwives' who were treated as untouchables in Burmese society.[24] The hereditary beggars were not beggars because of poverty. They were ordered by the king at some point in time to live as beggars. The following account made by a Christian missionary scholar, even after taking into consideration typical missionary prejudices, shows that the condition of the socially excluded was not different from those of such marginalized populations elsewhere in the world in general and in India in particular:

> These unfortunates did not become beggars because they were outcasts, but became outcasts because they were made beggars, not of choice, but by royal decree.... He is only reaping in this life what he sowed in some former existence. Therefore, he and his descendants forever are to be despised, and compelled to remain beggars, whatever their actual condition. Some of this beggar class are known to have become wealthy, but wealth secures to them no social standing. Outcasts they are, and outcasts they must remain.... The children of none of these outcast classes are permitted to enter the monastic or other schools.[25]

Here it is quite interesting to note that even after citing a paper that details untouchability prevalent in Myanmar against these communities, the Superintendent of Census operation for Burma S.G. Grantham I.C.S goes out of the way to deny the existence of caste in Burmese society. His reasoning was this:

> The use of the term caste with regard to the Burmese is a mistake, because that term has no meaning (except when it is used figuratively) apart from the whole Hindu social system. The Don, Hari and Hara are known only in Akyab and are Hindu descendants of mixed marriages between Hindus and the Chin hill-tribes, who in conformity with regular. Hindu practices occupy a low place in the caste scale.... The extension of the same term to the other classes mentioned is a different matter, because these are all Buddhists and entirely outside the Hindu social system.[26]

In his 1954 study of Burmese society, anthropologist Edmund Leach (1910–1989) pointed out that the lowest strata of the rural community in the Shan region consisted of 'fishermen, butchers, liquor dealers, pig keepers, etc., i.e., all those people who perform occupations which are improper according to the strict Buddhist code'.[27] It is important to note that the Shan region of Myanmar is surrounded by China, Laos, and Thailand, which suggests that this system did not have much Indian influence. However, the explanation of the British Census Superintendent, who absolved Burmese society of even caste divisions, shows how strongly colonial pro-Buddhist prejudices can shape the perception of historical and social reality.

The same is the case with Sri Lanka, where caste prejudices are particularly entrenched within Buddhist monasteries themselves. *Theravāda* text *Dambadeni Katikāvata* of the 11th century interprets the monks should be 'examined' as '*jātigōtravichārā*', that their caste and family clan should be taken into consideration before they are admitted into the Sangha. But even then, the feelings and connections were very much there. Examining Buddhism in Singhalese society between 1750 and 1900, historian Kitsiri Malalgoda writes:

> In theory, of course, Buddhist monks were 'casteless', for caste is a social category. and hence of no relevance to those who had renounced the society. Yet, in practice, this ideal was rarely realised.... On entering the order, monks showed no signs of losing their caste identities; on the contrary, they continued to be highly conscious of their caste.[28]

The Asgiri Vihāraya in Kandi is the centre of the Asgiriya Pārśvaya of the Siyam Nikāya, the monastic order that administers the most sacred of the Sri Lankan Buddhist places, including the Temple of the Tooth Relic, Sri Pada Peak, Kelaniya, and over 6,000 other temples. However, it is predominantly caste-based ordination of monks. As late as 1996, the Asgiriya monks of Siyam Nikāya expressed their disapproval of the ordination of Buddhist monks without consideration of caste, which was initiated by a reformist monk Venerable Sumangala. Venerable Sumangala himself, in an interview, stated that Chandānanda, chief monk of the Asgiriya temple, had instructed the Buddhist commissioner not to register the monks whose casteless higher ordination was done at from the Dambulla chapter because it was 'not a legitimate Buddhist organization'.[29] Anthropologists often argue that Sri Lankan society does not have both 'Brahmins' and 'untouchables' and the concept of 'pollution'.[30] Thus the caste system in Sri Lanka differs from that of India. There are untouchability and a strong sense of pollution present in the Sri Lankan society. The Rodiyas are a community of untouchable beggars, and Kinnaraya are an untouchable community of mat-weavers. This corresponds to the Buddhist classification of basket weavers as Hina Jāthi. Despite being in small numbers, these communities still face discrimination. There is inner stratification between Rodiya and Kinnaraya, even though both are untouchable castes. An account of this complicated relation made in 1905 explains:

> According to Armour's list, as well as that given in the 'Nitinighanduwa' (LeMesurier and Panabokke's translation) of the 18 wanam, the 'Kinnarayo rank one but the last and the Rodi' the last. This order of classification is disputed by the latter, who consider themselves superior to and claim a higher place than the former. In support of their superiority to rank and place they urge:
>
> - Firstly, that they are permitted to tie up their hair in a knot at the back of the head, a privilege not vouchsafed to the Kinnarayo' who have to cut their hair short, as a rule, or coil it up in rolls, and fasten round it a hempen fillet, which is a badge of their tribe.
> - Secondly, the Rodi women are allowed to suspend a handkerchief over the front portion of their body, securing it at the back of the neck by means of a knot, while the Kinnarayo' women only gird their breasts with a cloth band.

> To cite an every-day occurrence: A '"Kinnaraya" will not pass a Rodiya,' or vice versa, if they chance to meet on the road. One is as zealous as he is frightened of the other. It is a common saying that if a 'Kinnaraya' happens to meet a 'Kodiya', the former will stand on top of the slightest eminence, even be it a lump of dung or human excrement to indicate his sublime and exalted position as compared and that of his supposed inferior![31]

The picture that emerges from all these complicated webs of social relations and their evolution is this: whether in South Asia or abroad (Japan), Buddhism in its religious, sociological, or historical dimensions seems to have more a catalyst than an inhibiting factor in social stratification and inferiorizing certain hereditary communities.

Chinese Pilgrim Fǎ-Hiēn, who visited India during the Gupta period categorized Chāṇḍāla, fishermen and hunters as 'untouchables' and this he does in a completely Buddhist context. He describes the city of Mathura where the 'law of Buddha was still flourishing':

> The laws and ways, according to which the kings presented their offerings when Buddha was in the world, have been handed down to the present day.... Throughout the whole country the people do not kill any living creature, nor drink intoxicating liquor, nor eat onions or garlic. The only exception is that of the Chāṇḍāla. That is the name for those who are (held to be) wicked men, and live apart from others. When they enter the gate of a city or a market-place, they strike a piece of wood to make themselves known, so that men know and avoid them, and do not come into contact with them. In that country they do not keep pigs and fowls, and do not sell live cattle; in the markets there are no butchers' shops and no dealers in intoxicating drink. In buying and selling commodities they use cowries. Only the Chāṇḍāla are fishermen and hunters, and sell flesh meat.[32]

Fă-Hiēn's description of untouchability did not express revulsion, but rather Buddhist satisfaction with a society that upholds Ahimsa by stigmatizing communities involved in hunting, fishing, and meat-eating. It is important to note that the 'Brahminical' worldview, as expressed in the works of Kalidasa, does not consider the meat-sellers, fishermen, or hunters as Chāṇḍāla. Social historians Akepogu Jammanna and Pasala Sudhakar while studying the entry of untouchability into Andhra regions from a historical perspective point out the role of Buddhism and Jainism in the institutionalizing untouchability:

> The Jain texts also speak of Jati, jungitas (born untouchables) and Karma Jungitas (untouchables in body). Hunters, pointers, fishermen, tailors, and acrobats are classified as untouchables by birth. Those who reared birds like peacocks and fowls or animals like pigs, those who practised hunting, acrobatic exercises, and barbers work as vocations are called untouchables by conduct. Dumb, crippled, and hunch-backed people, dwarfs, and one-eyed persons are classified untouchables in body. All these peoples are shunned as untouchables by a holy Jain. Even Buddhist works speak of Hinajatis or degraded castes such as Chandalas, Venas (basket makers), Nishadas (fishermen), Rathakars (chariot makers), and Pukkasas (hunters). The idea of untouchables by birth and by conduct, found in the Dharmasutras, is incorporated into the Sanskrit (translated from Pali), and Buddhist texts. The doctrine of Ahimsa and Hindu ordained taboos seem to have played an important role in the proliferation of untouchability in India.[33]

The role of Buddhist values in stigmatizing certain trades and later making the communities associated with the trades lower castes is also documented in the field of historical anthropology. Reginald Edward Enthoven (1869-1952), a British colonial administrator and author of the three-volume *Tribes and Castes of Bombay,* worked within the framework of Aryan-Aboriginal binary framework, considering the so-called upper castes as generally Aryan and scheduled caste communities as indigenous. But even he, with respect to the community of Chambars, found out that they had enjoyed a special privileged status in Vedic and pre-Buddhist India so much that 'those who pursued it had a recognized guild of their own, with which kings always kept themselves in touch'. Such guilds, he observed, continued even now. However, situations started changing with the spread of Buddhism:

> About a century after the rise and dissemination of Buddhism, public opinion began to change. There is a passage in the Vinay-Pitaka which relegates leather-workers to the class of those who took to low crafts (him sippa); but even here it deserves to be noticed... that the profession of leather-working is classed under hina-sippa and not hina-jati (low castes), which comprised the Chandalas, Venas (rush-workers), Nishadas (bird-catchers), Rathakaras (cart-makers) and Pukkusas. The conclusion may therefore be safely drawn that, although the profession of leather-working had begun to fall into disrepute about a century after the prevalence of Buddhism or about 400 BC, those who pursued it were not yet looked upon as belonging to low castes (hina-jati); in other words, leather workers were even then regarded as standing within the pale of the Aryan society. But, once considered debasing, the profession must gradually have acquired more and more disrepute, until those who pursued it were degraded into a low-caste.[34]

Although Enthoven argues that only the Chambar community alone could claim such a pre-Buddhist higher status and that others were Aboriginal races, the truth is that almost every marginalized community in India has a claim to such a higher status originally and remembers vaguely a historical fall. There is no doubt in many cases, Buddhism and, to a significant extent, Jainism played a role here. Buddhism never challenged the

Hindu legal system or the Dharma-Shastra legal realm. None other than Dr Ambedkar admitted this as he pointed out that 'when the Buddha differed from the Vedic Brahmins he did so only in matters of creed, but left the Hindu legal framework intact and that He did not propound a separate law for his followers'.[35] However, what may have been a strange fact of history is that the strong conception of higher and lower, as well as the restrictions imposed on perceived low jāthi s in Dharma Shastras, could have been largely a consequence of unintended Buddhist doctrine.

Buddhism and Jainism, with their doctrinal upholding of absolute Ahimsa and strict moralism that often demanded the denial of all worldly pleasures, resulted in an ambivalent attitude towards communities involved in hunting, fishing, meat production, and also communities like bards and courtesans. The quasi-hierarchical varṇa system, which was more a social space than a birth-based system with Yajñá societal model of role allocation and redistribution processes, received a blow because of the impact of Buddhism and Jainism. It is highly improbable that Buddha or Mahaveera aimed for such a result. Nevertheless, this was an unintentional societal consequence. As a result, the artisan and working communities were divided into upper and lower communities. There was a proliferation of communities whose works got labelled as defiled. At the elite level, philosophical debates were happening with respect to the nature of Brähmanā or its absence, the nature of Sunya, etc. Definitely, the Vedic, Buddhist, and Jain religions competed for royal patronage and more often than not, the rulers patronized all the systems. But the society at large was becoming socially stagnant. Irrespective of philosophical affiliation to Buddhism or Jainism, the societal divisions and perceptions that these religions introduced became part of the psyche.

CHAPTER 8

Bhakti, Bhagavad Gītā, and the Beginning of the Movement

This chapter explores not only the spiritual and psychological concept of bhakti but also its social implications. Bhakti is a significant contribution to Hindu civilization that traces its roots back to the Vedic era. This chapter examines how bhakti is nurtured through various mediums, including the pan-Indian sacred texts such as the Bhagavad Gītā and Puranas, mainly *Śrī Bhāgavata Purāṇa*, as well as the mystic-bhakti literature in regional languages. The chapter further elucidates how bhakti seamlessly integrated the practice of Yajña, transforming it into an internal and societal ritual. Bhakti is portrayed as a remarkable civilizational endeavour aimed at rectifying any doctrinal corruption. It laid the foundation for future social movements in India, ranging from Khalsa to Gandhi. While social emancipation was not the primary objective of bhakti, it inevitably brought about societal liberation as a natural consequence with minimal or almost nil violence and sustained community elevation.

Bhakti: The Vedic Prelude

Tracing the roots back to the ancient scriptures of Vedic literature, if not older, bhakti, a religio-psychological phenomenon, has always been an important core of the social and spiritual life of India. The etymological root of the word is *bhaj* which means 'to partake', 'to participate', and 'to share'. *Rig Veda* differentiates between *bhaktam* and a-*bhkatam.*[1] Yāska, in his *Nirukta* with reference to the verse, uses the term 'bhaktini' as the share of agni. Traditional Vedic commentator Sāyaṇa interprets the terms bhaktam and a-bhkatam, as *sevamāna* and *a-sevanamāna* (those who serve and those who do not). Serving and sharing are related in Vedic verses and are thus traditionally associated with bhakti. Hence, often the Western and colonized Indologists who approached bhakti as a kind of monotheistic evolution from a polytheistic natural religion considered the term differently than the meaning in which the term is understood in Vedic literature. Nevertheless, the etymological root bhaj is used in *Rig Veda* by Ṛṣi Dīrghatamā in the context of partaking and sharing the results of collective praising of the Divine (in this case, Vishṇu): 'Hymners, propitiate that ancient Viṣṇu the indweller of *Ṛta* (ṛtasya garbhaṃ); realizing His greatness we celebrate His name; Viṣṇu, may we share the receiving of Your blessings (sumatim bhajāmahe).'[2]

Here Vishṇu as indweller of *Ṛta* is also associated with the phrase in *Aitareya Brāhmaṇa*, which speaks of Vishṇu as being born with Yajña (*yajño vai viṣṇuḥ:*).[3] Bhakti, as derived from bhaj, has not only a linguistic connection but also a deeper conceptual connection. It is the sharing of benevolent blessings (*sumatim*). If Yajña is co-creation, then when the Divine punishes those who hoard, He shares the auspicious wealth (*bhajati sūnaraṃ vasu*) with those who give through Yajña (*dāśuṣe*).[4] The later term *Dāsa* associated with bhakti, also shows a conceptual connection, even if not an etymological link, with *dāśuṣe,* which is an act of giving to the Divine.

However, Indological scholars, who continue to see bhakti through the still lingering colonial lens of Christian monotheism, regard it as a later development that was absent in what they perceived as the primitive conception of the Divine in the Vedic literature. This colonial scholarly perception has been around for two centuries now. For instance, Max Muller considered 'the idea of prayer as swelling or exalted thought may be true with us', there was 'little, if any, trace of such thoughts in the Veda'. Similarly, Austrian Indologist Moriz Winternitz (1863-1937) stated that there was 'nowhere [in the Vedas] any thought of devotion or exaltation of the divine'.[5] Moreover, Sir George Abraham Grierson, a British colonialist linguist, considered any semblance of bhakti in Vedas as 'incipient monotheism ... still-born' in Vedic poets. According to him, the source of bhakti should be seen elsewhere than from the 'Brahmans of Northern India', and that would be Nestorian Christianity.[6] However, later scholarship completely rejected this Nestorian or Christian influence on the Hindu bhakti movement that emerged in later centuries. Still, Vedas are considered as not having bhakti—either as a concept or as a religio-poetic expression. The reason is more the deep monotheistic bias in the colonial and still colonized academia than the actual nature of the literature.

Sanskritist and author Jeanine Miller (1930-2013) argues that bhakti as a literary mystic expression is definitely present throughout Vedic literature because for the Vedic hymns 'the inspiration was felt by the poets to be dependent on the graciousness and benevolence of the particular visiting deity' and 'therein lies plenty of room for the expression of a devotional attitude: the poets refer frequently to their heart, their yearning for the deity's favour and their exaltation in their vision'.[7] Miller highlights that bhakti, in its spiritual, psychological, and poetic manifestation, has a fullness as found within the Vedic hymns. However, the colonial and predominantly Protestant scholarship has overlooked its presence in the Vedas due to its bias towards monotheistic devotion as the benchmark for bhakti. Miller emphasizes 'monotheism' as a criterion of bhakti:

> Ignores the fundamental meaning of devotion which is inherent to human nature and can be shown to mother and father, brother and sister, and lover. The *ṛṣis* display true attitude of love to their gods which cannot be dismissed as 'still-born' only because it does not fit the monotheistic pattern. The evidence of devotion is obvious in the RV in many monologues and also in many dialogues between man and god. A personal relationship is established between them in the appeals, offerings and lively and loving or friendly communications which fully fall within the range of bhakti.[8]

In Vedic literature, bhakti exists in its most potent primordial (not primitive) form, involuting in it the seeds of all potential expansions we might encounter in later bhakti literature. Miller writes,

> That Being-sat or state of being-to which the sages referred simply as tat, 'That', 'whose shadow is death, whose shadow is immortality' (RV 10.121.2) is itself beyond worship, imagination and anticipation. But its representations in the seer's mind-as Varuna, the Lord of Cosmic Order; Agni, the ageless flame and friend of man; Indra, the munificent friend and man's own warrior; Surya-Savitr, the beacon of illumined understanding; and Soma, the king of exaltation and eloquence—*these could be accorded the highest devotion and worship man is capable of.*[9] (emphasis mine)

She points to the deeper meaning of the first two keywords, which are closely linked in the *Rig Veda*: 'vṛdh' (to swell, increase, expand) and 'Brahman', where the Brahman (not the Varṇa) is made responsible for invigoration (*vardhana*) and probably better translated as 'exalting'.[10] She envisions a technique for arousing the power, which is the 'Vedic Brahman'. It is 'the evocative power of the word or sound (*vāc*) which the seers found 'residing in their hearts' (10.71.3).

According to Miller, the later form of bhakti as such may not be related to the etymological root bhaj and its derivatives, such as 'bhajkamahe' or 'bhajati'. However, in the same paper, she points out how the same state of bhakti is an inalienable part of Vedic 'sacrifice' (Yajña). She believes that there is 'a spilling over of the devotional side of human nature into the structure of the sacrifice which is evident in the *Rig Veda* where this structure was not yet rigid and the performance of the sacrifice not yet mechanical'. With almost every Vedic deity, she brings out the presence of bhakti. Elsewhere she defines Yajña as not just sacrifice but also worship that involves 'the setting up of a communication between the within and the without and thereby the making "holy", so that the expanding without may be worthy of the within, may become a perfect mirror; hence the sacrifice in establishing a circuit of give and take, a balance, is the harmony'.[11] This worship that becomes the 'perfect mirror', 'circuit of give and take', which is the harmony (she also translates it as *Ṛta*), is not a transactional give and take but a co-creation of love. This then perfectly fits the definition of bhakti. In other words, bhakti is the inner process through which Yajña becomes an inner archetype and social ideational metaphor.

This Vedic-involuted bhakti unfolded itself throughout the historical time of Indian society. It challenged the social stagnation and status quo by questioning repeatedly the act of social exclusion. The Vedic episode of Kavaṣa Ailūṣa is a prime example of this. Here the famous Apnotrīya hymn of Kavaṣa Ailūṣa speaks of 'speeding for the brāhmanā', while Aitareya Brāhmaṇa speaks of 'how Saraswati flowed around him', i.e., the sacred waters of River Sarasvatī went to him, surrounded him, and embraced him (*enam kavaṣam parisasâra*) demonstrating the motherly love of the Goddess. This entire sequence of events formed a prototype for later bhakti movement instances where a devotee-mystic would be insulted on account of their birth and then they would burst into a hymn. The Divine would then reveal the greatness of the human irrespective of their birth or social status, thus challenging the social status quo.

Bhagavad Gītā as Harmonized Continuation of Vedic Bhakti and Yajña

The advent of Buddhism and Jainism inadvertently led to the karmic rationalization of social exclusion, with certain hereditary professions being deemed impure and others noble. However, the emergence of bhakti, expressed through individuals, ignited a sense of egalitarianism across all societal levels. It challenged the preconceived notions of nobility and defilement based on both occupation and birth, fostering a more equitable society.

The challenge came both through ethical-intellectual discussion and through bhakti. Bringing all these streams together and harmonizing the individual and the society with a vision of equanimity that springs from Vedic bhakti became the context and an important feature of the Bhagavad Gītā. For at least a millennium and a half, the Bhagavad Gītā remained a text of systemic unifier that had been discussed in the circles of spiritual philosophies of India. However, according to historian Prof. Vivekanand Jha, the social emancipation dimension of the Bhagavad Gītā led to its eclipse in the popular discourse until Mahatma Gandhi brought it into the spotlight:

> The Bhagavad gita, composed around the third-second century BC, definitely adopted a stance which was firmly and unequivocally opposed to that of the Dharmasutras and the Manusmriti on the issue of untouchability. Recognising the formidable and inescapable reality of the hierarchical and inegalitarian caste structure, which could not be uprooted or abolished wholesale, and seeking to reform the spirit of its working from within, it presented an idealized version of Varṇa and declared itself in favour of eradication of untouchability. The discerning

> Dharmashastra authors sensed the ominous nature of the work and its message and for centuries ignored both. This was the legacy of Gandhi, who drew his inspiration from the Gita and whose long and arduous campaign to eradicate untouchability and get justice for the untouchables from within the system could not be ignored and was therefore firmly opposed by the vested interests and the Sanatani Hindus.[12]

It is possible that the reason the Bhagavad Gītā did not become popular despite every acharya choosing to write detailed commentaries on it may be more because of the general elite nature of academia anywhere at any time rather than any deliberate attempt by the 'high caste' or elite authors of Dharmasastra to keep the text within a limited circle. However, what is important to note here is the recognition of the emancipatory nature of the Bhagavad Gītā by an academic who is from an academia that has heavy Marxist biases. The sudden popular spread of the Bhagavad Gītā predates Mahatma Gandhi. It is a strong possibility that the Bhagavad Gītā made the transition into a mass scripture from being a philosophical-spiritual guide with Sant Jñāneśvar (1275–1296). His commentary on the Bhagavad Gītā, called *Jñāneśvarī* or *Bhāvarthadīpikā,* was written in the Marāthi language. The work emphasizes the irrelevance of caste in the context of spiritual liberation while also speaking of carrying out the duties of the Varṇa one is born into. But in the larger context, being written by a casteless mystic in a non-elite regional language and with its emphasis on bhakti, the commentary took the Bhagavad Gītā to the masses.

> On one hand there was a handful of learned erudites, monopolising the entire Brahma-Vidyā and ruthlessly exploiting the ignorance of the vast sea of credulous, ignorant and simple-minded people of other castes. To the latter, human duties and relations and their value in shaping and moulding the life of the individual to serve the larger interests of the humanity at

> large, was a Sealed Book. Jñāneśvar, reminiscent of the tyranny of the orthodox and the bigoted exercised on these children of a sannyasi wrote his commentary in a spirit of developing universal consciousness and outlook and thus in a way democratised religion and opened the Gates of Immortality to all without any distinction of caste, creed or sex. He was the Pioneer among the galaxy of saints and reformers of Mahārāshtra and hence his greatness and the far-reaching effects impressed on the masses of population.

Since then, the Bhagavad Gītā has spread throughout India. As early as the 17th century, Māthai Thiru Venkatanathar, who ruled the south Indian Pandya kingdom on behalf of Madurai Nayakars, wrote a 'Bhagavat Gita lullaby' for his daughter. By the early 19th century in deep South India, the Bhagavad Gītā, with a Sankara-Vedantic monist interpretation, was significantly famous and by 1818, a non-Brahmin Vedanta monastery was established at a place called Thirukovillur. Therefore, one can say that the pan-Indian reach of the Bhagavad Gītā definitely predates Mahatma Gandhi. Its popularization in the Hindu psyche was a democratic process organically united with social emancipation.

Yet, the contemporary discussions of the Bhagavad Gītā, particularly in the colonial and post-colonial times, are characterized and criticized by a significant section of Indic scholarship as a text justifying birth-based social stratification, both through divine sanction and philosophical reasoning. One of the strongest criticisms of the Bhagavad Gītā in this regard was made by Dr Bhimrao Ramji Ambedkar. Dr Ambedkar was not only an eminent nation-builder and one who strove to emancipate Scheduled Castes communities but also a pioneering social historian of ancient India. He developed a strong criticism of the Bhagavad Gītā in his unfinished book *Revolution and Counter-Revolution in Ancient India* into a complete chapter titled 'Essays on the Bhagwat Gita: Philosophic Defence of Counter-Revolution: Kṛṣṇa and His Gita'. According to Dr Ambedkar, Bhagavad Gītā defends the Chātur-Varṇa system through the 'Tri-Guna philosophy of Sankhya' (with Satva, Rajas, and Tamas categories). In his own words:

> The Bhagvat Gita, no doubt, mentions that the Chaturvarnya is created by God and therefore sacrosanct. But it does not make its validity dependent on it. It offers a philosophic basis to the theory of Chaturvarnya by linking it to the theory of innate, inborn qualities in men. The fixing of the Varna of man is not an arbitrary act says the Bhagvat Gita. But it is fixed according to his innate, inborn qualities.... Similarly childish is the defence of the Bhagvat Gita of the dogma of chaturvarnya. Kṛṣṇa defends it on the basis of the Guna theory of the Sankhya. But Kṛṣṇa does not seem to have realised what a fool he has made of himself. In the chaturvarnya there are four Varnas. But the gunas according to the Sankhyas are only three. How can a system of four varnas be defended on the basis of a philosophy which does not recognise more than three varnas? The whole attempt of the Bhagvat Gita to offer a philosophic defence of the dogmas of counter-revolution is childish—and does not deserve a moment's serious thought.[13]

The intense criticism of the Bhagavad Gītā penned by Dr Ambedkar, of which only a part is published above, harsh as it may sound to the Hindu mind, cannot be brushed aside easily. Dr Ambedkar placed the Bhagavad Gītā in a specific historical context, namely the aftermath of the rise of what he terms as 'counter-revolution'. This 'counter-revolution' was the coup of Pushyamitra Sunga (185–151 BCE) against the last Mauryan emperor and the subsequent rise of 'Brähmanāical' rituals in the realm of the state as power symbols. According to Dr Ambedkar, after the 'counter-revolution' event, the Bhagavad Gītā was composed later during the time of Narasimha Gupta Bālāditya (470–535 CE).[14]

However, the historical milieu that Dr Ambedkar sets for the composition of the Bhagavad Gītā as a philosophical treatise aimed at subverting the Buddhist 'revolution' is not one of hostility towards Buddhism. Gupta emperor Bālāditya was so admired by the Buddhists that he was given the title 'Buddhapaksha'. The Gupta emperor was not the only one who raised the flag of resistance against the Hun massacre of Buddhists. Yaśodharman Vishnuvardhan, another 6th-century Hindu chief of Malwa, Central Indian region, also rose in revolt against the anti-Buddhist atrocities of the Hun. Both emperors belonged to the so-called 'Brahmanical' religion, yet they were inclined towards Buddhism as they were to the Vedic tradition. Had 'Brahminism' with royal patronage in the post-Sunga period strove to destroy Buddhism, then Mihirakula the Hun offered the best opportunity. But history stands as testimony to the fact that the Hindu kings of India stood by persecuted Buddhist monks and faced the ferocity of Huns on the battlefield.

More significantly, the famous Mandasor inscription (Mālava Year 589, i.e., 532 CE) of Yaśodharman invokes a stern Saivaite imagery in celebrating his victory against the anti-Buddhist Mihirakula:

> May that flying banner of *Śulāpaṇi* (Trident adorned Śivā) destroy the forces of your enemy, the banner that bears the Bull (Nandi), who in turn is marked by prints of the (vermilion or sandal paste dye soaked) five fingers of the Daughter of the Mountain (Pārvati), and whose bellowing reverberates in the farthermost quarters making the demons shiver with fear and whose horns split open the rocks of the valleys of *Sumeru* mountain, by the blows of his horns.

Indologist Hans Bakker refers to this proclamation as 'the language of war' and the beginning of the 'Śaiva Age'.[15] Therefore, one can be certain that despite the sectarian differences between the Hindu family of spiritual and religious traditions and notwithstanding the inevitable conflicts that would have existed, a full-fledged persecution, as it happened in the West, against Paganism with the ascendancy of Christianity or the mutual persecutions indulged in by Protestant and Catholic sects, was near absent in Hindu context. The same can be said for the much-flaunted persecution by Pushyamitra against the Buddhists. Even Historian Upinder Singh raises doubts about the complete veracity of any sustained Buddhist persecution during the Sunga period. There could be 'some historical basis' for Buddhist tradition to single out Pushyamitra, though the Buddhist account 'cannot be taken at face value':

> On the other hand, Sanchi and other Buddhist monasteries in central India continued to exist and flourish during the Shunga period. Was this in spite of Pushyamitra's persecution of the Buddhists? Was it because later Shunga kings discontinued his anti-Buddhist policy? Or should the Buddhist stories of Pushyamitra's persecution be considered exaggerated?[16]

According to her, accounts of violent religious persecutions 'form the exception than the rule' in ancient India and kings practiced what she calls 'inclusive sectarianism'.[17] So the physically violent religious persecution and suppression of Buddhism did not happen in ancient India. At the same time, the rise of Pushyamitra itself was against the varṇa system, as generally understood. It should have caused disturbance to believers in a birth-based hierarchical system. Dr Ambedkar was well aware of this.

> The revolution brought about by Pushyamitra created an initial difficulty in the way of the Brahmins. People could not be easily reconciled to this revolution. The resentment of the public was well expressed by the poet Bana when in referring to this revolution, reviles Pushyamitra as being base born and calls his

> act of regicide as Anarya. The act of Pushyamitra was properly described by Bana as Anarya i.e. contrary to Aryan law. For on three points the Aryan law at the date of Pushyamitra's revolution was well settled. The then Aryan law declared (1) that Kingship is the right of the Kshatriya only. A Brahmin could never be a king. (2) That no Brahmin shall take to the profession of Arms and (3) That rebellion against the King's authority was a sin. Pushyamitra in fostering the rebellion had committed a crime against each of these three laws. He was Brahmin, and although a Brahmin he rebelled against the King, took to the profession of Arms and became a King. People were not reconciled to this usurpation which constituted so flagrant a breach of the law that the Brahmins had to regularize the position created by Pushyamitra. This the Brahmins did by taking the bold step of changing the law. This change of law is quite manifest from the Manu Smriti.[18]

However, the transgression was assimilated by Dharmashastra writers who also enabled advantages for Brāhmanās and Kṣatriyas while creating legal disadvantages for Śūdra. As explained earlier, the disadvantage to Śūdra and other hereditary artisan guilds may be more because of the Buddhist influence than their adherence to Vedic values. Therefore, one may try to locate in the text of the Bhagavad Gītā the tension between social reality fashioned by rigid ahimsa-morality-related biases and Vedic values that advocate spiritual egalitarianism manifesting in social life.

The Mahābhārata,[19] the mother text in which the Bhagavad Gītā is embedded, provides an abundance of insights into this inherent tension. In Śānti Parva, there is a famous conversation between Ṛṣi Bhṛgu and Ṛṣi Bharadvāja, which Bhīṣma narrates to Yudhiṣṭhira. In this conversation, first, Bhṛgu bluntly states that the four categories of Brāhmaṇa, Kṣatriya, Vaiśya, and Śūdra are defined by four 'Varṇas' in the meaning of colours, namely sita (white), *lohita* (red), pītaka (yellow), asita (black), respectively. Here colour symbolizes the attributes. But Bharadvāja is sceptical and points out that all people have all attributes. Now answers:

> Na viśeṣo'sti varṇānāṃ sarvaṃ brāhmamidaṃ jagat |
> Brahmaṇā pūrvasṛṣṭaṃ hi karmabhirvarṇatāṃ gatam'
> There are no special differences between the Varṇas. All were innately Brāhmaṇas as emanated by the Brahman and through their work differentiation became different orders.

Then, he further states that those among the Brähmanās who had uncontrolled anger and were attracted to courageous venturing were unmindful of pious penances, were attracted to passionate pleasures, etc., and became Kṣatriya. Those who attended to agriculture and nurturing, as well as increasing the wealth of cattle, etc., became Vaiśya. The ones who were engaged in all kinds of activities for sustenance became the Śūdra.

Importantly the conversation uses the same format for the emergence of all the Varṇas:

- 'dvijā kṣatratāṃ gatāḥ': from the twice-born came the Kṣatriya
- 'dvijā vaiśyatāṃ gatāḥ': from the twice-born came the Vaiśya
- 'dvijāḥ śūdratāṃ gatāḥ': from the twice-born came the śūdra

And this has an important implication: *dharmo yajñakriyā caiṣāṃ nityaṃ na pratiṣidhyate* (members of all the four Varṇas should not be barred from doing the *yajñakriyā*). In other words, they have the right to participate in the Yajña and do the rituals. Bhṛgu then goes on to explain who a Brāhmaṇa is.

> The Brāhmaṇa are always devoted to the sacred texts and, mindful of vows and restraints, are capable of grasping the conception of the Divine. Their penances, therefore, never go for nothing. They amongst them are not Brāhmaṇa who are incapable of understanding that every created thing has in it.

One cannot but compare this with the statement of Buddha with respect to a similar question: 'Cattārome, vāseṭṭha, Vaṇṇā—khattiyā, brāhmaṇā, vessā, suddā'—(Vāseṭṭha, there are these four Varṇās: Kṣatriya, Brāhmaṇā, Vaiśya, and Śūdra). Some were aristocrats, mostly Kṣatriya. Then Buddha says that virtues and vices are present in all the members of each Varṇā. Then He goes on to explain the various Varṇā Maṇḍalas, which in this context can be construed as 'socio-eco spheres' rather than just circles. The Brahmins were simple living meditators. They begged for their food and then were immersed in meditation. But those who could not do this and came down to the society were looked down upon as reciters. Though the term reciter was a lowly term, now it is considered a noble one. Then 'some of those same beings taking up an active sex life, applied themselves to various jobs'. They formed the Vaiśya maṇḍala. The remaining ones with 'greedy and vile conduct' (*luddācārā khuddācārā*) took up menial jobs and formed the Śūdra maṇḍala. Then individuals from all four who were dissatisfied with their state declared that the individual would become an ascetic (*samaṇo bhavissāmī*).[20]

While the Mahābhārata emphasizes the twice-born nature of all the Varṇas, including the Śūdra and their rights in Yajña, Buddha speaks of becoming an ascetic in pursuit of truth. While the Mahābhārata considers *hiṃsā-anṛta priyā* (desirous of causing injury) (to other life forms) and attraction to disharmony (*anṛta*) as reasons for Brāhmanās taking up all forms of work (*sarvakarmopajīvinaḥ*) to become Śūdras, Buddha relegates the masses outside the first three Varṇas as 'greedy and vile conduct'. The similarity is striking. But the Buddhist enumeration terminates with the proclamation of the greatness of Kṣatriya as proclaimed by Brahmā Sanaṅkumāra. In the case of the Mahābhārata, it ends by defining again the conduct of a true Brāhmaṇa and a stern warning that if a Brāhmaṇa forgets the presence of the Divine in all beings (in the social context of human beings), then he would be born among ghouls and monsters (not other Varṇās as one would expect) —'*piśācā rākṣasāḥ pretā bahudhā mleccha jātayaḥ*'. The Mahābhārata also discusses the cardinal question 'Who is a Brāhmaṇa'?' In Vana Parva, Nahuṣa, an ancestor of Pāṇḍavas, who was cursed to be a serpent in the forest, captured Bhīma coiling around him. The condition of lifting the curse was that Yudhiṣṭhira, who was the wisest of the five brothers, should answer his questions. And the question was, '*brāhmaṇaḥ ko bhaved*?' (what makes one a Brāhmaṇa, and what is it that should be known?).[21] To this, Yudhiṣṭhira answered that a Brāhmaṇa is one who has truthfulness (*satyaṃ*), shares wealth with the needy (*dānaṃ*), has forbearance (*kṣamā*), has good conduct (*śīlam*), is impartial in proclaiming justice (*ānṛśaṃsyaṃ*), is self-restraint (*damo*), and has compassion (*ghṛṇā*).[22] However, Nahuṣa counters this by stating that these qualities are found in Śūdra too. To this, Yudhiṣṭhira gives an unequivocal answer. Drawing strength from definitely an already existing tradition, he declares, 'If in one (whom the society/custom considers as) Śūdra the virtues exist, then he is verily and surely known as Brāhmaṇa' (*vṛttaṃ sa brāhmaṇaḥ smṛtaḥ*).[23] But Nahuṣa persists. He says, 'If you state that by character alone a Brāhmaṇa is to be recognized, then what is the value of Jāti, i.e., birth in defining a Brāhmaṇa?' Here Yudhiṣṭhira points out that humans have long inter-married between categories because of sexual attraction. Further birth, sexual intercourse, and death are the same for all human beings. Then he cites Vedic authority (*idam ārṣaṃ pramāṇaṃ*, i.e., Vedic rishis have authoritatively stated) that whatever may be one's birth, all have the right in the celebration of Yajña. Hence it is character that takes primal precedence (*chīlaṃ pradhāneṣṭaṃ*) in defining whether one is a Brāhmaṇa or otherwise.[24]

In the definition of a Brāhmaṇa, an important value mentioned is *ānṛśaṃsyaṃ*. It means impartial justice irrespective of what is conducive to one's own personal benefits and profits. This would be brought out by Yudhiṣṭhira himself, both in theory and in practice, during the famous episode of Yakṣa Praśna. Here again, a question is asked as to what defines Brāhmaṇa nature (Brāhmaṇyam): whether it is birth, conduct, or *Svādhyāya,* which is a self-study for realizing the Self. In this context, this refers to the study of Vedic and Vedantic texts and, hence, being a Vedantic Pandit. The authenticity of this particular question and answer are contested because they are absent in the authentic manuscripts obtained so far. Nevertheless, what is important is that it gels with the overall spirit of the earlier text, and it has also been widely accepted by the collective civilizational psyche of India. For example, Padma Vibushan K. Balasubramania Iyer (1892-1970), a great Sanskrit scholar, in his translation and commentary of *Yakṣa Praśna,* includes this question. The answer of Yudhiṣṭhira is unambiguous:

> *Śṛṇu yakṣa kulam tata nasvādhyāya nacashrutam*
> *karanam hi dvijaṭve ca vṛttameva na saṃśaya:*
>
> Listen, Respected Yaksha, it is not ancestry (birth) or study or learning of Veda, or hearing or culture that is the cause of Brahminhood. Without doubt (na saṃśaya:), it is only conduct (Vṛttameva) that is the cause of Brahminhood. [25]

The Mahābhārata brings in the story of Dharmavyādha. Here a butcher is made the spiritual instructor of a Brāhmaṇa Brahmachāri Kauśika. Guided by a householder woman, he travelled to Mithila to the workplace of Dharmavyādha, who then imparts wisdom to the Brāhmaṇa. Historically the Mahābhārata is a layered text. There is a strong possibility that the concept of defiled trades based on excessive importance given to ahimsa and looking down on the hereditary Jātis are getting a strong rebuttal in this narration.

While the setting of the story itself is well-known, the way it is narrated repudiates the concept of untouchability. While the Buddhist worldview demanded that the butchers and meat sellers be considered untouchables, here, 'twice-born' people direct the Brāhmaṇa Kauśika to the meat shop of Dharmavyādha. The butcher considers the place unsuitable for a young Brahmin and hence invites (*gṛhaṁ gaccāva*) to his house. The butcher also respects the Brahmin and makes him walk in the front in the form of etiquette. Then in the house of the butcher, the Brahmin is offered water to clean his face and feet, which the twice-born accepts, says the text. When the Brahmin criticizes the work the butcher does and then expands a whole dialogue that becomes the celebrated Vyādha Gītā, the butcher says, 'I have inherited this from my father, and this is my hereditary profession.' Yes, the work he does is horrid (*karma goram*), agrees Dharmavyādha, but he himself does not eat meat. That is only his choice. He even avoids butchering animals and only sells meat. It might be part of his spiritual path even. But he neither looks down upon those who eat meat nor those who butcher animals. A butcher who butchers animals for a living can be a person of exemplary character (*prāṇi-hiṁsāratiścāpi bhavate dhārmikaḥ punaḥ*). He also gives the example of King Ranti Deva of old times. In his kitchen, every day, many animals would be slaughtered. But he distributed all that food and hence obtained a matchless good name (*atulā kīrti*). An explicit parallel is made between meat being offered in Vedic Yajña. It also rejects absolute ahimsa calling it impossible. Even the most pious persons, by the very act of living, unconsciously and inevitably harm other beings. At the same time, intentional injuring of all life should be rejected. Vyādha Gītā points out that any trade, including being a butcher, would not stand in the way of one becoming self-realized. No trade needs to be looked down upon. And on the self-realization of the individual, he or she becomes the Self, and even the hereditary Brahmins would have to learn from them. As Vyādha Gītā nears the end, the butcher reveals that in the previous birth, during a hunting expedition, he unknowingly injured a hermit because of whose curse he was born a butcher. This is the karmic justification of birth in a defiled trade community that is also common in the Buddhist-Jain literature. But at this point in Vyādha Gītā, the Brahmin states that he considers the butcher, even in this birth, as a Brahmin only because:

> *Yastu śūdro dame satye dharme ca satatotthitaḥ* |
> *taṃ brāhmaṇamahaṃ manye vṛttena hi bhaveddvijaḥ*
>
> A (person considered by the society as) *Śūdra* who is ceaselessly fixed in self-restraint, Truth and Dharma, him I consider as a *Brāhmaṇa* because it is through conduct (*vṛttena*) that a person becomes twice-born (*dvijaḥ*).[26]

In the Shanti Parva of the Mahābhārata, Bhīṣma narrates a dramatic event involving Tulādhāra, a trader of forest-derived herbs and herbal products at Vārāṇasī. Tulādhāra teaches the eternal dharma to a Brahmin ascetic named Jājali. According to Tulādhāra, Sanātana Dharma, which has existed since ancient times, means being friendly towards all living beings (*dharmaṃ sarahasyaṃ sanātanam sarvabhūtahitaṃ maitraṃ*). Although absolute non-harming of all creatures is ideal, Tulādhāra explains that in the case of necessity, the harm done to other living organisms should be as minimal as possible. Tulādhāra insists on three things: being compassionate and friendly to all living beings, causing no injury to them, and treating and viewing all as equal and doing everything in the spirit of Yajña. Explaining these to the Brahmin ascetic is done here by a trader. That is the ethical tension presented by the Mahābhārata in a society that predominantly functions on the basis of hereditary work guilds.

In the background of the notion of noble professions and defiled trades, the epic speaks for equal nobility within all professions and trades. Every trade can be a Yajña and in all birth-based communities, persons can be of Brāhmaṇa nature and become the authority for dharma. From them, others, however high-placed in the society they might be, should learn. It is within this value system of spiritual equality that the Bhagavad Gītā is placed. Bāl Gangādara Tilak, Indian nationalist, teacher, and independence activist, in his elaborate commentary on the Bhagavad Gītā, calls karma yoga 'the energetic path'. According to him, this is based on the 'spiritual knowledge, of continually performing all worldly affairs as pure duties with the idea of dedicating them to the *Parameśvara*, and thereby making a sacrifice to, or worshipping lifelong, the *Parameśvara*.' This is the path delineated by the Bhagavad Gītā and is known as the 'Bhagavata religion'. According to him, both the narrations of Dharmavyāda the butcher and Tulādāra the trader also emphasize the karma yoga of the Bhagavad Gītā.[27]

Now, coming to the text of the Bhagavad Gītā itself, one needs to estimate its possible time of composition. Even Kashi Nath Upadhyaya, who believed in the presence of Buddhist influence in the Bhagavad Gītā, dates it to 500 to 400 BCE. This well predates the assumed period of 'resurgent Brahminism arising against Buddhism', which would be from the 1st century CE. Dr Ambedkar believed that the triguṇa concept in the Bhagavad Gītā was 'a cruel perversion of the philosophy of Kapila'. On 3 October 1954, in a speech broadcast by All India Radio (AIR), he said:

> Every man should have a philosophy of life, for everyone must have a standard by which to measure his conduct. And philosophy is nothing but a standard by which to measure. Negatively, I reject the Hindu Social Philosophy propounded in the Bhagvat Geeta based as it is, on the Triguna of the Sankhya

> philosophy which is in my judgement a cruel perversion of the philosophy of Kapila, and which had made the Caste System and the System of Graded Inequality the law of Hindu Social Life.... My philosophy has a mission. I have to do the work of conversion; for, I have to make the followers of Triguna theory to give it up and accept mine. Indians today are governed by two different ideologies. Their political ideal set out in the Preamble to the Constitution affirms a life of Liberty, Equality, and Fraternity. Their social ideal embodied in their religion denies them.[28]

For Dr Ambedkar, the view of the Bhagavad Gītā was that its triguṇa concept is immutable, and through karma, it decides the birth in a particular caste. So, a person with *tamas* would be born in the Śūdra caste. Or those born in Śūdra castes are, by innate nature, *tamasic*. But the Bhagavad Gītā does not make the triguṇa immutable and totally innate.

As all these are the effects of the increase of the sattva guna, the differences in the effects of the sattva, the rajas, and the tamas have been described at length in order to convey the importance of acquiring sattva. In the celebrated *Gita Bhashya* by Ramanujacharya, the acharya makes it clear that no creature is free from the three gunas of the Prakriti 'either among men and others on earth or among the gods in heaven, that is, among all that are in association with the *Prakriti* from *Brahmā* down to immovable things'. The Bhagavad Gītā has 'described at length' the effects of 'the increase of the sattva guna, the differences of the effects of the sattva, the rajas and the tamas' only because increasing of *sattva* for the individual 'can be *acquired*'.[29] This means it is not decided by birth. Even more importantly, when Buddha speaks of those 'who do not strive', He imputes an innate inert and dense nature and then associates it with what He considers as 'Hina Jātis'. Yet the colonial and colonized traditionalist association of the caste system of the nineteenth and twentieth centuries with the Bhagavad Gītā is so strong that even a scholar of Dr Ambedkar's stature considers it as perverting Sankhya Tri-Guṇa as innate and immutable while the opposite is true.

But here, the responsibility for the harsh judgement of the Bhagavad Gītā by Dr Ambedkar lies more with the traditionalist Hindu leaders of the period (and to a significant extent even today) than with Dr Ambedkar. Even a reformist like Mahatma Gandhi, when explaining Bhagavad Gītā 4:13, wrote that 'guna and karma' are 'inherited by birth'.[30] This was the voice of a reformer contemporary of Dr Ambedkar. It should be remembered that Mahatma Gandhi was sincerely fighting the crime of untouchability. Yet this was his voice. Then, it can be imagined what would have been the interpretation of the Bhagavad Gītā by traditionalist religious leaders like the then-contemporary Shankaracharyas. It should be remembered that the good doctor started his reformist actions by basing his philosophy on that of the Bhagavad Gītā. An entry in *Encyclopaedia of Dalits in India* points out this historical fact:

> It is interesting to know that at the stage of the mid-1920s, Ambedkar understood that untouchables and caste Hindus belonged to one and the same religion and based his argument on the Bhagavad Gita, deemed as one of the sacred books in Hinduism. He argues that an agitation aiming at eliminating discrimination of Hindus by same Hindus is nothing less than satyagraha judged by any criterion given in the Gita and that though there is no denying that Gandhi is the first creator of the Satyagraha movement, Satyagraha does not always mean ahimsa and if possible and himsa (violence) if necessary, as it is in the end the moral nature of their conduct that determines whether or not it is Satyagraha. (*Bahishkrut Bharat*, 25-Nov-1927 in AACAS, 127–32)[31]

So, if such a scholar-activist and a thorough patriot as well as nation builder said that the Bhagavad Gītā cruelly perverted

Sankhya philosophy, then that necessitates searching the conscience of Hindu traditional religious leaders. That such criticism of the Bhagavad Gītā by Dr Ambedkar is legit can also be understood by the statement made by Belgian Indologist Dr Koenraad Elst, who is sympathetic to the Hindu Right Wing ideology in India. In a discussion thread on the topic at the online discussion forum of Religion in South Asia (RISA), a part of the American Academy of Religions (AAR), Dr Elst said that though he 'is in sympathy with the reformist agenda' he is sceptical that the Bhagavad Gītā was not in favour of birth-based division of the society. Referring to Verse 4:13, where Krishna states that the divisions were created based on 'Guṇa and Karma', Elst says the following:

> I am skeptical here for its sounds like a typical exercise in contrived exegesis in the service of an (admittedly laudable) agenda. The Gita does not say: 'not birth but work/karma and quality/guna', because one's work and quality could in their turn be determined by birth. Indeed, they are: qualities are to some statistically noticeable extent inborn, and a profession was traditionally taught in the home setting from father to son. So, nature and nurture conspired to make a succession from father to son in your work/karma the general rule, hence profession determined 'by birth', i.e. by the family that both generates and raises you. While this quote fails to disprove that caste by birth was the norm, other lines in the Gita positively confirm it.... To be sure, the Mahabharata was edited over a long period, and may have been twisted in the final round to suit the emerging casteist ideology which finds full expression in one of the younger parts, the Gita.[32]

The crux of Elst's argument itself rests not on Bhagavad Gītā 4:13 but on another verse, Bhagavad Gītā 3:24, where Kṛṣṇa uses the same term that Arjuna uses in Bhagavad Gītā 1:41. Taking into account all these verses, Elst makes his point:

> When Arjuna and Kṛṣṇa argue opposite viewpoints, viz. against and for the start of a fratricidal war, *both* conclude their argumentation with the warning that the opposite view will result in 'varna-sankara', 'mixing of castes'. If opposing viewpoints are justified with reference to the same value, viz. non-mixing of castes, this value must be a cornerstone of that society. Again, apologists will explain this away by saying that varna-sankara could also mean 'mixing of functions', e.g. a politician who ventures into religion or vice-versa would be a case of Brahman-Kshatriya-sankara. But that is too contrived and is refuted by the text's linking varna-sankara to 'immorality of women', i.e. a sexual mixing of castes.

So here we have a convergence between the points of view expressed by Dr Ambedkar in 1954 and Dr Elst in 2007. It is also important to note that many traditionalists would actually agree with the meaning that Elst gives to the Bhagavad Gītā verses. Only what Elst calls 'casteist', they would call it 'dharma'. However, a look into the verses of the Bhagavad Gītā, along with other verses in it, gives an alternative picture that is consistent with the spirit and values conveyed by the Mahābhārata and also the larger Hindu deep civilizational process. In pre-modern times, occupations were determined by birth and hierarchies based on birth were considered divine sanction, attributing 'casteist' ideology as even one of the motives of the Bhagavad Gītā is questionable. The question should be, then, does the Bhagavad Gītā have a viable and non-convoluted hermeneutic space not only for spiritual equanimity, a potent precursor for social egalitarianism, but also against the birth-based social aristocracy, elitism, and exclusion?

The first chapter of the Bhagavad Gītā is replete with notions of birth-based purity. In what can only be called an obsession, Arjuna, in a short span of seven verses, uses the term *kula* ten times. He regards kula dharma with great rectification as it is sanctified, ancient, and has been followed since time immemorial. The verses delineate a sequence where the war destroys the clan (*kula-kṣhaye*), which in turn results in the destruction of the dharma of the clan, which is ancient and eternal (*kula-dharma sanātanah*). Whoever is left of the clan turns to adharma. With adharma the women of the clan (*kula-striyaḥ*) become immoral (*duṣhṭāsu*), which in turn results in the mixture of Varṇas (*varṇa-saṅkaraḥ*). The mixture of Varṇa, in turn, leads to unwanted progeny, causing chaotic, hellish conditions in the society. As a result, oblations to the ancestors are lost, and with such misdeeds, the family traditions, birth-based dharma, and clan dharma (jāti dharma and kula dharma) are lost forever.[33]

The reason Arjuna attributes the immorality of clan women to the mixture of social divisions. He also uses the unambiguous term *varṇa-saṅkaraḥ* meaning mixing of social divisions and relates varṇa to kula and jāthi. Destruction of kula leads to adharma, which leads to the immorality of women, which in turn leads to a mixture of varṇa, which again results in the loss of kula dharma and jāthi dharma.

Dr Elst points out the use of the same term *saṅkaraḥ* by Krishna as an unwanted social phenomenon that would happen if He ceases to do His own action. Therefore, both Arjuna and Kṛṣṇa view a mixture of varṇas as a negative, unwanted phenomenon, despite having diametrically opposite stands. In this regard, Prof. Arvind Sharma, in the very same discussion thread at RISA, points out that while Arjuna uses the term *varṇa-saṅkaraḥ* 'in the sense of miscegenation (1.40-42), Kṛṣṇa seems to take it only in the sense of abandonment of duty (3.24)'.[34] He points out that the term has multiple meanings on the authority of *Manu Smṛti* (10:24). The verse clearly states three distinct reasons resulting in mixture or confusion, which are 'infidelity *among* the castes, by the marrying of women unfit for marriage and neglect of one's duties (*svakarmaṇāṃ ca tyāgena*)'. Therefore, the mixture means more confusion than intercaste marriage-based mixing. Here one should also remember that Yudhiṣṭhira has already stated that from very ancient times, there have been marriages among the different hereditary communities on account of which the varṇa of an individual cannot be based on birth but only on his or her conduct.

What Prof. Sharma says is consistent with the spirit of both what Kṛṣṇa says and the value system held positive by the epic at large. In the seventeen chapters of the Bhagavad Gītā, throughout His explanations, Kṛṣṇa never uses, even once, any of the terms repeatedly used by Arjuna, i.e., kula dharma or jāti dharma. Instead, He uses the term *svadharma,* and this arises out of *svabhāva,* which in turn comes from the triguṇa dynamics of the individual. This is consistent with what not only Yudhiṣṭhira says but many other positive characters say throughout the epic, that it is the individual character and conduct that constitutes one's varṇa. In contrast, Buddha encapsulated the definition of true Brāhmaṇā into His own sectarian doctrinal space conceptually and Sangha institutionally, Kṛṣṇa in the Bhagavad Gītā and the epic in general, in their own way, secularize and democratize the Brāhmaṇā hood and by consequence, the entire varṇa system.

Viewed in this context, the choice of words in the Bhagavad Gītā (4:13), *guṇa-karma-vibhāgaśaḥ,* (based on modalities and work) indicates a paradigm shift in a society stagnating because of world-views that categorized hereditary (kula/ jāthi) work-communities as noble and defiled because of the imposition of values like ahimsa as universal. If the text was casteist or pro-casteist, it could have unambiguously declared itself as *kula-janma-vibhāgaśaḥ* (based on clan and birth). That such is the value system of the Bhagavad Gītā is further fortified by the fact that the notion of one being high-born (*abhijanavān asmi*) and doing sacrifices and charity (*yakṣhye dāsyāmi*) is included as one of the Asuric qualities in chapter sixteen of the Bhagavad Gītā.[35]

From all the historical data, most historians construe that, in all probabilities, during the time of the Bhagavad Gītā, untouchability had not become institutionalized. There was social exclusion but no institutionalized untouchability. However, the mode of social exclusion did contain the seeds for the later evolution of this institution. It involves mainly an aversion to the body. In rural India and in the case of marginalized sections in urban settings, even today, untouchability is a persistent social evil. The Indian Constitution has declared it a crime with severe punishments. But it still persists. There are often atrocities committed against the former untouchable communities called Scheduled Castes. Many activist groups use the name 'Dalits'. Mahatma Gandhi used the term 'Harijans'. The Scheduled Castes themselves mostly abhor both the terms as demeaning.

The Bhagavad Gītā provides a critique of body-based aversion to others. It even provides an analysis of the psychological elements that result in such aversion. Kṛṣṇa says:

Ahankāraṁ balaṁ darpaṁ kāmaṁ krodhaṁ cha sanśhritāḥ
mām ātma-para-deheṣhu pradviṣhanto bhyasūyakāḥ[36]

The psychological drives of egotism, power, insolence, lust, and wrath are considered factors resulting in the harmful antagonizing (*pradviṣhanto*) of the Divine principle (ātma) in one's own and others' physical bodies (*deheṣhu*). In very secular terms, this can be construed easily as harming the fulfilment of one's human potential in oneself and others because of the aversion for the bodies, which in turn arises from egotism, power (political, monetary, communal, etc.), the excessive show of superiority, lust, and vengeful wrath (like old narratives of enmity, etc.). According to this verse, the aversion to body-based pollution arises due to the depreciation of the Divine Principle in one's own body, which, when it cannot be recognized, makes one fail to recognize it in others. Conversely, if one cannot perceive even in the faintest way the Divine in other bodies and has only aversion for others, then he will naturally be incapable of recognizing the Divine in one's own body.

This is complemented by verses in the chapter on Dhyana Yoga:

> The one who is fixed in Yoga (*yoga-yuktātmā*) is the one who sees all beings rooted in the Self (*sarva-bhūta-stham ātmānaṃ*) and the Self present in all the beings (*sarva-bhūtāni cātmani*) and hence views all with equanimity (*sama-darśanaḥ*).[37]

If it is the Self, then there is no need for a personal relation with all. The Self can be an abstract construct at the intellectual level. So, in the very next verse, that Self gets identified with *Kṛṣṇa* – a very tangible, adorable, personal Godhead.

> He who sees Me in all (*māṃ paśyati sarvatra*) and all in Me (*sarvaṃ ca mayi paśyati*), that person never is lost from Me and Me from that person.[38]

This could be objected to as '*sarva-bhūta*' here means all beings from ants and microbes to aliens and men. Hence, this need not necessarily mean equality of human beings. It has been pointed out that the subtle yet powerful transformation of ātmā in 6:29 into 'Māṃ' (here it refers to Kṛṣṇa Himself) in 6:30 makes the relation more realistic than abstract. This reaches even higher emphasis in the social setting. In 'Daivāsura-Sampada-Yoga' in the aforementioned very human setting with regard to the hatred for the physical bodies, Kṛṣṇa brings both terms together: *mām ātma-para-deheṣhu*.

Thus, the Bhagavad Gītā sets the high philosophical core for an egalitarian social renaissance that is deeply psychological and, hence, more holistically transformational than political ideologies and ideologies triggered revolutions. While most revolutions that defined the modern age—from the French Revolution to the Maoist Great Leap—have generated extreme human misery and violence, and their effects were short lived, the revolution that the Bhagavad Gītā was a part of, namely bhakti, became the most sustained social transformational movement against the human societal tendencies towards social stagnation and social exclusion. This unfolded through the history of India, through millennia, in a unique decolonized way.

CHAPTER 9

Bhakti, the Holistic Yajña Movement: Vedic to Early Medieval Period

Bhakti is a universal phenomenon. It is found in all religious cultures. In its pure form, it is a process of individuation that leads to self-transcendence. In Indian culture, from its very beginning, this phenomenon was understood in a very analytical manner and integrated into Yoga. It also became a strong influence on the society. Spiritual equanimity-based harmony in the society was emphasized over social stratification and even opposed to social exclusion. At the same time, this influence on society came from the outpouring of the very deeply individualistic process of bhakti. Thus, bhakti becomes the most potent link of creativity and justice between the society and the individual. It simultaneously affects the individual realization of inner potentials in a creative and transcendentally expansive nature while at the same time challenging the societal status quo, injecting vitality into social emancipation. This chapter explores how this transformative power of bhakti has operated throughout Indian history—from historical to medieval times.

The conventional model of the evolution of Indian society and its values posits that the bhakti movement was either a reactionary movement to Buddhism and Jainism or a rebellion against the caste system or both. Further, according to this model, the bhakti movement later atrophied and was appropriated by 'Brahmanical'

Hinduism. This chapter is a critical evaluation of this model and proposes an alternative that sets bhakti in its own autopoietic manifestation, contextualizing it as a universal spiritual movement within, i.e., the inner realm of the individual with an enormous impact on society. Though bhakti is a universal spiritual movement that can be identified in all human societies, it is in India that it has been recognized as a valid phenomenon, systematized as almost a science and has an enormous impact on society.

Bhakti: An Independent Co-Evolution

In 1958, Hindu intellectual savant Ram Swarup (1920–98) published a paper titled 'Hinduism vis-a-vis Buddhism'. In 1966 the eminent Indian statesman and freedom fighter Sri C. Rajagopalachari or Rajaji (1878–1972) commented on this paper in the magazine *Swarajya*. He wrote that the paper, apart from vividly explaining the affinity between Hinduism and Buddhism, also showed how Hinduism saved itself from 'the dangers of its own philosophical dialectics through the cult of Bhakti and surrender'. Ram Swarup made a respectful and detailed criticism of this stand of Rajaji. He wrote,

> Sri Rajagopalacharya agrees that there was a great affinity between the Vedanta and the Buddhist philosophy, but according to him Hinduism saw in it a danger of being misunderstood and identified with a school which denied God and soul; and it met the danger by developing the school of bhakti and surrender. I believe Hinduism sensed no such danger and it did not panic into bhakti and surrender because of any such danger. The fact is Bhakti and surrender even as a 'school' are older than Buddhism. They are great truths of the Spirit and, as is to be expected, they found their great expression in a comprehensive religion like Hinduism as did other great truths of the Spirit.[1]

This observation is important for two reasons. First, it highlights that even an erudite and learned scholar of Hindu dharma like

Rajaji was not immune to the influence of the standard model wherein bhakti was construed as a Hindu response to Buddhism. Second, it mentions an observation by Ram Swarup that bhakti predates Buddhism. Chapter 8 also demonstrated that bhakti does have Vedic roots. The text also refers to the flourishing of the Bhāgavata religion in the context of the Vedic God Viṣṇu during the rise and spread of Buddhism. Archaeological evidence supports this claim. The entry for 'The Archaeology of Hinduism' in the authoritative volume *Archaeology and World Religions* addresses this aspect:

> The earliest series is known as the Janapada (territories/principalities) coins, named after the principalities into which the subcontinent was divided during the sixth century BCE, the time of the Buddha. The symbols occurring on these coins have been studied and certain specific symbols or groups of symbols have been ascribed to individual principalities such as Magadha, Kasi, Kosala, etc. Five Saivite symbols can easily be located on such coins: the bull, footmark of a bull or Nandipada, trident, halfmoon, and the Lingam or phallic emblem itself. The solar motif in the form of a disc is common and may denote a sun-god or Surya. Similarly, the representation of spoked wheels sometimes found may suggest the discus of Vishnu, a peacock may stand for the god Karttikeya, a female figure standing on, or associated with, a lotus may be Sri or Lakshmi, the goddess of wealth. These symbols unmistakably indicate that a number of major Hindu cults had assumed their distinct identities during this period. The first Vishnu temples are found in the third century BCE. The evidence is limited but conclusive. At Nagari, the ancient city of Madhyamika in eastern Rajasthan, an inscription dating from the first century BCE suggests that at this place an extant stone-built enclosure was already associated with the worship of Narayana or Vishnu. Evidence for this earlier structure has been found archaeologically at 60 cm below the first-century BCE ground level of this enclosure where excavation revealed a structure.... This was the original Vishnu

temple mentioned by the inscription and can be securely dated to the third century BCE.[2]

Hindu temples have always been more than just spaces for congregational worship. They emerge as important conceptual and solidly architectural nodes connecting Yajña and bhakti. Indologist Stella Kramrisch (1896–1993) highlighted this in her authoritative work on Hindu temples:

> The living memory of the Fire Altar... has not only remained at the bottom of the temple where the *Vāstupuruṣamaṇḍala* represents its main residue, coterminous as it is actually or in principle with the Vedi, the total site, or with the extent of the *Prāsāda*.... The Vedic altar survives in the structure of the body of the temple, in its lowest and its highest part. In technique and name the *Prāsāda*, the Hindu temple shares in the name of the *Vedi* and *Citi*.... The architectural rhythms of the Hindu temple impart to each building its consistency and wholeness. They evoke in the devotee (*bhakta*) an adjustment of his person to its structure; his subtle body (*sūkṣma śarīra*) responds to the proportions of the temple by an inner rhythmical movement. By this 'aesthetic' emotion the devotee is one with the temple; and qualified to realize the presence of God.[3]

Rather than a reaction or response to Buddhism, bhakti can best be considered a parallel but independent and Vedic-rooted phenomenon. Even when Buddhism was in its very early centuries, still nascent, Vedic-rooted bhakti had evolved into a social phenomenon, as proved by the emergence of temples as places of communal worship.

Another important connection between Yajña and bhakti comes through the principle of Śraddhā. Vedic texts themselves speak highly of śraddhā. *Ṛig Veda* has a Sūkta (X.151) for Śraddhā which is addressed as a divine feminine, similar to how bhakti is personified in later literature. She is indispensable for

Yajña because it is she who kindles the Agni; it is Śraddhā who is the *Havis,* the sacred sacrificial offering poured into the Agni (*Sraddhaya hūyate haviḥ*); through the hymns, Śraddhā, who belongs to the family of Love, is glorified.[4] The Mahābhārata points out that a sacrifice loses its meaning if the spirit of Śraddhā is withdrawn. Śraddhā herself is the Yajña, the spirit that presides over all its attendant ceremonies. She is the goddess of the sacrifice.[5] This shifts, to a large extent, the centre of gravity of Yajña from ritual performance, without eliminating or replacing it, to the state of consciousness of the one who performs the Yajña. In the very later texts dealing with Indic aesthetic psychological principles such as *Saṅgitaratnākarā* and *Rasataraṅgiṇi*, it is stated that there is a minor school that considers bhakti as a *rasa* assigned to Śraddhā where the latter is a 'natural human disposition' (sthāyibhāva*)*. According to Indologist Minoru Hara (1930-2021), this suggests that Śraddhā is the permanent dormant or innate instinct, which, when stimulated by a particular stimulus, naturally develops into bhakti.[6]

Thus, the involuted transformational potential of Yajña serves as an archetype of an inner process of self-expansion rooted in non-dualistic universal empathy. This process permeates through the psychological, social, metaphysical, and mystical realms of the individual and binds together an emancipatory community through its force. This concept is already present in the Vedic literature, with Śraddhā serving as the vital link.

Thanks to Greek sources, we have a very clear picture of the religious landscape of the early Buddhist pre-Aśokan period. Megasthenes was the ambassador to the Indian emperor Sandrocottus, believed to be Chandragupta Maurya (350-295 BCE) from Seleucus I Nicator (circa 358-281 BCE). Most scholars agree that he visited parts of North India around 303 BCE. Although his original work *Indika* is lost, it has been quoted by many classical Greek historians. Indologist Edwin Bryant highlights how major Greek historians quoting Megasthenes had pointed out the existence of the devotional worship of Kṛṣṇa as an important Deity:

> According to Arrian, Diodorus, and Strabo, Megasthenes described an Indian tribe called the Sourasenoi, who especially worshiped Herakles in their land, and this land had two great cities, Methora and Kleisobora, and a navigable river, the Jobares. As was common in the ancient period, the Greeks sometimes described foreign gods in terms of their own divinities, and there is little doubt that the Sourasenoi refers to the Shurasenas, a branch of the Yadu dynasty to which Krishna belonged; Herakles to Krishna, or Hari-Krishna; Methora to Mathura, where Krishna was born; Kleisobora to Krishna pura, meaning 'the city of Krishna'; and the Jobares to the Yamuna, the famous river in the Krishna story. Quintus Curtius also mentions that when Alexander the Great confronted Porus, Porus's soldiers were carrying an image of Herakles in their vanguard.[7]

Greek historian Strabo writes about the presence of 'Dionysiac' elements in the worship of mountain communities in India, while 'Heracles' was worshipped in the plains. Art historian M.L. Varapande explains that the worship of 'Indian Dionysus' (likely referring to Śiva) and Indian Heracles (referring to Kṛṣṇa) involved dancing and singing:

> The Greeks struck upon the similarity between the Dionysian and Indian cults, particularly in the area of theatre. They must have come across various ancient Indian cults in which the rituals included dance and music like the Dionysian and other fertility cults of Greece.... The Indian Dionysus has satyr-like Ganas around him, half human, half animal, and the dark-hued Heracles of Methora is surrounded by fair girls who run in frenzy to him, to dance on hearing his flute.[8]

Strabo also says on the authority of *Indika* that in the plains, Heracles was worshipped by 'philosophers'. As late as 2021, Prof. Richard Stoneman, an expert in ancient Western history and Alexander the Great, stated that this should be an 'erroneous attribution of worship of "Heracles" to plain dwellers is still less to be associated with any philosophical position'.[9] That a popular worship with music and dance could be organically associated with 'high philosophy' and a philosopher at peace with such popular devotion still seems an uncomfortable thought for Western scholarship.

Similarly, the devotional and popular tradition of Śiva had strong philosophical roots. During the time of grammarian Pāṇini, there existed 'Śiva-Bhāgavatas' as per scholar-mystic Patañjali, as he revealed in his celebrated *Mahābhāṣya*. Patañjali also mentioned that the killing of evil Kamsa by Kṛṣṇa, a central theme in later bhakti literature, was performed through dance-drama for the public. This likely took place between the 3rd and 1st century BCE. R.G. Bhandarkar identified the Śiva-Bhāgavatas as the followers of Lakulīśa, a quasi-historical originator of a primary Śaivaite tradition. According to D.R. Bhandarkar, Lakulīśa likely belonged to the 2nd century CE and was more of a systematizer of an already existing tradition, probably pre-Common Era.[10] The chronicles of Alexander the Great also speak of the 'Siboi' people who lived in the 'Shorkot region in the Jhang district below the junction of Jhilam and the Chināb'. They were probably identical to the Śiva people mentioned in a passage of the *Rig Veda* (VII.18.7) and were one of the Vedic tribes who fought with King Suda of Vedic period. All of this indicates a long continuity in the tradition of Śiva worship.[11]

Archaeological evidence for the flourishing of a strong Vaishnava Bhāgavata tradition is attested by the famous Garuda-Pillar at Besnagar. Hēliodōrous was an ambassador to Indian King Bhāgabhadra from Antialcidas, an Indo-Greek king with Taxila as his capital (130 to 120 BCE). Hēliodōrous embraced the bhakti tradition and became a 'Bhāgavata'. He erected the famous 'Garuda Pillar' at Besnagar. The inscription on the pillar reads:

> This Garuda-standard of *Vāsudeva*, the god of gods, was constructed here by *Hēliodōra* (*Hēliodōrous*), the *Bhāgavata*, son of *Diōn*, a man of *Takhkhasila* the Greek ambassador who came from the Great King Amtalikita (Antialkidas) to King *Kāsiputra Bhāgabhadra*, the Saviour, prospering in (his) fourteenth regal year.... Three immortal path-steps (*Trini amuta—pādāni*)... when practiced lead to Swarga: self-restraint(*dama*) giving others (at the cost of one's own denial- *cāga*) and awareness (towards faultlessness) (*apramāda*).[12]

Here, one can see the inner bhakti is characterized by the socially relevant value of sharing one's wealth with others, even at the point of denying it to oneself. Thus, bhakti evolved parallel with Buddhism. Bhakti also became the corrective civilizational process that brought together individual self-realization and positive social values, namely egalitarianism, proactive removal of notions of superiority and inferiority, religious pluralism, and nation formation through theo-diversity.

The rise of Buddhism to popularity and as a state religion would happen with the Maurya emperor Aśoka and till the end of the Mauryan dynasty (268 to 185 BCE). This was followed by the Sungha rise. However, the first three centuries of the Common Era saw the establishment of the Kushan Empire Central Asian Yuezhi people. In the standard model of history, the Kushan empire is associated with Buddhism. Kanishka (127–150 CE), considered the greatest of all Kushan emperors, rapidly expanded his empire inside India from the so-called Gandhara region through Kashmir up to Bengal and even penetrated peripheral regions of China. During the time of

Kanishka, the fourth Buddhist Council was organized. At the same time, Kanishka was not a Buddhist. Less than 1 per cent of his known coins show Buddha. However, the Kushan period played a very crucial role in one of the important features of bhakti. During this time, Hindu-Buddhist iconography became highly standardized.

It may not be a coincidence here that along with the standardization of Hindu-Buddhist iconography, the theme of Yajña became an important symbol of the rulers. On the Kushan coins of Vima Kadphises, father of Kanishka, as well as those of Kanishka, there is an interesting change in the relationship between the ruler and the deity. For the first time, the ruler is shown making an offering at the fire altar. The shape of the fire altar resembles that of the Iranian fire altar. Historian Nayanjot Lahiri points out an important fact about this 'oldest representation of fire altar in Asiatic coins'.[13] Archaeologist Satya Shrava, in his detailed study of Kushan coins, considered that the fire altar, even though the imagery was Parthian, 'emerged from Indian customs'.[14] The Indian nature of the fire altar is further strengthened by the fact that in the famous Rabatak inscription of Kanishka, he called his 'grandfather Saddashkana the Soma sacrificer'.[15]

What is the importance of this? Many historians have argued that the Kushans brought to India the concept of divine kingship, citing as evidence 'epithets such as *devaputra* (son of a god/the gods), *bagopouro* (son of god), and *bagoshao* (god king)'.[16] A pop historian columnist in a web portal even went to the extent of making intentionally sensational claims that a deity that led to the worship of a deified Kushan king later got incorporated into the Hindu pantheon. However, the Yajña symbolism in the coins shows more of a Hinduization of Kushan polity. As Prof. Pankaj Jain, a scholar of religious studies and sustainability, points out, 'the major religious phenomena of Vedic India for *lokasaṃgraha*, activities for unifying Vedic society socially, religiously and politically'.[17] So, by the 1st century of the Common Era, Yajña definitely had become an important social archetype. Later in the modern era, this would give rise to the concept of what Mahatma Gandhi called 'trusteeship socialism'. But in effecting this, the bhakti movement played a decisive role. It is not a coincidence that cutting across specific tradition-based boundaries, bhakti emerged as a unifier. It unified across the horizontal boundaries of sects and vertical hierarchies of society.

This was also a pan-Indian phenomenon though the oldest direct literary evidence for this comes from the south.

South Indian Contribution to Bhakti

During the period of 300 BCE to 300 CE, we find that Caṅkam (Sangham) literature presents a culturally vibrant picture of Tamil Nadu. Pertinent to the present discussion is that the society shows the presence of Vedic Yajña well established in the society. In *Paripāṭal*, a verse provides the imagery of a Yajña and relates it to the form of the deity Viṣṇu (Thirumāl):

> You have as your high mast the birth of red-cued mouth (Garuda): the *Sruthi* chanting by the performers of *Yajña* become your form. You in the form of *Yajña Yupa*, have as food the animal tied for the sacrifice. As Brahmins through proper rituals, nurture and expand the sacred fire in the *Yajña*, Your form manifests. Even those who deny the Divine when witnessing this would affirm the sacred Divine presence.[18]

Here, we have perhaps one of the earliest expressions of connecting the divine form of a deity, which here is Viṣṇu. In *Paripāṭal,* most of the later expanded forms of bhakti expressions of the divine are present quite explicitly:

Thou art the five primordial elements (of the physical existence)
Of which You are realised as
One in space;
Two in air;
Three in fire;
Four in Water and
Five in land.
Thus from You emerged
All the realms
Thou art their primordial root
And also the Dharma
And the Time and Space, Fire and Wind.

It also resonates in content and style with the tenth chapter of the Bhagavad Gītā:

Thou art the radiant heat of the fire;
Thou art the fragrance of the flower;
Thou art the love in Dharma;
Thou art the strength in valour;
Thou art the Upanishad in the Vedas;
(Alternatively 'Thou art the Hidden essence of the Veda';)
Thou art the warm light of the sun;
Thou art the cool brightness of the moon;
Thou art all that is;
Thou art the inner essence of all that exists.[19]

Descriptions of nature and the way parallels are employed in Caṅkam literature provide a strong substratum for the later development of Śrī Vaiṣṇav Darśana. This development would energize social emancipation in a definitive and sustained manner. For example, His chest is compared to a dark green mountain, and His sacred *Yajñopavīta* is likened to mountain waterfalls that resemble white threads from a distance.[20]

Thy scorching valorous nature manifests in the sun;

Thy cool and benevolent nature manifests in the moon;
Thy benevolent showering nature manifests in the rain;
Thy ever-nurturing patient nature manifests in the earth;
Thy fragrance and cue manifest in Kāyā flower;
Thy expansive and deep nature manifests in the water;
Thy all permeating radiant nature manifests in the space;
Thy arrival and contractive nature manifests in the winds (Maruts).[21]

The episode of Prahlāda, which later became the pan-Indian model for spiritual resistance against temporal power, is described in one of the earliest literary references. The *Viṣṇu Purāṇa*, a text dating back to the 1st century CE and standardized no later than the 5th century ce, was the first in Sanskrit tradition to describe the passive resistance of Asura prince Prahlāda to his father Hiraṇyakaśipu, who insisted that only he be worshipped. In the story, Viṣṇu emerged from a pillar to show His omnipresence and protect His child devotee.

Divine Omnipresence as the Basis of Bhakti Equanimity

The account of this Purāṇic episode in *Paripāṭal* is described in an essentialist manner, making this literary reference significant. It raises questions about the traditional model of the emergence of bhakti as a response or reactionary movement. The spiritual foundation of the *Purāṇic* episode is fundamental to the later development of the *Śrī Vaiṣṇav Darśana*.

God with naturally reddened eyes!
As Prahlāda praised you,
Heart of his father fumed.
He subjected his son to
a variety of tortures.
To remove the suffering of
the tormented boy,

Who never forsake You
Even as his father hatefully abused You,
You emerged thunderously from the pillar.
You fought the Asura
Beat him with blows causing pain.
Vanquishing the enmity in his heart
You made him merge in you.[22]

The *Paripāṭal* emphasizes the immanent nature of the Divine in every aspect of physical existence. The Divine is the defining essence of the entire universe, present everywhere. This concept of omnipresence is a core vision of the Vedic religions, focusing on the all-pervading immanence of the Divine rather than a transcendent nature beyond the cosmos. The conflict between Prahlāda and Hiraṇyakaśipu questions this omnipresent immanence of the Divine. This immanent omnipresence of the Divine forms the basis for spiritual equanimity and promotes egalitarian values, challenging social stratification and social exclusion.

Sacredness of the Holy Feet

The divine feet of God now become the subject of the poet.

> His feet (because they offer liberation to the devotees), are greater than *Viṣṇu* Himself. They are Gods by themselves. Of course Your Divine Mystery are boundless which could be realised by the God-like Tapasvis who have realised the truth of the Upanishads but for us devotees, Your feet are enough.[23]

This was not an isolated reference. The connection of the Śūdra with the feet of the primordial cosmic person (Puruṣa often substituted with God) in the Puruṣa Sūkta of the *Rig Veda* is an example of a possible stigmatizing association. However, over time, this association with the feet came to be seen as a divine honour. Both Ācāryas (religious preceptors/leaders) and kings were given the title 'Bhagavat-pāda', which meant one who is at the feet of God. This, too, was a pan-Indian phenomenon.

In the 4th and 5th centuries CE, the Trikūṭa dynasty was a powerful ruling family in the Konkan region. One of their notable kings was Dahrasēna, who performed the Aśwamēdha sacrifice and took the title Mahārāja, which his father Indradutta also held. He referred to himself as 'Parama Vaiṣṇavā' (a devout worshipper of Viṣṇu') on his coins and as 'Bhagavat-pāda-karmakāra' (a servant of the feet of Bhagavān) in his copper-plate inscription. This proclamation was made in the year 456-57 CE after a successful campaign in the Southern Gujarat region.[24] So here we have a Kṣatriya with the origin story of emerging from the shoulders of the primordial Puruṣa, declaring himself to be the servant of the divine feet.

In 1987, a chance discovery led to the finding of copper plate inscriptions in the Bāleśvara Temple Complex, Sirpur, Chhattisgarh. Among the eleven inscriptions, nine copper plate inscriptions form a group. The temple was established by King Śivagupta Bālarjuna. His period was around the beginning of the 7th century CE. In the thirty-seventh regnal year of his rule, he granted a village for the maintenance of *Maiṭhikā*, which was associated with the temple to a Śaiva Ācārya named Vyāpaśiva, also known as 'Bhagavat-pāda', who taught shastras. The following year, another village was granted to the same Ācārya 'for the purpose of sponsoring continuous sattras and worship as well as teaching and initiations for the line of pupils and grand-pupils'.[25] These inscriptions reveal the presence of a spiritual teacher associated with the temple who imparts sacred knowledge to a lineage of students similar to the traditional role of a Brāhmanā, whose origins (not to be confused with the birth) are attributed to the head of the primordial divine person according to the *Puruṣa Sūkta* . The honorific title of the Acharya relates him to the divine feet.

In both instances, veneration of the Divine Feet counteracts any real or perceived stigma associated with the feet and the origin of Śūdra. Bhakti is an important force in reversing this perception of the feet, even though it is not its primary focus. This gives a clear instance of how bhakti works in societal values.

Impersonal and Personal Harmonized in Bhakti

The omnipresence of the Divine is also emphasized not just in impersonal terms but also through personal relations:

> (Your presence is there)
> In the Banyan and Kadamba trees
> Also amidst river stream dunes
> In the hillock tops with no winds
> And elsewhere
> There there you reside
> With names divine and diverse
> Whatever the places and whatever the names
> You are the One attained through all.
> You reside inside the folded hands (of your Bhaktas).
> You are also to them, a servant who heeds their demands as orders.
> You are the protection to the all the results of their work.[26]

The resonance with the famous *Rig Veda* verse of seer Dīrghatamas, '*Ekam sat viprā bahudhā vadanti*'[27] (truth is one: wise call it by many names) is unmistakable here. In these lines, Viṣṇu, from being the God who permeates the entire universe, becomes one who resides in the folded hands of His devotees and accomplishes their requests as verily a servant to them. Yet, He also is impersonal, transcendental, and impartial. You do not harm the unbelievers or those who do not consider You as great. But the bhaktas, to realize Him, project onto Him their mental categories.[28]

Historians have traditionally believed that the Kushan warlords from central Asia, who later established their empire, introduced the concept of the king as a divine figure. However, this view has been shown to be incorrect. In the Caṅkam literature, an alternative perspective on the divine nature of the king is presented. Here, the king is seen more as a temporal instance of the divine act of protection, similar to the protection provided by Maha Viṣṇu for all the realms, with His grace acting as the umbrella. When a ruler is compared with Viṣṇu, it is because the ruler, too, protects his subjects.[29]

The *Tirumurukāṟṟuppaṭai* written by Nakkīraṉār, belongs to the late Caṅkam age, though it is not later than the early centuries of the common era. The text illustrates the various forms of worship integrated into the spiritual tradition of Murugan-Skanda. It describes the worship of Murugan-Skanda by the twice-born Brahmins chanting Vedic hymns[30] as well as the Shamanic women priestess who offer rice mixed with the blood of a freshly sacrificed white goat.[31] Were these two groups of people from different ethnicities? Were the Brahmins a recent intrusion who either appropriated an existing ancient worship, or did they syncretize the existing worship with their own? According to the Brahmins who were worshipping Muruga-Skanda in the early morning with Vedic chants, they belonged to a very ancient lineage in Tamil province.[32]

Thus, by the 5th century ce, all the defining features of bhakti, which would vividly manifest in subsequent centuries, were in place, attaining what could be called the critical mass.

Social Emancipation through Śaivite Tradition

The Śaiva tradition emerged during the Bronze Age and there is a continuity in the evolution of *Śiva Liṅga* right from the Harappan times to the classical historical period. The roots of Śaiva sects like *Pāśupata*, *Kāpālika*, etc., can be traced back to a pre-Buddhist past. Historian Govind Chandra Pande (1923-2011) pointed this out:

> The earliest literary record in our history, viz., the *Ṛgvedasaṃhitā* clearly attests the worship of Rudra. The full sublimity of Rudra is, however, unfolded in the *Yajurveda* and even today the chanting of the Śatarudriya remains without parallel for its moving power. *Rudra-Śiva* is seen to be both Apollonian and Dionysian, the god 'who is shadowed in immortality and death'. In *Śvetāśvataropaniṣad* we find the first adumbrations of the philosophical aspect of Śaivism. Its connections with Yoga and Bhakti also become manifest here.[33]

By the 7th century, a strong Bhakti-Yogic was evident in the spiritual traditions of India. Siddhānta Śaivism, as it evolved, combined various forms of inner contemplations and emphasized spiritual equality. This evolution in *Śaivism* also led to the evolution of Śaivāgama texts, which had different graded approaches to traditional social stratification. Nevertheless, the overall direction was to reject social stratification. Dr Vishva Nath Drabu, a scholar of Kashmiri Śaivism (who incidentally had to leave his Kashmir home with a precious library of 1,000 books because of Islamist fundamentalism and spent his last years in a refugee camp), explains this:

> Śaivāgamas touched upon the most profound problems of human experience and far from advocating any theory of saṃnyāsa, (renunciation), suggest that the unitive experience of God or Sivahood can be accomplished through His grace and taboos of caste are redundant in the path of self-realization.[34]

During the pre-Kushan to Gupta period, the North-Western region of India saw the assimilation of numerous ethnic tribal communities. Kashmir at that time was a very vibrant place where various spiritual traditions, both Vedic and Buddhist, converged. Prof. Subhash Kak sees in this a 'Shaiva Psychology' that encompasses religion as well as a strict science of the mind and consciousness, with bhakti serving as the foundation of this evolving sacred science:

> Shaiva psychology is optimistic, scientific, secular, and liberating. At the personal level it emphasizes reaching for the spring-well of creativity (sakti) and the schema underlying this creativity (siva). The journey leading to this knowledge may be begun in a variety of ways: through sciences, the arts, and creative social activities. But this exploration of the outside world is to be taken as a means of uncovering the architecture of the inner world. Shaiva psychology also reveals that the notion of bhakti, which has played a central role in the shaping of the Indian mind during the past millennium, may be given a focus related to a quest for knowledge.[35]

The Kashmir Śaiva tradition incorporated various Śaiva sects and produced the *Śrīsvacchandatantra*, a religious text from the 5th century CE. The text takes the form of a conversation between the Goddess Devi and the fierce form of Śiva, known as Bhairava.

> *Brahmins, Kṣatriyas, Vaiśyas, Śūdras*, and others likewise, O Dear One, All of these have the same Dharma [—they have been enjoined in the Dharma of Śiva....
>
> Brāhmaṇāḥ kṣatriyā vaiśyāḥ śūdraścānye'thavā priye
> *Sarve te samadharmāṇaḥ śivadharme niyojitāḥ*
>
> They are remembered in the Smṛtis [Vedas] as having only one Jāti: that of *Bhairava Jāti*, imperishable and pure. ...
>
> *Ekaiva sā smṛtā jātirbhairavīyā śivāvyayā |*
> *Tantrametatsamāśritya prāgjātiṃ na hyudīrayet*

> Should a man mention the prior *Jāti* of a Putraka, Sādhaka, or of a Samayin, he would require expiation, O Goddess.
>
> He burns in hell for three of Rudra's days, five of Keśava's days, And a fortnight of Brahmā's days. Therefore, one must not discriminate, if he wishes to obtain the supreme goal.[36]

The reference here to *Smṛtis* as repudiating birth-based discrimination in the initiation into the spiritual path is significant.

Through the dīkṣā by the guru, a person, regardless of their caste, is initiated into the Bhairava jāthi. The use of the term dīkṣā is significant here. In the Vedic context, it meant initiation as well as specific austerities accepted by the Yajamāna before the Yajña and also the consecration of the sacrificer before the Sōma Yajña.[37] From the Vedic period, it also served as a deep spiritual concept that defied its ritualistic reductionism. It is associated with Satya and Ṛta and leads to Tapas and Yajña. It is the consecration gateway into the sacred and forms the bond between the sacred and the secular spaces. The *Atharvaṇaveda* in the first verse of its well-known *Pṛthvī Sūkta* states that 'Truth expansive' (Satyaṁ bṛhad), cosmic order/harmony intensive (Ṛtam ugraṁ), initiation/ consecration (Dīkṣā), austerities-penances (Tapō), prayerful contemplation (Brahma), and participatory-inner sacrifice (Yajña) sustain the earth (pṛthvī dhārayantí).[38] Here dīkṣā is placed between two supra-physical and three tangible actions, with Yajña being the final one. Elsewhere, the *Atharvaṇaveda* speaks of initiation as a ceremony of rebirth in which the spiritual teacher carries the disciple within, similar to how a mother carries the embryo in her body for three days, after which the disciple is spiritually reborn.[39] Thus, a practical and conceptual space has been created that generates a process to make an individual, irrespective of their birth in the prevailing social hierarchy, twice-born. A person given dīkṣā becomes twice-born.

In this tradition, an important development is the school of Saṁsiddha gurus, also known as Mahāmunis, mentioned in the *Rig Veda*. These munis, described as having long hair (*keśin)* and wearing a brown-red (probably saffron) dress, are said to possess the power of the Devās (devāso avikṣata) and the friends (sakhā) of every Deva (devasya-devasya). They are known to inhabit both the eastern and the western sea (*samudrāv ā kṣeti yaś ca pūrva utāparaḥ*), indicating their pan-Indian presence. They are considered the gatherers of all knowledge and are said to have once drunk poison with Rudra (*keśī viṣasya pātreṇa yad rudreṇāpibat saha*).[40] The Rudra nature of the ascetics drinking poison with the deity, a defining feature of Śiva in later well-established iconography, shows that the monk orders, in one way or another, are very old. Typically, in a binary fashion, the Western Indologists with the Aryan/non-Aryan framework depict the *Munis* as outside and inimical to the Vedic system.[41] However, in Vedic text, they are not opposed to Indra but Indra is their friend (*indro munīnāṃ sakhā*).In the context of *Saṁsiddha* gurus, the Munis were considered superior to all ācāryas, with their primary identification being Śiva bhakti.[42]

The spiritual egalitarian values of the society had a significant impact, challenging social stratification and exclusion. This empowerment was evident in the Siddhānta Śaivaite tradition, which was gaining strength in North India, with its spiritual roots in Kashmir and influence spreading to Central India. This tradition also underwent dynamic evolution in South India. Additionally, the term 'Bhagavat-pāda' shows how royalty in the Dakshina Kosala region granted village lands to Śaiva Ācāryas. The functional aspect of their institutions as *Brāhmanā* had been observed. At times, they also engaged in warfare, defending the chiefs who supported them, thus establishing themselves as powerful institutions.

Historian R.N. Misra uncovers various fascinating details in a detailed study of how Śaiva Siddhānta monastic networks functioned in Central India.[43]

The monastic networks were institutionally strong, and the munis (monks) were highly charismatic, earning the respect of the population through 'their life of self-discipline, frugal ways, spiritual pursuits and non-intrusive disposition towards the otherwise insuperable woodland community of *āṭavikas*...' points out Misra. *Āṭavikas* were forest chieftains of forest-based communities. These woodland communities were largely recognized for their autonomy within the Hindu political framework. According to Misra, *āṭavikas* 'seem to have acquiesced to their non-aggressive presence in the woodlands.' Further, they 'remained in allegiance to the munis and benefitted continually from their benevolence.' Perhaps it was this allegiance that paved the way for the munis to become a powerful institution, spiritually (in terms of religious and cultural dimensions) as well as socially (in terms of economic and military dimensions).

The munis were seen as selfless and loved by the people. One inscription describes Muni Kavacaśiva as the opposite of the negative stereotype often associated with monks. He was loved by the people because he did not avidly chase self-serving desires essentially to fill his belly. The munis gave refugee to people, dug wells and lakes for them, and engaged in works of charity. They were also great scholars and men of wisdom. For example, Vyomaśiva, the author of works quoted by other scholars, was an expertise not only in his own Siddhānta but also in 'Nyāya, Vaiśeṣika, Mīmāṃsā, Sāṅkhya, Lokyāta, Buddhism and Jainism'. The inscription also claims that he not only conquered Buddhists and Jains 'Jambūkas' in debates but also scattered the Mīmāṃsakas through his 'lion-like roar'. During the 8th to 10th centuries CE, in the Kalachuri state of Central India, R.N. Misra states that 'for a total grant of twelve villages and two fields to twenty-four Brāhmaṇās, the share of the endowment of villages to the Munis as phenomenal'. The monasteries were endowed with artisans and a strong and coercive contingent to enforce discipline and order. This contingent had 'Vīrabhadras' (protectors) and 'Vīramuṣṭhi' (warriors). With such a power structure, the munis 'could exercise executive and judicial functions' in comparison with which 'Brāhmaṇā pale into insignificance ... in every respect'. The 'power and force' they commanded 'tends to reflect a modified hierarchy in the varṇa-based social stratification—a hierarchy in which they seem to have emerged at the apex while Brāhmaṇā and the chief priest figure lower than them in precedence and privileges' thus 'repudiating the conventional Varṇa hierarchy on the one hand and granted supremacy to the ascetics on the other hand.' As 'the worldly connections of those graduating into the fold of ascetics were ritually renounced as they took to *sanyasa*.... Neither the stigma of a lower birth nor the prestige of a "higher" rank could be invoked in their respect.' However, there were occasional exceptions to these norms.

Till the Islamist invasions, the Śaivaite monasteries had enjoyed considerable influence in North India. After the Islamist invasions, the Śaivaite monasteries seemed to have lost their institutional ability to lead the resistance. Probably due to their proximity to royal power and the institutional structures they built, which served them well for centuries, became their fatal weakness with Islamist invasions. Now the resistance movement against monopolistic expansionism and the task of preserving indigenous Theo-diversity relied on the Śrī Vaiṣṇava Bhakti movement. It was more decentralized and non-institutionalized.

Social Emancipation through Śaivism in South India

In South India, the Śaiva Renaissance challenged traditional notions of hierarchy and defilement based on a person's occupation. Unlike in North India, South India boasts abundant literature primarily comprising musical and mystical compositions of the saints. These works offer a detailed insight into the worldview and values of the time.

Karaikal Ammaiyar—Pēy Ammai

The earliest known literary work of the Śaiva Renaissance in Tamil Nadu is attributed to Karaikāl Ammaiyār, who likely lived between the 5th and 6th century CE. Her real name was Punitavati and she belonged to a trading community. According to tradition, after a miracle showed that she was the recipient of the Arul of Śiva Perumān (as Śiva is called in Tamil Nadu), her husband prostrated before her and left her. She assumed the form of a pēy, often translated as a demon. Later Chōzha bronzes depict her with a skeletal frame and a divinely intoxicated expression. P*ēy* is a female supernatural entity that is said to haunt lonely places, especially burial grounds. There is a possibility that pēy shares etymological roots with the old French fay (related to fairy) and the old Germanic 'fey' (to die).

Her poetry has two important dimensions. First, it revives old musical traditions in South India. Second, it firmly places her Lord Śiva dancing in the cremation ground. The cremation ground was considered taboo, and work related to it was also considered defiled. However, she chose the cremation ground and transformed it into a sacred place.

This purely spiritual expression also holds crucial polemical implications on social planes as well.

In the post-Buddhist text of Brahma Sūtra (attributed to Bādarāyaṇa/Vyāsa), the author analyses the right of the Śūdra to study Vedas. He cites instances from the Upaniṣad, which serve as proof for denying birth-based Varṇa. One such instance is found in the *Chāndogyopaniṣad*, where Raikva, the Brahma-Jñāni, imparts Brahma-Jñāna to King Jānaśruti. Initially hesitant, Raikva addresses the king as a Śūdra. However, in *Brahma Sūtra,* Bādarāyaṇa argues that it was the sorrow in the mind of King Jānaśruti that made Raikva call the king a Śūdra and therefore this instance does not prove that a Śūdra has a right to Brahma-Jñāna. Similarly, he also cites the instance of Satyakāma, of unknown parentage, being initiated into Vedic studies by Sage Gautama. The same Upanishad also illustrates this point. In both instances, Satyakāma displays the characteristics of a Brāhmanā and Jānaśruti displays the characteristics of a Śūdra not because of their birth but because of their conduct. However, the author of *Brahma Sūtra* uses both instances to argue, citing *Smṛti*, to deny the right of the Śūdra (in a birth-based sense) to study Vedas. The instance of Raikva- Jānaśruti is even more striking because Raikva, the Brahman-realized-Jñāni, was not a Brahmin but a cart driver. He was found lying under a cart and scratching his itches when men working for King Jānaśruti discovered him. The two great *Bhāsyas* that emerged centuries after the composition of *Brahma Sūtra,* by both Śaṅkara (7th or 8th century CE) and Rāmānuja (7th or 8th century CE) cite identical *Dharmaśāstra* to strengthen the stand of the author of *Brahma Sūtra*. In doing so, both cite verses that call the Śūdras 'crematoriums.' According to Adi Śaṅkara:

> As for prohibition of hearing, we have the text, 'Then should he happen to hear the Vedas, the expiation consists in his ears being filled with lead and lac,' and He who is a *śūdra* is a walking crematorium. Hence one should not read in the neighbourhood of a *śūdra*. From this follows the prohibition about study. How can one study the Vedas when they are not to be recited within his hearing? Then there is the chopping off of his tongue if he

> should utter the Vedas and the cutting of the body to pieces if he should commit it to memory.[44]

Śri Rāmānuja also agrees with Śaṅkara on this point. Similarly, Śrikaṇṭa, usually considered a late contemporary or as belonging to a century after Śri Rāmānuja, also wrote a Bhāsya from Śivādvaita perspective. This also takes the same stand and quotes the same *Dharmaśāstra* verses denying Śūdra the right to learn Veda, Vedanta, or even hear Mahāvākyas.

While it is clear that what Śaṅkara or other commentators wrote might not have reflected the existing social reality of India of their times, their views did come from a powerful sociocultural and legal perspective that was taking shape. Even when considering the basic rule of not judging the ancient value system based on the present value system, the passages quoted are, to put it mildly, definitely problematic. This becomes even more pronounced because of two factors.

- The "*Parapakṣa*" that *Brahma Sūtra* author refutes and the refusal which the Bhāsya-makers agree and elaborate shows that based on pre-Buddhist Vedic-Upaniṣadic worldview, there existed a view that imparted Vedas to all deserving.
- The stand taken by the author and commentators goes against the value system and worldview implied by the acceptance of the Divine in all.

The elevation of the cremation ground in the hymns of Karaikāl Ammaiyār, also known as Pēy Ammai, should be seen in the context of pure mystic bliss rather than a social response. This elevation of the cremation ground in her poetry is a spontaneous outpouring and should be considered one of the aesthetic literary peaks of world spiritual literature. However, it has also created the powerful space for questioning the dehumanization of Śūdras in the *Dharmaśāstra*. This imagery of the cremation ground is not a new concept introduced by Pēy Ammai; it was already present in Mahābhārata. Indologist Stella Kramrisch comprehensively presents this aspect thus:

> His (Rudra- *Śiva*) abode was the burning ground, which was 'covered with hair and bones, full of skulls and heads, thick with vultures and jackals, covered with a hundred funeral pyres, an unclean place covered with flesh, a mire of marrow and blood, scattered piles of flesh, resounding with the cries of jackals' (MBh. 13.128.13-15). Indeed, in his wanderings all over the earth, the Great God had always been in search of a hallowed spot. 'There is nothing purer than a cremation ground,' Siva declared (MBh. 13.128.16). The hosts of ghostly beings that are his companions loved to dwell there, and Siva did not like to stay anywhere without them (MBh.13.128.18)[45]

Pēy Ammai, who would have the singular glory of being called the 'Mother of Śiva", absorbed this divine image of Śiva Perumān and anchored her mystic hymns onto Him and His preferred cremation ground. With ease, she puts forth Upaniṣadic wisdom:

> The Knower (in all) is He
> The Knowledge expressly obtained is He.
> The Knowing principle behind the process of knowing is He.
> The Knowable True essence (within all apparent knowledge) is He
> All the ever-dynamic existence is He Himself.[46]

She also points out that divine imagery that contains elements that might be considered socially unacceptable should not be judged from limited and conditioned knowledge. The meaning would come only when one realizes Him:

> From the bound perception, don't try to comprehend my Lord,
> For the way He roams around everywhere as a beggar and
> In the thick of night He dancing in the grounds of cremation.
> We will understand when we are revealed His form Divine.[47]

Here is an imagery of a crematorium she created:

> A child ghoul sits comfortably extending its legs in between the cactus that characterise the cremation grounds. It takes the last stick stuck to burn the dead body. Its ember is covered with ash and black soot. The ghoul wants to decorate itself and uses this black soot to draw its brow lines. The ember burns into the brow-line. In pain the ghoul throws the stick and as it gets up the cactus thorns further hurts it. It looks around the cremation ground knowing not what to do. It tries to comfort itself by applying the sand lying between the burning bodies to its self-inflicted wound. In that cremation ground stands and dances our Father Śiva. And that place is Tiruvālaṅkāṭu.[48]

Here the child ghoul symbolizes the humans immersed in the egoistic pursuits of Saṃsāra. The comfort zones created by egos are like the comfort the thorny cactus offered to the ghoul. The comfort was short lived and beneath it was always the pain waiting to strike. The soot-covered ember is the pursuits and vanities, physical, academic, psychological, financial, etc., with which we adore our egos. It is only a matter of time before the reality, like the ember, burns in through the vanity. Realization of the Saṃsāra as the wasteland leads to further meaningless acts like applying the dust, etc. Then the whole place is transformed into a sacred land, it is the place of Śiva's dance. Prof. Elaine Craddock points out how the self and society get organically linked by bhakti:

> In her poetry *Ammaiyār* performs her own devotion by building a vivid iconographic portrait of Íiva as a means of praising and focusing on him. At the same time her iconographic portrait serves to construct the emerging community of devotees 'and creates a tradition-specific subjectivity. This subjectivity is not individualistic but is itself a sign of the community and an expression of tradition. So while there is undoubtedly the development of interiority through text and ritual performance,

> this is not the development of a private self in contrast to a public self' (Gavin Flood, *The Ascetic Self: Subjectivity, Memory and tradition*, 2004, 221–222). The *bhakti* subjectivity that *Ammaiyār* projects in her poetry is constructed when the path becomes the goal, when the devotee lives everyday in perpetual service to Śiva in a community of devotees.[49]

It is not a coincidence that the Bhakti movement in South India surfaced with the mystic wisdom of a woman who was born in the Vaiśyā family. She came out of the family and used the most unusual and challenging imagery as her literary outpourings while at the same time reviving the ancient South Indian musical tradition. It is from her that the entire South Indian music tradition today popularly known as Karnatic music, flowers.

Thirujñāna Saṃbanthar

The 7th-century saint was born in the agricultural village of Sīrkazhi, which was located in the Cauvery Delta region of present-day Tamil Nadu. During the 7th century, it was part of the Chōla territory, just before the rise of the so-called Imperial Chōlas. According to Śaivaite accounts, the Jains received royal patronage in the Pāndya kingdom of Tamil province. Some factions of the Jains practiced forms of extreme untouchability known as 'un-seeability' and 'unhearability' towards the Śaivaites, as mentioned in Śaiva literature. It was believed that if a Jain saw a Śaivaite, they would consider themselves polluted and had to take a bath. Similarly, if a Jain heard about another Jain seeing a Śaivaite, they too would have to take a bath. There is no independent confirmation of this claim from the Śaivaite perspective. However, even today in colloquial language, the bogeyman equivalent used in Tamil Nadu to frighten children is 'Pooch-āndi' (ash-smeared-mendicant), which is a testimony to the aversion generated against Śaivaites in a forgotten past period of Tamil province.

The influence of Jain values extended beyond the borders of the Pāndya kingdom and transcended religious sectarianism. The strict adherence to non-violence and moral codes, which discouraged most forms of pleasurable activities, led to the stigmatization of various occupations. Traditional minstrels, bards, and performers, who were respected during the Caṅkam period, became 'untouchable' or defiled communities by the 7th century. *Cīvaka Cintāmaṇi*, a Tamil Jain classic written by Tiruttakkatēvar, a Jain ascetic poet, was composed nearly two centuries after the times of Jñāna Saṃbanthar. Its purpose was to demonstrate that Jains could compose literature with amorous themes, and it contains verses that shed light on the prevailing attitudes toward certain hereditary occupational groups at the time:

> Those who kill animals with bows and arrows,
> Those who have meat in between their teeth,
> Those fish hunters of the sea-side and such
> Defiled occupations and defiled clans
> One should escape and be born in good traditional clan.[50]

In the midst of a particular sociocultural setting, Jñāna Saṃbanthar started his mission. According to tradition, he was considered a child prodigy (given milk of wisdom by Goddess Parvāti). Accounts of his life include various miraculous events and sectarian conflicts with the Jains. These conflicts involved Jains setting fire to the place where he was staying and Saṃbanthar engaging in debates with the Jains, with the latter vowing to self-impale themselves upon defeat. The Śaiva tradition claims that Saṃbanthar emerged victorious in these debates. Later on, instead of preventing the Jains from self-inflicted harm, Saṃbanthar supposedly remained a passive witness when approximately 8,000 Jains impaled themselves. However, these claims are not substantiated by sources outside Śaivaite literature. There is no evidence of these events in contemporary inscriptions. Moreover, given the meticulous record-keeping of Jain monasteries in Tamil Nadu, the self-impalement of 8,000 Jains would have been a historical and traumatic event for the community and should have been recorded, but there is no such record. It was not until five centuries after Saṃbanthar times that the mythical impalement of Jains became celebrated in Śaivaite literature and temple sculptures.

Saṃbanthar's real disagreement appeared to be more with certain ethical excesses of Jains than with Jains as a religion. The fact that Jainism continued to flourish as a patronized religion for centuries also supports Saṃbanthar's argument. Further, the internal evidence in his verses clearly demonstrates that despite his animosity towards Jainism and Buddhism, he acknowledges their divine role in his own way. He states that both Jainism and Buddhism were created by Śiva. According to Saṃbanthar, Śiva is the mother of religions that negate Him. In his works, it becomes apparent that his criticism is not aimed at their negation and religious attacks on Śaivaism but rather at the fact that they live apart from society and promote that as superior. They oppose the Vedic Yajña, and when he mentions that they are against the Vedic Yajña, he means not only the ritual but also the view that all occupations are a form of Yajña. He also criticizes what he perceives as the inferior position of women in Buddhism and Jainism. Additionally, he almost always portrays Śiva as *Arthānārīśvara*.

> We can live in this very land a life of righteous happiness. Contemplate and see there is not even an iota of deficiency for the well-being. Because in this city (*Thirukazhumalam*) that pleases the eyes with all prosperity, inseparably with the best of the woman (Goddess Parvati) is our God magnificent *Śiva*.[31]

As against such glorification of the Divine Feminine, Jainism considers their initiated women as not worthy of the final liberation, so criticize Saṃbanthar.[52]

Thirunanipalli was a town 10 kilometres from the nearest coast. It had previously been a thriving hub for fish-related business, but its economic prosperity declined during the time of Saṃbanthar. The town was also the ancestral home of Bhagavatī, mother of Saṃbanthar. According to tradition, the people of Thirunanipalli lamented their socio-economic downfall. The town was more a Pālai (an eco-cultural zone with the desert as its centre) than a Neithal (an eco-cultural name for a coastal-life-based village). Upon hearing this, Saṃbanthar sang ten verses, which restored the town to its Neithal status. In his compositions, Saṃbanthar included an authoritative statement, 'I declare this as a command' (ஆணை நமதே). This authoritative declaration began with the verses sung at Thirunanipalli.

Scholars have debated about this 'miracle' performed by Saṃbanthar at Thirunanipalli. Dr Vai Irathinasabhapathy, an expert in Śaiva Siddhānta, notes that Nambiāndār Nambi (a 10th-century chronicler of the lives of Śaiva Nāyanmārs) had mentioned this transformation of a town, while the 12th-century composition *Periya Purāṇam,* the epic chronicle of Śaiva Nāyanmārs, composed by venerable Sēkkilār, a minister of Chola empire, is silent about the incident. This raised questions about the transformation. However, a 20th-century folk song tradition of the fishermen of Nagapattinam, located 50 kilometres south on the same eastern coast, reveals an interesting fact. An old fisherman's song, recorded in 1980, sheds light on this when he was a young fisherman:

The child who had seen the nation – Elelo elo
The child of pure wisdom – Elelo elo
The child of pure wisdom – Elelo elo

Sings Thevāram songs divine – Elelo elo
When he sings Thevāram – Elelo elo
Jain brat takes to his heels – Elelo elo
Oh woman so motherly – Elelo elo
Oh queen Mangaiyarkarasi – Elelo elo*[53]

The song clearly reveals a historical memory from the coastal community's point of view, which aligns with the 'miracle' of the transformation of Pālai to Neithal This transformation involved the lifting of restrictions and taboos that Jainism had imposed on fishing as an occupation and fish consumption. The song connects the mission of Saṃbanthar to the decline of Jainism and the resurgence of Vedic-Śaiva values, making fishing an honourable occupation once again. This was further supported by the legend of Athibhatha Nayanar.

Athibhatha Nāyanār and the Yajña of Fishing

Athibhatha, which means extreme devotee in Tamil, lived in Nagapattinam, an important port and fishing city at that time. His name is mentioned in the 'Thiruthoṇdar Thogai' [Group of Auspicious Servants (of the Lord)], which was a list of all the devotees of Śiva bhaktas from various walks of life. Sundarar, one of the three primal Nāyanmārs, sang this list in the 8th century. Therefore, Athibhatha must have lived before the 8th century and was likely a contemporary of Saṃbanthar.

He was a fisherman, the leader of a group of fishermen belonging to an ancient clan called 'Bharathavar'. Every day, he would select the best fish from his catch and release it back in the water, considering it as 'an offering to our Lord who performeth the cosmic Dance'. To test his dedication, Śiva Perumān limited his catch to only one fish per day. Despite the hardship, Athibhathar remained resolute in his devotion and continued to release that one fish back into the sea for the Lord. Eventually, Athibhatar's financial situation became dire, and he was unable to afford food. He 'nurtured himself with not food but love for Śiva', says Sēkkilār. One day, exhausted and in financial distress, Athibhathar cast his net into the sea and caught a fish adorned with priceless gems and shining with extraordinary brightness. His fellow fishermen suggested that he release one fish to Śiva as usual but keep this fish to gain infinite wealth.

The importance of Śaiva literature on Athibhathar is the glorious way in which the coastal fishing hamlet is described. It does not depreciate the occupation. Rather it glorifies and even romanticizes the occupation while realistically describing their habitat:

> The nets spread for drying near the houses of the fishermen look like they were meant to measure the very clouds. Near them one could see the gold coins brought for buying the fish, getting measured. Fish-like eyes of the fisherwomen observe the fish catches brought by the fishermen and gauge their prices by just observing.[54]

The height of the events unfolds when Athibhathar rejects the worldly sound advice, which was not wrong in itself and yet chooses to stand firm in his principle. Sēkkilār writes:

> He without hesitation threw that fish into the sea stating this would verily be fitting to my Lord and thus rejecting the way of the world, rejecting the sound economic sense, he severed and threw away the material bonds. In that instant *Śiva Perumān* appeared on His Rishaba before him and gave him the highest bliss of Śiva Loka with other devotees.[55]

The Śaiva literature does not project Athibhathar as an exceptional bhakta, thus voiding the act of inferiorizing his clan. Instead, the Śaiva tradition glorifies him in his occupational identity as a fisherman. In fact, his occupation involves murder (*kolaithozhil*), yet 'by standing in it firmly and through that very occupation, Athibhathar exhibited true devotion'.[56] The tradition urges everyone to prostrate at the feet of Athibhathar. When Athibhathar threw the fish into the sea, he showed that his work should be seen as a Śiva Yajña. This occupation and hereditary guild, once labelled as defiled and subjected to economic hardships, is now projected as an honourable occupation and a holy Yajña.

Reviving the Respect of Art Performers

The Caṅkam (Sangham) Tamil literature is known for its high regard for musicians and dancers. However, by the 7th century, the Pāṇars, the community of bards who could share seats with the chieftain rulers and musicians, became marginalized and were even considered untouchables. They were called Pāṇars because of their expertise in Paṇ, which is the Tamil equivalent of rāgā.

Although there were exceptional Jain musicians, the Jains looked down upon music and dance as impediments to liberation. They viewed them as distractions rather than art forms that could elevate one's self. Music was seen as related to Kāmam, and even the Jain ascetic Tiruttakkatēvar, who wrote the amorous epic, even went to the extent of calling Vīṇa the stringed musical instrument equivalent to Kāmam.[57] The Buddhist ethical code of conduct (Śilā) for monks forbids singing and dancing, and on special days, lay people too are asked to refrain from these activities. Even when compromises were made because of the natural evolution of musical traditions, particularly in the folk context, music was tolerated or, at best, enjoyed but not respected. Even today in Sri Lanka, one can observe how this fundamental perception of Buddhism, when revived with colonial Protestant purity, has been detrimental to local musical traditions:

> All members of the Sangha must, ideally, abstain from witnessing displays of dancing, singing, and instrumental music, and those who take the eight precepts on poya days make the same vow. Pali verses are always chanted, not sung.... Before the encroachment of Protestant Buddhism communal dancing, drumming, and singing were common in Sinhala village life, but men and women were segregated. Women's dancing, even their singing at harvest, and the tradition of playing the flat drum have practically vanished from village life today. In some areas, as Knox as well as contemporary anthropologists have noted, marriage rules and sexual mores were flexible before Sinhala culture was practically swamped by the puritan sexual ethic of Protestant Buddhism.[58]

Music was seen, at best, as entertainment and, usually, a phenomenon eliciting carnal pleasures.

Kāraikāl Pēy Ammai changed this perception by focusing on and reviving the music traditions of South India. She revived the Paṇ and used it in her innovation of the Pathiham format. Sēkkilār identifies Pēy Ammai, Saṃbanthar, and Thirunāvukarasar as gifted composers of musical verses. Pēy Ammai is considered to be earlier than the other two. Historian of South Indian music and music scholar Dr Gnanambikai Kulendran explains:

> When *Paṇ Isai* blossomed as what came to be called Carnatic music the form of composition called kirtana became popular. *Pallavai, Anupallavi* and *Charanam* combined together to form a *kirtana*. The pattern of the prose in the *Charanam* appears to follow the Padiham pattern. It is to be noted that even the rendering of the *Charanams* is akin to that of the Padiham mode of rendering.... The long traditional lineage of composition from Padiham to *Kirtana* owes their origin to *Ammaiyar*.[59]

It should be clear here that while the extreme moralistic worldview of world-negating religions eschewed music from the field of respectability, the phenomenon of bhakti, on the other hand, sacralized music in its own capacity. Saṃbanthar considers music as a spontaneous expression whenever there is love and does not differentiate here between sacred and secular. He states at one place that the cuddling and blandishment of children by their mothers create sweet music that attracts the celestials.[60]

The devaluation of music under world-negating religions had a significant impact on traditional communities of bards, wandering minstrels, dancers, and other performing artists in a society heavily influenced by the biases of puritanical and rigidly moralistic religions. The Pāṇars became an untouchable community. This devaluation of the community extended beyond religious boundaries and became an accepted norm in society.

Sēkkilār narrates the deep bond between Saṃbanthar and a highly talented Pāṇars contemporary, Thiru Nīlakaṇḍa Yāzhpāṇar. He was a genius adept at playing the stringed instrument Yāzh. His wife Mātaṅga Sūḷāmaṇī was also an equally talented musician. Yāzhpāṇar went to Madurai and performed hymns with his musical instrument, Yāzh. Musicians were considered a defiled profession and were not allowed inside the temple. However, Śiva Perumān appeared in the dreams of the devotees and instructed them to invite him reverentially inside. Finally, he was brought directly in front of Śiva, where he sang his hymns right in the temple. While singing, sitting on the floor right in front of the Lord, Śiva, through a disembodied voice, instructed the assembled to arrange a wooden board for Yāzhpāṇar, as the cool floor would affect the music.[61] This showed the respect and concern that Śiva Himself showed for musicians and their music. Later, when Yāzhpāṇar visited Thiruvārur, another of the holiest of Śiva temples, a northern decorative door was created especially in honour of Yāzhpāṇar.[62]

The couple were drawn to the mission of Saṃbanthar. When Yāzhpāṇar came to see Saṃbanthar, the latter went and met him right at the entrance of the town and greeted him.[63] From then on, wherever he went, he was accompanied by the musician couple. Whenever Saṃbanthar composed his musical verses, they were set to music by Yāzhpāṇar.

Another contemporary Śaiva devotee of the period was Thiru Nīlanakkar, a Brāhmanā known for his strict adherence to ritual purity. When his wife spotted a spider on the Śiva Liṅga (the aniconic sacred symbol of Śiva), she blew the spider off. On hearing this, Nīlanakkar expelled her from the house and sent her to her parental place. However, Lord Śiva Himself had to assure Nīlanakkar that his wife's act was down because of love and devotion. To prove it, Śiva showed Nīlanakkar that the places where his wife blew off the spider were free of inflammation caused by the spider bite. This *Purāṇic* incident shows the Puritanic ritualistic nature of Nīlanakkar.

When Saṃbanthar and his team of devotees, including the musician-couple, arrived at the town where Nīlanakkar lived, Saṃbanthar asked Nīlanakkar to host the musical couple in his house. Instead of just providing them with any space, Nīlanakkar had them sleep in the middle of the house where he kept the platform ('Vedikai') of the sacred ever-alive Yajña triple fire.

> There in the Vedi the ever-alive sacred red flame
> Spiralled rightward and ascended upwards as never before.
> The Brahmin with the sacred thread witnessed this,
> his heart filled with rapture as *Pāṇar* the master of Sakoda *Yāzh*
> went to bed with his wife.[64]

This represented a social revolution unprecedented in any part of the then-contemporary world. Despite this, it was not even recognized as a social revolution. The significance of a couple from a socially excluded community sleeping in the most sacred space of the ritual and being acknowledged by the Yajña flame had never been seen or acknowledged before.

Periya Purāṇam: A Unique Holistic Model of History

The *Periya Purāṇam* (The Great Purāṇa), also known as *Thiruttōntar Purāṇam* (Purāṇa of the auspicious voluntary servants of Śiva) is a 12th century Tamil work. It is a compendium of biographies of individuals who lived from the 5th century CE onwards. This work was composed by Sēkkilār, who served as the Prime Minister of Kulothunga Chola-II. Sēkkilār is actually a clan name. Sēkkilār's real name was Sēkkilān Māthēvadikaḷ Rāmathēvan, as mentioned in the king's inscription. The term 'Sēkkilār' referred to the owner of cattle wealth, and he belonged to the agricultural class, classified as the Śūdra varṇa. This is not an exception. It is worth noting that in the caste system, many ministers, army generals, and even local chieftains belonged to the Śūdra varṇa. This will be dealt with in detail in subsequent chapters.

The text discusses the lives of sixty-three devotees of Śiva Perumān venerated as Nāyanmārs. Each biography (modern scholarship may consider them as hagiographies) stands as a separate classic work, combining dramatic descriptive styles of epics with the supernatural sacralising nature of Purāṇas. The work shows detailed ground research, as Sēkkilār visited the native places and locations of mission and meditation of the Nāyanmār. He described features of fishing markets, Brāhmanā houses, crematoriums, wedding places, panchayats, and courts of kings in detail. Among the sixty-three Nāyanmārs, thirteen belonged to the agricultural clan, two to the cowherd clan, twelve to Brāhmanās, twelve to the warriors and rulers, four to Adi Śaiva, one to the Vaidhya-Māmatrar, one to the potter, one to the landless labourer-quasi serf, six to the trading community, one to the weaver, one to the hunter, one to the fisherman, and one to the washerman. Additionally, three of the sixty-three Nāyanmārs are women, effectively covering the entire spectrum of the society in the literature. Each Nāyanmār becomes the hero/heroine of that part of the literature, marking a departure from the literary convention of only portraying the upper sections of the society as heroes.

In the Purāṇam, individuals such as ThiruNāḷaiPōvār or Nanthanār, a landless labourer attached to large farmland, and Thiru Nīlakaṇḍa Kuyavanār, a potter, are portrayed as heroes. This literature has a significant impact, as seen in the construction of the famous Airavatesvara Temple at Dārasuram by Raja Raja Chōzha-II, with sculpted representations of the Nāyanmārs' lives. In every Śiva temple, the divine statues of the Nāyanmārs are placed with equal respect, regardless of their background. This work may be one of the earliest attempts to document the history of the common people, providing vivid descriptions of their lives, work, culture, and values.

Subsequent Śaiva Siddhānta Development and Social Emancipation

Further evolutionary branching from the basic Bhakti movement in Śaivism occurred. Tamil Nadu had always been in contact with Śaivaite schools from other parts of India. South India was familiar with and embraced Kashmiri concepts in the areas of dance, aesthetics, and Śaivism. Dr R. Nagaswamy, commenting on various works in South India on dance and aesthetics, found those works 'so close to Abinavagupta in point of time and... by the popularity of the Kashmiri school and its pan-Indian character'. Dr Nagaswamy also pointed to two inscriptions in the famous Śaiva temple near Śri Raṅgam called Thiruvānnaikā temple, which mentions a gift to the temple made by a lady from Kashmiradesa in the 13th century, showing 'the cultural migration from Kashmir to Tamil Nadu' in that period.[65] The mythical tradition of *Thiru Mūlar* being animated by a muni who came on a pilgrimage to South India from the North could actually be a Purāṇic way of indicating this interaction.

During the same period, the South Indian Śaiva Siddhānta school took a vibrant form as part of the Bhakti movement. This development was rooted in the Śaiva Darśana traditions across India. This is an important development in the evolution of Hindu philosophy. The Bhakti literature expressed the essence of a non-dual consciousness, and the systematic structure always referenced back to this literature to validate its components.

During the initial stages of development, the first text, *Thiruvunthiyār* was written by Sivayogi Thiruviyalūr Uyavantha Thēvar. According to tradition, he came from North India and settled here,[66] showcasing the cross-fertilization and pan-Indian nature of the evolution of deeply contextualized yet universal *Śaiva Siddhānta.* The verses are presented as being sung during a popular folk game that girls play, which involves holding each other's hands and then rotating in both right-hand and left-hand directions. One of the most famous late 9th-century Bhakti mystic poets, Māṇickavāchagar, first used this method to convey a deep spiritual experience. In 12th century, Thiruviyalūr Uyavantha Thēvar used the format to convey the spiritual essence of Śaiva Siddhānta in a systematized manner. Nevertheless, the text was anchored in the spiritual experience of Uyavantha Thēvar.

He had a disciple.

Disciples are chosen based on a scheme that involves the cleansing of what are called the three inner impurities. These are: Āṇavam (ego-self), Kaṉmam (Karma), Māyai (Māya). All beings have these three impurities. However, through proper conduct and 'Aruḷ', the inner impurities are slowly decreased and removed one by one. According to Śaivism, the process happens through various births. So, at any particular point in time, the sentient beings would be a mixture of those with all three inner impurities (called *sahalar*), those in whom one Māyā *Malam* is removed (*Praḷayākalar*) and those in whom both Māyā *Malam* and *Kaṉma Malam* are subdued (*Vijñānakalar*). Aruḷ is important for the reduction and removal of impurities. When evangelical Indologists studied the Tamil language and its religious classics, they translated this into 'grace'. But as Rajiv Malhotra has popularized the term 'Sanskrit non-translatable', in the same way, one can consider this as Tamil non-translatable. Grace is only a deficient approximation to Aruḷ. Don Handelman and David Shulman of Jerusalem University point out that while 'there is an unfortunate tendency to translate this critical term, in nearly every context, as "grace", with its heavy Christian connotations', Aruḷ actually 'approximates a notion of coming into being or freely becoming present, close, alive... a *Shakti* active and female aspect of Siva'. Pointing out that 'Aruḷ is not grace but an emergent presence', they elaborate that 'it or she is dynamic and oriented toward freedom...an experiential process of full, unconstricted potentiality'.[67] In *Śaiva Siddhānta,* the 'Aruḷ Śakti' of Śiva Perumān is His *Tirōdhāna Śakti* that veils the Jīva from its real nature, transforming into Anugraha Śakti that liberates the Jīva from its bonds thus making it realize its real nature, which is Śiva nature.

The state of being liberated from these fundamental inner impurities or having them subdued is referred to as mala paripākam. The Sanskrit term *paripāka* usually relates to the degree to which a food is cooked, but in this context, it signifies the readiness of the Jīva to receive the compassionate liberation awaiting it. Mala paripāka is not concerned with one's social class or caste. The guru appears and bestows dīkṣā to invigorate the evolutionary journey of Jīva towards liberation. As mentioned earlier, through dīkṣā, the recipient becomes 'twice-born' (dvija) regardless of their caste.

The disciple who received dīkṣā from Thiruviyalūr Uyavantha Thēvar was given the same name as the guru for his dīkṣā name. To distinguish between the guru and the disciple, the latter is called Thirukaṭavūr Uyavantha Thēvar. He wrote a work of a hundred verses to explain 'Thiruvunthiyār', the work of his guru, which consists of forty-five verses. Despite being highly appreciated for its erudition and clear explanation of the significant dimensions of *Śaiva Siddhānta,* there was opposition to treating the work as an authentic presentation of *Siddhānta* due to Thirukaṭavūr Uyavantha Thēvar being born in the Jāthi of goat merchants, which is considered a hīna jāthi. At the famous Thillai NatarajaNaṭarāja ChitambaramTemple, there are five silver steps with stone elephants on both sides, known as the sacred Pañchākṣarā steps or the elephant steps (Kaḷiṟṟupaṭikaḷ) due to the presence of stone elephants. It is believed that the text was placed there before Śiva Perumān, and according to tradition, the stone elephants came alive and took the palm-leaves manuscripts of the texts and placed them before the Lord.[68] Consequently, the text came to be called *Thirukaḷiṟṟupaaṭiyār* (auspicious book of the elephant steps). This text, along with *Thiruvunthiyār*, is part of the spiritually authoritative text for *Śaiva-Siddhānta.*

The next important development in Siddhānta was affected by 13th-century saint Meykaṇṭa Thēvar (a child prodigy born as Svēthavanaperumāḷ), who provided a comprehensive system through a text called *Śiva Jñāna Bōdham,* which consists of twelve sutras. Meykaṇṭa Thēvar belonged to the fourth varṇa and was known for his deep understanding of Vedas and Āgamās. One day, the young Meykaṇṭār was found teaching Siddhānta to other children. Initially, Aruḷ Nanthi Śivam was sceptical and thought the child was being haughty. However, upon questioning the child about the concept of 'Āṇava malam' (impurity of ego-self), he was astonished by the child's response. As a result, Meykaṇṭa Thēvar, became the guru of his family's guru, Aruḷ Nanthi Śivam, who belonged to the first varṇa.

The history of the seers in this lineage demonstrates how their spiritual tradition naturally challenged existing birth-based pride and prejudices and acted intrinsically against social stagnation. Maṟaijñāna Saṃbanthar, a Sama Vedi belonging to Parāsara Gōtra, became the disciple of Aruḷ Nanthi Śivam and continued the spiritual lineage of Meykaṇṭa Thēvar.

Umāpathi Śivam, a Brāhmanā and an important member of the priestly clan responsible for the daily rituals at the Chidambaram Temple, became the disciple of Maṟaijñāna Saṃbanthar. Apart from his duties at the temple, he was also a proficient scholar in both Tamil and Sanskrit. Due to his status, the Chola king honoured him by allowing him to travel in a palanquin accompanied by a formal retinue carrying fire torches. One morning, as Umāpathi Śivam's procession passed by, Maṟaijñāna Saṃbanthar, who was teaching his disciples, pointed at the procession and remarked, 'Look! There goes the morning-blind seated on a dead bamboo.' These words deeply affected Umāpathi Śivam, prompting him to jump out of the palanquin and request Maṟaijñāna Saṃbanthar to accept him as a disciple. However, this was not an easy feat, as Maṟaijñāna Saṃbanthar subjected the scholarly Brāhmanā to many tests, one of which is well-known in the Śaiva tradition.

Every day, Maṟaijñāna Saṃbanthar would go for alms. He would obtain alms from each and every house without discrimination. One day, he went to the street of weavers, accompanied by Umāpathi Śivam. In the house of a weaver, the guru received colloidal starch meant for clothes as alms and asked the weaver to pour it into his hands. As the starch started flowing, he drank it, uttering the words 'Śiva Prasātham' (blessed food from Śiva). As he drank it, the starch started flowing through the elbow and his cupped hands. Umāpathi Śivam drank that leftover starch from the hands of the guru as 'Guru Prasātham'. Thus, after ascertaining that the feeling of birth-based notions of superiority had been completely removed from him, Umāpathi Śivam was accepted as the disciple.

This had its own repercussions. Clearly, a lineage that traced its origin to a saint of the fourth varṇa should have been considered heretical. However, there had been no extreme punitive actions, as suggested by *Smṛtis* and *Dharmaśāstras*. On the other hand, the Vaīdīka Śaiva tradition has adopted a narrative that rejects and discourages any punitive action against all communities entering such a lineage. Maṟaijñāna Saṃbanthar was living in a place called Koṟṟavaṉkuṭi, near the Chidambaram temple. Informally excommunicated and terminated from performing pūja at the Chidambaram temple, Umāpathi Śivam moved to Koṟṟavaṉkuṭi. However, during the flag-hoisting (*Dvaja Ārohaṇa*) ceremony at the Chidambaram temple, the flag would not raise itself.

In Śaiva Siddhānta, the mast is a cylindrical structure column with thirty-two divisions representing the spinal path of Kuṇḍalinī, while the entire column symbolizes the Pathi or Śiva. The flag itself represents the Jīva and is bound by grass, symbolizing the thread that makes the flag cloth ascend, which is the Aruḷ Śakti. When the flag would not ascend, the priests of Chidambaram were worried. A disembodied voice declared that the presence of Umāpathi Śivam was necessary for the flag's ascent. When the priests requested that Śivam help, he spontaneously composed four hymns, which, when sung, made the flag ascend. Together, these hymns are called *Koṭi-Kavi* (hymns of the flag). The hymns spoke of the Jīva's need to liberate itself from bonds and realize its true nature, which is its Śiva aspect.

Light and Darkness share the same space.
When one exceeds, the other diminishes.
Yet both are not the same.
Inside the essence of essence of oneself
The radiant Supra-Intelligence exists and yet
Bathed in the primal impurities is the Jīva.
Raise the flag that this Jīva may commune with Aruḷ.[69]

In the first verse, the following three verses also focus on spiritual liberation. The process involves removing psychological constraints and transforming the ego-self into an expansive and all-encompassing self. This process also challenges the established social status quo and favours social emancipation over social stagnation. Another important incident further clarifies the interpretive space and the space of inclusive adaptability of *Śaiva Siddhānta.*

In India, many marginalized communities have a strong memory of a better past, where they were considered valorous, scholarly, prosperous, or all of these. The community known as 'Pulaiyar' (often also referred to as 'Paṟaiyar' and Śāmbavar) was one such community. During the 13th century, the community faced marginalization. One member of this marginalized community, Peṟṟān Sāmban, used to provide fuel wood to the monastery kitchen as a voluntary service without anyone's knowledge. When Sāmban faced an obstacle one day, causing a delay in the monastery's food preparation, Umāpathi Śivam learned about Sāmban's voluntary service. Impressed by Sāmban's dedication, Śivam wanted to meet him. The next day, when Śāmban arrived, he was brought before Śivam. As the guru asked Śāmban about his actions, a divine-looking grand old man appeared, handed a note to Śivam, and then disappeared. The note contained a verse in four lines that read 'The Dancer of the hall of consciousness who is humble to His devotees writes this note with His own hand, addressed to the head of *Koṟṟavaṉkuṭi* (monastery) declaring that it is (by order) proper to give Peṟṟān Śāmban, Dīkṣā with no discrimination.'[70] The words 'Dīkṣā with no discrimination' (பேதமறத் தீக்கை) became quite a Mahāvākya.

CHAPTER 10

Bhakti, the Holistic Yajña Movement: Pre-Modern Vaishnavaism in South India

The influence of Śaivism in the South seems to have originated from the North with its own unique developments. In contrast, the Vaiṣṇava tradition may have developed in the opposite direction. While from very early historical times, the presence of the Bhagavata Bhakta tradition that forms the proto-Vaiṣṇava tradition is attested in North India, a very significant core developed in this tradition from South India. In a post-Islamist invasion composition, probably 14th century to 15th century CE, 'Bhāgavata Mahātmāyām' bhakti is stated as having originated in Drāviṭa land (*utpannā Drāviṭesāhaṁ*).[1] This points to an earlier acceptance of the important emergence of a stronger bhakti phenomenon from the South. It has been observed that the Caṅkam (Sangham) literature incorporated three important components of later Vaiṣṇav bhakti: the omnipresence and theo-diverse nature of Viṣṇu (*Thirumāl*) as well as He being the master, form, and process of Yajña.

Pre-Āzhwār: Chilapathikāram Age

The epic-drama *Chilapathikāram*, which was written between the 3rd to 4th century CE, showcases a highly developed bhakti tradition that is both devotional and mystical, with robust Purānic elements permeating the entire Tamil society. In its description of Pūmpukār, a coastal city of the Chola kingdom, the author speaks of the smoke from the Yajña performed by the Brahmins, *impregnating the clouds with rain* even as the smoke-covered buildings of the city look like mountains surrounded by clouds.[2] This is very much the expression of the concept '*yajñād bhavati parjanyo*' (rains fall because of the performance of Yajña) in the Bhagavad Gītā.[3]

The epic unfolds the tale of Kōvalan and Kaṇṇagi, a young couple from the trading community of the Chola kingdom. Stricken by misfortune, they find themselves in Mathurai, the capital of the Paṇṭya kingdom. In a desperate attempt to alleviate their hardship, Kōvalan tries to sell his wife's anklet. However, the royal goldsmith falsely accuses him of stealing the queen's lost anklet, leading to Kōvalan's execution by the king's order. Upon hearing the tragic news, Kaṇṇagi goes to the royal court and breaks open her remaining anklet to reveal a trove of precious gems, different from the queen's anklet, which was filled with pearls. The king, realizing his mistake, falls from his throne in remorse and takes his own life. But Kaṇṇagi's anger is not quenched. She invokes a divine fire that engulfs Mathurai, sparing only the Brahmins, the righteous, the cows, the elderly, women, and children. This epic drama encapsulates the manifestation of the divine feminine fury through a human vessel.

Throughout the entire epic drama, one finds the fire of Yajña and the divine feminine as the flame of consciousness, a constant strand. Kaṇṇagi throws her breast, and the God of fire, Agni, appears before her as a Brahmin with a flowing beard and stomach that looks pale white – indicating his insatiable hunger.[4] This is very similar to how Agni appeared as a Brahmin before Kṛṣṇa and Arjuna when he desired to burn the Khāṇḍava forest.[5] In fact, there is a web of interconnected imageries here. In *Chilapathikāram*, Kōvalan left Kaṇṇagi for Māthavi, a dancer and then came back to Kaṇṇagi. In Mahābhārata, an ascetic Mandapalā who was reborn to beget children marries a bird Jaritā and begets four little birds. Then he abandons Jaritā for another woman Lapitā. Hearing about the forest fire, he came back and requested Agni to spare his children and Jaritā. So, they were left unharmed. In Mahābhārata, the text states six people escaped the fire: Māya the magical Asura architect, Aśvasēna the Naga, and the four little birds who had not yet developed wings. In *Chilapathikāram,* Kaṇṇagi explicitly asks Agni that six categories be not harmed: the Brahmins, righteous, chaste women, elderly people, and children.[6] The parallels are striking. This is more so because *Chilapathikāram* explicitly draws a parallel between the Khāṇḍava forest and the burning of Mathurai.[7] The Agni of Yajña brings nourishment. At the instance of injustice, the nourishing breast milk brings forth Agni that destroys the rulers who had wronged the powerless. Thus, in the overarching Yajñāgni Maṇdala of *Chilapathikāram,* we find some of the finest expressions of bhakti incorporated into community life.

The epic drama vividly describes the dance performed by the cowherd community girls. It took place when the cowherd women observed a bad omen. The song and dance performance harmonized advanced musical knowledge with Purāṇic narratives, mystic philosophical insights, and bhakti.

> Oh girls! When that Enchanter (Kṛṣṇa) who threw the calf over the woodapple tree to bring down the fruits, comes to our cow herd, will we not hear that most melodious music showering like the golden rain tree, from His flute!
>
> Oh girls! When that Enchanter (Kṛṣṇa) who churned the ocean with the serpent as the rope, comes to our cow herd, will we not hear that most melodious music as soothing as the beauty of waterlily, from His flute![8]

The dance commences with such lyrics. In this depiction, Kṛṣṇa is portrayed as Viṣṇu Himself, who was responsible for churning the cosmic ocean. As the dancing and singing continue, the poet goes beyond Joseph Campbell's functions of mythology to reveal the mystery of avatārhood, the cosmic divine becoming enshrined in a very localized, very human form.

> Making the Northern Mountain the churning rod and Vāsuki the Serpent the rope, the hands of the sea-cued One churned the womb of sea; those were the very hands tied by the ordinary ropes of mother Yasōda; Oh Lord having Lotus blooming navel! What *Māya* of Yours is this that mystifies us!
>
> Even as the celestials worship You as the ultimate Truth, You having no hunger yet ingest all that exists; And that mouth is the mouth which stole butter from the cowherd households! Oh Lord wearing Tulsi garlands! What *Māya* of Yours is this that mystifies us!
>
> All the Devas united worship red-lotus like sacred feet of Yours – the feet which with two steps removed the darkness of all the three worlds! Those feet were the same which walked the earth as emissary of peace for the *Pāṇḍavas*. Oh the Lion Lord who struck the enemy Asura! What *Māya* of Yours is this that mystifies us![9]

In each stanza, the poet combines a cosmic function of Viṣṇu in one of his supra human avatār with a very localized function of Kṛṣṇa as a very human avatār form. In the churning of the cosmic ocean, Viṣṇu's role is to stabilize the Axis Mundi with the cosmic serpent, preserving order. Some have suggested that this may be a Purāṇic rendering of an astronomical event—the precession of equinoxes. Here, the role of Viṣṇu is as the deity of preservation. This is contrasted with him being tied by very earth-based ropes. In the next stanza, he is the ultimate consumer of all words. He eats the worlds during the cosmic deluge not because he is hungry but because as all names and forms dissolve, he alone remains. This aspect is contrasted with the fact that he stole and ate butter, a deity who eats the multiverses. In the third stanza, the measuring of the three worlds by the strides of Viṣṇu is a cosmic function that should not be confused with the later Purāṇic event of Vāmana, though the latter is definitely derived from the former Vedic source. The strides of Viṣṇu are famous and are mentioned in the *Rig Veda*. They uncover the existence from chaos and hence are acts of creation. This is contrasted with him as Kṛṣṇa walking for peace. It is of interest to note that the poet sees it fit to present such integrated and whole aspects of Viṣṇu derived from Vedas and developed in Purāṇas with the interconnected paradoxical mystery of the Divine.

Historian Lavanya Vemsani has pointed out the involuted elements of later avatārs of Viṣṇu in her work:

> Vishnu is a cosmological deity in the Vedas, similar to the other Vedic deities. The Vedas contain short, crisp accounts of the qualitative representation of the major deities and their achievements with a connection to the creation. Hence the reference to Vishnu in the Vedas are short, but capture the most essential features connected with him. Only six verses of the Rigveda depict Vishnu (Rigveda 1.154-156; 6.69; 7.99-100). Vishnu appears as Vritrahan (killer of Vritra), the one who took three strides (Rigveda 1.154.1,4), and as *Gopa*, a cowherd (Rigveda 1.22.18; 3.55.10; 1.155.4), which connects him to Krishna, a cowherd in Vraja, described in the Harivamsa and the other puranas. Vishnu is therefore connected to three of the avataras: Narasimha (Vritrahan), Vamana(dwarf with three strides),and Krishna Gopala (cowherd). These references from the Vedas connect Krishna to several cosmological concepts connected with Vishnu. Three strides connect him to the cosmologic spread encompassing the three worlds (vikrama), the cosmic pillar (*skamba*) as axis of the world, and firther spread (vis, viraj) to pervade the entire creation.[10]

In the cowherd dance-singing of *Chilapathikāram*, various evolved integrations of Viṣṇu and Kṛṣṇa are presented as an integral part of the cowherd community life. Therefore, when bhakti is said to have emerged from the '*Drāviṭa Dēsa*' in later descriptions, there is a deep historical truth to it.

Āzhwār Bhakti and Social Emancipation

Nammāzhwār

With the passage of a few centuries, we find a society with strong notions of social exclusion and hierarchy. In terms of the development of Śrī Vaiṣṇav Darśana, Nammāzhwar was the most important of the Āzhwārs.

The historic periods of Āzhwārs are often debated. Based on traditional accounts, Nammāzhwār was born forty-three days after Kṛṣṇa left the earth, which would suggest a date of 3100 BCE through a literal interpretation. However, Mu Aruṇācalam, in his authoritative work on Tamil literary history, places Āzhwār in the ninth 9thcentury CE.[11] It is also suggested that he belonged to the 8th-century CE. By the time of Śrī Nāthamunikal (823-951 CE), the selective hymns of Nammāzhwār had become popular in certain temples, but they were not codified and were lost as a collection. Nāthamunikal learned about the hymns from being sung by some devotees who had come from Kannada province, and on hearing that they knew only ten verses out of more than a thousand, he set out on a quest to recover all of them. He travelled to the birthplace of Nammāzhwār, where he obtained instructions for recovering the texts from a disciple of another Āzhwār who was a contemporary and devotee of Nammāzhwār.

Nammāzhwār was born to Kāri, who was a minister of a local king, and his mother was Uṭayanaṅkai. The name given to him was Māṟan. He was born in a small town called Thirukuṟukūr in Southern Tamil Nadu. They belonged to the fourth varṇa.

Though there are claims of them belonging to Kṣatriyas, particularly by the local Nāṭar community, it is traditionally and historically accepted that he was born in the Śūdra varṇa. His varṇa is stated as a fact rather than in any way to characterize the Āzhwār. If at all his varṇa has any significance, it is only in a socially emancipatory manner. According to the Śrī Vaiṣṇava tradition, he was the emanation of Viṣvaksenā, who is the head of the divine forces of Viṣṇu.

The person who recognized the greatness of Nammāzhwār was Mathurakaviāzhwār, who was a Brahmin and scholar of Vedas and the Upaniṣads. Śrī Nāthamunikal made a single verse of praise ('*Thaniyan*') for Nammāzhwār, which brings out the importance and deep connectivity of Āzhwār to Vedic spirituality:

> The nectar to the Bhaktās, nourishing rain to the devotees, exposition of all the meanings (deeply embedded in the scriptures), that is the sacred words of *Saṭagopan* which is the core of all the Vedas is in the Upaniṣads and the concentrated essence of the Upanishads is this ocean that is the Vedic essence given in the *Drāviṭa* language.

It can be observed that this contradicts the literal and mechanistic application of *Smṛti* and *Dharmaśāstra* injunctions that the Śūdras are not entitled to Vedic and Vedantic knowledge. What is even more important is that in Vaiṣṇava tradition, Nammāzhwār is considered as Avayavi, meaning the one who possesses all the body parts or the life force, and other Āzhwārs are considered as his Avaya or body parts. This is reminiscent of Puruṣa Sūkta. However, the difference here is that no Jāthi or birth-based varṇa consideration is taken into account when assigning the different body parts of different Āzhwārs who were from various Jāthis. Bhūtatāzhwār becomes the head, Poigaiāzhwār and Pēiāzhwār his eyes, Periyāzhwār his face,

Thirumazhisaiāzhwār his throat, Thoṇṭaraṭipoṭiāzhwār his chest, Kulasēkaāzhwār and Thirupāṇāzhwār his two hands, Thirimaṇgaiāzhwār his navel, and Mathurakaviāzhwār his divine feet.[12]

Here are two Āzhwārs: one, King Kulasēkaāzhwār, and another Thirupāṇāzhwār, who were considered, due to rigid moralistic religious influence, to belong to marginalized or defiled caste. Yet tradition placed both of them at par, considering them to be as important as none other than an emanation of Himself. Mathurakaviāzhwār, a Brahmin pandit well-versed in Vedas, was considered the counterpart to Nammāzhwār's feet. This was not a conscious social engineering effort, as it would be seen today. Instead, this was a spontaneous expression of bhakti solidifying into a narrative well-anchored in the Vedic vision of non-discriminatory non-dualism, inherently challenging social stratification and exclusion without even making that its primary objective. Yet its impact is more powerful, pervasive, holistic, and sustaining through centuries than any conscious 'social revolution'.

It is believed that the four works of Nammāzhwār, namely *Thiruviruththam*, *Thiruvāsirium*, *Periya Thiruvanthāthi*, and *Thiruvāimozhi* represent the essence of *Rig*, *Yajur*, *Atharva*, and *Sāma Vedas*. The first ten verses are considered to contain the core vision, and it is said that Śrī Rāmānuja drew inspiration from this vision to write his celebrated *Śrī Bāṣya*. Śrī Rāmānuja made a pilgrimage to Thirukuṟukūr. There is a strong reverence for Nammāzhwār, to the extent that Śrī Rāmānuja wished to become Nammāzhwār's divine feet. It is part of Vaiṣṇava tradition that Viṣṇu Himself bestowed the name Saṭagōpan upon Nammāzhwārzhwār. In Viṣṇu temples, after the prasād of Tulsi leaves and sacred water, devotees receive a crown-like structure and the divine feet of Viṣṇu on their heads, known as Saṭāri, which is considered to be Nammāzhwār himself.

At Thirukuṟukūr, Mathurakaviāzhwār built a temple for Nammāzhwār and the divine feet of Nammāzhwār was called Mathurakavi as seen earlier. After Śrī Rāmānuja visited, the divine feet of Nammāzhwār became known as the Śrī Rāmānuja as he requested that he be made the divine feet of Āzhwār.[13]

It is important to view the commentary verses in *Vedanta Sūtra Bāṣya,* which contain an unjustifiable denial of Vedantic learning to Śūdras in the context of broader teachings of Sanātana dharma. These repeated verses found in commentaries from different traditions should be seen as a distortion of the past. Anantanand Rambachan, a scholar of traditional monist Vedanta of Śankara school, has relevant insights on these discriminatory verses that are urgently needed:

> Criticism of caste inequality, as far as the knowledge of Brahman is concerned, can also find justification in the Advaita teaching about the identity and sameness of self in all beings. It remains a matter of concern that the greatest historical exponent of this teaching remained untroubled by social inequality, a contradiction that is still not uncommon. There is still a tendency to offer mild explanations for Śankara's attitude.... There is a need, today, for the monastic orders and institutions associated with the tradition of Advaita to explicitly and formally renounce eligibility that is based on caste and gender and articulate an interpretation of Vedantic eligibility that is centered solely on the fourfold means discussed above. There are rich resources within the tradition for doing so, but it requires also a willingness to self-critically admit historical and contemporary injustices of caste and gender and to subject Śankara's endorsement to rigorous historical criticism.[14]

Though Rambachan's statement pertains to the monist Vedanta school of Śankara, 'rich resources within the tradition' permeate the entire ocean of Sanātana dharma throughout its history and through all its Sampradāyas.

Thirumazhisaiāzhwār

He came from the community of bamboo basket weavers. As seen in the earlier chapters from the ascent of the Buddhist value system, they had been made 'Hīna Jāthi'. In the traditional account of the life of this Āzhwār, three incidents convey the spiritual rejection of social hierarchy and exclusion by Śrī Vaiṣṇava sampradāya of Sanātana dharma.

The story goes that Azhwār, a revered figure in the Tamil tradition, had such a close spiritual connection with Viṣṇu that he could request commands from Him. Once, when a Pallava king of Kānchi asked him to leave the capital city, Āzhwār asked Viṣṇu to leave as well. To everyone's surprise, Viṣṇu followed Azhwār out of the city. Only when the king apologized, did Azhwār and Viṣṇu return. This story is not just about the supernatural but also about a bamboo weaver community bard challenging a king in a pre-modern society. Tradition holds that Āzhwār was given the name Bhaktisāra by Śiva Himself.

The second incident happened when the Āzhwār was in a village named Perumpuliūr which is on the way between Kānchi and Kumbakōṇam. There, he was resting on the front open veranda of a Brahmin's house called Thiṇṇai—a place where people used to sit, and wayfarers also would be allowed to rest. As Thirumazhisaiāzhwār was sitting there, there were a few Brahmins there chanting the Vedic hymns. They stopped the chanting as they considered the Āzhwār as 'low caste', and hence, Vedas should not be recited when he was around. Seeing their silence, Āzhwār left the place and went to another Thiṇṇai a bit away. The Brähmanās again restarted their chanting, and they could not remember the Vedas. They realized that they had committed sin against a bhakta. They went and apologized to Thirumazhisaiāzhwār, who took a black rice grain and split it with his nails. The gesture was related to the exact verse from which the Brahmins had to again start. The incident also contains quite significant aspects that a bamboo weaver could, without hesitation, walk and also take a rest in Brahmin houses. Nobody told him to leave. The only gesture the Brahmins did was that they stopped chanting. Dharma, however, sees even this passive discrimination as a violation. Thirumazhisaiāzhwār demonstrated that he had a complete mastery of the Vedas. He did not recite it, but he demonstrated his mastery. There was no punitive action against him as per the injunction of *Smṛti* and *Dharmaśāstra* that a person of low caste hearing the Vedas should be inhumanly punished, and if he had internalized, he should be fatally tortured.[15]

On the other hand, in the traditional Guru Paramparā Prabāva Sāram, Thirumazhisaiāzhwār is celebrated as the emanation of 'Sudarśana' or Chakrathāzhwār, which is the divine discus in the hand of Mahā Viṣṇu. Sudarśana, also known as righteous vision (Su-darśana, symbolizes the destruction of the darkness of ignorance.

The next incident involves a very learned and righteous Brahmin of the same Perumpuliūr. Upon hearing about the greatness of Āzhwār from the priest of Kānchipuram, he, along with the people of the village, wanted to honour Thirumazhisaiāzhwār. At that time, he was preparing for a great Yajña. So, he decided to give the Agrapuja, the highest respect paid to the most important person in an assembly, to Thirumazhisaiāzhwār. Consequently, Thirumazhisaiāzhwār was brought with all due respect and seated in a high seat. However, a commotion arose as some questioned how such high respect could be given to a Śūdra from the bamboo weaver caste, especially in the context of a Yajña and among Brahmins. The pious Brahmin tried to pacify the agitated individuals who were considered to be from the upper caste. Śrī Kāñchi Prathivāthi Bayangaram Aṇṇañkarāchārya Swāmi, one of the greatest authorities of Vaiṣṇava tradition, writes that the opposition from some Brahmin to the Agrapuja ceremony was similar to how Śiśupāla opposed Yudhiṣṭhira when he offered the first respect of the Rājasūya Yajña to Kṛṣṇa. The Dīkṣita, who had invited the Āzhwār, requested him to dispel the ignorance of those who were focused on caste distinctions and show them the true path of wisdom. Thirumazhisaiāzhwār sang the following verse:

> Of what use are these cries over the first respect!
> Will You not remove these conflicts bringing forth the Divine!
> Lord with hands holding Discus, make the ritualists humble!
> Manifest forth with radiance as You are within.

And then the Divine Discus of Mahā Viṣṇu started radiating in the body of Āzhwār, removing the caste-based pride and anti-Śūdra hateful prejudices.[16]

The parallel between Śiśupālaa and those who opposed the agrapuja to Thirumazhisaiāzhwār is quite meaningful. In both cases, the opposition arose because the opposers considered Kṛṣṇa and Āzhwār unfit for respect in the assembly due to their low-caste birth and low status (as cowherd/bamboo makers). In both cases, the Sudarśana Chakra was invoked. However, while Śiśupāla was physically killed, the Vaidikas, who were prejudiced based on caste, underwent a psycho-spiritual transformation, symbolizing inner ignorance being removed. This transformation indicates the form that later social affirmative and passive resistance movements would take, as will be seen later.

Nampāṭuvān17

During his time, singing was considered defiled. For example, in the context of Śaiva Nāyanmārs, singers were considered untouchables and were not allowed inside temples. However, the Vaiṣṇava tradition has two incidents to negate these disabilities.

Nampāṭuvān was a Pāṇār who was considered Chaṇḍāla during those times. His glory is presented in *Varāha Purāṇa* and narrated by Varāha Perumāḷ—the boar avatār of Viṣnu Himself, to His consort Goddess Earth. Although part of the *Varāha Purāṇa,* it holds independent significance as an important spiritual work known as *Kaiśika Purāṇa.*

Varāha Perumāḷ locates Nampāṭuvān at Sithāśrama, traditionally identified with Thirukuruṅguṭi in southern Tamil Nadu. He identifies Nampāṭuvān as Chaṇḍāla, a terrestrial social identification, while he is introduced to the Goddess as a great ascetic. Nampāṭuvān would come every very pre-dawn time called '*Brahma Mukūrta*' and sing devotionally in various rāgas from a distance, which he did for ten years. One Kārthikka month Dwadashi, as he was going to do his singing service, he was caught by a 'Brahma Rākṣasa', a cannibalistic demon, previously a Brahmin but reborn or transformed into a demon because of either a sin or a curse. The Brahma Rākṣasa harshly told Nampāṭuvān that it was going to relish his blood and flesh. Nampāṭuvān asked the monster to let him go and finish his singing service to the Lord, promising to return to the Brahma Rākṣasa, but the monster refused. Nampāṭuvān clearly states the importance of truth to his value system. He says:

> *Satya Mūlam Jagat Sarvam Lōka: Satyē Prathiṣtitha*
> *nāham mthyā pravaṣyāmi Satyamēva vathāmyaham*
>
> Truth is the origin of all this dynamic existence; It is sustained by the Truth.
> I shall never talk untruth; I always speak the Truth.

Nampāṭuvān was allowed to go since he was anchored in truth. He sang in front of Viṣṇu, and it could be inferred that he used to come and sing *Suprabhātam*, which was a service rendered to the temple. Upon his return to the Brahma Rākṣasa, Viṣṇu came in the form of a man and tested him by asking him to save himself, but Nampāṭuvān was firm. He told the human-formed

Viṣṇu that he would never deviate from the truth and made a profound statement:

> *Aham Satyē pravruthō vai Sīlam Satyē Prathiṣtitham*: Even if I (my temptations) deviate from the Truth, my inherent character makes me fixedly sustained in Truth.

As Nampāṭuvān returned and stood before the Brahma Rākṣasa, ready to be its food, the monster was astonished to see that Nampāṭuvān had returned. The Brahma Rākṣasa then changed his demand, asking for the benefits of Nampāṭuvān's singing in exchange for his life. Nampāṭuvān refuses, as he had promised to give his body and life and was determined to keep his word. The monster addresses him as a great devoted soul and begs that Nampāṭuvān give at least half the fruits of his singing before Viṣṇu. But Nampāṭuvān still refuses. He insists that only what was promised alone would be given. The Brahma Rākṣasa then asks for just a fraction of the time Nampāṭuvān sang, but Nampāṭuvān again refuses. Finally, he tells the monster that his music is in his blood and offers to give the music carrying blood to the monster. The Brahma Rākṣasa pleads with Nampāṭuvān to give him the fruit of one specific song that was sung in the early pre-dawn time in the presence of Viṣṇu ('Viṣṇu Samsathi'). He believes that this song has the power to free him from his current cannibalistic form and liberate him forever. Nampāṭuvān, feeling compassion for the Brahma Rākṣasa, queries how the Rākṣasa had transformed into his current state. Now it is revealed that in a previous birth, the Rākṣasa was a Brahmin who conducted Yajña out of greed and delusional lust (*kārayē Yajñam lōbhamōhaprapīditha*). This selfish conduct of the Yajña resulted in a negative karmic effect, and when he died before completing the Yajña, he was reborn as a cannibalistic Brahma Rākṣasa. Taking refuge (*Saraṇam*) in Nampāṭuvān, he implores for liberation. Nampāṭuvān grants him the fruit of a song sung in 'Kaiśika Rāga' that could hopefully deliver the Brahma Rākṣasa from his suffering.

After narrating this, Śrī Varāha Perumāḷ declares to Mother Earth: 'Those who with Bhakti sing Me in Kaiśika Rāga in My presence/temple (*Mama Samsathi*) I give them liberation just as how Nampāṭuvān gave liberation to Brahma Rākṣasa.'

The entire whole Purāṇic incident of Nampāṭuvān is a critique of social hierarchy at every level. A Brahmin who performed Yajña for selfish reasons transformed into a cannibalistic demon. He is redeemed through the Puṇya Palan (righteous fruits) of a single song sung by a socially excluded person. The demon explicitly expresses his desire for the fruits of Nampāṭuvān singing in the presence of Viṣṇu (Viṣṇu Samsathi). This raises the question of whether he was not allowed inside or if he was actually assigned the service of singing the early morning songs of the temple, which took place within the temple precincts but some distance from the sanctum where devotees usually stand. Later Viṣṇu Himself used the term (Mama Samsathi), which strengthened the possibility of Nampāṭuvān being inside the temple complex. Finally, God Himself equates His act of salvation to how Nampāṭuvān liberates the Brahma Rākṣasa.

For five hundred years, this drama was enacted in the temples of Southern Tamil Nadu in and around the vicinities of Thirukuruṅguṭi. It involved three actors: Nampāṭuvān and Nambi Kizhavan (Viṣṇu coming in human form) were portrayed by female temple dancers, and Brahma Rākṣasa by a male performer, usually from the hereditary temple security clan. This performance would start on the night of Kārttika month Śukla Pakṣa Ekādaśī and continue to the next day, Dvādaśī. However, during the colonial period, this tradition was endangered. Thanks to the efforts of scholar Prof. S. Ramanujam (1935-2015), a former professor of Drama at Tamil University, and dancer Anita Ratnam, this tradition was revived in the late 1990s. This revival represents a holistic approach from Sanātana dharma to challenge and reject social exclusion through Puranic as well as ritual-performance art.

Thirupāṇāzhwār

Thirupāṇāzhwār is venerated as the emanation of Śrīvatsa, the auspicious symbol in the chest of Viṣṇu, symbolizing the presence of Goddess Śrī, who is identified with Lakṣmī. Being born in the Jāthi of Pāṇārs, he was considered then as untouchable and defiled. He used to stand on the southern bank of River Cāuvery and sing with his entire consciousness absorbed in the bhakti of Śrī Raṅga, the holiest temple for Vaiṣṇavaites in South India. Lokasāraṅga, the archaka who used to take sacred water to the temple for bathing the deity, one day came to the banks to take water and saw Thirupāṇāzhwār immersed in his music and contemplation of Śrī Raṅga. Without understanding the noble state of Thirupāṇāzhwār, Lokasāraṅga threw stones at him. A few others also abused the Āzhwār. They were perturbed when Āzhwār, who was without body consciousness, did not respond despite bleeding. They understood they had not done the right thing. However, they did not give much to the incident except for momentary mental disturbance. But when they came to the temple, they found that the sacred idol of the Lord was also hit, and it was bleeding from its forehead, the exact place where the stone had hit Thirupāṇāzhwār. Then Lokasāraṅga and other priests were informed by a Divine voice of their sinful transgressions against the Āzhwār and were asked to repent by bringing him inside the temple. Lokasāraṅga, who was also considered highly pious and ritualistic, carried Thirupāṇāzhwār on his own shoulders. So, the Āzhwār is hailed as 'Muni Vahāna'. This incident, as we will see later in the book, provides a framework for how Hindu dharma heals the wounds of oppressed communities who suffered and continue to suffer from the injustice of dominant groups in the conventional social order. It is important to note that this order was based more on power struggles, economic relations, and cultural factors related to these than on dharma itself.

Textual Developments in Bhakti

The worldview of Āzhwārs was deeply rooted in the Vedic vision of divine omnipresence and drew from a variety of Purāṇic and proto-Purāṇic sources with pan-Indian characteristics. This contributed to a textual consolidation that played a definitive role in the bhakti tradition, *Śrīmad Bhāgavata Mahāpurāṇa*. The text acted as the spiritual mitochondria of social emancipation.

The text states that an outcast is revered and venerated more than the most learned Brahmin when the former has bhakti, surrendering all he has to Hari. By possessing bhakti, not only the individual outcast but also his future generations are lifted out of social exclusion and attain a higher social status or even the highest.[18]

The story also speaks about the greatness of Rantideva, who shared whatever food he had with those in need. He gave his food to a hungry Brahmin, not because he was a Brahmin but because Rantideva saw the Divine in all beings. Then he encountered another hungry person from the Śūdra varṇa. Now the king was left with the food meant for his family. Always immersed in the thoughts of the Divine, the king gave the food meant for his family to the hungry person from the Śūdra varṇa. Later, a person with his dogs arrived and asked for food for both himself and his dogs. The king showed respect and gave him the remaining food. Now only water remained. As the king was about to drink water, a Chaṇḍāḷa (considered low-born) came and asked for that water, specifically mentioning his low status. To this, Rantideva gave an answer that has become an important principle for Sanātana dharma:

> I do not wish to attain the salvation from the Supreme God (īśvarāt parām) nor for (liberation through) the eight-fold Yogic perfection; nor do I seek liberation from the cycle of births and deaths; I pray to be among those who are suffering and suffer on their behalf to remove the suffering so that all become free of all miseries (bhavanty aduḥkhāḥ).

Saying this, he gives the water to the Chaṇḍāḷa, even though the king himself was dying of thirst and hunger. At this point, the Chaṇḍāḷa disappeared, and the Gods revealed themselves and blessed him. Then *Śrīmad Bhāgavata* declares that all those who follow the principles of Rantideva naturally become Yogis and devotees of Nārāyaṇa (*nārāyaṇa-parāyaṇāḥ*).[19]

The text emphasizes there should be no discrimination among devotees and that the universal ethical principle of working for the welfare of all, irrespective of caste or creed, is important for becoming a true devotee. The text also highlights the collective singing (*saṅkīrtana)* of the glory of Kṛṣṇa as a Yajña in itself (*yajñaiḥ saṅkīrtana-prāyair yajanti hi sumedhasaḥ*).[20] Here the text also points out that one should not think of such collective bhakti worship as belonging to intellectually inferior people. Those who do that are highly intelligent (*sumedhasaḥ*).

Śrī Rāmānuja

The most important seer who galvanized bhakti and gave it a clear, flexible structure while spreading it throughout India was undoubtedly Śrī Rāmānuja (1017-1137 ce). Although some verses in his Bhāṣya for the Vedanta Sūtras of Bādarāyaṇa may seem offensive and appear to endorse the highly objectionable and inhuman discrimination found in the temporal laws such as *Smṛtis* and *Dharmaśāstras*, his well-documented life and the egalitarian principles of the philosophy of Bhāgavata empathy and communal values in Śrī Vaiṣṇava Darśana outweigh those few verses.

In his traditional life, incidents of caste discrimination were frequent. During that era, a great mystic, Thirukachi Nambi, also known as Kāñchi Pūrṇar, lived. Śrī Rāmānuja desired to be initiated by Kāñchi Pūrṇar, in line with his mother's wishes and also his own high regard for Pūrṇar. Pūrṇar, being a non-Brahmin, was initially hesitant but eventually agreed only to impart six precepts to Śrī Rāmānuja. Later, when Pūrṇar visited Śrī Rāmānuja's home for a meal, at the latter's request, it so happened that Śrī Rāmānuja was delayed due to work. After Pūrṇar finished his meal and left, Śrī Rāmānuja's wife, who had served him with respect, not only cleaned the place but also performed a purification ritual, as she believed the presence of a non-Brāhmanā had ritually polluted the area. Upon discovering this, Śrī Rāmānuja was distressed, as he believed that all food consumed or left behind by devotees should be considered sacred, irrespective of their social status or occupational community. This incident became the first major issue that eventually led to the couple's separation.[21]

Among the Bhakta community of Śrī Rāmānuja, there was Māraneri Nambi, who belonged to the so-called untouchable caste of that period. He was very sick, and another member of the Bhakta community, Periya Nambi, who incidentally belonged to the Brahmin caste, was taking care of him. Periya Nambi went to Māraneri Nambi's house every day and night, nursing him, including bathing him and so on. When Periya Nambi went to nurse Māraneri Nambi in the night, Śrī Rāmānuja would follow him for protection. One day, Periya Nambi accidentally found this out. When Māraneri Nambi passed away, Periya Nambi conducted the last rites and cremation, which caused quite an agitation. However, Periya Nambi's daughter Aththuzhāi was very happy and declared that it was through this gesture that she understood the greatness of her father. Yet to show to others the spiritual maturity of Periya Nambi and how divisions like caste become meaningless for great bhaktas like Māṟaneri Nambi, Śrī Rāmānuja requested Periya Nambi to remove the confusion and agitation caused by his action in the minds of many as to how could he, a Brahmin do the funeral rites of a Māṟaneri Nambi. The answer Periya Nambi gave is considered a classic guideline for the Vaiṣṇava value system:

> Śrī Rāma conducted the funeral rites of Jaṭāyu a bird treating it like His own father's elder brother; In which way am I superior to Śrī Rāma? In which way Māṟaneri Nambi is inferior to a bird? Yudhiṣṭhira conducted the funeral rites of Vidura treating him with equal respect due to any of his ancestors; In which way am I superior to Yudhiṣṭhira? In which way Māṟaneri Nambi is inferior to Vidura? You know the heartbeat of our Āzhwārs here.

The last reference was to Thoṇṭaraṭipoṭi Āzhwār's hymn that states:

> They may be Brahmins by birth who are well versed in the four Vedas and its six limbs, pious and disciplined in rituals; but if they were to abuse Your *Bhaktas* then they, at that very second, become the real untouchables.[22]

The term 'abuse' is defined as 'merely asking the Jāthi of any bhakta', and inquiring about the caste of a Vaiṣṇava is considered a sin. According to tradition, the act of discriminating against someone based on their caste would instantly make the discriminator a Chaṇḍāḷa, regardless of their birth status. Had it been said that such a sin would make them born as untouchables, then it would have become a karmic justification for untouchability and social exclusion. Vaiṣṇava tradition brilliantly avoided this pitfall by stating that those who show discrimination, as a punitive measure, would be considered untouchable irrespective of their status by birth in that very instant.[23] This tradition was upheld during a widespread agitation, and it was decided that Periya Nambi's family would be boycotted. During the chariot festival, Aththuzhāi, Periya Nambi's daughter, stopped the chariot and questioned the boycott not to the Brahmins but to Śrī Raṅganātha. Tradition says that Śrī Raṅganātha manifested in the form of an altered state of consciousness in the head priest and declared before all that what Periya Nambi did was dear to him, showing the world how to stand firm in the principles enunciated by the Āzhwārs and carry them forward as a movement.

Everyone knows the well-known story of Adi Śaṅkara Bhagavatpāda encountering a Chaṇḍāḷa in the streets of Kāsi and being enlightened by him about the importance of not showing caste discrimination. This encounter led to the creation of the famous '*Manīṣā Pañcakam*', which emphasizes that a person with knowledge of Brahman should be respected as a teacher, regardless of their caste or social status. When the disciples of the great Ācārya asked Chaṇḍāḷa to move, he instead asked:

> Oh! The greatest of the twice-born! With scornful 'Go-away Go-away' what is it that you want to move away from you? Is it one food-made (physical) body (of mine) from another (very same) food-made body (of yours)? Or is it the consciousness (that pervades in me) from the consciousness (that is in you)?[24]

The question is firmly based on the very monist Vedanta school that the Ācārya advocated, which makes the discrimination between the physical and spiritual aspects of existence meaningless. This made the most eminent Ācārya of monist philosophy exclaim in each stanza of the *Pañcakam* that follows the question 'whether the person of wisdom is Chaṇḍāḷa *or* twice-born that person is my Guru.'

A similar incident is recounted in the life of Śrī Rāmānuja. In this story, the great Ācārya encounters a Chaṇḍāḷa woman. The great seer was visiting Thiruvāzhi-Thirunagari, one of the 108

Divya Deśas (Divine provinces) of Vaiṣṇavaites. Afterward, he was visiting other sacred places. When Śrī Rāmānuja (and, in some versions, some of his disciples) asked the woman to move away, she answered back with a question:

> Aside! Which side? Towards you? The holiest of the *Brāhmanās*? Towards the sacred shrine of *Tirukkaṇṇapuram* behind me? To the right, towards the *Tirumananan Kollai* where *Parakāla* waylaid the Lord; or towards the Pipal tree used by him as a watch tower? Towards my left, where rests the Lord of *Thiruvāzhi*? Which way, Oh Soul of Parity, shall I turn?

The question here also assumes a deep understanding of the Viśiṣṭādvaita Siddhānta. According to this concept, the entire material existence is considered the sacred abode and body of Mahā Viṣṇu. Hence, all space is permeated by the same sacredness and cannot be polluted. The woman associated this idea with the sacred geography of the local temples and raised a profound question that struck at the root of discrimination. Upon hearing these words, the response of Śrī Rāmānuja is described in a scholarly biography of the great Ācārya:

> 'A thousand pardons, noble lady,' exclaimed the Master with sad humility. 'Length of years and shallow pedantry have but intensified that haughty pride of mine and cast a thicker veil over my eyes, which denies me even the sweet privilege of recognising the Lord's Elect. These Sacred Badges would become yon better than this proud idiot of a Sanyassin.' And he prayed her to grace the Vaishnava fold with her noble presence and take her legitimate place near the Lord in the temple, where you see her even unto this day.[25]

Here, the founder of Śrī Vaiṣṇava Sampradāya is depicted as asking a woman, whom the society had made an outcast, to accept the Pañcasaṃskāra or the five rites of initiation that make a person part of the Bhakta community. After receiving these rites, no caste discrimination can be observed, and a shrine is built for her.

Among the disciples of Śrī Rāmānuja was a wrestler named Villi-Dāsan (Skt. Danur-Dāsan). His wife, Hemāmba (Tamil: Ponnachi), was a courtesan. Both husband and wife became devotees of Śrī Rāmānuja. When Śrī Rāmānuja went to take a bath in the River Cāuvery, he would take the hands of Muthaliāndān, a Brahmin and a relative of the Ācārya, who was also a great scholar of Vedas and other sacred texts. Upon returning from the bath, Śrī Rāmānuja would take the hands of Villi-Dāsan for support. Usually, touching someone from a so-called low caste would necessitate a purificatory bath. But Śrī Rāmānuja made it a point that after his bath, he would take the physical support of the so-called low caste person. What was the reason? He stated that Villi-Dāsan did not have the sin of even thinking that he had become humble from being in a high position. Here Pi. Sri Ācārya, a great scholar of Tamil and Vaiṣṇava Siddhānta, points out that Muthaliāndān had no feeling of caste superiority at all at any time and hence the deeper meaning of what Śrī Rāmānuja said had to be contemplated upon. There are various incidents through which Śrī Rāmānuja made the Brahmins realize the greatness of Villi-Dāsan and Hemāmba, which are not presented here.

In this context, when pressed further about his perceived partiality to Villi-Dāsan and what was to be inferred by his disciples about it, in his discourse Śrī Rāmānuja made ten attributional and analogical distinctions between Brahmins and non-Brahmins:

1. Brahmins, because of their worldly-religious duties, had to toil in worldly affairs. The non-Brahmin Vaiṣṇavaites immerse themselves only in the bhakti of Nārāyaṇa.

2. Brahmins are like the ones holding the edge of the life-saving boat (bhakti of Nārāyaṇa) in a torrential river, half immersed in waters and just saving themselves. The non-Brahmin Vaiṣṇavaites are already inside the boat and comfortably saved from the danger of the waters.
3. Brahmins are like those Āzhwārs who initially were unaware of Hari's greatness but were later, through His grace, made to be His devotees. The non-Brahmin Vaiṣṇavaites are like Periāzhwār, who, right from birth by his very nature, was immersed in the bhakti and meditation of Nārāyaṇa.
4. Brahmins are in the stormy high waves of Samsāra, trying to get to the shore. The non-Brahmin Vaiṣṇavaites, through their unwavering bhakti, are already in that Terra-firma of the shore, safe and away from the stormy waves and that shore is of Nārāyaṇa.
5. Brahmins, because of their concerns about clan-based, birth-based, lineage-based pride, diminish themselves like atoms in front of the Meru-like magnificence of non-Brahmin Vaiṣṇavaites who have attained that greatness because of their prideless dissolving in the community of bhaktas and their bhakti.
6. Brahmins are like the sugarcane, for with Vedic studies and interpretation, the sugarcane had to be bitten and chewed and could cause injury to the mouth of the taster. The non-Brahmin Vaiṣṇavaites are the candy-like essence of the sugarcane. For they taste the essence of Vedas, which is the sweetness of all sweetness that is Nārāyaṇa.
7. Brahmins are like the soil, for when Nārāyaṇa comes to the soil, He displays His Līlāvibūthi, which is the playful divine grandeur that could cause fear and anxiety to those around. The non-Brahmin Vaiṣṇavaites are, on the other hand, like the celestial space where Nārāyaṇa exists in Nityabūthi,

His eternal splendour and they are like abiding in that, are without fear and anxiety and in peace and bliss.

8. Brahmins are struck in the darkness of (ritualistic maze of) Vedas and are hence lost. The non-Brahmin Vaiṣṇavaites walk steadfastly in the infinite radiance of Nārāyaṇa, verily like the Pāṇḍavas led by Kṛṣṇa.
9. Brahmins are like possessors of stones of not much value and perhaps of some medicinal curative values as they recite daily mantras like Gāyatri (which, through daily timely recitals, are like medicinal chemical stones) of limited value. But non-Brahmin Vaiṣṇavaites possess the valueless Ratna-like magical jewel of bhakti through which they obtain amrita or disease-less eternal life itself, which is Nārāyaṇa.
10. With ritualistic adherence to Vedic deities, the Brahmins are like women of inferior morality. But non-Brahmin Vaiṣṇavaites, having their heart abiding only in Nārāyaṇa, are women of high fidelity and ethics.[26]

In the passage above, Śrī Rāmānuja created an elaborate hermeneutic space that aimed to completely reject caste distinctions, whether the caste system persisted or faded over time. The devaluing of the Vedas should be viewed not as much a dismissal of the Vedas themselves but rather as an exaltation of the spiritually democratic bhakti as the condensed essence of the spirit and values of the Vedas. The Sants of the latter day Rāmānandī tradition, including Kābir, should be seen regarded as developments stemming from this fundamental philosophy of Śrī Rāmānuja.

Thus, Śrī Rāmānuja should be considered possibly the greatest spiritual emancipator of his time. He initiated a silent but perhaps the most sustained revolution in social emancipation. No other revolution in social emancipation has empowered so many communities over millennia with little to no violence, even in the midst of challenging circumstances such as alien invasions, forceful proselytization, colonial wealth drainage, and imperial subjugation of people. He was able to achieve this without the support of any empire or colonial surplus.

Subsequent Developments

Invasions, Escapes, and Restoration

Meanwhile, as the Delhi Sultanate expanded its Islamist empire southward, it was accompanied by unprecedented severity of temple destruction, large-scale massacre of civilian populations, and forcible conversion. The temples at Śrī Raṅgam and Chidambaram seemed to have emerged as special targets. In both temples, the Brahmins were specially tortured to reveal the whereabouts of the idols of deities of the temple, and then, despite horrendous tortures failing to extract the truth, they were massacred wholesale.

According to the chronicles of Śrī Raṅgam called 'Kōilozhuku' (The Stream of Temple History), in one day, 12,000 Brahmins were massacred at the temple of Varāha Swamy when the Islamist forces came to know that the idols of main deities had been successfully rescued by the devotees.[27] The statement of the sacrifice is quite famous among Tamil Hindus in general and Vaiṣṇava in particular, '*pannīrayiram tirumutitiruthtina pan̲riāzhwān mētu kalābham*'.

In the case of Chidambaram Natarāja Temple, Hazrat Amir Khusrau, in his *Tarik-i-Alai*, records the following incident that happened during the sacking of the temple by Malif Kafur:

> They saw a building (the temple of Barmatpuri (Brahmapuri i.e., Chidambaram) old and strong as the infidelity of Satan, and enchanting like the allurements of worldly life. The foundations of this golden temple, which was the 'holy-place' of the Hindus, were dug up with the greatest care. The

> glorifiers of God broke the infidel building, so that 'spiritual birds' descended down like pigeons from the air. The 'ears' of the wall opened at the sound of the spade. At its call, the sword also raised its head from the scabbard, and the heads of Brahmans and idol-worshippers came dancing to their feet at the flashes of the sword. The golden bricks rolled down and brought with them their plaster of sandalwood; the yellow gold became red with blood and the white sandal turned scarlet. The sword flashed where the jewels had once been sparkling, where mire used to be created by rose water and musk, there was now a mud of blood and dirt; the saffron-coloured doors and walls assumed the colour of bronze; the stench of blood was emitted by ground once fragrant with musk. And at this smell the men of Faith (Islam) were intoxicated and the men of Infidelity (Hindus) ruined.[28]

The pun that poetic Hazrat Amir Khusrau employed here should not be missed, the heads of the devotees danced in the temple of the Lord of Dances. Yet despite such treatment, the devotees never revealed the places where the idols had been hidden. Often, they were very near the places where they were being tortured. Prof. Job Thomas writes:

> Over eighty (hidden) images were found at Chidambaram: sixteen at Nallur. Most of the images belonged to the Chola period and no one knows when they were hidden. That they have remained unnoticed even in these busy temples would attest to the effectiveness of this method.[29]

The importance of highlighting this point here is because the colonial and continuing narrative of India's social history often depicts Brahmins as using religion as priestcraft to exploit the non-Brahmins. However, historical evidence shows that Brahmins were targeted, and, like other Hindu communities, they were among the main targets in non-Hindu invasions. In these situations, they chose to stand their ground and even accepted death deliberately for the deities they worshipped. This demonstrates that Brahmin rituals involved the adoration of and daily care of the deities rather than Brahmin acting as intermediaries between the devotees and the gods. They were the caretakers of the deities, which is a concept qualitatively different from the idea of 'priestcraft'.

During this time, the Bhakta community, which emerged with Śrī Rāmānuja Vaiṣṇava Sampradāya, transcended birth-based community boundaries and hierarchies to safeguard their deity from invaders. Their story is one of courage and sacrifice, demonstrating the social cohesion achieved by bhakti. Without this, Sanātana dharma would have been completely destroyed in Southern India. This historical event should be recognized as a remarkable achievement in achieving social justice and harmony anywhere in the pre-modern world. It stands as a testament to the intense human effort to uphold the cultural and spiritual values of a civilization against all odds.

Right during the invasion and occupation, the devotees were intimated, and their coming to the temple was violently discouraged. A temple dancer named Veḷḷāyi (meaning, fair/white woman) decided to enact an act of defiant resistance to the Islamist commander who was doing this. She seduced him and took him to a top temple tower, and then, as he approached her, she threw him down from the tower, which immediately killed the general. Then she herself jumped from the tower. She was fatally hurt and was in her last moments. When the nearby Hindus came to her trying to save her life, she said that she was happy she could do the supreme sacrifice for her people and that she and her community should be given the honour of getting fire for the rites from the sacred ovens from where the food for the Lord was cooked and that Prasād and divine-symbol honours should be given. That promise was made to her, and it was then being followed through generations.[30] One of the towers of Śrī Raṅgam is painted in pure white in honour of this dancer-girl.

The Bhakta community took an arduous and complicated route to escape from pursuing invaders. They travelled through the southern parts of Tirukkōṭṭiyūr, Kāḷaiārkōil, Thirumālirusōlai, then through Kerala, Kōzhikōṭu, Tirukkiṇāmbi (Mysore state), and Punganūr, until they reached the holy mountains of Tirupati. Here, they ceremoniously installed the idols safely and temporarily until they could return to Śrī Raṅgam.[31] This place was under the protection of Vijayanagar.

The arduous and dangerous exodus from Śrī Raṅgam was led by Piḷḷai Lōkāchārya, who was over a hundred years old at that time. One of his core disciples was a seer named Viḷāñchōlai Piḷḷai, who belonged to the Pullaiyar community. The Pullaiyar community came to be considered as defiled and as 'untouchable' with the advent of religions advocating rigid moralism and dogmatic non-violence.[32] During the exodus, before reaching the destination at a village called Jyōthishkui, Piḷḷai Lōkāchāchrya passed away. At that time, Viḷāñchōlai Piḷḷai was in southern Kerala. The next in line in the succession as Ācārya was Thiruvāimozhi Piḷḷai, who was well suited for tumultuous times as he was well-versed in spiritual disciplines and adept in dealing with the political forces of the time. However, his study of *Śrī Vaiṣṇava Vēdānta Rahaśyā* was incomplete. Rahaśyā does not mean secret but embedded divine insights in plain sight of a sacred text that could be illumined only through a guru or Ācārya. So Piḷḷai Lōkāchāchrya asked Thiruvāimozhi Piḷḷai to get these Rahaśyā from Viḷāñchōlai Piḷḷai. When Viḷāñchōlai Piḷḷai of the Pullaiyar community died, it was Thiruvāimozhi Piḷḷai, a Brahmin well-versed in Vedas, and then the Ācārya of Vaiṣṇava bhaktas, who performed the funeral rites 'as a son does to his father'.[33]

During the short-lived Madurai Sultanate (1334-1378), there were reports of extreme hardship in the society. Ibn Batuta, an Algerian Arab explorer, documented campaigns against 'idolaters' involving impaling the entire male population and slitting the throats of women and children.[34] The rise of the Vijayanagar empire established a strong foundation for Hindu Dharma and became a bulwark against the Islamist invasions. Vijayanagar prince Kumāra Kampaṇa Uṭaiyār brought an end to the Madurai Sultanate. His queen, Gangā Dēvi, in her Mathurā Vijayam, compares the tyranny of the Madurai Sultanate to the tyranny of the demonic King Kamsa.

As the forces of Kampaṇṇa Uṭaiyār humbled and vanquished the occupying invaders, Gopaṇa, his chief adviser and administrator, reinstalled the idol in the temple of Śrī Raṅgam 'in the Saka year 1293, AD 1370-71, in the year Paritapi, month Vaikasi, date 17.'[35]

Most of those who had experienced the traumatic period had passed away, and the survivors were very elderly. When a controversial dispute arose regarding the originality of the mūrti, the sacred form of Azhahiyamaṇavāḷa Perumāḷ, a visually impaired elderly washerman correctly identified the sacred form by the nature of water on the dress with which he was familiar. Similarly, the Kodava elders risked their lives to help in the safekeeping of Azhahiyamaṇavāḷa Perumāḷ. During the invasion, another warrior named Panchukoṇṭān displayed exemplary valour in fighting the invaders and became a 'Balidhāni'. These people from various occupations were honoured when the temple was re-inaugurated with the Lord reinstalled. The washerman was given the title 'Īraṅkolli' along with awards as if given by Vishnu himself. The Kodava were given the title 'Thiruthāzhvarai Dāsar'. The bards were given the title 'Isaiaṟiyum *Perumāḷ Kūṭṭam'*, meaning 'the Bhakta community singing for the Lord'. Panchukoṇṭān was honoured with special ceremonial respects each time Azhahiyamaṇavāḷa Perumāḷ would go out in His procession.[36]

The Dharmic supra-community network of Bhāgavata people united various hereditary communities across the boundaries of Jāthi and the framework of Varṇa. It was established and nurtured by bhakti and then further developed by Nammāzhwār and Śrī Rāmānuja. This structure later contributed to the sociopolitical stability and sustainability of Vijayanagar. Hari Saravanan, an ethnographer with a rooted Indic vision, highlighted this aspect while studying and documenting the marginalized communities in South India:

> Jati equations were remodelled under Vijayanagara empire. In the beginning due to the sole intention of uniting all practitioners of Sanatana Dharma numerous Jati-based distinctions and occupations were partially neglected and some newly created. Many communities like the Kuruba (Pastoralists), Golla (Pastoralists), Beda (Hunters), Madiga (Leatherworkers) and Viswakarma (artisans) took up military occupations. Inspired by the resurgence of Sanatana Dharma in South India numerous Brahmins took up active military service, like Gopanna, a Arvela Niyogi Brahmin. He was the leading general under Kumara Kampanna (second son of Bukka I) who had laid siege to Sri Rangam and Madurai and freed these two temple towns from Muslim domination and gave the final blow to the Madurai Sultanate in 1378 CE.[37]

In historical records, the participation of various communities and different professions, including battle-craft, as well as other vocations beyond their supposedly hereditary works, even in the pre-Vijayanagar period, have been documented. However, during the Vijayanagar Empire, there was a notable acceleration in this process. This was parallelled by the re-inauguration of the Śrī Raṅgam temple. Historian Ranjeeta Dutta from Jamia Millia Islamia discusses how different communities became connected through the temple, demonstrating the sociopolitical development that occurred in Vijayanagar and was prefigured in the Bhakti Siddhānta of Āzhwārs and Śrī Rāmānuja:

> This ensured patronage from diverse political groups and gave the honourable role of saviours to the community of devotees who were mostly tribal groups of the Irulas and Kodavars and marginalized occupational castes, such as temple singers, barbers, and washermen. In the narrative, they received honours and titles since they comprised the temple retinue and residents at Tirupati, where the idol was temporarily hidden from the sultan's army before being reinstated at Śrirangam.[38]

Evolution of Bhakti Schools

There have been philosophical developments in Bhakti school in South India during and after Śrī Rāmānuja. Śrī Nimbārkar (13th century) Śrī Madvāchārya (1238-1317) and Śrī Vallabāchārya (1479-1532).

Like all other 'orthodox' commentators, Śrī Nimbārka also, in his *BrahmaŚūtra* commentary *Vēdānta-pārijāta-saurabha*, seems biased against Śūdra. His immediately proximate disciple Śrīnivasa, in his *Vēdānta Kaustubha,* which in turn is the on the *Brahma Śūtra Bāṣya* of his guru, rejects even the moderate notion that the 'disqualification with regard to acts like sacrifices to be performed by means of fire,' by the Śūdra 'is not a cause of his disqualification for knowledge, as knowledge is mental, and as Vidura and the rest, as well as women like Sulabhā and so on, are found to possess the knowledge of Brahman' and unequivocally declares that 'a Śūdra is not entitled to the knowledge of Brahman.'[39] In the Darṣna of Nimbārkar Sampradāya, this strict orthodoxy gets seasoned by bhakti, though it does not completely obliterate the Śūdra exclusion. For example, Śrī Puruṣōtham Āchārya, one of the gurus in the Nimbārkar

Sampradāya, in his work *Vēdānta Ratna Mañjūṣā* makes Śūdra eligible for knowledge from the Purāṇa literature but not from the Upaniṣad.[40] All four Varṇas and women could be initiated into the Gōpāla Mantra. But while the first three Varṇas would be given a complete form of the mantra with eighteen syllables, the Śūdra and the women would be given a mantra of only ten syllables.[41] Despite such considerations to social status quo, Śrī Nimbārkar was one of the earliest Vaiṣṇava Āchāryas to bring forth Rādhā accompanied by Kṛṣṇa as the highest form of Divine to be meditated, devotionally loved, served and worshipped.[42] This form of the Divine now is perhaps the most beloved and well-known pan-Indian divine form as Rādhā-Kṛṣṇa. As Rādhā exists not just as a metaphor or spiritual symbol of meditation and devotion but also as a quasi-historical reality in the Hindu psyche, this has effects in making a strong woman-centred bhakti movement as would be seen in the later century Mīrābāi. Thus, whatever the puritanical position of Nimbārkar Sampradāya, it did become an important midwife in Dharmic social emancipation.

Śrī Vallabāchārya demonstrated that through devotion, a space for social emancipation of a far-reaching nature could be created, despite the limitations of the existing social conditions and dominant social values of a pre-modern society. Śrī Vallabāchārya, also known as Mahapurusha, welcomed followers from all social classes as his disciples. His Sampradaya (tradition) gained many followers in Gujarat. He appointed Krishnadas Adhikari, a Patel, to perform the ritual worship at the sect's shrine, the temple of Sri Nath. Among his disciples were celebrated devotees from all communities, such as Yadavendradas (a potter), Vishnudas (a tailor), Shyamdas (a carpenter), Kumbhandas (a weaver), and Khetu, Deepo, Rupo, and Toto of the fourth Varṇa.[43]

Vijayanagar Developments: Madvāchārya Lineage and Dāsas

In terms of social emancipation emanating from these Bhakti movement stands the striking phenomenon Hari Dāsas of Dāsakūṭam (commune of the devotee-servants of Hari). Of these, Purandara Dāsa is important with respect to musical tradition. In his compositions, he pointed out that Jāthi was not important for spiritual initiation, progress and realization. He sings:

> What if, of any caste? Let him be anybody; if he has realized the existence of God inside. If a sugarcane is bent, is its juice also bent?[44]

With the honorary revival of the musical tradition, he paved the way for the expansion of the Bhakti movement. His contemporary was Kanaka Dāsa.

Kanaka Dāsa

Belonging to a shepherd community (Kuruba) and named Timmappā, Kanaka Dāsa (1509-1607) rose to become a chieftain in the army. Because of his lucky nature of turning every venture golden (alternatively because he struck a golden treasure while digging), he was called Kanaka (golden), and because of his chieftain status, he was called Kanaka Nāyaka. He was drawn to the Vaiṣṇava tradition due to his interaction with a seer named Thathācharya. Kanaka Nāyaka built a temple for Ādi Kēśava, a form of Viṣṇu, on the primordial serpent.

After being severely wounded on the battlefield, he had a vision and wanted to get initiated. However, he was mocked and given a mantra meaning a buffalo by the then highly prestigious guru of the Madhvācharya tradition, Vyasarāja. Even though he was forming the Dāsakūṭam, he was hesitant to include a low-caste person due to social conditioning. So, in a light-hearted manner, he asked Kanaka to recite 'water-buffalo' as a mantra. Whether the mantra was given as an insult to the low caste of Kanaka or as a test of his devotion to his guru, Kanaka took to reciting the mantra sincerely. According to tradition, this led to superhuman strength or the ability to summon the buffalo mount of Yamā. With this ability, he was able to remove a gigantic boulder that was blocking a water body. Following this display of resolve, the guru initiated him properly. He came to be called Kanaka Dāsa. Whether or not the traditional incident is true, Vyasarāja included a man considered low caste into the Dāsakūṭam and Kanaka Nāyaka became Kanaka Dāsa.

Despite his devotion and belief in the presence of the divine in all life forms, Kanaka Dāsa was ridiculed by the upper-caste disciples of Vyasarāja. When a hungry dog took away bread from his house, he saw it as an opportunity to serve God and chased after the dog to feed it jaggery and ghee so that it could eat the bread with these as side dishes. Unfortunately, some people mocked him as Kunidāsa, which means 'servant of dog'. Vyasarāja, wanting to show the high spiritual state of Kanaka Dāsa, gave his fellow disciples banana fruits and asked them to eat them without being seen. All of them did as instructed except Kanaka Dāsa, who believed that he could not eat without god seeing him. Kanaka Dāsa experienced a visible rejection of social exclusion in Udupi when he was denied entry into the temple due to his caste. As a result, Kṛṣṇa's statue turned to face him, and a break was made in the wall of the sanctum.[45] To this day, that breach in the wall, now made into a small window-like structure, is called '*Kanakana Kindi*' or 'Kanaka's Window'.

Kanaka Dāsa spoke from his experience and hence his verses are authentic. Ramachandra Dattatreya Ranade ('Gurudev' Ranade, 1886-1957), one of the greatest scholars of Indian philosophy in his study of the bhakti phenomenon in Kannada literature, evaluates the poetry of Kanaka Dāsa thus:

> *Kanakadāsa* has given us a brilliant description of his cumulative spiritual experience.... In his song, *īsu dina ī vaikuntha estu dūra ennuttdde*, (before I had the vision, I used to say that Vaikuntha was at a very long distance), are described multiple experiences of a very high order, photic, chromic and morphic. 'For all these days,' says the poet, 'I was thinking that Vaikuntha, the city of God, was too far away. But when I saw it with the insight given by my Master, I found it here, in my heart, in the form of God Ranga, the Lord of creation.'[46]

From such authentic experience flows a rejection of social exclusiveness and birth-based pride. In his composition 'Rāmadānya Charitre', Kanaka Dāsa beautifully expresses a rejection of social exclusiveness and birth-based pride based on his authentic experiences. Rāma dānya or Rāma-grain is the name given to finger millet (also known as Rāgi or *Eleusine coracana*). The story is set in the context of Rāmā in the forest at the hermitage of the sages, where all the grains have been placed as part of the meals. Rāmā asks the sages assembled there which is the noblest grain, to which Sage Gautama answers that finger millet is the noblest of all the grains. Hanuman also favours Rāgi. This infuriates the rice grain, which is associated with the affluent sections of the society. The rice grain, called Bhaṭṭa, starts abusing Rāgi, calling it 'Śūdraṇṇā' (aṇṇā-elder brother). Rāgi, unable to tolerate the abuse, retorts by pointing out that rice, or Bhaṭṭa paddy, is given to the corpses as part of the final funeral rituals, devastating the rice grain. Finally, Rāmā consoles the rice grain by highlighting the significance of finger millet in helping the starving population during famines, thus challenging the tendency of social aristocracy based on ritualism. This composition also serves as a critique of the Dharma shastra statements that compare the Śūdra caste to a crematorium, providing a fresh perspective and challenging social stagnation as part of self-realization inspired by bhakti Śraddhā.[47]

The transformation here is continuous, unlike violent social upheavals and 'revolutions' of the West. It is not based on economic conditions but rather centres around the individual. Through the intense expansion of the self via mystical experiences, social stagnation and social exclusion are challenged. It should be noted that social exclusion and hierarchy are fundamentally challenged in this Indic model. When Timmappā became Kanaka Nāyaka, he clearly achieved upward social mobility in society, despite the so-called Jāthi and Varṇa not posing an impediment. However, it was Kanaka's self-transcendence and authentic mystical experience that led to his transformation from Kanaka Nāyaka to Kanaka Dāsa, making him the epicentre of a spiritual egalitarian renaissance that spanned centuries.

As late as the 18th century, Jagannātha Dāsa (1728-1809) in his work *Harikāthamruta Sāra* (13:4), stated, 'Let him belong to any caste, let him come from any country, let him follow any profession, if he worships Śrīnivāsa, He will accept him.'

A.P. Karamkar and N.B. Kalamdani, two scholars who made an authoritative study on *Haridāsās*, point out how the tradition sustained social transformation through spirituality for over 500 years till the advent of colonialism:

> In fact, the *Haridāsā* movement has done a great service to the masses in *Karnātak*. But unfortunately, mainly owing to the loss of political power and supremacy, a gradual decline of the *Bhakti* wave begins to take place after the middle of the 19th century AD Till then, the *Haridāsās*, while inculcating the doctrine of *Dvaita*, have also preached the doctrine of equality of status in society. Neither sex nor position in society could come in the way of the realization of the supreme Bliss. And eventually, we need not be surprised if we find the names of about three females in the list' of the *Dāsakūṭa*. Again for the attainment of the highest goal the ordinary barriers of caste and creed proved to be of no avail to the *Haridāsās*.[48]

Bhakti from the Vedic period poured into its Vaiṣṇava stream and soon became consolidated in the South Indian Vaiṣṇava tradition. Here, it created the conceptual space and sustained processes for social movements, which in turn were predicated upon spiritual humanism. This movement would later circumambulate the entire India through varied movements and diverse manifestations. Through processes spanning millennia, if not more, the Vaiṣṇava tradition created a strong spiritual value system that would inevitably affect social emancipation.

Śūdra: Spiritual Pride and Temporal Power

The bhakti movement had a significant impact on the fourth Varṇā, freeing itself from any association of stigma with the term and allowing the communities to attain temporal power. The bhakti movement mitigated the ritualistic stigma associated with the fourth by emphasizing all anchored in the divine. Notably, influential figures like Nammāzhwār and Appar had family members who were chieftains and army generals in the 7th century South India. Even during the time of later Chōlas, individuals from the fourth Varṇā, such as the minister Chēkizhār, held positions of influence, with the tradition depicting the Chōla king being humble and respectful towards him.

The transition from being chieftains and army officials to rulers was facilitated by the clans without denying their Śūdra heritage. This transition was greatly influenced by the effect of bhakti, leading to the high veneration of their heritage. The Pithapuram inscription of Pruthvīśwara II holds significant importance in illustrating this transition. Pruthvīśwara II belonged to the Velanāṇḍu Chōdas dynasty, which initially served as lower-level military officers in the Chōla empire. Under the rule of Chola emperor Kulōthuṅka Chōzha (1025–1122), the dynasty's first important ruler Gonka I, became a

Chōla vassal for the Velanāṇḍu region of Veṅgi. Over time, the dynasty emerged as a ruling clan, mostly allied with Chōlas against Kalyāṇi Chāḷukyas, except for a brief period.

Pruthvīśwara II reigned from 1186 to 1207 CE as the fifth ruler of this dynasty. In his inscription at Pithapuram, the harmonious coexistence of the dual Varṇa status is evident:

> The self-born, ancient, imperishable (Brahma, who was able to produce the living beings and the remainder of the visible world, appeared from the spacious apartment (which was) the lotus on the navel of Hari (Vishnu), who is the husband of Śri, who is the dwelling-place of the Vêdasiras, (and) who is engaged in protecting the multitude of worlds, which moves within his own belly.
>
> As the current of the Gangâ from the sole of the foot of Hari, the only lord of the three worlds,- the Chaturthanvaya was produced from the lotus- foot of him (viz. Brahmâ), which is praised by (the god) Mahêndra. In this (race) was born prince Indrasêna, who was praised by a wondering crowd of sages (and) who was adopted as son by king (Yudhishṭhira), the son of (the god) Dharma, who was pleased with (his) conduct in battle.
>
> ...This king, to whom king Dharma (Yudhishthira) had given all the emblems of a sovereign, ruled for a long time in that city, adorning the circle of the earth with the splendour of the glittering canopy of (his) great fame, making the minds of all learned men rejoice, (and) surrounded by an army of four members, as[3] the moon' by hosts of stars.[49]

In this passage, the origin of the Śūdra is not denied but rather elevated as originating from the sacred feet of the divine, which is also the source of the holy River Gaṅga. Similarly, the Kṣatriya status is portrayed as earned through bravery on the battlefield, emphasizing its worth-based nature. Notably, the status is conferred by Yudhiṣṭhira on the Purāṇic patriarch of the clan. One can note that this relation between Yudhiṣṭhira and Indrasêna in the Purāṇic time maps to Kulōthuṅka Chōla and Gonka I. The continued veneration of the divine feet in the Dharmic tradition, along with its permeation throughout the society through bhakti, makes the Divine feet-based origin holy and devoid of any stigma.

Further, the chieftains of this dynasty built temples and patronized Brahmins. As shall be seen in later centuries, these inscriptions reveal that there was no hesitation from Brahmins to serve in temples built by Śūdra landlords or affluent individuals, as seen in the case of Jāyāmbikā, the wife of Gonka III, and mother of Pruthvīśwara II. She, along with 'the daughter of one of the chiefs of Nādendla, who, like the chiefs of Velanâṇḍu, belonged to the Sûdra caste' not only built the temple of Kunti-Mādhava, a form of Viṣṇu bestowing grace to Kunti, the mother of Pāndavās. This temple is one of the most sacred of the five temples where Viṣṇu is worshipped in the form of Mādhava, the famous *Pañcha Mādhava Kṣētras*. The inscription reads:

> To Vishnu who fulfilled the desires of Kunti,' (and) who dwelt in the town called Sripitha (i.e. at Srîpîṭhapura), she built an assembly-hall (asthana- manḍapa), which was to enjoy a permanent income (bhôga), (and which was adorned) with pillars which bore splendid ornaments (and) were as lovely as sapphires.
>
> Having built to Him a temple which was adorned with an enclosure (prákára) and gate-ways (gopura), (and) having duly set up (an image of) Kamalâlayâ (Lakshmî), she obtained the desired rewards by propitiating Achyuta (Vishnu) together with her (viz. Lakshmî) by worship.
>
> She made manifest to men the beautiful name Hêmângai - which may be learn from the essence of all Vêdas (Sruti)- of the highest being which has assumed the shape of the lord of Śrisimhagiri in order to remove the distress of (His) devotees.[50]

The focus on Kunti-Mādhava by Jāyāmbikā was not a mere coincidence. The first popular prayer in the bhakti movement is from the *Śrīmad Bhāgavata Mahāpurāṇa*, known as the prayer of Kunti or Kunti stuti.[51]

One also finds the Śūdras occupying high offices in royal courts. Moreover, during the 13th century, Sōmanātha Daṇḍanāyaka, a general in the Hoysāla empire, not only built the famous Chennakēsava temple at Sōmanāthapura but also created an agrahāra or settlement of Brahmins. In an inscription inside the temple, Sōmanātha Daṇḍanāyaka acknowledges his ancestors:

> In the race born from the feet of Brahma arose Rudra, who was a minister of king Hermādi, lord of Kalyāṇa; his son was Mailaya-ṇāyaka; his son, Heggada-nāyaka, who was also a subordinate of the lord of Kalyāṇa; to him and his wife Rēvalā was born Sōma.[52]

Sōmanātha established an agrahāra which he named Vidyānidhi-prasanna Sōmanāthapura. This place became a hub for Vēdic culture, where every parrots could recite the Vēdic verses. He also built a Pañcha Liṅga temple with five Śiva Liṅgas, two of which were dedicated to his parents and one to himself: Rēvelēśawara, Pergaḍēśwara, and Sōmanātha.[53] This illustratesthe bhakti-based transformation of the feet-based Śūdra origin into a stigma-less and non-inferior divine origination, facilitating social mobility for the clans and individuals of the fourth Varṇa with passive acceptance and support from all levels of society, including the Brahmins.

The motif of Śūdra and River Gaṅga coming from the sacred feet of Viṣṇu has been a consistent means across the centuries to glorify the Śūdra origin of a ruler and seamlessly transform them into Kṣatriyas. For instance, the 14th-century Akkalpundi grant of Singaya Nāyak states:

> The Brāhmanās and next the Kṣatriyas, and Vaiśyās were produced from the face, arms and the thighs of Iswara and for

> their support the fourth Varṇa. That this Varṇa is purer than the other three is itself evident, for verily this (Śūdra) Varṇa was born along with the river Bhagīrathi (the Gaṅga which sprang from Viṣṇu's feet-the purifier of the three worlds). The members of this Varṇa are eagerly attentive to their duties, not wicked, pure-minded and devoid of passion and as such they only bear the burden of protecting the earth by helping those born in the kingly Varṇa. The cycle of Krita and other Yugas is rolling like the circumference of a wheel, the protectors of the earth are so likewise.[54]

The inscription reveals a different perspective of the Śūdra Varṇa, portraying them as not inferior but rather capable and resilient than other Varṇas within the bhakti framework. It offers a Hindu sociological understanding of societal dynamics and the temporal power associated with protecting the people among different Varṇa-clans. The impact of Bhakti is well-attested in this context, as Mummadi was a devoted Śrī Vaiṣṇava (as inferred from the content of Kōrukoṇḍa pillar inscription). The discovery of copper plates at Śrī Raṅgam establishes him as a disciple of Parāśara-Bhaṭṭa, whom he brought to Kōrukoṇḍa to spread the teachings of the Śrī-Vaiṣṇava Sampradāya.[55]

The specific date mentioned, 9 January 1358, was a Tuesday and amāvāśyā with a solar eclipse, which held significant religious importancc for Hindus. In the Śaka year 1280, during the month of Pausha, on darsa, Tuesday, and during the solar eclipse, King Ana-Vōta granted the village of Kōḍūru to sixty-one Brahmans of different *gōtras and sākhās*, renaming it Annavōtapuram, on the bank of the Maldpaha, along with the eight kinds of aiśvaryas and bhōgas. This grant, proudly attributed to King Ana-Vōta Reḍḍi, begins with the praise for his grandfather Prōlaya Vēma, who belonged to the fourth Varṇa originating from the sacred feet of Mahā Viṣṇu and accomplished various glorious deeds, including the construction of the 'the flight of steps leading to

Śrisaila'.[56] By the 15th century, the origin of Śūdras from the divine feet of Viṣṇu as a catalyst for social emancipation and mobility in temporal power structures was enshrined in the Bhimēśvara Purāṇa written by Telugu poet Śrīnātha where he depicts the Śūdra origin as 'pāvana' i.e. sanctified and life-giving.[57]

The trend continues well into the late medieval period and up to southern Tamil Nadu, where court poets of Nāyakkars of Tamil Nadu, in their poems of praise of their kings, referred to the Śūdra origin as a matter of pride, not stigma. For example, Cēmakūra Veṅkaṭakavi praised the 17th-century Thañjāvūr Nāyakka king Raghunātha Nāyakka, referring to him as the brother of Gaṅga due to their shared origin at the feet of Hari. The poet defined the Śūdra Varṇa as '*Vimala-śrī-ruchira-Varṇa*' – a Varṇa naturally free of impurities and with auspicious brilliance.[58] While various socio-economic and political factors contributed to the rise of these dynasties and clans, the cultural space itself for the proud Śūdra identity and the assertions of dual Varṇa leading to the status of a Kṣatriya was influenced significantly by bhakti. The widespread acceptance from all sections of the society (though there were some dissenting voices), including Brahmins, to this elevation of Śūdra clans demonstrates the power of bhakti as a potent and sustained force for social emancipation.

CHAPTER 11

Social Emancipation through Bhakti from Mahārāshtra to the Hindi Heartland

Bhakti tradition is a pan-Indian phenomenon with deep spiritual-psychological factors working to bring an integral individuation at the level of the individual seeker and, through such a powerful individual process, effect a strong social emancipation. Nevertheless, it manifests with strong local flavour and fervour. This is very clearly seen in the phenomenon of the Bhakti poets of Mahārāshtra, whose impact would soon reverberate beyond the geography of the province and galvanize the entire nation. Its impact would extend well into all the centuries subsequent to the Bhakti poets' period. Its imprint continues to energize the current social emancipation movement just as it impacted the National liberation movement of India.

Jñānēśhvar (1275–1296)

In the 13th century Mahārāshtra region was born Saint Jñānēśhvar (1275–1296). As his father re-entered family life after having obtained renunciation, all his four children were considered ex-communicated and not eligible for Vēdic initiation. A confrontation happened between a council of Brahmins and Jñānēśhvar. There are variations in the way traditional accounts depict the scene of Jñānēśhvar, his two brothers and a sister confronting the council. But in all the accounts, Jñānēśhvar is taunted by a Brahmin with respect to his name and that a buffalo, too, had the name but could it then recite Vedas. Then Jñānēśhvar makes the buffalo recite the Vedas, and Brahmins get humbled, realizing their folly. Here is the relevant passage from the famous *Śrī Mahā Bhakta Vijayam* by Mahipathi (1715-1790) as translated by an American Christian missionary working in Mahārāshtra in collaboration with Pandit Narhar Godbole:

> While they were thus speaking and saying among themselves, 'What is in a name?' one of the Brahmans remarked, 'A young male buffalo with a leather waterskin on his back is coming towards us. His name also is Dnyan.' Listening to this remark of the Brahman, Dnyandev joined his hands palm to palm, and said, 'Listen to my words. I cannot see the least difference between this male buffalo and myself. The ātma (soul) that pervades everybody is alike in every creature. If an infinite number of jars are filled with water, the sun would be reflected in all of them. So the All-pervading, the Holder of the disk (Krishna) is alike in every creature. There might be eighteen kinds of vegetables, but the water that feeds their roots is the same for each. Just so the Lord of Bama (Krishna) is alike in every existing thing. The gold is the same in all ornaments, but the ornaments are seen to be different. So God pervades all existing things alike. One thread is used in the weaving, but the cloth woven appears in different forms. So the Holder of the disk (Krishna) pervades all existing things alike.' A Brahman hearing him say this remarked, 'You are needlessly talking too much.' Then taking a whip in his hand, he angrily struck the buffalo. That made Dnyaneshwar violently tremble, and the welt appeared on his own back. When the twice born (Brahmans) saw this, they exclaimed, 'If there is no difference between you and the buffalo, then let it recite the Veda." Hearing these words of the twice-born (Brahmans), the *bhakta* who knew no differences did as follows. He went up to the buffalo, and placed his hand upon its head, saying, "Recite at once the Rig Veda, and satisfy these earth-gods (Brahmans).' As soon as he said this a most extraordinary thing happened. The young buffalo recited the Vedas with proper intonation.

> The buffalo then recited all four of the Vedas and gave pleasure to the Brahmans.... All the Brahmans were full of astonishment, and they felt repentance in their hearts.[1]

Below is the translation of Tamil translation as given by 'Guhapriyai' and this translation was endorsed by Śaṅkarāchārya Pītham of Kāñchi. The improvising in Tamil translation shows how the Hindu narrative organically evolves and it naturally gravitates towards social emancipation in a sustained manner. In this version, the scene is more confrontational:

> The chief of the Brahmins got enraged and said We have nothing to discuss with you, just get out and go the way you came. Nivarthināth (brother of *Jñānēśhvar)* countered this by saying: 'Oh! *Bhū-Suras* (*Dēvas* on earth)! Did those *Ṛṣis Vyāsa*, *Vasiṣṭha* and *Viswāmitra* who delivered the Vedas in a systemic manner, achieve their noble venerated position through birth or due to their great deeds?' At that time a buffalo came with water bags loaded on it. Seeing that animal *Jñānēśhvar* remarked to the Brahmins: Your equal is this buffalo. You would have possessed wisdom that is inherent in the Vedas only if you had sincerely chanted the Vedas. It is better to converse with this buffalo than argue with you. The Brahmins retorted that indeed *Jñānēśhvar* was fit only to debate with a buffalo. *Jñānēśhvar* answered that only if those Brahmins had a thousandth of a fraction of the wisdom of the buffalo, then they indeed could be venerated. This was too much. The head of the Brahmins got enraged. The Brahmins said You have made a statement that we do not have the even a fraction of the knowledge of that buffalo. You should right now prove it or we will order your execution. Now a huge crowd had gathered before the assembly. *Jñānēśhvar* brought the buffalo and spoke to it: 'Oh! Buffalo! Is a man a Brahmin by birth or a Brahmin by his deeds? Is a man twice-born through Karma or is he twice-born through *Jñāna*. Tell it clearly.' At this the buffalo started talking and talking in Sanskrit. It first chanted the Vedic verses and then finally stated the following four verses:

> All are born Śūdras by birth. It is through the deeds that one becomes twice-born. What defines a Brähmaṇā is understanding of the Vedas and realising of the Brahman.
>
> The great Ṛṣi *Nārada* came from the womb of *Dāsi* (servant woman). Through *Tapas* he became a *Brähmaṇā*. So never consider the Jāthi of a person (in evaluating his worth.)
>
> The great *Ṛṣi Vasiṣṭha* came from the womb of *Ūrvasi* (courtesan). Through *Tapas* he became a *Brähmaṇā*. So never consider the Jāthi of a person (in evaluating his worth.)
>
> The great *Ṛṣi Sounaka* came from the womb of she-dog (possibly a reference to socially excluded dog-eating community). Through *Tapas* he became a *Brähmaṇā*. So never consider the Jāthi of a person (in evaluating his worth.)
>
> The Brahmins now realised their folly.[2]

The exhaustive quoting of this text is because *Śrī Mahā Bhakta Vijayam* transcended linguistic barriers made it to the houses of millions of Hindu families in South India through the last three generations, the colonial discourse defines Hindu Dharma through selected passages justifying or advocating social exclusion in texts that are not common in Hindu households. Further, the version of *Śrī Mahā Bhakta Vijayam*, which was published (and saw multiple reprints) and blessed by a Brahmin monastery, contains in it a version of events that are a harsher critique than found in the other versions. These all show the natural direction and nature of the core discourse of social emancipation in Hindu society. Jñānēśhvar wrote a detailed commentary on the Bhagavad Gītā in Marātti. The impact of this regional language translation had already been discussed in the section on the Bhagavad Gītā.

Nāmdēv

Nāmdēv (1270-1350) belonged from a Mahārāshtrian tailor community. He is credited with the invention of abaṅga form of poetry. The earliest biography of the saint was *Parichai* (Familiarizing), written by Anantdās in Hindi in 1587 CE. It mentions miracles attributed to Nāmdēv, including the turning of the temple at Nagnath. Nāmdēv himself alludes to this in one of his Hindustani verses. Initially, he laments his birth in a class considered inferior in society, but subsequently, he regains strength and questions such divisions that are meaningless spiritually and hence socially:

> I am low and poor by caste, Oh *Paṇdari Rāi*! Why did you make *Nāmā* a tailor! He made *Nāmā* with the gongs, came to the temple; The Brahmin priest drove him out; *Nāmā* said '*Alakh*' (Invisible a cry of devotion towards the invisible form of the Divine innate in all Divine forms) behind the temple; The temple began to turn round wherever *Nāmā* turned;
>
> Cows are of many colours, milk is of one colour; How are you *Brahmin* and how are we *Śūdra*? My mind is the needle, my body is the thread Nama the tailor bows at the feet of Kēsavji.[3]

As he and the people of all castes following him were not allowed inside the temple, the temple itself turned its direction towards Nāmdēv. In his, he writes:

> Some are blinded by the power of the pelf; They do not remember how are they surrounded by Death; Some are proud of this learning and their high caste; But they are taken to the underworld by the dark qualities-Falsehood, greed, avarice and delusion The whole life-span is wasted in these *Nāma* says kindly come and emancipate Such a life Oh Keshav! My Father and Mother.[4]

Here, one can see clearly the resonance with

> Hari's name is caste; Hari's name is sub-caste; Hari's name is revolution; In the whole life

In one of the abaṅga, Nāmdēv infuses his tailoring work with spiritual symbolism:

> Why should I bother about caste or sub-caste? I serve *Rāma-Nāma* day and night· My mind is the measuring rod; My tongue the scissors; With *Rāma's* grace cut the knot of *Yama;* Let me stitch the coat of Ananta's name, stitching which the fear of *Yama* is gone; It would stitch in such a way. How can I live without *Rāma*? With the needle of memory, the thread of love, *Nāma's* mind is attached to *Hari*.[5]

A Junior contemporary of Jñānēshvar, he also refers to the buffalo miracle that Jñānēśhvar performed.[6]

Nāmdēv also initiated another great bhakta of India, Chōkameḷa, who belonged to the Mahar community, which was then socially excluded. When Chōkameḷa died when a building he was working on collapsed, Namdev, highly saddened, went and recovered the remains and had a shrine constructed for him at Paṇdārpur temple, a very sacred temple for the Vaiṣṇavas of Mahārāshtra region.

Chōkameḷa

Perhaps the most important focus in this entire series of Mahārāshtra bhakti saints should be on Chōkameḷa (1273-1338). A Mahar, he was a great devotee, and he was initiated into Bhakti sadhana by none other than Nāmdēv himself. Yet he was humiliated and physically attacked by upper castes.

> When the dainty food has been cooked in the house of a Brahman, dogs are not allowed to sit by the ceremonially clean plates. So out-castes have no authority to worship Pandurang. How can beggars enter into the pleasure-house of kings? Therefore Chokhamela should not go into the temple.[7]

However, that night itself, Chōkameḷa was taken inside the innermost sanctum by none other than Pāṇḍuraṅga Himself (a form of Kṛṣṇa standing on a brick for his devotee: worshipped at Pāṇḍaripūr). Brahmins, including the priest of the temple, witnessed this and yet were prejudiced against the bhakta, and their anger increased. They told him to depart from Pāṇḍaripūr. The reason they said, as given by the text, is interesting. They did not accuse Chōkameḷa as having entered by deceit or even magic but that if Chōkameḷa were to stay in Pāṇḍaripūr, then Pāṇḍuraṅga would again take his bhakta inside the sanctum.

The writer wanted to show that it was not the non-recognition of the greatness of Chōkameḷa that made the birth-privileged orthodoxy act against him. It was precisely their understanding of the greatness of the saint that made them behave inhumanly towards him. In other words, it was not ignorance, but it was their jealousy and hatred coming from that jealousy. They also accuse him of polluting God. Here the text makes Chōkameḷa give a reply to the Brahmins, which becomes the strong argument exposing the meaninglessness of pollution affected on the Divine by the so-called untouchables entering the temple:

> That I have defiled the Husband of Rukmiṇī (*Kṛṣṇa)* is a false charge. If an out-caste and a Brahman both bathe in the Ganges, one should not blame the Ganges. The earth is regarded as pure and on it all castes walk. How is it defiled? And in what Shastra is it written that it can be defiled? If the wind strikes an evil man, his evil qualities will not attach themselves to the wind. It is a wrong thought to blame the wind. . It space fills the washerman's vessel and an earthen jar, still it is quite detached from the two. It is not entangled in them. So to God supreme, the Lord of Rukmiṇī, all castes are alike. How can you think that He is defiled? The Lord of Vaikunth fills all the universe but is unattached to it.[8]

This only serves to further increase the anger of the Brahmins, who compare the 'low caste' man teaching the 'upper caste' to the locust teaching the eagle and shepherds teaching the guru of the celestials. Chōkameḷa leaves the village, and when he is on the other side of the river, Pāṇḍuraṅga still comes and spends time with him.

One day, Pāṇḍuraṅga was having food in the house of Chōkameḷa when his wife Soyarābāi (who is also venerated as a Sant) spilled some curds on the traditional yellow dress of the God. Chōkameḷa rebuked his wife for this. The Brahmin priest of Pāṇḍaripūr, who happened to pass by, heard this conversation. He thought that he was enacting this conversation just to insult the priest. He entered the house and then slapped him hard on his face. Then, he went to the river and had his bath to remove his physical touch of the 'outcaste'. When he went back to the temple, he saw the curds spilled on the dress of the idol. Astonished, he saw the face of the Lord and was shocked to see the cheek was so swollen that the eye of the Lord had closed because of the swelling. The Brahmin priest, at this point, realized the sin he had committed: 'Just as when an evil man troubles an infant, and this troubles the mother, so when anyone persecutes a Bhakta, the Lord of the world becomes sorrowful.'[9]

The narrative ends with the Brahmin priest going and ceremoniously inviting Chōkameḷa into the temple with all the respects and Chōkameḷa having Darshan in the temple.

However, Chōkameḷa's work was normal. Even after he was publicly recognized as a saint, he continued to work as a labourer. He died while working on the construction of a building that collapsed. Upon hearing the news of his death, Nāmdēv travelled from a distant place, collected his remains, and then constructed a shrine next to the main temple of Pāṇḍaripūr.

An Important After-note

It is a tragic example of how, despite the principles of dharma advocating for universal emancipation, social stagnation and exclusion continued to grip society.

Chōkameḷa's gentle bhakti transformation had such a profound impact that the entire Pāṇḍaripūr community agreed to build a shrine of Chōkameḷa by Nāmdēv. This transformation should also have affected the Hindavi Swarājya established by Śivāji. Mahar oral traditions have preserved memories of positive associations with Śivāji. During the time of the rise of Śivāji, the Mahars served as village guards. However, Śivāji started employing them in the military services.

In a proclamation made in May 1784, the Government of the Peshwas established the following as one of the seven rules for regulating worship at Pāṇḍaripūr:

> There is a stone-image of Chokhamelā (untouchable saint of the 14th century) to the north of the (main) temple (dedicated to Vithoba, an incarnation of Vishnu), and there the untouchables (atishüdra) frequent for worship. The place is so narrow and crowded that the visitors are touched to one another and the Brahmins are opposed to this. Therefore the untouchables should perform worship from near the stone-lamp (in front) of the image of Chokhameḷā or from a nearby untouchable hamlet (mahār vada). They should not approach the temple (of Vithoba). Those who do shall be punished.[10]

However, untouchability was not observed in military campaigns, and the Mahars were not only employed in military services of the Marāttas, but they also enjoyed privileges and earned land grants because of their exemplary services. This was an important secular achievement for social mobility in pre-modern societies. After the setback in the third battle of Panipat, the supremacy of the Hindu confederacy of Marāttas was re-established only through the battle of Kharda, in which the Hindu army won a decisive victory against the forces of Nizam. In this battle, the following incident occurred:

> Shidnath Mahar came to Kharda and pitched his tent beside those of the Brahmins and Mahrattas. Naturally the Sardars did not like it. The complaint ultimately reached the ear of Sawai Madhawrao. Hiraji Patankar, an old Mahrayya Sardar, was sitting next to the Peshwa. The Peshwa listened to the complaint and looked at Patankar. Patankar said, 'This is not a dinner party. This is a party of warriors. There is no pollution or untouchability here.' The Peshwa gave his decision. The camp of the Mahars was to remain where it was.... In the battle of Wasai, Tuknath Mahar fought gloriously and was amply awarded by the Peshwa. The researches of Aba Chandorkar have definitely established that the untouchables had many Pathaks or units of their own in the army.[11]

When the British came, they continued this Indic tradition to an extent by enlisting Mahars in their army. However, by the early 1890s, Mahars were systematically removed from the British army and their recruitment was banned because of the British concept of 'martial races'. The observation of D.D. Gholap, the first 'untouchable' representative of the Bombay Legislative Council in 1921, is very important in this regard:

> None dare say that even the most tyrannical and Brahmanical Peshwas were unquestioned enthusiasts in preserving and encouraging the martial spirit of the Mahars, whose regiments served the Mahratta Empire no less patriotically than what the Tommies do for their fatherland-England. The hereditary military services not only enhanced the civic value of our race and furnished life with unique promises for generations together, but simultaneously did they raise the standard of our culture and polished habits, to make our forefathers quite easily overlook the petty handicaps of socio-religious prejudices. In the British regime we have been systematically deprived of all these avenues of ambitious careers, leaving the Mahars and other untouchables without any scope to make their life worth living.[12]

Freedom fighter Bāl Gangādar Tilak, who was also a historian and often considered a conservative with respect to social issues, corroborates what D.D. Gholap has said:

> It was the custom and the privilege of the Mahar Chief to have his tent put up by the side of the Peshwa. Once, it so happened that Nana Phadnavis got his tent pitched in the place of the Mahar chief. The chief when arrived, refused to be re-encamped anywhere else and would not get down from his horse, when ultimately Peshwa Sawai Madhavaro had to unpitch the tent of Nana Phadnavis.[13]

Here, we see both the effect of the Bhakti movement and the continuing struggles of social emancipation that the movement continues to confront. It was an organic movement for liberation. It is likely that without colonial interference, the 'outcastes' could have evolved into a warrior community and eventually secured their rights to enter temples. However, colonialism and modernization changed the situation drastically. The bhakti-inspired social emancipation had to operate in a completely changed social milieu with pressing new challenges.

As late as 1932, *Kesari*, considered a conservative newspaper, wrote this heartful agonizing plea in its editorial:

> More than 500 years ago there lived a simple Maharashtrian saint named Chokhamela who it seems was not allowed to take the vision of Vithoba. After him were hundreds and thousands of Mahars, Mangs and Chambhars who became Varkaris, the chief devotees of Vithoba at Pandharpur. They played their instruments, lifted high their banners, founded their guilds, and in the very vicinity of the god built even their schools. But these were all compelled to satisfy their hungering hearts by bathing in the sacred rivet Chandrabbaga nearby and by gazing from a distance at the spires of Vithoba's temple. Why should not this three hundred years penance of gazing at the temple spires now have its due reward? Why should they not now be permitted

> to look into the holy of holies where the God abides in serene contemplation, standing on the sacred brick with band on hip, beneath those spires on which they have feasted their eyes for generations past? May not Vithoba Himself lie weary with the long vigil as he beholds their distress? Why should not these untouchables now be reckoned to have completed their long probation?[14]

In post-independent India, there has been systematic overlooking of the voice of bhakti saints, particularly Chōkameḷa, in what is predominantly called the 'Dalit' literature and social movements. Scholar Jayasree Gokhale-Turner, who studied the Dalit movement closely, pointed this out as early as the 1980s:

> The teachings of Chokha Mela have been almost completely repudiated, and the bhakti tradition's understanding of caste and the solution to Untouchability is now seen as an ideological mystification perpetrated by the higher castes and succumbed to by the lower castes. In their place, a new explanation of caste and a different resolution to untouchability, are offered by the writers of Dalit Sahitya. And Chokha Mela as a historical figure is also almost completely ignored; or in company with the other saints, is roundly condemned.[15]

A major reason can be attributed to reluctance than the inability of the dominant Hindu communities to explore the socio-spiritual space created by bhakti and its implications for social emancipation. Bhakti saints define dharma more than the shastras. To paraphrase an old Sanskrit adage, our dharmic value systems should follow the footprints of Bhakti saints as the calf follows the hoof marks of its mother cow. They are not the exceptions; they are the Sanatana Dharma in action.

Secondly, the dominant stranglehold of anti-Hindu forces in academia and media has been systematically working for close to a century to sideline the voices of bhakti as voices of a bygone era and as voices of a failed rebellion. However, there have also been voices pointing out that ignoring bhakti voices is erroneous. Gokhale-Turner highlights this issue:

> Yet, according to a leading Dalit intellectual, even if the Dalit writer does not feel that there is a direct bond between himself and Chokha Mela, he still ought to recognise the contributions of the Mahar saints and the bhakti tradition as a whole. For within its own historical context, the poet-saint movement was fully as revolutionary as the dalit movement is today.... Thus, from the standpoint of providing some features to a seemingly blank past, as well as questioning the notion that Untouchables were invariably supine, the figures of Chokha Mela and the other lower caste saints would constitute, it would seem, a source of identification and pride to the dalit writer today.[16]

In fact, the Bhakti phenomenon is age-old, perhaps as old as the Vedic civilization itself, and is a strong, defining, and living strand of Sanātana Dharma. The presence of the voices of Bhakti saints from classes and clans of social exclusion as the authentic voices of dharma makes the Hindu religion perhaps the world's only 'subaltern' religion.

The dharmic narrative presented in texts like *Bhaktavijayam* addresses the issue of social exclusion and prompts society to examine its conscience. It contrasts the unwavering devotion of the socially excluded saint with the arrogant behaviour of the social elite. The text emphasizes the position of dharma, embodied by Pāṇḍuraṅga, over the rigid application of certain scriptural words and highlights the eternal spirit of dharma manifested in Pāṇḍuraṅga's actions. It suggests that societies that have followed this principle have progressed in sustainable and just ways, while those that have not had experienced conflict and suffering.

Dr Bhimrao Ambedkar's writings also acknowledge the untapped spiritual potential of Bhakti saints in the following treatise on the history of untouchability: 'Inscribed to the memory of Nandanar, Ravidas, Chokhamela, three renowned saints who were born among the untouchables and who by their piety and virtue won the esteem of all.'[17]

Ēknāth

Ēknāth (1533-99) was a Rigvedi Brahmin and a disciple of Janardhan Paṇdit. He had a vision of Dattātrēya asking him to translate both Rāmayaṇa and Bhāgavata into the Marātti language. Ēknāth used to conduct collective devotional singing (kirtans), and one of the attendees was an outcast named Rāṇyā. Rāṇyā invited Ēknāth to his house, arranging a feast for him, and Ēknāth removed his hesitation by reciting *Bhāgavata* verse 7.9.10, which angered the upper castes. They were further incensed when Eknath went to Rāṇyā's place for meals. Another incident involved an outcast who had become a thief because of hunger. Ēknāth fed him, and the thief, who was a fugitive, obtained a pardon and became a part of the bhaktas. Another incident is narrated differently in different versions.

According to one version, Ēknāth took a child from an outcast community, consoled the child, and helped reunite the child with its parents. Later, a Brahmin afflicted with leprosy who was performing penances for the removal of the disease at the temple of Tryambakeśvara was asked by the Lord to go to and ask for the blessings he had earned because he had lifted the outcast lad out of misery by carrying him to his mother on his shoulders. Without hesitation, Ēknāth was ready to give the merits of all his deeds, but the Brahmin asked only for this. Due to the blessings earned by Ēknāth through carrying the outcast child on his shoulder and taking him to his mother, the Brahmin was cured of leprosy.[18]

The other version is that during the Śrāddha ceremony of offering food to Brahmins in remembrance of their ancestors,

Ēknāth heard a woman from a marginalized community expressing her desire for the delicious food being offered to Brahmins. In response, he gave all the prepared food to the members of the 'untouchable' community, with the help of his servant Khaṇdyā Kṛṣṇa. This servant was believed to be Lord Krishna himself, who was staying in Ēknāth's house to enjoy his devotional songs. Upon learning of this, the Brahmins became angry and decided to boycott Ēknāth. However, Khaṇdyā Kṛṣṇa assured Ēknāth not to worry and prepared another feast for the Śrāddha ceremony. This time, the gods themselves came in person and accepted the offerings. Despite this, the Brahmins still demanded that Ēknāth should perform an atonement ceremony for the 'sin' of giving the food meant for Brahmins to the untouchables. At that moment, a Brahmin with leprosy approached and informed Ēknāth that in order to be cured, he needed the blessings obtained from feeding a single untouchable child during the feast.[19]

In the text, the leprosy of the Brahmin becomes symbolic of the disease of the mind, which is called caste supremacy and related to social exclusion in the form of untouchability. By giving priority to the needy over the socio-traditional aristocracy and removing the inner disease of birth-based discrimination, it ultimately benefits the entire society by making it healthy.

Thukā Rām

Belonging to the agriculturist caste (considered Śūdra), Thukā Rām (1608-1650) lived during one of the most cataclysmic and yet nebulous times in Hindu history. The era was marked by Mughal invasions, constant wars, famines, and ill effects of social stratification. Bhālacandra Nemāḍe rightly points out that the 'loss of freedom leads to loss of self-corrective social system and to stagnation of social institutions.'[20] In his spiritual practice

(Sādhana), Thukā Rām was influenced by four seers. In one of his famous melodious verses, he gives their names:

> *Nāmadēva*, the boy of a tailor, who played without faltering with the Divine; then, *Jñānadeva*, who with brothers and sister danced around the Divine; then *Kabīra*, the disciple of *Rāmānanda*, who was a worthy partner to these; and finally, *Ēkanātha*, the child of a Brahmin, who gathered about him a number of devotees. These played, says *Tukārāma*, the game of spiritual life, and the game never affected them.[21]

It is worth noting that in choosing the preceptors, Thukā Rām did not discriminate, showing respect to all saints. He also considered himself part of a grand pan-Indian Dharmic phenomenon.

Ramēśwar Bhatt, a Brahmin, harboured a strong dislike for Thukā Rām and subjected him to torment. At one point, all the poems composed by Thukā Rām were thrown into River Indrayani, leading to Thukā Rām becoming dejected and deciding never to compose poems again unless assured by God Viṣṇu. As fate would have it, Viṣṇu appeared before his devotee, and Thukā Rām documented his experience of divine vision after thirteen days of depressed penance in his Abhaṅg:

> Compassionate as you were, you divided yo in two places, near me and in the river, and saved both me and the books.... There is nobody who can be compared to you in point of compassion. Verily, my words fail to describe your greatness![22]

But the persecution continued. Boiling water was poured on him. Thukā Rām recorded the physical and mental pain he endured in his bhaṅg-3956. Ramēśwar Bhatt himself then suffered bodily anguish. Bhatt later mentioned in his writings that Jñānaēśwar appeared in his dream and asked him to seek forgiveness from Thukā Rām. He did so, and Thukā Rām healed him with his Abhaṅg.[23]

Thukā Rām, like other bhakti saints, points out the irrelevance of *Jāthi*:

> The cow eats all kinds of dung; but it is yet holy. The brooks that enter into a river become identified with it. The holy *Pippala* is born of the crow's excreta. The family of the *Pāṇḍavas* was not a holy one...*Ajāmeḷa*, *Kubjā* and *Vidura* were not born of a high caste. *Vyāsaḥ*, *Vasiṣṭha*, *Viswāmitra* and *Nārada* cannot boast of a high lineage. Whatever unholy deeds are committed by men and women, when they remember God with repentance, they become free from sins.[24]

It is interesting to see that all the Bhakti poets critiqued Jāthi discrimination by highlighting natural processes that unite diversity and render discrimination meaningless. They emphasized the spiritual insignificance of birth-based discrimination and social exclusion. They then showed the spiritual meaninglessness of such birth-based discrimination, particularly social exclusion.

In one instance, Thukā Rām, in a Tamil version of his life, gave a saree belonging to his wife to an 'untouchable' woman on the auspicious day of Ekadashi. This act angered his wife, who intended to smash Pāṇḍuraṅga's feet with a grinding stone. However, when she reached the temple, she realized that it was Goddess Rukmiṇi who was wearing her saree. This revelation transformed her perception.[25]

Even after Thukā Rām passed away, he continued to be an inspiration. In the 18th century, a Ṛigvedic Brahmin had a mystic vision. He received the mantra dīkṣā from Thukā Rām. He became a poet and a bhakta himself. He wrote the famous *Śrī Mahā Bhakta Vijayam* in 1762 and *Bhaktalilāmrit*in 1774 CE.

Challenging Social Exclusion in Śrī Mahā Bhakta Vijayam

In the book *Śrī Mahā Bhakta Vijayam*, there is a significant portrayal of societal trauma and the spiritual foundation of social liberation through the life of Śrī Dāmāji Paṇdit. He was a Brahmin who worked as a subedar under the Muslim ruler of Mangalvedha.

The Deccan region of the time often faced devastating famines due to the failure of monsoons. One of the most severe famines was the Durgā Dēvi famine, also known as *Dwādasa varsha Panjam*, which lasted from 1393 to 1408. led to a significant decrease in population between the Gōdāvari and Krishnā rivers, causing a complete collapse of the administration. It took almost forty years for the region to recover from the aftermath of this famine.[26] The famine coincided with a dry period in the decadal hydrological cycle of the Asian monsoon region,[27] leading to increased social hierarchy rigidity. The Mahar community was among the socially excluded groups during this period. In the 18th century, the writer of *Bhakta Vijayam* identified the Mahar community as a socially excluded group from the 14th and 15th centuries. Consequently, the word 'Mahar' in Bhakta Vijayam represents a socially excluded community. In 1460 the region faced another famine, commonly referred to as the Dāmāji Pant famine. This famine is named after Dāmāji Pant, who initiated a widespread food sharing movement by opening two government grain storehouses to the entire population. The act of sharing food is documented in the *Mahā Bhakta Vijayam*:

> The Brahmans, Kskatriyaa, Vatshyas, Shudras, grocers, Gondhalis, the helpless and the poor all came to Mangalvedhe, took grain and then went back. The carpenters, labourers and others of various castes, potters, barbers, and those without much understanding, hearing of Damajipant's fame came

> to carry away grain. Masons, milkmen, workers in stone, fishermen, workers in copper and gardeners all hastened to Mangalvedhe and took away grain as much as they desired. People from Gujarat, dyers, salt manufacturers, yogis, saints and mahanis exclaimed, 'The Husband of Rukmini is pleased with us and has entered into Damaji's heart.' Tailors, washermen, workers in stone and an endless number of castes and out-castes came and took an unlimited amount of grain. Hearers may have a doubt and say, 'Why was it necessary to bring there all castes? Why did he not attempt to select those who were worthy?' But all who lived at the sacred city of Pandhari should be considered alike, so the ancient verses composed by the saints say, therefore you should not have any doubts in your mind. There are ninety hundred thousand water animals in the midst of the sea, but the sea looks alike on ail of them, so the Lord of the world looks with mercy upon all castes.[28]

This account holds significance for three reasons: Firstly, during times of widespread social distress such as famine, the social structure tends to favour those who hold higher status in society, leaving those at the bottom of the societal hierarchy to endure the greatest suffering. While this prioritization may have been accepted in medieval times across the globe, it is specifically acknowledged and rejected here. Secondly, the explanation provided emphasizes that the sanctity of Paṇdarpūr places the divine presence in all individuals—the fundamental divine egalitarianism—above all other societal distinctions and hierarchies. Thirdly, this principle is then extended to all humanity through the non-partisan compassion of Viṭṭalā, the deity in Paṇdarpūr. He is the substratum in which all beings are immersed showing no favouritism. Consequently, his devotee Dāmāji Pant could not uphold any discrimination based on birth despite the social norm of honouring a birth-based Brahmin. Then the narrative in *Śrī Mahā Bhakta Vijayam* narrative shifts to the part where the Sultan summons Dāmāji Pant. Expecting to face capital punishment, Dāmāji Pant first visits the temple to worship Viṭṭalā before going to the Sultan's court. Viṭṭalā takes on the form of a Mahar and appears at the Sultan's court, resolving the issue of the government's grain stores' value by providing the equivalent amount of money. The Mahar also insists on getting a receipt. *Mahā Bhakta Vijayam* explains the scene in the following way:[29]

> The Lord of Pandhari assumed the form of an out-caste, for on account of His bhaktas, the Pervader of the world feels great joy in His heart. He wrote a request to the king in Damaji pant's handwriting, and becoming Damaji's messenger. He hastened to Bedar (Sultan's place). The Husband of Rukmini fastened on His head tattered garments, placed around His neck a black cord and in His ears the *pagar* earrings (the ornaments worn in the ears of Mahars). Around his waist was a loin cloth and He had a staff in His hand. Rukmini remarked to Him, 'What is that the Lord of the world is planning to do?' The Lord of Vaikunth replied, 'My Bhakta Damaji has been carried to Bedar in order to be put to death. For his sake I have become an un-namable (or out-caste), When My bhaktas fall into distress I am never ashamed to help them.'

Then Viṭṭalā enters the court of the Sultan and makes a salute in the way Mahars' salute.

> The Lord of Pandhari then saluted him with the word Johar (the Mahar word used in salutation). This may seem very strange to us. He whose glory is not understood by even the Vedas and Shastraa which describe Him, He bowed His head low and saluted the king with the word Johar. He, to attain whom the eighty-eight thousand rishis perform austerities, He addressed the Muhammadan king with the words, 'You are My mother and father,' for His bhakta who was accused of wrong.

Then Viṭṭalā introduces himself:

> I am the Mahar servant of Damaji of Mangalvedhe. I call Myself his hereditary slave. You will perhaps ask, 'Would He who lives on the sea of milk and reclines on the serpent Shesha use such obsequious words? But you should not keep in your mind any question or doubt about this; for when He, Krishna, was protecting the cows at the bouse of Nanda He openly called Himself a cowherd, and when He was at the house of Dharma, the King of the Yadavas (Krishna) gladly removed the used-up dining plates; when He was Arjuna's charioteer He washed his horses with His four hands; therefore the Husband of Rukmini without any hesitation called Himself the hereditary slave of Damajipant. When the king's minister asked the Mahar his name He said, 'My name- is Vithonaik, an adopted child of Damaji.'

It is important to recognize that Viṭṭalā takes on the appearance of an outcast and refers to himself as a hereditary slave. In this context, the hereditary aspect does not pertain to the 'slave' as this Divine slave is not subject to birth or death. Viṭṭalā chooses to serve the hereditary line of Dāmāji Pant because Dāmāji Pant had served all of humanity. Viṭṭalā could have assumed any form, such as a Brahmin priest, an accountant, or a headsman, but He chooses the form of an outcast in society. Additionally, He proclaims Himself as the adopted son of Damaji Pant. By declaring Himself as the adopted son of a Brahmin as a Mahar, Viṭṭalā establishes a specific Bhakti context for social exclusion. Bhakti and the Yajña of Sēva (the distribution of food for the needy without discrimination) enable the breaking of rigid social hierarchy barriers and the challenging of social exclusion. Even when socially marginalized communities were forced into quasi-slavery, Bhakti emphasized that the Divine prefers to manifest in the form of the socially excluded and suggested that in the community of Bhaktas, the relationship between such marginalized individuals and the affluent could resemble that of a family.

Śrī Pāda Srī Vallabha Dattārēya (1320-1351)

The Dattārēya Sampradāya has deep ancient roots. According to the Markaṇṭēya Purāṇa, Dattārēya was believed to be the incarnation of Viṣṇu, born to the sage Atri and his virtuous wife Anusūyā. The Purāṇa portrays Him as the greatest of Yōgis, unaffected by worldly dualities. He deliberately engaged in activities that were unexpected of a revered sage, such as consuming intoxicants and socializing with women. When the dēvas approached Him to lead the battle against the asūras in the spiritual realm, he initially declined, citing his addiction to drink and impurity. However, the dēvas persisted, acknowledging him as their refuge despite his unconventional behaviour.[30] The practice of presenting oneself in a negative light to both seekers and society while maintaining purity at heart was a defining characteristic of Pāśupata mendicants. It is important to note that in the early Pāśupata tradition, Dīkśa, or initiation, was believed to be exclusively conferred upon Brahmins. However, G. Vasudeo Tagare, a scholar of religious history, revealed in his extensive study of Saivism that as early as the Mahabhārata texts, Pāśupata Dīkśa was granted to Vāsudēva Kṛṣṇa by Ṛṣi Upamanyu, despite Kṛṣṇa not being a Brahmin. Furthermore, non-Brahmins were documented to have received Pāśupata Dīkśa throughout the centuries, as established by non-Saivaite sources.[31] The Dattārēya Sampradāya, with its emphasis on His Avadūta nature, serves as a remarkable harmonization of the Saivaite Yōgic tradition with its roots in Pāśupata, along with subsequent Yōgic developments, including Nāth Yōga, Siddha traditions, Shākta Tantrism, and Vaiṣṇava Bhakti. Naturally, this spiritual movement posed a challenge to social stagnation through its emphasis on spiritual unity.

In the Dattārēya Sampradāya, an esteemed saint revered as Dattārēya Himself is Śrī Pāda Srī Vallabha. His life and influence were mainly centered in the present-day state of Andhra Pradesh, but his impact extended across the entire Deccan region. A brief account of Śrī Pāda Srī Vallabha's life can be found in the work *Guru Charitra*, authored by the late 15th-century poet Saraswati Gaṅgādhara. However, the primary focus of the work was the biography of Śrī Nṛusimha Saraswati, believed to be the next incarnation of Śrī Pāda Srī Vallabha. Consequently, a detailed biography of Śrī Pāda Srī Vallabha is not available.

In 2001, Malladi Govinda Deekshitulu, a descendant of the maternal grandfather of Śrī Pāda, unveiled a Telugu version of a Sanskrit biography that takes the form of a travelogue chronicling the pilgrimages undertaken by Śrī Pāda. This narrative also portrays the encounters of Śrī Pāda with various sages and disciples. The author, Saṅkara Bhat, was a contemporary and an ardent devotee of Śrī Pāda, infusing the travelogue with numerous Purāṇic elements. The text encompasses significant aspects crucial for societal liberation through spirituality and is known as Śrī Pāda Srī Vallabha Charitāmrtam (SPSVC).

Bhat, a Brahmin, is depicted in the travelogue as refusing cooked food from a tribal village and instead opting for honey and fruits when he was hungry. After being bitten by a snake, he was saved by washermen who transported him on a donkey, and then he was cured of the deadly snake bite by a leather worker-physician. Bhat recounts this experience in his writings:

> I stayed in the leather worker's house throughout the night. The leather worker was chanting 'Datta Digambara! Datta Digambara! Sripada Vallabha! Datta Digambara!' throughout the night. I was lying on a cot. My heart bloomed on hearing that most melodious name. As this leather man was a Guru-relative because of soul relation, I developed love towards him.

> The next moment I felt sorrow because I was born in a higher Brahmin family and he was a leather man.

As these thoughts crossed Bhat's mind, the leather worker, Vallabh Dās, revealed himself as a disciple of Śrī Pāda. He then proceeded to explain to Bhat the importance of every Varṇa performing their work without pride and with love. Vallabh Dās further elaborated on how individuals, based on their abilities, could change their Varṇa. However, he emphasized that devotion to the Divine and the love showered by the Divine know no discrimination. Moved by Vallabh Dās's words, Saṅkara Bhat underwent a profound transformation:

> With that friendly teaching by Sri Vallabha Das, my brahmin ego had come down. The feeling that Vallabha Das belonged to fifth caste vanished and I developed a brotherly affection towards him like a blood relation. After taking Vallabha Das' hospitality for three days, I started from that village

Saṅkara Bhat also recounts a conversation between an argumentative Brahmin named Narasāvadānulu and Śrī Pāda. Interestingly, the Brahmin was a relative of Śrī Pāda. It is worth noting that Śrī Malādi Bāpannāvadāni, who was Śrī Pāda's maternal grandfather and the head of the Brahmin council in his village, held the belief that the Vaiśya Varṇa could undergo the 'Vēdōkta Upanayana' ritual, including the investiture of Yajñōpavītam and Vēdic chanting. He also supported the 'Purāṇōkta Upanayana' for the Śūdra Varṇa. Narasāvadānulu was greatly troubled by this stance and questioned Śrī Pāda, stating that his maternal grandfather's position went against the *Dharmaśāstras*. In response, Śrī Pāda vehemently rejected the notion of one Varṇa arrogating divine authority while denying it to others, emphasizing that although the *Dharmaśāstras* were a guide, the words of saintly individuals with pure and selfless hearts held the same weight as Vēdic injunctions:

> Not only Brähmanās Kṣatriyas and Vaiśyās but also Śūdras, are eligible for 'Vēdōkta Upanayana'. If they follow austerities with upanayanam, the third eye (eye of knowledge) should get opened. The 'antahkaraṇa' (the inner cognitive organs) should get purified and the mind should concentrate on '*Brahma Jñāna*'.... When the topic related to *Brahma Jnana* comes, I am a Brahmin. While doing darbār and listening to people's prayers and gracing them, I am a Kṣatriya. Every 'jeevi' will have a salary decided by the sins and merits done by that jeevi. I have the salary of every one with me. While calculating how much to give to whom, I am a Vaiśyā. While attracting the difficulties and problems of devotees onto me and doing service by giving peace and happiness, I am a Śūdra. While washing the sins of Jeevas, I am a washerman. I am burning to ashes the bodies of jeevas and granting them new higher births. So I am the 'katikapari' (manager of burial ground). Now tell me to what caste do I belong?

In his teachings, Śrī Pāda Dattārēya emphasizes the importance of implementing spiritual equanimity at the societal level, highlighting that non-discrimination is the ultimate reality in the spiritual realm. According to him, there exists only Oneness and Non-dual consciousness, known as Brahman. Additionally, Śrī Pāda Dattārēya makes a profound statement by internalizing all the functions of every functional group (Jāthi) and every societal archetype (Varṇa).

As Saṅkara Bhat made his way to a place called Kurungadda, where Śrī Pāda was staying, he arrived at a hermitage belonging to a sage named Nāmānanda. Nāmānanda shared the story of how he, born into a Vaiṣṇava Brahmin family, was approached by the Divine in the form of a Chaṇḍāḷa, causing him great distress. Despite realizing that the Chaṇḍāḷa was Śrī Pāda, the Brahmin accepted Him as his Guru, even in the form of a social outcaste. This decision had significant repercussions within the community, which Nāmānanda explained to Saṅkara Bhat:

> I was hungry. I was not getting food in any house. People used to talk about me strangely. 'He is a mad man. A chandala came drunk and extracted guru dakshina from him. Though he is a Brahmin, he accepted a chandala as Guru. So, he is an untouchable. So to give bhiksha (food) to him is against "dharma shastra."'¼ I was so weak that I could not utter the words 'Bhavathi Bhikshan Dehi' with my weak throat. Meanwhile, Sripada Srivallabha opened the door and came out with food in plate. He made me sit on the floor and with His own hands fed me. He wiped my hands and mouth with His own hands.

The account of Saṅkara Bhat sheds light on a society and era in which Śrī Pāda Srī Vallabha emerged, with the Datta Sampradāya being the most influential in that region. Saṅkara Bhat encounters a seer named Śrī Bhāskara Śāstrī, who, after elucidating the Śāktic dimension of Śrī Pāda, narrated an incident where a greedy Sanyāsi pretended to give Datta Dīkṣā (spiritual initiation into Datta Sampradāya) and was receiving Dakṣiṇā from everyone. The villagers were captivated by the pious appearance of the Sanyāsi. This led to a debate about who was eligible for the initiation. It was found that the three non-Śūdra Varṇas were eligible, but Śūdra people were required to pay the Dakṣiṇā without receiving initiation, as their spiritual welfare would be taken care of by the austerities performed by Brahmins with Dīkṣā. However, Śrī Malādi Bāpannāvadāni opposed this stance. He advocated that Datta Dīkṣā should be given to all communities without discrimination. He also objected to the mandatory Dakṣiṇā and proposed that it should be voluntary.

Upon witnessing these events, Śrī Pāda visited the home of one of his devotees, Veṅkaiāh, who was a peasant. It was there that Śrī Pāda commenced imparting Datta Dīkṣā without requiring any Dakṣiṇā. Numerous individuals, including Brahmins, Kṣatriyas, and Vaiśyās, sought initiation. The fact that this initiation was conducted in a Śūdra's home caused significant distress among the Brahmins, prompting them to consider seeking the intervention of the local Śaṅkarācharya. However, before any action could be taken, Śrī Pāda had already transcended into the Divine realm. Subsequently, when a Brahmin was afflicted by severe physical and mental ailments, the farmer who hosted the Datta Dīkṣā ceremony provided the Brahmin with 'Mantrākṣata' or sanctified grains. This Brahmin had previously received Dīkṣā from a self-serving Sanyāsin. He thought:

> Veṅkaiāh tells me to take the *Mantrākṣata* from a Śūdra's house. May be it is to be taken like that. Normally, Brahmins give *Mantrākṣata* to Śūdra. But Śūdras will not call Brahmins home and give *Mantrākṣata*. Veṅkaiāh, being a good natured person, may be calling me, only keeping my welfare in mind.

The Brahmin accepted the sacred grains and went in peace. The narration ends with a huge ritual of dinning for people of all communities without discrimination.

The original Sanskrit travelogue of Saṅkara Bhat may have been lost, but the manuscript translated from Sanskrit to Telugu by Śrī Malādi Gōvinda Dīkṣitalu was discovered and published as late as 2001. This discovery raises thought-provoking questions about social stagnation and exclusion while also offering institutional solutions to overcome these challenges. At the core of this exploration lies the self-realization and divine persona of Śrī Pāda Śrī Vallabha, who represents the pinnacle of the Datta Sampradāya. The concept of internalizing all occupational groups and societal archetypes, as well as the reversal of the flow of blessings in the form of Mantrākṣata from a Śūdra to a Brahmin, signifies a radical and monumental social emancipation achieved with spiritual grace by Śrī Pāda. Despite being overshadowed by historical factors, this spiritual emancipation remains a potential force against social stagnation.

After the Samādhi of Śrī Pāda Srī Vallabha, a Brahmin named Vallabesh made a vow to feed 1000 Vedic scholars at Kuruvapūr as a penance for seeking a child. However, he was attacked by dacoits and gravely injured on his way. According to tradition, he was miraculously revived by Śrī Pāda Srī Vallabha. Vallabesh later became the ancestor of the Hedgewar clan, from which emerged the founder of the Rashtriya Swayamsevak Sangh (RSS), Dr Kesav Baliram Hedgewar. The RSS, as per its constitution, is committed to combating divisive tendencies in society and striving to uplift all Hindus regardless of caste. In 1969, the RSS adopted a resolution denouncing untouchability in Hindu society and advocating for the inclusion of all Hindus. It can be said that the organization carries the influence of the Dattārēya Sampradāya in it.

Chaitanya Mahāprabhu

Chaitanya Mahaprabhu (1456-1534) was born in Māyāpūr, in the Navdeep region, which is now located in modern West Bengal. His parents were a pious Brahmin couple named Jagannāth Miśra and Śacī Devi. He was given the name Viśvambhara Miśra and was also known as Nimāii. Chaitanya was a scholar in the Nyāya school and became a teacher of Sanskrit treatises. Navdeep was a centre of Nav-Nyāya Darśana during his time, and this legacy still continues to this day. Chaitanya had his first spiritual experience in Gaya while standing before the sacred icons of the feet of Viṣṇu. A scholar-seer named Īshwar Pūri, whom he had previously ridiculed, now appeared to him as a great saint who would lead him to liberation. Soon, Chaitanya became a bhakta and started gathering a following. He was initiated into the tradition of Bhakti by Kēśav Bhārati, who also initiated him into ascetic life, giving him the name Chaitanya. Ishwar Pūri gave him the sacred syllable for chanting. Both Kēśav Bhārati and Īshwar Pūri belonged to Mādhavendra Puri (1420-70), who reinitiated the tradition of commune-devotional singing.

Chaitanya had such a traditional lineage to his Bhakti. In the 14th century in Bengal, there lived a poet Bhakt Chaṇdi Dās, who wrote a devotional work on Kṛṣṇa and Rādhā called *Śrī Śrī Kṛṣṇa Kīrtan*. His love for Rami, a washerwoman, is legendary, and his writings indicate that the love was intensely mystical as well as very human.

Chaṇdi Dās, Sahajiyā Mārg, and Chaitanya Bhakti

According to tradition, it was Goddess Bāśuli who made Chaṇdi Dās realize that only through the love for Rāmī could he attain liberation. Bāśuli herself is a forest goddess. The first forest goddess is mentioned in Indian literature in the Vedas as Araṇyāni.[32] Bāśuli is also associated with mountains. In a quasi-historical tradition, she took birth as a Brahmin woman and came to live with the fishermen of Bengal.[33] She instructed a highly depressed Chaṇdi Dās:

> Love this woman, my son, it is your fate that you should do so—nay, this love will sanctify you; neither I nor hundreds of gods and goddesses like me will be able to give you a glimpse of that higher life which this woman's love will teach you.[34]

Bāśuli is also revered as the mountain goddess. She is highly respected in Odisha, where the sacred mountain Gōvardhan holds great significance in the life of Kṛṣṇa. In the Sahajiyā Vaiṣṇava tradition, which is popular in Bengal, more than one text attributed to Chaṇdi Dās speaks of Bāśuli spreading the Sahajiyā Mārg in rural Bengal.[35] One commentator associates Yogamāyā (associated traditionally with Viṣṇu) with leading his spiritual awakening.[36] Chaṇdi Dās, the Bengali poet, is one of the trinities of Sahajiyā Mārg, along with Jayadēva, who composed in Sanskrit, and Vidyāpathi, who composed in Mithili.

The love Chaṇdi Dās shows for Rāmī, never leaving its human nature, also becomes profoundly mystical. Bengali Historian during the colonial times Dinesh Chandra Sen explains:

> (Chaṇdi Dās) says, 'Though I am a Brahmin and you are a washer-woman, you are to me holy as Gayatri.' He rises above caste-prejudices, and sees good in love far more than in his Brahminical blood or in the scriptures. He declares Rami to be as adorable as Parvati, the giver of fortunes, as Lakshmi, the giver of luck and as Saraswati, the goddess of fine arts and learning... Chandi Das saw one temple in the whole universe, that was the cottage of the washer-woman near Basuli's courtyard, and he became the high priest there. His love was not limited by any conventional idea. He calls Rami his 'pitri matri' i.e., 'father and mother.' No lover ever spoke such a language. Love to him was a homogeneous and undivided whole.[37]

According to Prof. Dinesh Chandra Sen, this tradition is very unique in India and can be considered as having 'trampled upon all conventions of Hinduism about caste and religion'. However, this view is not accurate. This is uniquely Indian. In the conventional worldly tradition, a wife is seen as capable of becoming a mother for her husband. In the sacred realm, Goddess Shakti is believed to have given birth to an aspect of Śiva while also being his consort. The ability to distil the maternal element in the marital relation is not considered incestuous but rather a transformation from the worldly to the sacred. There is an intriguing connection to this phrase in Vaiṣṇava's bridal mysticism from the South, and it is also implicit in the Bhagavad Gīta. Dravidologist Dennis Hudson, in his paper speculating on the possible Tantric rites in the Bhakti poetry of Āṇdāḷ, a Vaiṣṇavaite poetess from the 6th or

7th century in the Tamil region, whose poetry is rich in deeply spiritual bridal mysticism, also explores this connection:

> Vasudeva-with-Laksmi (Tirumal) is the primordial 'Father-Mother,' the highest mode of Narayana that beings can worship. Through maya, Vasudevawith-Laksmi makes formations (vyuhas) of himself to produce the cosmos and us, and differing forms (murtis) to act for us and to be served by us. Notable among these are three goddesses (devis) called Sri (kingship), Bhumi (the material realm), and Candika-Durga (victorious conquest); three gods (devas) called Visnu (pervading sustenance), Siva (destruction), and Brahma (emanation); and two humans called Balarama and Krsna.... As the Bhagavan in the form of Krsna said to his friend Arjuna, 'My womb (yoni) is the transcendent brahman, and I plant the embryo (garbha) in it; the arising of all living beings comes from that, O son of Bharata. In all wombs, O son of Kunti, whatever comes into being with a form, the transcendent brahman is the womb, and I am the father who gives the seed' (Bhagavad Glta [BG] 14.3-4). Just as the fetus resides within the womb of a pregnant woman, the universe resides inside God as if God were a pregnant king.[38]

The passage in a paper unrelated to Chaṇdi Dās surprisingly makes several interesting connections. It starts by associating the name Chandi with one of the divine feminine energies of Viṣṇu and Yogamāyā. Additionally, it connects an androgynous parental figure in the context of bridal mysticism in a strongly Vaiṣṇavaite imagery. It is important to note that the poetry of Āṇḍāḷ and its spiritual vision greatly influenced the Vaiṣṇava traditions that flourished in Vijayanagar, from where many bhakti traditions spread northwards.

It is important to note that Chaitanya was influenced by Chaṇdi Dās. The earliest mention of Chaṇdi Dās comes from *Chaitanyacharitāmrita*, written by Kṛṣṇadās Kavirāj, who was a contemporary of Chaitanya and is considered the most reliable of his biographers. According to Kṛṣṇadās Kavirāj, Chaitanya, in his later years, found spiritual inspiration in the songs of Chaṇḍi Dās, Jayadēva, and Vidyāpathi.[39]

Chaitanya Bhakti against Social Stagnation

Two important disciples of Chaitanya were Nityānanda and Advaitāchārya. The latter was an elderly leader of Vaiṣṇavaites. The devotional movement gathered into its commune people of all castes. It is said that even at a very young age, Chaitanya told his mother that in the worship of Kṛṣṇa 'all rituals such as initiation and taking the sacred thread are quite unnecessary, everyone is free to worship and caste is no barrier'.[40] An important innovation of Chaitanya was that 'he resuscitated the pastoral tune of boatmen's songs adding to it a lovely musical mode which was quite original' and 'this was the origin of the famous Manoharshai' form of music.[41]

His declaration on the acceptance of renunciation was filled with heightened empathy for the liberation of all without discrimination. Prof. Dinesh Chandra Sen gives that declaration as below:

> I shall wander from house to house giving the holy name of God to all. The Chandals—the lowest caste—women and children all will stand with wonder and love to hear His name. Even boys and girls will sing His praise. The Aghore Panthis and other vicious tantriks will be attracted by His sweet name. The banner of His name will wave high in the air. Princes and poor men alike will sing His glory. If I do not turn a sanyasi how will the sinners and those that are stung with the world's sorrows be saved? My heart weeps to see the misery of the people around.[42]

One can note that Chaitanya, as quoted in the above passage, wanted to break the barriers of not only social stratification and reach out to the social outcasts but also wanted to ignore the barriers among the Sampradāyas and reach out to all. This has a remarkable similarity to the lines written in a letter written (original in Bengali) in 1894 by Hindu monk Śwāmi Vivekānanda:

> Let some of you spread like fire, and preach this worship of the universal aspect of the Godhead – a thing that was never undertaken before in our country. No quarrelling with people, we must be friends with all.... Spread ideas-go from village to village, from door to door-then only there will be real work. Otherwise, lying complacently on the bed and ringing the bell now and then is a sort of disease, pure and simple.... Through the Lord's will, out of your lips shall come millions of Vedas and Tantras and Puranas.... Go from village to village, do good to humanity and to the world at large. Go to hell yourself to buy salvation for others. There is no Mukti on earth to call my own.... We are Sannyasins, who have given up everything-Bhakti, and Mukti, and enjoyment, and all. To do the highest good to the world, everyone down to the lowest – this is our vow. Welcome Mukti or hell, whichever comes of it.[43]

Despite the differences in external appearance, there is a notable similarity between the thought processes of Chaitanya and Śwāmi Vivekānanda, despite the four-hundred-year gap that separates them. Chaitanya also faced the challenge of writing a commentary on the *Brahmasūtra* to further consolidate his religious authority as an Ācharya. However, doing so would have limited the movement's appeal to only the upper sections of society, hindering its outreach to all sections. Nevertheless, it would have elevated Chaitanya to a celebrated intellectual ascetic, earning him a considerable reputation. When Chaitanya was questioned by Prakāśānanda Saraswati, a renowned Sanyāsi scholar of Saṅkara school, Chaitanya gave an explanation. This explanation became part of the movement's stance, asserting that 'the *Bhāgavata Purāṇa* is the natural commentary of the *Brahmasūtra* because the author of the Vedas, Vyāsa himself, accepted the *Bhāgavata Purāṇa* as such'.[44]

According to Prof. D.C. Sen, Chaitanya 'found the caste system eating into the vitals' of the social fabric. While this statement may be an exaggeration, there is empirical evidence to show that the Bhakti movement led by Chaitanya naturally broke down caste barriers in terms of non-egalitarian relations and emphasized a spiritual fraternity that transcended social barriers. The Sanghīrthan movement provided a nascent societal form to go beyond social stratification, particularly addressing issues of social exclusion such as untouchability and the categorization of people as 'Chandala'. Prof. Sen states:

> (Chaitanya) said 'He that eats a meal cooked by a Dom becomes pre-eminently entitled to the grace of God.' The Dom is certainly the lowest caste in Bengal. The motto of the Vaishnavas was (that) 'even a Chandal should be held higher than Brahmin if he has devotion for God' and this is a well-known text of the Naradiya Puran. 'If a Muchi (cobbler) prays to God with devotion I bow a hundred times to his feet', said Chaitanya.... Chaitanya not only preached the equality of men but sometimes advocated a somewhat forward step in the practice of this doctrine. We find in the last chapter of Charitamrita that one Kalidas, an uncle of the celebrated apostle Raghunath Das of Saptagram, used to eat the refuse from the plates of low-caste men. Kalidas was born of a Kayastha family of high status and was himself a great scholar.... He had resolved to eat the refuse simply to give a rude shock to the popular prejudice that the man of an unclean caste was not worthy of touch – the food touched by him was unclean. When the caste-rules were so stringent Kalidas's conduct was certainly held heroic by the reformers. Once at Puri there lived a man named Kanai, who belonged to the sweeper caste, one of the lowest castes in Bengal, but a cleanlier man than Kanai did not exist in the country in respect of morals and devotion to God. Kalidas called on Kanai one day and bowed to him, at

> which that very humble soul mildly protested saying that as a Kayastha he should not have bowed to a sweeper. Kalidas offered him a mango, and when Kanai had partaken of a part and thrown away the remnant, Kalidas picked it up and began to taste it. This was a horror to all, a Kayastha eating the refuse of a sweeper. But when Chaitanya heard of this he praised and blessed him saying that God's grace would be on him, since he honoured merit and not caste. In him, since he honoured merit and not caste. In his own life his treatment of Haridas, Rupa. Sanatan and Ram Ray showed that he was no respecter of caste. At a test held at Puri he ordered that Haridas, the Mahomedan convert, should he first served. In the Vaishnava community the highest respect, generally shown to the most exalted Brahmins, used to be shown to Haridas even at religious functions. Chaitanya often touched Haridas saying 'I feel myself purified by your touch'. And when Haridas died he made all the good Brahmins drink water touched by his foot.... In the humble huts of the peasants and other low-caste people, praises and tributes of worship are offered to him every night and the song; 'Praise unto Chaitanva the god-man of Nadia, the friend of the fallen and one who does not l) believe in caste' is often sung in chorus.[45]

Chaitanya chose two brothers to formulate Gauḍīya Vaiṣṇava Darṣna. They were Sanātana Gosvāmī and Rūpa Gosvāmī.[46] Both had been excommunicated by the orthodoxy (as said to have been reconverted from Islam) and hence should have been considered as being verily outside the Varṇa system itself. Prof. Sen shows how even into the 20th century, the feeling of ritual impurity and the spirit of social ostracism continued with orthodox Hindus with respect to Sanātana Gosvāmī:

> A tank dug by Sanatan in Jessore still exists, the water of which is held unclean up to this day by the Hindus, because it is associated with the name of one who had once adopted Mahomedan ways.[47]

Yet it was them Chaitanya chose to be the formulators of the wisdom of his movement after him.

Melville Kennedy, the warden of Calcutta Young Men Christian Association Student Hostel of Calcutta, also a missionary scholar of the Chaitanya movement, could not accept this radical characterization of Chaitanya by Prof. Sen. As could be seen right from the Vedic times through Āzhwars and the medieval Bhakti movement, Chaitanya movement is very much consistent and in harmony with the pan-Indian deep Hindu spiritual phenomenon of challenging continuously the social status quo particularly opposing social exclusion through the vision of spiritual unity of all existence. Kennedy, in an attempt to dilute such a depiction, even posits a kind of rift between Chaitanya and Nityānanda Prabhu, the one who chiefly took forward the movement and spread it.[48] But it is more unconvincing and speculative than factual. Within the movement, Nityānanda Prabhu is venerated as a divine avatāric colleague of Chaitanya. Nevertheless, Kennedy's work presents empirical historical facts that demonstrate the movement's importance in absorbing social outcasts.

Right from Sahaja tradition, one of the spiritual streams that fed into the river of the Chaitanya Bhakti movement was Buddhist Tāntric elements. There indeed was a stranded Tāntric Buddhist community in Bengal who were considered outcasts. They were mostly Tāntrics. With the semi-permeable nature that characterizes the boundaries between the Hindu family of religions, there has been a free flow of ritual and philosophical elements and cross-fertilizing between Shakti and Buddhist systems. The community mostly consisted of Bhikṣūs and Bhikṣuṇis (male and female Buddhist ascetics). They were outside the Saṅgha. From the traditional biographies of Chaitanya, it is clear that the Buddhist philosophers were a respected school and Chaitanya had to engage in debate with them. Still, even such 'proper' Buddhist institutions seemed to have shunned the Tāntric Buddhist mendicants, both male and female. They were social outcasts. It was to the credit of the Chaitanya movement that they were accepted. It did not happen during the time of Chaitanya himself. But it was the son of Nityānanda Prabhu, Śrī Vīrabhadra, who accepted 1,200 Bhikṣūs and 1,300 Bhikṣuṇis (called *Neṛās* and *Neṛīs*) into the fold of Vaishnava at Kardaha, a small village now in West Bengal.[49]

This incoming of *Neṛās* and *Neṛīs* into such a mass movement as that of Chaitanya, along with other pre-Gauḍīya Vaiṣṇav streams, revitalized the Baül movement in West Bengal. However, in the 20th century, Western Indology considered this integration to be an unwanted addition to the Chaitanya movement. Melville Kennedy wrote about the Kardaha absorption of Buddhist mendicants as 'a distinct legacy which it (i.e., Gauḍīya Vaiṣṇava movement) could well have done without'. He described these mendicants as 'degraded bhikshus and bhikshunis of decayed Buddhism...and their own moral condition was not such as to make them welcome in any orderly society... and were looked upon as outcastes' and Kennedy believed that they were the source of 'degrading influences that have not been surmounted to this day'.

> The colonial view suggested that the Baul movement was not significant, but in reality, it became one of the strong decentralized spiritual networks in Bengal and Bihar. It even drew in spiritual seekers from Islam despite conventional Hinduism's religious boundaries. Kshiti Mohan Sen (1880-1960), a Tagore scholar, provides a suitable description of the historical continuity of this spiritual movement in his work on Hinduism thus: There are many similarities between the poems of the Bauls and those of the North Indian mystics.... However, the Bauls are less organized and have not crystallized themselves into fixed orders. It is probable that they were influenced by the medieval mystics of North India, but simple

> Bhakti tradition is so deeply rooted in the soil, springing up in every age in different parts of the country, that it is really very difficult to trace the origin of these movements. There is some similarity between Baul beliefs and those of some of the cults mentioned in the Atharvaveda, so that movements of this sort may well have appeared in India throughout her history.[50]

One can say that into this continuity, entered the streams of Buddhist Tantra and Bhakti. Buddhist Tantra, which was viewed by the then institutionally weakened Saṅgha and also generally by the society that was constantly under siege from Islamist invaders, led to the social exclusion of the mendicants of both genders. Thus 'many Bāuls, whether Hindu or Muslim, mention Vīrabhadra as their ādiguru, '"original preceptor", who gave legitimacy to their sexual sādhanā'.[51] Chaitanya Bhakti movement, headed by its head Śrī Vīrabhadra around the 17th century, injected new life and vigour into the Baul movement. Chaitanya himself had been inspired by Bhakti through one of the sacred trinities of the Sahaja Baul movement, Chaṇdi Dās, who could have absorbed directly or indirectly the Bhakti movement from the South. In a detailed paper, Prof. Kshiti Mohan Sen demonstrated how the Yogic-Tantric and Bhakti streams have harmonized so thoroughly throughout Indian history that they have always acted as a potential force of creative liberation:

> The inter-relations of man's body and the Universe have to be realized by spiritual endeavour. Such endeavour is called Kaya Sadhan (Realization through the body).
>
> One process in this Kaya Sadhan of the Baüls is known as Urdha-srota (the elevation of the current).... The currents of jiva (animal life) must be converted into the current of Shiva (God of life). They form a centre round the ego; they must be raised by the force of live. Says Dadu's daughter, Nanimata:
>
> 'My life is the lamp afloat on the stream.
> To what bourne shall it take me?

> How is the divine to conquer the carnal,
> The downward current to be upward turned?
> As when the wick is lighted the oil doth upward flow,
> So simply is destroyed the thirst of the body.'
>
> The Yoga Vaishta tells us: 'Uncleansed desires bind to the world, purified desires give liberation.' References to this reversal of current are also to be found in the Atharva Veda (X.2.9:2.34). This reversal is otherwise considered by Indian devotees as the conversion of the Sthula (gross) to the Sukshma (fine).
>
> The Baül sings: Love is my golden touch. It turns desire into service: Earth seeks to become Heaven, man to become God.
>
> Another aspect of the idea of reversal has been put thus by Rabindranath Tagore in his Broken Ties: 'If I keep going in the same direction along which He comes to me, then I shall be going further and further away from Him. If I proceed in the opposite direction, then only can we meet. He loves form, so He is continually descending towards form. We cannot live by form alone, so we ascend towards His formlessness.... One comes from freedom into bondage, the other goes from bondage into freedom; only thus can they have their communion. He sings and we hear. He ties the bonds as He sings to us, we untie them as we listen to Him.'[52]

Prof. K.M. Sen demonstrates the continuous, pan-Indian, and ever-vibrant socio-spiritual process of the Baüls. He highlights the influence of the spiritual poetry of Rabindranath Tagore in the modern 20th century sphere. The Chaitanya movement, through Bhakti, brought about strong social emancipation and revitalized the Baül movement by embracing the socially excluded *Neṛās* and *Neṛīs*. This led to the extreme democratization of spiritual experience-based authority and brought about a literary renaissance that extended well into the 20th century.

Now let us consider how Prof. Romila Thapar, a doyen of Marxist historians, viewed and wrote about the phenomenon of Chaitanya Mahāprabhu:

> A Bengal school-teacher, Chaitanya (1486–1533), became a devotee of Krishna after experiencing a strange hysterical trance. He held devotional meetings where hymns were sung and the meaning of Vaishnava belief was expounded. He travelled through the country inspiring people with Vaishnava teaching through the cult of Radha and Krishna. Chaitanya was concerned almost solely with bringing Vaishnava teaching to as many people as possible, and he was motivated by purely religious feelings.[53]

The above passage by Prof. Thapar on Chaitanya is a textbook instance of how deep-rooted colonial influences in the field of historiography in Independent India, combined with vested ideological interests, devalue the essential Indian aspect in culturally significant phenomena such as Chaitanya. This indoctrination, then presented as 'the history', is reinforced by the institutional control of the state.

Mahāpuruṣa Saṅkara Dēva

Saṅkara Dēva (1449-1568) was born in a Kayasta family in Assam and became a leading figure in the Bhakti movement in the Northeast. He was orphaned early and raised by his paternal grandmother, where he exhibited exceptional physical strength and leadership qualities. Despite initially showing no interest in education, his grandmother encouraged him to join a traditional school, and he soon became proficient in letters, composing a short poem full of bhakti upon learning the alphabet. That first poem was on Kṛṣṇa, adoring Him as Mahā Viṣṇu. Mastering all Sanskrit literature in a short period, he then practiced Yōga, although he found that Yōga without Bhakti was not for him. His path became clear after being given the *Śrīmad Bhāgavata Mahāpurāṇa* by Jagannāth Miśra, a Brahmin reciter of the holy book at Puri who was instructed by a vision to bring the book to Saṅkara Dēva. Immersing himself in *Bhāgavata Mahāpurāṇa*, Saṅkara Dēva proclaimed his realization not as an enlightenment of Gnosis but as the descent of compassion of the divine for the bhakta:

> Oh Lord Supreme Being the redeemer of Bhaktas, the Supreme Lord of my heart, Thou art my Guru. I pray Thee the great Guru Hrishikesha. I have realised the ever conscious Supreme Brahma through the grace of Sri Krishna.[54]

It is said that Saṅkara Dēva hand-decorated every element in a drama to give the audience a vision of Vaikuṇda, the non-material supreme realm of Mahā Viṣṇu . Enacting dramas of Bhaktas became an important component of the Saṅkara Dēva movement.

His bhakti became a major source for the renaissance of Assamese literature. He produced exquisite poetry, enchanting lyrical dramas, and devotional Mantric hymns that invigorated literature and performing arts in the region. His disciple Mādahva Dēva continued the literary and artistic tradition with equal energy. He composed the entire poetic translation of the tenth Canto of *Bhāgavata* in one night, titled *Gopee Uddhava Sambad*, which he used to give diksha to his disciples of all castes.[55] According to a traditional biographic verse, 'Bhuyans, Brahmans and other people became blessed through initiations'[56].

Who was the Guru of Saṅkara Dēva? According to the tradition, he considered every bhakta as his guru. Thus, ordinary lay persons, men and women, from every social strata of the society, if a bhakta, was venerated by him as a guru. When seen in the context of orthodoxy essentialized as Hinduism, this statement appears quite unique. For example, Rustom Bharucha, a writer and dramaturg, writes about ordinary Bhaktas venerated as the guru of the originator of an important Bhakti tradition as 'an extraordinarily nuanced position that compels one to rethink the political beyond the controversies and immediacies of the realpolitik today'.[57]

However, in the context of pan-Hindu Bhakti traditions from all over India, where tradition equates every bhakta, particularly from socially excluded or downtrodden classes, as equal to God himself, this is the most natural and spontaneous statement for the originator of a bhakti tradition. All the bhakti saints, belonging to various periods and linguistic provinces of India, have often stated in their own languages that a social outcaste, when brought into the fold of bhakti, becomes equal to all others and, in fact, becomes superior to a socially upheld caste which in the Indian context would usually be a Brahmin.

Similarities across various linguistic bhakti traditions throughout India in emphasizing spiritual equality, rejecting social stratification, and social exclusion		
Thirunāvukarasar	Thoṇdardipodi Āzhwār	Saṅkara Dēva
Period: circa 7th century CE	Period: circa 8th century CE	Period: late 15th to mid-16th century
Language: Tamil	Language: Tamil	Language: Assamese
Region: South India	Region: South India	Regions: Assam (northeastern India)
A person infested with leprosy and his limbs are decomposing, and the person belongs to the outcastes who skin the dead cow and eat its meat, even such a person is verily the God I worship if he is the loving Bhakta of Siva who adorns his locks with Ganga.	Lord of Sri Raṅgam commands the chastest of the Brahmins who are well learned in the four Vedas thus: Whom the society considers as out-caste, if they are My devotees, then exchange with them and treat them as Myself.	An outcaste reciting and meditating on the Name of Hari is superior to a Brahmin.

Appar Thēvāram: Thirumuṟai: VI; 95.10	Thirumālai: 42	*Prahalāda Caritrā*

The ritualistic Brahmins saw Saṅkara Dēva spiritual movement as a challenge to the theo-aristocracy and they filed a complaint to the ruler of the Assamese province where he was residing. At that time, Assam was ruled by two powerful kings. Initially, he resided in the territory of Ahom king Suhummung Sargadeva (1497-1539). The Brahmins complained to the king and Saṅkara Dēva was summoned. But Saṅkara Dēva managed to convince the Pundits and the court scholars of the Vedic sanction to his spiritual movement. Later, the relationship between the Ahom king and Saṅkara Dēva became bitter due to an entirely non-religious matter involving the king's capture of wild elephants. As a result, Saṅkara Dēva left the kingdom and went to the land governed by Koch kings, with Narnārāyaṇ as the ruling monarch. A similar dispute occurred there, and once again, Saṅkara Dēva proved the scriptural authority of the Bhakti tradition. This time the king was so impressed that he expressed a desire to embrace the path of bhakti. But to his credit and vision, Saṅkara Dēva declined royal conversion and instead worked to build a people's movement of bhakti. Towards that end, he revived an ancient system of institutions in Assam, which remains important in the cultural and social life of Assam even today.

Sattra Institutions: A Multi-dimensional Yajña in Bhakti

Sattras have their origins in Vedic literature. Originally, they were special Vēdic Yajña sessions, which were long and performed by priests for their own worldly benefits, without a Yajamāna. Indologist Michael D. Willis points out a 2nd-century CE Mathura inscription commemorating a twelve-day-long

Sattra. Eventually, the term that originally meant a ritual Yajña became the name for 'charitable almshouse'. Willis explains this transformation and its continued similar usage thus:

> How a sacrificial session could turn into an almshouse is explained by the elaborate homologies built around the human body and sacrifice. This long-standing current in Indian thought led to the conflation of eating and sacrificing, the point being that the stomach and the sacrificial fire are insatiable consumers of the food poured into them. This is how the Hitopadesa could make the seemingly bizarre assertion that 'one should honour the sacrificial fire with the stomach.' If eating was a sacrificial act, then hospitality was, in fact, a sacrifice. This shows that the sattra of the inscriptions can be aligned with Manu's atithi, the reception of guests, also described by Manu as manusyayajha, the offering or sacrifice to men. To put the matter in practical terms, the community of Brahmanas – the primary readers of Manu's text – had an obligation to support fellow Brahmanas, especially those who might be on hard times. The offering of alms to passing mendicants and the poor was equally recommended because it deflected threats and added to one's spiritual merit.[58]

Willis brilliantly elucidated the spiritual vision behind the transformation of Sattra from a ritualistic ritual to a metaphorical ritual. Nevertheless, the connection is even stronger than Manu alone. It goes back to *Taittirīya Upaniṣad* and later in the Bhagavad Gītā (4:30). Willis gives further instances of how Sattra evolved as an institution associated with temples: the 5th-century inscription of a Sattra built by a Brahmin Dhruvaśarman associated with a temple of *Kārttikēya;* a mid-5th-century pillar inscription at Poḍāgarh where along with a temple of the sacred feet of Viṣṇu, a *Sattra* was built to feed 'Brāhmaṇas, wandering ascetics, and the destitute.'[59] In the 6th century, a minor Hindu king Bhūta of central India donated two villages to a temple of Vishṇu built by his Queen Mother. In the copper plate inscription of the grant, he speaks of an institution associated with the temple, which would be supported by the grant for medicine and restorative food to be given here to parivrājakā (wandering ascetics) and to Dāsis and Dāsās of the Deity as well as 'those bereft of food, clothing, etc., who come to the habitation acquired'.[60] The Dāsis and Dāsās are translated directly as female and male slaves of God by Willis, but in this context, they represent the Bhaktas. According to Willis, it is amply evident that 'the description of a habitation (avasatha) handing out medicine and restorative food (bhaisajapathya bhojana) can only refer to a sattra' which was 'a building attached to a temple ... that the intended recipients were the destitute, wandering mendicants and – if circumstances required – brahmanas' and that 'sattra provided an institutional place and space for those practices and knowledge that stood outside the tightly circumscribed ambit of the old Vedic schools'.[61] In other words, Sattra was a flexible institution of service to humans conducted as a Yajña, and this was conducive to the Bhakti movement.

In *Bhāgavata Mahāpurāṇa*, Sattra is the Yajña that was conducted by the sages at the forest of Naimiṣāraṇya, and it was this assembly of sages that set the stage for the telling of *Bhagavata*.[62] The spiritual movement Sankara Dēva, called *Eka-Hari-nāma-saraṇa-Dharma*, combined the *Atithi*-oriented Sattra with the Brahma Sattra of *Bhagavata* and revived it as an institutional network in Assam. According to Dr Pradip Jyoti Mahanta, a scholar who has studied the Sattra institution, it evolved from its 'initial notion of *Harikathā* ... transformed into centres of permanent institutions ... the centre for sustaining the tradition of religion, learning and the new social life born of the renaissance' which 'together present an inner structural wholeness'.[63]

Śrī Kamal Chandra Gōswāmi, a head or Sattrādikār of Ādi Elangi Sattra of Assam, explains the egalitarian nature of the structure and functioning of the Sattra institutions:

> A Sattra is a public institution of the Trinity – the Gurus, the Bhaktas and the Shishyas. The basic tenet of the Bhakti sampradaya thus indicates that this path, irrespective of any caste and creed is subservient only to Bhagwan Sri Krishna and to the universe, the sole creation of God the almighty.... In the matter of such traditions and customs no discrimination can exist relating to any caste or creed, high and low consideration. Even no members or sons of the Guru family will be allowed to perform any duty of the Sattra, internal or external, until unless he is or they are formally initiated or qualified for that purpose. A democratic element can also be noticed in the preferential treatment in day-to-day or occasional performance of Nam-Prasangha. No distinction or priority exists in the seating arrangement in the Namghar save and except for the Head Guru, the Satradhkar who is adorned with a special respect by all concerned. Thus equality to all as far as possible and collective voice of each and every one is based purely on the democratic process.[64]

He traces this institutional egalitarianism to the spiritual oneness that Saṅkara Dēva stresses in many of his devotional-mystic compositions, as in Kīrtana Ghōśa, where he says that the entire existence is permeated by Hari, and hence one should treat all beings as Viṣṇu: '*Samasta bhutate byāpi āso moi Hari; Savāko mānibā tumi Biṣṇu buddhi kari.*'[65] According to Saṅkara Dēva, a person is said to have attained equanimity and bliss of the Self only if he treats a person of high caste and outcaste equally, a thief and a charitable person with no judgement but love; treats the one considered sacred and one considered non-pious as of having the same spiritual essence and hence with equal reverence: '*Brāhmaṇānara chaṇḍāḷara nibichāri kula; Dātāta chorata yena driśti ekā tulā; Nichata sādhuta yāra bhaila eka jnāna; Tāhākese paṇdita buliyo sarbajana.'*[66] Even after Saṅkara Dēva, the progressive evolution of Sattra continued. A century after him, Kanagalatā Ai, a woman, became Sattra head and spread the movement further. She established Vaikuṇdapuri Sattra, which had to be relocated because of Islamist invasions. She was instrumental in discovering the birthplace of Saṅkara Dēva at Bordowa, which had been forgotten because the saint himself had moved out.[67] The sacred place or 'Śthān', which in Assamese is called 'Thān', became an important pilgrimage centre and centre of activities.

Though Sattra itself became a centre of various activities, it was a self-sustained community with porous borders. But it was not a gated community or a cult in isolation but rather engaged itself in active interaction as well as exchange of goods and services with the outer economic and cultural life of the society. Saṅkara Dēva himself employed outside labourers and not his Bhaktas in doing works like carpentry, etc. They were paid for their services. In his work *Ureṣā-Varṇana*, Saṅkara Dēva listed professionals like painters (citrakāra), medicine men (baidya), actors (naṭa-bhāṭa), dancers (narttakī), singers (gāyana), Brāhmaṇa or vipra, etc. When he invited a Brahmin, Brahmānanda Bhattacharyya, for a month-long Gītā recital, he paid the Brahmin in gold, which he emphasized was not dānā (a donation) but a dakshina (payment).[68] Thus, Sattra institutions became not only centres of religious and cultural renaissance but also economic development for regions around. Sattra is thus Yajña institutionalized through Bhakti and evolved to serve the spiritual, cultural and socio-economic developmental needs of the community.

Even into the 20th century, Sattra's institutional network became active in the national freedom movement. From the time of the Bengal partition to the 'Quit India' movement, the Sattra institutions and the trustees of the Sattras, the Sattrādikārs, helped the freedom movement dynamically. Assamese historian Dr Sagar Barua writes:

> Accompanied by Krishnachandra Dev Goswami, the Deka Sattradikar of Garmur Sattra, Sri Sri Pitambaradeva himself visited neighbouring villages including the Mising inhabited areas, propagating Gandhiji's message and enrolling Congress volunteers. When the Congress leaders were arrested Sri Sri Pitambaradeva took the leading part of the Congress in Jorhat. The active participation of the Sattradhikar of Garmur Sattra was a cause of alarm for the Government and hence it immediately imposed restrictions on the movement of Sri Sri Pitambardeva, confining him to the Sattra.... In protest against it, Krishnachandra Dev Goswami of Deka Sattra came out to the streets and addressed large gatherings and advised people to make the (Quit India) movement a success.... The Sattradhikar was put in jail and was detained for two years.... The arrest of Sri Sri Pitambaradeva Goswami produced an unprecedented situation. The disciples of the Sattradhikar and people of the neighbouring villages took our processions holding flags and singing Viswa Bijayee Na-Jawan of Jyotir Prasad Agarwala.[69]

Sattra institutional networks also played a vital role in organizing Hindus in Assam and making them aware of the dangers of the Cabinet Mission Plan, placing Assam in the Class C category, which would make the state part of Pakistan. Hemachandra Gōswāmi of Auniati Satra played an important role in forging Hindu unity appealing against casteism and untouchability. Haridev Gōswāmi of Dakshinpat Sattra made the society aware of the dangers of the Cabinet Mission Plan and played a role in integrating the state with the secular Indian Republic.[70]

One should remember here that the Sattra institutions, with their ancient Vedic roots, were a conscious innovation by Mah Puruṣa Saṅkara Dēva in which he made Bhakti-based commune activities and social emancipation verily a Yajña. This is a powerful combination of Bhakti Yōga, Jgñāna Yōga, and Karma Yōga brought into the Yajña enclosure and making it an epicentre of community life. This is a model that will be tremendously important for social emancipation in the coming years with digital connectivity, cost-effective technologies, and concepts of sustainable development.

Rāmānandis

A few centuries after Śrī Rāmānuja, even as South India got fortified against violent invasions, North India was still struggling. Now, the spiritual movement that he initiated spread out slowly and steadily into North India. The different Bhakti streams coalesced into a strong movement.

The person who took it forward remains a mystery figure to historians and scholars, though, to common Hindus, the differing traditional accounts regarding Śrī Rāmānanda are more real than what ivory tower historians might tell. These accounts agree upon one thing. With Islamist invasions and proselytization, there came a need to accommodate those who had been forced to leave Hindu Dharma but yearned to return. An institutional process was needed. It is from the Śrī Sampradāya of Śrī Rāmānuja came the response in the form of Śrī Rāmānanda. However, it seems such reconversion had made the orthodox elements, even in the Śrī Sampradāya, uncomfortable. This resulted in the emergence of Rāmānandi Sampradāya. One of their main creed statement was that 'Do not inquire from any Bhakta his caste or sect; whoever worships Hari, belongs to Hari.'[71] While there is no text-based 'evidence' for Śrī Rāmānanda having said this, it is more than clear that this should have been too axiomatic and common base that it had become part of the organic core of the movement to be written in a text.

Indologist Prof. Purushottam Agrawal points out that while this statement is made in Hindi ('*Hari ko bhaje so Hari ka hoi, jat paant poochhe nahin koi*'), verses expressing the same spiritual value are present in the Sanskrit work *Vaiṣṇava Matha Bāskar* attributed to Śrī Rāmānanda:

> God in his grace does not care for the caste, purity or the power of anyone seeking refuge in Him. (ślōka:100)
>
> - The sages and the scriptures enjoin those born in the higher Jāthis to serve Vaiṣṇavā, even those belonging to the lower Jāthis. (ślōka:107)
> - Those belonging to the Dwjā-castes must seek liberation in Hari, who does not care for either rituals or caste. (ślōka: 125)
>
> Those who carry the five Vaiṣṇavā marks on their body, whether twice-born, Śūdras, or women – are epitomes of piousness. In fact, they are manifestations of Viṣṇu Himself. They are the essence of the holiness of holy places. They purify the place in which they dwell. All sins go away merely by looking at these noble souls. (ślōkas:149–50)[72]

According to Prof. Agrawal, Śrī Rāmānanda is considered the most important source of inspiration for the spread of 'non-caste Hinduism' in the whole sweep of Indian—certainly north Indian—religious history.[73] Another work *Rāmārchanapaddhati* attributed to Sri Ramananda places him as the twenty-third in the line of the Acharyas of *Śrī* tradition. But here, the tradition starts with Śrī Rāmāchandra and Sītā instead of Śrīman Nārāyaṇa and Śrī Lakshmi. The next eight Āchāryas are the same in both lineages, which include Śrī Rāmānuja. The first three Āchāryas belong to the transcendental realm of *Vaikuṇda*. The first human Āchārya in both traditions is Sadagōpa or Nammāzhwār, who belonged to the so-called fourth Varṇa. In the subsequent developments, particularly early 20th century,

Rāmānandi Sampradāya decided to consider themselves a separate lineage from the Śrī Sampradāya because the latter saw the all-caste inclusive Rāmānandis as inferior. In this, they pushed the period of Rāmānanda by a century. According to Dr Agrawal, this had an unintended consequence making a more Sanskritic Rāmānanda, who differed from the till-then traditionally held more-Hindi rooted Rāmānanda, who was acknowledged by Rāmānandis till the 1921 Ujjain Kumbha Meḷa when they declared Rmānanda as Śrī Rāmānandāchārya.[74]

Nevertheless, Śrī Rāmānuja had created enough hermeneutical space in Śrī Sampradāya itself to repudiate caste distinctions, as has been shown in the superior positioning of non-Brahmins over the Brahmins. Here it is apt to observe a parallel development in Śrī Sampradāya of South India. Almost around the same period as Śrī Rāmānanda, in South India, strong criticisms of any consideration of caste of Śrī Vaiṣṇava bhaktas emerged with definite employment of the so-called 'Brahminical' or Sanskritic literature like Gitā in support of their caste-negation position. In the 13th century, Śrī Azhakiya Maṇavāḷa Perumāḷ wrote such a critique in his work '*Āchārya Hrudayam*' (The Heart of the Āchāryas). In this, he made a detailed denial of following birth-cased social stratification in Vaiṣṇava communities. Even a stronger commentary was made on the text by the celebrated Śrī Maṇavāḷa Māmunikaḷ (1370–1450) for this work. Śrī Maṇavāḷa Māmunikaḷ was considered by his followers as the very re-emanation of Sri Ramanuja, and Māmunikaḷ wrote the commentary for Āchārya Hrudayam from his deathbed. So the venerable centrality of the text to the *Sampradāya* cannot be overstated. The text makes a distinction between attaining Brahminhood and Vaishnava-hood. The former may be (by the then prevailing conditions) predicated upon birth and caste. But the latter is open to all. The latter stands on its own and the former is of no value if it does not have in it the latter. The text states:

> By studying all the Vēdās and following all the rituals and mastering Mīmāsā etc., one acquires Brahmaṇa nature. By (experiential) mastering the divine verses of *Āzhwars* one attains Vaiṣṇava nature. Without the latter the former is of no use.
>
> ...
>
> Those who value (birth-based) four-fold Varṇa, when they enter into the discussion of the (fourth) Varṇa status of the *Āzhw*ār to negate it as a treatise of Vēdic essence, then they acquire the sin of those who consider the Divine worshipful sculpture of Viṣṇu (*Archāvatāra*) only as a metallic object and discuss the nature of the metal of its make. They are equivalent to those who seek to query about the genitalia of their mothers.
>
> If one rejects the Vēdic Gnosis contained in the Pāsurams because of the (fourth Varṇa) origin of the *Āzhwār*, then one should reject *Mahābhārata* accepted as the fifth *Vēda,* because Vyāsa was born of *Macchagandhi* the woman with the odour of fish and also one should reject the six-times-three chaptered *Bhagavad Gītā* as *Śrī Kṛṣṇa* was a cowherd.[75]

At one point, the author goes to the extent of comparing the fish-odour-filled birthplace of Vyāsa and butter-odour-filled place of Kṛṣṇa with the Tulsi odour-filled place of origin of Āzhwār and considers the latter superior to others. This is a typical hyperbole of Bhakti, where Bhakta is considered superior to even God and the scripture. The text continues:

> Even if a person of *Milēcha* origin (i.e. uncultured-uncivilised person) becomes a Vaiṣṇava, then those Brahmins who have mastered the four *Vēdas* should consider him as equivalent to the Deity of their clan and wash his feet and consider that water sacred.
>
> ...
>
> Those who consider the birth based superiority and discriminations (in the community of Vaiṣṇava), however learned they might be in scriptures and however high-born, all their pride of clan as well as their knowledge are as vain as the use of sacred vermilion to a donkey that carries it or the decoration made to a dead body.[76]

The radical and unconventional ideas found in Rāmānandi Sants and Kabir can be traced back to the Vēdic literature. However, this parallel development is often overlooked by scholars studying the division between the Rāmānandi and Śrī traditions. Anthropologist Daniela Bevilacqua provides an insightful perspective on this issue in her study of Hindu ascetic traditions, offering a less biased view of the historical Rāmānanda compared to the Christian-colonial prejudices often found in traditional Indology:

> There were several critical moments in the construction of Rāmānanda as an historical figure, perhaps first as a Sant and later as an ācārya. Whereas the Sant Rāmānanda only exists in the Sants production, another Rāmānanda, associated with nirguṇa-yogic practices, lives in the tapasī branch of the sampradāya, together with a saguṇa Rāmānanda who can be found in all the branches. Perhaps all these Rāmānandas are evolutions of the original Rāmānanda. The saguṇa school of thought, followed by the rasik component of the sampradāya, could have later needed the construction of a proper ācārya Rāmānanda. To support this portrait, the connection between Rāmānanda and Rāmānūja stressed in earlier texts such as the Bhaktamāl was initially used, while during the twentieth century, it had to be neglected to prove the independence of the sampradāya and of Rāmānanda as its founder.[77]

If one replaces in the above passage terms like ‘production’, ‘needed a construction’, ‘initially used’, etc., with a framework of involuted potentialities existing simultaneously and evolving out organically (which is also suggested but not fully explored by the author of the passage above), then one can see the range of potentialities that the Bhakti contains within it—harmonizing the spiritual aspirations of the individual and the socio-spiritual needs of the society for its social emancipation in a sustained way.

The text *Bhaktamālā* is one of the most sacred texts of Rāmānandis. It was composed by one of the Āchāryas of the tradition, Śrī Nābhādās, reverentially called Śrī Nābhādās Gōśwāmi. The accepted date of composition is around 1580 CE. According to tradition, Śrī Nābhādās was born blind. Hence, he was abandoned by his parents during a famine. He was adopted by two Sadhus, Kīlhadās and Agradās. According to generally accepted convention, Śrī Nābhādās Gōśwāmi belonged to the basket-weavers community called Ḍoms. Internal evidence in Bhaktamālā states that the compilation of the devotees was done on the orders of Agradās. The poet narrates the lives of the great disciples of Śrī Rāmānanda. Twelve Bhaktas primarily emerge. Of these twelve disciples, Kabir was a weaver (and a Muslim); Raidās or Ravidās was a cobbler; Dhanā was a farmer; Sēna was a barber; Padmāvati and Surasuri were women. The others, Anantānand, Sukhānand, Narharyānand, Bhavānand, and Sursurānand (whose wife was Surasuri), were Brahmins. Among these, the most important with respect to the present subject is Raidās or Ravidās.

Śrī Bhaktamālā was written in a very concise style. Consequently, Nābhādās Gōśwāmi himself requested Śrī Priyadās Gōśwāmi to compose a detailed version of *Śrī Bhaktamālā,* which resulted in *Śrī Bhaktirasa Bōdhini.* Some scholars have criticized Priyadās for showing bias towards Brahmins. For example, when discussing Sant Ravidās, who was a cobbler, he recounts a tradition claiming that Ravidās was originally a Brahmin disciple of Śrī Rāmānanda, but due to a mistake he was born in the socially excluded Jāthi. Dr Darshan Singh elaborates on this further:

> *Priyadāsa*'s amplification of *Nābhādāsa*'s Bhaktamālā provides useful information regarding life and teachings of *Ravidāsa,* but being a committed Brāhmana he does not recognize *Śūdra*'s right to be initiated into spiritual life. *Ravidāsa,* according to

> him succeeds in seeking initiation not because of his devotional bent of mind but because of his high Varṇa and association with *Śwāmi Rāmānanda* in his previous life.[78]

The fact that Priyadās, a pious Brahmin, willingly accepted a supposedly lower-caste saint as his Guru, Nābhādās Gōśwāmi, who came from a basket weaver community, contradicts the accusation that he could not accept a Śūdra as his guru. The idea that Ravidās was a Brahmin in a past life and was born into harsh circumstances in this life is likely a reflection of oral tradition rather than Priyadās' bias. Priyadās himself accepted a guru from the basket-weaver community, undermining the claim that he would not accept Ravidās as his guru. This claim seems to reflect modern anti-Brahminical prejudice rather than reality.

In his commentary, Priyadās demonstrated a casteless approach by introducing a significant tradition. While Nābhādās Gōśwāmi mentioned only one Vālmīkī, referring to Ṛṣi Vālmīkī, Ādi Kavi, and the composer of Rāmāyaṇā, Priyadās Gōśwāmi added another Vālmīkī, Upa-Vālmīkī, who was socially excluded and considered untouchable. This Vālmīkī, resembling a character from Purāṇic tales, lived during Dwāpara Yuga and was known as Śvapāca (dog eater: outcast) Vālmīkī.

Once, the emperor and the eldest of the five Pāṇḍavās, Yudhiṣṭhira, organized a grand Yajña. The success of the Yajña depended on a magical conch that would blow loudly when the most auspicious aspect of the Yajña was completed. However, the conch remained silent until the end. Distressed, they sought guidance from Kṛṣṇa, who instructed them to follow His guidance without hesitation or mental inhibitions. He asked them to invite a perfect devotee, a Bhakta, to partake in the Yajña. Only then would the Yajña be complete and the conch would sound the benediction. However, finding such a devotee was a rare occurrence. Luckily, such a devotee existed in their kingdom, but he was known to be devoid of ego and might leave if his devotion was revealed. Despite this, due to the Pāṇḍavās' distress, Kṛṣṇa made an exception and revealed his name, Śvapāca Vālmīkī. Kṛṣṇa cautioned Arjuna and Bhīma that true bhakti was rare. Both princes approached Vālmīkī with respect, requesting him to partake in the food and share the remains as prasāda. Hesitantly, Vālmīkī agreed and as he started eating, the conch began to make an auspicious sound, though not loudly. Kṛṣṇa instructed the conch to make the auspicious sound for every rice that Vālmīkī consumed, but the conch instead asked Kṛṣṇa to inquire Draupadi for the reason. Draupadi revealed that when she watched Vālmīkī eat, caste pride entered her thoughts, believing that he, being of a low caste, was not cultured enough to appreciate her cooking. When Kṛṣṇa asked Vālmīkī for an explanation, he shared that he saw the food as prasād and, therefore, mixed all the delicacies into one, as one should not have any preferences in blessed food. This showcased the greatness of Śvapāca Vālmīkī.[79] Vālmīkī's action demonstrated the principle that having a preference for one dish over another would imply considering one as high and another as low, which would amount to insulting the food and the sage should not insult sacred food. This resonates with the Taittirīya Upaniṣadic value that food should never be insulted, which is a life-vow.[80]

The influence of the Rāmānandi tradition can be observed in the transmission of this memetic component to its various Sampradāyas and Panths. The Śvapāka Vālmīkī incident, as narrated in *Bhaktarasa Bōdhini*, undergoes a slight alteration in the Kabirpanth, as depicted in the Sukhsāgar, one of the works of Gharibdās (1717-78), a revered Sant from Haryana in the Kabirpanth.[81]

In this version, the hermit is known as Śvapāka Sudarśana. The change in name to Sudarśana connects to an older, geographically distant tradition. This parallels an incident in the tradition of Thirumazhisai Āzhwār, who embodied Sudarśana Chakra. When traditional sections of society objected to honouring him first in the Yajña, he manifested the Sudarśana Chakra. This combines both Śvapāka Vālmīkī and Thirumazhisai Āzhwār. This may be the Purāṇic way of emphasizing the pan-Indian continuity of Bhakti Sampradāya.

In addition to the name change, there are several other updates in the latest version. Initially, Bhīma was disrespectful, and the five-faced conch did not produce the auspicious sound because the Yajña was incomplete, as the Pūrṇa Puruṣa did not partake in the sacrificial offering. Śvapāka Sudarshan mentioned that Yudhiṣṭhira needed to provide him with the Puṇya of a thousand Yajñas they conducted before he would partake in the Yajña-offered food due to the aftermath of a terrible war. Bhīma, frustrated by this request, reported to Kṛṣṇa, who then took the Pāṇḍavās to the hut of Śvapāka Sudarshan. After paying their respects, they sat with him, and Kṛṣṇa shared the famous Kabirpanth words, 'Sant milan kō chāiyē, taji mōh māyā abhimān Jayōṅ Jayōṅ pag āgē dharaē, kōṭi yajña samān,' which means that seeking the auspicious company of a sant is equivalent to ten million Yajñas. Following this, Draupadi repented her actions, washed the feet of Śvapāka Sudarshan, and drank the water as a ceremonial act known as Charaṇāmrit or nectar of the feet.

Rāmānandi movement through Kabirpanth also gave rise to various spiritual sampradāyas such as Satnāmīs, Rāmnāmīs, and Dādupanth. Awadesh Kumar, a social historian from Punjab University, explains Rāmānandi influence in the subsequent religious landscape of North India thus:

> It was largely owing to the influence of Ramanand and his followers that Hindi became a literary language. His disciple Kabir, who flourished in the fifteenth century, was even more bold and outstanding. His influence spread widely and deeply and led to the emergence of numerous religious panths. Sikhism,

Dadupanth, Satnam and a host of minor religious panths are attributed to the powerful influence of Kabir's teachings and Kabirpanth's ideology.[82]

After the time of Kabīr, the Rāmānandi movement spread rapidly, bringing communities together through the power of Bhakti. These communities were able to create social and economic networks, offering an alternative for preserving their identities and achieving social liberation during challenging times of invasions, aggressive conversion efforts, and social stagnation. They also provided a local resistance to external political and religious pressures.

Throughout centuries and across diverse linguistic traditions in various regions of India, the consistent presence of Yajña in these narratives illustrates its significance as more than just a metaphor. It serves as a potent force challenging social stagnation, embodying a deep spiritual archetype that facilitates social liberation and individual growth.

Event	**Source**	**Sampradāya**	**Period**
Saraswati demonstrates the greatness of Kavaṣa Ailūṣa when he was expelled from Yajña because he was an Abrāhmana.	*Aitarēya Brāhmaṇa* (2:19)	Vēdic	Circa 1200 BCE
Gñāna Sambanthar made Nīlakaṇṭa Yāzhpāṇar and his wife Mataṅga Cūḷāmaṇi sleep besides the Yajñavēdi.	*Periya Purāṇam* (32: 30-31)	Vēdic Saivism	Period of event: 7th century CE Period of composition: 12th century CE

Event	Source	Sampradāya	Period
Sōmāsi Māra Nayanār witnessing Siva entering the Sōma Yajña.	*Kuñjitāṅghristavam* (verse: 170)	Vēdic Saivism	Period of event circa 7th century CE Period of composition: 13th century CE
Thirumaṅgai Azhwār manifests Sudarsana Chakra when some Brahmins denied him the first honour of the Yajña	*Guruparampara* chronicles	Vaiṣṇavaism	Circa 7th century CE
Narration of Śvapāka Vālmīki as the one most eligible person for the consumption of food for the completion of Yajña	Bhaktirasa Bōdini	Rāmānandi Vaiṣṇava	Circa 16th century CE
Śvapāka Vālmīki as Sudarshan	*Sukhsāgar*	Kabirpanth	17th century CE
During the Vēdic period and up to the 17th century, popular spiritual narratives from Hindu Sampradāyas have consistently challenged social stagnation while advocating social emancipation. The common connecting theme throughout these narratives is the practice of Yajña.			

Guru Ravi Dās

Perhaps the best testimony to the social emancipation potential of the Rāmānandi Bhakti movement comes from the phenomenon of Ravi Dās or Rai Dās (1471-1575). It is believed that he lived during the same time as Guru Nānak and Kabīr. By 1604 CE, forty of his devotional-mystic verses were added to the Adi Granth, which was consolidated by Guru Arjan Dev, the fifth Guru of the Sikhs. This demonstrates the immense influence Rai Dās had in spiritual and devotional domains, even centuries after his samadhi. Ravi Dās belonged to the sub-caste of Dhed among the Chamārs. The family used to remove the carcasses of cattle, and Ravi Dās was a cobbler. He lived in Vāraṇāsi. His Sādhana moves easily into both nirguṇa and saguṇa Brahman. Thus, he sang in Viṣṇu Bhakti in his Pȧc Vāṇi:

> Life of the worlds Kṛṣṇa Murāri!
> You are shiny red silk, Four-armed,
>   I am a wretched silk-worm.
> Drinking the nectar from the flowers on the branch,
>   through company with elixir I became a bee.
>
> You are a sandal-tree,
>   I am a wretched castor-oil plant,
>   that grows near You.
> As your fragrance pervaded my bad smell,
>   I turned from a low plant into a lofty tree.
>
> My caste is low, my birth is low,
>   my trade is low,
> I am in the refuge of King Rām,
> says Raidās the wretch.[83]

Here very clearly, Rai Dās appeals to the Saguna Brahman whose highest realization in Vaiṣṇava Bhakti tradition is made in the form of four-armed Viṣṇu. At the heart is the mapping of the spiritual and the social. As an individual Sadhak, he portrays himself as being still in the grip of Samsara or worldly bonds and, hence, in the pit of the Kārmic web. This is how a bhakta, irrespective of the social division to which he or she belongs, portrays oneself. But with Rai Dās, this is also fully pregnant with another message that Bhakti, whom the society considers low, can be transformed, liberated from the oppressing social stratification and social elimination. When that divine will for transformation is acquired through Bhakti, then the social forces of the status quo should bow down before this transformation and acknowledge it or fight the divine, in which case they transform into asūric forces.

Tradition has it that he became the spiritual Guru of Mīrābāi, the famous Bhakti saint and princess of Mēwār, who led her from sa-guṇa worship to nir-guṇa Advaitic realization. According to historian Darshan Singh, the possibility of this tradition being true could not be ruled out.[84] Also important is the disciple-hood of Jhali Rāṇi who was the wife of Mahā Rāṇā of Chithūr. She openly declared her acceptance of Sant Ravi Dās as her guru. This is how BhaktaMālā of Śrī Nābhādās Gōśwāmi gives the following Bhakti-traditional account of the consequences:

> Amongst the disciples of Raidas was Jhali, the Rani of Chitore: her adopting a chamar, as her spiritual preceptor excited a general commotion amongst the Brahmans of her state, and, alarmed for her personal safety, she wrote to Raidas to request his counsel and aid. He repaired to her, and desired her to invite the Brahmans to a solemn feast. They accepted the invitation, and sat down to the meal provided for them when between every two Brahmans there appeared a Raidas...from this his enemies and revilers became his disciples.[85]

The life of Satguru Rai Dās thus comes with many insights into the social impact of Bhakti and its potential for social emancipation. Thc individual Sadhana here brings out the potential of Bhakti to transform society against its stagnant mindset. One should note here that the queen and princess accepting Rai Dās as their guru has been accepted both by society and tradition. It is also well preserved in the tradition and repeated in the Bhakti literature elsewhere. In all these, we find that the Sanātan Dharma disconnects itself from the side of social stagnation and proactively initiates and catalyses social emancipation.

Equally important is the way the chieftain of Vāraṇāsi accepted the Divine nature of Guru Ravi Dās.

According to the tradition tale, Sant Ravi Dās once gave a coin to a Brahmin and requested him to offer it to the River Goddess Gaṅga. After bathing in the river, the Brahmin placed the coin in the water. To his surprise, the hand of the River Goddess emerged and presented him with a diamond-studded bracelet. The Brahmin chose to keep it. Eventually, when he attempted to sell the bracelet, he encountered suspicion due to its extraordinary value. This led to a series of events, including a court summons and, ultimately, the revelation of the bracelet's divine origin.. When the local ruler heard the whole incident, he asked if Ravi Dās could produce the other pair. Ravi Dās had a water-pot used in his cobbler trade. He prayed to Hari and River Goddess Gaṅga emerged from the pot with the diamond bracelet. Thus, the chieftain of Vāraṇāsi eventually acknowledged the divinity of Sant Ravi Dās.

Continuity of Dharmic River

In the next century, in distant Tamil Nadu, there was a remarkable incident involving Śrīdara Vēṅkatēsa Iyyāvāḷ (1635-1720), an Advaitic seer-scholar. He generously offered food meant for ritualists conducting the Śrāddha ritual to a hunger-stricken social outcast. However, the Brahmins, who were supposed to conduct the ritual, refused to do so after learning that the food had been given to an 'untouchable'. They even demanded that Śrīdara Iyyāvāḷ bathe in River Gaṅga. When Iyyāvāḷ explained that it was impossible for him to travel such a great distance, the Brahmins mockingly suggested that he should ask the sacred river to come to his village, Thiruvisainallūr. In response to this humiliation, Śrīdara Iyyāvāḷ sang Gaṅgāshtakam (eight verses on the River Goddess). Miraculously, as he reached the fifth verse, River Goddess Gaṅga started torrentially pouring out of his backyard well with such force that the Brahmins feared a devastating flood. Fearing the consequences, they asked for forgiveness and the river subsided back.

The stories of river goddesses playing a pivotal role in social liberation are deeply ingrained in the cultural fabric of India. Whether it is the tale of River Saraswati aiding Kavaṣa Ailūṣa, the emergence of the sacred River Gaṅga from a cobbler's pot in the case of Sant Ravi Dās, or River Gaṅga's presence in the backyard well of Śrīdara Iyyāvāḷ, these enduring narratives symbolize the timeless values that flow through the riverine spaces, bridging the ancient Purāṇic traditions with the evolving dynamics of society.

Ravi Dās also provides spiritual meaning to the different Varṇas.

The concept of Brāhmaṇā in Hindu philosophy involves recognizing (in all) Brahman Ātman. A true Brāhmaṇā is characterized by freedom from Kāma (lust), Krōdh (wrathful anger), Madh (bloated ego), and Lōbh (greed). Similarly, a Kṣatriya is one who gives his own life to remove the sufferings and miseries of others. One who earns his wealth and conducts his transactions with integrity and truth, such a person Ravi Dās calls Vaiśyā. A person with a pure nature is considered a Śūdra. Ultimately, these distinctions are meant to illustrate the unity of all people, and it is important never to discriminate based on a particular Varṇa.[86]

This perspective aligns with the internalized Varṇa definition given by Śrī Pada Śrī Vallabha (1320-51).

Whatever form the present-day Ravi Dās movement takes, it has been a strong force of social emancipation through all sociopolitical churning that has been happening right from the Mughal occupation, through the British colonialism, to mildly Hindu-phobic Nehruvianism, and the constant shape-shifting forms of Christian evangelical attempts.

Satnāmī Sampradāya

Of particular importance here is the Satnāmī movement. The first historical mention of Satnāmīs comes in the hagiographical account of the reign of Mughal ruler Aurangzeb, which was between 1658 and 1707 CE. *Maāsir-i-Ālamgiri* written by Sāqi Mustad Khan mentions a fierce Satnāmī rebellion against the Mughal forces and a massacre of these people. It happened in 1672 CE. According to Sāqi Khan, the Satnāmīs were 'a rebellious horde of low people like goldsmiths, carpenters, scavengers, tanners, and members of other menial professions, who are naturally weak and foredoomed to slaughter'.[87] Here Marxist Historian of Medieval India Irfan Habib, who also is sympathetic to Islamist politics, states that 'the goldsmiths could hardly have been placed among the status-less or menial castes as to be classified with carpenters, sweepers and tanners' and explains this away as a misreading. Though the text reads zargar (goldsmith), it was a wrong omission of a dot and should have been barzgar, cultivators.[88] However, there is a Hindu Purāṇic linking both carpenters and goldsmiths as descendants of the Viswakarma. The description of Sāqi Khan further speaks of the fierce battling nature of Satnāmīs as inspired by the war scenes of Mahabharata.[89] Despite having no arms or ammunition, they gave stiff resistance and killed many Mughal soldiers but were eventually slaughtered. Another description of them was made by a Brahmin, Ishwardas Nagar, who was a loyal official of the Mughal empire and was, for a long time, a Qazi. In his work *Futuhat-i- Ālamgiri*, written in 1731, almost sixty years after the Mughal massacre of Satnāmīs, he mentions that 'if a dog had eaten from their bowl they would not abstain (from eating from the same bowl) or showed (no) revulsion'.[90] This particular behaviour was repulsive to a noble who had internalized Mughal values; nevertheless, it may show a religious value that could have been derived from Bhagavad Gītā, where a truly wise does not differentiate between a learned pious man, dog, dog-eater, cow, and elephant.[91] Actually, all accounts of Satnāmīs who survived the massacre and resurfaced characterize them as religiously abstaining from meat. But the author of *Futuhat-i- Ālamgiri* states that they ate pork. Perhaps the chronicler, who was a Brahmin-turned-Qazi, was trying to please his masters by depicting the rebels as unclean from an Islamist point of view, or the chronicler himself had internalized the Mughal value system.

Conventionally, historians trace the founding of the Satnāmī tradition to Bir Bhan and also to a trinity of Jōgi (Yōgi) Dās, Udai Dās, and Bīr Bhan. Of these Jōgi (Yōgi) Dās and Udai Dās are considered by some scholars as one and the same. In the Guru-Śiṣya lineage, Bīr Bhan was the disciple of Udai Dās, who in turn was the disciple of Ravi Das. Generally, it is held that Bir Bhan founded the tradition in 1657 CE in Narnaul of Eastern Punjab. A contemporary historian Abu'l Fazl Ma'muri provided a description of Satnāmīs:

> There is a group of Hindu mendicants, known as *Satnāmi* who (are) alaso called Muṇdiyas.... Although these Muṇdiyās dress like mendicants yet their livelihood and profession is usually agriculture and trade in the manner of small merchants with small capital. Living according to the ways of their own community they aspire to reach the status of a good name (nek-nām) which is the meaning of the word *Satnām*. But if anyone should want to impose tyranny and oppression upon them as a display of courage and authority, they will not tolerate it; and most of them bear arms and weapons.[92]

In 1818, a Christian missionary named Henry Fisher heard an account from Jai Singh Sadh, a Satnami from a Punjabi village, about Jōgi (Yōgi) Dās, who was considered one of the founders or a proto-Guru of the sect. According to the account, Jōgi Dās, the son of Gopal Singh of Bindair, lived around 160 years prior (around 1658 CE). He was a commander in an army and was severely injured in a battle and left for dead. However, a mendicant who came to the scene revived him:

> The stranger led him away to the solitudes of a distant mountain and there detained him in the diligent study of those sacred truths which it was intended he should disseminate among the people. As soon as he was adjudged sufficiently qualified for the labours of his mission, the mendicant stranger returned him to his friends, with a commission to inculcate the doctrine which he had received.... He chose Bheer Bhan (Birbhan) to attend him on a circuit, which he began to make in order to propagate his new opinions.... Jogee Das continued to propagate his tenets for twelve years.[93]

According to historian Jadu Nath Sarkar, the nearest historical approximation he could get to this account of Jōgi (Yōgi) Dās was 'the Raja of Dholpur at the time is Maha Singh, Raja of Bhadawar (a place some miles east of Dholpur), who was a trusted general under Dara Shukoh and fought in the battle of Samugarh in 1659.'[94] One can surmise that from an NDE and the transformative spiritual experience of a military official, the movement was born. According to Sarkar, the Sādhs, who emerged in the later century after the extermination of rebellious Satnami and called themselves Satnāmis, belonged to the same Sampradāya, and they had evolved quite a strong institutional network for themselves.[95]

In the early 1890s, Prithi Lāl, a Sādh, was baptized into Christianity at Farrukhabad. The missionaries made him an informer about his community and obtained from him a version of how Sādh/Satnāmīs view their own Sampradāya and its founder. This document was obtained in 1894 by a missionary, Dr H.D. Griswold, and was translated only in 1922 under his supervision with the help of four different Hindi pandits. According to this account, Udai Dās guided two brothers, who were worshippers of Saligram, to spiritual awakening. He transformed the brothers, Bīr Bhan and Jōgi (Yōgi) Dās, to become like Rama and Lakshman. Additionally, he renamed Bīr Bhan's wife as Sīta. Udai Dās later travelled to Delhi, where he helped many people convert to the Sadh Sampradaya. Finally, this resulted in a confrontation with the Mughal emperor Aurangzeb, who killed Udai Dās with an arrow.[96] The period subsequent to the tragic encounter with the Mughals saw the emergence of Guru Ghāsidās (1756-1850) revitalize the order. According to many traditions, he was initiated by Guru Jagjīvandās (1669-1760), who was a wandering mendicant Satnāmī. Ghāsidās met Udai Dās during the pilgrimage to Pūri.

Jagjīvandās was born into a Rajput/Thakur family soon after the Mughal massacre of Satnāmīs. Tradition has it that while grazing the cattle one day, he met a most holy faqir, Bulle Shah, in company with a still more holy man, Govind Sahib.[97] They later revealed to him that they had come to initiate him and make him a spiritual master.

The presence of Bullhe Shah (1680–1757) in this narrative is quite important. Bulle Shah was a mystic poet whose mystical-poetic universe was infused with the following vital Hindu elements: *Trikuti* and *Anāhad Sabdh* from *Nād Yogis* as well as Vaiṣṇava Vēdāntic Bhakti. Islamic scholar N. Hanif, in his authoritative biographical encyclopaedia of the Sufis of South Asia, explains:

> He accepted the Vaishnava idea of the Grace of God.... According to Ijadist Sufism, the scope of God's Grace is limited in its sphere. It begins after the man has won over the nafs and is no more a defaulter in the observance of the religious obligatories at any stage. But the Vaishnava Vedantic pantheist's notion of God's Grace is much wider. He believes that God showers His Grace not only on the noble and those who have won over the nafs but even on the sinful.... Thus, under the Vaishnava impact Bulhe Shah emerged as much more clear in the quandary of justice and grace than any other Panjabi Sufi poet.[98]

He had been excommunicated by the religious establishment as Kafir. Fortunately, his creative period and his geography of work coincided, respectively, with a period and province where Mughal power had declined, and Sikh power had become stronger. He had met the tenth Guru of Sikhs, Guru Gobind Singh and had, with pain, heard 'the atrocious deeds of Muslims in decapitating Hindu saints'.[99] His association with the main Guru Jagjīvandās related to the Satnāmī revival is thus an important linkage. Jagjīvandās became a Satnāmī guru and lived mostly in jungles. It is also said he was a Rāmānandi. After the divine encounter Ghāsidās had, he revived the Satnāmī tradition in his community. He forbade meat consumption and emphasized a great veneration for the cow so much so that they should not be used for ploughing, and generally, after mid-day in the hot sun, there should be no ploughing. There should be only the veneration and worship of Satnam. The guru position passed from father to son, and among the Satnāmīs, there was no caste distinction. Even in 1890, it had been recorded that the Satnāmī Guru made the conventional travel (*Dig-Vijaya*) 'in great state, with elephants, camels and a large retinue'. By 1901, though the Satnāmīs were predominantly Chamars, one of the Scheduled Castes communities to which Ghāsidās belonged, there were 2000 Satnāmīs belonging to all communities.[100]

The consolidation of colonial power in India, along with widespread famines catalysed by increased colonial connectivity and changes in land ownership, etc., created a lot of strife between the landed caste communities and agricultural labouring communities, most of whom were Satnāmī. The landed 'upper' castes tried to subvert the equal status that Satnāmīs Sampradāya provided the labourers who were more and more getting divested of their small land holdings and were increasingly economically exploited. This erupted in the form of opposition to the Satnāmī tradition of wearing the *Yajñopavīta*. The son of Ghasi Das and the next Guru, Guru Bālak Dās (1809-1850) defied this sectarian appropriation of the sacred thread.

He was mortally attacked by the 'upper castes' for this. But he succeeded in making *Yajñopavīta* a part of Satnāmī initiation.

Meanwhile, the missionaries tried to convince targeted sections of *Sādhs/Satnāmīs* that the Satnām was the name of Jesus, and they held that Satnāmīs were somehow a lost, isolated community of Christians. Christian missionaries and mission scholars made repeated studies of the Satnāmī community. They tried to pass the translated Christian Bible as the sacred book of Sādhs. When this attempt was made in a Sādh temple by missionaries and a few converted implants, a local Sādh preacher exposed the missionary deception and pointed out that it was the book of the 'Sahebs'. Further, the strong taboo Sādhs had against beef eating made them resistant to conversions.[101] Such fraudulent evangelical attempts and aggressive proselytization of Sādhs were also one of the reasons that fed into the uprising of 1857 CE.[102]

A fanatical Christian missionary, Oscar Lohr of the German Evangelical Mission Society, came to Central India determined to convert Satnāmīs. In this, he was highly aided by Colonel Balmain. Balmain, who was on 'a civilizing mission', did not only facilitate the missionary acquiring land but also placed the British colonial machinery in the service of evangelism. Col Balmain was notorious for his attempts to forfeit the properties of influential Indian leaders whom he suspected of supporting the 1857 uprising and sentencing them to rigorous imprisonment or exiles, which even the higher British authorities often found unjustified.[103] Lohr was also running a school at Raipur for in which there were thirty-five students.

Lohr went to the headquarters of Satnām Panth on the most sacred day of their festivities, Satnāmī Guru Puja. It was celebrated on the occasion of Dusshera or *Vijaya Dasami*. He rudely disrupted their festivities and preached Christianity while claiming that without accepting Christ, they had no right to call themselves Satnāmīs. Contrasting this Christian arrogance, Satnāmīs reciprocated with typical Hindu kindness and tolerance. They offered him refreshments. A gentle stroking of his beard by a Satnāmī elder was taken as a sign of their acceptance. The next day, he also continued his evangelical crusade. In 1868, a thousand Satnāmīs were made to attend the Christmas function celebrated by the missionary in which many colonial officials also participated. The next Sunday, it was announced that three Satnāmīs would get baptized. At this point, Lohr wanted them to remove their *Yajñopavīta*. The Satnāmīs got agitated. The students in the missionary school also protested and they returned only after Lohr assured them that there would be no forced conversion. Anthropologist Saurabh Dube writes:

> The missionary command to the Satnami converts to remove the janeu before baptism, on the other hand, challenged a principle of faith within Satnampanth. The initial millenarian hopes of Lohr were dashed. The Satnamis became wary of the missionary enterprise.[104]

But 1868–69 was a period of famine. This led to a successful harvest for the mission enterprise. However, most Satnāmīs who had converted during these difficult years as a survival strategy in a time of need and misery eventually returned to 'the fold of their religion'.[105]

In 1870, apart from receiving the land papers for his mission, he also purchased an entire village called Ganeshpur and became the 'malguzar' of two villages. This meant that he had proprietary rights over the distribution and use of land within them, as well as the responsibility to determine and collect taxes.[106] Balmain, who had previously been involved in confiscating the properties of well-known Hindu leaders, informed Lohr that a large area of government wasteland, totalling 1544 acres, was going to be auctioned off to the public. Balmain then ensured that the missionary was able to acquire the land with financial support from himself and other British officials.[107] The missionaries used a variety of strategies, but they were not successful in getting baptisms. Pro-missionary scholar Chad M. Bauman has acknowledged that the missionaries attempted to establish a Christian-Satnami connection as a 'marketing strategy'. This approach only worked to a certain extent; it helped in getting Satnāmīs to listen to the stories of Jesus, etc. However, when it came to baptism, the Satnāmīs were not receptive. This was the case even in 1935. Bauman writes,

> There is no question that Lohr and others – for the same confusion would later plague the Disciples of Christ missionaries – understood Christianity to be a religious tradition entirely distinct from Hinduism. Yet they tried strenuously to forge connections with Satnami and Hindu modes of thought. They understood these adaptations as superficial adjustments, mere marketing strategies. But the adaptations were effective to the extent that, at least at first, Satnamis understood Christianity to be a panth, a school of thought or way of spiritual praxis that could be investigated and explored without compromising their connection to the Satnami community.... Missionary reports, letters, and books are saturated with stories about Satnamis who liked to listen to missionaries, attended church, read the Bible, and spoke lovingly of Christ but yet who displayed no interest in baptism.[108]

Satnāmī Spirituality beyond Evangelical and Marxist Frameworks

Marxist historian Irfan Habib repeatedly emphasizes the monotheist nature of the sect. This may be because of the deep theo-colonial coda of Marxism, in which monotheism is a superior development. Habib's monotheistic emphasis could also be partly because of his unconscious (or consciously covet) religious bias. However, a look into the religious literature of the movement finds that they define their spiritual universe in strong Purāṇic cosmological terms, and ontologically, it is more aligned with Hindu Bhakti. The rejection of all textual authority for the authority of guru and Bhakti is typical of Hindu devotional tradition.

In the Satnāmī worldview, in Satya Yuga, the twin Divine principles of Govind and Paramēshwar emanated from Mahādeo and Shakti-Pārvati. In Dwāpar Yuga they were succeeded by Rāmā and Lakshmana. In Trētā Yuga, they were succeeded by Kṛṣṇa and Balarāma. In Kali Yuga, they were succeeded by Jōgi (Yōgi) Dās and Bīr Bhan.[109]

The sacred book of the Satnāmī tradition is 'Nirvaṇa Gyān'. The book was a closely guarded sacred text of the Sampradāya. It was through almost a decade of acquaintance and fellowship with the Sādhs that Gwalior-based American Presbyterian missionary W.L. Allison got access to the reading of the text. He wrote,

> There are 247 pages in this book, sixteen lines of handwritten Hindi poetry on each page. It contains a total of 4,200 lines, most of which are couplets, while the others are quatrains. Its 33,000 words make a book about equal in length to the first two Gospels.[110]

Laxmi Narayan Sādh, a spiritual leader of the Satnāmī commune, recited and explained. With the help of Hindi Professor Badri Narayan of Gwalior, the missionary was able to make translations of some verses. The verses contain a list of devotees both from recent history and of the Purāṇic past: Mīrābāi, Prahalād, Lakshmaṇ, and Jōgi (Yōgi) Dās and Bīr Bhan. 'They sent the cup of poison to Mīrābāi; She drank, knowing [its contents]'; 'Prahalād depended upon Truth for his support, And thus he escaped from the fire.'; In an interesting formation-narrative of the Sampradāya, they were those who refused to take meat when one Brahmin asked others to take meat after he had tasted it. Those who refused to eat goat became Sadh/ Satnāmi. 'The Truth is Yoga itself.' Though 'Nirvaṇa Gyān' speaks of Allah as the only existence, it rejects the prophet of Islam: 'Although God created Muhammad yet, Muhammad did not experience the vision.'

According to Allison, this gels with the worldview of Sādh/ Satnāmī, as according to him, Sādhs did 'not look upon Muhammad as an incarnation, nor as occupying the position of the True Teacher'.[111] One of the Sādh writings shows that the masters of the Sampradāya were aware of Jesus and even Mary. But they categorically rejected the Christian-Islamic theological stream:

> By the power of devotion, Lakshman escaped from weapons, Parhalad escaped from the fire, Mira Bai escaped from the poison, but Mahatma Yisu (Jesus) did not escape from the cross... Mary, Jesus and Mohammed were all ordinary people.... The Vedas, Puranas, Quran and the Gospel are words of men; the true secret of devotion came from the True Guru.[112]

The above verse quoted by Allison shows two important aspects: the primary importance given to Bhakti and not to scriptural text. Even if the instances of Bhakti come from the sacred text, the text itself could have man-made elements and could be subjected to interpretations that are human constructs. But Bhakti was paramount and could elevate itself to planes of consciousness untouched by human biases and prejudices as well as likes and dislikes. So, the miraculous elements of Jesus' life gets dismissed too because they are more out of God-commanded supernatural events than the result of Bhakti. This is a very nuanced but powerful original Hindu perception in the encounter of these two religions of non-Hindu family religions.

The colonial characterization of the Bhakti-based Samprādayas and/or Panths is that they are 'reform' movements in a Lutheran sense, as moving towards a Protestant or Islam-like monotheistic anti-idol worshipping religion, who often 'relapse into Hindu superstitions like idol worship', etc. But this misses the core Hindu spiritual context of the emergence and functioning of the Bhakti-based Samprādayas. While Kabīr may stress the importance of the all-pervading nir-guṇa Brahman aspect of the divine to be achieved through the Bhakti of anchoring to the Nāmā or the sacred Name of the divine, they did not launch a campaign against the worship of sacred sculptural form or idol. This allows the Sampradayas to navigate easily between the nir-guṇa and sa-guṇa aspects of the divine. Bhakti becomes the bridge in the socio-cultural context of accessing the larger cultural circles in which the particular Bhakti Sampradāya or Panth is embedded.

In the instance of Satnāmīs, this can be clearly seen in the following description given by colonial scholar Geo. W. Briggs, in his work on Chamārs:

> Jagjiwan Das preached the worship of God under the name 'Sat Nam' and taught that the Deity is both cause and creator of all things, but conceived of him in popular Vedantic terms. His followers prohibit the use of meat, red dal (masur ki dal), egg-plant, and intoxicating liquors. Satnamis do not worship idols; but they do worship Hanuman, and pay reverence to what they consider manifestations of the nature of God visible in avatars, particularly in Rama and in Krishna. They observe most of the Hindu festivals, and honour the family and caste customs of the members of their sect.[113]

However, the missionary observers saw with irritation how, despite their evangelical efforts backed by the might of the British Empire in particular, the Satnāmīs 'reverted to popular Hinduism'. Bauman quotes the following part of a report sent by a missionary William Baur which was sent from a Satnāmī Mela of 1930:

> Finally I discovered one well-fed Brahmin walking about with a Satnami Mahant. This Mahant was boasting about the fact that the Satnamis were really Hindus. And the Hindu brother was smirking and smiling and seemed to be happy that the Satnamis were so well Hinduized again. The Mahant did not realize how true his words were. For Satnamiism has again reverted to popular Hinduism and Hinduism has once more demonstrated its power to neutralize and absorb anything like a reform which starts from within.[114]

Both Sanskritization and 'reverting' or 'reabsorbed' perception of such so-called 'Hinduising' miss the deeper spiritual-cultural continuities the Bhakti Sampradāyas have with the rest of the pan-Hindu organism to which they belong.

Social Emancipation through Reconnecting to the Roots

During the Indian freedom movement, the famous Hindu social reformer from the Scheduled Castes community Ganesh A Gawai (1888–1973) was instrumental in forming the Akhil Bhāratiya Satnāmī Mahāsabha. In this, he was greatly assisted by Gandhian freedom fighter and social reformer Pt Sunderlal Sharma. Gawai, one of the much-forgotten social emancipation leaders, was in alliance with Veer Savarkar and Dr Balakrishna Shivram Moonje of Hindu Mahāsabha. The freedom movement period also saw Saint Bābā Rāmchandra (1864–1950) take the cause of Satnāmī Sampradāya. A Maharashtrian saint, he had emerged as an important organizer of landless agricultural labourer communities and launched political agitations for their economic rights and against their exploitation. He was equally concerned about the spiritual strength of the communities and reinforcing them for social emancipation. He was instrumental in consolidating the Satnāmī sacred literature for the challenges they were facing under colonial rule, particularly aligning their rights with the national movement for liberation. In a way, the Bābā Rāmchandra was only dipping into an entirely different context which makes him very much an insider in a cultural ecosystem: 'Baba Ramchandra was very much part of that Ramanandi, Vaishnava ethos, a fact that contributed substantially to his immediate and positive reception by landless and land poor peasants in the countryside.'[115]

Even in post-independent India, the Satnāmīs still face aggressive proselytizing with the same dubious methods. In the 'Report of The Christian Missionary Activities Enquiry Committee' of 1956, there were many instances of missionaries using the impoverished conditions and health traumas of the Satnamis for conversion to Christianity. The report observed,

> Mahant Nayandas, M.L.A., and Secretary, Akhil Bharatiya Satnami Sabha (Raipur, No. 23), stated from his personal knowledge how pressure was brought to bear on the patients in hospitals to get converted to Christianity. He cited an instance of one Kejha of Modpa, Bilaspur district, who was an in-door patient at Mungeli. He was asked to become a Christian, if he wanted to be cured. Similarly, Bodhan Satnami of Dhawra Bata, an in-door patient of Bilaspur Hospital, was pressed to become a Christian and was actually converted. One year after he was out of the hospital, he approached Mahant Nayandas to take him back into his own Satnami fold and he was reconverted.[116]

The fictitious story of Christianity being the true 'Satnāmī' religion was also used. The report stated,

> A pamphlet published at Raipur entitled 'Satyanami Panth' contained a veiled suggestion that the first Guru of Satnamis, viz., Ghasidas, had derived his inspiration to preach Satnam from a Christian preacher. As Ghasidas died in 1850 at the age of 80 (page 100, C. P. Gazetteer, 1870), it is very unlikely that he could have come in contact with the Missionaries.[117]

A local lawmaker from the Satnāmī community also produced a Christian pamphlet that claimed that one of the famous 19th-century Satnāmī spiritual leaders was a Christian and his preachings were indeed Christian religion.[118] The resistance to proselytization displayed by this relatively small sampradaya was against all odds. Despite the impoverished conditions of the community, which is the cumulative effect of the four centuries of battle against the Mughal empire, the ill effects of social stagnation as well as the allurement offered by the diverse activities of British missionaries with the support of the British Empire, the community has stuck to its Dharmic tradition. However, the current sociopolitical narrative of the 'caste-Hindu' versus 'tribal/Dalit-as-non-Hindu' coupled with the amplification of social malaise of institutionalized untouchability under the British, which continues into post-independent India, maybe finally severing the Dharmic ties of the community with the larger Hindu body.

Anti-Sanyāsin Stereotypes Mainly against Rāmānandi, Dasnāmi, and Derived Sampradāyas

The Sanyāsins, in general, were under growing doubt by the colonial Empire that was consolidating itself in India. Major-general William Henry Sleeman (1788-1856), who ran a dreadful manhunt against the so-called 'thuggery'wrote contemptuously of the all-caste nature of the monk's orders in India. In the pilgrim routes crisscrossing India, apart from lay pilgrims, he noted most of the pilgrims he met were 'of the two monastic orders of Gosains, or the followers of Śiva, and Bairagis, or followers of Vishṇu, and Muhammadan Fakirs'. He also observes the strategic importance of such an informal network:

> *A Hindoo of any caste may become a member of these monastic orders.* They are all disciples of the high priests of the temples of their respective gods; and in their name they wander over

> all India, visiting the celebrated temples which are dedicated to them. A part of the revenues of these temples is devoted to subsisting these disciples as they pass; and every one of them claims the right of a day's food and lodging, or more, according to the rules of the temple. They make collections along the roads; and when they return, commonly bring back some surplus as an offering to their apostle, the high priest who has adopted them. *Almost every high priest has a good many such disciples, as they are not costly; and from their returning occasionally, and from the disciples of others passing, these high priests learn everything of importance that is going on over India, and are well acquainted with the state of feeling and opinion.*[119] (emphases added)

The criminal nature that Sleeman ascribed to 'three-fourths of these religious mendicants' was greatly more out of prejudice and bias than from empirical data. He states that they did 'rob and steal, and a very great portion of them murder their victims before they rob them' and yet 'not any of them as a class been found to follow the trade of murder so exclusively as to be brought properly within the scope of our operations'. Then he also relates to an operation in 1833 in Rajasthan in which 'several gangs of Hindoo mendicants who had been guilty of the most atrocious crimes' were arrested 'but in despair of being able to convict them before any of our courts of any specific murder or to bring them legitimately under our jurisdiction' they were 'ultimately obliged to release the whole, though satisfied that they were in reality murderers and robbers'. In other words, they had more prejudice and aversion than solid evidence against the mendicants. However, this arrest was used to justify custodial arrests of 'in different parts of India many gangs of these mendicants under different denominations who were evidently robbers, and who frequently murdered their victims' and so on. Sleeman concluded that 'almost all such mendicants' who would do 'any species of crime throughout India' 'were really men in disguise, for Hindoos of any cast can become Byragees and Goosaens' and so on.[120]

Such colonial hate-filled 'anti-Hindoo' stereotypes should be taken into consideration in what would also emerge as strictures against all caste Hindus becoming Sadhus, a defining feature particularly in Rāmānandi tradition. As late as the 19th century, the Rāmānandi tradition ran into trouble again. Rājā Rām Singh II (1833-1880) of Jaipur, who ruled under the British, came in the lineage of the famous ruler Jai Singh II (1688-1743). Jai Singh II had used the weakened Mughal empire after the death of Aurangzeb, to wrestle considerably his own autonomy and assert his Hindu identity. He used his newfound assertiveness to make the Mughals remove the hated *Jizya*, the discriminatory and humiliating tax imposed on non-Muslims and the pilgrimage taxes imposed on Hindus and performed the Vedic Aswamēdha Yajña, which, in a way, served as a statement of Hindu political sovereignty. His spiritual preceptors came from Nimbārka Sampradāya of Vaiṣṇava Bhakti Vēdāntā. He tried to regulate the functioning of Rāmānandis. Despite the pro-birth-based-Varṇa stratification stand of the king, not much had changed with respect to Rāmānandis, who mostly ignored such strictures. In 1864, seven years after the 1857 uprising, Rājā Rām Singh II became pro-British and considered a reformist, convened a Dharma Sabha. A major accusation against the Vaiṣṇava Sampradāya was that they 'allowed Śūdras to join the sampradāya and to perform tasks intended for Brahmans.'[121]

So, one can say that throughout the history of their sampradāya, the Rāmānandis mostly kept their spiritually energized and social emancipation intact against all odds of monopolistic invasions, subsequent persecutions, economic exploitations, and also the intimidations arising from social stagnation.

All these movements, through the spiritual realization of one guru, affected the social emancipation of an entire community in the Hindu social ecosystem formed by the networks of communities. This spiritual movement outwardly used Jāthi to destroy the oppressive elements of the Jāthi-based social system. In this, they also used the Varṇa system in a nuanced manner. While Jāthi is birth-based, Jāthi-based Varṇa created a seemingly concrete system of what Dr Ambedkar calls 'graded inequality'. Here, the Rāmānandi movement and most of the Panths that emanated from it anchored themselves in the spiritual realization of the divine essence in whatever form (personal or impersonal), in the divine form or formless, and subtly rekindled the Brahmin hood of non-birth-based idealistic worth-based Varṇa system. Most miracle-filled biographies of the founders of the panths are, in a way, restating the ideal Brahmin as one who realizes the divine oneness of all existence, and before that, the birth-based religious authority bows down. In a social corollary, the Panths could form martial sanctuaries and, using the political turmoil and opportunities, climb the social ladder while securing for themselves Kṣatriya-hood. The social emancipation process was sustained and powerful, with Bhakti culture and tradition at its core. This, in turn, allowed individuals to realize their true selves and become the epicentre of social emancipation, mostly avoiding the human misery created by 'secular' sociopolitical revolutions.

CHAPTER 12

Dharmic Social Emancipation from 19th Century to the Present

India's journey over the past two centuries has been a tale of two epochs. The first, a colonial era that began in the 19th century, was followed by a period of post-colonial modernity that has spanned the seventy-five years since India's independence. Throughout this time, Hindu spirituality and the dharmic framework have dynamically shaped the social emancipation movement. However, due to the pervasive colonial narrative that persists even in post-colonial historiography, this significant contribution has been overshadowed. Furthermore, Hindu spirituality and the dharmic framework have often been unjustly stereotyped as being opposed to social emancipation. This chapter aims to continue the legacy of '*Periya Purāṇam*' and '*Śrī Mahā Bhakta Vijayam*', shedding light on both the major and lesser-known yet regionally significant contributors to social emancipation. It is a testimony to the enduring power of spirituality and dharma in shaping society, even in the face of adversity.

Iyyā Vazhithe Path of Iyyā

In the middle of the 19th century, just before the 1857 uprising, the princely state of Thiruvithāṅcūr (Travancore) in southern India was in chaos. At the close of the 18th century, Tipu Sultan of Mysore invaded Malabar and Thiruvithāṅcūr kingdoms twice between December 1789 and May 1790 CE. In the first attempt, Tipu Sultan was defeated. During the second invasion, the then king of Thiruvithāṅcūr, Kārthika Thirunāḷ Rāma Varmā, sought assistance from the East India Company (EIC), which had gotten a foothold in both Bengal and Madras. This allowed the EIC to get strong control of the militarily weakened Thiruvithāṅcūr by making the state enter into a 'subsidiary treaty' of 1795 CE[1] and soon become its de facto ruler while the Thiruvithāṅcūr dynasty became the proxy ruler. Within decades, crucial changes were made in administration, particularly taxation.

The British Regent compelled the Thiruvithāṅcūr government to pay the British Rs 800,000 annually as a protectorate. This resulted in the Thiruvithāṅcūr government levying new taxes. In 1807 CE alone, Rs 18,523 was collected as palm tree tax. Communities like Ēzhavās, Chānnars, Cherumārs, Sāmbavās, and Pulayās, which were already disadvantaged politically and economically, had to pay individual head tax for individuals between the ages of 16 and 60. Under this tax, Rs 163,000 was collected annually. The Nāiars, Veḷḷāḷas, Muslims, and Kanmalas communities were exempted from paying these taxes.[2] Incidentally, this discriminatory taxation with respect to communities had nothing to do with Varṇa or even the *Dharmaśāstra* injunctions. In a strict conventional pre-modern birth-based Varṇa categorization, the Chānnars should be considered Kṣatriyas and Veḷḷāḷas were Śūdras. Nāiars were an important martial community and a strong supporting pillar of Thiruvithāṅcūr. However, the Chānnars considered Nāiars derisively as Śūdras claiming for themselves Kṣatriya status. In many literatures of the time, to insult or provoke Nāiars, they were called Śūdras. This proves how political changes rather than the dictates of *Dharmaśāstra* largely decided the social ranking during that time.

EIC started pressing the princely state for vast amounts of money, which led to the famous Vēlu Thampi Daḷawāi's (1769-1805) uprisal:

> The burden of land revenue was heavier on the lower sections of the peasantry owing to inequality in assessment and the disparity between the market prices and Government rates. The tribals like Kurichiyas and Kurumbas also lost their small land holdings on account of their participation in the Pazhassi's revolt, because most of the properties of the rebels were confiscated by the British government. The action of British is the violation of the right to property and hence it is a kind of human rights violation that took place in Kēraḷa. Vēlu Thampi Dalawa also took up arms against the British rule and his famous Kundara proclamation had called out clearly about the human rights violations caused by the colonial British. He came to Kundara on January 11, 1809 and made a stirring call to the people in order to get their whole-hearted support. This proclamation is an epoch-making document in the anti-colonial struggle in South India.[3]

In his famous *Kuṇṭara* proclamation made on 11 January 1809, Vēlu Thampi stated how the social system was thrown into chaos by economic depredation unleashed by EIC while at the same time how the colonial-evangelical system was making full use of the chaos and social stagnation:

> It is the nature of the English nation to get possession of countries by treacherous means and should they obtain ascendancy in Tiruvitamkur, they will put their own guards in the places, sircar buildings and the fort gates, destroy the royal seal, do away with horofic Palanguin and other distinguishing marks; suppress the Brahmanical communities and worship in Pagodas, make monopolies of salt and every other thing, measure up and make themselves the absolute owners of waste lands, impose exorbitant taxes on paddy lands, coconut tress etc., get low caste people inflict heavy punishments for slight

> faults, put up crosses and Christian flags on Pagodas, compel inter-marriages with Brahman women without reference to caste or creed, and practice all the unjust and unlawful things which characterise *Kaliyuga*.[4]

But Vēlu Thampi's rebellion was short-lived and crushed by EIC. What is important in the proclamation is how Thampi saw a connection between the heavy taxes and the social unrest in the state.

The colonial economic draining of the princely state had a cascading effect on the society, leading to a range of responses from violence to cultural abuse and subjugation of vulnerable sections. This, in turn, made the vulnerable sections hostile to the princely state and the religion it professed, i.e., Hinduism and made them gravitate towards Christianity. This, in turn, was subtly and sometimes explicitly encouraged by the officials of EIC. Around 1815 CE, then Thiruvithāñcūr regent Col Manroe reduced the market price of food grains without proportionately lowering the taxes for paddy producers, particularly affecting the agricultural class, mainly the Veḷḷāḷas. Additionally, the inter-community feud between Chānnars and Nāiars regarding Kṣatriya status, in which the Nāiars were favoured and Chānnars being imposed with humiliating disabilities by the Thiruvithāñcūr princely state, played well into the hands of EIC and the evangelical missionaries. This created fertile ground for rapid conversion to Christianity among the Chānnar community.

It was at this point that in the Chānnar community, a child was born and named Muṭi chūṭum Perumāḷ, which means 'Mahā Viṣṇu who shall wear the crown'. However, the royal officers promptly ordered that the community should not have such names indicating royalty, so the child was renamed 'Muthu Kuṭṭi', which means endearing pearl. The child grew up and as a youth he had a life-changing vision after a brief illness. He declared himself as an *avatār* of Mahā Viṣṇu. He was venerated with the name 'Iyyā Vaikuṇṭar', meaning Venerable Lord of Vaikuṇṭa. The movement he started, called 'Iyyā Vazhi' became a radical movement, gathering people from all jāthis. His mystic outpourings were collected into a comprehensive sacred text called '*Ahila Thiraṭu Ammānai*', which contains perhaps the most penetrating critique of colonialism, proselytization, and social stagnation. The entire critique is couched in Purāṇic language.[5]

The narrative establishes continuity in the Asūric villainous elements *in* every *Yuga* from Rāvaṇa to Sūra Padman—the Asuric Egoistic element in *Skanda Purāṇa*. The social stagnation and the collaboration that the Thiruvithāṅcūr royal state had with the EIC became the Kali-Nēcha (asūric low-natured Kali), and the British EIC became the Veṇ- Nēcha (asūric low-natured white ones). *Ahila Thiraṭu Ammānai* explains how the Chānnar became the special target of tax collectors who used the most violent methods to extract the taxes. It also states the highly noble nature of these people; instead of asking them to rise violently, it asks them to organize themselves and, through non-violent spirituality, overcome their tormentors. Dharma is defined thus in the text: 'Dharma is protecting the powerless and downtrodden as one's own self!'

He asked all, irrespective of the caste, to come together and have *Satsangh* together, then dine together and drink from the same well. This included the communities of 'Chānnars, shepherds, traders, Thulu Bhatta, Shudra, Brahmins, Pariahs, farmers, Kuravar (tribals), Maravar, fishermen, Chakkliyars' and so on. The worship combined devotional singing in congregations with a light lamp held before a mirror signifying the *Ātman* in all people. This is rooted in one of the ancient wisdom traditions of India 'as in a mirror, so within one's self'.[6]

What Iyyā Vaikuṇṭar did was certainly against the social restrictions of Thiruvithāṅcūr at that time. He challenged the rules of caste-related taboos in dining and sharing water resources. The proselytization by British Protestant missionaries, which was facilitated by EIC, posed a challenge to the social hierarchy of Thiruvithāṅcūr of that day. But Vaikuṇṭar considered proselytization destructive to the societal harmony and spiritual heritage of the land. He could see in it an ulterior motive as part of the larger colonial process that had been destroying civilizations:

> Poisonous demonic (Western) low-natured ones who had been destroying the worlds all around, also destroyed the Dharma of the noble *Chānṟōr* and transgressed against them. He destroyed their works of charity.... Turning the communities against each other, he destroyed the boundaries of cordiality of the *Jāthis*.

The mission engaged by Vaikuṇṭar naturally created problems for the missionaries. In many places, there were re-conversions. The criticism of the colonization made by Iyyā Vaikuṇṭar in the Purāṇic language reached the population. Vēlu Thampi, who had once welcomed the British EIC and later went against it, mainly communicated his dissatisfaction with the colonial expansion with communities like Nāiars and landowners. However, the criticism of Iyyā Vaikuṇṭar, being more wholesome and efficiently communicated to more people, alarmed the EIC administration.

In the 1840s, Robert Caldwell (1814–91), a Scottish missionary of the Society for the Propagation of Gospels (SPG), was working in Tirunelveli, which was then mostly under direct EIC control with its administrator (collector). He recorded the following in 1844:

> Mootoocootty and his disciples, originally twelve, the inspired representatives of this deity, profess to foretell all events, to

> avert calamities, and to cure all diseases by giving the sick persons copious draughts of cold water. The person was an apostate Christian, and did his best to induce the people to think of him 'the great power of God.' Heathens flocked to him from every quarter in considerable numbers and some Christians in the neighbourhood, partly from curiosity, were tempted to visit him. When the delusion was at its height, the prophet began to prophesy the overthrow of the Company's government and a golden age of light taxes. This led to the interference of the authorities and the prophet's downfall.[7]

In another report, the alarm that EIC felt with respect to the rapid growth of the movement and its forcing of Thiruvithāṅcūr state to take action against Vaikuṇṭar and his movement is well brought out:

> This impostor's name was Muttukutty. By some clever artifice, he contrived to get himself talked of as a worker of miracles, and, as his fame spread abroad, numbers flocked to him. He announced himself as an incarnation of the god Naraiyanan; forbade idolatry and said that men were to worship only himself. He also sent out disciples, two and two, into Travancore and Tinnevelly, to proclaim his miraculous powers and set up his worship in such villages as were disposed to receive them. One of the disciples pretended to be an incarnation of Hanneman, the monkey-kind so celebrated in Hindoo mythology and in a village not far from Courtallam, used to sit up in a tree all day and run about the village in the evening. Persons and parties went in consequence to the chief impostor from many places, prostrated themselves before him ... and I regret to add, that a few individuals among the converts in both Missions, suffering from diseases which they had tried in vain to remove were also tempted to resort to him. Some cures no doubt were performed, as in such cases they have often been:...His fame continued to increase, and.... Growing bold also, by his successes and perhaps believing his own lie, he and his disciples began to teach sedition, declaring that the man was born who would put

> an end to the rule of the East-India Company in India. Reports of these things spreading in Tinnevelly, reached the ears of the Collector; who felt it his duty to inquire into the statements which had been circulated and to ascertain with whom they originated. Having communicated the result of his inquiries to the Travancore government, the Rajah caused Muttukutty to be apprehended and put in confinement; from which time the delusion gradually died away.[8]

Thus, EIC had both economic and evangelical interests in the colonies, which led to punitive action against Vaikuṇṭar. According to *Ahila Thiraṭu Ammānai*, at the court of Thiruvithāṅcūr, the king expressed scepticism about Vaikuṇṭar's divine status, questioning why a supposed incarnation of Viṣṇu was born among the Chānnar community rather than the high castes like Brahmins and Śūdra (i.e., Nāiars). Among the council of advisors to the king, there was a person named Pūvandar who belonged to the cowherd community (and in Thiruvithāṅcūr, they are called '*Kṛṣṇavahai*', i.e., community of Kṛṣṇa). He pointed out to the king that divine incarnations had appeared in various communities in the past, and humans could not decide which community a divine avatar would be born into. The king nevertheless sent his troops (mainly of soldiers of EIC). They beat and humiliate Vaikuṇṭar, including throwing him into a pit of urine and human excreta. However, he remained calm and bore all with serenity. The elites overseeing the persecution eventually caused the death of an onlooking Brahmin, prompting the shocked king to cease the torture. Vaikuṇṭar was released but asked to restrict his activities to his communities.

However, the claims in the reports of both Caldwell and Petit that the movement was somehow reduced in strength and importance seemed to have been falsified. Subsequent reports from the missionaries complain of the movement being a strong impediment to proselytizing. Seven years after the samādhi of Vaikuṇṭar, a missionary report observed this:

> There is a widow living at this place who was a follower of Muthukutti. She was also a fortune-teller and pretended to cure diseases by incantations. She allowed her hair to be matted like that of Pantaram, abstained from fish on Tuesdays and Fridays, performed ablutions in the sea, sang for four or five hours together in honour of her swami and was occasionally under the influence of the devil.[9]

Unwittingly, the report shows how the movement empowered women to assume community leadership roles in the spiritual domain. In 1864, a missionary report called it 'a modern sect greatly in increase'.[10]

When it became evident that Iyyā Vazhi could not be purged as the missionaries desired, they attributed its ability to attract people to alleged Christian elements in it. Samuel Mateer (1835-91) was a zealous British missionary in Thiruvithāñcūr, joyfully and sincerely documented the systematic destruction of Hindu shrines in villages where the proselytization was complete. In 1871, Mateer characterized Iyyā Vazhi as 'a curious phenomenon in the religious history of Travancore' and as 'an absurd medley of Hinduism and Demonolatry, with a slight tinge of Christian element'. Labelling it a 'superstition', he called Vaikuṇṭar 'a poor Palmyra climber who laid claim to be an incarnation of Vishnu'. Then, he acknowledged that 'this singular people display considerable zeal in the defence and propagation of their religion', which he again characterized as being full of 'destructive errors'.[11] A missionary report from 1874 called this spiritual stream 'Muthukuttyism' and saw in it 'a great power of darkness':

> It was in the village comprising this (Thamaraikulam) section that the gospel gained its earliest conquests in South Taravancore. Progress was rapid. Congregation were formed

> and adherents come over in great numbers. In 1821 there were upwards of 1,200 converts in these places. It seemed as if the whole population would soon be brought under the influence of the cross. But a terrible check was given to our operations by the rise of Muthukuttyism. Lastly, a car festival was instituted at Kottayady to which thousands are annually drawn from the towns and villages far and near. This cunning contrivance of Satan has much impeded our progress in these parts and is still a great power of darkness against which we have to wage unceasing war.[12]

So, what is the truth? Is Iyyā Vazhi a separate non-Hindu religion? Or is it part of the Hindu family of spiritual paths which all energize social emancipation? The answer is that Iyyā Vazhi is a socio-spiritual phenomenon that is anchored in Hindu spirituality.

While missionary reports always characterized Vaikuṇṭar as an illiterate impostor and a false prophet, the modern academia, who are in a way conceptual extensions of the evangelical scholars of yester-centuries, reduce Vaikuṇṭar as a phenomenon that should be reduced to the result of the socio-economic conditions of the middle of 18th century—at best a rebellion clothed in religious terms. What is ignored here is that the Vaikuṇṭar phenomenon always manifested with a spiritual core that transcended the socio-economic barriers of the specific time periods. Epigraphist S. Ramachandran and community historian Ganēsan Nādar explain the historical continuity of Hindu spirituality deeply encoded in the Dharma preached and lived by Vaikuṇṭar:

> *Iyyā Vaikuṇṭar* calls his people 'Children of the eye'. This is not simply a call of endearment· but has a *Purāṇic* motif weaved into it. Ancient inscriptions speak of *Chāṇṇārs* as 'Eye-*Chāṇṇārs*'. *Upamanyu Bhakta Vilāsam* calls them as 'Witnessing Clan borne Nobles'· 'Preceptors of (martial) arts' etc. It is this tradition

> that is being recognized and revived by *Iyyā Vaikuṇṭar*'s call of 'Children of the eye'. *Iyyā Vaikuṇṭar* attained *Mahā Samādhi* on 1851 June 3 (Kēraḷa Calendar: Vaikāsi 21 Kollam 1026). During his last days' he was at a village called *Osaraviḷai* where he established a temple similar in its numerical dimensions to the Chidambaram Temple – which was the traditional coronation centre of *Chōzha* kings. Similar to the Lingam of ether or space in *Chidambaram*, *Iyyā Vaikuṇṭar* established a roof with 96 fittings, symbolizing the *Chithākāśa* (space of Consciousness) beyond the 96 principles in *Śaiva Siddhānta. Vaikuṇṭar* proclaimed his Dharma Yuga rule – rule of the righteous eon from this village. He had already condemned proselytizers as being ignorant of *Chithākāśa* concept which pervades all existence. His establishment of this place of worship with such symbolism was a reaffirmation of this truth.[13]

The uprising of 1857 and subsequent changes ensured that the British could not further interfere with the movement. This movement could be considered one of the earliest, entirely Indic deep criticism of colonial operations and their social manipulations. It differentiated Indic social emancipation from the manipulative colonial 'reforms' which superficially appeared to liberate people. Actually, it helped to consolidate colonialism by psychological acceptance of the civilizational superiority of the British. The movement infused the marginalized or disadvantaged communities of South Thiruvithāṅcūr with confidence, coordination, and emancipatory energy.

When one compares the 1809 Kuṇṭara proclamation with the Iyyā Vazhi response to colonialism, one can see how dharmic emancipation stands as holistic and deep compared to a mere political/power response to colonialism (Table 1).

Table 1: Comparing Two Early Responses to the Problems of Colonialism

Colonial Problem	'Kuṇṭara' Proclamation	Iyyā Vazhi
Taxation	High taxation is a problem	High taxation and cruel tax collection from people are a problem
Proselytization	A big threat to culture and society: mentions only Christianity	A huge threat because of the monopolistic nature of Christianity and Islam
Caste related problems	Destruction of caste barriers and imposed intermarriages was a threat	Destruction of caste relations is a problem. Colonial demons (*Veṇ-ṇīsan*) destroyed societies all over the world. Fall of the community is seen in this overall context
Call to people	To raise in armed rebellion: Aimed mainly at landed agriculturists and martial communities of the society	All people, irrespective of caste, unite and organize common spirituality- eat and share water. Resist tyranny with patience, justice and unity

While the '*Kuṇṭara*' proclamation is undoubtedly patriotic and inspiring, it still belonged to the braveheart of a bygone era. In the organic response of Iyyā Vaikuṇṭar, space is created for a holistic sustained response with the involution of democratic forms of resistance to power.

Vaṭalūr Vaḷḷalār Rāmaliṅga Swāmigal

Vaḷḷalār was born Rāmaliṅgam (1823-74) in a traditional Śaivite family. A child prodigy, he had a consistent spiritual yearning, culminating in mystic experiences. Soon, he launched himself into creating a movement that aimed at adapting the ancient social and cultural components to the challenges of the colonial era emerging around him.

He concentrated particularly on alleviating food insecurity caused by frequent famines resulting from the increased control of EIC in southern India. Providing food for the poor and needy from the ever-burning oven became a symbol of dharma for Vaḷḷalār. To this day, the large oven continues to burn to feed the needy at Vaṭalūr, the movement's headquarters. This should be seen in the context of colonial developments and Hindu institutional encounter with the colonial power structure in a disadvantaged manner.

The traditional institutions such as 'Chatrams', which provided food and other services like education to all members of society, were significantly weakened by the British due to centralization. Tanjore king Sarfoji Bhonsle II (1777-32), in a letter to British EIC Regent Benjamin Torin, dated 20 January 1801, requested him to allow the Chatrams to function, detailing the good services they were providing to the people:

> I will now explain to you the nature and extent of the Charities dispense by them (*Chatrams*) – all the travellers from Brahmins to Pariahs inclusive, pilgrims of every descriptions including *Jogues, Jungums, Ateets* and *Byragis* are fed with boiled rice, those who do not choose to eat the boiled rice, receive it unboiled with spices etc. These distributions continue till the middle of the night when a bell is rung and a proclamation made requiring all who have not been fed to appear and take the rice prepared for them.... In each *Chetrum* a teacher to each of the four *Vēdams* is appointed and a schoolmaster and doctors, skilful in the cure of disease, swelling and poison of reptiles; all orphans and of strangers, who may come to the *Chetrum* are placed under the care of the schoolmaster – they are also fed three times a day, and once in four days, they are anointed with oil – they receive medicines when they require it, clothes are given to them and utmost attention paid to them. They are instructed in the science to which they may express preference,

> and after having obtained a competent knowledge of them the expense of their marriage are defrayed.[14]

However, the British colonial administrators were 'under pressure to curtail the expenditures and to abrogate the resources thus freed to revenue of the British state'.[15] Another important consequence of the British takeover was its impact on the inter-community relations and the governing value system of Indian villages.

Mike Davis, in his authoritative work on the creation of colonial famines, which he calls the 'Victorian Holocausts', points out how British colonialism systematically ignored the traditional water management/harvesting systems of India while encouraging railways, which were mainly for the commercial and military interests of the Empire. In the case of Tamil Nadu, a well-knitted traditional irrigation system was in place. Davis quotes Col J. Anderson of Madras Engineers (1878) with regard to the merit and efficiency of the traditional Indian irrigation network created by Hindu rulers of South India:

> In no other part of the world has so much been done by ancient native rulers for the development of the resources of the country. The further south one goes, and the further the old Hindoo polity was removed from the disturbing influence of foreign conquest, the more complete and elaborate was the system of agriculture and irrigation works connected with it.... Every available source of supply was utilised, and works in advance of supply have been executed, for tanks [reservoirs] have been very generally constructed, not only for general rainfall, but for exceptional rainfall.... Irrigation from rivers and channels, or by these and combined, was also carried on.[16]

Such a system involved not only material engineering but also a network of communities to take care of the water bodies.

These village-based community networks were respected so much that they were associated with Dēvēnthra; when they lost their respected role during the colonial times, they were reduced to landless labourers and became reduced in stature. This mainly happened during the colonial times. The dehumanizing of bonds between communities through colonial intervention possibly made a respected and important water-managing community into an untouchable one of landless labourers. This community, which is today fighting to come out of being categorized by the government as a 'Scheduled Castes community', has among its traditional names such as '*Nīr Mūppar*' (Elders of the water) and '*Dēvēnthra Kula Veḷḷāḷar*' (Agriculturists of Dēvēnthra clan).[17] That they became deprived of their traditionally respected place in the deprived state of landless agricultural labourers shows how disastrous colonial interventions were in terms of community relations in India.

Maintenance of irrigation structures was abandoned in the changed agricultural system, where the emphasis was only on revenue collection. This also brought changes in the way land and water were owned. This dealt a blow to the Yajña value system that harmonized the spirit of collective good with individual entrepreneurship:

> Within half a century of the British conquest the village communities were divested of their cohesion and vitality, and they were fragmented into discrete, indeed, antagonistic social groups which had formerly enjoyed an intimate relationship of interdependence. Likewise in the districts of the Madras Deccan, the 'development of private property rights and the dissolution of landowning collectivities ... destroyed the investment capacity of mirasidar assemblies altogether.' British rule, in various ways, emancipated local political chiefs and big men from the obligation to invest in community resources and public institutions such as tank systems. The shortfall was not made

> good by the government's own public works.... British policies, however Smithian in intention, were usually Hobbesian in practice. In the case of Gujarat ... the new property forms freed village caste-elites from *traditional reciprocities* and encouraged them to exploit irrigation resources to their selfish advantage [18]

What Davis states with respect to Gujarat is also very much true for colonial Deccan, particularly for Tamil Nadu. The 'traditional reciprocities' come from the Yajña spirit. This is just one instance of the dehumanizing and abusive transformation of inter-community relations with the abandonment of the Yajña system for a revenue-oriented system.

This consistent destruction of food security and replacement of the educational system with a colonially intended new system would not have escaped the attention of Vaḷḷalār. He also observed how the colonial system encouraged killing animals for food. Non-vegetarian food was nothing new to India. However, now it was becoming a theo-civilizational statement – that non-human life had no worth in itself and eating animal life was not wrong. Particularly, the cow veneration was targeted and projected as a 'Hindoo superstition'.

Vaḷḷalār envisioned what he called '*Ānma Nēya Orumaipāṭu*' (unity based on atman grounded empathy). This emphasized the fraternity of all living beings, including humans and non-human living beings.

The humanitarian foresight of such an institution can be gauged from the fact that in the two years after Vaḷḷalār 'merged with the all-pervading Divine Light', 1877-78 saw one of the worst famines that ever visited humanity in its history. The Madras Famine or Deccan Famine wiped out nearly six to ten million South Indians. The actual contribution of this particular institution during the famine in providing food to the needy and saving the lives of Indians, though not at all documented, could very well be more than a few million.

In 1867, he established a school, 'Sanmārga Bōdhini', where education was given to all, from children to adults. Here, Vaḷḷalār followed the three-language teaching Tamil, Sanskrit, and English. He considered Sanskrit and Tamil to be the mother and father of the Hindu family of languages. Yet he considered the mystic *Śaiva* hymns in *Tamizh* to give the true gnosis that is so shrouded in symbolic secrecy of the Vēdas in a lucid and accessible manner to all seekers. Further, according to him, Sanskrit learners should be extra-cautious of being affected by pride in knowledge, an impediment to realizing the truth. Yet he made it clear that Sanskrit should be learned to understand the spiritual context of the culture. English should be learned for the coming colonial era when one had to earn a worldly living. Thus, it was Vaḷḷalār who first brought in the three-language formula. Further, whether it is the never-idle oven for *An̲n̲a-Dhān̲am* or the education, he did not seek government assistance. Rather, he wanted the community of his *Sanmārga people* to finance them.

Vaḷḷalār, while universal in his approach to all religions, contrasted the difference between Dharmic religious systems and others. He rejected the religious differences within the Dharmic spiritual traditions. He called this conflict-free spiritual goal-oriented universal path as '*Sutha Samarasa Sanmārgam*' (pure, harmonious, all-encompassing divine path). But he clearly distinguished between 'Hindu systems' and 'others'. He said:

> Only in *Hindu Vedāgamas* the two *Siddhis* – *Yēma Siddhi* and Jñāna Siddhi – have been told. Other religions do not speak of these two Siddhis and do not speak of the knowledge of immortality. If a religion is found to speak so then it should be approximation of what have been told in the *Vedāgamas* [*Upadēsa Kur̲ipukaḷ: Vēdāgama Chirrapu, 1872*].[19]

Vaḷḷalār institutionalized a universal, pure-non-dual sādhana of Jōthi worship and harmonized it with the social service movement—particularly food security and national education. But it was his heart-cleaved bhakti towards what he experienced as the only Truth, Cosmic compassion which he, in his 'final teaching' (made a few months before his 'merging with the Jōthi') declared as 'the gain of *Ātman* the *Śivānubhava*' which defined his movement. In the same final interaction, Vaḷḷalār explained the symbolism of the flag that he had designed. The design was based on the consciousness movement through the mystic chord (*Nāṭi*) between the navel and the middle of the eyebrows. He made the representation of this yogic experience the flag of his movement. Perhaps this was the first time in a socio-spiritual movement that the Yogic movement inside the human body was made the symbol of a flag. It was a grand statement uniquely Indic.

This movement is a crucial step in adapting ancient systems to the new challenges of colonialism. The adaptation was not made with the overt intention of reacting to the colonial challenge, but rather, it was a spontaneous spiritual movement that generated the needed response naturally.

Ārya Samāj of Śwāmi Dayānanda Saraswatī

Śwāmi Dayānanda Saraswatī (1824-83) was born Mūl Śaṅkar Tiwāri. With spiritual seeking, he became a wandering mendicant searching for a guru. His own autobiographical notes stop around 1856 CE. According to Lala Lajpat Rai, he witnessed the 1857 uprising during his wandering.[20] But we do know that he witnessed a famine ravaging where he was (Narmada basin) in the year 1860-61, soon after the uprising. Finally, he found his Guru Swāmi Virjānanda, who, though blind from birth, was also a great Sanskrit scholar who had defeated many eminent Sanskrit scholars by mastering *Pāṇini* to refute most other grammatical works with deficiencies. Thus, we have here a call to go back to the roots to appreciate the constructive evolution and unwanted deviations from the source – a defining characteristic of the worldview of his most famous disciple Swāmi Dayānand. Soon, he would preach and debate extensively across India. In 1874, before the proper starting of the movement Ārya Samāj, he established a Pādasāla and announced:

> Purvamimanaa, Vaiaheshik, Nyaya, Patanjali and Vedanta, the ten Upanisads, Manusmriti, Katyayana and Grihasutra will be taught in the pathshala, and later the Vedas and their branches will also be taught; that a grammarian will teach Ashtadhyayi, Dhatupath, Ghanpath, etc. Nighaotu and Nirukata will also be taught and *people of all Varnae (castes) will be admitted.* A paper named *Aryaprakash* will also be published as an organ of the pathshala.[21]

In 1875, Ārya Samāj was founded, and his magnum opus *Satyārtha Prakāsh* was published. In it, he condemned the salt tax fifty-five years before Gāndhi started his campaign defying the British salt tax.[22] The meeting happened in Rajkot, with the members of Prārtanā Sāmaj assisting in organizing. *Dayānantha* mainly toured North India and princely states, winning supporters for his movement, never compromising on his values, despite facing strong condemnation in some places. In Pune (Maharashtra), those who opposed him conducted a procession, parading a donkey, giving it name 'Gardabhanand (donkey) Saraswati'. British police often took a tactical anti-Dayanand stance.[23] During this time, the British had removed the Baroda king on charges of attempting to poison the British Regent, leading to agitations. At that time, Dayanand came to Ahmadabad. There in the meeting, Gatulal, a famous Sathāvathāni (a person capable of a hundred cognitions simultaneously) came and composed instant poetry. In that poetry, he criticized the

British for their action with respect to the king of Baroda. The British government took action on all those who conducted the meeting, most of them being Ārya Samāj office bearers, which greatly affected the newly launched movement.[24] Nevertheless, the movement grew rapidly through the almost cyclonic travels and lectures of *Dayānantha*. In 1877, a magazine from Lahore had this to say about him:

> His views are more advanced even than those of the English educated people. We expect great progress and reform by his teachings. He desires not only religious reforms but wants social reforms and removal of such evils as child marriage and the caste system. He wishes that women should become free and educated. He says that until the women are educated and become free from the. bonds of the Purdah, it is useless to hope for any perceptible progress in the country.[25]

But it was not only among the English-educated people of India that his views were more progressive. Yuval Noah Harari points out that his views have been found 'surprisingly liberal', like supporting 'for example equal rights for women long before the idea became popular in the West'.[26] Probably in the 19th-century context, the primacy of Vedas advocating the Vedic religion as 'eternal' or 'Sanātan Dharma' could have been first done by Dayanand.[27] Meanwhile, in the West, a spiritual movement had been created by a remarkable Russian woman, Helena Blavatsky and her spiritual collaborator Col Henry Steel Olcott. Olcott would later play a decisive role in creating a strong Buddhist identity, as in a previous chapter in this book. Theosophical Society was growing rapidly in the West. Blavatsky and Olcott came to know about Dayanand. They were so impressed by him that they thought of amalgamating Theosophical Society with Ārya Samāj. It would have been a great temptation for any ordinary social reformer or religious leader who had founded a new movement. However, Dayanand 'found them naïve and too interested in occult phenomena' and 'insisted on disaffiliating the Ārya Samāj from the Theosophical Society'.[28] As later events showed, this was a remarkable foresight that Dayānanda showed. Later, Blavatsky wrote that in him, 'there was a total absence of everything like degrading sycophancy and toadyism towards foreigners from interested motives'.[29]

After his death, his spiritual vigour energized the movement to empower the marginalized and downtrodden. Āryas, as the *Samājists* called themselves, were at the forefront of fighting against caste inequalities and untouchability and also in various famine relief measures. From the investiture of sacred thread to the so-called untouchable *Jāthis* to inter-dining and inter-marriages, the *Āryas* were strongly catalytic in social transformation. Here is an excerpt from a report by the *Samāj* as quoted by freedom fighter Lajpat Rai in his book on the movement (1915):

> The Arya Samajists reclaim these depressed classes by admitting them to the privileges of the Dwijas. They administer Gayatri to a select number, invest them with the sacred thread, confer on them the privilege of performing Homa, and start inter-dining and in a few cases even inter-marriage with them. This startles the Hindus.... In the territories of the Maharaja of Jammu and Kashmere the whole strength of one of these castes (in one pargana), about 10,000 souls, has been admitted into the Arya Samaj. This is the result of about three years' work. The agitation is now subsiding and things are resuming their normal condition. In another district (Sialkote) over 36,000 of another caste have been similarly raised. A special organization has been formed to look after their education, etc., called the Megh Udhar Sabha (a society for the uplift of Meghs), which maintains a Central School and several primary schools. The Central School has a splendid building of its own, the foundation stone of which was laid by the Collector of the District, and on which they have spent

> some forty thousand rupees. In another district (Gurdaspur) Pandit Ram Bhaj Dat has reclaimed several thousands within the last two years. The orthodox party is still agitated there, and no organization has yet been formed to look after those reclaimed. In another district (Hoshiarpur), thousands have been reclaimed and there is a regular organization looking after their educational and other needs.... There is hardly a district in the province where some work in connection with the uplift of the depressed classes is not being done, though in most cases it only forms part of the general programme of the Arya Samaj.[30]

In some places, Āryas persuaded the orthodox sections to see reason and touch their conscience. The excellence in their education services was such that the schools they ran for the depressed sections attracted the so-called upper castes, the cited report states:

> In Lahore and some other places we find that nigh caste Hindus have no scruples in sending their children to the schools which we maintain mainly for the depressed classes. The children mix quite freely and on equal terms.

But more often than not, Āryas and their family members were made outcastes by upper castes. One such family was that of Lālā Somnāth. They were denied access to the clean waters of the village well, which affected the health of his mother. When *Somnāth* was ready to compromise and apologize to the 'upper' castes, his mother refused to compromise. She fought against caste distinctions and had to pay with her life.[31] This particular aspect of Ārya Samāj was recorded by Sidney Webb (1859-1947), a socialist and co-founder of the London School of Economics, in 1914:

> These two remarkable institutions, the Dayananda Anglo-Vedic College at Lahore and the Gurukula at Hardwar, represent... only a fraction of the educational work of the Arya Samaj. Throughout

> the Northern provinces of India its branches are engaged in every type of educational service, from propagandist lectures for adults down to special schools for the children of the low castes and criminal tribes whom orthodox Hinduism refuses to touch. I retain in memory the picture of a little wooden building in an obscure village of the State of Baroda. Here a Brahmin and his wife and children, with another Brahmin as assistant, both men of high intellectual attainments and social position, were living, day and night, with a score or two of children of the lowest and most despised castes. These children were not only being gratuitously supported, and physically and mentally trained, but were also being initiated into the Vedic rites, and invested with the sacred thread, for hundreds of years restricted to the 'twice-born.' This is only a sample of the educational work, and the educational work is only a small part of the social service that the Arya Samaj is doing in Northern India-to the perplexity of the average unimaginative and somewhat 'unspiritual' British official, who cannot understand 'what it is that these people are after!'[32]

Herbert Butler was Lieutenant Governor of Oudh and North-West Provinces, and as such, he had praised the Ārya Samāj contribution to education and famine relief work in public. Still, in a private letter to Sir James Dunlop, he cautioned and made an urgent appeal:

> What will be the end of the Arya Somaj (sic)? What will be the upshot of female education? If the Government is not quick it will find the women of India educated by Arya Somajists (sic). Now is the time, it seems to me, to get out ladies from England in numbers as Inspectresses and teachers to guide female education.... To me that our position in the country will be almost hopeless, if the women are trained up in hostility to us. The Arya Somaj is a dangerous movement because it combines an appeal to national feeling with a tendency to elevate the low castes. Shivaji did this. So has every great Hindu leader.... They swept in new forces by promoting the low castes to be Rajputs and Brahmans.[33]

Butler had made the correct civilizational connection here. The colonial administrator understood the danger the movement posed to colonial presence. However, with the colonial empire fossilizing the castes into solid categories and making the hierarchical relations concrete, amplifying its inhuman and abusive elements, Ārya Samāj was facing quite an uphill task. One such instance is the famous 'Dola Palki' movement.

'Dola Palki' movement[34]

In Uttarakhand (formerly British Garhwal), a significant movement took place during the fight for independence. Here, the Dom community faced marginalization and social exclusion, being relegated to the status of untouchability. Kushi Ram, one of the community leaders of these marginalized people, came in contact with Ārya Samāj worker Ram Prasad. Together, they formed an organization and invited Lala Lajpat Rai to their place. On the auspicious day of Baisaki in 1913, Lala Lajpat Rai visited Sunkia village in the Nainital district. He praised the community's artisan skills and societal contributions, advocating for the Shilpakar community to be treated equally with other Hindu communities. Under the guidance of the Ārya Samāj, the community began wearing the sacred thread, which influenced the thinking of the educated Hindus. From within the community itself, other leaders, important among them Jayanand Bharati, Bacchi Ram, and Baldev Singh Arya, also emerged from Ārya Samāj. One of the repressive discrimination the Shilpkar community faced was the denial of the right to use Dola-Palki, which were the palanquins used by the bride and bridegroom on the day of marriage despite being the traditional craftsmen who sculpted them for all communities.

On 16 January 1920, Kushi Ram Arya organized a Shilpakar marriage party with a dola-palki. Except for a minor quarrel, the marriage procession proceeded peacefully. In 1923, however, thc procession was stopped by the regional dominant caste—the Bith community and they were joined by Muslims. In the incident, a Muslim youth named Haider led the dominant caste mob with a double-barrelled gun and the palki was set on fire. The sacred threads were cut by force. Fortunately, the marriage party escaped and returned home after three days. More than 300 ceremonial marriage processions of Shilpakars were stopped by the 'upper castes' because of 'Dola-Palki'. On 24 March 1929, 5,000 strong Shilpkars decided to convert to Christianity and marched to the local Christian Mission home. Jayanand Bharati brought the issue to Mahātma Gāndhi's attention. Gāndhi visited Nainital in July 1929. He gave a speech in which he said:

> (The second key to swaraj) is to remove untouchability; otherwise the Hindu religion itself will be wiped out. How can any Hindu practise untouchability when he proclaimed faith in Advaita? It is (as true Hindus) our first and foremost duty to remove untouchability.[35]

In 1929, Mahātma Gāndhi lamented:

> We say this man is high, that is low. Sciences, both physical and metaphysical, tell us that we are all identical both physically and spiritually. Scientists, having analysed the human body, state that our bodies are made up of the same physical elements, there being no difference on account of origin, race or sex.... The Upanishads and the scriptures teach us that our inward view will reveal only one soul pervading us all. In spite of knowledge of these facts, the stress on the high and the low is not as pronounced in any other society as it is in the Hindu society.[36]

Here, one can see that Gāndhi was employing the updated and adapted version of the same logic/argument that the Chaṇḍāḷa put forth in his encounter with Śaṅkara.

During Gāndhi's visit to the region again, the issue was taken to him.

Meanwhile, the Shilpakars started fighting for their rights legally after a particularly violent attack on the marriage procession in 1933. Though the judgement favoured the dominant caste in the lower court, in Allahabad High Court, the Shilpakars were able to get justice. Still, the attacks continued. Jayanand Bharati faced physical assaults several times. Gāndhi announced that even as the entire India was joining the freedom movement, British Garhwal region leaders would not be allowed to participate in the freedom movement till the attacks on Shilpakars continued and their right to Dola-Palki was denied. At the same time, in January 1941, Jayanand Bharati started individual Satyagraha against the dominant castes' attacks on marriage processions using palanquins. Finally, on 14 May 1941, a conference of all community leaders passed a resolution recognizing and respecting the Shilpakar right to use the palanquins in the marriage processions.

Thus, one of the most intense and long movements for social emancipation in India right during the freedom struggle itself was fuelled by Ārya Samāj with impressive victories, though even now, occasionally violent transgressions continue. But again, it should be noted that this was completely because of the inhuman injustice of local social hierarchy and social exclusion. Yet the blame always ended upon Hinduism. This is even though it has been Hinduism and Hindu values which had fought the injustice. Though the vision of Dayānanda was Vedic and that of Gāndhi was Advaita with an emphasis on the Bhakti Sampradaya of Vaiṣṇava tradition, the Ārya Samāj workers who spearheaded the movement did not hesitate to approach Gāndhi, nor did Gāndhi ask them to abandon the principles of Ārya Samāj. this injustice.

The Spiritual Fire of Dayānanda

Many consider the Vedic vision of Śwāmi Dayānanda to be very similar to the Christian monotheistic view. In this comprehension of Śwāmi Dayananda, his spiritual vision is reduced in its importance, and his movement is only seen for its social reforms, hence placing it within the particular period in which it existed. However, Śri Aurobindo (1872–1950), whose Vedic interpretation is considered highly mystical and in line with the vision and values of the hymn-givers, wrote about Śwāmi Dayānanda thus:

> Amidst the chaos and obscurity of old ignorance and age-long misunderstanding (Dayananada's) was the eye of direct vision that pierced to the truth and fastened on that which was essential. He has found the keys of the doors that time had closed and rent asunder the seals of the imprisoned fountains.[37]

It was a spiritual pragmatism that characterized his work, according to Śri Aurobindo, which he placed decisively in the spiritual essence of Indian culture and civilization:

> And the whole sums itself up to mean a powerful impression of spiritual practicality. The combination of these two words, usually so divorced from each other in our conceptions, seems to me the very definition of Dayananda.... In Dayananda's life we see always the puissant jet of this spiritual practicality. A spontaneous power and decisiveness is stamped everywhere on his work. And to begin with, what a master-glance of practical intuition was this to go back trenchantly to the very root of Indian life and culture, to derive from the flower of its first birth the seed for a radical new birth![38]

Thus, Ārya Samāj, which at its core is a Vedic spiritual movement with the supra-human personality of Dayānanda initiating it, transformed the social conscience of India and effected an organic transformation. It was quite successful in its service, particularly in the Northern and North-Western parts of India. One should remember that the movement gave its best when India was under colonialism and received more hindrance than assistance from the powers. From Anglo-Vaidic schools to famine relief, they served the nation enormously. Given all these aspects, what Ārya Samāj achieved in making Indians spiritually and ethically conscious of the problems of social stagnation should be considered an inspiring model for holistic social emancipation.

Śri Rāmakṛṣṇa, Sārada Dēvi, Rāṇi Rāsamaṇi, and Swāmi Vivēkānantha

Śri Rāmakṛṣṇa (1836-86) was born Gathāthhar Chattōpadhyāya. He was born into a very orthodox Brahmin family. His father took pride in the fact that he had never performed any ritual for any Śūdra family. These prejudiced values were passed on to the children as well. It is important to understand the context here. Pre-colonial Bengal was not so obsessed with *Smṛti* and *Dharmaśāstra* restrictions and was relatively liberal due to the influence of the bhakti movement. Still, the colonial rule and judicial system enforced strict rules based on religious texts, which intensified prejudices within a generation. Within a century and a few decades, a generation had come up and nurtured in virtues of prejudice. However, it is worth noting that many Śūdra communities were economically well-off. So, adhering to such principles was more of a burden for poor Brahmins and their families rather than a demonstration of superiority. In fact, their day-to-day engagements with members of other communities were cordial and unprejudiced. Yet Gathāthhar would face his very first trial against this social stagnation right when he would be wearing the sacred thread.

Dhani was the village nurse who delivered Gathāthhar. She belonged to the caste of blacksmiths, which was considered a 'lower caste'. Gathāthhar used to have food in her house, and it seemed nobody objected. As the boy's ninth birthday approached, his sacred thread ceremony was being planned. Some time ago, Dhāni had told Gathāthhar that it would be a great blessing for her if he, during his investiture, got his first alms from her and called her mother. Moved by her maternal love, Gadadhara readily agreed. When Gathāthhar was to undergo the Brahminical initiation ceremony, it was his elder brother Rāmkumār who was in charge of the family as their father had passed away. Gathāthhar was firm in his decision that he would get the first alms from Dhani, even though it was against the rules to receive the first alms from a non-Brahmin woman, especially one belonging to a lower caste. Gathāthhar, *in turn, argued that if he failed to keep his word,* then that would go against Satya, the greatest Dharmic principle, and hence he would not be qualified to wear the sacred thread. As the nine-year-old Gathāthhar would not compromise, everything came to a standstill. A friend of their father and a Shasric man, Dharmadās has to be consulted. The official and most authentic biography of the saint *Śrī Śrī Rāmakṛṣṇa Līlāprasaṅga* has to say this about the incident:

> When the news reached the ears of Dharmadas, he tried to reconcile the difference. He said to Ramkumar, 'Although this has never so far happened in your family, it has been done in many good Brahmin families elsewhere. Therefore no blame attaches to those who allow it. You must also consider the question of satisfying Gadadhar's conscience and his peace of mind.' At these words of their father's friend, wise old Dharmadas, Ramkumar and others refrained from raising further objections. Gadadhar then, with a cheerful heart, put on the sacred thread in accordance with the scriptural injunctions and applied his mind to performing Sandhya, worship, etc., as

> befits a Brahmin. From now onwards, Dhani also considered her life to be blessed on account of her new relationship with the boy.[39]

However, the caste-prejudice as virtue was very much entrenched in the social atmosphere and it permeated the entire colonial Bengal. In such a setting, there emerged a woman provincial ruler, Rāṇi Rāsamaṇi (1763–1861). She was the widow of Babu Rajachandra Dās, a wealthy Zamindar from the fishing community.

Rāṇi Rāsamaṇi

The life of Rāṇi Rāsamaṇi challenges many myths and stereotypes about traditional Hindu society in colonial Bengal. Despite discrimination and inhuman social malaise like untouchability, the non-Brahmin communities and the so-called lower castes flourished in both economic and political power in the society. Though more than the Vedic tradition, the dogmatic religions with an emphasis on non-violence led to categorizing the fishing community, *Smṛti* and *Dharmaśāstra,* far from challenging these social prejudices, further sanctified and cemented them. Still, they did not wield the same kind of authority as the Mosaic Law, Canon Law, or Shariat. However, with the colonial era, written texts started becoming the law, leading to the fossilization of social prejudices inherited from the rigidly moralistic and dogmatic non-violent religions of the past.

Rāṇi Rāsamaṇi clashed with the British authorities to gain the legal rights of the fishing community in River Gaṅga.

When the British government imposed a tax for catching fish in River Gaṅga, Rāṇi Rāsamaṇi made a smart and bold move. She took on a lease that part of the river where fishermen used to catch fish by paying a large sum to the government. Rāṇi Rāsamaṇi then placed chains across the river in various places, making it impossible for British ships to pass through that area. When the British protested, she said she had the legal upper hand. She negotiated with the government, offering to give up her lease rights if they removed the taxes on fishing for the fishermen.[40]

Rāṇi Rāsamaṇi had a vision of Mother Kāḷi, who commanded her to build a Kāḷi temple at Dakṣinēṣwar. However, she could not find a priest to perform daily worship at the shrine as Brahmins were reluctant to work in a temple built by a woman whom they considered Śūdra. This was a difficult situation, and at this point, a suggestion was made that the temple be ritually made a property of a Brahmin (although the control of the property would be for all practical purposes with Rāṇi Rāsamaṇi and her descendants) so that Brahmins would not object. Finally, the temple was consecrated in 1855. It was Rāmkumār, the elder brother of Śri Rāmakṛṣṇa, who made this suggestion. Rāṇi Rāsamaṇi then requested Rāmkumār to be the priest of Dakṣinēṣwar Temple, and he consented. Śri Rāmakṛṣṇa Paramahaṅsa objected to this. SSRL described the situation:

> He reminded his brother that their father neither officiated in the sacrifices of the Sudras nor accepted gifts from all and tried to dissuade him from that course. It is said that Ramkumar tried to vindicate his action to the Master in various ways with the help of reason and scriptures, but nothing touched his heart. [41]

With all logic failing before Śri Rāmakṛṣṇa Paramahaṅsa, a traditional method called '*Dharmapatra*'—diving through taking lots before the Deity through a child—was used. The answer came in favour of Ramkumar. Śri Rāmakṛṣṇa Paramahaṅsa agreed, half-mind yielding to what he thought was the Divine will. Still, he could not bring himself to consume the food offered or food prepared in the temple complex.

> But he (*Gathāthara)* could not be made to agree to take Prasada in the temple in spite of Ramkumar's loving persuasion. He said, 'It is a temple and the food is cooked with the water of the Ganga; besides, it has been offered to the Mother of the universe; it will not be reprehensible for you to take it.' But these words were not to the liking of the Master (i.e., *Gathāthara*). So Ramkumar said, 'Then take uncooked provisions from the temple store, cook them with your own hands on the sands of the Ganga under the Panchavati and have your meal. Don't you accept that the Ganga purifies everything on its banks and bed?' The Master's strict principle regarding food had now to yield to his devotion to the Ganga.[42]

Still, he had not come to peace entirely with respect to the problem of food from the 'low-caste' woman. Here is an eye-witness account of how he felt when he consumed even the prasad from the temple:

> He took his food under the *Panchavati* and I had *Prasada* in the temple. But I made all preparations for his cooking before I parted. His principle regarding food was so strict then that he felt no peace of mind although he took food cooked by himself. He cooked his midday meal of rice etc., himself, but like us, he took *Ludhi* offered at night to the Mother of the universe. I noticed on many occasions that his eyes became filled with tears when he took Luchi and heard him say sorrowfully to the divine Mother, 'Mother! Thou hast made me take food from a *Kaivarta (fisherman caste woman).*'

Later, Śri Rāmakṛṣṇa himself explained his mental attitude in those days just prior to becoming the priest in that temple:

> I felt extremely afflicted to think that I should have to take food from a Kaivarta. Even many of the poor indigent people did not come to the Kali temple of Rasmani to take their food for that reason. As many people could not be procured to take the cooked food offered to the deity, cows were fed with it and the rest had to be thrown into the river.[43]

At that time, the collective mindset of Bengal was deeply influenced by prejudice, which was considered a virtue. Śri Rāmakṛṣṇa Paramahaṅsa illustrates how he overcame caste prejudices through his devotion to Mother Kāḷi. His spiritual experience had a significant impact on others, particularly Narendra Nath Dutta (later Śwāmi Vivēkānanda), and played a pivotal role in changing the course of India's history. It emancipated millions from social stagnation and exclusion.

Soon, through sadhana and immense bhakti, Gathāthara transformed into Śri Rāmakṛṣṇa. These notions of social discrimination and prejudice-as-virtue mindset began to be replaced with a clear sense of non-dual vision in which these notions were realized as mere social conventions and unrelated to spiritual self-realization. He later explained to his nephew Hriday why he would remove even the sacred thread during the meditation, which shocked Hriday:

> The sacred thread also is a 'bondage', for it is a sign of the egoism, 'I am a Brahmin and superior to all.' When one calls on Mother, one should discard these 'bondages' and call on Her with a concentrated mind. This is why I have put off these. I shall put them on again when I return at the end of meditation.[44]

Soon, Śri Rāmakṛṣṇa would practice even tougher sādhanas to remove even the tinge of the sense of superiority from him. Here is how *ŚŚRL* describes these sādhanas and the effect they had on his vision of equanimity:

> With a view to having the firm conviction that all things and persons without exception from Brahma down to a blade of grass, were the manifestations and parts of the divine Mother, the Master partook of the leavings from the plates of the poor and cleaned the place where they took their food. For the purpose of completely removing pride and egoism from his mind and of having the conviction that he was not superior in any way even

> to the object of universal aversion, he cleaned, like a sweeper, the abominably dirty places with his own hands;[45]
>
> No sooner had he cleaned with his own hands those abominably filthy places, at whose contamination people could not rest satisfied without a bath, than his mind gave up the egoism due to his Brahmin birth and he became convinced for ever that he was in no way superior to those persons who were regarded in society as untouchables.[46]
>
> He carried on his head the leaf-plates, out of which the poor people had taken their food, threw them outside the temple, and washed clean the place. At one time he partook of even the leavings of those people, regarding them as Narayana Himself. Again, he washed and cleaned with his hair' the place where the temple servants answered the calls of nature and prayed earnestly to the divine Mother, 'Mother, see that I may never entertain the idea that I am superior to them.'[47]

The initial social prejudice and social exclusion inculcated as virtue gave place to true discrimination awakening in him, which put away all the social exclusions. Later, Śri Rāmakṛṣṇa did practice food restriction, but it was not based on caste but on the spiritual maturity and righteous conduct of the person who brought the food. Śwāmi Premānanda (1861-1918), one of the direct disciples, documented this:

> As regards caste, the Master used to say that the devotees formed a class by themselves. They did not need to observe caste rules with each other. But he could not eat from the hands of a person of evil character, though the latter might have been born into a high caste. He could not even sit on a seat spread on the floor by such a person. On the other hand, he was once going to touch the leaf-plate from which someone had eaten. That person at once cried out: 'Sir, what are you doing? I have eaten forbidden food. Please don't touch my used leaf-plate.' The Master replied: 'There is no harm in it. Your mind is pure.'[48]

He also ate from the hands of Premānanda, who was not a Brahmin. Premānanda further records the incident of him cleaning the toilets of the so-called untouchables with his hair to remove even the least sense of caste-based superiority in him:

> When the beggars finished their meals at the Dakshineswar temple garden, the Master carried their dirty leaf-plates on his head. And in order to eradicate any sense of superiority over the untouchable sweepers, he cleaned the toilets of the temple garden with his long hair.[49]

Śwāmi Vivēkānanda also discussed this incident in his lecture '*My Master*'. The importance of this incident can only be understood by understanding Gathathara's stance on the issue of caste and how unwaveringly he held that position. It was solely through his spiritual journey and experiences that he reached a point where no discrimination would be shown, and any sense of pride or aversion based on birth would be eradicated.

At the same time, this gentle approach, full of humility, was also too radical for those who had assumed the suggested laws of *Smṛti* and *Dharmaśāstra* as canonic laws in an unchanging society. Śwāmi Raṅganāthananda (1908-2005), who was the thirteenth president of Rāmakṛṣṇa Mission and Math, in his commentary on *Manisha Panchakam*, narrated the following interaction between a traditionalist Hindu Pontiff and a Śri Rāmakṛṣṇa bhakta, with respect to this Jāthi negating sādhana of Śri Rāmakṛṣṇa:

> A university registrar went to a Maṭādhipati and in the course of a talk, told him about Sri Ramakrishna and the local Sri Ramakrishna Ashrama. He referred to this sadhana of Sri Ramakrishna – that he went and washed the latrine of an untouchable. As soon as the Maṭādhipati heard this statement, he could not bear to hear anything more. 'Stop, Stop. Don't tell it. Don't tell it.' The gentleman said, 'But he did it.'

> 'Even if he had done it, don't tell it to others. Don't tell it to others. It is degrading to the Brahmana,' said the *Mathadhipati*. The gentleman replied, 'I find it to be the greatest act for a Brahmana.'[50]

Even during his time, Bengali Hindus who were modernized by European education had difficulty understanding the phenomenon that was happening through Śri Rāmakṛṣṇa. For example, Pratap Chandra Majumdar (1840-1905), who was a scholarly intellectual, could not explain what was so attractive in 'this man' who seemed to be an antithesis of his intellectual grandeur:

> My mind is still floating in the luminous atmosphere which that wonderful man (*Śri Rāmakṛṣṇa*) diffuses around him whenever and wherever he goes. What is there in common between him and me?... I, a Europeanized, civilized, self-centred, semi-sceptical, so-called educated reasoner, and he, a poor, illiterate, unpolished, half-idolatrous, friendless Hindu devotee. Why should I sit long hours to attend to him to Disraeli and Fawcett, Stanley and Max Muller, and a whole host of European scholars and divines? I who am an ardent disciple and follower of Christ, a friend and admirer of liberal-minded Christian missionaries and preachers, a devoted adherent and worker of the rationalistic Brahmo Samaj. Why should I be spellbound to hear him?.... A Hindu saint is always particular about his externals. He wears the ochre cloth, eats according to strict rules, refuses to associate with men, and is a rigid observer of caste. He is always proud and professes secret wisdom. He is always guruji, a universal counsellor and a dispenser of charms. But this man is singularly devoid of such claims. His dress and diet do not differ from those of other men except in the general negligence he shows towards both, and as to caste, he openly breaks it every day. He most vehemently repudiates the title of guru, or teacher. He shows impatient displeasure at any exceptional honour which people try to pay to him and emphatically disclaims the knowledge of secrets and mysteries.... He has nothing extraordinary about

> him. His religion is his only recommendation. And what is his religion? It is orthodox Hinduism, but Hinduism of a strange type.

But for the Hindu psyche, it is easy to understand and accept the sadhana of Śri Rāmakṛṣṇa. The Hindu civilizational and social milieu became the receptacle as well as the web for the emergence of Śri Rāmakṛṣṇa phenomenon. At least one writer in the West had tried to understand how the phenomenon of Śri Rāmakṛṣṇa, which he too understood not completely yet better than many Western scholars, benefitted from the Indian cultural environment. Colin Wilson (1931-2013), in his celebrated work *The Outsider* (1956), pointed out:

> By way of comparison with the Western mystics we have been dealing with, we might turn to the life of a great Hindu mystic, Ramakrishna. Here the environment is different. India has its tradition of contemplation and 'self-surmounting' (although at the time of Ramakrishna's birth, 1836, Western ideas were pushing that tradition into the background). Here we can see what happens when the Outsider can slip into a tradition where he ceases to be a lonely misfit.[51]

Śri Rāmakṛṣṇa was not a lonely misfit in Hindu society. He was one of the peaks and creators of Hindu civilization and history. He was also the distilled essence of millennia of the best of Hindu civilization's most dominant socio-spiritual phenomenon called bhakti.

Sārada Dēvi

Sārada Dēvi (1853-1920) was born Sāradāmaṇi Mukhōpadhyāya. She was a child bride and 'nun-wife'[52] of Śri Rāmakṛṣṇa and rose to become the Holy Mother and guide of the nebulous movement. Sārada Dēvi displayed gentle yet unwavering spiritual authority.

Unlike her husband, she did not have to undergo intense spiritual practices to address social exclusion and stratification. Her natural, spontaneous maternal love combined with her stamp of authentic spirituality was recognized and accepted by all the direct disciples of Śri Rāmakṛṣṇa . She defied social taboos of exclusion and was recognized for 'the extraordinary spiritual greatness...hidden under her rural simplicity'.[53] Śri Rāmakṛṣṇa devotees and monks addressed Sārada Dēvi as 'Holy Mother'.

While growing up as a poor Brahmin girl in Jayrāmbāti, a Bengali village, she showed caring empathy for all, transcending caste barriers. During the 1864 famine, when she was merely 11 years old, her family, despite being poor, shared their khichuri (a dish made with pulse and rice) with the poor people around them without any regard for caste distinctions. When a so-called 'low caste' child came in hungry, little Sārada invited her in and shared her khichuri.[54]

As seen earlier, Śri Rāmakṛṣṇa demonstrated, through his own spiritual practice, how caste prejudices ingrained as virtues could be overcome through spiritual self-persuasion. However, he discriminated based on the virtue and conduct of persons, particularly with respect to food. He would not accept food from people whom he considered led 'impure' (lustful, unethical, or materialistic) life. However, Sārada Dēvi did not make this discrimination. She showed that her maternal universal love encompassed all, regardless of their conduct, pure and impure. Her biographer Swāmi Tapasyānanda narrates an incident:

> One day. as the Holy Mother was bringing the Master's plate of food, she saw a lady standing near the Master's room. She hurriedly came to her and wanted to be allowed to carry the Master's food that day. The Holy Mother gladly handed over the plate to her. Afterwards, when the lady had left, and the Holy Mother was fanning the Master during his meal, he told her that he found it very difficult to take that food as the woman

> who carried it was not pure in life. The Holy Mother admitted that she knew about it, and requested the Master to take his food somehow that day. When she was thus appealing to him, he asked her to give word that she would never hand over his food to anybody in future. At this, the Holy Mother laid aside the fan and said with folded hands, 'That I cannot; for if anyone wants something of me, I feel I must grant it. But anyway I shall try my best to carry your food myself.' Sri Ramakrishna at once understood the nobility of her outlook, and said nothing more on the subject. He continued his meal, talking joyously with her on various subjects. [55]

She did not care about 'losing caste' when it came to feeding people. Here is an incident from her life. Once, some Muslim construction workers were doing construction work for her house at Jayrāmbāti:

> Among these Mohammedans, there was one named Amjed whom the Mother took into her house for a meal. He was seated in the verandah and Nalini, her niece, was serving him. Owing to caste scruples, Nalini was standing at a little distance from him and throwing the various items of food into his plate. At this the Holy Mother remarked, 'If you serve a person in this way, can he eat with relish? You give the things to me, I shall serve him.' After he had finished eating, the Holy Mother herself washed the place where he had taken food. Nalini was shocked at this and exclaimed, 'O aunt, you are going to lose caste.' The Holy Mother snubbed her with the remark 'Keep quiet. Even this Amjed is my son, exactly in the sense that Sarat (*Swāmi Sāradānanda*) is!'

She herself was brought up in an orthodox village setting. She never moved much out of her veiled apartment. However, she could understand and support many modern movements that the Western disciples of Śwāmi Vivēkānanda initiated for women empowerment. Her biographer records:

> She blessed Sister Nivedita in her great efforts for the education of women. She encouraged Sister Sudhira to continue Nivedita's work and even allowed her to finance her boarding home for girls by undertaking tuition in families. She permitted a girl disciple of hers to study midwifery on the ground that she would thus be useful to many, although conservative women like Golap-Ma objected to the idea of a high-caste Hindu girl working in a hospital, however noble the motives behind might be.[56]

She also repudiated the idea that Śūdra and women should not be ordained as monks:

> Speaking about the objection of certain people that some of Sri Ramakrishna's Sannyasin disciples being Sudras, are not entitled for Sannyasa, according to orthodox rules, the Mother said, The disciples of Sri Ramakrishna are Jnanis and therefore Sannyasins. A Jnani can be a Sannyasin. Take the case of Gaurdasi. A woman cannot be initiated into Sannyasa, but is Gaurdasi a woman? She is more than a man! How many men are there like her? See what she has achieved – built a school, acquired horses, a carriage and so forth."[57]

In all these, she was not being radical or reformist in an activist sense of the term. Śwāmi Tapasyānanda, her biographer, explains:

> Indeed, this breaking of the bonds of caste consciousness was another achievement of her maternal consciousness. She was not a breaker of caste in the manner of social reformers. For it was never her intention to give a violent shock to anyone by breaking long-established traditions. What happened was that before her maternal love the impediment of narrow rules and restrictions automatically gave way.[58]

It is through this spiritual nourishment and mentoring that Śwāmi Vivēkānanda emerged and burst forth upon an India suffering from social stagnation aggravated by colonialism.

Śwāmi Vivēkānanda

While the biography of Śwāmi Vivēkānanda (1863-1902) is quite well known, the purpose of this book is not to present his life story. Instead, it explores his vision, values, and appeal impact on social stratification and exclusion. In this regard, Śwāmi Vivēkānanda is widely recognized as a leading figure in raising awareness about social exclusion in India. However, there has been recent criticism of Śwāmi Vivēkānanda, accusing him as a votary of caste. Jyotirmaya Sharma, a Professor of Political Science and the Dean of the School of Social Sciences at the University of Hyderabad, published a book in 2013 focusing on the religion and social vision of Śwāmi Vivēkānanda, coinciding with the 150th birth anniversary of the saint.[59]

In this, he concluded that Śwāmi Vivēkānanda was a votary of the caste system. He substantiates this with the following passage from a letter written by Śwāmi Vivēkānanda on 3 January 1895:

> Now, take the case of caste—in Sanskrit, Jâti, i.e. species. Now, this is the first idea of creation. Variation (Vichitratâ), that is to say Jati, means creation. 'I am One, I become many' (various Vēdas). Unity is before creation, diversity is creation. Now if this diversity stops, creation will be destroyed. So long as any species is vigorous and active, it must throw out varieties. When it ceases or is stopped from breeding varieties, it dies. Now the original idea of Jati was this freedom of the individual to express his nature, his Prakriti, his Jati, his caste; and so it remained for thousands of years. Not even in the latest books is inter-dining prohibited; nor in any of the older books is inter-marriage forbidden. Then what was the cause of India's downfall?—the giving up of this idea of caste.

He then quotes from the same letter the following:

> The present caste is not the real Jati, but a hindrance to its progress. It really has prevented the free action of Jati, i.e., caste

> or variation. Any crystallised custom or privilege or hereditary class in any shape really prevents caste (Jati) from having its full sway, and whenever any nation ceases to produce this immense variety, it must die. Therefore what I have to tell you, my countrymen, is this: That India fell because you prevented and abolished caste. Every frozen aristocracy or privileged class is a blow to caste and is not—caste. Let Jati have its sway; break down every barrier in the way of caste and we shall rise.

From these quotes, he concludes the following:

> In practical terms, caste designated individuals to perform certain actions according to their natures, their prakriti. As long as they continued to perform those without locating their actions or varna-prescribed vocation in custom, privilege or heredity, caste functioned smoothly. So, the cobbler, the peasant and the sweeper, despite an education, will continue to do their jobs and do them even better as long as they got the sympathy of the upper castes. This, in sum, is Vivekananda's argument till now.[60]

However, here Sharma has left out the most important part of what Śwāmi Vivēkānanda said in the quoted passage:

> Now look at Europe. When it succeeded in giving free scope to caste and took away most of the barriers that stood in the way of individuals, each developing his caste — Europe rose. In America, there is the best scope for caste (real Jati) to develop, and so the people are great. *Every Hindu knows that astrologers try to fix the caste of every boy or girl as soon as he or she is born.* That is the real caste—the individuality, and Jyotisha (astrology) recognises that. And we can only rise by giving it full sway again. *This variety does not mean inequality, nor any special privilege.* (Emphasis added)[61]

Here, Śwāmi Vivēkānanda provides a new definition of Jāthi. He takes it to mean the individuality inherent in each person. To him, this is exactly how individual worth alone is considered in the modern West. This reinterpretation represents a significant departure from the traditional understanding of the word Jāthi. In many Hindu households, the family astrologer provides a specific caste (actually a Varṇa to a child), regardless of the community into which the child is born. The present writer does not believe in astrology and considers it a pseudo-science and perhaps born out of a genuine yearning to connect with the universe or, at best, an intuitive way to understand the psychological makeup of humans and, hence, more to do with the mind than the stars. Nevertheless, what is important is that this recognizes that the child born can have a completely different aptitude and interest than the community in which he or she is born. Now, this emphasis on individuality, which could differ from the community-ordained vocation and his harsh criticism of hereditary elements, makes the Jāthi that Śwāmi Vivēkānanda speaks more akin to democratic individualism than the clan or community-inherited work.

While Śwāmi Vivēkānanda says that astrology recognizes the fact that a child's caste is his or her individuality and also endorses this idea of recognition of an individual's individuality, elsewhere, he has rejected astrology as a 'sign of a weak mind'.[62] This is further evident when he uses the term 'caste' to mean what existed in India of his time-birth-based compartmentalized units with social hierarchy, social aristocracy and social exclusion—his statement comparing that caste to its absence in the West further clears his statement that has been quoted just above. In this context, he said harshly to his countrymen:

> In Western countries there is no botheration of caste. Those on whom Fortune smiles for their industry and exertion, are alone regarded as leaders of the country and the controllers of its destiny. Whereas in your country, you are simply vaunting your

> superiority in caste, till at last you cannot even get a morsel of food![63]

If one goes through the complete works of Śwāmi Vivēkānanda and distil the essence of his conception of society, which in turn is based on the spiritual vision and tradition that he inherited from his 'Master' then this is what we get:

To him, caste as a social institution has nothing to do with religion.[64] As every human being embodies eternal knowledge, bliss, and existence, it has ethical implications for equality. However, the concept of special privilege operates against this. Here, Śwāmi Vivēkānanda creates a sound basis for an applied science of Hindu social science and ethics:

> Two forces, as it were, are constantly at work, one making caste, and the other breaking caste; in other words, the one making for privilege, the other breaking down privilege. And whenever privilege is broken down, more and more light and progress come to a race. This struggle we see all around us.[65]

Here Śwāmi Vivēkānanda goes into the core of the problem and points out what can be considered an archetypal continuity. He points out that while individual variations are to be respected and even nurtured, the system of privilege and, by extension, exclusion, which justify themselves with the excuse of preserving variations and individuality, should be opposed. A lecture delivered at Sesame Club, London, on 12 June 1896 provided a framework that is rooted in the Hindu value system but which could be used to understand the social emancipation movements throughout the world:

> Absolute sameness of thought and feeling would produce mental decay and degeneration. Sameness, therefore, is to be avoided. This has been the argument on the one side, and it has been urged in every country and in various times, with only a

> change of language. Practically it is the same argument which is urged by the Brahmins of India, when they want to uphold the divisions and castes, when they want to uphold the privileges of a certain portion of the community, against everybody else. The destruction of caste, they declare, would lead to destruction of society, and boldly they produce the historical fact that theirs has been the longest-lived society.... On the other hand, the idea of oneness has had its advocates throughout all times. From the days of the Upanishads,... down to our present day, in the new political aspirations, and in the claims of the oppressed and the downtrodden, and of all those who find themselves bereft of privileges—comes out the one assertion of this unity and sameness. But human nature asserts itself. Those who have an advantage want to keep it, and if they find an argument, however one-sided and crude, they must cling to it. This applies to both sides.... One side wants us to keep to the phenomenal, to all this variation, and points out, with great show of argument, that variation has to remain, for when that stops, everything is gone. What we mean by life, has been caused by variation. The other side, at the same time, valiantly points to unity. Knowledge would be impossible without that unity. Without the idea of sameness there would be neither perception nor knowledge. So both run side by side. That all men should be the same, could never be, however we might try. Men will be born differentiated; some will have more power than others; some will have natural capacities, others not; some will have perfect bodies, others not. We can never stop that.... But what can be attained is elimination of privilege. That is really the work before the whole world. In all social lives, there has been that one fight in every race and in every country.... The enjoyment of advantage over another is privilege, and throughout ages, the aim of morality has been its destruction. This is the work which tends towards sameness, towards unity, without destroying variety.[66]

When combined with his discussion of 'caste' as individuality, it becomes clear that he demonstrated how Vedantic concepts, experienced through bhakti, could bring about social emancipation by harnessing individuality for the welfare of society and, at the same time, destroying the system of prestige and social exclusion.

While talking to his Western audience, he might approach some of the social conventions with understanding (not justification) so that the colonial prejudices would not be reinforced on Indians, when talking to the Indian audience he minced no words. He famously turned the contemptuous words that the author of Brahma Sutras had used against them and said:

> However much you may parade your descent from Aryan ancestors and sing the glories of ancient India day and night, and however much you may be strutting in the pride of your birth, you, the upper classes of India, do you think you are alive? You are but mummies ten thousand years old! It is among those whom your ancestors despised as 'walking carrions' that the little of vitality there is still in India is to be found; and it is you who are the real 'walking corpses.'... In this world of Maya, you are the real illusions, the mystery, the real mirage in the desert, you, the upper classes of India![67]

The orthodoxy did not remain idle either. He was called a Śūdra, and the legitimacy of his Sannyāsa itself was questioned. In his response, Śwāmi Vivēkānanda made two points. One was that the Jāthi to which he belonged was not Śūdra that was a factual mistake he pointed out. But the more important point he made was that he did not take offence to it:

> I just refer to this, but I am not at all hurt if they call me a Shudra. It will be a little reparation for the tyranny of my ancestors over the poor. If I am an untouchable, I will be all the more glad, for I am the disciple of a man, who—the Brahmin of Brahmins, wanted to cleanse the house of an untouchable. Of course the untouchable would not allow him; how could he

> let this Brahmin Sannyasin come and cleanse his house! And this man woke up in the dead of night, entered surreptitiously the house of this untouchable, cleansed latrine and with his long hair wiped the place, and that he did day after day in order that he might make himself the servant of all. I bear the feet of that man on my head; he is my hero; that hero's life I will try to imitate. By being the servant of all, a Hindu seeks to uplift himself. That is how the Hindus should uplift the masses, and not by looking for any foreign influence.[68]

Śwāmi Vivēkānanda was driven by a strong sense of mission for the upliftment of the downtrodden. Before gaining worldwide fame with his address at the World Parliament of Religions in Chicago, he travelled throughout India as a wandering monk, engaging with both royalty and the poor. He broke caste taboos and often placed himself at the charity of the poorest of the poor. In a letter to his friend and disciple Azhasiṅgha Perumāḷ from the United States, he expressed deep concern for the suffering of millions of oppressed people in India:

> And, oh, how my heart ached to think of what we think of the poor, the low in India. They have no chance, no escape, no way to climb up. The poor, the low, the sinner in India have no friends, no help—they cannot rise, try however they may. They sink lower and lower every day, they feel the blows showering upon them by a cruel society, and they do not know whence the blow comes. They have forgotten that they too are men. And the result is slavery. Thoughtful people within the last few years have seen it, but unfortunately laid it at the door of the Hindu religion, and to them the only way of bettering is by crushing this grandest religion of the world.

He envisioned a renaissance of Sanātana Dharma where youths fired by the Vēdantic ideal of non-dual unity would take the fire of spiritual equality and, through it, would bring social emancipation:

> A hundred thousand men and women, fired with the zeal of holiness, fortified with the eternal faith in the Lord, and nerved to lion's courage by their sympathy for the poor and the fallen and the downtrodden, will go over the length and breadth of the land, preaching the gospel of salvation, the gospel of self; the gospel of social raising-up – the gospel of Equality.

What Azhasiṅgha Perumāḷ envisioned became true in the form of the Rāmakṛṣṇa Mission, which carved out a name for itself in serving the downtrodden so much so that Dr Ambedkar cited the Rāmakṛṣṇa Mission as a model for the Buddhist Sangha. This article is particularly noteworthy because it was published in the April-May 1950 issue of the *Maha Bodhi* magazine, which was meant for Buddhists all over the world, particularly outside India:[69]

> When the idea of service to suffering humanity comes to one's mind everyone thinks of the Ramakrishna Mission. No one thinks of the Buddhist Sangha. Who should regard service as its pious duty the Sangha or the Mission? There can be no doubt about the answer. Yet the Sangha is a huge army of idlers.[70]

So, we have here a Hindu Vēdantic inspiration for Buddhism as a model in service to humanity that too shown by Dr Ambedkar a great humanist and also a bitter critic of Hinduism. No wonder the very same Dr Ambedkar said that in recent centuries, the greatest man that India had produced was not Gāndhi but Śwāmi Vivēkānanda.[71]

Śrī Chattampi Śwamigal

During his life as a wondering monk (*Parivrājaka*), Śwāmi Vivēkānanda had a meeting with a sanyāsin in Kerala. After witnessing the kind of inhuman and irrational caste restrictions that the *Nambūḍiri* Brahmins had imposed in the society and passed it on as part of religion, Śwāmi Vivēkānanda was deeply shocked. He was so disgusted that he called it a 'lunatic asylum'.[72] In such a state, a spiritual renaissance was taking place through completely detached mendicant sanyāsin. His name was Śrī Chattampi Śwamigal(1853-1924).

At a very young age, Iiyappan, affectionately called Kunjan, had to support his family. He collected wild vegetables and sold them to women to make some money. Even though he was not a Brahmin, he used to overhear the Vedic lessons of Brahmin boys in a Vedic school (*Vēda Pādasāla)* in his village near Trivandrum. When the tutor of the Pādasāla noticed 'his surreptitious attempts at educating himself', he was impressed by the 'high standards of the young aspirant's attainments, he allowed him to attend his classes'.[73] This helped Kunjan gain a sound Sanskrit foundation. This datum is important because even in the morbid social stagnation that Kerala Hindu society was under, acts of individuals in a truly Dharmic way could create great societal changes. Later, he attended a traditional school run by his uncle, where he mainly studied secular education. It was here that he gained the name 'Chattambi' (monitor). He always had a spiritual yearning and used to meditate in a dilapidated Kāḷi temple. Meanwhile, along with his native Malayāḷam, he also became a master of Tamil.

His biographer, K.P. Menon explains how spiritual awakening happened to him:

> At *Vadiviswaram* (a village in Nagercoil· Kanyakumari district then South Travancore) he saw an aged beggar merrily licking the remnants of food from the leaves thrown away after a feast. Around him were a pack of street curs with whom he shared the refuse. The proceedings roused the interest of some mischievous boys who reacted by raining stones on the old man. But he ignored the missiles that fell on him· and continued his

> fellowship with his canine brethren. The docile obedience of the dogs convinced Chattambi that the old man had some strange power. He looked intently at him· and the beggar noticing it got up and walked away. When Kunjan Pillai followed him· he quickened his pace. As Chattambi started running· the beggar entered a thick forest and disappeared. The helpless and disappointed youth fell down in a swoon. The old man noticed the spiritual light that gleamed on his pursuer's face. He knew that the young aspirant was fit to receive his mystic advice. The sage picked up the unconscious youth and communicated to him the effluence of his divine virtue. When Chattambi came under the touch of the holy man he saw before him a luminous halo of super-mundane effulgence. The spiritually enfranchised sage blessed Chattambi by initiating him into the divine mystery through the *Praṇava Mantra*.[74]

The mantra is said to be *Bāla Subramaṇya* mantra.[75] Soon, he became known as a Siddha with a basket of varied skills from Siddha medicine to mastery of Yogic sciences to capturing snakes and curing snake bites. He was also a wrestler and taught wrestling to the youths, irrespective of caste. After initiation, his name became Shanmugha Dāsan.

In an alternative version, according to historian S.N. Sadasivan, 'Chattampi travelled extensively and found a saint Atmananda Śwāmi (originally Kumaraswami belonging to the Channar or Nadar community) who made Marutvamala in the descending range of the Western Ghats his abode' and 'Chattampi stayed with him and learned Agastya Yoga, a variant of Tantra Yoga in which he became proficient'. Then he came back as Chattampi Śwāmi.[76]

His work '*Vēdādikara-Nirūpaṇam*' (Proof on the Authority of Vedas), which he had been writing in his personal papers, was eventually published as a book in 1921. Though a significant part of the work is said to have been lost, it remains a concentrated redeclaration of Vēdāntic spirituality. Śrī Chattampi Śwamigal meticulously examined Vedic texts, Purāṇic lore, and *Smriti* injunctions, bringing out inherent contradictions related to the exclusion of Śūdras from Vedic learning. He also scrutinized passages attributed to Ādi Śaṅkara in his *Bhāṣya* of *Brahmasūtras* and showed how the great Acharya showed inconsistency and contradicted his own words:

> Sri Sankara Bhagavadpadar himself, in his commentary on the very first of the sutras of Brahmasutra, says: 'Going through Upanayana and possessing hands-on knowledge of sacrificial rites are not pre-conditions for following the path of Liberation/ Self Realization. The only requirement is that the person must possess a certain 'quartet of instruments or means' called 'Saadhana chatushtayam', irrespective of the order in which one follows the other. But it is baffling that contrary to his own expressed view, given above, the Bhagavadpadar himself had stipulated the order in which the above things should happen, in his aforementioned commentaries on Sutras 34 to 38.[77]

Honoured 'Śrī Vidyārāja Chattampi Śwāmigaḷ' was the vital link in the continuity of the rṣis of Sanātana dharma. With clinical precision, he went into every argument of caste supremacists, who often cited the scriptures, and he proved how their stand could not at all stand a knowledgeable scrutiny:

> Sage Paraashara, the son of a boat-woman, and sage Vyasa, the son of a fisherwoman have authored the Vedas. But they were considered Brahmins.... The fact of the matter is that both of them were born of lowly wombs. They became Brahmins because their fathers were Brahmins. Let us see if at least this principle holds. If it holds, Pandu, Dhritarashtra and Vidura, the sons of Vyasa, the Brahmin, should have been Brahmins. But on the basis of their mothers' caste, if Pandu and Dhritarashtra became Kshatriyas how is it that Vidura became a sudra. If such questions are decided on the basis of one's mother's caste, then Vyasa and Paraashara should have been considered as non-brahmins.[78]

His conclusion was unmistakable:

> Of course· Sudra's position in society today is lowly and degraded. But that does not mean· some day in future· they are not going to occupy positions of stature and power. And, therefore, it should be accepted that all that is required for Vedic learning is only right desire and conduct on the part of the aspirant. If one who refuses food to the starving can be called inhuman· what would you call one who refuses the Veda to the deserving.[79]

The meeting between him and Śwāmi Vivēkānanda occurred before the latter went to the United States, around November or December of 1892. Even then, because of his personality and deep spiritual knowledge, he attracted many people around him. At that time, he was in Ernakulam where Chattampi Śwāmi was also staying. When the latter came to meet Śwāmi Vivēkānanda, because the place was crowded, he left without meeting. When Śwāmi Vivēkānanda heard about this, he said that it was only proper that he should go and meet such a great man and went to the place where Chattampi Śwāmi was staying. Here is a description of what happened:

> While at Ernakulam, Swamiji met Chattambi Swamigal (1853-1924) the scholar-saint of Travancore, and a close associate (and according to some the Guru) of Sri Narayana Guru (1856-1928). A great soul and an equally brilliant mind. Chattambi Swamigal was a remarkable peripatetic. On the day of meeting, he was at the residence of Rama Iyer, the Dewan Secretary, who was himself a great admirer of Chattambi Swamigal. The two great sannyasins spoke in Sanskrit. Swami Vivekananda introduced the topic of *Chinmudra* in the discussion and the illuminating way in which Chattambi Swamigal discoursed on the subject enabled Swamiji to have a glimpse of 'Kēraḷa Pratibha'. They had another edifying discussion on the next day. Swamiji is reported to have described Chattambi Swamigal as a 'wonderful man'.[80]

Here is another account of how Chattampi Śwāmi explained Chinmudra to Śwāmi Vivēkānanda:

> Swami Vivekananda was searching for a person who can explain some aspects of 'Chinmudra' on which he was not satisfied with the knowledge he had acquired. So understanding Swami's knowledge and advanced Yogic practices he introduced the topic of "Chinmudra" into their discussion.... By quoting authentic, very rare and detailed commentaries on Brihadarnyakam and his own experience Swami explained in Sanskrit how that position of the fingers vibrate some specific nerves how it arouses the power of Kundalini, and how it reaches Sahsrarapadma breaking different levels taking one to the ultimate experience. 'You have explained it well. Now I can understand that. I have travelled from Bengal to these southern most parts of India. I have met many sadhus and sanyasins. I asked the same question to them. But till now I could not get a satisfactory answer.' So saying Swami Vivekananda embraced Chattampi Swami. He took both hands of Swami and placed it on his head to express his satisfaction and respect.[81]

In 1882, Chattampi Śwāmi, known for his spiritual humanism, met a Malayāḷi youth who had already become known for his spiritual humanism. That youth *Nāṇu Āsān* and Chattampi Śwāmi became collaborators in spiritual sadhana and through non-dual spirituality catalysing social change. Their interaction led to a socio-spiritual revolution in Kerala. Both Nanu Asan and Chattampi Śwāmi received Yogic training from another spiritual person named Thaicadu Aiyāvu. Chattampi Śwāmi introduced Nāṇu Āsān to Thaicadu Aiyāvu. Later, Nāṇu Āsān become known as Śrī Nārayana Guru. Was Chattampi Śwāmi then the Guru of Śrī Nārayana Guru? As both belonged to two different communities, a heated controversy was generated. But both Chattampi Śwāmi and Śrī Nārayana Guru were above such petty controversies. They considered each other as spiritual collaborators.

There was a disciple whose house Chattampi Śwāmi used to visit in Kerala. There was a three-year-old toddler whom Śwāmi used to take in his arms, and it was as if some secret communication passed between the child and the saint. The mother of the child wondered aloud, 'What exactly are you telling him, and what is the language you both use?' Śwāmi would answer, 'He understands it all, why do you interfere with us?' The child later grew up and was himself white-bearded and wondered in 1967 thus:

> Is there communication possible between a silver-bearded Master and an uninitiated infant? Whatever else there might have been in my early life, there was no spirituality or religion apparently evident and yet twenty-five years ago, when I was in my early twenties, I can look back now and declare that, suddenly, from nowhere a spiritual urge and a religious hunger took me by storm, and in one tidal wave sustained me for ten short years in Utterkasi, only to leave me back again on the shores of the Indian Hindu metropolis, to preach, to serve and to convert the Hindus to Hinduism.[82]

That child later became famous in the world as Śwāmi Chinmayānanda (1916-93).

Śrī Nārayana Guru

Born in the highly oppressed Jāthi of Ēzhavās, Śrī Nārayana Guru (1856-1928) provided perhaps the most sterling instance of how spirituality could affect a tremendous social uplift of an entire community and hence make the whole society more just and more humane. It is an interesting phenomenon again that in Keraḷa, despite the worst epidemic of social malaises arising out of social stagnation and tyranny of social privileges and inhuman characteristics of social exclusion, Sanskrit knowledge was widespread through Ayurvedic texts among the Vaidyas who were mostly of Ēzhavā community. The community made Sanskrit a kind of lingua franca of the Vaidya fraternity.[83] Thus, Nāṇu Āsān was well-versed in Sanskrit, Tamil, and Malayalam when he set out on his spiritual quest. Apart from being a genius in indigenous medical tradition, he was also a gifted poet.

As we have already seen, he practised Yōgam, along with *Chattampi* Śwāmi under Thaicadu Aiyāvu. This deepened his spiritual quest, and he engaged in intense penance inside a cave at Marthu-vāzh-malai (which means 'hill where herbs live'. This small mountain is rich in herbs and has a local Puranic tradition that it was a pebble that fell from Sanjivini that Hanuman was carrying). It is a preferred mystic mountain near Kanyakumari, where spiritual seekers used to meditate in caves.[84] Due to his spirituality, he was hyper-alive to the human conditions around him. One of his disciples had recorded this:

> When fishermen gave him fresh· uncooked fish· he would accept that too· and take it to an old woman· living along with her only daughter on a hillock close by. The old woman would cook the fish and serve a meal with fish and a portion of her own meagre food. Noticing the dire poverty of the family· he taught them how to prepare coconut fibre out of husk· helping them thus to eke out their paltry income.[85]

During this time, he recorded in his hymns the 'over-whelming influx of ecstasy he experienced as he plunged into the depth of divine love'.[86] After his spiritual experience of realizing the non-dual essence that pervades all, he came to a place called Aruvipuram. He became known as Śrī Nārayana Guru. Though he remained invisible as much as possible, his spiritual radiance attracted disciples. An ashram came up where he started guiding people in spiritual sadhana.

In 1888, Mahā Śivarātri – the great night of Śiva – was on 10 February. There was a spiritual gathering at the ashram. Among the audience, he saw a particular phenomenon. Some people were sitting separately. Naṭarāja Guru, a direct disciple of Guru, explains what happened that night:

> A group of women and children, more sunburnt than the rest of the crowd, sat segregated from the others. They were poor peasants, who, after a day's hard work, had come in search of consolation to the festive scene. For ages these poor labourers and their ancestors had tilled the soil for the richer people who took advantage of their goodness. On the basis of their caste, these people had been condemned to age-long suffering, and were segregated and spurned. The Guru's watchful eyes lighted on the group. He asked the orators to wait a moment. He asked the crowd if these people should be segregated. Why should they not come and feel equality with the others? The Guru arranged that two of the boys from the crowd be brought on the platform, and seated them, after kind questions, one on either side of him. 'They are God's children as much as the others,' he murmured, and tears of compassion more eloquent than speeches carried home his silent message to the crowd. Even they who would have growled at such a departure from tradition, could not resist the winning power of the Guru's eyes.[87]

While Ēzhavās themselves were a suppressed community, they had their own social exclusion of castes, which they deemed 'untouchables'. This is the dreaded inhuman trap of 'graded inequality' that Dr Ambedkar pointed out.[88] In response, Śrī Nārayana Guru created a sacred space open to all, emphasizing that he belonged to all humanity. Here is what happened next:

> At dead of night Swami had a dip in the river. He came up after some time with a Sivalingam in his hands and walked into the make-shift temple and stood there with his eyes closed in deep meditation, his hands holding the *Siva lingam* to his chest,

> tears flowing down his cheeks, completely lost to the world. For full three hours, he stood still in that asana (posture) while the entire crowd rent the midnight air with continuous cries of, '*Om Namah Sivaya, Om Namah Sivaya*' for full three hours. The whole lot of them appeared to have only one mind, one thought, one prayer among them. '*Om Namah Sivaya* – Obeisance to Siva.' At three in the morning, Swami placed the *Sivalingam* on the pedestal, consecrated it, and performed *abhisheka*.[89]

Predictably, there was outrage among the upper castes, particularly Brahmins. But Guru simply disarmed those who confronted him by stating that the Śivan he installed was Ēzhavā Śivan and not 'their' Śivan. Today, some interpret Guru's words as a form of rationalization for the segregation of castes and temples, suggesting that each community could have their own temples and Gods. However, they either intentionally or ignorantly miss Guru's point. Śivan, as the ultimate divine, cannot be restricted to being Ēzhavā Śivan or Brahmin Śivan. Śivan is Śivan. Śivan is beyond caste and social divisions. Guru's response was a form of spiritual satire at its highest. This is further attested by the words that Guru inscribed in the temple: 'Without the prejudices of caste walls and religious hatred, let this be the model abode of worship.'

Whenever he installed temples, an outpouring of hymns occurred as Guru entered an exalted state of non-dual consciousness. Guru opened and consecrated more than sixty temples in various parts of South India, not just Kerala. In many temples, he introduced innovations with deep aesthetic and spiritual symbolism, which naturally uplifted the vision of equanimity in society.

> In 1912 when he started building a temple for Sārada Devi at Sivagiri in Kerala. Along with the temple he also opened up a Vēda Pādasāla for the study of Vēdas and Upanishads for all Jāthis.

- In 1921, at Murukkumpuzha Kālakaṇḍēswara Temple, he installed a sculpted stone with *Praṇava Mantra* (Om) along with the words '*Satyam*', '*Dharmam*', '*Daya*' (compassion) and '*Santhi*' (peace).
- In 1927, just a year before his *Mahā Samādhi,* he consecrated an *Artha-Nārēswara* temple at *Saktiswaram* of *Azhapuzha* district of *Kēraḷa.* Here, during the consecration, a controversy erupted with radical reformists under Western influence abhorred what they considered 'idol worship' and did not want installation of 'idol' by the Guru. The traditionalists, afraid that Guru, as he was considered as a spiritual revolutionary, might also avoid the installation and consecration of *Mūrti*, were so frustrated that one old man even stated that he would commit suicide if consecration by Guru did not happen. As confrontation threatened to destroy the beauty of the occasion, Guru came with a wonderful solution. He installed as the *Mūrti* a mirror with a lamp and 'Om' inscribed on it. He explained this as symbolic of both '*Aham Brahmāsmi*' (*I am Brahman*) and also '*Tat Tvam asi*' (*Thou art that*)—the Upanishads' *Mahā Vakyas*. [Here, it is pertinent to remember that according to Dr Ambedkar, despite his bitter criticism of Hinduism, the Upanishads' *Mahā Vakyas* form the spiritual basis for democracy as a way of life and not just as a political system.][90]

One should remember that during the time of Guru, the Protestant colonial mindset was strongly prevalent among the educated youths. The same youths were also attracted to Guru because of their Hindu cultural milieu. They found in him a space where their modernity could meet with Indian spiritual tradition. Guru could not and would not abandon their hopes. At the same time, he had to point out to them the holistic nature of mūrti worship and its final destination. Through his various installations with varied symbolic-spiritual innovations, he was restating the Upanishadic dictum that those who worship the Divine as one with form enter the darkness while those who worship the Divine only as formless enter greater darkness and the wise realize the Divine through both as with form and transcending the form.[91]

Initiating Literary Renaissance

Equally important is the Guru's contribution to initiating a great literary renaissance rooted in its core, Advaita's spiritual-social vision and values. Śrī Nārayana Guru recognized the exceptional literary potential in a 17-year-old boy named Kumaran. Born in 1872, Kumaran was a child prodigy. By the age of eight, after just a year of attending a local traditional school, he had already mastered the alphabet and arithmetic tables. These traditional schools, called Kudipaḷḷikūdams, were typically meant for specific communities in a given area. They provided education in the mother tongue, basic arithmetic, and Sanskrit for talented youth, as well as vocational skills such as medicine and astrology. However, these schools gradually lost their relevance as the mass schools introduced by missionaries overshadowed them. In regions such as Thiruvithāñcūr and other Princely states, as well as regions under direct British administration, there was a push for mass schooling, which favoured dominant castes and disadvantaged marginalized castes. This paradoxical nature, with traditional education being segregated and decentralized and colonial institutionalized education being non-egalitarian, centralized, and mass-uniform, should be understood in the discussions of social emancipation. The traditional system lost relevance because it lacked networking, integration, and modernization with the current knowledge systems. On the other hand, the modern system failed to incorporate the decentralized nature and traditional knowledge systems present in these cost-effective traditional schools. Despite hailing from a socially excluded caste, Kumaran was taught Sanskrit treatises like

Amarakōsam and Raghuvamsam and treatise on indigenous medicine.[92] Kumaran, eventually known as Kumaran Āsān because of his teaching service and skills, flourished as a renowned poet. One very crucial piece of advice Guru gave the young poet was to sublimate the libidinal tendencies that arise into spiritual ones. Historian Sadasivan comments:

> The advice of the Guru has full justification physiological, philosophical and spiritual. The source of all human energy remains one and the same. It is the sexual energy that is sublimated into intellectual activities and finally into spiritual attainments. The nature of sexual energy is to seek frivolous, ephemeral, mundane pleasure and unless it is sublimated, higher intellectual achievements would become impossible. The process of sublimation begins with strict discipline to control the mind and body for the acquirement of virtues. It is a method of transforming the transient into the transcendent. The Guru knew that the poems depicting the voluptuousness of the female body composed widely by the Malayalam poets, neither did elevate them mentally or intellectually nor did serve the ethical values necessarily to be promoted in society. The Guru had therefore reasons to caution his disciple not tread the facile conventional path of fickle pleasure but raise his mind by self-regulation and self-instruction to the world of attributes to be receptive as well as expressive of higher thought.[93]

Here, one can observe the concept of Tapas or discipline in achieving a higher purpose by sublimating raw psychological energies. This is the foundation for individual spiritual liberation, manifesting as high art and aesthetic achievements rooted in universal ethics and empathy, fuelling social emancipation.

Kumaran Āsān's romantic poetry also reflects this sublimation, demonstrating an inner spiritual aspiration. Kumaran Āsān spent three years accompanying Śrī Nārayana Guru and was even referred to as 'Chinna Śwāmi' (Little Master), almost second in the lineage to Guru. However, both Guru and disciple recognized that Āsān was not meant for renunciation. Āsān married Bānumathi, a woman who fell in love with him while he was teaching her Sanskrit despite the significant age difference sparking controversy. Āsān sought Guru's blessings through four verses composed in Sanskrit. Guru gave his blessing. A Brahmin Krishna Iyer functioned as the purohit.

The Sree Narayana Dharma Paripalana Yogam (SNDP) was set up in 1903 by Dr Padmanabhan Palpu a close disciple of Guru. Guru, however, distanced himself from the organization when he found the Ēzhavā casteism infiltrating into the organization and he condemned it. He was deeply pained when he witnessed some Ēzhavās joining forces with the so-called Savarnas against the Pulayas, fighting for their religious, educational, and civil rights. Furthermore, SNDP supported more marginalized Jāthis in their fight for rights. Āsān served as its General Secretary till 1919, even though he also distanced himself from the movement around 1915. However, he was called upon to address its session in 1916. His experiences with the organization were expressed symbolically in a poem (*Grāma Vrikshatile Kuyil*: 'The Cuckoo of the Village Tree', 1919). The poem depicted the torments of a cuckoo in a tree nurtured by a Yogi in a village. The cuckoo suffers from the villagers after Yogi leaves the village, with the departure of the Yogi symbolizing the Guru's distancing himself from SNDP:

> This place you may leave now; this huge tree
> Does not deserve a tear. His penance fulfilled
> The sage has left his abode,
> For great men are not attached to any thing for long.[94]

In SNDP, particularly among its leaders, there was a strong tendency to move away from mainstream Hindu Dharma, which they identified with what they considered as inhuman

Brahminical caste humiliations and imposed disadvantages. In the context of the mid-20th century Kerala, it was more real than perceived in terms of the dominance of social stagnation. Cultural historian and author explains how the movement towards conversion was very much grained in the ideological and strategic dimensions of SNDP:

> The cry for conversion incessantly heard from the inner camps of the Yogam throughout the early decades of the twentieth century also betrays the missionary orientation genetically inlaid in its organisational and ideological constitution. Proselytization was held as the most fashionable gesture of reform by the English educated Eezhava elites who manoeuvred the official programs of the Yogam. It was found to be a shortcut towards the attainment of social status, power and wealth, generally believed to be the indices of social progress. Conversion was upheld as a panacea for all grievances of caste, a compensative measure for the suffering undergone by the community in the past under the Brahminical casteist regime. Moreover it was deployed as one of the profitable and strategic means for bargaining for more rights, powers and status with the religious regimes of the period. At times it was used to threaten and blackmail the authorities of the Hindu society domination by Savarnas and at times, it was used as means of bargaining with the forces of market on the whole-sale selling of the community to the major religious orders of the period.[95]

They were particularly attracted to Buddhism. However, the presence of Guru, through his soft admonitions, gentle discussions, and spiritual guidance, had a strong inhibitory effect on the move towards conversions. Āsān was against such a move. He had written a very popular and highly spiritual literary work, 'Karuṇa', based on the unsolicited love of courtesan Vasavadatta for Upagupta, the Buddhist. Upagupta comes to her not when she was beautiful, but when she was accused of murder, disfigured, and thrown out, and gives her salvation.

Despite such a strong literary portrayal of a Buddhist theme and making it massively popular among all sections of society, Āsān refrained from conversion to Buddhism. In this connection, he wrote a letter to C. Krishnan, a reformist who was in favour of conversion to Buddhism. This letter was later published as a booklet titled *The Alchemy of Conversion* (Matha Parivarthana Rasa Vātham), a sarcastic title. He pointed out to those desiring to convert to Buddhism the presence of a very living Master rooted in the ancestral Dharma of Hinduism. He wrote:

> I could certainly say that Swamy Trippadangal, (a respectful reference to Śrī Nārayana Guru by mentioning not his name but his feet considered auspicious and sacred by the devotee – a practice universal in India), who has solid foundation in spiritual matters would not change his religion even if compelled by some of us who crave for conversion. I feel sorry to say it is an act of disrespect to Guru on our part, to persuade our Spiritual Guru for conversion. It is my humble opinion that it is disastrous to run after the priests of Ceylon or Tibet leaving a great Teacher who has been instrumental for the whole progress of our community till this time, the one who is universally acclaimed by whole of us and whose presence we proudly held as the fortunate accomplishment of the community; it is like running after fortunes throwing away the gold possessed by one self.[96]

In fact, Guru himself held conversations with those desiring conversion. He never stood in the way between personal beliefs or conversions driven by conviction, as well as those motivated by material or social reasons. He understood and even empathized with their suffering and feelings, yet he tried to gently discourage them as much as possible. During a detailed conversation he had with Sri. C.V. Kunjuraman, who had partially converted to Buddhism, Guru listened to his arguments for conversion with empathy and even agreed with certain points of view before explaining his own thoughts in detail:

If the religion of those who live in Hindustan is Hinduism, then the religion of Christians and Muslims who presently live in India is also Hinduism. But nobody says so and nobody agrees. Now Hinduism is the common name for the religions indigenous to Hindustan. This excludes Christianity and Islam which came from outside. For this reason, some people say Buddhism, Jainism etc. are also Hinduism. If it is not irrational to call different religions such as Vaidika, Pauranika, Sankhya, Vaisheshika, Meemamsaka, Dvaita, Advaita, Shaiva, Shaktheya and Vaishnava commonly as Hinduism, how is it irrational to call all religions together as 'Eka Matam'?... When Mahatmaji came here, he pointed out in his speech how all its branches and leaves were different from one another in a mango tree in the yard. Similarly all personalities in the human world will also be different from each other. As long as these differences exist, the faith of people would also be different. What Mahatmaji said is true. But if it is examined in the view of dialecticians (Naiyyayikas), it has to be accepted that there is a separate religion for every individual.... For twenty billion Hindus, there would be twenty billion religions. Although the truth is so, people can be treated as belonging to a single religion since there are certain aspects that are common in the faith of all people. In the same way, as there are certain common aspects in the religions of the world, they all belong to a single religion. No religion can exist without basing it on some eternal dharma or truth.... However, brotherhood is dependent on love, and love dependent on brotherhood. Without realizing it, argument arises about brotherhood being greater or love being greater. Well, it is only a futile argument. The eternal dharmic principles are equal in importance. Depending upon place and time it might become necessary to give importance to any one of them.... What is the need of India today? Freedom from rivalry between castes and religions! Let people study all religions giving equal importance and equal devotion. Let the awareness gained thus be exchanged with mutual love. Then it would be understood that the reason for rivalry is not religion, but conceit and arrogance. The enthusiasm for religious conversion would also end then.[97]

At the same time, Guru also welcomed those who had been converted away from Hinduism back into the ancestral fold. In Neyyatrinkara, a place near Trivandrum, he reconverted the important leaders of Ēzhavā Christians to Hinduism.[98] His biographer writes:

> A Thiyya in Kannur had embraced Christianity owing to some family problems. However, he strongly desired to return to Hinduism. But the Thiyyas refused to accept a Christian into their fold. The convert approached the Guru. Guru immediately called his relatives and community leaders and advised them to accept him as a member of the Thiyya community. They accepted his advice and took him back into the community. There were a few Ezhava Christian families near Neyyattinkara in South Travancore. They were Ezhavas by caste and Christians by faith. Even at present, there are some such families in that area. Seeing the prosperity and reform in the community under Guru's leadership, a lot of people among them wanted to become Hindus again. So they approached Guru. Guru happily welcomed them back to Hinduism.[99]

The venerable Guru himself indicated this. Though he had distanced himself from SNDP, he still remained their spiritual inspiration and mentor. In 1926, he asked SNDP members to rise above the identities of their caste and sectarian identities. In the annual convention, he gave them what could be considered his final message:

> Religious reform should not become an attempt to leave any particular religious group and embrace another religious group. Our organization should be one that accepts all people equally. Our community structure should be one that brings all people together. Our religion should be one that allows freedom of faith, acceptable to all cultured minds and that leads humanity to a noble ideology. The Sanatana principle, 'One Caste, One Religion and One God for Humanity' is such a religion. I feel the

> ideal principle for the Yogam would be to accept all equally who believe in this Sanatana Dharma. Those who think that without religious conversion inequality, and difficulties would not end, acceptance of Sanatana Dharma as their religion would be their religious conversion and proclamation of freedom.[100]

Despite such gentle persuasion and a clear indication of the direction towards which his own heart gravitated towards, conversion remained a strong attraction for some of the influential community leaders. But the way Guru created a universal space for all through his updating and adaption of the Sanātana dharma model for the inclusive brotherhood of all humanity reduced most of his followers' enthusiasm for conversion.

Another great literary personality who Guru inspired was Mūlūr S. Padmanābha Paṇickar (1869-1931). Popularly known as Mūlūr, he met Guru in 1905. This encounter had a profound impact on his life. Through his poems and activism, he advocated for the abolition of caste-based discrimination between Jāthis and within each Jāthi. Dr Ambedkar highlighted the issue of graded inequality as a great bane of Hindu society. A sub-group of the Ēzhavā community 'Kurup' felt that the non-Kurup Ēzhavās were marginalizing them. In fact, there were Ēzhavās who considered Kurup as non-Ēzhavā. Some in the Kurup community even considered converting to Christianity. When Mūlūr came to know about it, he requested Guru to declare the Kurup as fully part of the Ēzhavās.[101] Even though Guru was not limited by community barriers and not bound by identities, given this importance, he consented to the request. The event was conducted with great enthusiasm, and for the first time in the history of Kerala, intra-caste discrimination was removed. Mūlūr also challenged the cultural hegemony the socially privileged communities had in the domain of literature and culture. When Kodungallur Kunjikuttan Thambiran, a doyen of Malayāḷam literature, wrote a historico-literary compendium of the language *Kavi Bhāratham* and left out important Ēzhavā contributors, Mūlūr came out with an alternative compendium, *Kavi Rāmāyaṇam*. that included all the great contributors to literature irrespective of caste.[102] Mūlūr also oversaw the construction of the famous Mezhuveli Anandabūthīśwara Temple. The sacred deity form was consecrated by Guru himself.

Guru's Critique: Deciding (Nirṇayam) and Definition (Lakshaṇam) of Jāthi[103]

The famous statement attributed to Guru and widely known among his followers is that when one cannot decide one's Jāthi by physical appearance, then why ask? In 1914, Guru gave a holistic critique of deciding one's Jāthi and defining it.

In determining Nirṇayam, Guru made clear that 'Jāthi' simply refers to species and is biological. The human species is compared with other species, highlighting that the variations within a species do not prevent them from breeding within that species. This is a very physical reality, and the biological process of birth is the same for every human being, regardless of social order. The differences in character and other variations exist only at the individual level. In this, Guru combines the concept of individuality (Swabhava-Swadharma) emphasized in Bhagavad Gīta while expanding upon the questions asked at the beginning of Manisha Panchakam.

> Humanity marks out,
> Of what species humans are.
> Even as bovinity
> Does with cows.
> Brahminhood and such
> Do not do so in this case.
> No one does realise, alas!
> This apparent truth.

Of one kind, one faith, one God is man;
Of one womb, of one form
Difference here is none.

Within a species does it not
Offspiring truly breed?
The human species, thus seen,
To a single species belongs.

Of the human species
is a Brahmin born
As is an excluded one too.
Where is caste difference then,
Amongst the human species?

Of a socially excluded woman
was born the great sage
Parasara in those old days.
And even the sage who
Condensed the Vedic secrets
Into great aphorisms
Was born of the daughter
Of a fisherman.

Species-wise, does one find,
When considered,
Any difference between man and man?
Is it not that
Difference exists apparently
Only individual-wise?

In the case of the definition of Jāthi, he begins with the biological oneness of the human species. Then, there are individual differences that we know about. So, asking a person his or her caste is futile. The species is the basic mould of human beings. Further deep, all existence, like waves emerge from the ocean of primal consciousness. So, either way, it is fallacious to ask one's

Jāthi—for physically, we are all human species, and spiritually we are all Brahman:

All that mate together
And beget offspring
Belong to one species;
Those that do not material
Together are not so.
Those of the same species
Are often seen in pairs as well.

Each species does have
Its own bodily form.
Its own way of sound-making,
Its own smell and taste,
Its own bodily temperature,
Please remember that.

Following all these,
There exists in each
Their own distinguishing features,
Therefore It is that
We know various things
One different from another

Ask for the name,
Placc and calling
(Of someone you meet).
Do not ever ask
'Who are you (by caste)?'
Because the body itself
Tells you of that truth.

The body that pertains
To the species tells you,
Of what species you are.

Those who think, and
Those who have eyes,
Therefore will not ask,
'Of what kind (Jāthi) you are.'

As in the case of
Males and females,
Differentiating species
Is to be done with.
The sole help of
Distinguishing marks.
Such is the proper way
We should know things.

Species is the mould.
For all are apparent forms
To emerge from the ocean
Of primal Consciousness.
The rows of water-waves
Are really nothing but
The one-root-cause-water.

Species (Jāthi) speculated on,
is found to be a mould
Devised by a moulder
Called pure Consciousness.
All that has come to be
Moulder thus, will
Come back again
Moulded all anew.

It is called 'species'
Because it enables you
To know something specifically.
Unless thus specified
Species-wise, there would be
No knowing that
This is such and such.

It is thus with scientific precision and spiritual insight Guru rejected entire caste as created by the society within human species as absolutely irrelevant and delusional at every level.

Guru, Vaikom Satyāgraha, and Mahātma Gāndhi

In September 1921, T.K. Mādhavan, a disciple of Guru and a leader of the Indian National Congress (INC), met Mahātma Gāndhi in Tamil Nadu and explained to him the widespread practice of both untouchability and unapproachability in Keraḷa. Guru was an inspiring and guiding spiritual presence for what unfolded as the most visible Satyagraha for the rights of the socially excluded communities to win their basic rights of walking on the public streets. His followers, led by T.K. Mādhavan, pioneered the Satyagrāha at Vaikom, a temple town where 'lower castes' were not allowed even on the public roads adjoining the temple streets. This was in 1924-25. The INC, under the guidance of Mahātma Gāndhi, was strongly advocating temple entry for the 'Harijans' (the Scheduled Caste Communities). INC took the fight here and Gāndhi decreed that only Hindus should take up the fight. Mahātma Gāndhi was clear regarding the goal of the movement. While the immediate goal was to open the road for all citizens, irrespective of caste or creed, to use, the ultimate aim was to make the temple entry for all Hindus, irrespective of their castes a reality. Meanwhile, even the roads which once accessible to the 'lower castes' were also barricaded. Gāndhi characterized the mindset of the 'upper-caste' Hindus of Travancore princely state as that of 'tyrant'. He compared it to the mindset of General Dyer, the villain of the Jallianwala massacre. Gāndhi wrote in *Young India* dated 1 May 1924:

> I fasted to reform those who loved me. But I will not fast to reform, say, General Dyer, who not only does not love me but who regards himself as my enemy. I am assured that the use of

> the road is the final goal of the Satyagrahis.... The one who is in sympathy with you is the 'lover'. In my opinion, in the Vykom movement, opponents of the reform are the ' tyrant'. The State may or may not be that.... It is however not to be denied that the present movement throughout India is to throw open to the suppressed classes all the public roads, public schools, public wells and public temples which are accessible to non-Brahmins.[104] (*Young India*, 01 May 1924)

There were reports that Guru wanted the volunteers to remove the barricades. Gāndhi received from upper-caste Hindus veiled threats that the situation might take a turn like the one at Chaurichaura, where the Satyagrahis ended up killing policemen and the whole movement had to be called off. Citing the reports of Guru, the upper castes wanted Gāndhi to call off the Satyāgraha in the name of the principle of Ahimsa. But Gāndhi was unwilling and saw through the trick, even though he had no means of verifying whether the method suggested by Guru, as alleged in the report, was true. Even taking the report at its face value, Gāndhi wrote:

> His Holiness Shri Narayan Guru, spiritual leader of the Tiyas, is reported to have disapproved of the present methods of Satyagraha at Vykom. He suggests that volunteers should advance along barricaded roads and scale the barricades. They should enter temples and sit with others to dine. Though I have compressed the interview I have reproduced almost the exact words.... A friend who has sent me the press cutting recording the interview suggests that by reason of the violent advice of the Guru I should ask the local Congress committee to call off Satyagraha. The friend cites Chaurichaura as an illustration. In doing so, he has betrayed confusion of thought or ignorance of facts.... If Congressmen connected with the Vykom movement entertain the suggestions said to be favoured by the Tiya spiritual leader, there would be a case for penance and therefore suspension but not otherwise.[105] (*Young India*, 19 June 1924)

In reality, it was the 'upper-caste' Hindus who were against the opening of roads around the temple to all Hindus decided to use the vows of the Satyāgrahis to intimidate them. Satyāgrahis had taken the vow of not appealing to the State because they deemed it unjust with respect to the road-entry movement. These Hindus, who called themselves 'Savarna' threw all kinds of obstacles in the way of the Satyāgrahis. Even as the Satyagrahis would complain of such ill-treatment, their vow prevented them from appealing to the government. Such uncivilised low-level tactics were used by the 'upper-castes'.[106]

In 1925, Gāndhi came to Thiruvithāṅcūr. He met the Satyagrahis and was with them for two days. Then he came to meet the Guru on 12 March. He stayed in the ashram. The next day, there was a conversation between Guru and Gāndhi. Guru spoke in Sanskrit. Gāndhi spoke in English. A legal luminary N. Kumaran acted as the mutual translator.[107]

> Gandhiji: Swamiji, do you think untouchability is enforced in any authoritative Hindu scriptures?
> Swami: No.
> Gandhiji: Do you have any difference of opinion about the Satyagraha Movement for eradication of untouchability?
> Swami: No.
> Gandhiji: Do you feel that something should be added or something should be changed in that movement?'
> Swami: It is going on very well as far as I know. I do not think any change is required.

With respect to conversion, Guru was of the view that those who got converted did so for material benefits, and they could not be blamed, though he stated that there was no need for conversion for spiritual salvation: 'For spiritual liberation, Hindu religion is more than sufficient.'

Guru did not consider inter-dining and inter-caste marriages as wrong. Instead, he did not prioritize them. 'They could wait', he said, 'the opportunities for social uplift should be available for the socially excluded communities.' Then, another probing question was asked by Gāndhi:

> Gandhiji: Some people are of the opinion that use of force is required for getting the rights and peaceful Satyagraha is useless. What is Swamiji's opinion?
> Swami: I do not think use of force is good.
> Gandhiji: Use of force has been advised in Hindu dharma shastras?
> Swami: The puranas say it is necessary for the kings and all and they had used it. However, for ordinary persons, use of force will not be right.

Gāndhi thus had a first-hand account of Guru's views and values and should have understood that the reported interview was mischievous and not true. After his return, Gāndhi wrote in *Young India* more forcefully and more committed to social emancipation:

> I am impatient because I am a Hindu, because the State is a Hindu State, because its Dewan is a Hindu, because the people are educated and because the evil is acknowledged. If it was the British Government, it could certainly plead neutrality if it wished. But since it is a Hindu Government and in this case and in such cases it is not dominated or influenced—not so far as I am aware—by the British Government, it cannot plead or profess neutrality. It must take the side of reform and oppose blind orthodoxy or superstition even as it would take the side of the robbed and come down upon robbers with a heavy hand. A Hindu sovereign is the custodian of the dignity and protection of Hinduism against assault from without and disintegration and corruption from within. It can remove abuses that have crept into Hinduism without any difficulty or even in spite of it.[108] (*Young India*, 26 March 1926)

The impact of Guru on Gāndhi's stand is subtle yet powerful. Gāndhi had always insisted that change should be made within society. However, he suggested that with the kind of inhuman humiliation of fellow human beings, such as the phenomenon of untouchability and unapproachability, the state should use power. One can see that this correlates with Guru's statement that according to Hindu Sastras, the force could be used by a just ruler but not by ordinary citizens.

Gāndhi further wrote that according to the Satyagrahis, the vast majority of the so-called Savarṇa Hindus favoured the reforms of opening the public roads of Vaikom to all Hindus, including the so-called 'unapproachables'. He had also met the opponents of the reform. They accepted the fact that only the socially excluded caste members were not allowed in the streets and not Christians or Muslims. These 'upper-castes' made two claims: one was that this custom was handed over to them by Adi Shankara himself and the second was that 'the unapproachables, were so born as a fit punishment for their misdeeds in the past incarnation and that the taint was indelible during their present incarnation'. Gāndhi outright rejected the second view as against Hinduism and humanity. With regard to the first, he wanted them to 'produce Shankara's authority in support of their contention'. In that case, he said he would ask the satyagrahis to withdraw Vaikom satyagraha. Yet he stated that it would not bind him 'for all places for the simple reason that even if Shankaracharya held the view in his time, he would not be bound by what appeared to him to be contrary to religion and humanity.'[109]

At this point, the 'upper-castes' brought before Gāndhi a Sanskrit work called 'Śaṅkara Śmriti', which purportedly validated the above restrictions. Gāndhi did not know the Sanskrit written in Malayalam script. At this point, a Nambūdiri youth, Kṛṣṇan Nambūdiri (later Śwāmi Āgamānanda), who was a recognized expert in Sanskrit, was introduced to Gāndhi for examining the validity of the given text. He not only translated into English but also pointed out the glaring grammar mistakes in the text, which clearly falsified the claim of its authorship by Śaṅkarācharya.

Then Gāndhi wrote about his meeting with the Guru and also the Diwan of Thiruvithāṅcūr and recorded this:

> I waited also upon His Holiness Shri Narayan Swami Guru. He entirely approved of the satyagraha movement and said that violence would never succeed and that non-violence as the only method. The next day I waited upon the Dewan Bahadur. He too said he was entirely on the side of reform. His only difficulty was that as an administrator he could not legislate unless there was strong and clearly expressed public opinion.[110]

Thus, the interaction with the Guru made Gāndhi realize the gravity of how social exclusion in Hindu society had assumed an inhuman form, intolerable to anyone with basic humanity present in them. The followers of Guru consider the starting of the magazine *Harijan* in 1933 and also his change of views on inter-caste dining and inter-caste marriage, which he opposed earlier and accepted later, to this meeting with Śrī Nārayana Guru.

In 1927, Gāndhi again took a tour of Kerala in connection with the eradication of untouchability. At this point, many marginalized community leaders were contemplating converting to Christianity. On 15 October 1927, Gāndhi met two groups of socially excluded community teams fighting for justice. These were the Depressed Classes Mission led by C. Seshayya and the Ezhuvas led by T.M. Chamiappan, Sukumaran, and P.C. Gopalan. While P.C. Gopalan strongly advocated for conversion as an alternative, Chamiappan, who was also representative of the same community, informed that most of the Ēzhavās did not wish to be converted to other faiths, barring a few. Gāndhi said that instead of leaving Hinduism, these marginalized communities should fight the cause with all reasonable force. According to Gāndhi, 'the utility of Hinduism' far outweighed 'the persecution of the so-called higher castes' so much that the latter amounted to 'nothing'. Based on these interactions, he visited 'to His Holiness Shri Shankaracharya of Kumbakonam Mutt, to have an interview, with a view to converting the Swamiji, if he could, to his view in the matter of the removal of untouchability'. But 'His Holiness Shri Shankaracharya of Kumbakonam Mutt', while expressing 'appreciation of Gandhiji's efforts to spiritualize politics' was equally firm that the 'temple-entry for Harijans... might amount to a form of himsa to wound the feelings of those who still believed in the supremacy of Shastras and tradition'.[111]

The struggle would go on for another nine years till the temple entry proclamation would be made by the Thiruvithāñcūr princely state. Two years later, a similar act was passed in the Madras Legislature by C. Rajagopalachari. Śrī Nārayana Guru attained Mahā Samādhi on 20September 1928.

The following historical contextualizing of the spiritual phenomenon by Nataraja Guru, that happened through Śrī Nārayana Guru, which in its transcendental essence defies contextualizing, approximates it in both its historical and spiritual dimensions:

> Dayananda stressed the importance of the Vedic and Aryan virtues of equality; Vivekananda defended Hinduism primarily in the name of mother-worship of Kali; Gandhi stressed Vaishnava democratic notions in public life; and Tagore sang songs breathing something of the freedom of the Upanishads across modern India—all of them aiming at raising the status of India in the world. The silent Guru of Varkala, sitting on a hill-top at the southern extremity of Mother India, steeped in the silence of non-dual unitive vision, integrated all the contributory

views and visions into one whole, brought all within the scope of one contemplative Word-wisdom, by which human dignity could be held high everywhere and all mankind become free.[112]

Mahātma Iyyankāḷi

Another great soul who took forward into society the dhārmic fight for equality was Mahātma Iyyankāḷi (1863–1941). When he was a child and was playing, the ball fell into the ground of a Nair community person. The Nāir sternly warned the little boy against entering the ground. This was a shock for the boy because, after all, he and his community had been working in the fields of Nāir people. Iyyankaḷi belonged to the Pulaya community. At the same time, another Nāir, Parameswaran Pillai, the landlord on whose farm the father of Iyyankāḷi, Iyyan, worked, appreciating his hard work and high character, registered eight and a quarter acre of land in Iyyan's name. This created quite a stir locally. But this gesture made Iyyankāḷi from a landless labourer under the mercy of landholders into a landholder himself. So Iyyankāḷi had seen both the stagnant and malicious nature of society and how individuals could stand apart against it by their sheer humanist nature.

He started organizing youths in his village (Veṅkānūr). He himself directed a drama Harichandra and it acted out. Iyyankāḷi was unlettered, yet the dialogues for the drama were extraordinary.

When Iyyankāḷi was twenty-five, in 1888, on the night of Shiva Ratri of that year, Śrī Nārayana Guru installed defying the caste restrictions of orthodoxy. This became a great guiding light for Iyyankāḷi. In 1893, Iyyankāḷi bought a bullock cart. That a Pulaya could buy a bullock cart itself was unheard of in those days. Then he rode in a bullock cart with a bow-like bamboo roof called *Villuvaṇdi,* considered a status symbol-drawn by two white bulls through a public road that, till then, the Pulaya community could not even walk on. The biographer C. Abimanyu of Iyyankāḷi describes the march of the bullocks in the so-called *Savarṇa* streets (though they were public streets) as similar to the unstoppable running of 'Yajña Aswa'.[113] The Pulaya youth movement formeḍ in Veṅkānūr was emboldened and inspired by this event.

Meanwhile, Christian missionaries were doing impressive work among the humiliatingly suppressed communities in Kēraḷa. They too were fighting for the right of the depressed communities to be admitted to schools. Many relatives of Iyyankāḷi had converted and were working in missionary organizations. The conversions were playing a havoc in the community unity. Salvation Army was working among the Pulaya community and converting to Christianity meant education as well as a strong sense of liberation for the oppressed. But the converted looked down upon their own Hindu Pulaya community. They called them 'Mada Pualaya' (Stupid Pulaya). Seeing the natural leadership qualities in Iyyankāḷi and with families on his maternal side being converted to Christianity, Salvation Army's local 'Colonel' Clara Case asked him to come and attend a prayer meeting. Iyyankāḷi was given a special seat, and he explained the problems faced by his community. Clara Case explained what she considered the liberating nature of Christianity and its importance to Pulaya's social emancipation. He was still undecided with respect to collaboration with the missionaries. Even as he was hesitating, the special seat was laid under a coconut tree and a coconut fell on his head. Fortunately, he survived that hit but became unconscious.

Between converting to Christianity and fighting for the rights as a Hindu, Iyyankāḷi decided in favour of the latter. He also petitioned the king of Thiruvithāṅcūr, who was under British Regent, that forcing conversions should be banned in the state. A royal proclamation was made. It stated that forceful conversions should not happen, and genuine conversions of individuals should not be stopped.

The decisive point came for the mission of Iyyankāḷi when his maternal uncle Thomas 'Vāthiyar' (Master) heard the speech made by a monk Śwāmi Sadānanda at the place called East-fort in Thiruvananthapuram. Śwāmi Sadānanda, before his renunciation, belonged to the Nāir community. He was pained by the way the so-called upper castes treated the suppressed communities as quasi-slaves and with added religiously shaded humiliations like untouchability and unapproachability. In addition, there was unseeability – meaning when the king or men of very 'high birth' went around the regions, certain communities should ensure they remained invisible. If a high-born happened to see a person of such a community, that person would be canned or punished worse.

Śwāmi Sadānanda spoke against these customs. While such practices are unthinkable today, they were the norm then. Thomas Master took an interest in the speech of Śwāmi Sadānanda. Śwāmi Sadānanda conducted a Hindu Unity Convention. Thomas Master attended the convention without revealing his identity. Convinced that the concern of Śwāmi Sadānandawas genuine about uplifting the humiliatingly oppressed communities of Thiruvithāṅcūr Princely State, he met him along with Iyyankāḷi. They invited him to Veṅkānūr. Śwāmi came and decided to start a branch of his movement, 'Brahma Nishta Sabha', under the name '*Chit Sabha*'. On the *coming Vijaya Dasami* day, the Pulaya community decided to see the king and convey to him their grievances. Śwāmisaid that they should go as a procession holding high a painting of the king. Any 'upper-caste' person trying to attack them would damage the portrait of the king, and that would be considered sedition. This way, they succeeded in meeting the king and airing their grievances. The taboo of 'unseeability' was broken.

Śwāmi Sadānanda incidentally was also the sage who inspired and initiated Subramaṇya Śivam (1884-1925), who was a freedom fighter and one of the chief organisers of 'Coral Mill' workers' strike (1908) of Tuticorin against the British administration. It was one of the earliest workers' movements in India, and it succeeded in achieving its objectives. Unfortunately, beyond a few mentions and references, the biography of this sage is unavailable for study.

In 1907, Iyyankāḷi decided to create a wide movement encompassing the community's cultural, political, and economic welfare. Towards this end, '*Sādhu Jana Paripālana Saṅgham*' (Association for the Welfare of the Sādhu', SJPS) was established at Veṅkānūr. The choice of the word 'Sādhu' is important and has deep meaning. It means a calm-meek person who can endure hardships with a smile not because of his or her weakness but because of the *Sātvic* spiritual quality in the person. South Indian adage states that 'if a Sādhu ever gets angry, then even a forest of opposition could not stand it'. Initial demands included six workdays per week and Sunday as a holiday. Every member of the Sangha had to pay a small amount, and a ground was purchased for the Sangha.

In 1907, Thiruvithāñcūr state announced another important decision that schools should not deny admissions to children belonging to marginalized communities like Pulayas and Kuṟavas. Already another suppressed community, the Ēzhavās had fought because of Śrī Nārayana Guru, from 1896 onwards, for the rights of their children to attend the new system of common schools created by the government. In 1905, their fights bore fruits.

Now it was the turn of the Pulaya community.

Despite the 1907 proclamation, 'upper castes' made sure that the proclamation was so muted that the beneficiaries were not even aware of such a proclamation. This was made known to Iyyankāḷi by Diwān P. Rājagopālachāri in 1909. A traditional and dharmic Brahmin, Diwān P. Rājagopālachāri was committed to the upliftment of the depressed Jāthis. Armed with this information, SJPS made the demand that the children of the Pulayas be allowed in schools. The officials in charge of education made it clear that they would not abide by the order. The logic was 'if your children get educated, then who would labour in our agricultural fields in the next generation?'

Iyyankāḷi organized what would be the first strike of agricultural labourers in the history of Kēraḷa. The agricultural labourers, mainly women, stopped working. As the agitation continued, the Pulaya families had to face the problem of feeding their families. Iyyankāḷi brilliantly networked with the fishermen communities; each boat would care for one Pulayas family. The landowners, mainly Nāirs, tried to break the agitation by working the fields. Years later, in 1916, Iyyankāḷi reminisced that six Nair males took several days to finish the work that one Pulaya woman would take merely a day. With the sympathies of Diwān P. Rājagopālachāri on the side of striking the Pulaya community, the landowners were forced to find a solution. Finally, the Pulaya community children started attending schools. When things got settled, the Pulaya community children got the right to attend schools where Ēzhavās community children were also taught. The role British chief educational officer Dr Mitchell and Diwān P. Rājagopālachāri played a crucial mediatory role in favour of Iyyankāḷi.

Another great man who fought along with Iyyankāḷi for the welfare of the Pulaya community was P.K. Govindan Piḷḷai. Belonging to the Nair community, he was the representative of the Pulaya community in Śrī Mūlam Prajā Sabhā (SMPS), the legislative assembly of Thiruvithāṅcūr. He often stressed the need to make the people of the Pulaya community landowners. He said that the government should register land and give it to the

Pulaya people who had been landless agricultural labourers. On 13 February 1911, he made a historical statement. He stated that instead of him representing the Pulaya people in the assembly, a Pulaya leader should do it. This was accepted. On 5 December 1911, the Government Gazette of Travancore announced that 'Respected Śrī Iyyankāḷi of *Sādhu Jana Paripālana Saṅgham* had been made the honourable member of *Śrī Mūlam Prajā Sabhā*.' This was a monumental occasion in the history of Kerala. Śrī Iyyankāḷi entered the royal legislative assembly of Travancore as a representative of the Pulaya people. But he was representing the voice of all the voiceless or oppressed communities.

But such a position did not stop Iyyankāḷi from working the ground zero for the rights of his people. In 1912, Iyyankāḷi asserted the Pulaya people's right to buy vegetables and fish in the common markets at a place called Nedumangādu. The 'upper-caste' and Muslims planned an organized attack on him and his people. Iyyankāḷi himself was a martial artist and had a team of well-trained disciples. So, they retaliated and defended themselves with valour even though outnumbered. At a coastal place called Kazhakkoottam, local Muslims launched another organized attack on Iyyankāḷi. But with ferocious retaliation from Iyyankāḷi and his men (also called Iyyankāḷi 'padai' or army of Iyyankāḷi), the confrontation reached the proportion of a riot. Because of the timely intervention of local police inspector one Mr Daniel, it did not become a communal riot.[114]

In 1913, a magazine was started for SJPS. Called Sādhu Jana Paripālini, many dharmic-minded 'upper-caste' Hindus came forward to support it.

Talks of Iyyankāḷi in the legislative assembly are filled with passion for the upliftment of his people in a holistic way. It was not caste politics he talked about. Untouchability was a disease that was eating into the vitality of dharma and society. If society is to become healthy, then social exclusion should go. Thus, by sounding the clarion call for the upliftment of Pulayas, Iyyankāḷi was raising the ethical and spiritual health of the entire Hindu society. His priorities were educating the next generation, land rights, and creating spiritual infrastructure.

He pointed out: 'A Pulaya student today, could have been seen only a few years back, would have been seen as just a Pulaya boy and not a student.' (1919 December). He explained with statistics what ails Pulaya students in the current educational system in the state. Of the three lakh Pulayas in the state then, only 12,381 alone were going to schools, and in this, only 136 had been pursuing their education beyond the fifth standard. Only seven persons had succeeded in the common examination. He suggested that there should be education on physical work. Along with the scholarships, there should be a system of instalment paying fees. The only way to make sure that Pulayas attained literacy was to make education till the fourth standard compulsory (2 March 1920). In his speech on 10 March, 1924, Iyyankāḷi made a plea for the mid-day meal schemes for the children. Most Pulaya children came from households of abject poverty. A mid-day meal, even the most basic meal of just gruel, would go a long way in increasing exponentially the literacy rate among the children.

In his speech on 21 March 1923, he expressed concern that in the current population of close to four lakh Pulayas, a considerable percentage had been converted to Christianity:

> The main reason for conversions are poverty and untouchability. This untouchability has no divine sanction. My people have no proper homes and have no access to temples. So in these matters the Government should proactively help than to those of affluent communities. Construct for us temples and water wells. Members of Pulaya community should be at least in small numbers, should be employed as officials in judiciary bodies and government offices. Encouragement in terms of increased

> salary should be given to first standard and second standard school teachers who teach Pulaya children.

The response of the State, which was officially a 'Dharmic State or Hindu State', was that such temple constructions would not come under the purview of the government. Iyyankāḷi was quick to answer that if the state could not construct religious places, it could donate us land and resources with which our own people would build the temples.[115]

In his speech made on 26 February 1924, he pointed out the problems faced by marginalized sections in the agrarian field. Though agricultural land had been given to the Pulaya people, they got occupied illegally by 'upper castes'. Approaching courts was beyond the capability of poor Pulayas. So, they should be exempted from court fees.

In 1930, again, Iyyankāḷi had to organize a strike by the Pulaya agricultural workers. This time the landlords tried to evict the Pulaya workers from their holdings. In a large meeting of Pulaya men and women held on 30 September of that year during the strike, the Salvation Army, who too influenced the Pulaya community, told that the agitating workers should return to work. Iyyankāḷi-led Pulayas made it clear that they would go to work provided their proposed scheme for regular work for their uplift was met. Again, they were able to wrestle significant rights for their emancipation.[116]

The same year, the annual meeting of SJPS was conducted. It was presided over by the then Dewān VS Subrmaniya Iyer, which was unthinkable just a decade ago. Iyyankāḷi made a passionate welcome address in this meeting:

> Long ago, ignoring all consideration of caste, Lord Subrahmanian (Kartikeya the son on Siva) married a low caste Kurava girl. Likewise, we are able to go to schools and other public places like markets without fear. We have reached a stage where we can speak

> our mind to the government about our needs. This honourable gentleman from the upper caste helped us put an end to untouchability to a very great extent. That is why I consider today's Dewan-ji not as Subrahmanya Iyer but as Lord Subrahmanyam himself. I am sure my people also think likewise.[117]

By the 1930s, the fight against untouchability and for the entry of all Hindus, irrespective of their Jāti, to enter the temples continued in Kerala. Gāndhi extended his support for the temple entry movement, including the famous temple of Guruvāyūr. The fierceness of the fight could be understood from the following efforts made by a famous Pontiff in Tamil Nadu against the entry of 'Harijans' into the temples:

> With our Swamigal's complete blessings, a group of Sanatanis left for Kerala on 10-12-1932. The group included legal experts such as T.R.Ramachandra Iyer, Thirpugazhmani T.M. Krishnaswamy Iyer, Sivaramakrishnan, Rajagopala Iyer, S.Subramania Iyer as well as legislators such as M.K. Acharya and V.Somadeva Sharma. They were accorded welcome by Palghat municipal Chairman S.K. Ramaswamy Iyer. There was a public meeting at Palghat on December 10th and one in Guruvayur on December 11th. The Guruvayur meeting was led by Kodakkal Raja. Palghat Dr.Sankara Iyer and Thekadi Govinda Menon also made speeches at the meetings. Many resolutions were passed against the Harijans' entry into temples. The opposition to entry into temples for Harijans was gathering momentum in Kerala where even women participated in the demonstrations.[118]

In 1933, Iyyankāli declared and stressed the right of all Hindus to enter the temples. Ultimately dharma prevailed. Maharaja Chithira Thirunal Balarama Varma issued the Temple Entry Proclamation on 12 November 1936. Diwān C.P. Rāmaswamy Iyer played an important proactive role in this historical proclamation. Temple entry was a major victory in democratizing spirituality in a land plagued by social stagnation of the worst kind. In a thanks-giving message to C.P. Rāmaswamy Iyer, 'Sree Narayana Dharma Samrakshana Sangham' an organization based on the principles of Śrī Nārayana Guru, wrote:

> The glorious Temple Entry Proclamation which liberated millions of Non-caste Hindus from age-long social and religious tyranny and guaranteed their equality has given Travancore an international reputation and she, has been enabled thereby to establish her hegemony among Indian States. It is confidently hoped that the Temple Entry Reform will soon develop into its logical and natural perfection by the opening of the Devaswom Department to all denominations of Hindus.[119]

The magnificent spiritual and social renaissance set by the spiritual impulse in society continues and progresses steadily.

In 1983, a Vishal Hindu Sammelan (VHS Grant Hindu Convention) was organized by Rashtriya Swayamsevak Sangh (RSS) in Ernakulam, Kerala. The chief Tantrik of the main puja conducted in the sammelan was an Ēzhavā, and his assistant was a Nambūdiri. The same year saw the founding of the Thanthra Vidya Peedham (TVP) by a senior life worker (pracharak) of the RSS, P. Madhavji (1926-88), along with eminent Vedic scholars. Since then, TVP has been an integral part of the sociocultural movement that has today culminated in the appointment of priests from all Hindu communities without any discrimination. The Peetham trains youngsters in all traditional knowledge domains to become qualified priests in Kerala, irrespective of their caste. In a public ceremony, the certificates were given to the students trained in TVP by none other than the junior acharya of Kanchi—Sri Jayendra Saraswathi.[120]

Thus, in Kerala, modern social emancipation arose from strong spiritual seeds and their subsequent natural development. Again, the standard model historiography provides little attention to the spiritual seed component of the social emancipation movement and often sees it as merely a convenience adopted by the pioneers of the social movement. In reality, in the historical context of continued spiritual processes vitalizing social emancipation in India, the struggle for social emancipation by marginalized and depressed communities in the state should be viewed as the manifestation of this important dimension of Hindu spirituality in the context of modernity and the colonial situation.

CHAPTER 13

Dharmic Emancipation through Bhakti and Advaita in Modern Age: Tradition, Individuals, and Lineages

Colonialism brought with it two important factors, modernity and impoverishment. Impoverishment made society stagnant and amplified the social evils in society. Modernity brought in new structures and challenges. Mass education through an institutional chain under the centralized state authority created immense challenges. This, in turn, created an imaginary conflict between the oppressive indigenous system of ignorance versus the enlightenment brought by the colonial project. The dharmic organism of the nation responded to this challenge in ways more than one. This chapter explores such responses from individuals rooted in dharma, as well as authentic traditions and lineages. Having no State to support them, and having not much capital, unlike the colonial forces, these dharmic forces rose and played a very important role in social emancipation.

Śrī Karapāthira Śivaprakāsa Śwāmigaḷ (1874-1918)

Karapāthri is a famous name for a specific order of monks known for their strict adherence to a vow of owning no material possessions, not even a begging bowl. Instead, they receive alms directly into their hands. The name 'Karapāthri' originates from the combination of 'kar' (meaning hands in Tamil as well as Sanskrit) and 'pāthra' (meaning bowl), signifying that the monk's hands serve as their begging bowl, hence the name 'Karapāthri. This concept is mentioned in the Natṟṟiṇai, a *classic* Saṅgam-era literature dating back to 1,800-1,500 years ago. It describes penance-performing monks who receive food only in their palms.[1] In other words, the practice of Karapāthri monks is a pan-Indian concept, representing a characteristically Hindu phenomenon uniting the nation through the ages.

Born in a Vīra Saiva family in Tamil Nadu in the 19th century, the parents named their child 'Śivaprakāsa'. Later he would become Karapāthri Maharāj. It is said the child showed an almost miraculous interest in spirituality even as an infant. For example, the lore has it that instead of using the usual first words 'Ammā' (mother) and 'Appā' (father), the child started uttering the words 'Umā' and 'Śiva' to the surprise of all.[2]

When he was sixteen, Śivaprakāsa's father died, and his elder brothers made him take up the trade of betel leaves. During this time, Śivaprakāsa became attracted to both the Śankara, a school of Advaitic Vēdāntā, and the Advaita School of Śaiva Śiddhāntā. His teacher of Vēdāntā was Ratna Dēsikar, hailed as Vēdāntā Bānu' (radiant sun of Vēdāntā). Soon, Śivaprakāsa persuaded his family, gently but firmly, to allow him to renounce the world. When his mother insisted that he marry and give her a grandchild, he agreed, in his own way, by choosing to marry the life of renunciation and giving her the child of wisdom and liberation, which would bring her true joy.

This method of passive response to the opponent arguing against and then slowly working to change the mind of the opponent became a characteristic feature of the Śwāmigaḷ. Before renouncing worldly life, he ceremoniously received the food in his hand during a final food-serving ceremony by asking for the plantain leaf to be removed. Then he entered ceremoniously into the 'Karapāthri' tradition. After the passing of Ratna Dēsikar, he found a spiritual mentor in Śwāmi Krishnānanda Yatīndra, a saint of the Ādi Śaṅkara tradition.

Similar to Ramaṇa Mahaṛṣi, he gained followers and devotees despite his penance in solitude.

Among those who came to Śwāmi was a young boy, Munusāmi. He exuded spiritual knowledge and sought truth. Earlier, he had excelled as a student in a missionary school. Munusāmi came from a poor background and belonged to a Scheduled Castes community. Missionaries, recognizing his talents, tried to convert him to Christianity and gave him a new name, but Munusāmi refused. As a result, he was humiliated and forced to discontinue his education.

The reason Munusāmi refused to convert was because he had a strong Hindu spiritual inclination. He was later initiated into Vēdāntic studies by a spiritual institution guided by Karapāthri Śwāmi of Tamil Nadu at that time—Thiruthuruthi Indra Pīthām Karapāthri Satchitānanda Maharāj. Here, Śrī Nīlamēga Śwāmi trained the young boy in Vēdānta. Munusāmi then came to Śrī Karapāthria Śivaprakāsa Śwāmigaḷ.

Śrī Karapāthria Śivaprakāsa Śwāmigaḷ recognized the spiritual potential of the youth and arranged for the best talents in Tamil and Sanskrit grammar, Nyāya and Vēdānta available in the province to teach Munusāmi. Many who came to see Śrī Śwāmigaḷ were zamindars, a feudal class that had grown powerful under the colonial government and the educated power elite of colonial Madras. They were surprised to see the extremely favourable attitude of Śrī Śwāmigaḷ towards a Scheduled Caste community youth. However, Śrī Śwāmigaḷ made him the most intimate disciple, much to the chagrin of these so-called upper castes.

Murugēsa Mudaliyār, an expert in Nyāya Sāstra, was initially reluctant to teach Sāstra to the youth. However, Śrī Śwāmigaḷ insisted, and as Mudaliyār started teaching the young boy, he realized the brilliance of his student. Mudaliyār later admitted that teaching Munusāmi could benefit the entire society. He movingly confided with Śrī Śwāmigaḷ that the very purpose of Mudaliyār learning Nyāya Sāstra was fulfilled only by teaching Munusāmi. Śrī Śwāmigaḷ then initiated Munusāmi into the life of renunciation, service, and sādhana, giving him the name Śwāmi Sahajānanda.

In colonial Madras, the notion of colour-based casteism, influenced by European racism and the Indian caste system, had started percolating into the collective psyche of elite Indian people. When a devotee murmured about the dark complexion of Śwāmi Sahajānanda, Śrī Śwāmigaḷ replied:

> What is in colour? Cannot you see his character and intelligence? If colour is the criterion for nobility then the British should be considered as the noblest which is not the case. So bless this boy who is learning and do not judge by colour.[3]

Here, the passage illustrates how traditional Hindu Vēdāntic humanism rejected the idea of colour-based superiority, borrowed from European colonialism and mixed with the Indian caste notions.

When some of his disciples suggested that he should accept a disciple from a non-Scheduled Castes community and ask Śwāmi Sahajānanda to go, Śrī Śwāmigaḷ responded with Vēdāntic satire: 'Yes, he should be made to go. He came from somewhere, and he will have to go somewhere. He cannot stay.' Then, when the casteists began to settle in, Śrī Śwāmigaḷ explained to them the futility of caste-based notions. These were superficial affiliations, he said to them. But if one looks deeper, were we all not born of women, and are we all not divine? Thus, gently but firmly, Śrī Śwāmigaḷ worked to remove caste biases and notions of superiority and inferiority in the devotees around him.

In a collection of poems he brought out on Vēdānta, titled '*Vēdānta Manana Sinthāmaṇi*' there are verses that demonstrate the futility of caste and true Brahminhood. Again, these ideas are integral to the traditional spiritual discourse. Yet, in the context of social stagnation eating into the vitals of the nation, they naturally served social emancipation:

Those who know the truth of
Non-discriminatory oneness primordial
Would they even consider Jāthi and clan?
Higher are ones who possess wisdom venerable
Inferior are all others. [*Amrita Sāram*][4]

Do not get disheartened and disillusioned by Jāthi;
Who knows what Jāthi is who for all bodies are the same;
Jāthi to know is those who know their true self as Śiva
They alone are the high Jāthi, so the *Vēdā*s declare the Truth.
[*Śivānanda Bōtham*, verse 8][5]

Even one well versed in *Vēdā*s
If devoid of undivided Jñāna
Jñāna that accomodates no differences,
They then are no Brahmins,
Their upavīta just a caste mark
Not a tool of Brahmanatva.
When adorned with
Non-Differentiating Para-Brahman
Verily as the true upavīta
One becomes a Brahmin,
A true liberated one.
[*Ribu Gīta*, verse 191][6]

From Upaniṣads to Thirukkuraḷ to *Manīsha Pañchakam*, he would cite and make the assembled disciples realize the fallacy of their caste-based objections to Śwāmi Sahajānanda.

For instance, when a person questioned, in an offensive way, whether children from the scheduled community children could really study, Śrī Śwāmigaḷ simply asked Śwāmi Sahajānanda to recite a difficult verse and explain its meaning. After doing so, the questioner realized his mistake and acknowledged that Jāthi, etc., were merely a social construct. Śrī Śwāmigaḷ possessed a rare copy of the *Ribu Gīta*. He had received it from his guru. Out of all his disciples, he chose to gift this sacred text to Śwāmi Sahajānanda, signifying the spiritual and social significance of the gesture.

Not all his disciples took to such praise of Sahajānanda easily. One Natēsa Nāyakar wrote a letter to Śrī Śwāmigaḷ that if he did not send the seer away, Nāyakar would be forced to kill Śrī Śwāmigaḷ by poison. Even after this letter, Śrī Śwāmigaḷ treated Nāyakar with love but did not flinch in his love and concern for Śwāmi Sahajānanda.[7] Śwāmi Sahajānanda was a very calm personality but economically poor. When one made a remark on this, Śrī Śwāmigaḷ said that he was actually a very (spiritually) rich person. And when someone made a comment on the young seer being always silent and calm, Śrī Śwāmigaḷ stated that Śwāmi Sahajānanda was an equivalent of Ādi Śaṅkara himself.[8]

Later, Śwāmi Sahajānanda aimed to establish social and spiritual institutions to uplift the marginalized and exploited sections of society in Chidambaram. Naturally, there was opposition from the so-called upper castes who wanted to prevent the establishment of such institutions. Śrī Śwāmigaḷ not only supported the saint but also contacted Parañjōthi Śwāmi of an influential Śaivaite Mutt in Chidambaram. Initially, this swami was not supportive of establishing the institutions, but Śrī Śwāmigaḷ convinced him to assist Śwāmi Sahajānanda in overcoming the opposition as well as in establishing the institutions.[9]Although born in the Vīra Saiva family, Śrī Karapāthira Śivaprakāsa Śwāmigaḷ found his truth in Ādi Śaṅkara, particularly in the universal inclusiveness and non-dual Gnosis displayed in *Manīsha Pañchakam*. On every birth anniversary of Ādi Śaṅkara, Śrī Śwāmigaḷ performed a grand worship of the Ācharya. Additionally, in Vyāsarpādi, Chennai, where he had established a Vēdānta Saṅgha, he also placed the sacred idol of Ādi Śaṅkara, who was carried in a procession.

Śrī Karapāthira Śivaprakāsa Śwāmigaḷ attained mahāsamādhi in 1918.

Maharṣi Vitthal Rāmji Shiṇdé

The strong socio-political movement against untouchability can largely be attributed to the influence of Vitthal Rāmji Shiṇdé (1873-1944). He was a calm, determined, soft-spoken, scholarly figure, born in a small village now in northern Karnataka. His father Rāmjibābā held a clerical officer and teacher position. Despite the prevailing reluctance to send girls to schools at that time, he persuaded families across the social spectrum to send their daughters to school. This resulted in a diverse student body, including eight Brahmin girls, four Marāttā girls, and three Muslim girls.[10] Shiṇdé witnessed his father becoming particularly religiously attracted to Varkari during economic hardship. He observed the strength his mother derived from her Vaiṣṇava tradition-inspired bhakti throughout her extremely difficult life. When the family fell into very desperate conditions due to his father's alcoholism, Shiṇde saw how his mother's individual-level bhakti helped her maintain an unbelievably positive outlook while running the household:

> Even after we were somewhat more grown she would alleviate the stark painfulness of our poverty by singing such songs and narrating tales about Krishna and Gopis. Mother must have learned in Algur, even before her marriage, to keep observances and perform household rituals and fasts just like Brahmins.[11]

He witnessed his mother enduring economic hardship, her husband's alcoholism, and the cruelty of her mother-in-law, yet she raised the family with strong character. This deeply fascinated him with the spiritual power of religion and made him feel the strong need for reform in Hindu marriage. He also observed that his Sanskrit teacher, Ganesh-Shastri Joshi, never discriminated against him based on his caste. As he evolved into a brilliant student, he also imbibed the teachings of Dnyansehwari, the poetry of Tukaram, Ashtakas of Dattatreya, and the Bhakti saints of both Kannada and Marathi. As an intelligent and inquisitive young man, all these began to churn within him. His biographer writes:

> He believed that religion and other mundane matters were essentially related. He thought that the religious impulse in the human being is also a matter of natural growth and evolution. In his thought of course evolutionary principle occupies an important place. Eating, drinking, reading, study etc., happen as a matter of natural development; they do not require a divine gift or inspiration. Similarly in his opinion, religious awareness and evolution do not need divine intervention.... Just as one sees a course of evolution from prehistoric man to civilized man in notions of religion, so may one see a growth in an individual's religious feeling from childhood to maturity.[12]

As he grew intellectually, he gradually moved from scepticism to a fascination towards religious rituals and tradition. Although he became an active member of Prarthana Samaj of the Brahmos, his Vaiṣṇava Bhakti remained strong. Mahārāshtra of the times was in turmoil, with Tilak and nationalists on one side and Phule and Ranade, etc., on the other side. This too influenced him. However, he was always concerned about the lack of focus on religion as a phenomenon. He was in favour of the reformists and critical of Tilak's negative or indifferent attitudes towards reforms. Yet before embarking on his journey abroad for higher studies, he then, an unknown student, a sincere Brahmo, and a pro-reformist, made it a point to get an appointment with Tilak. This was due to his admiration for Tilak's selfless patriotism despite their differences. To his surprise, he obtained an appointment. Tilak was sitting on the floor in a traditional manner, and he made Shiṇdé sit by his side like a well-known friend.

> He gave me affectionate advice that I must learn to compare Eastern and Western ways and ideas without allowing my mind to be warped by the divisions and schisms in the Hindu religion such as Dvaita, Advaita and Visishta Advaita and different modes of worship such as Shaiva, Vaishnava and Shakta. He suggested that I ought to emulate the bravely independent minds that had characterised Hindus of the Upanishad Era. I was pleasantly surprised at this outcome of our meeting.[13]

Shiṇdé studied comparative religion at Oxford between 1901 and 1903. During this time, he had some mystic experiences in the settings of nature. This is how he described one such experience:

> Everything was so still even the thinnest leaf did not stir. I watched this kingdom of peace with my eyes. The army of progress had been driven far away. Ideas such as emancipation and progress did not occur to the mind here. The peace without enabled the voice of my deepest inner being to be heard.... Here one did not even remember one's dearest relations. Awareness of the surroundings did not impinge on one's mind. I had departed altogether from the world. Who was this magician in the inner sanctum of nature who in moment forced us to surrender to it! Once I entered this highest spiritual state I was powerless to return from it.[14]

While in Scotland, he climbed up the 3,000-foot Ben Lomond and had a similar spiritual experience. He described this experience using the term 'samādhi'. In a personal letter, he explained the terms as he used them. Interestingly, Shiṇḍé found similar expressions in non-human animals. Although not exactly as Shiṇḍé had interpreted them, such religious experience in non-human primates would be recorded by primatologist Jane Goodall almost a century after Shiṇḍé wrote these lines:

> In the above letter I have termed 'purely personal' experiences such as prayer, encounter or meeting and 'samadhi.' These are serious words. A reader may think that in using them I am glorifying myself. And he may think that the description is exaggerated. But it is not.... Furthermore even lower animals whose consciousness is developed may experience beauty in the manner I have called 'samadhi' which is a condition of oneness or communion.[15]

After returning to India, working extensively with Brahmos and Prārthana Samāj, as well as touring throughout the country, he felt compelled to work for the upliftment of all sections of society. In this, he was supported by two individuals from Arya Samāj—Dr Ruben and Śwāmi Swātmānanda of Karachi. Through his journeys, organizing conferences, and meeting all sections of society, Shiṇḍé became acutely aware of the importance of fighting untouchability. While there were regional efforts to eradicate this social evil, Shiṇḍé realized that addressing untouchability required a pan-India approach due to its widespread nature.

He identified the religious dimension of the problem:

> The evil is rooted here in the religious system, founded upon the Varna distinction. Everyone believes that this order with the sanction from religion and scriptures cannot be changed. To emancipate the untouchables, the religion that created the category must be essentially modified; notions it has engendered

> must be eradicated if untouchability should be eradicated. Rituals and conduct based on religious sanctions would need to be modified and superstitions and notions based on them must be rooted out. Only then would the mind of the people be revolutionised.[16]

After extensive networking and convincing prominent leaders, the 'Depressed Classes Mission Society' was established on 18 October 1906. Sheth Damodar Sukhadwala generously donated a significant sum of Rs 1,000. In its first year, the Mission organized nine public lectures, four kirtans, and five readings from the Purāṇas. This also helped to dispel the notion that they were Christian missionaries. The Mission also ran a lodge for Scheduled Castes community students, and one of the students, Ganesh Akaji Gavai, went on to become a prominent activist for the rights of the suppressed and a Hindu Mahasabha leader. The Mission achieved remarkable success and made rapid progress. In 1909, a founding day event was organized in Pune, where the Mission had not yet firmly established itself. The meeting took place at the famous Kirloskar Theatre and was attended by prominent personalities cutting across the political spectrum, such as L.B. Bhopatkar and N.C. Kelkar, Dharmanand Kosambi and Islamail Bahadur. Surprisingly, even Śaṅkarācharya of Hampi expressed his sympathy through a representative of the Math present at the meeting, Mr Harkaré.[17] Despite facing challenges and insults, the Mission received substantial help from Hindu society at large, including a significant contribution from Shreemant Tukojirao Holkar, the prince of Indore, who donated a cheque of Rs 20,000 for the construction of a building in Poona, with the condition that it be named after his illustrious ancestral matriarch, Ahalyabai Holkar. As a result, the building in Poona became known as Ahalyashram, bearing the name of the esteemed matriarch.[18]

Gradually, the voice of the Depressed Classes Mission began to gain more serious attention at the national level. As the idea of home rule or Swarajya was becoming a reality, it became necessary to pass an official resolution against untouchability as a sin towards humanity. Shiṇdé and his association tirelessly worked for the passing of this resolution in the Congress. At its annual session in Calcutta on 26 December 1917, Dr Annie Besant passed a resolution against untouchability, marking an important victory for Shiṇdé. Additionally, Nationalist Congress leader from Madras Presidency and a publisher of nationalist literature Ganapathi Agraharam Annadhurai Ayyar Natesan, supporting the resolution, said:

> Until today this question has been placed on the agenda of other organisations. It is being placed here now keeping in view of the special nature of the national Congress. We have drawn out a blueprint of Swadeshi or Home Rule. To carry it out it is necessary we attend it now. It is our first duty to remove inequality and injustice from our society first. The main thrust of this resolution is to remove the unjust, harsh and lowly condition imposed on this class of people. On one hand as we are demanding the rights of British citizenship, how can we deny some people amongst us the basic right to treatment as human beings.... We must keep in mind that it is from amongst the same six crore people came saints like Nandanar, Chokamela and Rohidas. They have such implicit strength and superior morality.... When we are elevating them, we are elevating humanity in India. When we obtain responsible self-rule, we ought to be able to say with firmness it is for all classes and everyone has equal social rights.[19]

It is worth noting that Dr Besant's role in moving this resolution was significant. In 1909, Annie Besant strongly opposed the entry of students of Depressed classes with the 'caste Hindu' students. Her writing in the February 1909 issue of *Indian*

Review is worth quoting in some detail, as it illustrates how British social prejudices played a large role in their perception of Indian reality:

> In every nation we find, as the basis of the social pyramid, a large class of people, ignorant, degraded, unclean in language and habits, people, who perform many tasks which are necessary for Society, but who are despised and neglected by the very Society to whose needs they minister. In England, this class is called the 'submerged tenth,' forming, as it does, one-tenth of the total population. It is ever on the verge of starvation, and the least extra pressure sends it over the edge. It suffers chronically from under-nutrition, and is a prey to the diseases which spring therefrom. It is prolific, like all creatures in whom the nervous system is of a low type, but its children die off rapidly, ill-nourished, rickety, often malformed. Its better type consists of unskilled labourers, who perform the roughest work, scavengers, sweepers, navvies, casual dock-labourers, costermongers; and into it, forming its worse type, drift all the wastrels of Society, the drunkards, the loafers, the coarsely dissolute, the tramps, the vagabonds, the clumsily criminal, the ruffians. The first type is, as a rule, honest and industrious; the second ought to be under continued control, and forced to labour sufficiently to earn its bread. In India, this class forms one-sixth of the total population, and goes by the generic name of the 'Depressed Classes.' It springs from the aboriginal inhabitants of the country, conquered and enslaved by the Aryan invaders.... What can be done for them by those who feel the barbarity of the treatment meted out to them, by those who feel that the Indians who demand freedoms should show respect to others, and give to others a share of the consideration they claim for themselves? Here, as everywhere, education is the lever by which we may hope to raise them, but a difficulty arises at the outset.... Ought the children of families in which good manners and courtesy are hereditary, to be robbed of their heritage, a robbery that enriches no one, but drags the whole nation down? In England, it has never been regarded as desirable to educate boys or girls of all classes side by side, and

> such grotesque equalising of the unequal would be scouted. Eton and Harrow are admittedly the schools for the higher classes; Rubgy and Winchester are also schools for gentlemen's sons, though somewhat less aristocratic. Then come a number of schools, frequented chiefly by sons of the provincial middle class. Then the Board Schools, where the sons of artisans and the general manual labour classes are taught; and below all these, for the waifs and strays, are the 'ragged schools,' the name of which indicates the type of their scholars, and the numerous charitable institutions. A man in England who proposed that ragged school-children should be admitted to Eton and Harrow would not be argued with, but laughed at. Here, when a similar proposition is made in the name of brotherhood, people seem ashamed to point out frankly its absurdity, and they do not realise that the proposal is merely a violent reaction against the cruel wrongs which have been inflicted on the Depressed Classes, the outcry of an awakened conscience, which has not yet had time to call right reason to guide its emotions.[20]

The above passage shows not only how much the British prejudices played into the perception of Indian society but also how the characterization of Indian society as dominantly controlled by a unique ethically deficient religion, i.e., Hinduism, was hypocritical on the part of the Western missionaries, though their work definitely helped the marginalized communities in India. It is worth noting that the Hindu social reformers then outshine their British counterparts in their commitment to human equality.

Even such a prejudiced person as Dr Besant was converted to passing a resolution against untouchability was in itself a testimony to the persuasive power of Shiṇdé. A significant supporter of the resolution was from a Malabar Brahmin named Ram Iyer. He argued that Indians could not be 'liberal in political terms and tyrannical and custom-ridden in social terms'. Once the resolution was passed in Calcutta, every state and then every district Congress Committee would have to follow suit. In this, again, Shiṇḍé played an important role. At the Lonavala provincial meeting, the resolution against untouchability was passed unanimously and to everyone's surprise, Tilak, considered by many as conservative, supported the resolution.

Resolution against Untouchability

The next most important milestone for Shiṇḍé was conducting a conference on the eradication of untouchability in 1918. King of Baroda Sayajirao Gaekwad presided over the conference. It was attended by eminent leaders like nationalist leader Bipin Chandra Pal, Hindutva leader Barrister Mukundrao Jayakar, and eminent jurist Chandravarkar. Rabīndranāth Thākur and Śaṅkarācharya of Karvir sent telegrams extending their support to the Conference. King Gaekwad, in his speech, pointed out the similarity between the 'Hinain class in Japan and the lowest of the untouchable class in India'. But in Japan, the young emperor had abolished the inhuman practice 'by one imperial order', he said. 'With no such possibility of an imperial order in India, we have to solve the problem through education and change of conscience by appealing gradually to the mind of the population.'

> It is easy to point to empirical proof here in India of the fact that the new so-called Antyaj people, or Panchamas, as they are termed in Madras, are not uniformly feeble in spirit or mentality. It is a commonplace that the depressed classes in every part of India have produced saints of nation-wide reputation respected even by Brahmins; for example, Nanada in South India, Ravidas in Oudh, Chokamela in Maharashtra, Haridas Thakur in Bengal. There are current examples too numerous to mention of outcaste boys who have passed the highest tests of the universities both in India and abroad.[21]

Then he gave instances from the not-so-old history:

> That this idea of untouchability is only a later refinement, born of ignorance and conceit and nurtured by self-complacency, which the luxury and ease of a settled life of peace and order rendered possible, is well illustrated by the manner in which it was allowed to be smoothed over and ignored on the battlefield. The story of the Shilledar Shidnak, who was a Mahar, whose tents were pitched amongst those of the Brahmin and Maratha officers, and who rubbed shoulders with them on the plains of Kharda, proves the adage that necessity knows no law. Religious scruples of untouchability were cast to the winds when the people were hemmed in under enemy pressure.

In the closing address, he pointed out the incompatibility of caste discrimination with the knowledge of the Self as revealed in the Bhagavad Gītā:

> The highest knowledge is knowledge of the self, and it is this knowledge that reveals to us the essential unity of the Supreme Being manifesting Himself in various embodiments which it is only an illusion to regard as inherently differing in kind. It is unwise to over-emphasize differences. Nowhere is there any authority for the view that varna is by birth and that, whereas personal merit counts for nothing, the accident of birth is everything. I exhort you to seek inspiration from the noble teaching of the Bhagavat Gītā: 'To me all creation is equal; there is no like or dislike.'

In this appeal of Gaekwad, one can see how the instances of Bhakti saints from throughout India, as also the knowledge and realization of Self in all as revealed in the Bhagavad Gītā become anchor points to argue for human equality, particularly in terms of the intellectual and spiritual equality of all communities. This sets Hindu social reformers apart from the Western approach to uplifting marginalized communities. Gaekwad himself was very conscious that Indian social emancipation should not ape the West.

It was Hindutvaite Jayakar who proposed the first resolution that 'untouchability... be eradicated immediately' and towards this end, 'the important and thinking leaders in each region should make a public declaration that the (depressed) class be given unrestricted access to schools, hospitals, law offices, public institutions funded by government money, wells, tanks and other public sources of water, all places of ordinary business, temples and similar places'. An important message was given in the speech made by Mahant Mohandas Maharaj, the spiritual leader from the 'untouchable' Dhed community. He gave the instances of 'Satyakama Jabala, Kavasha Ailusha, Swami Ramanand, Kabir, Sena Bhakta, Rohidas and Nabhaji in the Hindu religion and pointed out that the real twice-born was not by birth'. Unfortunately, Tilak did not sign the declaration that followed. It is dealt with separately in the sub-section that follows this section.

With the ascendancy of Mahatma Gandhi and Dr Ambedkar, Shiṇdé slowly moved towards the sunset of his life. It was clear that Dr Ambedkar and his movement did not trust him, which saddened him. To them, Shiṇdé was, despite his efforts, a non-untouchable caste Hindu, and hence, they viewed him with reservation. Despite this, he accepted the situation. When Pandit Māḷaviā expressed regret about he being a defeated hero, Shiṇdé replied that a hero should be, by necessity, defeated. He nevertheless continued to participate in the national liberation movement. In 1930, he was arrested and received a six-month rigorous imprisonment for participating in the Civil Disobedience movement. The harsh punishment of a fifty-seven-year-old social revolutionary drew widespread condemnation, but he entered prison with equanimity, reciting lines from the famous Maharashtrian spiritual treatise Dhyaneswari.

The pain that he felt in his life was evident in the starting passage of the autobiography of Shiṇdé. It also showed how deeply spiritual his worldview was that even pain manifested as

Bhakti. Shiṇḍé, in his introduction, quotes what Prahlād says to his grandson Bali.

> Softness can conquer hardness; softness can conquer softness too; nothing is impossible for softness; that is why compassion is sharper than the sharpest weapon. (Mahabharata: Vanaparva: 32)

Shiṇḍé continues:

> The sloka is the emblem of Mahatma Gandhi's Ahimsavada. Ever since I became aware of the world, such has been my experience at least in public work. I do not mean to say that my native tendency is to be compassionate. How can I say what is not true!... My innate nature was hard certainly not soft as defined by the above sloka. But in my adult life, whatever work I undertook, whenever I put on the yoke of religious mission on my weak shoulders, a truthful and loving duty I encountered harshness. Consequently I have become softer to some extent if not altogether compassionate. And I consider that the reward of my service and thank not only the Ruler of the Universe but the universe itself.[22]

After a fruitful life of selfless service and advancing the cause of social emancipation, he died on 2 January 1944.

Tilak Controversy[23]

On 24 March 1918, freedom fighter Lōkamānya Bālagaṅgādhar Tilak (1856–1920) passed a resolution that the Indian National Congress include representatives of untouchable castes. He aimed to involve them in discussions and obtain their cooperation and support for the national cause. During his emotional and impassioned speech at the conference, he stated that there was no sanction for untouchability in the Vedas. He emphasized that if Vedas supported untouchability, he would reject them. He also expressed that if God sanctioned untouchability, he would reject

God himself. Tilak then narrated incidents from his personal life wherein he had defied untouchability:

> In 1894 in Poona a Chambhar had set up a public Ganesh idol during the annual festival. At that time work that Shiṇdé is doing was not happening. No one was willing to allow the Chambhar's Ganapati to join the procession. So after talking to him I brought his image of Ganapati to my cart. [loud clapping.].... At home I do not maintain untouchability. [Loud clapping.] Some followers of Chokha Mela came to my house for some work. They wished to consult me about something. I had them sit with me in the house.... I declare unambiguously that I oppose untouchability. I believe that the custom of untouchability must go. It is a mere custom and must be eradicated.

This should have created a stir among the conservative followers of Tilak. As a follow-up action, a declaration was drafted. The declaration stated that for a unified nation, the eradication of untouchability was imperative.

> It is the duty of every son and daughter of India, every person who is proud of his religion, to rid himself of the customary restraints and strive to his utmost to bring to hundreds of thousands of victims of the custom the succor they need.

Then the second part read:

> Similarly we the signatories declare that when in our personal lives occasion presents itself to do so, we shall put this resolution into practice as our individual duty.

Among those who readily signed this declaration were Rabindranath Tagore, Bipin Chandra Pal, Hindutvaite Barrister Jayakar, and staunch Tilakaites N.C. Kelkar, B.S. Moonje, Namdar Karpade, and others. When Shiṇdé took the resolution to Tilak, he initially moved to sign it, but Dadasaheb

Karandikar got in his way. Tilak requested that he be given some time. However, Shiṇḍé insisted, and Tilak pleaded with folded hands that he would consider it after his London trip. Tilak ultimately did not sign the declaration. Shiṇḍé wrote to Tilak in June, but Tilak did not reply. After Shiṇḍé persisted, Tilak finally sent a reply in August, stating that he was unable to sign the declaration due to the second paragraph, which made it a personal duty to fight untouchability. Nonetheless, Tilak assured that he was in total agreement about the necessity of eradicating untouchability.

Despite this one unpleasant episode, the relationship and respect between Shiṇḍé and Tilak remained cordial. With 300 eminent persons from all over India supporting the declaration, Shiṇḍé linked the eradication of untouchability with Śwarāj. At the Lonavala district political conference, when a resolution was to be passed on obtaining Śwarāj, Shiṇḍé made it a precondition that a resolution on abolishing untouchability should also be passed. Lavaté, a staunch follower of Tilak, opposed this vehemently. Shiṇḍé made Lavaté visit Tilak. Tilak gave the following advice to Lavaté:

> The time to refuse eradication of untouchability with a religious excuse is now gone. If, by persuading Shiṇḍé you wish to pass your Swaraj resolution unanimously, then his anti-untouchability resolution also should be passed unanimously. If this does not suit you then you (Lavaté) should leave the conference marquee.

This brought Lavaté to accept the anti-untouchability resolution, and both resolutions were passed simultaneously and unanimously.

There is evidence that Tilak did not observe caste barriers in his personal life. V.O. Chidambaram Pillai, also known as VOC, a freedom fighter from South India who belonged to the non-Brahmin community, attended the Surat Congress session in 1907, where he met Tilak, whom he considered his guru. In his writings, VOC always referred to Tilak as his guru. He had the opportunity to meet Tilak in person for the first time at the Surat Congress in 1907.

> [O]ur noon meal was waiting for us for a very long time as my Guru was not able to leave the crowds that were coming by thousands to kiss his feet. At about 3 p.m., one of our Surat friend asked the crowds to wait for a few minutes and took my Guru, Babu Arabindo, myself and a few others to a back room to have our meals. Having known that we belonged to different castes and creeds and thinking that my Guru might not like to sit and take his food with us, that Surat friend asked my Guru 'May I arrange to serve you the meal in the next room?' My Guru promptly replied 'All patriots are of one and the same caste and creed' and sat amidst us and took his food with us. That is his so-called Orthodoxy![24]

One should note that the events mentioned occurred before the Untouchability Eradication Conference. In 1908, VOC was convicted of sedition and initially sentenced to life in the Andaman Islands, which was later reduced to six years of rigorous imprisonment in the mainland. He was released in 1912. During this time, 'his Guru' was also awarded rigorous imprisonment and released from Mandalay jail in 1914. In 1915, when VOC visited Poona at the invitation of Tilak, it coincided with the death of Gopal Krishna Gokhale, who was perceived as Tilak's main political rival. Tilak attended Gokhale's funeral and returned late at night, discussing Gokhale's greatness with VOC. Tilak was aware of a plan by a group of Indians abroad to use the First World War to liberate India through an armed uprising with the help of Germany. Tilak expressed his doubts about the success of this plan, given the dynamics of European politics. He also conveyed that due to India's vast diversity, the path to Indian freedom might not be the same for all Indians. However, he emphasized the importance of unity in the aim of achieving freedom, despite the diversity of methods. VOC also inquired about social reforms and Tilak's response was documented:

> He said that it was a very good movement. If it was so, I asked him, why did he not take any active part in that movement. He replied that one should have one object in view, and that he should concentrate all his attention and energy to attain that one object. If he allows himself to have more objects than one in view, his attention and energy will be diffused and consequently he cannot accomplish any one of those objects. I asked him, if the present caste system does not stand in the way of unity among the people of the country. He replied 'Yes, It does stand. Several men including those that are in Government services are working to root out the evils in the present caste system. Why should we interfere in their work, when we have more than enough work to do in another direction?'[25]

Again, this statement was also made by Tilak two years before the conference, and it is consistent with his behaviour at the conference. He was too truthful, like the legendary Harichandra, and did not care about his reputation. He opposed untouchability while opposing untouchability was not part of his mission. But in his personal life, he never cared for caste, as the following testimony of VOC shows:

> I fear I will be wanting in gratitude if I do not express a word it treatment that was accorded to me during my stay with my Guru. For a few days in the beginning he used to sit with me during my morning and evening tea and during my noon and it meals and to take his drink and diet with me. His drink and diet were those of diabetic patients. Although I did not like the flavour and taste, he used to ask me to taste a little of them any time he drank and ate with me. When I got acquainted with his

> relations and friends in his house, I preferred to go, sit and my noon and night meals with them. Even then he used to come and ask me how I liked the meals etc. Neither he nor of his relations or friends ever asked me to what caste I belonged. In short, every one of the inmates of my Guru's house including my Guru treated me as the master of the house.[26]

This was the typical behaviour one would expect from a patriot who had no awareness of caste distinctions. So, when he said in the conference that he never practised untouchability in his house, he was only partially truthful. The actual truth was that he never had any caste barriers, including untouchability, in his house. He only mentioned this at the conference to inspire people, as he never emphasized this positive aspect of himself anywhere else to portray himself as progressive.

Understanding Tilak to Understand 'De-colonization' Fallacy

The period in which Tilak emerged was filled with motivated anti-Brahminism, which allied itself with the social reformist movement. The local community ego-clashes began to have a new colour and added constructed dimensions under British rule.

Chitpavans as the Brain of Anti-British Agitations

The British viewed the Chitpavan Brahmins as a threat to their rule in India. This was the same caste to which Tilak belonged. The British-controlled English press in India consistently perpetuated negative stereotypes against them. Even before the British consolidated their hold in Western India through the second Anglo-Maratta war, 'Brahminical' Peshwa Bajirao-II (1775–1851) showed that the sense of freedom could go beyond caste considerations. He risked war with the British to avoid handing over his trusted high official, Trimbkaji Dengale, a non-Brahmin who had been accused of killing Gangadar Sastri, a Brahmin who was a minister and envoy from the pro-British side. Peshwa refused to hand over Dengale. Elphinstone, who was known for his aversion towards Brahmins and Hinduism, wrote to Peshwa to hand over Timbkaji: 'You are a Brahman and the head of a Brahman State. An open murder has been committed of a Brahman which you will agree, cannot remain without investigation.'[27]

Before the decisive defeat of the Marathas in the third Anglo-Maratha war, Trimbkaji, with the support of Peshwa and princes like 'Sindia, Holkar, the Raja of Nagpur', etc., was organizing a fighting force consisting of 'the Bhils, Kolis, Ramoshis, and Mangs of Khandesh Nasik, and Ahmadnagar'.[28] All these communities were later, under the British, declared as either criminal tribes/castes or Scheduled Tribes/Castes.

Between 1826 to 1850, there were continuous but unsuccessful rebellions in the Maratta region against the East India Company. The British attributed these rebellions to 'Brahmans, Deshmukhs and other hereditary officers, and discharged soldiery'. In 1826, Ramoshis, a nomadic community known as 'warrior tribes', rose against the British. Traditionally, the Ramoshis were 'hunters, gatherers, and guardsmen' and were spread throughout the Maratha-dominated regions, which are today Karnataka, Maharashtra, and Madhya Pradesh.[29] Wherever they settled, they were employed as village watchmen, responsible for protecting the standing crop in the village and the village property through the Baluta system, a Maratta variant of the Jajmani system.[30] Their rebellion was led by Umaji Ramoshi. The British finally had to concede defeat and compromise with them in 1827. The Company agreed to employ them as hill police and granted them land.[31] However, within fifty years, in 1871, the British declared the community 'criminal tribes' and imposed many disabilities on them.

However, the unrest did not die down. The next uprising was even more systematic. In 1839, Kolis—fishermen community rebelled—against the British. Men of all castes joined the rebellion, which was led by three Brahmans, Bhau Khare, Chimnaji Jadhav, and Nana Darbare. They aimed to re-establish Peshwa Raj. The desire to bring back the 'oppressive' and 'Brahminical' Peshwa Raj was puzzling, as it was not just Brahmins but all people who desired this. The British suppressed the revolt, hanging a Brahmin and a Koli. Twenty-four rebels were pardoned, while others were punished, some with life transportation. The idea that Brahmins instigated the rebellion seemed to be more of a British construct, as seen in the 1844 Koli rebellion, led by the sons of a Koli jamadar, Raghu Bhangria and Biipu Bhangria. The sons of Ramoshi leader Umaji, Tukya, and Manbala also joined the rebellion.[32] The British viewed Brahmins as the villains who crafted the rebellions against the British. The uprising of Vasudeo Balwant Phadke (1845–83), although not supported by Tilak, further cemented the British animosity towards Brahmins as mischief makers. Weeks before Phadke's arrest, in two confidential letters written on 3 July 1879 and 9 July 1879, Richard Temple, the Governor of Maharashtra, expressed to Viceroy Lytton his deep-seated prejudice and fear about what he considered the treacherous nature of Chitpavan Brahmins:

> Now the Chitpawun tribe still stands in vigour and prosperity. They are inspired with national sentiment and with an am bition bounded only with the limits of India itself.... If you were to count heads among our best native employees all over the Deccan and the Concan, and even among our humble village accountants, you would be surprised to find what a hold this tribe of Chitpawuns has over the whole administrative machinery of the country. And this position is won over not by favour but

> by force of merit. For among prize men and honours holders in the schools and graduates of the University the Chitpawuns are predominant.... But nothing that we do now, by way of education, employment, or advancement in the public service, at all satisfies the Chitpawuns. They will never be satisfied till they regain their ascendency in the country, as they had it in the last century.... They esteem it their charter from on high to rule over the minds of the Hindoos. ... Their past to them- their glorious past—survives in their mind.[33]

In the second letter, he wrote:

> Barely sixty years have elapsed since the Chitpavans ceased to be rulers—the memory of all this is still to this day comparatively fresh in the minds of the Natives, fresher far than the memory of most of the great political events of Indian history. Now the Chitpavan tribe still exists in vigour and prosperity. They are inspired with national sentiment and with an ambition bounded only with the bounds of India itself.

Historian B.R. Nanda brings out the fundamental fear that Elphinstone had, expressed in those letters: 'Just as the Marathas under Brahmanical guidance "beat the Mahomedan conquerors bit by bit, inch by inch, out of the Deccan", so some day the British would be made "to retire into that darkness where the Moguls have retired."'[34]

The British skilfully intertwined anti-Brahminism with the educational institutional changes they brought into the society. When combined with the Aryan race theory, anti-Brahminism became a powerful framework to view society. While definitely the Brahmins had the first advantage in accessing the English educational system and employment, the 'orthodox' and 'reform' divide was not much different in Brahmin society; it was prevalent in other societies as well. However, Brahmin orthodoxy was more visible.

Shahu Maharaj and Lōkmānya Tilak

Quarrels between the Brahmins and non-Brahmins were perceived differently. Shāhu Maharāj (1874-1922), the descendant of Shivāji and the king of Kolhapur under British rule, was insulted by his Brahmin priests by being called a Śūdra. This incident led him to introduce job and institution reservations for non-Brahmins. The social emancipation process was also motivated by his anger towards the Brahmins. In 1899, the reformist Brahmin Prof. Rājārām Shāstri Bhagwat alerted the king to this ritualistic discrimination. In 1902, Shāhu reserved fifty per cent of all administrative posts under his control for non-Brahmins. With already some serious differences in previous legal cases with the king, Tilak, in his *Kesari* newspaper, supported the Brahmin priests' claim that the king was a Śūdra, further complicating the situation. This controversy helped Shāhu Maharāj project these issues in a way advantageous to him and to the British. While he was not completely anti-Brahmin, as alleged by *Kesari* and though he was in favour of Brahmins who supported him, the attacks by Tilak in *Kesari* helped him to project the whole issue from a different angle. Historian Gordon Johnson points out how these elite ritualistic and legal quarrels took on entirely new dimensions in a rapidly changing society whose educated sections were rooted in a colonial worldview:

> But Shahu's anti-Brahminism was always selective: it was only his enemies he wished to get rid of, and, throughout his reign, 'loyal' Brahmins in Kolhapur had no difficulty in finding jobs or in keeping their land.... Shahu looked towards Poona, too, and in that city, where everyone who mattered was a Brahmin, his propaganda against that caste was no asset. Instead, he fell in with the existing party lines: if Tilak was against him, then he was for the other side.... The Maharaja of Kolhapur's declared intention of employing non-Brahmins in his state, his moves

> against his feudatories, and his action over the properties of the Rajopadhye, the Shankaracharya of Sankeshwar and Baba Maharaj were the fuel with which the anti-Brahmin movement in western India was fed. The Bombay government, for its own ends, made selective use of the Kolhapur intrigues: it was convenient to be able to show from an independent Indian source that Brahmins as a class were not to be trusted in politics.[35]

Thus, Tilak's career in his initial public years could be seen as unconsciously split between threats to the socio-economic interests of his own caste and an increasing ethnic hatred against his caste, on the one hand, and his pure patriotism to secure liberation for the motherland, on the other hand.

Disappointment with Social Reformers

On 4 October 1890, Tilak, along with Ranade and Gokhale, attended a tea party held in the house of a Christian missionary, which caused a major uproar. Tilak was called to appear before the religious court of the regional Śaṅkarācharya. He agreed to accept any required ritualistic atonement but managed to avoid the situation through expert legal manoeuvring.

In 1889, Pandita Ramabhai, a strong advocate for women's education and liberation, established Sarada Sadhan, a school for girls' education. This faced strong opposition, with Tilak being critical of Christian evangelists being involved in women's education. However, when Ramabai assured him that there would be no proselytizing, Tilak publicly supported the school. However, within months, in December 1889, illustrated *Christian Weekly*, an evangelical magazine, revealed that two of the seven child-widows in the school had volunteered to get converted to Christianity, which left Tilak feeling betrayed. It became evident that Sarada Sadan, which received most of its funds from American evangelical philanthropists, was viewed as a Christian mission work. This led prominent reformists like

Justice Mahadev Govind Ranade and Bhandarkar, who also supported Ramabai's work, to resign from the committee due to the strong Christian influence.[36] Historian of political science, Prof. Jai Narain Sharma explains the consequence of these two resignations from the perspective of social reform versus radical nationalism as represented by Tilak, with its bias towards social conservatism:

> The controversy about the Sarada Sadan widened the split between Tilak and the social reformers which was growing ever since 1886-87. Tilak's argument was that once the real proselytising motivation behind the Sadan had been revealed. Ranade and Bhandarkar should have severed their connections with that institution and exposed the designs of Ramabai.... However, the resignation of Ranade and Bhandarkar served two purposes. First, it vindicated that Tilak's perceptions about the real intentions of the founder of the Sadan were correct. Secondly the resignation definitely pointed out that, at the most, Ranade and Bhandarkar were social-reformers and men of comprehensive toleration but certainly they were not anti-Hindu. They could not reconcile themselves to the game of the conversion of the Hindus.[37]

All these influences, too, should be taken into consideration when one looks into the behavioural pattern of Tilak. His hesitating approach to social reforms, despite his realization of its importance being as vital as a political cause, could be summarized in the following passage that he had written in *Kesari* in 1892:

> There is considerable resemblance between our difficulties in the political field and those in the social one, neither the political administration nor the structure of our society completely satisfies us. We want to reform both. The English administration as well as the Indian society have solid foundation. We are, therefore, bound to proceed with caution. Now, if people are willing to accept political reforms in a spirit of conciliation and

> compromise, we fail to understand why we should like to proceed with social reform in such an arrogant and defiant manner. If we are prepared to make compromise when the Parliament passes the Council's Act 1892, why should we not do so with respect to questions like widow remarriage? Fanatical opposition might occasionally be successful but as a rule, in political as well as social matters, fanaticism is suicidal.[38]

Tilak strongly opposed child marriage, but he did not want the ban imposed by legislation. He was also critical of widow remarriage and opposed to widowed men remarrying as well. At times, Tilak aligned with obscurantist forces in quite a few instances, which caused a divide between the National Liberation Movement and the Social Reformation Movement. These instances were related to his career as a lawyer and his knowledge of *Smṛti* and *Dharmaśāstra*, which the British legal system treated as equivalents to the canonical laws of Christendom. This created a conflict between the enlightenment values of the West as its civilizational essence and that getting pitted against the *Smṛti* and *Dharmaśāstra* through the British legal framework—a fallacy that even present de-colonizers fall into.

Bhagavad Gītā to the Rescue

Most enlightenment values of the West, taken out of the Western context, still remain universal values and resonate with the dharmic values. The binary is a deeply enshrined colonial view in which deconstruction becomes adherence to the stagnant values of *Smṛti* and *Dharmaśāstra* as if they were strict constitutions. This results in a stagnation of the *Smṛti* and *Dharmaśāstra* production process. On the other hand, through the Vēdāntā spirituality and Vēdāntā-inspired patriotism, there was a gradual shift towards embracing an egalitarian worldview of social emancipation. As seen earlier, Tilak could completely ignore caste rules for inter-dining with fellow nationalists of other castes. His clarity in vision with regard to the eradication of untouchability as well as caste as a problem came from his profound study of the Bhagavad Gītā.

Tilak's detailed commentary on the Bhagavad Gītā, titled *Śrīmad Bhagavdgītā Rahasya* (SBR), was published in Marāthi in June 1915. The text challenges birth-based social stratification in SBR and emphasizes individual worth and spiritual equality through bhakti.

Even at the outset, Tilak recognizes that Chātur Varṇa has undergone a devolution in India into a mere birth-based division, forgetting the duties. Then he explains it as more an archetypal classification than a rule to be imposed. He states:

> The ancient *ṛṣi* had created the institution of the four Varṇa which was in the nature of a division of labour in order that all the affairs of society should go on without a hitch,... without any particular person or group of persons having to bear the whole burden. Later on, people belonging to this society became '*jātimātropajivi*' that is 'persons, who forgetting their respective Varṇa duties, belonged to a particular caste merely by reason of birth' and became mere nominal *Brāhmanās, Kṣatriyas, Vaiśyā* or *Śūdra*;... There are numerous societies in the Western hemisphere, which have come to prominence notwithstanding that they do not have the institution of the *Chātur-Varṇa*. But we must not forget that although the institution of the four castes may not be in existence among them, yet all the duties of the four castes are seen being performed in those societies, if not in the shape of castes, at any rate by some other arrangement in the shape of professional divisions or classes. In short, when we use the word '*Dharma*' from the worldly point of view, we consider in what way society will be maintained (*dhāraṇā*) and benefited.[39]

Regarding the question of the spiritual authority of 'Adhikāra', he does not make caste the basis of it. On the other hand, it could be by birth, which means more the circumstances of birth rather than the caste, or it could be acquired as well. According to him, 'if one considers minutely and independently what this qualification is, and how it is acquired' then it comes with:

> every human being, as a result of the arrangement of four castes, or of any other social arrangement consistent with the division, of inherent qualities, acquires, by birth, the high or low qualification of maintaining and uplifting society, according *to his or her own powers*, and proportionately with whatever intellectual capacity, authoritative capacity, financial capacity, or physical capacity is naturally possessed by him, or can be *acquired by him* having regard to his status in life.[40]

So, while the caste one is born into may have been a social reality of a particular time, it gets superseded by individual qualities and efforts through which one acquires 'whatever intellectual capacity, authoritative capacity, financial capacity, or physical capacity'. In other words, he changes the entire Chātur Varṇa system as predicated upon individual capacity. On the whole, in SBR, Tilak shifts the emphasis from the birth-based caste system to the individual as well as the duty a person has towards society, which in turn is acquired by the innate and acquired potentials of the individual. Further, while the orthodoxy might consider the societies without explicit Chātur Varṇa as '*Milecha*', Tilak includes all societies as having Chātur Varṇa as archetypal divisions.

In conclusion, when considering the line '*swa-dharme nidhanaṁ śhreyaḥ para-dharmo bhayāvahaḥ*' (BG 3:35), which is often translated as Kṛṣṇa asking Arjuna to adhere to his caste/clan/birth-based Varṇa duty even if he finds the duty of another Varṇa more appealing, Tilak takes a different view. According to him, Swadharma does not necessarily come from one's caste or birth-based varṇa. It could be according to the

Chātur Varṇa system or 'according to any other arrangement of society which may be applicable to it, that duty which has fallen on one's shoulders or which, being possible, may have been taken up by one as a duty, of one's own choice.'[41]

The central theme here is the belief in the spiritual equality of all humanity as superior to all divisions. Here Tilak even transcends religious barriers and sees the spiritual equality explained in the Bhagavad Gītā, as revealed in Buddhism as well as Christianity. Although Tilak's language may not be considered 'politically correct' in today's socio-political context, one can still discern the tension between the influence of the colonial worldview, which introduces the concept of races, and the Hindu view perspective spiritual equality that is forcefully emphasized in bhakti:

> To the Parameśvara, women, or the lowest of mixed tribes, or Brahmins are the same. 'The Parameśvara craves (only) for your Faith'. He does not care for symbols, or for the black or white colour of the skin, nor does He care for the difference between men and women, or castes like the Brahmins or the Chaṇḍāḷas (tribes born of the mixture of Brahmins and Śūdra). The saint *Tukārāma* says that:
>
> Brāhmanās Kṣatriyas, Vaiśyās and Śūdra, I
> and the Chaṇḍāḷas, all have the right I
> As also children, women, men, and oven prostitutes II
> Tukā says that he has found by experience I
> That even others, who are devout I
> experience happiness by their good fortune II (Gā. 2382. 5, 6)
>
> Nay; it is a doctrine of the Gita, that 'however sinful a man may be, if he surrenders himself to the Blessed Lord, wholly and solely, even at the moment of his death, the Paramesvara does not cast him off' (Gi. 9. 30; and S. 5-8). Seeing the word 'prostitutes' in the above stanza, some learned persons, who parade their purity, might feel offended; but it must be said that

> such persons do not understand the true principle of Religion. This doctrine has been adopted not only in the Hindu religion, but also in the Buddhist religion (Milinda Prasna 3.7.2); and there are stories in Buddhistic religious treatises, that Buddha initiated a prostitute by name Amrapali, as also a thief by name Angulimala ... and the Lord Christ has Himself said in one place that even prostitutes, who put faith in His religion would obtain, salvation (Matthew 21:31; Luke 7:50).... When one considers and takes into account the sense of Equality appearing in the Philosophy of Devotion taught by the Gita, and its capacity to enable all equally, to easily grasp the Knowledge of the identity of the Brahman and the Ātman mentioned in the Upanishads, without sacrificing the ordinary activities of worldly life, and without establishing any difference between the four Varṇas or the four stages of life, or the communities, or even between men and women, one 'understands the true import of the summing up of the Religion of the Gita made by the Blessed Lord'.[42]

Even then, the old traditions remained, but they were not as strong as before. They were considerably diluted. For example, in 1918, when Vithalbhai Patel (1873–1933), a freedom fighter and elder brother of the famous 'Sardar' Vallababhai Patel (1875–1950), introduced the 'Hindu Marriages (Validity) Bill' that legalized marriages between Hindu castes, Tilak opposed it. Yet this time, the opposition was more nuanced and the arguments more centred around the chaotic effect it might cause on society. Then, on 13 December 1919, he wrote that his opposition was not based on any religious or social ground but because the bill would create problems in the Hindu Succession Act.[43]

When assessing the impact and views of Tilak on social emancipation, we must consider his immense and deep knowledge of law, scriptures, and history, as well as his strong patriotic fervour for liberating the nation from foreign colonialism. It is important to acknowledge that some of his staunch followers revered him for his patriotism while disagreeing with his conservative social views. Additionally, we should note that while his internalizing of *Dharmaśāstra* texts within the British legal framework led him towards rigidly socially conservative attitudes, his love for the Indian nation and the study of the Bhāgavad Gītā made him more receptive to values of equality and social emancipation.

Vithalbhai Jhaverbhai Patel and His Marriage Bill

As seen earlier in the discussion of the continued inhibitions of Tilak with respect to inter-caste marriages, freedom fighter Vithalbhai Patel introduced the bill legalizing inter-caste marriage. The validity of such marriages has been recognized in Hindu tradition, as evidenced by both *Rig Veda* and Rāmāyaṇa. The Ṛṣi Śiśuḥ Áṅgirās, who introduces himself as a poet-praiser of the Divine, with his father as a physician and mother an agricultural worker, states that despite coming from diverse professions, spiritual wealth is desired by all souls in this earthly life.[44] The Vālmiki Rāmāyaṇa also speaks highly of Yajñadatta, the son of a Śūdra mother and a Vaiśyā father, who established a forest āśram and recited sacred texts in sweet voice.[45]

Yet later, inter-caste marriages were forbidden when Hindu *Smṛtis and Dharmaśāstras* were placed in the strongly text-based legal structure of the British legislative system. Before that, inter-caste marriages, though not much encouraged, did exist in significant numbers, and when Jāthis moved into the Varṇa matrix of social space, there were marriages. However, British legislation brought about a peculiar combination of the social stagnation features of Hindu society, passing off as the civilizational essence of Hinduism. This served the British by portraying an enlightened civilizational superiority while also catering to the anxieties of status-quo conservative elements in Hindu society by resisting the modernist changes that were inevitably entering the society and irreversibly changing it.

Vithalbhai Patel challenged this stagnation by introducing the Hindu Marriages (Validity) Bill in the Imperial Council (1918) to legalize inter-caste marriage. This elicited both support and opposition from various quarters. It has become common to categorize those who opposed the bill as 'Hindu orthodox' and others as reformists. In reality, there were Hindus who religiously adhered to their religion and were firm in the opinion that the social emancipatory legislations were correcting a wrong. They would have self-defined them as truly orthodox in tune with the injunctions of the Vedas and Bhakti traditions.

Vithalbhai Patel himself came from a highly devotional Vaiṣṇava tradition. The authoritative biographer of Vithalbhai Patel, Gordhanbhai Patel, points out the heritage and influence of this tradition in Vithalbhai's value system and politics:

> Both the parents of Vithalbhai, Jhaverbhai and Ladbai, were devoted followers of the Swaminarayan sect – a semi-reformist off-shoot of the Vaishnava Sampradaya.... Vairagya (renunciation) and Bhakti (devotion) are the most important parts of Swaminarayan's teachings.... It was this religious background, which his parents had made their own, that materially influenced Vithalbhai's outlook on men and matters. The deeply religious atmosphere in which Vithalbhai was brought up was probably responsible for that subdued earnestness which he evinced in such large measure in the critical and stormy junctures of his public life.[46]

So, his reformation zeal should also be attributed to a significant extent to this Vaiṣṇava tradition. He was also influenced by such Hindu thinkers as Śri Aurobindo and Ārya Samājists. Additionally, he preceded Gandhi in uplifting the 'Harijan' community, a fact acknowledged by Gandhi himself.

The bill received support from Lālā Lajpat Rāi, a fearless freedom fighter, staunch Hindu Saṅghatanist, leader of both Ārya Samāj and Hindu Mahāaabha, and a prominent Congress leader. In a message sent in support from New York, he regarded the bill as an 'extremely small measure of reform based on actual legal necessity' and expressed 'a sense of shame and humiliation' at the opposition to the bill. He pointed out that the authors of the very *Dharmaśāstras*, which those against the bill were using as a basis, had made 'a liberal provision for necessary changes in social life and customs in accordance with the needs of place and time (*Desha Kal*)'. He also highlighted the stagnant situation in Hindu legislative evolution because of the colonial framework:

> The Shastras made ample provision for the legal recognition of these changes. It is the rigidity and absurdity of the Judge-made law of the British Courts that has brought about the existing impasse in the marriage laws of the Hindus. A change such as is contemplated is an absolute necessity. Opposition to it is based on short-sighted partisanship and false notions of Dharma.... It is sheer dishonesty to oppose this reform on the ground of its being dangerous to Vamashrama Dharma, while the latter is a mere caricature of its original self. Unless we propose to live for ever and ever in our present degraded condition, it is absolutely necessary that our ideas of Vamashrama Dharma should be radically changed. Political democracy is a myth unless it is based on social and economic justice.[47]

Śri Aurobindo's Support for the Bill

In his book, *Caste Pride: Battles for Equality in Hindu India*, author Manoj Mittal discusses the bill proposed by Patel and the debates that surrounded it. Mittal argues that the lack of remembrance today has 'engendered a nationalist myth: that India's political freedom finally empowered Hindus to enact the caste reforms that they could not have carried out earlier'.[48] Towards this end, Mittal seemed to have misinterpreted the response of Śri Aurobindo with reference to this bill. Singling out the response of Śri Aurobindo among the supporters of the bill, he writes:

> Aurobindo Ghose's support was, however, a qualified one: 'I should have preferred a change from within the society rather than one brought about by legislation.' At the same time, 'it would appear', he said, that 'the difficulty created by the imposition of the rigid and mechanical notions of European jurisprudence on the old Hindu Law' could only be 'removed by a resort to legislation'.[49]

In reality, Śri Aurobindo's support for the bill was complete, taking into account the historical context of colonialism and its impact on the way Hindu scriptures were losing their dynamic nature and stagnating into a very mechanical literal-textual manner—that too incompletely.

Vithalbhai Patel was part of the administrative circle of a newspaper called *The Hindustan*, which was run by Sheth Ranchoddas Lotewalla, a staunch Ārya Samājist and a warrior of social emancipation. In 1918, when Patel introduced the bill, Lotewalla wrote to Śri Aurobindo for his comment. At that time, Śri Aurobindo had moved away from politics and was concentrating on his sādhana. Yet he wrote back a detailed response, demonstrating the importance he attached to this issue. With his characteristic insight, Śri Aurobindo recognized how colonial jurisprudence had impacted the interpretation of Hindu scriptures and that the remedy for this particular malaise was very much a legislative one. Here is his complete reply:

> In answer to your request for a statement of my opinion on the inter-marriage question, I can only say that everything will have my full approval which helps to liberate and strengthen the life of the individual in the frame of a vigorous society and restore the freedom and energy which India had in her heroic times of greatness and expansion. Many of our present social forms were shaped, many of our customs originated, in a line of contraction and decline. They had their utility for self-defence and survival within narrow limits, but are a drag upon

> our progress in the present hour when we are called upon once again to enter upon a free and courageous self-adaptation and expansion. I believe in an aggressive and expanding, not in a narrowly defensive and self-contracting Hinduism. Whether Mr Patel's Bill is the best way to bring about the object intended is a question on which I can pronounce no decided opinion. I should have preferred a change from within the society rather than one brought about by legislation. But I recognise the difficulty created by the imposition of the rigid and mechanical notions of European jurisprudence on the old Hindu Law which was that of a society having and developing by an organic evolution. It is no longer easy, or perhaps in this case, possible to develop a new custom or revert to an old – for the change proposed amounts to no more than such a revision. It would appear that the difficulty created by the legislature can only be removed by a resort to legislation. In that case, the Bill has my approval.[50]

In the support given to the Bill by both Lajpat Rāi and Śri Aurobindo, there exists the critical observation that the colonial jurisprudence had an adverse impact on Hindu legislative tradition in terms of creating a support base for social stagnation.

The constant prompting of Hindu social reformers like Vithalbhai Patel and Ārya Samājists had its own impact on the British system. The diversity and flexibility of Hindu Dharmaśāstric tradition began to be recognized in the system. Instead of seeing the Hindu legal system as an oppressive, stratified prison tolerated in deference to native religious sentiments, the British started appreciating the real dynamic nature of the Hindu system. This shift was evident in the detailed analysis that Sir George Lowndes, the then Member-in-charge of the Imperial Council, offered in response to criticism of unchanged Hindu ethics being destroyed by the inter-caste marriage bill:

> Therefore, I think, the Council ought to understand that when we hear talk of the foundations of the Hindu religion being disturbed, it is not the foundations of the old Hindu religion, but the foundations of modern custom which has supplanted the old religion since the 16th century. And this, I submit, is a point of considerable relevance.[51]

The viewpoints of Lajpat Rāi and Śri Aurobindo converge regarding the stagnation in the evolution of Hindu legislative texts. Lowndes also shares this view, although he attributes the stagnation more to the chaotic times of the 16th-century Mughal invasions than to the British colonial times. As will be seen, Dr Ambedkar also resonated with the views of Lajpat Rāi and Śri Aurobindo in his own way, particularly in his debate on women's property rights in the Constitutional Assembly debates in Independent India.

Dr Moonje's Sanghathan Postscript

In the wake of the Moplah pogrom against the Hindus in 1921, which involved murders, violence, abduction of women, and forced conversions, a commission headed by Dr Balakrishna Shivram Moonje (1872–1948) was sent to study the situation. The commission's report titled 'Forcible Conversions in Malabar' was published on 4 August 1923. In this report, Moonje highlighted that the caste system had weakened Hindu society by creating 'so many water-tight compartments, each having a social culture and life of its own' because of which there was 'hardly any association between them in the wider field of social activities.' He suggested that inter-caste marriage could help bridge the divisions and preserve the true purpose of the four Varṇa system. His report states:

> (Hindu society) must give up its system of water-tight compartments of caste and bring about a real organic unity

> between the four sections of the society which can be done by again bringing into vogue the system of marriage of what are called the *Anuloma* and *Pratiloma Paddhati* as provided in our *Dharmashastras* with a view to bind the four sections of the society in blood connections and thus bring about organic unity out of the very diversity of sociological functions allotted to these four original varna or castes.[52]

Hindu-phobic scholar Christophe Jaffrelot has tried to explain away Moonje's recommendation of both *Anuloma* and *Pratiloma* (marriage between the woman of the so-called upper caste and the man of the so-called lower caste) with a strange and convoluted logic:

> But for a Hindu nationalist theorist the mere mention of these practices in texts as prestigious as the *Dharmashastras* is enough to legitimise an innovation that his project demands: the promotion of a sociological model suitable for reinforcing the Hindu community by adopting some of the socio-cultural strengths of the aggressor-under the pretext of a return to the prestigious Vedic era. This diversion into a fictitious version of history allows for the legitimisation of the caste system in an amended form.[53]

However, a close examination of the development of social emancipation within the Hindu tradition itself suggests that Dr Moonje's recommendation for accepting Pratiloma has precedence in Hindu legal tradition, even in modern times. Dr Moonje had witnessed a similar argument made by retired Justice Naryan Ganesh Chandavarkar in support of Vithalbhai Patel' s bill. When N.G. Chandavakar was a judge, he had invalidated a Pratiloma marriage on the work of Vishvanath Narayan Mandlik (1833-1899), one of the earliest Indians to be familiar with English and civil law and who served as a government pleader. After retirement, Chandavakar studied the work of Gopalachandra Sarkar Sastri and came to the understanding 'that, despite the passages in the Smritis, which "by implication prohibit" pratiloma,' they were 'more of moral obligation only'. So even if such marriages were discouraged, Sastri contended that nevertheless 'if such a marriage does in fact take place' for the *Dharmaśāstras*, 'the same must be regarded valid as between the parties to it, and the issue legitimate'.[54]

Given the facts that this legal churning had happened several years before Dr Moonje recommended using both Anuloma and Pratiloma Paddhati and happened right where Moonje and his activities were happening, one needs to conclude that Dr Moonje's recommendation was based more on a solid grounding of recent Hindu legal history than 'a fictitious version of history' or 'a return to the prestigious Vedic era', as stated by Jaffrelot.

Sayajirao Gaekwad III

Another important aspect of the bill and the debates surrounding it highlighted how the Hindu princely states spearheaded social emancipation far better than India under direct British rule. Tej Bahadur Sapru (1875–1949), a freedom fighter, Liberal Party leader, and also a Kashmiri Pandit, strongly supported the bill. He cited the fact that the Hindu princely states 'had taken a lead in this matter', i.e., inter-caste marriage. He pointed out that such laws existed in both Indore and Nepal. Ten years before Vithalbhai Patel tabled his bill, Sayajirao Gaekwad III (1863–1939), the king of Baroda had passed a law approving inter-caste marriage. Earlier to this the Brahmo Marriage Act (1872) allowed both inter-caste marriage and widow remarriage, but the condition was that the couple should declare themselves as non-Hindus. Sayajirao Gaekwad III modelled his law on the Brahmo Marriage Act, nevertheless removing the requirement of renouncing Hindu dharma. Earlier in 1901, he passed the 'Infant Marriage Prevention Act', which raised the minimum age of marriage for girls to twelve and boys to sixteen. In 1904, he enacted the 'Age of Consent' law, which further fortified this law.

The difference between Shāhu Maharāj and Sayajirao was that while Shāhu became excessively friendly with the British because of his anti-Brahminical mindset, however justified it could be, Sayajirao harboured no such prejudice, though he too had his own share of opposition from the status-quoists. When Shahu extended full loyalty to the British, partly because it was his duty and mainly because of his hostility to the nationalist movement, which he perceived as a movement of Maharashtra Brahmins,[55] Sayajirao more often than not took a confrontational path towards the British rulers.

Sayajirao engaged in a war of letters with Lord Curzon regarding his restriction of foreign tours. The letters were drafted by Śri Aurobindo, who briefly period served as the Secretary to His Highness. When Curzon's term as Viceroy ended, Sayajirao did not attend the send-off party organized by the princes of other principalities. Instead, he sent a telegram: 'Bon Voyage, may India never see the like of you again.'[56] The British administration always had suspicions about Sayajirao, and they were not entirely wrong. His personal barber, Shankar Wagh, was warned by British officials as 'an undesirable character' because he was associated with Vinayak Damodar Savarkar.[57] In 1908, Sayajirao delivered a lecture at Poona's Sarvajanik Sabha, whose secretary was N.C. Kelkar, a well-known disciple of Tilak. A 'confidential' intelligence report on his visit to this 'extremist society in Poona' observed that his speech was 'a thinly veiled disparagement of the British rule'. The reports of him and his wife meeting various anti-British Indian revolutionaries or radicals, including Madam Cama and Taraknath Das, who was editor of *Free Hindustan*, also alarmed the authorities.[58] In 1909, Curzon Wyllie was assassinated in London by Madanlal Dhingra, who was part of the 'India House' radical group. However, this did not prevent Sayajirao from visiting Shyamji Krishna Varma, who was the brain of 'India House'. In 1911, when Sayajirao met Crewe, the then Secretary of State for India, at the latter's residence, Crewe warned the king of his 'special sympathy with the India House Gang' and meeting Krishnavarma and Madam Cama. While denying the sedition charges or even knowledge of activities related to sedition, Sayajirao did admit to meeting Krishnavarma and Madam Cama.

In fact, he was able to remarkably balance both the nationalist movement and the social reform movement. This is exemplified by his employment of two great personalities of modern India—Śri Aurobindo and Dr Ambedkar. This confluence had wide ramifications for India's civilizational stride both during the freedom struggle and after, as shall be seen in the section of Dr Ambedkar. He hired Ārya Samāj teachers in schools for socially excluded community children and established an Ārya Samāj school for women. He was also invited to many of the events of the organization and addressed them.

He even recognized Ārya Samāj as a more effective institution for social emancipation than Satyashodhak Samaj of Jotiba Phule. He obtained Ārya Samāj activist scholar Pundit Atmaramji to establish a branch in Kolhapur in 1918, and, with his backing, established schools and began to spread its work in the princely state.[59] In 1920, he founded the Shivaji Kshatriya Vedic School with the aim 'to root out the superstitions which have been mixed up with the Vedic religion, and to restore the purity of the Vedic system'.[60] Moreover, Shahu Maharaj, influenced by the Baroda impact, seemed to have been sympathetic to the Gandhian movement in a reluctant way. While making it clear that he did not support the political motive of the movement, he saw in Gandhi 'a holy person' and 'a solitary instance of a personality that claims out tribute of love and respect'.[61]

In his implementation of what could be called the 'whirlwind implication' of social reforms and institutional processes for social emancipation, while acknowledging the positive need to learn from the social emancipation movement from other societies, the king insisted that there should be no blind copying. In 1904, at the inaugural address of at the National Social Conference of the Indian National Congress, the king set out his vision of social reform with clarity and depth:

> There is, of course, some truth in the position that reform must work along lines natural to the country and our national characteristics. There are some features in our environment which are sufficiently powerful to modify the practical application of any idea, and these account for certain tendencies in national history which persist even through long centuries of foreign influence. *It is also true that servile imitation is no reform and is often worse than the original evil.* But the great truth behind the phrase is, that it is the general advance of the nation which is the aim of reform: that only is national reform which subserves national interests. It matters nothing where the truth comes from. If it serves a national purpose or helps national ends, then it is national whether the form in which we find it is modern or Vedic, European or purely Indian. And we must be eager to find this knowledge and apply it whether it has the sanction of the older ideas or not.... What we need now is action—common-sense practical measures—and not discussion as to whether this or that reform is justified by older traditions or the sacred writings of our ancestors.[62] (emphasis added)

He implemented action-oriented reforms that were influenced by global experiences and tailored to fit India's conditions. The British authorities noted the significant social progress under his rule, but they felt it could not be replicated in the rest of British-administered India. On 31 March 1908, in the House of Commons, the then Secretary of State of India John Morley was asked if he was aware of the progress that was happening in the princely state of Baroda and if that could be implemented in the rest of British administered India. Morley confirmed the progress in Baroda but attributed the inability to implement similar reforms in the rest of India to the unwillingness of Indian princes. Historian Manu Bhagwan, Professor of History and Chair of the Human Rights Program at the Roosevelt House Public Policy Institute, explains why the British did not adopt the Baroda Model of social reforms:

> This exchange betrays British duplicity. The British freely interfered in the rights and powers of native rulers whenever they saw fit.... Yet when it came time to apply successful reform measures to other states, the British demurred. Any application of the Baroda measures, it was feared, would recognize the benefits and usefulness of said reforms. Since these steps were taken by a native prince, this would imply a recognition of the benefits and usefulness of native administration. That is, the Baroda reforms might be perceived as original and superior to anything thus far done throughout the Empire. If the English adopted these steps, they would implicitly have to accept native ability to progress and this would strike at the very nature of the colonial project. Mimicking the native was not possible, especially when claims were made that the native reforms were copies of British ideas. The discussion in the English parliament proves there was a recognition that there was something new, and thus something 'not Western', about Baroda's reforms. The British could thus not use Baroda's reforms out of strategic consideration.[63]

The king died on 6 February 1939. He decisively showed that the social reform movement and the national liberation movement, which had been depicted as being at loggerheads in Maharashtra and Madras, could be harmonized into a powerful unity serving the national cause in a synchronized manner. As will be seen, the efforts made by the king of Baroda changed the course of the history of social emancipation dramatically, accelerating it in a positive direction.

Gajānan Bhāskar Vaidya

A contemporary of Sāhu Maharāj and Lokmānya Tilak, Gajānan Bhāskar Vaidya (1867–1921) belonged to the Kāyasta community settled in the Thana district. A religious youth who sought knowledge from all the sources, he combined his devotion with his brilliance. One of his notable achievements was reviving a failing girls' school that was run by an organization called Students' Literary and Scientific Society'. Prominent figures like Dādābhāī Navrojī, Candāvarkar, and Telang had supported girls' education through this school. Vaidya took on the cause of the failing school, raised funds, and soon 'a commodious and beautiful building was built in the populous Girgaum area', revitalizing the school's presence and serving women's education.[64] He was a strong advocate of women's equality and opposed child marriage while supporting widow remarriage. He even confronted a prominent figure, Justice Ranade, when he remarried a young girl instead of a widow after the death of his first wife. Justice Ranade humbly acknowledged Vaidya's leadership in the reform efforts and called upon Vaidya to lead from the front.[65] He did lead from the front.

In 1917, he founded the Hindu Missionary Society with the aim of preventing conversions and bringing back those who had left Hindu dharma. Where he differed from Ārya Samāj was in replacing the word 'Shuddhi' with 'Upanayan'. In this, he was supported by Raghunathrao Khedkar, who later became the first president of the Hindu Missionary Society of Pune. In his insightful thesis on the evolution of the 'modern Hindu self' during the colonial period, scholar Rahul Sarwate brings out 'a mysterious tale' from the childhood of Khedkar: 'When he was about 7–8 years old, a Sanyasi had approached the Khedkar family. He told them that Raghunath was part of them: the Vedic Sanyasis and he prophesied that Raghunath will become a missionary of Vedanta.'[66]

Sarwate points out that Khedkar became 'an important bridge between Shāhu Maharāj and the larger non-Brahmin network with the Tilakites in Pune'.[67] The Hindu Missionary Society benefitted from the association of such daring personalities. Khedkar was a great exponent of Vēdānta. While studying medicine in England, he conducted a Bhagavad Gītā study circle.

The Hindu Missionary Society had as its cardinal principles the following:

- Anyone who calls oneself a Hindu should be considered Hindu.
- Anyone who wishes to join Hinduism would be welcomed.
- The religious rights of every Hindu are equal.

Later, as will be seen in the coming sections, a Saṅkarāchārya would petition the British government to legally declare the Hindu Missionary Society to be outcastes of Hinduism. Apart from Khedkar, Vaidya had the support of Keshav Sitaram Thackeray (1885-1973). Together, the three spearheaded a nuanced movement. This movement harmonized radical social reform, and as rooted in Hinduness, it removed to a large extent vitriolic anti-Brahmin hatred that often stereotyped Brahmins as vicious, ethnically different aliens, not different from the way anti-Semitism stereotyped the Jews.

The colonial template contained a social reform movement that viewed the social stagnation as indicated by the behaviour of Brahmin clans through the prism of the Āryan-non-Āryan binary. It mostly created negative stereotypes and more rhetoric than real achievements. On the other hand, the indigenous social emancipation movement facilitated by Bhakti and Vēdic-Vēdāntic rejuvenation achieved considerable social emancipation, even while fighting mostly in an uncompromising manner against the ill effects of social stagnation. There were also times when both had their boundaries blurred. Mostly, the works of the Khedkar-Vaidya-Thackeray trio had a moderating influence on the emancipation work of Shāhu Maharāj, transforming the anti-Brahmin nature of his deeds into non-Brahmin emancipation.

Innovation of Shāhu Maharāj and Its Impact

As noted earlier, Shāhu Maharāj, influenced by Ārya Samāj, introduced structural innovations that helped democratize Hindu institutions. On 8 July 1920, he founded the Shivaji Kshatriya Vedic School, which included teaching the recital of the Vēdic Mantras, conducting Vedic rituals, and educating students in musical recitals of religious themes. The students were then employed in the family temples of non-Brahmins and in the palace. In his final two years, he also aimed to create a non-caste-based seat of Jagadguru, a title that was mostly used by sanyāsins of caste-based orders.

The concept of 'Jagadguru Peeth' or dharmic authority was defined as 'the ascetic ideals of the 18th-century saint and the Vedic ideals of the Kshatriya, not as caste but an order without reference to birth or race, holding its own in matters spiritual as well as secular'. The Jagadguru of this order could marry and have a family, but the successor to the seat could not be the biological descendant of the 'Jagad Guru'.[68] The Patagon Math, founded by a Mauni Baba during the time of the great Sivāji, was selected for the title of 'Jagadguru' for its tradition and history. Sadashivrao Patil of Benadi, also called Benadikar, was made His Holiness Kshatra-Jagad Guru Benadikar. Apart from the knowledge of sāstras, he also had a college education. Though installed by Sāhu Maharāj, the king addressed him respectfully once he occupied the chair. In a letter dated 24 January 1921, he addressed him as 'Your Holiness' and requested him for a prospectus of a Vedic school to be started at Patagon and ended the letter with humility, addressing himself as 'an ignorant disciple'. When George Llyod, the Governor of Bombay and a conservative imperialist politician, visited the king showed his respect to 'Jagad Guru' as he 'threw himself, as was customary, at his guru's feet.'[69]

The king himself was becoming strongly anti-Brahmin, but His Holiness Kshatra-Jagad Guru showed himself to be remarkably free of such hatred and was all for pan-Hindu unity. His chief patron was not well disposed in favour of Tilak, but Jagadguru Benadikar highly appreciated Tilak's *Gītā Rahasya*. He even went to the extent of calling Tilak a closet-non-Brahmin because he had criticized Saṅkarācharya's Gītā commentary. He worked closely with Hindu Sanghatan leaders, including B.S. Moonje, Veer Savarkar, and Dr Hedgewar. In 1938, he attended the Hindu Youth Conference. It was presided over by Dr Hedgewar, the founder of the RSS. *Kesari*, the magazine founded by Tilak, felicitated Jagadguru Benadikar, who was on the side of Sāhu Maharāj, who Tilak bitterly opposed.[70] This is another instance of the indigenous dharmic spirit overcoming caste prejudices, hatred, and feelings of supremacism on both sides of the Brahmin-non-Brahmin divide created by the colonial-Indic composite complex.

Kāvya Kāntha Vāsiṣṭha Gaṇapathi Muni

The first (and perhaps the only) talk delivered in Sanskrit at the All India Congress Session was at Belgaum in 1924. The speaker, Vāsiṣṭha Gaṇapathi (better known as Kāvya Kāntha Vāsiṣṭha Gaṇapati Muni, 1878–1936), delivered a speech condemning casteism and untouchability in pure Sanskrit. He used Vedic texts to argue against the support of untouchability as part of religion.

He had written a comprehensive treatise in Sanskrit covering various subjects, including Parliamentary democracy and astronomy and authoritatively proved that there was no place for caste discrimination and untouchability in Vedic Hinduism. His deep knowledge of Sanskrit led him reject all forms of discrimination.

Freedom fighter Varahaneri Venkatesa Subramaniam Iyer (1881–1925), popularly known as V.V.S. Iyer, established a gurukul-type residential school in southern Tamil Nadu in 1922. Called 'Tamizh Gurukulam', it was run by an ashram called Bharadvāja Ashram, led by V.V.S. Iyer. Influenced by the educationist Booker Washington (1856–1915), Iyer modelled the institution after Washington's methodology but with Indic content. Students of all castes studied and lived there. Iyer and other teachers ate with all the students, and food was prepared by a Brahmin cook. However, two Brahmin students wanted to eat separately. Instead of informing the parents about the collective dining arrangement, Iyer made the two students eat in a storeroom. The parents of the two students had made significant financial contributions. The incident became an opportunity for emerging non-Brahmin leaders to further their cause, or perhaps they were genuinely concerned that this would lead to more discrimination. They demanded that Iyer make everyone eat collectively and hire a non-Brahmin cook or resign from his position due to financial contributions from the Indian National Congress. Iyer reacted harshly to these demands but pointed out that, including himself and all children and teachers in the ashram dined together without discrimination and that he could not impose collective dining on the two dissenting students. The conflict escalated by 1924, with prominent non-Brahmin leaders Varadarāja Nāidu and E.V. Rāmasamy Nāicker (EVR or 'Periyar' to his followers) leading the anti-Iyer group. It was at this time that Vāsiṣṭha Gaṇapati came to Tamil Nadu and was made the head of the Tamil Nadu Congress Session's welcome committee, which was headed by EVR. Both individuals spoke in favour of egalitarian collective dining in their lectures.

Both V.V.S. Iyer and Varadarāja Nāidu met Mahatma Gandhi and said their side of the controversy. After hearing both the parties, Gandhi wrote a letter to Nāidu, which seemed to vindicate the position of Iyer. It was published in *The Hindu* dated 21 March 1925:

> In so far as the present brahmacharis are concerned, if the parents of the Brahmin boys insist on their boys being allowed to dine separately, their scruples should be respected. But, for the future, it may be announced that no brahmacharis would be accepted whose parents would not let their boys dine in the same row with the others. I understand from you that the cook at the Gurukul would be always a Brahmin. What you object to (and that properly) is the separating of non-Brahmin boys from the Brahmins. I do think that all the boys should sit in the same row whilst they are taking their meals.[71]

The controversy arose during the Vaikom Satyagraha in 1925, where the Satyagrahis won a significant, though partial, victory in opening the roads to all Hindus, irrespective of castes, including the marginalized. EVR was one of the leaders deputed from the Madras Presidency Congress to participate in the Vaikom Satyagraha. He sent a telegram to the Mahārāni of Thiruvithāñcūr, 'heartily' thanking 'her Highness for removing the ban on Vykom roads' and saying that 'Shri Padmanaba may bless Her Highness and young Maharajah with all prosperity.'[72] Overall, a strong section of Congress leadership was against any form of discrimination, real or perceived.

Even with Gandhi's intervention, no agreement was reached. It seemed that V.V.S. Iyer's opponents wanted him to resign, and Iyer agreed to do so. However, the opponents continued to increase their demands, insisting on interfering in the management of the ashram. Both Iyer and his opponents sought the help of Vāsiṣṭha Gaṇapati in 1925. The seer visited the gurukul with Iyer and his opponents, mainly Varadaraja Naidu and EVR. He proposed a solution, suggesting that the food should be prepared by a cook from the so-called untouchable community. With Vāsiṣṭha Gaṇapati's intervention, both parties softened their stances. A solution seemed within reach until 4 June 1925, when tragedy struck. Iyer and his daughter Subadra visited Courtālam Falls. Subadra fell into the raging stream and Iyer jumped in to save her. Their bodies were recovered four days later.

The drowning of Iyer was a great loss for the vision and the initial steps towards a mission for a renewed and comprehensive national education. This approach aimed to break down caste barriers and elevate Tamil student society to greatness by integrating the best aspects of both Indic and modern educational systems. To this day, no similar effort has been made since Iyer's. Unfortunately, jealousy, blind hatred towards Brahmins, and a hunger for control from Iyer's opponents led to the demise of this dream. Iyer was a talented swimmer, and it is likely that on that fateful day, his failure to survive was due in part to the breaking of his will to live, caused by the venom of caste-based hatred that he never expected from the society for which he had given his all. Those leaders who freely spread hatred of Iyer did not physically force him and his daughter into the deadly waters, but their actions may have contributed to the tragic outcome.

Grief struck, Muni quoted an ancient sloka to express his heart:

> As the night set in, the lotus closed with the black bee in it. The bee was thinking 'the night will pass-the day will dawn and the sun will rise up making the lotus blossom. And I shall fly out.'

> Then suddenly an elephant came to the lake, pulled out the louts and stamped over it, killing the bee in it.[73]

On 25 February 1927, in Hyderabad, there was a significant social conference organized by Bhagya Reddi and Baji Kishen Rao, who were a prominent leader of social reforms. The meeting was presided by Prof. Veerabhadrudu, and the main speaker was Vāsiṣṭha Gaṇapati. He spoke about various social issues and emphasized that the reform movement was in line with Vedic principles. While some pandits were unhappy with Gaṇapati's criticisms of certain societal customs, many educated Hindu reformists and activists were pleased to have the support of such a prominent Vedic scholar. It was at this conference that Vāsiṣṭha Gaṇapati was given the title Muni.[74]

After the conference, Vāsiṣṭha Gaṇapati faced numerous questions and asserted that wherever possible, equality should be pursued. He emphasized the importance of unity and moving towards equality while acknowledging that inequality would exist in areas with significant differences, such as dietary choices between vegetarians and non-vegetarians. However, he believed that certain rituals, such as upanayanam (sacred thread ceremony), could be common to all.

> Q: Must caste differences exist?
> A: Everyone should become a Brahmin. Till then, the inner differences inside the castes must be removed. There should not be grades of merit inside a caste. The unity of customs alone brings about Brahmin-hood. Customs started by those who have realized God have to be accepted as authoritative. Equality means that the customs like upanayana have to be common to all. Inequality in other things, like customs, have to be removed. Because there is a difference between a vegetarian and non-vegetarian, inequalities cannot be removed in the food habits.
>
> ...
>
> Q: Are castes good?
> A: If there is discrimination, it is certainly bad.

> Q: Can Smritis be written afresh now?
> A: They can be.[75]

To a question on removing untouchability, he recommends that the so-called untouchable communities be made Śūdrās. Taken literally, this might be misinterpreted. But there are two aspects here. One is that in South India, Śūdra Jāthis are mostly affluent, land-owning communities. They also have strong monasteries. Secondly and most importantly, he was against *Smriti* injunctions that Śūdrās should be barred from studying Vedas:

> Q: How to solve the problem of Brahmins and non-Brahmins?
> A: By giving the right to study Vedas to all.
> Q: In certain Smritis, Sudras are barred from access to the Vedas. How do you reconcile this?
> A: They are temporary injunctions. When such things are written on the basis of jealousy, they are not to be taken as the standard. Smritis which go against the Vedas need not be taken as standards. The Sutras which are written denying access to the Vedas are hatred oriented. They are against Vedic pronouncements and so need not be taken as the standard.[76]

The Indian National Congress passed a resolution against untouchability, causing a stir among those orthodox sections who conflated untouchability with Varṇāśrama dharma. The Madras Varṇāśrama Dharma Saṅgha planned to hold a conference with leading authorities on scriptures to condemn the Congress's anti-untouchability programme. However, they wanted to keep a semblance of a fair, objective discussion by inviting numerous scholars, most of whom supported untouchability. However, something unexpected occurred. In his biography of *Gaṇapathi Muni,* Gunturu Lakshmikantam writes:

> The organising committee instructed their secretary to invite such pandits who supported their move. But the secretary came to know that pandit Madanmohan Malaviya would be in Madras on the day. He chose to invite Malaviya knowing full well his attitude. The idea of inviting Ganapati Muni came as an afterthought. Since Ganapati Muni and Malaviya were friends, the Secretary thought it appropriate to send an invitation to Ganapati Muni also. It was not as though the secretary was ignorant of the progressive ideas of Ganapati Muni would it not be delightful to find all these Vamaashram pandits dodging under a mask of petrified silence in the formidable presence of Ganapati Muni?[77]

The pro-untouchability pandits were surprised to see Vāsiṣṭha Gaṇapati and Madan Mōhan Māḷaviā at the gathering. When the two friends innocently started chatting after a long time, the Pandits were clearly uncomfortable. Once Vāsiṣṭha Gaṇapati and Māḷaviā realized this, they left the place. Fortunately, Māḷaviā arranged for Vāsiṣṭha Gaṇapati to give a lecture at Hindu High School that evening. Then, Māḷaviā invited Vāsiṣṭha Gaṇapati to give a lecture at the Hindu Maha Sabha conference that same night. At the conference, Vāsiṣṭha Gaṇapati proclaimed that untouchability was against Vedic dharma.[78]

A genuine seeker of spiritual realization, Vāsiṣṭha Gaṇapati was admired by spiritual giants like Ramaṇa Mahaṛṣi and Śri Aurobindo. In 1936, Kāvya Kāntha Vāsiṣṭha Gaṇapathi Muni attained samādhi.

Despite his strict adherence to Vedic values and code of conduct, Vāsiṣṭha Gaṇapati's original outlook was not accepted by the orthodox elite. When Dr S. Radha Krishnan, then Vice-Chancellor of Andhra University (1931–36), tried to establish a Sanskrit chair in Gaṇapati's name, traditionalist members of the university academic committee 'were so thoroughly worked against the social outlook of Gaṇapati that they would not listen to such a proposal'. They believed that social issues should not be mixed with spiritual matters and that associating Sanskrit with broader social issues would lead the youth away from the traditional path of dharma. Their opposition left Dr S. Radhakrishnan feeling disgusted and left the meeting.[79]

Subramaṇia Bhārati

In Tamil Nadu, Subramaṇia Bhārati (1882–1921) is a well-known poet who is considered the father of modern Tamil poetry. He was rooted in Vēdāntic wisdom and deeply influenced by Śwāmi Vivekānanda, Sister Nivēdita, and Śri Aurobindo. He considered Sister Nivēdita his guru. He had extensive interaction with Śri Aurobindo when he moved to Pondicherry, where Śri Aurobindo had been staying and practicing his Yōga. Bhārati also had the guidance of some siddhas, and his worldview became Shāktic Advaita.

The poet was fiercely multidimensional in his poetry. He sang about various topics, such as the comets and the mystery of existence, and even anticipated in his art quite a few developments in the worldview influenced by New Physics. Despite living in a remote corner of South India and facing economic hardships, he sang about the uprising of the agricultural workers in Tsarist Russia, likening it to 'the graceful eye glance of Mother Kāḷi'.

In terms of the social situation in India, he prioritized social liberation equally with political liberation in his songs

In 1915, he wrote a long song for children titled 'The Baby Song' (*Pāpā Pāṭṭu*). In simple lyrical lines, he encoded the highest wisdom of India for children. The verses, simple and sweet, imparted a strong physical culture, appreciate and enjoy nature, love for all life forms, a daily routine of study, music, play and worship, inspirational devotion to overcome defeats, companionship with all children, never to exclude any child, love for Tamil, love for Hindustan and in the penultimate verse he wrote: 'There are no Jāthis, my dear child; Attributing higher and lower notions by birth is a veritable sin; Those imbued with values of justice, wisdom complete and love for all, alone are people high.'

Initially, he wrote, 'There is no pride in Jāthi', and later, in 1917, he changed the words to mean 'There are no Jāthis'. This was published by his very close friend Parali. Su. Nellaiappar, with an added verse, said this nation 'undivided Hindustan' is the land of Vedas and valour and should be worshipped as Divine.[80] The same spirit is also shown in other poems of him as well. When he sings about the freedom of the nation, he specifically speaks of the freedom of marginalized communities.

Bhārati dons the role of a traditional fortune teller who roams the streets and asks for alms in exchange for fortune telling. These traditional fortune-telling beggars go around with a small drum and announce they are coming with the words 'Auspicious times are coming'. They are called 'Kōṇaṅki'. Now, such wandering, alm-seeking communities have considerably decreased, but in the time of the bard, they were a common sight. Needless to say, they were part of the lower rungs of the society. Bhārati sings as a new 'Kōṇaṅki' and sings of the coming auspicious times of the entire 'Bhārat', which he calls 'Vēdāpuram'. He invokes the power of 'Sakthi Mahā Kāḷi' to infuse him with the power of telling the future of the nation. The sequence he constructs is quite evolutionary. At the outset, he says, 'Jāthis unite; Conflicts fade.'

His prose writing is equally filled with vigour and is uncompromising in its approach to the birth-based system of discrimination. He wrote a novella titled *One in Six Shares*, which was proscribed by the British in 1911. He dedicated the novella thus:

> One Jāthi. One life force! All three hundred million people of Bhārat belong to one Jāthi. There can be classes. There can be divisions. There may be different occupations and trades. But there can be no birth based discriminations. There can be different religions. But there should be no religious hatred. This realisation alone will give us freedom and immortal greatness. There is no other way. I dedicate this work to the pure-hearted Vaiśyā communities which are the Paraiar and Paḷḷar communities who nurture us with food.[81]

The dedication shows a historical insight and uses that insight to empower and emancipate marginalized communities. In the novella, through one of the characters, he described the humiliations Indians faced abroad and linked them to the way socially excluded communities were treated by Indians in India:

> What we do in the forenoon, we shall reap in the afternoon. What we do to our socially excluded communities in India, we experience upon us in foreign lands. If our Śṛngēri Śaṅkarācharya and Vānamāmalai Jīyar were to go to Natal or Transvaal, they would have to stay only in slums. They would not be allowed to use the public pathways which others (whites) use. They should walk deliberately away (from public roads). They cannot even think of using palanquins or other carts. In summary: we treated a section of our own people as inferior. Now the world thinks of us as the most inferior of all the nations. We called a section of our own people as untouchables. Now the world considers both Hindus and Muslims from India are seen as untouchables. All races in the world have divisions. But if they become permanent divisions dividing the nation, then it becomes easy for others to disrespect us.

He expressed strong opposition against the caste system in his articles. Through poetry, essays, and fiction, he addressed this complex issue. In 1917, he wrote an essay in the form of a quasi-fictional conversation during a morning walk by the seashore and humorously titled it, 'Conference on Varṇāśrama by a Seaside Bridge'. The conversation involved a Brahmin as the speaker, the poet as the moderator, and an audience consisting of a lone fisherman and later an elderly Pariah. The Brahmin proclaimed that he would have no objections to marrying his daughter to the educated son of the fisherman. Shocked, the fisherman thought the Brahmin was insane. The Pariah, on the other hand, expressed more concern over economic matters than untouchability or public road usage. However, he believed in an imminent spiritual revolution that would eliminate the false caste systems, giving rise to a new era.[82]

In yet another article titled 'Jāthi Confusions' (1920), Bhārati states that economic poverty and the caste system are twin major problems in India. From 1918 to 1920, there was a famine in the province of Odisha (Orissa). Bhārati wrote that the marginalized sections of the society, usually the scheduled caste communities, bore the brunt of the famines, while the upper sections of the society, mostly made of upper castes, showed apathy to the suffering. He attributed this to the caste divisions and pointed out the deep-rooted, unrealistic, and pseudo-scientific notion of Jāthi and Varṇa. In a temple, three mahouts were employed to look after an elephant. Two of them were Brahmins and the other was a 'Ōthuvār' (a traditional singer of sacred Tamil hymns at temples, mostly derived from the land-owning Veḷḷāla caste). All three of them were doing a profession that was not theirs 'by birth'. Bhārati saw one of them beating the elephant mercilessly and told the mahout to train the elephant with love. The mahout responded by claiming that the elephant was a Śūdra and started 'a blabbering lecture of fabricated Śāstric rules' about classifying the elephants and other animals as per Varṇa, claiming there were Brahmin, Kṣatriyas, Vaiśyā and Śūdra elephants. Similarly, this pseudo-scientific taxonomy was extended to planets, gems, plants, and other animals. Bhārati says:

> I am saying this to show how deeply this caste feeling is entrenched in the psyche of our people.... In a country where such a caste system is deep rooted, is it easy work to inculcate feelings of human liberty, equality and fraternity? How many *Jāthis!* And within each *Jāthi* how many internal divisions! And each will not inter-dine and intermarry!...Joke! Joke! What a great joke we have made of ourselves!.... All should be given good education and all would then be equal in their mental abilities. Those who become vegetarians should be made Brahmins.... Entire India should be made a Brahmin nation this way.... Whatever the *Jāthi* anyone who becomes a vegetarian should be given the sacred thread and Gāyatri Mantra and should be considered a Brahmin. This is the path shown by Vivekananda. This is surely a good way to removed caste differences. But even a better way is for the so-called upper class people to forget their notion of superiority and mix with all.[83]

In 1908, Bhārati fled from arrest in British India to the French-governed Pondicherry, where he lived for a decade. In 1912, he was invited by the members of a youth club called 'Progressive Union Cricket Club' in Pondicherry, which consisted mainly of Scheduled Castes community youths. They wanted him to deliver a lecture. Many of the boys also belonged to families that had converted to Christianity. When he asked, 'What shall I talk about?', one of the youths, Kanakalingam, later reminisced that he immediately said, 'on caste distinctions'. Saying that their wish coincided with his own thoughts, he agreed. Despite the boys trying to keep it a low-profile affair, the speech attracted a significant number of attendees and the attention of the CID department. At that time, revolutionary V.V.S. Iyer, a one-time colleague of Savarkar, had become a friend of Bhārati and joined him at the event. Later, at the instigation of British CID, a court penalized the organizers with each fined five francs, and the person who provided his house as the venue fined twenty francs.

Kanakalingam became a lifelong disciple of Bhārati and was welcome to his house at any time. He was very affectionate towards the poet's young daughter, who used to sing her father's songs and visit Kanakalingam's house to sing for his family members. Then, one day, Bhārati calmly informed Kanakalingam that he had decided to perform the Yajñopavita ceremony for him. At that time, Bhārati was plagued by poverty, but he had organized a small ceremony in his house, inviting some important patriots. In his memoirs of Bhārati, Kanakalingam emotionally recalled the ceremony later thus:

> Bharathiyar told me one day: 'We have decided to perform the sacred thread ceremony for you. Get up at dawn; have a bath; wear clean clothes and come here. Do not wear a shirt.' Accordingly I went to Bharathiyar's house the next morning. As I went in and saw, there were Bharathiyar's friends who were Brahmins and non-Brahmins. The great savant VVS Iyer majestically sat there. Thiru. Srinivachachariyar, Thiru Naryanaswamy Iyer, Kuvalaikannan, Thiru Govindarajulu Naidu and others were there.... I understood that a gathering had assembled for the sake of the sacred thread wearing ceremony to be conducted for me. I paid my obeisance to savant VVS Iyer and to others with all my heart. They also paid their respects to me and blessed me by chanting '*Vande Mataram*' (*Mother! We Bow to Thee*!) Bharathiyar was busy plying between the hall and the kitchen. 'It's getting late. Let's proceed!' said VVS Iyer in a ringing voice. 'I am coming immediately,' said Bharathiyar in a voice, which echoed sharp and clear like a bell. Bharathiyar came up on the scene with a dot of kumkum adorning his forehead.

There were portraits of the deities Lakṣmī, Saraswati, and Kṛṣṇa in the hall. Bharathiyar adorned them with flowers. There was a curved dagger under Kṛṣṇa's portrait. He decorated it with a dot of kumkum. For some time, he sang, meditating in prayer to Shakti, the Mother Supreme.

Then he told me to sit facing the East. As I sat down, my Guru smeared my forehead, arms and chest with marks of sacred ash. Then he told me to kneel. Taking the thread in his hands, and worshipping the sun, and prolonged prayers, he adorned me with it. Immediately, I touched his feet respectfully and prostrated myself before him. He blessed me and declared in his stentorian voice: 'From today you are a Brahmin. Hereafter, if anyone asks you as to what caste you belong, boldly say "I am Brahmin."'[84]

Bhārati was a great devotee of the Divine Feminine, particularly in the form of Mahā Kāḷi. He had written many songs about Kāḷi and Shakti. He was particularly fond of *Dēsamuthu Māriamman* temple at a place called '*Uppaḷḷam*'. This temple belonged to the Scheduled Castes community. The temple's priest was from the Valluvar community, known as the priest clan of Paṟaiar Jāthi, and his name was Nāgaliṅga Paṇḍāram. He also worked as a carpenter in the same office as Kanakalingam, who was a clerk. When Nāgaliṅga Paṇḍāram learned that Bhārati had performed the Gāyatri Mantra initiation and investiture of the sacred thread for Kanakalingam, he wanted the same initiation from Bhārati. Initially, when Nāgaliṅga Paṇḍāram met the poet, he thought Bhārati was a madman. However, as they grew closer, Nagalinga Paṇdaram came to realize the greatness of Bhārati's inner richness. He used to visit Bhārati on Sundays and hence Bhārati affectionately called him the 'Sunday student'. At Nagalinga Paṇdaram's request, Bhārati initiated him in Gayatri Mantra, performed the ceremonies, and made him wear the *yajñopavīta*.[85]

On one occasion, when Nāgaliṅga Paṇḍāram visited Bhārati's house, Bhārati asked his daughter to bring a harmonium and then instructed her to sing the song he had composed about the Goddess Dēsamuthu Māriamman of the Uppaḷḷam temple.

Today, the song Bhārati sang for this Goddess is an integral part of the rich Tamil culture:

> In You Dēsamuthu *Māri*
> Taking refuge surrendering me
> after all the quest many!
> Remove all negativities and
> Bless with every boon asked!
>
> Singing I surrender at Your feet
> Attachments binding, Remove all Thee!
> Countless blessings You will shower!
> All deficiencies (in us) You will dissolve!
>
> One ever in sorrow is indeed a sinner
> Willing I shall do Your work
> And flourish I shall by Your grace Divine!
>
> Praising Shakti ever in Tamizh poetry
> Filled with Bhakti Singing Her glory
> All fears vanish and get destroyed!
>
> Rooted in Shakti we exist in Her.
> So declare the scriptures precious
> We will do any work and every
> And all works are that of
> She the Goddess Divine!
>
> Let us forget the falsehood that
> Misery is the truth of existence;
> Bliss alone we shall seek and
> Duty-bound She is to give us all we ask.
>
> Trust Her and She will never forsake you;
> So say all the Vedas four;
> Take refuge in Goddess Ambikai
> Gain boons countless!

Nāgaliṅga Paṇḍāram was ecstatic. The poet requested the priest to sing it in the temple. Later a night school and an informal library were established for the Scheduled Caste community nearby. Sudhānanda Bhārati, another poet and a Yogi, who was briefly part of the budding commune of Śri Aurobindo Ashram, named it 'Bhārati' library. Bhārati left Pondicherry at the end of World War I. He was briefly arrested by the British. Then he settled in Madras. When he died due to illness in 1921, he was not even forty years old. Till the last year of his life, he continued writing articles and poems rich in spirituality, calling for social emancipation and national liberation.

When Bhārati's collection of poems was published by his widowed wife, the title of this poem was written as *Uppaḷḷam Dēsamuthu Māriamman*. However, in some editions published by others, there was a brief attempt to remove or dilute the identity of the Goddess, particularly the temple to which She belongs. R. Kanagalingam writes:

> When (Bhārati) sought refuge in Pudhuvai (another name for Pondicherry), in many temples there – whether one of Shiva or of Vishnu or of Kali – fanatic casteism was intolerably rampant. My Guru (Bhārati) used to boldly remark that 'in such temples there was no God!' He also did not wish to sing of such Gods. This was a secret known to all. Therefore, he sang heartily of only, the Goddess of the Nadupathi Muthumariamman Temple of Uppalam belonging to Harijans. In the first pary of the book, 'National Songs' originally published by Tmt. Chellamal wife of Bharathiyar, these songs were published under the title 'Uppalam Muthumariamman'. That alone is correct. For some reason, in later editions, only the name, Muthumariamman appears as the title on top.[86]

In 1947, decades after the song was written, Sri Kanagalingam wrote movingly about the ever-vital impact of the song:

> Ever since his singing of this song, it has offered us, Harijans, great consolation to this day. This confidence and the power of Bharathiyar's poetry have led greatly to the movement of nationalism in general and to Harijan upliftment in particular, in Tamil Nadu. The movement for 'Temple Entry' has come to a happy conclusion in our land, with the entry of Harijans to the Tirupathi temple. It is my belief that all this is because of the divine blessings of Desamuthumari, celebrated in song by Bharathiyar.[87]

Śwāmi Sahajānanda Paramāchāya

Born Munuswāmy in a Scheduled Castes community household and in a family battling poverty, Śwāmi Sahajānanda Paramāchāya (1890-1959) was made to discontinue his studies at Arcot Missionary School. The young Munuswāmy was brilliant and had been marked for conversion by the school authorities. When he refused to become a Christian. he was sacked from the school immediately and the complete fees was demanded by the missionaries in a merciless manner.

Munusāmy and his family eventually moved to Kolār where his father became a contract worker (a slightly better form of indentured labourer). Fortunately, Kolār Gold Fields had a strong network of organized welfare activities springing up from the initiative of labourer leaders, who were mostly from Scheduled Castes communities. A lot of indigenous religious institutions had come up. There would be frequent traditional 'telling' performances or Kathā-*Kālakshepa,* and Munuswamy would listen to Rāmāyana and Mahābhārata stories told in Upanyasas in the evening. He was determined to practice dharma in a steadfast manner like Rāmā and walk the path of the Bhagavad Gīta. In 1905, the parents moved back from Kolār Gold Fields to their native place, where they, along with the boy, again started working as quasi-indentured labourers in the farms of local landlord, Subbaiāh Nāidu.

Ray of Light from an Inclusive Advaita Pītam

At that time, a monk arrived in that village. His name was Śrī Nīlamēga Śwāmigaḷ. He found the boy to be calm and with a different kind of aura around him. So, he called the boy and asked who he was. The boy astonished the monk when he answered that he was 'Para Brahman'. Soon, the Śwāmi found himself in a deep discussion with the boy about the spiritual field. He realized that the boy was born to uplift the nation through spirituality. Meanwhile, Śwāmi speaking to an 'untouchable'boy became a problem for the 'upper castes'.

Śrī Nīlamēga Śwāmigaḷ was from a village called Munugapattu. He came in the lineage of Śrī Jagat Guru Śrī Satchithānanda Śwāmigaḷ. Śrī Jagat Guru Śwāmigaḷ was born in the community of potters and grew up in Shaṇmugajñānapuram, a village near Madras. He was taught grammar and literature by Saranavaperumal Iyer, a Brahmin scholar in the village. Iyer directed him to a great Advaitic seer of that time, Jagat Guru Śrī Piṟasai Aruṇāchala Śwāmigaḷ. This Śwāmigaḷ came in the lineage that traced itself to Ādi Saṅkara. According to this tradition, Indra Pītam at Thiruthuruthi, a place in the Cauvery Delta region, was one of the four Pītams founded by Ādi Saṅkara. In this, there was a great saint called Jagat Guru Dattātrēya Śwāmigaḷ, and in this lineage of Jagat Gurus Śrī Piṟasai Aruṇāchala Śwāmigaḷ was fifth from him. Soon the boy became a bright disciple and eventually his spiritual successor. He was so immersed in the non-dual state that the people used to call him 'Brahman' Itself. He was against Karma-Kāṇḍa-based divisions and insisted on the search and realization of pure Advaitic-Vēdāntic Gnosis. He wrote a commentary (Bāṣya) for Advaitic texts *Kaivaluanavanītham*, Upaniṣads, *Vēdānta Chūḷāmaṇi*, and Bhagavad Gīta (not published).[88]

Śrī Nīlamēga Śwāmigaḷ was the disciple of Śrī Jagat Guru Śrī Satchithānanda Śwāmigaḷ. He got the boy released from the quasi-bonded labour of the landlord and took the boy to

Thatchṇā Śwāmigaḷ at Kāñchi. After teaching the boy all that he knew in Vēdānta, he directed the boy to Śrī Karapāthira Śivaprakāsa Śwāmigaḷ. From this point to his spiritual sojourn in the ashram of Śrī Karapāthira Śivaprakāsa Śwāmigaḷ (1874-1918) has already been dealt with in the section on Śrī Śwāmigaḷ.

Munuswāmy to Śwāmi Sahajānanda

Here he got the initiation and became Śwāmi Sahajānanda. Śwāmi Sahajānanda read *Śrī Mahā Bhakta Vijayam*, the compendium of the saints and sages of Vaiṣṇava tradition (mainly from the Deccan region), which has been seen in detail in the previous chapter. These saints also challenged all kinds of social discrimination. Śwāmi Sahajānanda realized his path. He decided to fight against all discrimination in society and purify society of the evil of the caste system.

With the help from the seers like Śrī Karapāthira Śivaprakāsa Śwāmigaḷ, he established Nandanār Ashram at Chidambaram. However, the feudal caste-ridden bureaucracy created hurdles for the establishment of the institution. Reformist leader M.C. Rājāh cited this incident to show how the bureaucracy operated to thwart every social emancipatory attempt. In his work *Oppressed Hindus*, he wrote:

> Swami Sahajanandam, an Adi Dravida Saint, a highly cultured Sadhu, applied for a piece of Government waste land for his Nandanar Free School in Chidambaram. His application for the grant of this land was sent to the subordinate Government Revenue Officials. These caste-ridden officials did not recommend the assignment. Whereupon, the application of Swami Sahajanandam was rejected. The Swami did not step there. He went up to the District Collector who is an Officer of the Indian Civil Service, and requested him. To personally inspect the site, before finally rejecting his application. The District Collector was a sympathetic officer, he went up to the spot, inspected the site and assigned it to our Swami.

Then he quoted what the collector actually saw with respect to the objection raised by the local mirasdar:

> Assignment-land-Chidambaram Taluk-Kallipadi village-Sahajanandam-Manager-Nandanar School—Chidambaram.
>
> ...
>
> The mirasdar Mr. V. Velayudam Pillai is the chief opponent of the assignment. Knowing that I inspected the land he gave up the contention that the Northern portion is required for water spread and says that it is required for village site. The contentions of persons who offer contradictory arguments of this kind are worth nothing.
>
> (Sd.) R.F.B.L. Guppy, Ag. Collector. [89]

This model ashram also involved itself in running schools and residential hostels for children of all communities without discrimination, including, and mainly, the Scheduled Castes community students, both boys and girls. In 1957, two years before his death, in his Madras legislative assembly speech, he pointed out that in 1920 when the Government asked for Scheduled Caste community graduates to come for government jobs, there were only two and of the two as one had embraced Buddhism (C.N. Sivaraj) only one got eligible. But in 1955, when the government called for Scheduled Castes community graduates, 400 eligible Scheduled Castes candidates applied, of which 100 students were ones who studied from Nandanār educational institutions that Śrī Śwāmigaḷ started.[90]

Between 1926 and 1932, he was a nominated member of the Madras Legislative Assembly, and he made a passionate contribution to the advancement of the welfare of the Scheduled Castes community in particular and social justice for Hindu society in general. He was again elected between 1936 and 1947. After Independence, he was elected to the Assembly from the Chidambaram constituency and continued as a member till his Mahā Samādhi in 1959.

Śwāmi Sahajānanda advocated modules on the Indian knowledge system in schools. He particularly advocated dedicating at least one period every week to familiarizing children with local herbal knowledge in the form of first-aid medicine so that in case of medical emergencies, local resources could be used to save lives or minimize harm. His legislative speeches show the battles he fought on multiple fronts for social emancipation.

In 1938, the Provincial Congress Government in Madras, under the Premiership of Chakravarti Rajagopālachāri, better known as Rajāji, enacted a temple entry bill for the Malabar region. Then, the most prominent Scheduled Castes community leader and social reformer, M.C. Rājah, expressed his bitter disappointment at the government not taking up a much stronger temple entry bill that he had billed in 1932. In sad irony, the bill was initially supported by the same Rajāji, who helped even draft the bill, but later, Rajāji hesitated and thought it would unnecessarily anger the orthodox sections of Tamil regions. Here, then, is an instance where the ethical Hindu in Rajāji wanted temple entry, and the shrewd politician in him made an ethical compromise which, in hindsight, does not favour well the reputation of this sage-like politician. Yet after expressing all his bitterness, M.C. Rājah expressed his support for even this diluted bill. Śrī Śwāmigaḷ spoke eloquently about the bill, both its deficiencies and merits and also, more importantly, the need for temple entry. This speech made at Madras Legislative Assembly, during the discussion of 'the Malabar temple entry bill, 1938', shows the pain of a spiritually advanced politician at the unkind treatment that emanated from the 'caste Hindus', which degraded the humanity of entire Hindu society:

> This bill has started a new era. We have been trying to bring a similar bill for many years. In the previous assembly our leader MC Rajah brought a bill for temple-entry. Now the government

itself is bringing the bill for which we are extremely happy.... But this bill could have been brought up in another manner as has been done in Bombay legislation by enabling the Trustees to effect temple entry. Recently when I took a noble person (from Scheduled Community) to a famous Siva temple, the trustee welcomed him respectfully with garland and asked him to go inside and worship. He simply said not to reveal the caste. Both in Madras and other parts of Tamil Nadu there are many temple trustees waiting for a legislation to open the temples for Harijan temple entry. This bill should have been enacted in a different manner. It is now the duty of the Government to implement temple entry enabled by the legislation. Our people have strong belief in the presence of Divinity in the temples. That we are not allowed to enter the temples have hurt us strongly and we have lamented in our hearts why were we destined to be born as Hindus.... The temples belong to God and we are the children of God. Then do not we have a right in the temples of God who is our father? This is our question. There is provision for this bill to be enacted.... No Vēdā and no true śāstra prohibits the temple entry of Harijans. No scripture tells us not to enter the temples. Some religious heads have issued statements. Sriṅgēri Sāṅkarācharya, Kumbhakoṇam Sāṅkarācharya, Vānamāmalai Jīyar Śwāmigaḷ – they have issued statements. But if one can look into their heart of hearts, they are anxiously waiting for Harijans to make temple entry. They why they are saying contrary outside is because they expect the orthodox sections creating unnecessary troubles. In reality they have no objection to temple entry. Here one should remember one thing. Both our Premier and health minister are Śrī Vaiṣṇavaites. In Śrī Vaiṣṇava religion there is no concept of pollution. Once a person is initiated with the holy water then the caste should not be seen. Vānamāmalai Jīyar Śwāmigaḷ follows this in his daily rituals. All these show that when one is a Bhakta then he has no pollution. In fact, I would go to the extent of saying that the temples are exclusively for Harijans. Because according to an Ācharya, one who considers himself high-born or superior to others has no love for God while one who is considered lowly has his place in the Divine realm of liberation (parama patham).

> So Harijans can enter the temples. But if someone calls himself an upper caste then he cannot enter the temple. They say that the Harijans are unclean. But what matters is the uncleanliness of heart and character. There is no scripture that is against the entry of Harijans into the temple.[91]

The speech is one of grace and broad heartedness. When Śrī Śwāmigaḷ states that the Sriṅgēri Sāṅkarācharya, Kumbhakoṇam Sāṅkarācharya, Vānamāmalai Jīyar Śwāmigaḷ as expecting the temple entry in their hearts while remaining the prisoners of circumstances, Śrī Śwāmigaḷ arose to become verily a Kṛṣṇa in the Kurukshetra of social emancipation, addressing these traditional Hindu heads, to realize how forgetting their spiritual strengths and duties, they had entangled themselves in the bondages of traditions that had nothing to do with Sanātans Dharma. He goes on to quote the Bhagavad Gīta to support his argument.

In his speech next year at the Legislative Assembly, made during the discussion on education, he made a revolutionary proposal. The schools are inside the villages. Mostly Harijans are made to live outside the villages in slums. If they go to schools in the villages, they are harassed. There are schools in Harijan habitations. Even though only Harijans studied there, the government showing poor enrolments started closing these schools and integrating Harijan schools with the schools inside the village where mostly so-called 'caste Hindu' children studied. What happened was whenever there was an inspection, the Harijan children would be allowed in these 'inside village' schools, but from the next day onward, they would be harassed. Pointing out this practical painful reality, Śrī Śwāmigaḷ proposed:

> Instead of abolishing low enrolment schools in the slums and integrating them with the schools inside the villages, let the schools inside the villages be abolished and let them be

> integrated with the schools in the Harijan areas. Let all caste children come to the schools in Harijan habitations and learn.[92]

He pointed out that the boarding schools were run in Madras Presidency with financial support from the government. He made a personal investigation into how the funds were allocated by the Government to the boarding schools. Then he pointed out the following:

> Now after our Congress ministry has been formed in Tamil Nadu, they are doing a noble deed. They are giving scholarship to college going Harijan students. I express my heartfelt gratitude for that. Harijan students studying in high school are demanded fees. How could they pay it? Many Harijan students suffer because of this. So from elementary school to college the education for Harijan students should be without fees.... Another strange happening should be told here. Two years ago, rupees two lakh was allocated as boarding grand. This year this has been increased to three lakhs and eleven thousand. This increase is appreciable. But there is a deep secret here. Five to six years ago I made an enquiry. Among the boarding schools how many are run by the missionaries; how many by the Hindus; how many by Muslims and how many boarding schools are run for Adi Dravida students. There were totally 173 boarding schools of which 157 belonged to missionaries, 11 belong to the Hindus and 5 to the Muslims. So there is none for Harijans. Missionaries work well but there is a problem. From my village my friend and myself were studying in the elementary boarding school run by missionaries at Tindivanam. They asked me to convert to Christianity and when I refused to convert, I was asked to pay for the food. I incurred expenditure. If Hindu students go to missionary run boarding schools then there is no way they can return back as Hindus. But the fund for the missionary boarding schools come from the government here. Still they do not feed the Hindu students and the Harijan students. They feed only the Christian students.... Harijan communities do not have money to run boarding schools and

> there is no way a Harijan student can remain a Hindu and study in a missionary boarding school. If it takes Rupees four for a single Harijan student to study from a boarding school then the government should pay that amount. Only if we have such a scheme then only we can have boarding schools where Harijan students shall come forward to study.[93]

As seen earlier, a significant number of Scheduled Caste community graduates selected for government jobs came from the schools of Nandanār educational institutions. That was in 1957. But it was not an easy achievement. In his 1952 speech at the legislative assembly, we learn that there were intentional bureaucratic hurdles and even possible destruction of applications because of casteism. He also demanded that 'Harijan' representatives should have an increased number of hours in the legislative assemblies because their people relatively face more problems that need urgent as well as sustained solutions.[94] In 1957, he proposed that in the model of a five-year plan, there should be a five-year plan for 'Harijan' upliftment. He wanted an increased number of hostels for Harijan's welfare and wanted private players to be allowed to create the hostels.[95] A close study of his speeches in Independent India shows that he had observed how the bureaucratic hurdles towards running educational institutions and related institutions like hostels and boardings, which continued even after the independence, actually hurt the welfare of 'Harijan' students.

Śwāmi Sahajānanda Paramāchāya attained Mahā Samādhi on 1 May 1959.

CHAPTER 14

Dharma as Liberator: From a Neo-Buddhist Bodhisattva to an Advaitic Paramacharya

More often than not, Dr Ambedkar is projected as a hate figure for the so-called upper-caste Hindus, while for others, he is considered a liberator. The person hailed as the Chief Architect of the Indian Constitution had spoken exhaustively against Hinduism. In more than one way, the dominant castes of the Hindu society and those people who were its traditional leaders were responsible for the righteous bitterness that Dr Ambedkar displayed towards Hinduism. Yet what is missing is the deeper Hindu spiritual impact on Dr Ambedkar's worldview. Equally important in the history of Dharmic emancipation is the contribution of M.C. Rājāh a staunch believer in Hindu spirituality and social justice. He framed his approach to social justice through Dharma. This chapter also looks into the tough task taken up by C. Rājagōpālachārya popularly known as Rājāji worked on the programme of Temple Entry through legislation and people's movement, getting brickbats from all sides. This chapter also explores the much-underreported contribution of the non-sectarian Advaitic schools of South India, which played a pivotal role in social emancipation and also the role of the Śrī Rāmakṛṣṇa-Vivekānanda movement – particularly Śwāmi Chithbavānanda.

Dr Bhimrao Ramji Ambedkar

Dr Bhimrao Ramji Ambedkar (1891–1956), a polymath and a warrior for social justice, was also a bitter critic of Hinduism. Through his speeches, articles, and books, he repeatedly emphasized that Hinduism, in its essence and historical consequences, was detrimental to the spiritual and social well-being of the nation. However, upon closer examination of his work, it becomes evident that his harsh criticism was intended as a necessary corrective measure of the so-called 'upper castes' and traditionalists who were perpetuating social stagnation in the name of dharma. Behind his harshness lay a genuine concern for humanity. He often stressed that the annihilation of caste and liberation of socially excluded communities from hierarchical tyranny were fundamental prerequisites for the survival and prosperity of Hindu society in the future. This message was forcefully conveyed in his harshest (and even a seemingly unjust below-the-belt) critique of Hinduism, notably in the infamous *Riddles of Hinduism*.

To fully comprehend this, one should start with Dr Ambedkar's most severe criticism of Hinduism: 'The Hindu social system is undemocratic not by accident. It is designed to be undemocratic. Its division of society into varnas and castes, and of castes and outcastes are not theories but are decrees. They are all barricades raised against democracy.'[1]

Such ruthless criticism is expected of Dr Ambedkar. So, did the good doctor find the entire Hindu Dharma undemocratic? Immediately he springs forth a surprise:

> From this it would appear that the doctrine of fraternity was unknown to the Hindu Religious and Philosophic thought. But such a conclusion would not be warranted by the facts of history. The Hindu Religious and Philosophic thought gave rise to an idea which had greater potentialities for producing

social democracy than the idea of fraternity. It is the doctrine of *Brahmaism*.[2]

'Brahmaism', as Dr Ambedkar acknowledges, is a term he borrowed from Indologist Edward Washburn Hopkins, who used it to denote 'a belief in the All-soul without necessarily implying a concomitant doctrine of Illusion, Māyā'.[3] It is important to note that of the triune values which form the heart of what may be considered as the enlightenment humanism of the West, 'liberty-equality-and fraternity', Dr Ambedkar always considered fraternity as the most valuable and higher among equals. Yet here, he was considering Advaitic value as having 'greater potentiality' than even fraternity for social democracy. This will be discussed in a more elaborate contextual setting subsequently.

All these may be pointing towards a deeper yet indirect influence that was not realized consciously by Dr Ambedkar himself. It could have come from Sri Aurobindo.

Sayajirao Gaekwad III played a pivotal role in the connection between Aurobindo and Baroda. In 1892, the Maharaja met Aurobindo and asked him to take a teaching position at Baroda University. Śri Aurobindo spent thirteen years in Baroda from February 1893 to February 1906, serving as both the vice-principal of the college and the king's personal secretary. In this capacity, Śri Aurobindo also wrote speeches for the king. During this time, Sri Aurobindo also contributed to magazines for freedom fighters in Bengal. The British authorities were suspicious of the Maharaja's sympathy for Hindu revolutionaries, and Aurobindo's association with the princely state exacerbated their concerns. Despite the British pressure, the Maharaja remained defiant. For example, he provided military training to Jatin Bannerji, one of Aurobindo's friends, and allowed him to join the Baroda cavalry, in direct opposition to the British ban on Bengalis joining the military. Attempting not to cause further problems for the Maharaja, Aurobindo eventually left Baroda. Although the Maharaja urged him to stay, Aurobindo was resolute and took up a lower-paying job in Bengal. Even after Sri Aurobindo left, the British regarded the Maharaja with suspicion. In his secret letter to the British government, Viceroy Hardinge traced the hostility that the king had for the British 'to the pernicious influence of the Poona Brahmins' who 'with a concerted object ... kept up a constant glorification of the Gaekwad'. The letter also speaks of the influence Aurobindo had on the Maharaja even years after he had left, observing that 'his employment in the State gave a great impetus to the anti-British movement.' Then there was an 'akhara', a wrestling club in the heart of Baroda that was run by Hindu monks, which, the report pointed out, was where 'sedition has been openly preached ... without any opposition from the State police'. As seen earlier, the intelligence reports of the British also spoke about Shankar Wagh, a barber in the employ of the palace who was 'known to be an extremist and a great friend of V.D. Savarkar'.[4]

It was this seditious king of Baroda under the 'pernicious influence of the Poona Brahmins' and Śri Aurobindo, who also gave a young Bhimrao Ambedkar a scholarship initially for his studies in India. In 1913, aged twenty-two, the young Ambedkar was supported by the Baroda State Scholarship of £11.50 per month for three years, for his post-graduation in Columbia University. Later, when Dr Ambedkar returned to India, the Maharaja nominated him as a member of the Baroda Legislative Assembly and implemented a special electoral law allowing Scheduled Castes communities to participate in the assembly elections. This sheds light on the potential influence Śri Aurobindo had on Dr Ambedkar.

Views on Caste: Original Conception and Later Devolution

We have discussed in the previous sections the views held by Sayajirao III on caste and untouchability. Historian Dr Ruma Bhattacharya summarizes the approach of the king towards the caste system and untouchability thus:

> (Sayajirao) disagreed with the view that the rigid caste system with its concomitant out-castes was a part of the Hinduism in the old Vedic times. In fact, society was then divided into four classes on the basis of division of labour and these four classes were not castes. One could improve his quality and ability and get into the next higher class. He expressed his views that the ideas of untouchability are only a later refinement born of ignorance and conceit and nurtured by self-complacency. He pointed out the fact that untouchables were not feeble in spirit or mentality. As an example, he mentioned the names of some famous saints of India, who were respected even by the Brahmins. Such as Nanda in South India, Ravidas in Oudh, Chokamela in Maharashtra, Haridas Thakur in Bengal.[5]

The thought process does have what can be considered an 'Aurobindonian' signature. In 1907, in his magazine *Bande Mataram*, Śri Aurobindo wrote,

> The division of castes in India was conceived as a distribution of duties. A man's caste depended on his dharma, his spiritual, moral and practical duties, and his dharma depended on his svabhāva, his temperament and inborn nature. A Brahmin was a Brahmin not by mere birth, but because he discharged the duty of preserving the spiritual and intellectual elevation of the race, and he had to cultivate the spiritual temperament and acquire the spiritual training which could alone qualify him for the task.... Essentially there was, between the devout Brahmin and the devout Sudra, no inequality in the single virāṭ puruṣa of which each was a necessary part. Chokha Mela, the Maratha

> Pariah, became the Guru of Brahmins proud of their caste purity; the Chandala taught Shankaracharya: for the Brahman was revealed in the body of the Pariah and in the Chandala there was the utter presence of Shiva the Almighty.[6]

One can see very well a continuity of the same stream of thought in Dr Ambedkar:

> The essence of the Vedic conception of varna is the pursuit of a calling which is appropriate to one's natural aptitude.... While I reject the Vedic varnavyavastha for reasons given in the speech, I must admit that the Vedic theory of varna as interpreted by Swami Dayanand and some others is a sensible and an inoffensive thing. It did not admit birth as a determining factor in fixing the place of an individual in society. It only recognised worthwhile caste is based on the principle of each according to his birth. The two are as distinct as chalk is from cheese. In fact, there is an antithesis between the two.

Even the rejection of *Varṇavyavasta,* for which Dr Ambedkar elaborated, mainly on the practical impossibility of classifying people belonging to 'four thousand castes based on birth'into four categories based on worth, is anticipated in Sri Aurobindo's thought process.

In 1926, a few years before Dr Ambedkar wrote *Annihilation of Caste*, Śri Aurobindo highlighted how the fourfold system can be viewed as a kind of failed experiment that 'sought to develop different types and marriage within the same caste was intended to help this system':

> Gradually the whole thing has become meaningless and the classification into castes serves no purpose — still the religious samskāra acts against its abolition. It is said that instead of abolishing the caste the proper course would be to restore it to reality. But that is not possible. There are Vaidyas who show

> natural fitness for Shastras, there are Brahmins who show no aptitude for Brahmins.[7]

Sri Aurobindo also introduces another notion—that of dynamic psychological types, which are more fluid and flexible and more individualistic than social—a dimension that Dr Ambedkar ignored.

However, there is a striking similarity between the way Śri Aurobindo and Dr Ambedkar see how the system became more and more rigid with the passage of time. Śri Aurobindo scholar and psychiatrist Dr Soumitra Basu explains,

> Unfortunately, with the passage of time, the psychological and ethical ideas ceased to be the guiding principles and the typal life became fixed, conventional, hereditary and traditional ... the plasticity of the typal stage was replaced by, a fixed and formalized arrangement. Sri Aurobindo points out that the conventional stage is born when the outward supports of the ideal become more important than the ideal itself. In the evolution of castes, the outward supports that hold the four#fold order comprised primarily of (a) birth, (b) economic factors, (c) religious ritual and sacrament and (d) family custom.[8]

This process is also narrated by Dr Ambedkar, in his own way, through a scholarly speculative scenario:

> In the transformation of Varna into Caste three stages are quite well marked. The first stage was the stage in which the duration of Varna i.e. of status and occupation of a person was for a prescribed period of time only. The second stage was a stage in which the status and occupation involved the Varna of a person ensured during lifetime only. The third stage was a stage in which the status and occupation of the Varna became hereditary.
>
> ...

> First it shows that Varna was determined by an independent body of people called Manu and Saptarshi. Secondly it shows that the Varna was for a period after which a change was made by Manu.... The determination of the Varna was done in a rough and tumble manner. This system seems to have gone into abeyance. A new system grew up in its place. It was known as the Gurukul system.... Upanayan by the Acharyas was the new method of determining Varna which came into vogue in place of method of determination by Manu and Saptarshi. The new method was undoubtedly superior to the old method. It retained the true feature of the old method namely that the Varna should be determined by a disinterested and independent body. But it added a new feature namely training as a pre-requisite for assignment of Varna. On the ground that training alone develops individual in the make up of a person and the only safe way to determine the Varna of a person is to know his individuality, the addition of this new feature was undoubtedly a great improvement.... Varna instead of being Varna for a period became Varna for life. But it was not hereditary.[9]

Not taking into consideration the micro-factual mechanical correspondence between the two, what is common to both is a narrative of the gradual rigidity setting into the Varṇā system.

Caste Rigidity against Democracy

This is the next more striking parallel. The core of Dr Ambedkar's criticism of the caste system is that it is fundamentally undemocratic and hence against the very spiritual basis of what he called 'Brahmaism' based on the Upaniṣad Mahāvakyās. One of the earliest Indian seers of the last century to make this connection was Śri Aurobindo. Writing in 1907 in the nationalist magazine *Bande Mataram*, Śri Aurobindo wrote the following about 'the unHindu spirit of caste rigidity':

> No monopoly, racial or hereditary, can form part of the Nationalist's scheme of the future, his dream of the day for the advent of which he is striving and struggling.... The Nationalist does not quarrel, with the past, but he insists on its transformation, the transformation of individual or class autocracy into the autocracy, self-rule or Swaraj, of the nation and of the fixed, hereditary, anti-democratic caste-organisation into the pliable self-adapting, democratic distribution of function at which socialism aims.[10]

Here, one can note that Śri Aurobindo viewed the rigidity of the caste system as an inherent anti-democratic element, which he considered to be 'un-Hindu'. Sayajirao-III similarly criticized the 'rigidity' of the caste system that led to 'ignorance and superstition'. He saw caste as an obstacle to the emerging 'national consciousness'. The critique of the caste system, formed by Śri Aurobindo, which also influenced Sayajirao III, anticipated many of the ideas later developed by Dr Ambedkar. Sayajirao rejected the essentialist argument that caste is unique to Hinduism and its core. According to him, Kṛṣṇa, if he had lived in the modern era, would not have tolerated 'the rigidity of the caste system that sentences millions of our fellow men to a life of misery, subjugation, and degradation.' Dr Ambedkar expressed similar sentiments, in his own words, describing the caste spirit as anti-democratic. However, he viewed the core spiritual values of ancient India, enshrined in the Upaniṣadic Mahavakyas, as the very basis of democracy.

Democracy and Fraternity

In his final speech to the Constituent Assembly on 25 November 1949, Dr Ambedkar defined social democracy and emphasized its importance. He said:

> What does social democracy mean? It means a way of life which recognises liberty, equality and fraternity as the principles of

> life. These principles of liberty, equality and fraternity are not to be treated as separate items in a trinity. They form a union of trinity in the sense that to divorce one from the other is to defeat the very purpose of democracy. Of all these three values, the greatest importance he attached was to fraternity.[11]

To him, 'without fraternity, equality and liberty will be no deeper than coats of paint.' This led Dr Ambedkar, who had rejected both the words 'socialism' and 'secularism' in the preamble of the Constitution, to introduce the word 'fraternity' in the Objective Resolution, which is now permanently enshrined in the preamble of the Constitution.

It is again amazing how closely this resonates with the vision of Sri Aurobindo. In his work, *Ideal of Human Unity* (1915–18), Śri Aurobindo stated that 'freedom, equality, brotherhood are three godheads of the soul.' Of these, fraternity formed 'the real key to the triple gospel of the idea of humanity.' According to him, the people's movements that did not make fraternity their basis had ultimately failed. Taking the French Revolution as an example, in 1910, he explained:

> It (freedom) is the goal of humanity, and we are yet far off from that goal. But the time has come for an approximation being attempted. And the first necessity is the discipline of brotherhood, the organisation of brotherhood; for without the spirit and habit of fraternity neither liberty nor equality can be maintained for more than a short season.[12]

In his Bengali writing on fraternity, again written in 1910, Śri Aurobindo elaborated upon the primary importance of fraternity among the triune principles. Then he went on to explain what could form the basis of fraternity as an energetic value:

> The Socialist errs in trying to establish fraternity on equality, instead of establishing equality on fraternity. It is possible to have

> fraternity without having equality; but equality without fraternity cannot last and it will be destroyed by dissension, quarrels and inordinate greed for power. First we must have complete fraternity and then only complete equality. The brotherly feeling is an outward condition: if we all remain full of brotherly feeling, have one common property, one common good and one common effort, that is fraternity. The external condition is based on the inner state. Love for the brother infuses life into fraternity and makes it real. There must be a basis even for that brotherly love. We are children of one Mother, compatriots; this feeling can provide the basis for a kind of brotherly love; though this feeling becomes a basis of political unity, social unity cannot be achieved in this way. We have to go still deeper: just as we all have to overpass our own mothers in order to worship the Mother of our compatriots, in the same way we have to transcend and realise the Universal Mother. We have to transcend the partial Shakti in order to reach the Shakti in her completeness. But, just as in our adoration of Mother India, though we overpass our physical mother yet we do not forget her, in the same way, in our adoration of the Universal Mother we shall transcend Mother India and not forget her. She too is Kali, she too is the Mother. Only religion provides a basis for fraternity.[13]

Incidentally, in his highly popular *Pakistan or the Partition of India* (1946), Dr Ambedkar pointed out the link between fraternity and spiritual unity in the context of national unity: 'If unity is to be of an abiding character it must be founded on a sense of kinship, in the feeling of being kindred. In short it must be spiritual.'[14]

From political and social fraternity, Śri Aurobindo further saw the triune principles of liberty, fraternity, and equality as having a deep spiritual basis. In 'The Ideal of Human Unity' serialized in the magazine *Arya* between 1915 and 1918 and published in 1919, he wrote,

> When the soul claims freedom, it is the freedom of its self-development, the self-development of the Divine in man and in all

> his being. When it claims equality, what it is claiming is that freedom equally for all and the recognition of the same soul, the same godhead, in all human beings. *When it strives for brotherhood, it is founding that equal freedom of self-development on a common aim, a common life, a unity of mind and feeling founded upon the recognition of this inner spiritual unity.* These three things are in fact the nature of the soul; for Freedom, Equality, Unity are the eternal aspects of the Spirit.[15] (emphasis added)

Both Śri Aurobindo and Dr Ambedkar derived the cardinal principles of 'liberty, fraternity, and equality' from Indic and not Western sources. Dr Ambedkar was born in the Kabir-panth, which in turn derived itself from the Śrī Rāmānuja tradition. Thus, on the one side, he had the influence of Vaiṣṇava tradition of socio-spiritual influence and on the other side, through his early benefactor, supporter and inspirer, the Maharaja of Baroda, he seemed to have been also influenced by Śri Aurobindo's socio-spiritual thoughts.

Dr Ambedkar might have explicitly rejected the Bhagavad Gītā as the text of counter-revolution, but he very clearly insisted on what can only be called Karma Yōga. Very radically, he uses the argument to criticize Hinduism itself as emphasized by the dominant socially stagnant sections of the society. On 30-31 May 1936, he adds an audience of thirty-five thousand in a conference organized by the All- Bombay District Mahar Conference. In this he said,

> Unlike the drop of water that merges its existence with the ocean in which it drops, man does not lose his entity in the society in which he lives. Man's life is independent. He is born not for the service of the society but for his self-development. For this reason alone, in developed countries one man cannot enslave another. A religion in which an individual has no importance is not acceptable to me. The Hinduism does not recognise the importance of an individual, and therefore it is not acceptable

> to me. I do not accept a religion in which one class alone has a right to gain knowledge, another has only a right to use arms, the third one to trade and the fourth, only to serve. Everyone needs knowledge. Everybody needs arms. Everyone wants money. The religion, which forgets this, and with an intention to educate a few, keeps the rest in darkness, is not a religion but a conspiracy to keep the people in mental slavery.[16]

The lecture addresses the significant influence of social inertia that has historically been considered traditionalist Hinduism and, to a large extent, still persists today. However, as demonstrated by Śwāmi Vivekānanda, Śri Aurobindo, and many other scholars, Hinduism, in its unchanging aspect, emphasizes the importance of the individual over society. The pursuit of complete self-development takes precedence over even social obligations and responsibilities. The *Brihadāraṇya Upaniṣad* states that all connections and affections, including those within the family, a fundamental unit of society, exist for the sake of self's development and realization. In a way, this sentiment echoes the words of Dr Ambedkar, who emphasized that every man needs knowledge, resources, and physical work and that these aspects are inseparable. Similarly, the Upaniṣad encourages looking for the qualities of Brāhmanās, Kṣatriyas, etc., within oneself.[17] By advocating for the preservation of the self and rejecting the hierarchical classification of society through pseudo-religious authority, Dr Ambedkar carries forward an ancient and dynamic tradition into the modern context. It is important to note that the concept of self is not present in Buddhism.

Vedic Maitri, Buddhist Metta, and the Preamble of Indian Constitution

It is well known that Dr Ambedkar focused heavily on the principle of fraternity among the triune principles of liberty, equality, and fraternity. He stated that he derived this principle neither from political science nor from the French Revolution, but from religion, specifically from the teachings of Buddha. Additionally, he pointed out that these principles are also present in the Upaniṣads and suggested that the spiritual basis of democracy (and we can deduce, hence fraternity) in ancient India was contained in the Mahāvakyās of the Upaniṣads. In the original document of the Preamble of the Constitution of India, the word 'Nation' is linked to the principle of fraternity and hence, it is also capitalized:

> WE, THE PEOPLE OF INDIA, having solemnly resolved to constitute India into a SOVEREIGN DEMOCRATIC REPUBLIC and to secure to all its citizens JUSTICE, social, economic and political; LIBERTY of thought, expression, belief, faith and worship; EQUALITY of status and of opportunity; and to promote among them all FRATERNITY assuring the dignity of the individual and the unity of the Nation; IN OUR CONSTITUENT ASSEMBLY this twenty-sixth day of November, 1949, do HEREBY ADOPT, ENACT AND GIVE TO OURSELVES THIS CONSTITUTION.

Although the preamble was loosely based on Jawaharlal Nehru's 'Objective Resolution', the profound aspects of it can be attributed to Dr Ambedkar, with regards to 'Fraternity'. Dr Ambedkar underlined the need for spiritual national unity and linked this spiritual feeling to the principle of fraternity. He made a connection between the principle of fraternity and the unity of the Nation. Later, in his works on Buddhism, he considered the term 'fraternity' as inadequate and instead opted for the term 'Maitri'. In one of his most notable criticisms of Hinduism in 'Riddles', he wrote:

> What sustains equality and liberty is fellow-felling. What the French Revolutionists called fraternity. The word fraternity is not an adequate expression. The proper term is what the Buddha

> called, Maitree. Without Fraternity Liberty would destroy equality and equality would destroy liberty. If in Democracy liberty does not destroy equality and equality does not destroy liberty, it is because at the basis of both there is fraternity. Fraternity is therefore the root of Democracy.... The foregoing discussion is merely a preliminary to the main question. That question is—wherein lie the roots of fraternity without which Democracy is not possible? Beyond dispute, it has its origin in Religion.[18]

A comparative analysis of the views of Śri Aurobindo and Dr Ambedkar can potentially shed light on the remarkable parallels between the thought processes of these two influential figures in Indian history.

A comparison of the views of Sri Aurobindo and Dr Ambedkar on Caste and Varṇas:

Śri Aurobindo	Dr Bhimrao Ramji Ambedkar
First, we must have complete fraternity and then only complete equality. And the first necessity (for equality) is the discipline of brotherhood, the organization of brotherhood; for without the spirit and habit of fraternity neither liberty nor equality can be maintained for more than a short season. (1910)	These principles of liberty, equality and fraternity are not to be treated as separate items in a trinity. They form a union of trinity in the sense that to divorce one from the other is to defeat the very purpose of democracy. Of all these three values, the greatest importance he attached was to fraternity. (1949)
First, we must have complete fraternity and then only complete equality. The brotherly feeling is an outward condition: if we all remain full of brotherly feeling and have one common property, one common good and one common effort, that is fraternity. Only religion provides a basis for fraternity. (1910)	The foregoing discussion is merely a preliminary to the main question. That question is—wherein lie the roots of fraternity without which Democracy is not possible? Beyond dispute, it has its origin in Religion. (1955)

There is yet another unity which is as yet only dimly symbolised in the ceremony of the Rakhi ... the unity in national comradeship of the children of one mighty Mother, whatever their class or condition—Indian fraternity based on ***Indian liberty and Indian equality. (1909)***	You must give a new doctrinal basis to your Religion—a basis that will be in consonance with Liberty, Equality and Fraternity; in short, with Democracy. I am no authority on the subject. But I am told that for such religious principles as will be in consonance with Liberty, Equality and Fraternity, ***it may not be necessary for you to borrow from foreign sources, and that you could draw for such principles on the Upanishads. (1935)***

While Dr Ambedkar finds the term fraternity inadequate and substitutes the Buddhist term 'Maitree', one wonders why he did not use the more Buddhist, Pāli term 'Metta'. The answer may be because the good doctor finds in what he calls Vedic 'Brahmaism'. In fact, it is in the context of the inadequacy of the term 'fraternity' that he introduces the term 'Brahmaism' itself: 'The Hindu Religious and Philosophic thought gave rise to an idea which had *greater potentialities for producing social democracy than the idea of fraternity*. It is the doctrine of Brahmaism' (emphasis added).[19]

So, it stands to reason that though Dr. Ambedkar starts the unpublished manuscript of 'Riddles' with an extremely negative labelling of the Vēdās as 'a worthless set of books', he still had imbibed the Vēdic values when he used the word 'Maitree'.

Maitri comes from *Mitra*, the Vēdic deity.

Many experts on ancient Indian religion have pointed out the continuity of Vēdic Mitra and the continuity of Mitra-function in the later developments of Buddhism. Famous Dutch Indologist Jan Gonda (1905–91) explains:

> As far as Mitra and maitra are concerned, it may be recalled that the idea of maitra continues to play an important part in post-Vedic religious thought. It implies 'ideas' such as helpful benevolence and radiating influence for good. The (later) Vedic occurrences of this term foreshadow the well-known Buddhist idea of maitra, maitri, maitrya (Pãli mettã) which is translated by terms such as active interest in others, love and amity, active good-will.[20]

In yet another paper, Jan Gonda describes this Vēdic deity thus:

> (Mitra) is the god who, while peacefully maintaining the fundamental and universal order (rta), keeps its manifestations in the right condition, puts things right, regulates the contacts between men and the divine powers, stabilizes, redresses, adjusts, restores, appeases, unites men; he represents the idea of benevolence, active goodness and friendliness and maintains special relations with fire and sunlight.[21]

One can see clearly how the qualities 'benevolence, active goodness and friendliness' along with Rta actually make fraternity very well part of this realm of qualities. Another eminent scholar of Buddhism, Dr Martin Gerald Wiltshire, explains why it is important to look into the Vēdic roots of Buddhist Metta:

> Since the pre-eminent Buddhist ethical value is the principal of conciliation or avihimsa, made religiously potent by means of the meditational technique of metta, etc. and since the practice of metta itself is archaic, we shall examine some of the significances of the Vedic figure Mitra, a name etymologically linked with the word metta (Skt. maitri).[22]

He points out that in the Vedas, the term 'ahimsa' is mentioned twice, with one occurrence being in association with Mitra. The *Ṛig Veda* V.64.3 states Mitra practices 'ahimsana', and the Satapatha Brahmana mentions that 'Mitra injures (himsati) and is injured by no one, for Mitra is everyone's friend'. According to Dr Wiltshire, Varuna and Mitra 'epitomize' the twin requirements of true Kshatriya status: 'sovereignty' and 'conformity with reality or natural law' and points out that these are 'exactly the two principles which the Buddha as dharma-raja embodies'.

The term fraternity, associated with the unity of the nation in the Constitution's preamble, is deeply and holistically connected with Maitri. Through Vedic Mitra, Maitri is associated with the Rashtra-Rajya conception of ancient India. Maitri is the civilizational democratic impulse that correlates with fraternity. This underscores the civilizational genius of Dr Ambedkar, who associated fraternity with 'the Nation'.

While Dr Ambedkar could have harshly criticized Hindu religion, due to the inhuman perversion exhibited by the orthodoxy, he emerges as a person of compassion and wisdom, akin to the attributes attributed to the Bodhisattva in Buddhist texts. He upholds, in an uncompromising manner, the true vision of Vēdic Ṛṣis, displaying deep insights and compassion despite the social stagnation perpetuated by the perversion of religious ideology.

Mylai Chinna Thambi Piḷḷai *Rājah*

Popularly known as M.C. Rājah (1883–1943), he worked for the upliftment of the socially excluded communities in every domain – from temple entry to the labour movement.

Born to a poor Tamil family in Madras, he entered politics after graduating from college and became a leader of Paraiyars (a Scheduled Caste community) in the Justice Party. But he left the party in 1923 over the treatment of Scheduled Castes communities and allied with Dr B.R. Ambedkar.

In 1926, at Nagpur, an 'All India Depressed Classes' Leader Conference' was held. This created the first all-India organization of the 'All India Depressed Classes' Association. M.C. Rājah was the President of this organization.

Rajah Moonje Pact[23]

Before the Poona pact between Dr Ambedkar and Mahatma Gandhi (A-G pact), Dr Moonje and Rājah formulated a pact called the Rajah–Moonje pact (R-M pact). Historians Meenakshi Jain and the late Devendra Swarup made a detailed study of this forgotten pact and how it served to thwart the British plan to completely separate Scheduled Castes communities from the larger Hindu body.

It is a historical fact today that the R-MP was the first-ever agreement on the reservation between the so-called 'caste Hindus' and the Scheduled Caste communities. Later, M.C. Rājah pointed out the significance of the pact as the one between 'the only central organization of the depressed classes' and the 'organized body of Hindus taken as a whole'. He also hailed the 'hand of fraternity' extended by 'our co-religionists, the Caste Hindus'. At the heart of the problem was the issue of joint or separate electorates for the so-called depressed classes.

Dr Ambedkar had returned from the Round Table Conference and started vehemently supporting separate electorates for the Scheduled Castes communities. On the other hand, M.C. Rajah was in favour of joint electorates. The then British Prime Minister Ramsay MacDonald had favoured separate electorates through the 'Communal Award' by which the separate electorates, hitherto given to the Muslims, would now be extended to the Scheduled Castes. Gandhiji perceived this as dividing the Hindu society and responded with the announcement that he would launch a fast unto death if separate electorates for the Scheduled Castes were not withdrawn. But Dr Ambedkar considered the communal award 'a priceless privilege' and declared that with the dual vote and separate electorate, the 'untouchables would have been in a position to determine if not dictate the issue of the general election'.

However, Rajah pointed out that the communal award actually took more than it gave. While the Simon Commission gave 117 seats out of 1,436 in the provincial legislature for the Scheduled Castes, and 237 under the minorities pact (which Dr Ambedkar himself had signed), 90 seats according to the recommendations of the Indian Central Committee, the communal award gave Scheduled Castes communities just 71 seats. Rājah further argued in favour of the joint electorates with reservation for Scheduled Castes from the point of view of a healthy democracy and social empowerment:

> I do not know why the Prime Minister calls the scheme of joint electorates with reservation of seats as impracticable. It is already in force in local bodies in Madras and some other provinces and has worked very satisfactorily. ... I am surprised at the argument of the Prime Minister that there is no segregation because we can vote for Caste Hindus who will have to solicit our votes. But, Sir, how can we bring about a common ideal of citizenship when Depressed Class representatives are not to solicit the votes of (so-called) higher castes?

Then he went on to argue the need for reforming the Hindu society from within and not by alienating it through separate electorates. This is a principle to which Rājah would adhere all his life—that Scheduled Castes are an inalienable and even primary component of Hindu society. Hence, his opposition, apart from his political differences with Dr Ambedkar, also reflects his perception of the nature of the Scheduled Castes community:

> We Depressed Classes, feel ourselves as true Hindus as any Caste Hindu can be and we feel that the moral conscience of the Hindus have been roused to the extent that our salvation lies in

> bringing about a change from within the main body of Hindu society and not segregating ourselves from them.

The British were over-concerned about the R-MP, and the secretary of state for India from London asked the viceroy if he could send 'any estimates' regarding 'the extent to which the pact is likely to receive general acceptance by the interests involved'.

In Tamil Nadu, K. Bashyam, a Gandhian leader who was active in an anti-untouchability campaign, met Rajah and expressed his support for the R-MP. This was duly noted by British intelligence (under Secretary's Safe File No 804) in 1932. The British interest was not interested in social justice but more in gaining advantages through a divide-and-rule policy. Political anthropologists Frank de Zwart and Bas van Gool point out how the 'concern' for the Scheduled Castes communities was, actually, a camouflage in their appeasement of pan-Islamist separatism in India, which in turn, was part of their larger divide-and-rule policy:

> The primary targets of this colonial divide and rule strategy were the Muslims (at the time around 23 percent of the population. The Untouchables (estimated at that time at 15 percent of the population) were added, however, because, as Secretary of State L.S. Amery put it, there were 'politically very considerable advantages in having two substantial minorities to whom consideration has to be paid, and not to be put in the position of being merely labelled pro-Muslim and anti-Hindu'.[24]

The opposition to the pact was violent and vehement. In the All-India Depressed Classes Conference held at Kamptee in 1932, a prominent Schedule Castes leader, Raj Bhoj, who supported the R-M pact, was attacked physically by the supporters of a separate electorate and was hospitalized. However, there was also widespread support for the R-M pact. In the *Hindustan Times*, dated 29 February 1932, the special correspondent reported that the R-M pact was sent to the Prime Minister of England. On 9 March, the paper reported the support of the Hindu and Sikh members of legislative assemblies to the R-M pact. On 17 March, the pact was hailed by Schedule Castes leaders on behalf of Shraddhanand Memorial Trust. *The Tribune* from Lahore, in its issue dated 25 March 1932, hailed the pact as 'the best solution' and wrote:

> If only the other minorities in India had the same wisdom, clear-headedness and sagacity that Mr Rajah and his Association possess they would have come to exactly the same conclusion to which the latter have come. If the depressed classes are socially an integral part of the Hindu community, the Muslims and other non-Hindu Minorities are politically an equally integral part of the Indian nation.

The Statesman, dated 30 March 1932, reported that in New Delhi, *All India Shradhanand Dalit-Uddhar Sabha* took out a procession in support of the pact. They raised the 'Bharat Mata ki Jai' slogan and carried banners that declared 'We are Hindus of Hindus'.

Thus, the R-M pact, often forgotten today, laid the groundwork for future social liberation frameworks. When Gandhiji and Dr Ambedkar signed the Pune Pact, Rājah fully supported it without ego, despite its resemblance to the R-M pact. In a speech given at the legislative assembly on 13 September 1932, he wholeheartedly supported the A-G Pact. Swami Sahajananda, another social reformer and a Scheduled Castes community representative, also supported him in this.

It is worth noting that although Dr Ambedkar later became a sharp critic of the Poona Pact, partly because of his anti-Congress politics and largely because of the way unyielding anti-Schedule Casteist stance of traditional Hindu leaders and Hindu society at large, his writings on minority rights (social minorities, not religious minorities) reflect the spirit of the R-M pact. He viewed reservations as provisions for unifying the majority and minorities. On 4 November 1948, Dr Ambedkar stated this in the Constituent Assembly: 'In this country both the minorities and the majorities have followed a wrong path. It is wrong for the majority to deny the existence of minorities. It is equally wrong for the minorities to perpetuate themselves.'

Rājah had placed hopes and aspirations of the Schedule Castes as the responsibility and duty of the larger Hindu society, though it did not meet with the expected success. Dr Ambedkar, reminding the social majority of their duty, stated that 'the minorities in India have agreed to place their existence in the hands of the majority' and emphasized that 'the moment the majority loses the habit of discriminating against the minority, the minorities can have no ground to exist' and that 'they will vanish'.[25]

In hindsight, the R-M pact saw through the British plan to perpetuate minorities in India for their political advantage and opted for joint electorates with reservations as a means to achieve social integration. Later, Dr Ambedkar also came to the conclusion that social minorities should merge with the majorities, with the latter removing the discrimination. Reservations are seen as tools towards this end, but should also be supported by religious tools that negate the religion-based discriminations and social exclusions.

Opposition to Conversion

Dr Ambedkar announced conversion as a means of social emancipation in his famous speech at Yeola on 13 October 1935. His statement that he was born a Hindu but was determined not to die as a Hindu sent shock waves cutting across the political spectrum. Almost immediately, on 11 November 1935, in a meeting of Scheduled Caste communities organized by Adi Draivda Mahajana Sabha of Madras, Rao Bahadur M.C. Rājah said that there was no better religion than Hinduism and that one should not leave the caste for fear of not getting one's grievances redressed, but should get one's rights by being in it.[26] Then, on 12 November, M.C. Rājah, as the leader of the All India Depressed Classes' Association, issued a statement on the issue[27]:

> While I fully share in the resentment which many of our men feel at the treatment meted out to cur people in many parts of the country by the so-called high-caste Hindus, I would at the same time request them to compare conditions existing now with what they were away 15 years ago. Conditions have improved considerably today. A large section of educated Hindu India has come to condemn the practice of untouchability and has thrown its weight on the side of reform. I venture to say that in view of the awakening of the Hindu conscience that has been noticed in regard to our condition and status, the days of untouchability as practised toward the community are now numbered. It should be remembered that in the course of a decade things have changed considerably in favour of the depressed classes and there is also a very strong awakening among the depressed classes themselves.

What was the real solution if it were not for conversion? Rājah emphasized legal battles through secular and democratic means.

> The immediate remedy ... is the total withdrawal of the legal and administrative recognition to the superstition of pollution. The law~ as they are administered today uphold these superstitions under the guise of preserving peace and punishing the untouchables who attempt to enforce their civil rights. On September 26 last I introduced in the Legislative Assembly a Bill called the *Removal of Social Disabilities* among certain classes of Hindus. Bills like this, if passed into Act, will go a long way to

> remove civil and secular disabilities from which the depressed classes are suffering under the existing laws. *This Bill will also remove the obstacles created by the British India courts giving legal recognition to certain social customs and usages which enlightened public opinion regard as unjust, anti-social and irreligious*. (Emphasis added)

By shedding light on how the colonial judiciary system has embedded 'unjust, anti-social and irreligious' customs and practices into traditional Hindu Law, Rājah introduced a powerful concept here. He suggested that the fight to end social disadvantages faced by marginalized communities was also a profound decolonization effort. He ended the statement with the following emotionally surcharged words:

> Hinduism is our religion and it is sacred to us. It is our duty to preserve it and purify it. We do not want to cut away form the Hindu fold. We want better recognition-a recognition of the fact that we are men equally with the caste-Hindus. Our goal is to remove untouchability and our aim is to become unsegregated and an unquarantined part of the Hindu society.

In June 1936, Dr Moonje and Dr Ambedkar engaged in a profound discussion regarding the potential exploration of Sikhism as a as a viable option for conversion within the Indian cultural context. This display of mutual trust and alignment of values between Dr Moonje and Dr Ambedkar contradicts the portrayal by scholars with anti-Hindu sentiments, such as Christophe Jaffrelot who suggested that Moonje's actions were solely motivated by concerns over Hindu numerical strength. Historian Prof. Rohit Wancho, in his detailed analysis of the conversion dilemma of 1935 following Dr Ambedkar's call, wrote:

> Assertions by scholars like Christophe Jaffrelot and Keith Meadowcroft that Moonje only wanted to 'defuse their [Dalit]

> new militancy' are half-truths or overstatements. If there had not been a long history of Hindu anxiety about Dalit conversions and widespread acknowledgement of the necessity for reform the Moonje–Ambedkar proposals would never have triggered a major debate in which leaders as diverse as Madan Mohan Malaviya, Mohandas Karamchand Gandhi and Rabindranath Tagore participated. Decades of work by Swami Dayanand Saraswati, Swami Shraddhanand and Lala Lajpat Rai had created the climate in which Moonje and Ambedkar could contemplate mass conversion to Sikhism.[28]

When Moonje presented this proposal to Rājah, the latter firmly opposed it. In his letter to Moonje dated 20 July 1936, Rājah expressed that the Scheduled Castes community people were 'no sheep and cattle to be bartered away in this fashion driven from one political fold to another as a result of a bargain between the leaders of different communities'. Besides the issue of 'bartering', he also accused the Mahāsabha leader of seeking an easy way out by attempting to exclude socially marginalized communities from religious Hinduism instead of working towards reforming Hindu society and eradicating the problems of untouchability and other social injustices:

> One would expect you, as President of the Hindu Mahasabha, to ameliorate the social condition of the Depressed Classes by removing civic and social disabilities of these classes, not to speak of securing for them the right of worship in Hindu temples on an equal footing with other worshippers, and to further the Harijan movement started by Gandhiji all over the country. Instead of doing this, what is it that you are doing? You are dissecting the Depressed Classes and affiliating them religiously to the Sikhs while retaining them politically as Hindus.[29]

After the Poona Pact, M.C. Rājāh focused on drafting legislation to eliminate discrimination in Hindu society. The first bill he worked on was the Removal of Civil Disabilities Bill, which he mentioned in his 1935 speech. In his speech, he thanked C. Rājāgōpālāchariār, also known as Rājāji or CR, for his assistance.[30] However, this relationship soured when Rājāh felt that CR was intentionally delaying the temple entry bill. He even suspected CR of supporting the so-called Sanātanists. Rājāh's disappointment with Gandhian gradualism in social emancipation led him to believe that the Poona pact was not the right solution. He argued that the socio-political interests of the so-called caste Hindus were entirely different from those of the Scheduled Castes communities, a position similar to that of Dr Ambedkar.

'Oppressed Hindus'

M.C. Rājāh was a prolific writer and a deep thinker. He had written some of the most pioneering and popular children's literature in modern Tamil literature. As the former Superintendent of Wesley College Lower School, Madras, he, along with Smt. Raṅganāyaki Ammāḷ, the Hony. Superintendent of A.D.C. School, Madras. published a collection of rhymes titled *Kindergarten Room*. The manuscript obtained by the Tamil Heritage Foundation was the third edition published in 1930. It was published digitally in 2017.[31] This collection contains many popular children's rhymes that are sung in homes even before children start school and also in schools. The cultural components in the books show a complete organic unity with the rest of the society. For example, the book talks about what cows contribute, giving importance to cow dung for ceremonial cleaning of houses and as fuel, as well as for milk. The book also encourages children first to go to the temple and then to school. The lullaby in the collection refers to the child as the gift of Śrī Raṅga Śwāmi. The lullaby indicates a unity between the Śaiva and Vaiṣṇava traditions by saying that the child was formed in the womb of the mother by the grace of the Lord who wears the moon. 'You are the parrot that seeks to hear music in this land that reverberates with the Vēdās.' It suggests that the child is the result of 'Tapas and Dhāna'. All these are values and cultural sentiments common to pan-Hindu society, beautifully expressed in songs for children.

The most significant work by M.C. Rājāh was the book *Oppressed Hindus,* written around 1925. This book is important for many reasons. It demonstrates how the so-called caste Hindus developed distinct socio-economic and political ambitions under British rule based on their community interests. As a result, the Brahmins, non-Brahmins, and the Scheduled Castes communities became clearly defined categories, each viewing the other as oppressors and encroachers. The socially excluded communities were the most vulnerable in this colonial situation. They saw the 'native' sociocultural milieu as oppressive and saw the British rule as creating a liberating space for solutions. At the same time, the enlightened leaders of the community, such as M.C. Rājāh, also saw the umbilical cord of culture and spirituality not just uniting them with the rest of the Hindu society but also saw the Hindu religion as having played a primary historical role for them, which was denied by the so-called caste-Hindus. Meanwhile, the colonial 'secular' history provided an Aryan-race framework in which the Brahmins were seen as Aryans. The cultural and political behaviour of the so-called upper caste Hindus seemed to reinforce the racial view of Hindu civilization brought in by the colonialists. All these aspects are expressed in the work *Oppressed Hindus*. The book begins with a dedication to the 'Members of British Parliament and their representative here ... for their earnest endeavours to promote the interests of the Depressed Classes in India.'

Despite such a pro-British dedication, that book commences with a deep criticism of colonial education which served to create a class that was neither rooted in Hindu values nor in the enlightenment values of modern European society:

> That educational system modelled on the old University of London, a mere examining body, has now been condemned as soulless and as having produced merely sensitized specimens of humanity. The products of that system were types that had cut themselves adrift from all their old moorings of 'Dharma and Ahimsa' and had not assimilated the British ideals of Justice and Fairplay. They were with a few honourable exceptions, merely free-lances abroad armed with a smattering of Western knowledge in a vast population of varying degrees of culture from the fifth century to the fifteenth and mostly took to the predatory professions and fished in troubled waters of their own creation.... All this fell with the greater intensity on those classes that are classified as the 'Depressed' and riveted their social. Disabilities on them, for the Indian official was almost entirely drawn from the higher castes with their notions of inherent superiority.[32]

The book provides an explanation of the term 'Ādi Drāvida'. The term was used by the prominent Scheduled Castes community leaders. The Anglo-Indian community had opted for the name 'Anglo-Indian' instead of 'Eurasian'. Similarly, 'the Non-Brahmin caste Hindus had opted for the name Dravidian or 'Ādi Drāvida', instead of the name Sudra to distinguish themselves as a separate sociopolitical class. M.C. Rājāh explained the deep cultural rootedness of the term, providing detailed historical data with authentic substantiation as to the organic way in which the Schedule Castes communities were an integral and respected part of the rest of the Hindu community throughout history; he points out their undeniable equal rights in the Hindu society. Here is the explanation:

> Adi means original, pure and unalloyed as in 'Adi Saivas, Adi Sankarachariar, Adi Lakshmi, Adi Bagavan, Adi Sivan,

> Adi-Narayan, Adi-Kesavan, Adimulam' etc.... In an inscription of the eleventh century AD, we find recorded the decision of one Vesali Parian and his Councillors to be a final one in a civil case concerning the ownership of a piece of land belonging to a temple in the village of Mudepakavar. Even in the North it is so, for the evidence of the Mhar is required in every dispute. 'Should two cultivators quarrel respecting the boundaries of their fields,' says Mr R.N. Goddine, 'the Mhars' evidence ought to decide it, and should a similar quarrel happen between two villages, the Mhars are always the chief actors in it and to their decision alone it is sometimes referred.' Mr W.F. Sinclair calls the Mahar as the guardian of boundaries and of public peace and health.... The special privileges that the Adi Dravidas enjoy even to this day, point to their former greatness. At the annual festival of the tutelary Goddess of George Town in the premier city of Madras, the thali or marriage badge is tied round the neck of the Goddess by an Adi Dravida in the name of the entire community. The Adi Dravida in question is clothed gorgeously and fed in the temple as the accepted bridegroom of the Goddess as long as the festival lasts. Drums are beaten in his honour when the idol of the Goddess Egathammal is carried round the city and a copper coin is placed in his hand and another copper coin on the hand of the Goddess by the officiating priest when the Kappu ceremony is performed. The Adi Dravida, officiates as priest at the Bull Games at Dindigul. During the great Hindu annual festivals at Conjeeveram, one of the sacred cities of India, and at Srivilliputtur, Kumbakonam, Tiruvottiyur and other holy places, Adi Dravidas are permitted to pull the ropes of the huge cars containing the idols.... During the festival of Siva at Tiruvalore in the Tanjore District, the Adi Dravida headman is specially honoured by being placed on the temple elephant along with the God and made to carry the chowry in his hand to fan the idol.[33]

Then he gives the list of Bhakti saints from all over India:

> Among the twelve Alwars of Vaishnavaism, the famous Tirupan Alwar was an Adi Dravida. Among the sixty-three Nainars

of Saivitism, the well-known Nanda was an Adi Dravida. In the sacred work Manushya Panchakam of Jagat Guru Sree Sankaracharya, the founder of the four Sankara Pedams, the seats of learning, it is stated that this Great Jagathguru publicly accepts one Visvanadhan as his guru and received initiation from him. This Visvanathan is an Adi Dravida and is held in high esteem by his followers who are Smartha Brahmins. In Bakthavijayam—Lives. of Vaishnavite Bakthas or Devotees of North India—Chokka melar, the great baktha who was accepted as a guru by the learned Brahmins of Pandaripur, was an Adi Dravida.[34]

He also singles out and highlights the work of Thiruvaḷḷuvar:

In the galaxy of the eminent poets and scholars of the period the holy Thiruvalluvar stood first and foremost. His famous work Thirukkural is a code of morals expressed in poetical aphorisms. Even after a lapse of more than 1,800 years it has lost none of its original admiration and popularity among the tamil people and it is still considered as a standard authoritative work in Tamil literature.[35]

Then he dwells into the Ithihāsās and Purāṇas and brings out the Purāṇic connectivity of sacred characters with the communities now considered Scheduled Castes:

Subramanya, the son of Siva, is credited with having chosen a South Indian girl called Valli as his wife. She was an Adi Dravida. Parvati, the wife of Siva is even worshipped as an Adi Dravida woman in her disguise as Matangi[36].... Arunthathi is the wife of Vasishta, the Brabma Rishi, one of the Saptha Rishies and a Vathaparangadha. She is famous for her chastity and that is why she is worshipped by the bridegroom and the bride of all Hindu communities on marriage occasions. When Arjuna's son Abhimanyu was hit by an arrow and was at the point of death, his mother Subhadra invoked the blessing of Arundhathi and her son recovered. This shows the high veneration with which

> she was held by women of all classes. She is now said to exist in the form of a star.[37]

He speaks of Jāmbavan as the clan patriarch of the Sāmbava community, another name for the Paṟaiyar community:

> Samban is also a title borne by some Adi Dravidas in the tamil country. The word Samban is a corruption of the word Jambavan, who though described in Ramayana as a bear and having a following of his own species, is said to be the first born of the God Brahma, the creator. It is also found in Ramayana that Jambavan, the Adi Dravida, was the custodian of all ancient learning and was a mighty warrior though called a bear in Ramayana by the Aryan poet in his conceit.... Then again, Jambavan was a faithful devotee and the commander of the army of Sreeman Narayana. And it was Jambavan that proclaimed to the world, by means of tom tom, the victory of Tiruvickarama, God Narayana, who redeemed the worlds from the cruel tyrant, Mahabali. Jambavan was also holding the office of a Chief Judge. As it is the custom: even now for the crier, to announce the arrival of a Judge in the public court, the crier during the days of Jambavan used to announce the arrival of Judge Jambavan by crying out Mthadigai, which means, the Great is coming. This term Mahaligai is now converted into Madiga and signifies a section of the Depressed Classes.[38]

Here, we can see how the colonial narrative about Hindu sacred texts contradicts the actual and traditional implications of the texts. Vālmīki himself is traditionally believed to have been a tribal hunter, and to this day, his name is associated with a community that Rājāh himself would categorize as one of the communities of 'oppressed Hindus'. Yet he states that Vālmīki as 'Aryan poet in his conceit' called Jāmbavan a bear. The primary data of Jāmbavan as a mighty warrior and a great man of wisdom emerges from the very Rāmāyaṇā. It is of further importance to see that Rajah also points out that it was the patriarch of the

Scheduled Castes community, Jāmbavan, who announced to the world the dethroning of the 'cruel tyrant, Mahabali'. Elsewhere in the colonial knowledge system inspired deconstruction of Hindu mythology, particularly by the pro-British non-Brahmin narrative of Jyotirao Phule (1827–1890), *Mahābali* was radically reconstructed as an egalitarian and just ruler and his dethroning was seen as disposing a non-Aryan king through deceit by cunning Aryan-Brahmins. One can contrast the above passage of M.C. Rājāh with the way Aryan versus Non-Aryan was constructed out of Hindu *Purāṇic* literature by pro-British Phule school reformers. The latter is given in a detailed manner by Gail Omvedt, a scholar perpetuating a pro-colonial school of social emancipation:

> Gulamgiri was written in dialogue form, as was true of most of Phule's writing with the exception of Shetkaryaca Asud (The Cultivator's Whipcord). Using raw and powerful language, he lost no chance to scorn and mock the 'Irani Aryabhats' who were seen as the enslavers of the masses. The first avatars, fish and tortoise, were said to represent invasion by sea. Then came the boar, apparently over land; then the direct confrontation with non-Aryans, as Aryans managed to win over some of them (Prahlad), and used deception to destroy the best of them, King Bali. Indeed, it was Bali Raja who provided the main symbol for Phule. Bali, remembered by the masses as an ideal king, who could make 'troubles and sorrows go,' was for Brahminic theory a 'demon,' upholder of adharma simply by the fact that he dared to violate his own demonic dharma to be a good king. Even the puranic stories depicted Bali as a good king; it was simply that an asura was not supposed to be dharmic, and in being so, his kingdom rendered Indra and heaven unnecessary.[39]

Hindu Purāṇas actually make the Asūra kings mostly virtuous and make their fall the result of one of their ignoble tendencies. Thus, they are not all evil. In the case of Mahābali, he was made indeed a benevolent king in most narratives but a man who did all charities with an ambition of grabbing power. This became the cause of his downfall. This characteristic feature of not making completely evil villains out of the Asūra kings but fallen noble hero-villains was most probably a technique employed by the authors of Purāṇic literature to caution the seekers of spiritual paths against pitfalls. However, colonialists gave this a historical twist in a racial manner. But the writings of Rājāh show that in the traditional account of Scheduled Castes also, Mahābali was not seen as a benevolent king but as a cruel one, and his dethroning was actively seen as a liberation of the Scheduled Castes community. In traditional sculptures of *Trivikrama*, the full-blown manifestation of *Vāmana, Jāmbavan* is indeed depicted as triumphantly rejoicing along with other celestial Gods in the subduing of Mahābali by Viṣṇu as in the Pallava cave temples of Mahābalipuram or Māmallapuram.

Thus, the book provides an extraordinary historical and cultural insight into the traditional self-perception of the socially excluded communities, which falsifies the vested-interest-induced claims of certain communities being 'untouchables' and relating it to age-old religious customs. This vested interest induced behaviour on the part of not just so-called caste-Hindus but also by the traditional religious heads like Saṅkarāchāryas, Śaivaite Ādhīnams, and Vaiṣṇavaite Jīyars compounded the divide leading to an embracing in various degrees the colonial deconstruction of Hindu texts through a racial prism. The so-called caste-Hindu behaviour rooted in pseudo-religious vested interest reinforced the colonial pseudo-historical interpretation of India's social evolution.[40]

M.C. Rājāh died on 2 August 1943.

Gandhian Movement

The Gandhian movement played a crucial role in achieving social emancipation by breaking free of the constraints of social stagnation and exclusion. Rooted in the spiritual essence of Hindu civilization, the movement against untouchability, in particular, was fuelled by a deep religious conviction shared by many of its participants. In Tamil Nadu, the Gandhian movement produced numerous influential leaders, some of whom are highlighted below, each driven by a profound spiritual purpose that led to tangible social progress.

P. Kakkan41

P. Kakkan (1908–81), also known as Kakkanji, is still celebrated as a symbol of unwavering integrity. He courageously advocated for the water rights of Scheduled Castes communities in Tamil Nadu, inspiring people from all backgrounds. When members of a dominant community attempted to prevent scheduled caste community members from accessing water from a common source, leaders from the same dominant stepped up to support the rights of their Scheduled Castes community brethren. Born into a Scheduled Caste Community, Kakkan belonged to a priest clan that performed pūja in the village temple of Badra Kāḷi. His father was deeply committed to his Hindu heritage and reacted strongly upon learning that a potential bride for Kakkan was rumoured to be a Christian. However, the situation was clarified when it was revealed that the girl's full name was Sorṇam Pārvathi and that she was, in fact, a Hindu who had simply attended a Christian school.

Inspired by the teachings of Gandhi, Kakkan joined the Congress. Sri Vaidhyanātha Iyer served as his mentor, and he was known for his dedication to the Congress and his advocacy for temple entry. Iyer was responsible for leading the historic temple entry into Madurai Meenakshi Temple on 8 July 1939, and Kakkan was among the five persons chosen to participate in this significant event to enter the temple. Throughout his involvement with the Congress, Kakkan faced imprisonment multiple times for his participation in various Satyagrahas of the Congress, including individual Satyagraha and the 'Quit India' movement. His dedication led to physical hardships in jail, where he endured beatings each time he uttered 'Vandē Mātaram'. His granddaughter, Ms Rajeswari, who is now an IPS officer, vividly recalls witnessing the scars on her grandfather's body from these beatings and hearing his accounts of why he was beaten for chanting Vandē Mātaram and for going on hunger strikes.[42] During his time in jail, Kakkan found solace in reading Tilak's commentary on the Bhagavad Gītā and deepened his understanding of Thirukuraḷ.

He established a hostel for students of all castes in an Agrahāram, a Brahmin residential area. During a challenging time, Chief Minister Kamaraj (1903–1975) made a significant and symbolic gesture by involving the education department, rather than the Harijan welfare board, to address the issues. This action sent a clear message that the education of any section of society cannot be compartmentalized and alienated. Serving as the Home Minister of Tamil Nadu from 1963 to 1967, Kakkan played a key role in implementing strict laws against caste-based atrocities. Well-versed in both the Bhagavad Gītā, which he studied during his imprisonment and Thirukural, Kakkan was part of the movement that facilitated the entry of Scheduled Castes communities into the Meenakshi Amman temple. Even before India's independence, Kakkan served as the minister for agriculture in a Congress ministry and was instrumental in the construction of numerous irrigation dams in Tamil Nadu.

V.I. Munuswāmy Piḷḷai

V.I. Munuswāmy Piḷḷai (1889-1953) was a member of the Madras Legislative Council right from 1926. He was a representative of the 'Depressed Classes'. In 1932, during a tumultuous year when Gandhi went on a fast against the communal award of a separate electorate, he presided over the national executive meeting of the All India Depressed Classes Federation. In the stormy year, he was instrumental in convincing several Scheduled Castes leaders to agree to the Poona pact between Dr Ambedkar and Gandhiji and was one of the signatories to the pact. A fervent supporter of the temple entry bill brought by Rājāji, which was strongly opposed by orthodoxy, he stated that the temple entry bill removed the 'blemishes that are a blot on Hindu religion' and would 'go a long way to show the world how sacred our religion is and how pure its worship'.

> I must say a word of praise to the calibre and capacity of the Chairman of the Drafting Committee, Dr B.R. Ambedkar. (Loud cheers) Coming as I do from a community that has produced Dr Ambedkar, I feel proud that his capacity has now been recognized, not only by the Harijans but by all communities. The scheduled castes have produced a great Nandanar, a great devotee, a Tirupazanalwar, a great Vaishnaivite saint, and above all a Tiruvalluvar, the great philosopher whose name and fame is not only known throughout the length and breadth of India but of the whole world. To that galaxy of great men of Harijans now we have to add Dr Ambedkar who as a man has been able to show to the world that the scheduled castes are no less important.[43]

Then he pointed out how the Constitution has made untouchability a criminal offence and temple entry for all communities has been affected:

> Great avathars and great saints tried their level best to abolish untouchability but it is given to this august Assembly and the new Constitution to say in loud terms that no more untouchability shall stay in our country. Again, Article 29 gives power to the would-be Government throwing open all Hindu religious institutions to all classes and sections of Hindus. At

> one time dogs and swine might enter the sacred precincts of temples but the shadow of an untouchable was considered a great abomination. I feel proud, Sir, that by this article that slur has been removed away. Due to this discrimination of not allowing a certain section of Hindus, my people have been converted to various faiths and thereby our population has dwindled as also their merit, but today I am proud that under Article 29 not only all Hindu religious institutions have been thrown open to all classes and sections of Hindus but all educational institutions maintained by the State or are receiving aid from Government will be thrown open to all the sections of the people.[44]

Then he expressed his happiness over the inclusion of the protection of cow and her progeny in the Directive Principles of the Indian Constitution:

> Article 46 gives the Scheduled Castes and Scheduled Tribes a very important place and I welcome that. Another, Article 48, deals with the preservation of milch cow and prohibition of cow slaughter. As a Hindu I feel that the great value of a cow is felt in India and it is a religious sentiment that the cow must be preserved and I feel happy that an article has been brought in this Constitution.[45]

In the concluding part of his speech, he reiterated the hope that the social minorities, namely the disadvantaged sections of the society, would finally get socio-economically and emotionally integrated with the rest of the society through the affirmative programme of reservations:

> The great thing in this Constitution, that is before the House, is that the word 'minorities' has been removed. I know, as a matter of fact, it is not the desire of myself or of my community to be ever called a minority or Scheduled Castes, we want to merge with the thirty crores of people in this country. As Mahatma

> Gandhi rightly said, it is the change of heart that is required. The caste Hindus and those people who predominate in this country only show that change of heart, it will be time, Sir, that we ourselves merge into the great community of Indians and I do not want to perpetuate this seclusion for ever.[46]

One should note that this is exactly what Dr Ambedkar said about minorities and majorities in the future of India. He envisioned that 'the moment the majority loses the habit of discriminating against the minority, the minorities can have no ground to exist' and that 'they will vanish.'[47]

Babu Jagjivan Ram

One of the eminent leaders hailing from the Scheduled Caste community, Babu Jagjivan Ram (1908–86), made significant contributions to the struggles for national freedom and social emancipation.

His house exuded a powerful spiritual atmosphere. Jagjivan Ram's father, Sobhi Ram, was employed in a British military mess, but he eventually left his position after refusing to apologize to a British officer. Jagjivan Ram was initiated into Śiva Nārāyaṇī Sect, which was established in the 19th century by mystic Saint Śiva Nārāyaṇ. This sect emphasized a blend of Bhakti and nirguṇa Brahman meditation, sparking an all-inclusive spiritual movement that attracted many economically impoverished and socially excluded communities, although it was not limited to them. Jagjivan Ram was born on 5 April 1908 and initially named Budh Ram by a pandit, but his name was changed to Jagjivan Ram by his father after consulting a sacred book. Indrani Jagjivan Ram, the wife of Jagjivan Ram, described the rural environment and the socio-religious nature of her father-in-law:

> Our village had a large number of households, most of whom did farm work. There was a number of Brahmins and a few

> Kayasthas. As most of the people of our caste were poor, they tilled the land for the Brahmins and Kayasthas. There were no Thakurs, Muslims, Kahar, Dhobi, Pasi, Badhai or Lohar. Social relations were amicable in the village. However, the well was in the are of the upper castes and to draw water from the well, people from our caste had to do some work. My father-in-law consulted a Babaji who told him that the solution was to dig a well in his own house, but my father-in-law got the well dug outside the house so that the entire community could draw water from it. The water of the well was so sweet that even Brahmin girls came there to fetch water for cooking.[48]

His father had a premonition of his death. He made Jagjivan Ram, who was just six years old at the time, perform the final rituals, even though he was the younger son. The rituals involved Bhajans, Havan, and making a Samadhi. For ten days, Jagjivan Ram had to eat saltless food, which he adhered to. The household had a very devotional atmosphere, and evenings used to be filled with Bhajans, particularly on Kṛṣṇa. One evening, while Jagjivan Ram's was singing a Bhajan about mother Yashoda waiting for the return of lad Kṛṣṇa addressed as Murāri, the elder brother entered the house and said that her Murāri had returned home. At that time, as Jagjivan Ram was elsewhere, the mother answered, 'Yes! But what about the other Murāri?'. Such was the intense devotion that was part of the basic maternal bonds of the family.

According to Indrani Jagjivan Ram, the Brahmins of the village not only had good relations with the so-called untouchable castes but also went out of their way to help them during times of need. The village schoolteacher 'Guruji' Kapil Muni Tiwari, made sure that Jagjivan Ram attended the classes. Once, when Jagjivan Ram went out and climbed a tree to avoid coming to the class after an altercation with the other boys, 'Guruji' personally went and persuaded him to come back to the class. Unlike the

Thakurs in other villages imposed a custom that 'untouchable' castes should not ride in carts in their streets, the Brahmins never imposed such customs. When there was flooding of the river in the village and Jagjivan Ram's house was flooded, 'Guruji' Kapil Muni Tiwari vacated a room in their house and accommodated the family for weeks.[49]

Interestingly, Jagjivan Ram's fight against social exclusion began with an act involving water. He persistently shattered the separate pitcher designated for 'untouchable' students, in the town school he studied. Initially there were two pitchers—one for Muslim boys and the other for Hindu boys. However, when Jagjivan Ram used water from the 'Hindu' water, it was deemed impure, and a new pitcher for Hindu boys was provided while the old one was labelled 'polluted'. Jagjivan Ram continued to break this pitcher as a form of protest until the school management relented and put an end to the practice of having an 'untouchable' pitcher.[50]

During the Bihar earthquake of 1934, Gandhiji noticed the potential of this promising young man who was both intelligent and with natural leadership and organizing qualities. Soon he became involved in the Harijan welfare programme of the Congress and received a generous monthly salary of seventy-five rupees. Surprisingly, he allocated forty rupees of his earnings towards the education of a Bengali 'Harijan' student. The ascent of Jagjivan Ram in public life, particularly his championing of social emancipation was tumultuous. It was through his efforts that the 'Akhil Bharatiya Dalit Varga Sangh' was established. Dr Ambedkar, disillusioned with the insincerity of the 'caste-Hindus' and the slow progress in implementing measures for emotional integration and confidence building, announced his decision to renounce Hinduism. This sent shock waves throughout India, prompting strong opposition from Jagjivan Ram, who was staunchly against such conversions. Instead, he encouraged Dr Ambedkar to join his Dalit Varga movement, declaring, 'Hindu society will not be divided'.

Jagjivan Ram was clear in his vision. He believed that the Scheduled Castes masses considered themselves Hindus and that they had sacrificed much for the cause of Hinduism. At the same time, he through his organization 'pressed for special representation in the legislature and in the services in order to enable the Scheduled Castes to raise themselves to the level of the rest of the country'.[51] In February 1936, he passed a resolution at All India Ravidas Sammelan stating that religious conversion was not a wise decision and that 'Dalits'/'Harijans' would remain within the Hindu fold and fight for their rights. In May 1936, an all-religion summit was organized at Lucknow to discuss the idea of conversion as to which religion the 'suppressed castes' should get converted for optimum social emancipation. Despite heading an all-India organization for Dalits, Jagjivan Ram and his followers were not invited. Recognizing the hidden agenda of the conference, Jagjivan Ram decided to send five of his colleagues to attend the conference. The pro-conversion activists wanted immediate action, but Dr Ambedkar, who took almost two decades to get converted, was not enthusiastic about immediate conversion. Jagjivan Ram's colleagues succeeded in passing a resolution that called for the establishment of a committee to study four or five religions and study them in detail to assess the pros and cons of each in relation to the conversion of the 'Depressed' classes. The committee did not submit any report, and the conversion movement, as anticipated by Jagjivan Ram, fizzled out. Similarly, it was his towering personality and dedicated activism that prevented the conversion movement from gaining traction in Bihar.[52]

In a report (SECRET 1934/34 S.B. Memo No. 39-Bihar-37) from the British CID of Bihar province, dated 9 March 1937, a letter written by Jagjivan Ram to Dr Bhimrao Ambedkar is mentioned. In the letter, Jagjivan Ram addressed Dr Ambedkar as 'my dear Doctor Saheb', and cautioned against a certain 'Mr Baldeo Prasad Jaiswal of Allahabad', stating that no person of Bihar was supporting him and that he operated his office from a Catholic Church, with everything being managed by missionaries. Jagjivan Ram also expressed his objection to Mr Jaiswal's method of inviting a large number of Muslims and Christians to gatherings while ignoring genuine depressed classes conferences.'[53]

Jagjivan Ram was addressed with respect as 'Babuji', and he served as the Labour Minister in the Interim Government formed in 1946. He retained the same post in the cabinet of free India. In 1977, he resigned from the Indian National Congress when Indira Gandhi was Prime Minister. He then joined the Janata Party and served as the Defence Minister after the party's victory. In January 1979, he became the Deputy Prime Minister. After the fall of the Janata experiment, he contested and won elections twice from a non-INC ticket. In 1984, he won an election against the Congress party despite the sympathy wave following the assassination of Indira Gandhi.

Jagjivan Ram was not only a political leader but also a fighter against social inequalities. He was also a great scholar who kept himself updated with the research into ancient Indian social history. In 1970, Jagjivan Ram, who was then the Central Minister for 'Food, Agriculture, Community Development and Co-operation', wrote a foreword. In it, he appreciated the importance of the thesis that the 'Śūdras were one of the Aryan communities of the solar race, a part of the Kṣatriyas Varṇa, and that their subsequent degradation and descent into the fourth varna of the Hindu society was essentially due to their continued feud with the Brahmins'.

While appreciating 'the undoubted intellectual prowess and depth of scholarship' and also how Dr Ambedkar 'brought to bear all the gifts of his towering intellect and dynamic personality' for the championship of the downtrodden people, nevertheless Jagjivan Ram pointed out that since the book was written 'social sciences and social history have made a significant progress' which had shed 'new light on Dr Ambedkar's hypothesis and scholars may not completely agree with some of the details'.[54]

Throughout his life, he displayed great love for India, her civilization, and Hindu Dharma. For him, the true essence of Sanātana Dharma, as opposed to the societal Jāthi system and its undemocratic, unjust core defined by birth-based stratification and exclusion, was a great force and resource for emancipation. A chief nation-builder of the modern Indian State, he was a profound spiritual person. In 1974, when the magazine *Illustrated Weekly of India* asked him why he was a Hindu, he gave an elaborate reply that deserves to be reproduced here in full:

> I was born a Hindu and I am proud to be one. I have read Hindu scriptures with various commentaries and I have come to believe that Hinduism, as revealed in the Vedas and the Upanishads, is such as can claim to be a religion of eternal modernity.
>
> A fascinating feature of Hinduism is that it not dogmatic or authoritarian. More than a religion it is a way of life. Although Hinduism has been inhibited by the Varna system of which caste is a necessary corollary, it has managed to survive as a great force. It has shown great resilience in many adverse circumstances.
>
> Hinduism teaches the Divinity of Man through its three basic formulae, viz. 'I am the Brahman', 'That art thou', and 'All around us is the Brahman'. All men are equal for they are all Divine. The Hindu believes that he is a spirit or Atman. The sword cannot pierce him, nor fire burn him. Death is only a change from one body to another.
>
> The entire universe is an expression or manifestation of God. Attachment to perishable things is the cause of sorrow. Here we have a vision of God as well as a rule of life. Liberation or

moksha is not a hypothetical state to be attained after death but is realisable in this very life. The Upanishads say: 'When all desires that the harbours are gone, man becomes immortal and attains the Brahman here.' Hinduism also implies to me the threefold path of Jnana Yoga, Bhakti Yoga and Karma Yoga. Jnana Yoga is the path of knowledge or spiritual insight Into the nature of God and the universe. Bhakti Yoga is the way of love – way of devotion – and it takes different forms according to the relationship established with the Beloved – the Creator and in wider perspective the creation. Karma Yoga means work as a path to perfection in which the doer loses all attachment to work or its fruits. Success and failure make no difference to him.

The greatest merit of Hinduism is its catholicity and spirit of accommodation. The widest freedom is allowed in matters of faith and worship to suit every individual's aptitude and inclination and thus it attains the status of a federation of faiths. Hinduism recognises different levels of religious experience and puts them in that order–from crude forms of worship to contemplation of the Formless or the Abstract who is all-pervasive. Out of the broad spectrum of Hindu though, each one can accept what he needs at his particular stage of development and thus progress from one step to another. Hinduism prescribes to each according to his need. The Upanishads declare that cows of different colors yield the same white milk, so all the different paths lead to the same goal.

Hinduism means to me Yoga – the competence and skill for action and the simultaneous development of body, mind and spirit which it implies. Yoga is known to the West only in its rudimentary form which is nothing more that exercises for development and purification of various parts of the body externally and internally. Yoga literally means union with the Divine. The yogi can attain perfect health and perfect bliss. The West has now begun to realise the value of Yoga and we have a continuous stream of seekers from the West anxious to learn the wisdom of the East.

Hinduism conceives of the world as one family and each individual as part of the Indivisible Divinity with all its attributes and hence the equality of all animates. It has displayed the ability

> to absorb into its fold – through sheer love – waves and waves of invaders from the north-west. It lays the greatest stress on non-violence. Truth has to be searched and passed on to others only through non-violent means.
>
> Hinduism does not look down upon any religion. It believes in the sanctity and equality of all religions, sarvadharma *samatvam*. The one truth has been spoken of by the wise in different ways – *Ekam sat viprah bahudha vadanti*.[55]

Such was the enlightened love Babu Jagjivan Ram had for Sanātana Dharma. From his childhood till the end, it was part and parcel of his being, galvanizing him into action as his own sadhana. One also needs to see the spiritual convergence of the thoughts cutting across political differences. Babu Jagjivan Ram highlighted as important the very same three *Mahā Vākyas* of the Upaniṣads ('Aham Brahmāsmi', 'Tat Tvam asi' and 'Sarvam Kalvitham Brahmam') that Dr Ambedkar hailed as the basis of the spiritual basis of democracy. On 6 July 1986, he breathed his last. His birthday every year is observed as 'Equality Day'.

Temple-Entry Gandhian Social Emancipation: A Case Study

While some extraordinary individuals were instrumental in inspiring social change through their spiritual dedication, the Gandhian movement encountered significant challenges along its path. Through remarkable means, it succeeded in bringing about profound societal and personal transformations. Firmly grounded in the Vaiṣṇava traditions of the Hindu nation, the Gandhian movement initiated enduring social progress and liberation, achieving this with a remarkable degree of nonviolence, unlike its dominant Western civilizational counterpart. The movement's advocacy for temple entry and associated legislative actions stands as a notable example of its impact.

Temple Entry: From Rājāh to Rājāji

After the Poona Pact, the issue of temple entry became a crucial topic for discussion and liberation in both the legislative assemblies and society. Following an initial period of harmony and collaboration between M.C. Rājāh (MCR) and C. Rājagōpālāchāri (also called Rājāji, hereafter CR), there ensued a bitter clash. Looking back, the partnership, conflict, and legislative as well as activist movements towards temple entry demonstrate how MCR and CR, despite their disagreements, ultimately advanced the cause of social liberation.

CR had initially supported MCR in passing the 'Removal of Civil Disabilities Act' authored by MCR, which was originally introduced in the Central Assembly in 1936. Unfortunately, political developments prevented the bill's progress. However, the then Government of India Act gave the provincial governments power to deal with the issues tackled by the bill. Taking advantage of this, CR introduced and passed the bill in the Madras Assembly.[56] This law provided the basic legal framework for the inhuman social exclusion that existed within Hindu society.

The Temple Entry Bill drafted by MCR marked a turning point in his relationship with CR and the Congress Party. MCR had previously clashed with CR over a bill for total prohibition in Madras Presidency, as CR favoured gradualism. This disagreement strained their relationship.

However, it is important to note the context behind these events. In retrospect, one should say that CR was pre-empting some important colonial strategies that would thwart reforms. This proactive approach began five years earlier.

In 1933, Ranga Iyer, Har Bilas Sharda, and Bhai Paramanand introduced a Bill in the Central Assembly for the entire British India, which was supported by CR. The bill called 'the Hindu

Temple Entry Disabilities Removal Bill' demonstrates how the Colonial Government exploited social stagnation within Hindu society to impede reform and the national liberation movement. The Bill was formulated by members from different parties and organizations. Ranga Iyer belonged to Indian National Congress. Harbilas Sarada, a Hindutvaite, belonged to Arya Samaj. R.K. Shanmukham Chetty belonged to the Swarajist Party. Bhai Paramanand, a freedom fighter who had toiled in Andaman Jails, was then the President of All India Hindu Mahāsabha. K.C. Niyogi also belonged to Hindu Mahāsabha. Niyogi was later part of the Nehru Government ministry and quit it because of the Nehru-Liaquat pact of 1950.

Systematic British Sabotage of an Indigenous Emancipation Attempt

The British Government employed various tactics to delay the process. Additionally, it required that the bill draft be distributed to all segments of society, particularly those considered important stakeholders, mainly the orthodox and religiously conservative sections. In a confidential communication dated 20 July 1934, Harry Graham Haig (1881–1956), the official responsible for strategies to dismantle Gandhi's Civil Disobedience Movement, explained how the British administration perceived the Bill:

> In my view the whole move in connection with the Temple Entry Bill was essentially political. The object was to get the Bill passed on a wave of temporary enthusiasm, and on the one hand to secure the support of the depressed classes, and on the other hand to turn the resentment of the orthodox against Government, who in the general estimation would be responsible for allowing the Bill to be passed.[57]

Then he went on to explain how the British defeated the plan by roping in the forces of social stagnation within the Hindu community:

> We have allowed discussion and this has led to violent antagonism between the orthodox and Gandhi; the depressed classes have shown little interest and generally recognise that the Bill is going to do them little or no good; the Government remained uncommitted, and so far by insisting on full discussion and preventing the Bill being rushed through have appeared in the character of preservers of religion. For this the orthodox are grateful.[58]

The British had already made a decision regarding sanctioning the Bill. In a telegram sent by the Legislative Assembly Department to the Secretary of State dated 24 July 1934, probably Maurice Garnier Hallett (1883–1969), who was mainly responsible for countering the bill, explained that they would not support the Bill. Even while sanctioning the Bill for introduction in the Central Legislative Assembly and discussion, Hallett made it clear that the British Indian Government 'retained a free hand to take at later stages such action as may, upon a full consideration of the circumstances, appear necessary to recommend that it should be vetoed if passed.' Thus, he explained three alternatives: to remain neutral and allow the Bill to be decided by votes, to postpone the decision by allowing the Bill to be talked out, or to oppose the Bill and make a definite statement to that effect. Hallett favoured the third alternative and explained why. He argued that there were 'political advantages in taking up a definite attitude' and making it clear that the British opposed the Bill. The government would 'earn the real gratitude of the orthodox' and that was 'a factor of appreciable political value.' This would also have the orthodox 'learnt the lesson of the necessity of taking steps to protect their interests'. Winning over the orthodoxy, representing the conservative element in Indian society, might 'conduce to the smooth working of the constitution and prevent the adoption of revolutionary proposals either in economic or religious matters'.[59] The Secretary of State replied through a telegram on 31 July 1934:

> While recognising force of your arguments in favour of definite opposition to Bill, I feel nevertheless that there are grave objections to such a course. We shall be accused of refusing to allow Legislature to come to its own conclusions in a matter of which it is best judge and of deliberately obstructing a much needed reform.... A fourth possible alternative, namely, to refuse facilities now for present Bill on ground that mandate of existing Legislature has nearly expired and that it is not right that a matter of such importance should be settled by Assembly at the very end of its time. Facilities could be promised for a new Bill in new Legislature if there is a demand for it. This may, it is true, be merely postponing issue but it will have effect of making the orthodox realise that they have got to organise their opposition to the Bill and developments in interim may simplify problem of Government's decision as to line to be adopted.[60]

The British government's exercise of gathering the opinion of various sections of Hindu society throughout India unwittingly provided us with a clear map of who stood where in the process of social emancipation.

Patterns in Hindu Responses to 'Hindu Temple Entry Disabilities Removal' Bill of 1933

The government, while appearing unbiased in seeking the viewpoint the opinion of the Hindu society through local governments, sent instructions 'asking them to satisfy themselves that the circulation of the two Bills, particularly to the orthodox section, is adequate and effective'.[61] When the office of a Shankaracharya, who was the 'President of Dharmacharyas' Conference of Guruvayoor' which in turn was against temple entry, queried about 'proper steps to elicit the opinion of the Sanatanists who... though are highly cultured ...

are often illiterate', the Government in its reply let it out that 'apart from the initial instructions issued to local Governments to secure the widest circulation of these Bills in order to ascertain all shades of Hindu opinion from as wide an area as possible, the Government of India recently addressed local Governments asking them to satisfy themselves that the circulation of these two Bills, particularly to the orthodox section is adequate and effective.'[62]

Despite the government's manipulative strategies and biases, the reports from local governments reveal clear patterns regarding the response of the overall Hindu society to the issue of temple entry of all Hindu communities. This marks a decisive step in social emancipation.

In both the Congress and the Swarajist party, there were important leaders and provincial voices that opposed the Bill. The majority of organizations identifying themselves as 'Sanatanists' were against the Bill, though there were notable exceptions. Additionally, many feudal non-Brahmin 'upper caste' leaders also opposed the Bill.

One Shankaracharya in particular, known as 'His Holiness Shree Shankaracharya of Sankeshwar-Karvir Peeth' fervently supported the British Government in order to prevent the Scheduled Castes communities from entering the temples. He offered a legal roadmap to the British to overcome the problem. Claiming that 'the Reformers of the Sanatana Dharma, like Ram Mohan Roy, Dayanand Saraswati, Dr Bhandarkar, or Pandit Madan Mohan Malaviya, Mr. Gandhi, the Pandits of Vai Pradnya Path-Shala, etc., have propounded new principles through their institutions, e.g., Brahmo Samaj, Arya Samaj, Prarthana Samaj, Hindu Mahasabha, Satyagrahashram, Hindu Missionary Society Wai Pradnya Path-Shala, etc.', he claimed that those principles were 'entirely opposed to the ancient Sanatana Dharma'. So he asked the British government for

> legal recognition to this new or Protestant Hinduism and separate pro-changers completely from the old Sanatana Hinduism by legislation as they are looked upon as out-castes and renegades from Hinduism by their Sanatanist caste people according to the Shastras and in accordance with the injunction of the respective Acharyas, though they may be still passing off as Sanatanists.[63]

He almost echoed what was in the minds of the British strategists working against the Bill and proposed the above legislature as the sure means to cut the strength from under the Civil Disobedience Movement:

> Besides, we should like to bring to the notice of Government that most of the political agitators belong to this pro-changer class, and the agitation gathers strength, because the Sanatanist masses are led to believe by these pro-changers that they (pro-changers) are Sanatanists. Further this distinction of the Hindus not being clearly declared and established by any enactment, the agitators can mislead the people as well as Government by their professions of being leaders of all Hindus. If Government were to bring home to the masses that the agitators who are anti-Government in the political field are also against Hinduism and that they do not belong to Hinduism, or as a matter of that, to any established religion at all. the masses would not join their agitation. Their claim to speak in the name of all Hindus will be gone, and the agitation would then lose all its force. The whole country would be saved from a great deal of unrest, expense, trade depression and the consequent general distress caused by their agitation.... So we are requesting Government to save the whole country from this tyranny and distress by legally recognising the pro-changers as belonging to a new and separate religion by taking the necessary steps to rush a legislative measure through the legislative assembly. Only by so doing, Government will be able to protect the loyalist Sanatanists from the encroaching of the non-Sanatani disloyal agitators upon the Sanatanist institutions and establish peace

> and prosperity in the country by making it impossible for such anti-Government and anti-God agitators to get any backing in the country for their schemes.[64]

Then His Holiness went on to make the most ingenious argument as to how 'untouchables' kept as social capital would serve the economic and imperial interests of the Empire and how the National movement liberating them would jeopardize at a fundamental level, the safety of the British.[65]

The argument presented by 'His Holiness', despite his respected position, not only disregards basic human dignity but also goes against the fundamental belief in the sacredness of life emphasized in Hindu dharma. It serves as an example of how socio-economic interests, stemming from social stagnation and colonial influence, can be disguised as religious tradition and perpetuated. His Holiness concluded his response with a warning to the government:

> If Government do not take immediate steps to stop this anti-religious propaganda of Mr Gandhi and his followers, the masses who are mainly Sanatanists would be led into the belief, rightly or wrongly, that Government is helping, directly or indirectly, this attack on their religion and once this belief gets rooted in the minds of the masses, whose religious fervour is just as strong as ever, the consequences will be very serious and the Government will be creating in no time a situation far more awkward than what Mr Gandhi would have been able to create after even 50 years of intensive Civil Disobedience Movement.[66]

Contrary to this, 'M.R.Ry.K. Kuppuswami Ayyar Avargal, Agent to His Holiness the Jagadguru Sri Sankaracharya Swamigal of Sri Kanchi Kamakoti Peetam, Kumbakonam (Camp), Karnool' presented a different argument that was less offensive but still had a similar impact. The statement began with the observation made by the Pontiff that 'throughout his tour of fifteen years in

South India, His Holiness had found that there were more pious Hindus among the men and women of the so-called "excluded communities" than among other communities'. Then the statement conflated Varṇa with Jāthi:

> The basic and distinctive feature of the Hindu religion is the 'Varna Dharma', that is, that every Hindu has some duties and injunctions ordained by his religion, based on birth in his respective caste. The faithful observance of such duties and injunctions elevates him not only spiritually, but contributes to the collective welfare of all Hindus, nay even the whole of humanity, and *he, in so doing, is not spiritually inferior to any other person born in any other caste having greater or lesser responsibility imposed by such duties and injunctions.* In short, the Hindu Dharma mainly rests on 'jathi ' which in Sanskrit means 'birth'.[67] (Emphasis added)

Unlike most other orthodox religious leaders, the Pontiff accepted the equality of all professions and saw no superiority or inferiority in their vocations. However, he pointed out that these vocations were 'imposed' on the communities by birth. This birth-based vocation and derived rights and limits formed the basis of Hinduism according to this Ācharya highly venerated by the influential and powerful South Indian upper castes. His Holiness then rejected the notion that the 'Depressed Classes' were excluded from the temples. He argued that the Agama Sastras actually outlined graded access to temples for every community in which the so-called excluded communities could derive the same spiritual benefit from just viewing the towers of the temples from the outside:

> Every respective 'jathi' was allotted a different place of worship from which it was to derive its spiritual benefits of worship, and in that spiritual arrangement of worship some castes were to derive the benefit of worship from the outskirts of those

> temples, looking with veneration on the visible 'Vimanam' or 'Gopuram ' which was as much specially sanctified as the central deity under the 'Gopuram'.[68]

Then he went on to explain that all the communities had their own community temples in which other communities had to stand outside:

> The Pariahs or the so-called depressed classes, the Visvakarmas, the Sourashtras, the Ezhuvas, the Lingayats, the Konkinis of Malabar have all their respective temples. In the Konkini temples of Malabar, not even the Nambudri or Tamil Brahman is allowed to enter. In the temples of the Pattar Brahman of Malabar, not even the Nayars and Rajas are allowed. Pious Pariahs would not allow Brahman into their colony or into their temples. All these arrangements have not been resented but all along for centuries faithfully followed by the Hindus.[69]

The Pontiff, or technically his agent on his behalf, ended with a prediction of 'natural death' for the movement and an appeal to the sanctity of the proclamation of 'Gracious Queen':

> It is to be repeated here that the political reformers now agitating on this question are verily a very small minority though their present agitation initiated by political expediency and backed by the political press may loom large in the eyes of the unsophisticated public and it is doomed to die a natural death.... Lastly, the Bill violates the pledge of religious neutrality vouchsafed by the Gracious Queen's Proclamation and is a departure from the wise policy of non-interference in religion guaranteed by Parliamentary statutes and followed by the British Government.... His Holiness feels it His duty, according to the traditions of His mutt, as His predecessors have done, to tender in the same spirit, to the Sovereign His Majesty and to his accredited representatives, the Viceroy and Government of

> India, the advice, that the Bill should not in any circumstances be passed into law.[70]

The officials of the Hindu Religious Endowment Board were also overwhelmingly opposed to the bill. M. Sambanda Mudaliyar Avargal, the commissioner of the Hindu Religious Endowment Board, described the bill as 'the first move in the attempt to do away with the Hindu religion altogether'. Among other things, Sri Sambanda Mudaliyar argued:

> It is well settled law that members of a community for whose worship a particular temple is designed have a legal right to make their worship undisturbed by interference by polluting and other castes. This civil right is sought to be taken away by implication by this Bill by conferment of the right to enter, on such excluded castes under this Bill.

He concluded that the Bill sought 'to legalize sacrilege'.[71]

Dr S. Muthulakshmi Reddi (1886–1968), a pioneering female doctor in India and the first woman legislator of British India hailing from Madras, expressed her full support for the Bill. She dismissed the use of ancient texts to justify the exclusion of certain Hindus, highlighting the lack of historical evidence to suggest that the temple-building kings excluded any particular community from entering the temples. Dr Reddi underscored the dynamic nature of Hindu law texts, contrasting them with the unchanging nature of the Bible or Koran.

> The Hindu scriptures have been written and added to, from time to time, according to the needs and conditions of these periods. They are not like Bible or Quran—the expression or the preaching of one prophet. In fact Hindu religion embodies the thoughts and experiences of ages. Therefore Manu laws cannot be made to apply to all times. It will be simply intolerable if such a state is allowed.... According to the right definition of a

Brahman in the Sastras there are very few or none at all in these days.... To call a normal human being an untouchable is a sin and to argue for the continuation of that state of affairs in any society is, in my opinion, a crime and wrong against humanity.

She also asked the non-Hindus to express their solidarity with the Bill in the interest of larger humanity.[72]

Sanghathan Response

As a pan-Indian organizational network with considerable provincial freedom and diversity, Hindu Mahāsabha surprisingly came with a strong and consistent response to the Bill. Government Industrial Surveyor Delhi, in the confidential report he submitted, stated,

The volume of opinion received in this office, weighed in the balance, is definitely on the side of the orthodox section who are opposed to the proposed enactment. This opinion has the strength that it derives from the religious convictions of the Hindu community. The most important organisation among the supporters of the contemplated legislation happens to be the Hindu Mahasabha the accredited representative body of the Hindus.[73]

Central Hindu Mahāsabha, Head Office, New Delhi, made the following response:

For the opinion, of the Hindu Mahasabha on the questions of temple-entry and the removal of disabilities on the so-called untouchables, regarding public schools, public wells and other sources of drinking water, public meetings, public roads, please refer to resolution No. 22 of the printed copy of the resolutions passed by the fifteenth Session of the Hindu Mahasabha, held at Ajmer in October, 1933, under the Presidentship of Bhai Parmanand, M.A., M.L.A.

Resolution No. 22. Untouchability.

> The Hindu Mahasabha declares that the so-called untouchables have equal rights with other Hindus to study in public schools, to take 'water from public wells and other sources of drinking water, to sit with others in public meetings, and to walk on public roads'. The Mahasabha calls upon all Hindus to remove such restrictions as may be existing any where at present in the way of the so-called untouchable Hindus exercising these rights. The Mahasabha appeals to Hindus that facilities for worship be offered equally to the so-called untouchables in all temples and places of worship open to the public. The Mahasabha calls upon Purohits (priests), barbers and washermen to offer their services to all Hindus irrespective of any caste. The Hindu Mahasabha is of opinion that every Hindu to whatever caste he may belong, has equal social and political rights.[74]

In his report to the government, E.A.R. Emstace, Deputy Commissioner, Shimla, expressed support for the bill, observing that the Hindu Mahāsabha always favoured 'such progressive measures which contribute towards the removal of disabilities of the depressed classes in respect of entry into Hindu temples' and hence 'supports the bill'. Similarly, Simla Kali Bari 'the oldest Hindu religious institution in Simla' pointed out that as far as worship in the temple was concerned, 'no Hindu was regarded as an untouchable by reason of his birth and that those who were so regarded elsewhere have the same and equal rights as other high caste Hindus in regard to the entry into the NatMandir and Parikran of the temple' and hence Simla Kali Bari had 'no special observation to make in regard to the provision of the Bill'.[75] The All India Hindu Mahāsabha Working Committee member Ram Rakha Mai Bhandari considered the Bill 'very mild' and as 'only first step towards a very urgent reform' and hence welcomed it.[76]

Advocate Rai Bahadur Diwan Khalinda, as President of Hindu Sabha, Multan Division, gave detailed and spirited support for the Bill:

> All the religions of the world describe God pre-eminently as the Friend of the friendless. Help of the helpless and Protector of the weak. The rest of the world apart, in India who can be more friendless, helpless or weaker than the forty millions or more Hindus of India who are classified as 'untouchables'? If, therefore, any body of people can be fitly described as men of God, they are surely these helpless, friendless and despised people.
>
> ...
>
> Interdining and intermarrying may hasten the removal of untouchability, but if they are not preceded by and founded upon spiritual principles in which man's religion is involved, we will create new problems and the evil of 'untouchability' will manifest itself in new forms. Temple-entry is a powerful and a potent force, a true spiritual move in which will be found numerous opportunities for improvement of all classes.... Temples are the citadels of orthodoxy and, if we manage to get admission there, the cruel and inhuman practice of untouchability will be exterminated from our land once for all and we will be enabled to use all other public institutions, roads, wells and tanks. If untouchability is completely removed through temple-entry, our economic condition will be improved as they will be getting work in Hindu quarters.... However educated and independent some of the Harijans are at present, they have to undergo several inconveniences owing to the practice of untouchability among the Hindus. Dr. Ambedkar and some others of his class have to pocket several insults from the caste Hindus.[77]

He also refuted arguments like Harijans themselves did not want temple entry.

The British colonial strategy cleverly exploited the trepidations of traditionalists towards modernization to achieve two main goals. First, it significantly diminished the zeal among the conservative factions within society for the Swarajya—self-rule—advocated by the national movement. Second, it engendered a sense of mistrust within the progressive segments of Hindu society towards the Swarajya, fearing it would usher in an era governed by laws steeped in severe social marginalization.

In his autobiography, Jawaharlal Nehru made an insightful observation regarding the bills proposed by Indian Nationalists and social activists inspired by Gandhi, who had a strong sense of justice. This sheds light on the colonial strategy of making imperialist civilizational capital out of every manifestation of social stagnation in India to morally justify its rule over India:

> There was a great agitation for removing the barriers to temple entry, and a Bill to that effect was introduced in the Legislative Assembly. And then the remarkable spectacle was witnessed of an outstanding leader of the Congress going from house to house in Delhi, visiting the members of the Assembly and canvassing for their votes for this Temple Entry Bill. Gandhiji himself sent an appeal through him to the Assembly members. And yet civil disobedience was still going on and people were going to prison, and the Assembly had been boycotted by the Congress and all our members had withdrawn from it.... I was amazed at Gandhiji's appeal, under the circumstances then existing, and even more so by the strenuous efforts of Rajagopalachariar, who, a few weeks before, had been the acting President of the Congress.... The Government attitude to this Temple Entry Bill, then and subsequently, was very revealing. It put every possible difficulty in the way of its promoters, went on postponing it and encouraging opposition to it, and then finally declared its own opposition to it, and killed it. That, to a greater or lesser extent, has been its attitude to all measures of social reform in India, and on the plea of non-interference with religion, it has prevented social progress. But this, it need hardly be said, has not prevented it from criticising our social evils and encouraging others to do so.[78]

The actions of the reformers within the Indian national liberation movement shed light on the deep strategic challenges they faced, while also revealing the unfortunate role played by the colonized 'traditionalists' who identified as 'Sanātanists' and unwittingly supported their colonial rulers. The British intervention facilitated the dominance of the upper castes and conservative beliefs across India. This provided the British with leverage to obstruct the freedom movement if nationalists pursued social reforms. Furthermore, without social reforms, the national movement risked being confined to the upper castes, thereby legitimizing British rule as more benevolent to the masses compared to a Hindu Raj that enforced caste divisions. MCR and CR were walking into this complex and hazardous territory.

Backstabbing by CR?

In 1934, MCR introduced Bills for temple entry and the Removal of Civil Disabilities Bill in the Madras Legislative Assembly. During that period, the Justice Party, a non-Brahmin party, held power. Despite the Justice Party's claim to be pro-social justice, the bills were not passed. It was under Congress rule, with CR as Premier, the bill proposed by MCR for the removal of civil disabilities was successfully passed. Emboldened by CR's support, MCR introduced the temple-entry bill, 'A Bill to remove the Disabilities of the so-called Depressed Classes in regard to Entry into Hindu Temples' (L.A. Bill No.7 of 1938), to be enacted as law. During the assembly session, he urged the passing of the bill, emphasizing that it was not legally binding but aimed at reforming the attitudes of the 'caste Hindus':

> Let me point out at the outset that this Bill is not a piece of compulsory legislation.... The Bill does not throw open the doors of temples to depressed classes all at once, whether the worshippers like it or not. This is a kind of Local Option Bill for removing the legal impediments to reform and puts no compulsion whatever on the caste Hindus. The Bill seeks to give every congregation of Hindu worshippers the right of deciding

> the question of opening the temples to Harijans instead of being dictated by a minority.[79]

However, at the floor CR backed out of supporting the Bill. He explained that this was more a change of strategy than a change of heart:

> In all seriousness, I tell you, Sir, that till a week ago, it did not flash across my mind that we could adopt a line of action which I will presently state; and as soon as it flashed across my mind, it was a struggle of 'Shall I do this? Will it not look like retraction? Will it not look like a change of mind, like showing the white feather? Shall I not look like a betrayer?' Oh yes, it may be so. But one must be true to oneself and to the cause that one holds dear. These misinterpretations will pass like the mist at some time or other before the sun. We should not be frightened by possible misinterpretations or even slander. This cause is dear and it is just as dear to me and my colleagues even as Hinduism is dear, and may failure in this cause is a failure for our civilization and for our religion which we hold dear. Therefore, the fear of misinterpretation is nothing before that.... Government have decided to introduce a measure for Malabar. The measure of Travancore carried forward to the British area in Kerala, very rightly will be a Government measure and it will be a measure on the same lines, because they are the lines which we all have examined and found to be the best.... And after Malabar, the next step will be easy. I ask friends to be patient. It is easy to be enthusiastic, but it is difficult to accomplish things. We have not failed, we have not shown cowardice, we have not shown unwillingness and if we succeed in Malabar, we shall have avoided many difficulties.[80]

Still, he could not convince 'Harijan' leaders of his own party. Generally soft-spoken Śwāmi Sahajānanda responded to the suggestion of postponement with uncharacteristic harshness, showing the deep angst and the pain of betrayal the 'Harijan' members of Congress felt that even years after the Poona Pact, the 'caste-Hindu' dominance still prevented as fundamental a right of a Hindus as temple-entry:

> Mahatma Gandhi had assured us that once Swarajya Government was formed then temple-entry would be accomplished. It was with trust in this promise of Mahatma that thirty (Harijans) had entered the Legislative Assembly (on behalf of Congress).... If this Bill is postponed now, as suggested by the Premier, then that would amount to breach of faith. Hence I request that the Bill be passed immediately. In Kerala where there used to be cruel treatment of Harijans, the upper castes had been made to open the temples for Harijans by the order of the Rajah. The same way if the Government made this a law then none is going to oppose it. If this Bill is postponed now, then how would we feel? Are we sinners? Do not we need to worship the God coming inside the temples? What kind of cruel sinners, those who refuse entry into the temples for us, should be! If some humans stop fellow human beings from entering the temple then should not they be considered more as monsters than as humans![81]

One significant 'Harijan' leader who supported and stood by CR was V.I. Munuswāmy Piḷḷai, a member of the legislative assembly and who also served in the ministry. While recognizing 'the need for the legislation as indeed very great', Piḷḷai viewed the method proposed by CR as 'really good'. He highlighted that 'greater atrocities were being committed towards Harijans for their merely asking entry into the temple' and that 'Harijans' were 'treated worse than dogs, for the simple reason that they want to worship the God which others also profess to worship'. Piḷḷai had no doubts about the sincerity of his colleagues in safeguarding the interests of the Harijans, without which he would not even occupy the cabinet seat he held. He requested MCR 'to agree to this measure being taken to the next meeting and then if the Government failed in their duty to bring in a new

Bill covering mostly all the provisions contained in the Bill now before us, then he would be justified in thinking that he (Piḷḷai) was insincere in making the plea'.[82] MCR responded to this with justified agony and righteous anger:

> Sir, the Hon. the Prime Minister (CR) ... says that I had introduced this Bill with his consent and at his request. Quite so; but what was the request? When he handed over the draft Bill to me, he told me and he told the country that the country was ripe for this measure. And now, six years afterwards, he comes and asks me to withdraw the Bill or withhold the Bill. Is it right for him to do so, Sir? I have been deceived in this matter. (Cries of 'Oh' from all sides of the House.).... Sir, six years ago the Hon. Mr. C. Rajagopalachariyar told me that the country from the Himalayas to Cape Comorin was ripe for a Bill like mine. Did he not say so, Sir? But now when I want to introduce this Bill, not for the whole of India, but for a smaller area, our province, he comes and says 'No.no. You cannot do it.... I am standing here all alone and they think they can play their tricks with me.... For ages we have suffered like this.... They think by this they can suppress me. They are mistaken.[83]

The event singularly shattered the faith MCR had in Congress. He wrote to Gandhi who in turn wanted MCR to trust CR. The advice did not help. Bitter, he rejoined Dr Ambedkar. When the Malabar-Temple Entry Bill was launched, MCR gave dignified support to the Bill while at the same time asking in which districts the Bill would be extended and applied:

> Sir I agree with this Bill so far as the principle of temple entry is concerned; but as far as the machinery set up and the limited locality for the application of the measure are concerned the Premier alone is responsible for them.... I want the Hon. Premier to give us an indication as to what district he is going to take up next for extending the application of this Bill.... Sir, I support the motion and I wish the Bill success.[84]

CR answered,

> 'What districts next?' asks Mr. Rajan and wants an answer at once.... I want a great many favours from him in the future and therefore request him not to put such a question.... I tell him as a brother and a colleague that it would make our work very difficult and I hope it is not his intention.... With regard to what may follow after Malabar, we need not go district by district. If Malabar succeeds, there is no reason to think of districts. We have crossed the Rubicon and it may very well be the conquest of the whole Province.[85]

CR again explained the reason for choosing Malabar, this time emotionally and finally concluded, emphasizing the civilizational importance of the Bill:

> Why did I do it?... Where did we work as satyagrahis in connexion with the opening of these temples? At Guruvayur. Where did Kelappan fast? At Guruvayur. And where is Guruvayur? In Malabar. If for no other reason, for no other argument, for no other considerations of wisdom and forethought but only for this emotional attachment, it is a good setp that we have taken.... We cannot afford to lose in this battle. If we do, not only the Government, not only the Congress but Hinduism as a whole will have been defeated.[86]

The references made here are important. The tradition of denying temple entry to large segments of Hindus due to social stagnation, masquerading as tradition, had been spiritually challenged by the Advaita movement, which had its root in the spirituality of Śrī Nārayaṇa Guru. This movement drew the attention of Gandhiji and subsequently Dr Ambedkar–Gandhiji Poona Pact further accelerated social emancipation with respect to temple entry, despite any perceived drawbacks of the pact. The subsequent introduction of the Bill, along with the manipulative tactics and exploitation of orthodoxy by the British was countered by the genuine essence t of spirituality. Therefore, the acknowledgment of the Kēraḷā Vēdāntic movement by CR, even if unconsciously, revealed the spiritual foundation of social emancipation in India with the passing of the legislative measure on 8 December 1938. Subsequently, the bill became law, followed by more significant events.

Subsequent Events

CR and his team consistently pursued the Malabar Bill. They engaged in mass communication and propaganda against untouchability and conducted numerous public meetings advocating the entry of Harijans into temples. A systematic campaign was launched for the entry of all Hindu communities, including the so-called 'untouchables', irrespective of caste differences. From the national Harijan movement, Rameshwari Nehru came to the Madras Presidency to participate in the campaign. In his account of this part of the movement for access to temples, author Manoj Mitta gives a very subtle twist to CR's concern. He writes,

> [Rameshwari Nerhu's] first-hand experience in both places helped her see that Rajaji was being more wary than the maharaja had been. Despite giving 'his wholehearted support to the cause', Rajaji was 'very keen' that temples be thrown open 'without the aid of law' and 'by the voluntary free will of the people'. Her reading was that he desired a situation where trustees, rather than waiting for legislation, brought about temple entry on their own with the assurance that caste Hindus were willing to worship alongside Harijans.[87]

Rameshwari Nehru (1886–1966) had dedicated herself to 'Harijan' emancipation. For Gandhiji she was the right hand in his Harijan-oriented activities and organizations. In 1934, she joined All India Harijan Sevak Sangh, which had been founded by Gandhiji in 1932. Soon she became its Vice President. In this capacity, she undertook a trip to South India to promote the Harijan's emancipation works. Her own observations of what CR and his team had done paint a very different picture than the one given by Mitta. Mitta provides a description that cleverly suggests that 'despite' his 'wholehearted support', CR expected the trustees to gain entry into the temple.

But what she had actually observed and recorded do not suggest such a behaviour or thought process in the case of CR. The word 'despite' was a clever twist of words. In fact, Rameshwari Nehru's observations showed admiration for the clear vision and clearer roadmap that CR had facilitated for the temple visit. Far from that, she saw in the movement 'the possibility of the Hindu ideals supplying to the world the secret of making democracy effective'. Moreover, he had achieved more than halfway in this mission, namely, popular support from all sections of society. Rameshwari Nehru recorded the following:

> The most significant feature of this event was that it was accomplished peacefully without the pressure of law or police or authority. Sri Rajagopalachariar, who gave his whole-hearted support to the cause, was very keen that temples should be opened without the aid of law by the voluntary free will of the people. Consequently a campaign similar to the Travancore one was organised by the Harijan Sevak Sangh. Scores of meetings, which were attended by thousands, were held all over Tamiland. *I had the honour of presiding at most of these meetings, where I beheld the joyful spectacle of all sorts of men vying with each other in giving their support.*[88] (Emphasis added)

As the italicized line indicates, popular support from congressional staffers was already a fait accompli at the state level. Now the temple entry movement was focused on the Śrī Meenākhi Sundarēswar Temple in Madurai. It was one of the most sacred of the Hindu temples in South India. On 13 June

1939, a large pro-temple entry conference was held in Madurai. According to an eyewitness account, 20,000 to 30,000 people attended the conference, and all but a single vote was in favour of entering the temple.[89]

During this time, CR also made a promise to the people that he would ensure that the movement became a mass movement that would win over a large section of Hindu society across all communities, and he would give it legal protection. This was a well-crafted move where legislation would be brought in line with a collective people's movement, reducing the strength of the opponents to an ever-decreasing court-hopping fringe, an observation that Rameshwari Nehru also made.[90] Thus, CR promised the activists of the pro-temple entry movement:

> If by persuasion you can convince the people, you can bring about this improvement, you can tell the priests, the trustees and the local people to get the Harijans and others introduced into the temples end worship openly and publicly there and if you can maintain it without disturbance or disorder, surely it would not be difficult for the legislator to make the necessary law.[91]

With such confidence infused by CR, Sri A. Vaidhyanādha Iyer (1890–1955), who was the head of Harijan Seva Sangh of Tamil region, planned a temple entry into Śrī Meenākhi Sundarēswar temple of Madurai. After securing the support of all sections of the society, the temple entry was planned with caution and responsibility. It was nothing less than a social revolution – the abolition of a custom that was in reality only a few centuries old and prescribed by the *Smṛti* and *Dharmaśāstra* texts interpreted within the framework of British legal system. People were also tired of mere legislative reforms, which often resulted in clashes rather than societal transformation.

One of the campaigners for the temple entry programme was R.T.P. Subramaṇian, a Congress worker belonging to Nādār community. The Nādār community, an affluent trading community in the Madurai region, had epigraphical evidence and also oral literary tradition as to their Kṣatriya status.[92] Nevertheless, they were declared untouchables or even 'unapprochables' in certain regions, mostly due to pre-modern political rivalries. The community has special ceremonial rights and ritual turban honour in Śrī Meenākhi Sundarēswar temple. However, this ritual turban honour symbolically performed with a coconut due to untouchability. Despite such treatment, the Scheduled Castes communities were treated with disdain by most Nādār communities. R.T.P. Subramaṇian himself narrated how as a nationalist he brought in 'Harijans' into his house and how his mother was horrified and extremely depressed because of that.[93] He understood very well the psychology of such untouchability and the deep-rooted, multi-layered phenomenon they were fighting against. He recorded in detail how the entry into the temple- came about and the subsequent responses. The following sections on the temple entry, strategies employed by CR, and subsequent developments – up until the response of Gandhiji – are based on R.T.P. Subramanian's account: [94]

The team arrived at 6:00 a.m. and assembled at the house of Vaidhyanādha Iyer. Iyer was an expert in Vēdāntic and Bhakti literature and with his deep knowledge rejected untouchability as non-Hindu and insisted on Temple-Entry as genuinely Dharmic. On the day of Temple-entry there were five 'Harijans' including the famous Sri Kakkan who would later become state minister and Sri L.N. Gopalswamy the secretary of Harijan Seva Sangh of Tamil Nadu. R.T.P. Subramaṇian was selected to represent the Nādār community. But he declined as he was then a youth and suggested community elder Sri Shaṇmuga Nādār. All had taken bath already and had applied Holy Ash (*Vibūti*). The atmosphere scintillated with sacred fervour. Then they drove in taxi to the temple. The time was then around 7:45 a.m. Temple executive officer (EO) Barrister R.S. Nāidu welcomed them with respect and took them right before the sanctum where the Goddess was present. The Brahmin priest (*Bhaṭṭar or Śivāchārya*) did the *Pūja* and provided the holy *Prasād* to all with love and respect. Entire Madurai was jubilant over the successful and peaceful Temple entry.

The sections of orthodoxy tried to create a semblance of strike by locking all the inner doors and leaving the city with the keys, thus trying to stop the daily *Pūja*. In a cruel irony, after the Islamist invasions, the section of orthodoxy who self-labelled themselves as *Sanātanists* obtained the dubious reputation of trying to stop the daily *Pūja* at Madurai temple. But Iyer brought in willing *Bhaṭṭars* from nearby famous temples. The locks were broken and *Pūja* was performed without any interruption. With every day after temple entry, the self-styled *Sanātanists* found themselves getting dwindled in numbers and were reduced to a motley group of court-hoppers clutching to British-made Hindu legislation. Here too CR acted fast and brought in the legislation which prevented any legal persecution of those who committed what was then a 'legal violation' i.e., temple entry.

R.T.P. Subramaṇian had documented the three important precautions that CR took regarding temple entry. First, he wanted the date and time of temple entry to be kept as much as a secret and within a small circle; second, he asked the team to make sure that the temple entry happened on a day when the priests in charge of the sanctum were those who were the most supportive for temple entry; third, in case any group of the temple priests resorted to not doing the Pūja, the team was to have backup Bhaṭṭars ready to replace them and perform the puja properly. All these instructions proved useful in managing the situation. After the temple entry, when the self-styled sanatanists tried to arouse passion through rallies, which were countered by the proponents of temple entry Hindus and counter-countered by the other side, CR understood that this would only polarize the society. He urged the temple proponents to stop the counter-rallies, arguing that without counter-rallies, people would lose interest in such circus events and the other side would fade further into the background. CR was proved right.

Usually, emotions ran high among those who opposed CR. This was especially true among the non-Brahmins. After entering the temple, these feelings of hatred seemed to have changed (at least temporarily). R.T.P.S reported that one person who had previously said that he would assassinate CR if given the opportunity, apologized after entering the temple and said that he would now prostrate before him. As mentioned earlier, the custom tying the ceremonial turban to the tender coconut to honour a person from the Nādār community changed after entering the temple and the Bhaṭṭar now tied the ceremonial turban to the respected person from the Nādār community. A sage, Śwāmi Karuṇānanda, who belonged to the Scheduled Castes community in his pre-Sanyas days, entered the temple and was so filled with spiritual feeling that he went into deep meditation. Later, overwhelmed with emotions, he said that CR was indeed an avatar who had come to uplift the downtrodden. All in all, it was a great success brought about by CR, whose politics always predicated itself on his Hindu spirituality.

Gandhiji wrote triumphantly on 12 July 1939:

> The Proclamation opening the State temples of Travancore was no doubt a very big step. But it was the prerogative of the Maharaja. He had in his Dewan a wise adviser. The Maharaja, the Maharani and the Dewan brought about the transformation. But the opening of the celebrated temple of Madura is a greater event in that it is the popular will that has brought about the happy consummation. It reflects a decided conversion of the temple-goers of the Meenakshi temple. Shri Vaidyanatha Aiyar and his co-workers deserve all the praise for the ceaseless effort that they have put forth in educating public opinion,[95]

The Madurai temple entry had a massive cascading effect on the state. On 9 July, the Sri Soundararaja Perumal temple, located just a few kilometres away from the Madurai temple, was opened to all Hindus irrespective of caste. Then on 16 July, the famous Tanjore Brahadeswara temple was opened. On 26 July, Sri Tirukuttalanathaswami temple near the famous Kuttalam waterfalls was opened. Then on 27 July, Sri Kasi Viswanathaswami temple in Tenkasi was opened for all Hindus irrespective of castes. All these did not happen by chance. They were well planned, as CR explained later in the Legislative Assembly. They took place in the heart of regions that were considered orthodox, 'not only..., viz., the Brahman communities are concerned, but where many other communities belonging to the non-Brahman classes as they are called, are concerned, who are equally orthodox and sometimes more orthodox.'[96] It is clear that CR and his team had done a lot of groundwork to bring about such a rapid change.

In reality, CR was very clear and realistic in his expectations. He was sure he would get the approval of the vast majority of the Hindus, including the Brahmin and non-Brahmin communities. He achieved that too. But he had no illusions about the hearty approval of the leading citadels of orthodoxy and did not mince his words when he even referred to Sankaracharyas as 'fundamentalist':

> I have no doubt whatsoever that there is no member who can say once for all that the Ahobila Mutt, the Sankarachariyars and Jeeyars, the Vanamamalai Mutt and the orthodox Hindus of India will withdraw all objection, provided you take votes and prove it, and that they would abide by that decision. I have no doubt whatsoever that there is not one man who has that capacity and the position and influence to say that on behalf of the fundamentalists.

In the debate in the legislative assembly CR who was the Premier pointed out that the rules laid down for ritualists, sculptors, carpenters, or various professions associated with the temples were not the 'the truly fundamental tenets of Hinduism' but that such principles were contained in the Vedas and Upaniṣads. He argued that the rule of social exclusion from the sacred space of the temple, which charged a 'man without guilty mind' who offers worship, as a defilement of the temple and punishes him, should be abolished. For he argued that such a custom made into a law was only 'a custom ... opposed to the principles of Hinduism ... opposed to the fundamental doctrine to which Hinduism is welded ... opposed to the welfare of society, a custom which has been converted by judge-made-law into a rigid statutory piece of legislation'.[97]

CR thus pointed to the peculiar situation that the colonial legal system had created by freezing and essentializing Hindu laws out of social stagnation. This was an argument that cardinal Hindu principles or the truly fundamental teachings of the Sanātana Dharma and the enforced laws of colonial times were at odds with each other. The temple-entry legislation achieved by CR was more organic and the triumph was civilizational, even against the deeply colonized neo-orthodoxy of his time.

Thus it may be said, far from betraying M.C. Rājāh, C. Rājagōpalachāriyār made temple entry by taking into account all dimensions: the social, the peculiar colonial legal stagnation of Hindu law and mentality,, the importance of social emancipation for national liberation, the social harmony achieved without compromising on social justice, the healing of society from the social evil of untouchability, not only by the astute manoeuvres taken by C. Rājagōpalachāriyār with his absolute conviction in social justice but also through the role of constructive, completely justified, aggressive criticism and relentless efforts of M.C. Rājāh. Today, access to temples is taken for granted by all Hindus, but this self-evident democratization of spiritual space was brought about by the greatness of such selfless individuals, all inspired in their own way by Sanātana Dharma.

Śrī Rāmakṛṣṇa-Vivēkānanda Vēdānta Movement

In South India, Śrī Rāmakṛṣṇa-Vivēkānanda Vēdānta played an important role in emancipating socially excluded communities. Here, the contributions of three saints from this stream of the Vedantic movement are presented.

Śwāmi Vipulānanda

Śwāmi Vipulānanda (1892-1947) was born on 27 March 1892 in a traditional Saivite family in Batticaloa, Sri Laṅka. His parents named him Mayilvāhanan-.

A prodigy, Śwāmi Vipulānanda passed the Cambridge examination for senior college even before turning sixteen. The same year, he became a tutor and served in that capacity for two years. With varied interests, he mastered ancient Tamil classics and the works of Shakespeare and obtained a diploma in natural sciences in 1916. During this period, he was introduced to the Vivēkānanda movement and passed the Tamil Pandit exam conducted by the Madurai Tamil Society. His chemistry lectures were popular, and he later obtained a Bachelor of Science degree from London University.

Śwāmi Vipulānanda had a transformative encounter with Śwāmi Sarvananda of Śrī Rāmakṛṣṇa Mission in Madras, who visited Sri Lanka. Pandit Mayilvahana met the Swami, which resulted in a significant change in the Tamil pandit. This encounter inspired him to dedicate himself to service and spirituality.

As a knowledgeable individual in the sciences and classical Hindu languages such as Tamil and Sanskrit, he was approached by prominent citizens to become the principal of the Hindu College. In addition to teaching chemistry, he also taught Latin and Shakespeare. Amidst all this, he also aimed to instil an appreciation for the richness of the Tamil language in his students. In 1922, Śwāmi Vipulānanda joined Śrī Rāmakṛṣṇa Math in Chennai. Shortly after, he became the editor for both the Tamil and English magazines of the Math, 'Śrī Rāmakṛṣṇa Vijayam' and 'Vedanta Kesari', respectively.

Furthermore, Śwāmi Vipulānanda was a vocal opponent of untouchability, a widespread and deeply entrenched social exclusion practice. Citing Vivēkānanda, he made his disapproval of untouchability clear in his writings:

> The first lesson which Vedanta teaches to both men and women is their potential greatness: 'The greatest error, says the Vedanta, is to say that you are weak, that you are a sinner, a miserable creature, and that you have no power. and you cannot do this or that'.... This idea arises from the knowledge of the divine in man. God is both transcendent and immanent. In His immanent aspect he is the Soul of all souls.... The true philosophy of service. Karma-Yoga was formulated by the great Swami. In his wake, modern India has earnestly taken up the work of uplifting the untouchable and the downtrodden.[98]

In his worldview 'all castes can produce exceptional individuals who rise above the conventional limitations set to the particular castes in which they were born'.: 'The Svabhava of an individual is a better criterion for determining his Svadharma. Mental attitudes and capacities may differentiate individuals more than accidents of birth and shades of colour in the complexion.'[99]

All religious binaries were to 'the vestiges of old tribal vanities'. They should go. Hinduism, to him preached the 'divinity of man, perhaps much more emphatically than any other religion does', and yet Hindus were 'branding one group of the adherents of their faith as untouchables': 'Renascent Hinduism should take immediate steps to remove the curse of untouchability and do social justice to all adherents.'[100]

What he wrote he practiced in his life.

In 1925, he returned to Sri Lanka and began giving lectures. The same year, he started a school for girls' education in Jaffna called Śārada Vidyālaya. In 1927, he organized a student conference in Jaffna and met Mahatma Gandhi, who was visiting Sri Lanka. Śwāmi Vipulānanda encouraged and organized student groups to study Tamil and Sanskrit. He believed that knowledge of Sanskrit was essential to understanding and appreciating Tamil in its depth. He established a residential school to cater to the educational needs of all sections of society, particularly the marginalized. In 1931, at the request of Rājā Sir Aṇṇāmalai Chettiār, the founder of Aṇṇāmalai University, Swami moved to the newly founded university at Chidambaram, where he provided extraordinary educational and social services. He also conducted a night school for children from the Scheduled Castes community whose families could not afford regular school education. Swami himself purchased the essential books for the children. During the convocation ceremony of 1933, while the Union Jack was hoisted on every house top, Swāmi hoisted the Śwadēsi tricolour at his residence, leading to a police investigation, which did not deter him.

Śwāmi Vipulānanda is best known for his reconstruction of ancient classical Tamil musical instruments. These instruments, well-known in the past, were lost due to various invasions and cultural changes. Their memories were preserved in ancient classical texts dating back at least 1,500 to 1,000 years. In the 1920s, he interacted with the famous Mahapadhyaya Sri U. Ve Swaminatha Iyer, the grand old man of the Tamil Renaissance who dedicatedly saved ancient classical Tamil literature. Swami combined his knowledge of music, ancient classical literature, and mathematics to recreate a working model of the ancient string instrument. His research culminated in the book *Yāzh Nūl* (The Book of Yāzh; Yāzh was the ancient lost Tamil musical instrument), which was submitted to scholars for critical evaluation and approval on 5th and 6th June 1947.

The traditional Hindu way of releasing a book took place at the Thirukollamputhūr Vilawāraṇīswara temple, which was a fitting location for the occasion. A devotee of Ganesha at this temple, named Nambiāṇdar Nambi, played a crucial role in rescuing and reorganizing the sacred Tamil literature of Vedic Saivism a thousand years ago. At the function, during the event, the reconstructed musical instruments were demonstrated by the renowned string instrument musician of that time, Ka Po Sivānandam Piḷḷai. The reconstruction and revival of traditional Tamil music by a Vēdāntic monk was a statement against the decline of music and related traditions in moralistic dogmatic religions.

He passed away on 19 July 1949, at the age of fifty-seven.[101]

Śwāmi Āgamānanda

Śwāmi Āgamānanda was born on 27 August 1896 in the prominent Nambūdiri family of Putumana Illam in Kerala.

Puthumana Nārāyaṇa Paramēswarar, his father was a prominent authority on Vēdic rituals and Puja ceremony. The name given to Āgamānanda by his parents was Krishnan Nambudiri, who also mastered Vedic chanting and rituals at a very young age. Initially, the young Krishnan was shielded from English education and received only traditional education. While studying astrology, he came into contact with Chavara Math Krishnan Asan, who was a classmate of Śrī Nārāyaṇa Guru. In 1912, the young Krishnan discovered Śwāmi Vivekananda, or more precisely his talk '*My Master*', which was about his illiterate Guru Śrī Rāmakṛṣṇa. He felt more and more attracted to his school of Vēdānta. He had previously joined a spiritual anti-idol worshipping spiritual group in Kerala. But the Śrī Rāmakṛṣṇa-Vivekananda literature offered him an alternative that was more rooted in the cultural reality of socio-spiritual life around him. He received his *Mantra-Dīkṣā* from Śwāmi Brahmānanda who was the first president of the Śrī Rāmakṛṣṇa Math. Nevertheless, he seemed to be mainly pro-caste in terms of social views. He founded a Brahmin organization for the Brahmins of Kerala. When he moved to Madras to study BA Sanskrit, he met friends who were staunch Vēdāntins of the Vivekananda tradition: Chinnu, who would later become Śwāmi Chithbavānanda, and also Avināsilṅgam Chettiār, who later became the Education Minister of Tamil Nadu. The three used to discuss spirituality and society with Śwāmi Brahmānanda at Mylapore of the Math. By 1924, Krishnan Nambūdiri was so broad-minded and out of the clutches of casteism that, as a Sanskrit scholar, he demonstrated to Gandhiji the unreliability of the work *Saṅkara Smṛti* and proved that Ādi Saṅkara could not be its author. This gave a great moral boost to the Satyagrahis in Vaikom when the above-said text was used to justify the refusal to allow the marginalized sections of Hindu society to use the roads around the temple. In 1928, he joined the Śrī Rāmakṛṣṇa Mission. Soon, he was conferred full monkhood with the name Śwāmi Āgamānanda.

He started the tradition of giving spiritual lectures at temple functions, starting with Vaikom in 1935. In his lectures, he emphasized the spiritual necessity of social emancipation. He emerged as a strong Vēdāntic voice against social stratification and stagnation. He said:

> What is the nature of the caste madness? Someone arrogates due to the birth in a certain race or group which had already lost its nobility, if it had so. It is cruel.... All these identities are in the body. If the caste is a reality, where does it exist? Can I see? The caste of human being is his humaneness, that is, 'Manushatvam'. Yet we say, 'I am the highest and you are the lowest.' This is madness. Sri Ramakrishna demonstrated that one cannot attain liberation without abandoning the caste identity. He cleaned the nightsoil of a person belonging to 'untouchable' caste. That is the beginning of Harijan upliftment.[102]

Many of Śwāmi Āgamānanda's writings and speeches on the subject are in line with those of Dr Ambedkar. They both believe that the value-based Varṇā system eventually devolved into rigidly birth-based system. In the devolving of Varṇā into a birth-based system, Śwāmi Āgamānanda sees the Pūrva Mīmāsa as having played an important role by giving primacy to rituals. He also writes that the original purpose of the system was to assimilate the various warring and even ethnically different communities and make humanity evolve spiritually. Unlike the Western civilization that destroyed entire populations of conquered people and decimated them, here Varṇā system assimilated them and made the entire society grow. In this mission over historical time the system in its 'positive, extensive and proper practice and theory, it was complete, wonderful and not found in elsewhere'. According to him, the basic philosophy of Varṇā is the 'prosperity of the weak'.[103] He completely rejected the *Smṛti* literature as authoritative due to its mutually contradictory, unreliable, and often interpolations. His earlier brush with the dubious *Saṅkara Smṛti* made him highly sensitive to the unreliable nature of this genre of literature. His aim was social transformation through education which, according to him, should be given 'to manifest the Divine which is as much shining in the downtrodden masses as in the affluent sections of the society'. If that education is given to express the complete potential then the depressed sections might accomplish great deeds than the presently affluent sections, he said.[104]

He took an active part in temple entry Satyāgraha at Vaikom and later Guruvāyūr. He gave a series of highly spiritual lectures that took the spirit and values of Advaitic Darshana to every listener irrespective of their background – from high scholars to illiterate people. The Divine, according to him, is 'eternally pure, limitless and utmost humble and can never be defiled'. So, there are no caste differences. It is among those who adore It. Vēdās, the most sacred of the Hindu sacred texts, actually permit that all can enter the sacred space to worship the Divine that is in the Deity. Any other text to the contrary can be discarded.[105] Apart from Kerala, he also campaigned for the opening of temples to all Hindus in Mysore. The sections of society in the grip of social stagnation retaliated with boards in some places declaring 'No Entry for Avarṇa and Āgamānanda.'[106]

The spiritual institutions he started centred around Kāladi, the legendary birthplace of Ādi Saṅkara. In 1936, he started at Kāladi, a Sanskrit school Brahmānandōdayam, which admitted students from marginalized communities in favoured numbers. In 1940 a Harijan students' hostel was started. Along with the school, he started Śrī Rāmakṛṣṇa Gurukulam. He admitted children, irrespective of caste, to study the Vēdās. Gupthan Nāir and Chandrasekharan Nāir, in their compilation of the work of Śwāmi Āgamānanda, explain:

> Agamananda announced that every child would became Brahmana, if they learned Veda, and he instruct the depressed children. He earned money for their food and education by begging and religious speeches throughout Kerala. The early teachers of his school were great scholars.[107]

He also went to the Harijan colony in the place called Mattur and started night schools there. An educationist extraordinary, he considered *Chintanam* (ability to contemplate and generate original thoughts), *Smriti* (good memory) and *Saṅkalpam* (willpower/determination). His Āśrama at Kāladi had three components which were Gurukulam, residential school and Vēdāntic school. He explained the purpose of each of these institutions:

> Gurukulam aims to provide proper character nourishing education to the students with both Eastern and Western knowledge systems. Vēdāntic school is unique because this is the only institution that teaches the four Vedas, six systems of philosophy, various religions, as well as western philosophies along with Eastern Darshanas in Kerala. If highest standard religious knowledge is to be disseminated we need institutions with such a vision. Āśrama also publishes the Advaitic works of Saṅkara into Malayāḷam.[108]

He emphasized Sanskrit education in a holistic way. He pointed out that it was children from poor families who came to study Sanskrit while the affluent families sent their children to English medium schools. But Sanskrit was a must for understanding Indian culture. As such, its knowledge is needed for every child, he said. To this effect, he cited what Gandhiji said in 1927 that every Hindu child should have a Sanskrit education. For Śwāmi Āgamānanda, Sanskrit studies should be supported by philanthropists, the government, and organizations like that of the followers of Śrī Nārāyaṇa Guru.

His efforts were opposed from all sides. Proselytizing Christian missionaries saw his institutions as a hindrance to their work. Hindu orthodoxy opposed a religious institution where untouchability and other caste rules were not followed. Having little support, Agamananda gave lectures, and whatever little was earned was spent for the food of then the initial six to seven students who were in the Āśram. Even in the days they had rice and vegetables they had no good cooks. During rainy days, the ashram thatched roofs leaked, and they struggled to find a place to sleep. Yet they went on overcoming the difficulties.[109] His educational efforts among the marginalized sections of the society bore fruit as Kuttappan, the first Indian Administrative Services (IAS) officer to come from the once excluded Jāthis of Kerala, came from the Harijan upliftment efforts of Śwāmi Āgamānanda.[110] It was not only in secular civil services but also in spiritual services he broke the caste barriers. He provided training and made spiritual seekers from the so-called Avarṇa Jāthis in conducting pujas. Vavakuttan Master, well known for his Sāstric knowledge and ritual excellence, was one of those pujaris trained by Śwāmi Āgamānandanda. Hailed as 'Vivēkānanda of Kēraḷa', Śwāmi Agamānanda attained Samadhi on 17 April 1961 at Kāladi.

Śwāmi Chithbavānanda

Born in a wealthy agricultural family in the Coimbatore district, Tamil Nadu, on March 11, 1898, Chinnu (the name given by their parents) was a brilliant student. The family planned to send him to London to prepare for the Indian Civil Service. When in Madras to process his passport-visa documents, he came across Śwāmi Vivēkānanda's '*Lectures from Colombo to Almora*'. The book transformed him. He changed his plans about going to London. Instead, he joined Presidency College in Madras so that he could remain in constant touch with Śrī Rāmakrishna Math in the city. In 1922, he finished his junior graduation (BA degree) and at once went to Belur Math and became a Brahmachari. In July 1926, Śwāmi Śivānanda, who was a brother-disciple of Śwāmi Vivēkānanda, bestowed complete monkhood upon Chinnu and gave him the name Chithbavānanda. This ceremony took place at Ooty, a famous hill station in Coimbatore district. Ooty became the centre of his activities or the Bhūmi of Śwāmi Chithbavānanda, where he served from 1926 to 1940. In 1930, he became the head of the Math centre at Ooty until 1940.

Even before becoming a monk, in 1921, as a student, he had the opportunity to meet with Śrī Ramaṇa Mahaṛṣi. After joining Math, the opportunity to meet with Śrī Ramaṇa Mahaṛṣi. Śwāmi Chithbavānanda explained the non-dualistic experience he had through the silence of Ramaṇa Mahaṛṣi :

> I gazed at him and he gazed back at me. What followed was indescribable. His body seemed a glass case from which a blissful brilliance streamed out. More than half an hour passed in this way. It was an experience unique and unforgettable. It confirmed [for me] Sri Ramakrishna's statement that spiritual experience can be transmitted from one person to another in the manner in which material things are handed over.[111]

Śwāmi Chithbavānanda met another spiritually realized soul Śrī Nārayana Guru in 1926. Guru showed the young sānyaśin how Vēdānta could be a great emancipating force. The young seeker had doubts about self-effort and self-surrender as they appeared contradictory to him. Guru asked him how many selves were there and directed him to study Tamil sacred text, probably of the 9th century CE, Thiruvāchagam of Saint Māṇickavāsagar. Guru also inspired Chithbavānanda to write a commentary on it. Chithbavānanda took the assignment so sincerely that it took him three and a half decades of study to write a voluminous commentary on this sacred text. Today, this commentary is considered an authoritative Advaitic commentary on Thiruvāchagam. The speciality of the commentary is that apart from Upaniṣads and other sacred texts, he also used the famous *Gospel of Sri Ramakrishna* in his commentary. An incident in the life of Guru that Chithbavānanda loved and often quoted in his lectures was about a *Nambudiri Brahmin* who asked the guru his caste; The Guru asked in return if the *Nambūdiri* could not know it by just seeing. When the *Nambūdiri* replied in negative, then the Guru said: 'If it (Jāthi) cannot be known by seeing, then how can it be known by hearing?'[112]

Thus, Śwāmi Chithbavānanda had the non-dualist or Advaitic confluence in him of Śwāmi Vivekānanda, whose non-dual universal vision galvanized the nation through his 'Practical Vedanta', Sri Ramana Maharshi, whose non-dualist, ever-abiding, and apparently withdrawn silence dissolved conflicts and spread the experience, and Sri Narayana Guru, whose non-dual experience flowered into petals of social emancipation, literary evolution, and spiritual realization for an entire region. All these made him simultaneously a spiritual visionary and socio-spiritual missionary. His meeting with V.V.S. Iyer, who was a great educationist, also highly inspired Śwāmi Chithbavānanda. Though, because of the untimely death of Iyer, the interaction lasted only for a brief period, it left its impact on Śwāmi Chithbavānanda, who was then just a brahmachāri. V.V.S. Iyer was so impressed by the youth that he almost indicated him to be the heir of his educational work. Śwāmi Chithbavānanda had also interacted with Śwāmi Vipulānanda, who was also an educationist. This influence also shaped him as an educationist.

When in Ooty, he worked mainly with the Baduga tribal community and Scheduled Castes community children. Despite the lack of transportation facilities, Śwāmi used to walk to Baduga villages early in the morning. He never criticized or judged their habits, which earned him great goodwill within the tribal community. At Ooty, he held weekly classes for the Scheduled Castes community children and conducted night schools for illiterate adults, with an average attendance of fifty.

Avināsiliṅgam Cheṭṭiyār, a philanthropist inspired by Vivēkānanda Vēdānta, wanted to start an orphanage and a school. He sought advice from Śwāmi Chithbavānanda, and on the auspicious Vijayadasami day, 12 October 1929, they began planning. On 3 February 1930, Śrī Rāmakrishna Vidyālayā was launched. Its first enrolled student was a boy from the Scheduled Castes community. In 1934, the institution was officially affiliated with Śrī Rāmakrishna Mission. The school admitted students of all castes. Despite facing difficulties due to the frequent arrests of its main donor, Avināsiliṅgam Cheṭṭiyār, for his association with the Gandhian freedom movement, Chithbavānanda ensured the steady development of the school into a vibrant educational institution. In 1934, Gandhiji visited the Madras Presidency as part of his untouchability eradication program. His constant travels and lack of proper sleep had greatly affected his health.

In 1934, Gandhiji visited Madras Presidency as part of his untouchability eradication programme. The constant travels and lack of proper sleep had greatly affected his health, and he needed to take a break at the hill station Coonoor, very close to Ooṭy, between 30 January and 5 February. During this time, the young monk wanted to meet him, and ten minutes were allocated for their discussion. The conversation was brief and revolved around Varṇāśrama.

The young monk asked Gandhiji if Varṇā was based on birth. Gandhiji agreed affirmatively, stating that birth-based Varṇā was a reality, but discrimination in civil life was criminal, and the notions of superiority and inferiority were sinful. However, Śwāmi Chithbavānanda completely rejected this notion of birth-based Varṇā, emphasizing that Varṇā was purely individualistic and not based on birth, a concept that was emphasized by

Śwāmi Vivēkānanda. Śwāmi Chithbavananda told Gandhiji that even four children born to the same parents would not belong to the same Varṇā. Among the siblings, one could be a Brähmanā, another Śūdra and yet another Vaiśyā or Kṣatriya based on their innate nature and manifest behaviour. Although Gandhiji did not agree at that time, he later completely repudiated the birth-based notion of Varṇā. However, he agreed to visit the works of the Mission in and around Ooty.[113]

On the evening of 4 February, Gandhiji arrived at Ooṭy Math. The students, who were mostly from Scheduled Castes communities, performed bhajan in which Gandhi participated. Śwāmi Chithbavānanda then took him to Śrī Dakshiṇāmūrti Pītham or Math at Kānthal, a small place. In the previous generation, the Math was reigned by Ādimūla Śwāmi, a saint who, before monkhood, was from the so-called 'untouchable' caste. The Pītham traced its origin to Ādi Saṅkara and Vidyaraṇya and was called Asala Pītham. After his demise, it was looked after by Śrī Ōm Prakāsa Śwāmigaḷ, with whom Śwāmi Chithbavānanda was in close contact. Here the teachings and personality of Śrī Ōm Prakāsa Śwāmigaḷ need to be briefly looked into.

Non-Exclusive Network of Saṅkara Non-Dualism

Śrī Ōm Prakāsa Śwāmigaḷ was a great Vēdāntin who initiated many people across Tamil Nadu into the path of self-realization. He himself was initially guided and inspired by Saṅghu Siddha Sivaliṅga Nāyanār (1835-1900). Saṅghu Siddha Sivaliṅga Nāyanār was born to a Brahmin father and a Scheduled Castes community mother. He worked as a house assistant in the house of a Britisher named Simpson, who was a director in a firm called Benny and Company in colonial Madras. The Britisher seemed to have understood the deep spiritual nature of his house-help. The household members also seemed to have experienced a few miraculous events. Saṅghu Siddha Sivaliṅga

Nāyanār had as his Guru Kaṇṇudaya Vaḷḷalār, who had written a treatise on self-realization called 'Ozhiviloduukam'. His time was estimated to be around the 15th century. The text speaks of pure non-dualism. Kaṇṇudaya Vaḷḷalār strongly indicated that he was the disciple of Thiru Jñāna Sambandar, the 6th-century Śaiva mystic-poet. Saṅghu Siddha Sivaliṅga Nāyanār had both Thiru Jñāna Sambandar and Kaṇṇudaya Vaḷḷalār as his inner Gurus and practiced his sadhana. Soon disciples from all sections of the society came to him. Sanghu Nayanar wrote in the form of Tamil verses about his spiritual experiences, titled Pūraṇānanthōthayam. Śrī Satchitānanda Śwāmigaḷof Indra Pītham, who adheres to the Ādi Saṅkara lineage, gave a benedictory verse to this work. Indra Pītham traced its lineage to Ādi Saṅkara and Dattātrēya and had as its acharya, the meritorious of the disciples of the presiding acharya irrespective of Jāthi.[114]

Śrī Ōm Prakāsa Śwāmigaḷ was initiated by Saṅghu Siddha Sivaliṅga Nāyanār. Unfortunately, the life and teachings of Sri Om Prakasa Swamigaḷ are not well-known to the outside world, except to a small circle of his disciples and their gnostic descendants. He wrote treatises on Advaita, one of which is 'Śrī Satsambāshiṇi', written in 1915 in the form of a dialogue between a seeker and a guru. It is a catechism text for Hindu spirituality that brings together various traditions with a liberal harmonizing of modern science. Śrī Śwāmigaḷ living in a remote mountain village in South India's colonial wilderness, effortlessly combined the wisdom of the Upanishads and the knowledge of Thomas Huxley in his exposition of Dharma. Though a misattributed quote, Śrī Śwāmigaḷ was surprisingly open to the science of evolution. His followers had established 'Asala pītha ulōkōpakāra Vidyādhāna Sabhā' (association for the distribution service of wisdom for world welfare) and published his works. In this, they were supported by the disciple of Śrī Karapāthira

Śivaprakāsa Śwāmigaḷ who was Brahma Śrī Kāsivāsi Sivānanda Yatindra Śwāmi.[115]

His disciple Śrī Jñāna Yōgi Ratna Śatguru (1905-86) wrote a traditional commentary for the works of his guru, titled 'Satha Prakaraṇam'. This work contains a critique of the notion of birth and body-based varṇa and was published posthumously:

> Is the notion of one being Brähmanā – the 'Brähmanthva' – an outcome of the manifest body? If so the manifest body is also present for those who are called the Śūdra. If it is the tuft of hair and the sacred thread, then it is also universally seen in communities like the carpenters, Chetty, Vaiśyā. Is it because of the body components? There different names for different body parts. So one should realise that the notions of higher Varṇa including considering one as Brähmanā etc., is more like the name-calling child-play than the real attribute at any time to Ātman. Understanding this completely eliminate the differences practiced in the name of Jāthi, Varṇa, sect etc.[116]

Gandhi was impressed by the sanctity of Math and registered his pleasure regarding the way the age-old institution was functioning. After having heard completely apartheid-like strictures against the socially marginalized communities in the name of Ādi Saṅkara in Kēraḷa, it should have been a great joy for Gandhi to see such flourishing Advaitic schools of Ādi Saṅkara which did not care about even Jāthi leave alone untouchability. It should have been the greatest proof that untouchability had nothing to do with religion and was not central in any way to the practice of Sanātana Dharma. The intention of Chithbavānanda in taking Gandhiji to this Math was perhaps to make him see for himself that Brahminhood exists across birth-based communities and was more an individualistic phenomenon. The Swami then took him to the Vinayagar temple at Kodappamund. Gandhi declared the temple open to all Hindus, including 'the Harijans'.[117]

Charting His Path: Education and Emancipation

After the samadhi of his Guru Śwāmi Śivānanda and the passing of other direct disciples of Śrī Rāmakrishna, Śwāmi Chithbavānanda Chithbavananda established Śrī Rāmakrishna Tapōvanam at a place called Thirupparaitturai, on the banks of River Cauvery. Here, he led the temple entry movement of socially excluded communities despite facing strong resistance.[118] In his various writings, he emphasized the need to remove social stratification infringing on the religio-spiritual space. He rejected the belief that women and the Shudras should not recite the Gāyatri Mantra. In a paper explaining the Mantra, he stated that these restrictions arose during a time of societal stagnation. He pointed out that Śrī Rāmakrishna considered Sāradā Dēvi as 'Para Jñāna Satguru' and initiated disciples based on their inner spiritual quality and not their caste. He argued that the restrictions on the Śūdra and women with regard to the Gāyatri Mantra should be abolished and that it should be considered the national mantra, accessible to all, regardless of caste or gender.[119]

While court cases have been fought about whether or not a Śūdra has a right to monkhood, Śwāmi Chithbavānanda categorically declared that those who have the notion of caste superiority are ineligible for monkhood. He wrote:

> When Śwāmi Vivekānanda was a wondering monk, he visited a famous traditional monastery and started a dialogue with the head of the monastery. The conversation was in Sanskrit. The first question that the head of the monastery asked was what Jāthi Śwāmi belonged to. Vivēkānanda silently left the place. A person who asks about the Jāthi of a monk, according to him, was neither a monk nor a Vēdāntin. We should remember this. .... A person who holds on to the feeling of Jāthi could never be a monk. He should be above this imaginary notion of caste with which society has conditioned one. He should be above all sectarianism.[120]

Regarding the concept of Varṇāśrama and regarding the Brahma Śūtra commentators citing Smṛti and Dharmaśāstra and calling the birth-based Śūdra as not only ineligible for Vēdāntic knowledge but similar to a bipedal crematorium, Śwāmi Chithbavānand rejected such notions categorically:

> In the universe all life moves towards the ultimate Truth. The purpose of Vēdāntā is to help such all life wherever necessary. Belittling any life or any aspect, or preventing the knowledge cannot be the doctrine of Vēdāntā. Many thousand years Vēdāntā has been helping all life in many stages of spiritual development to realise spiritual life of self-realisation in appropriate ways. Hindu religion or Vēdāntā recognises discrimination in authority for handling of Vēdāntic knowledge. Instead of feeding the Brahma Vidyā uniformly each person should be given the knowledge depending upon the internalising strength of the individual. This system has worked successfully for all these thousand years, in imparting spiritual knowledge to all. Vedas have two parts – Karma Kāṇdam and Jñāna Kāṇdam. In entering Karma Kāṇdam a person needs to be qualified for it. He should have Samskārā. Upanayanam channelises the person towards the target (of self-realisation). Among such channelised disciples the foremost is the Brahmin, the next comes Kshatriya and finally the Vaishya. One who is in no way qualified is the Sudra. These are the four categories which are present in all societies. Understanding this and handing the methods is how the wise impart knowledge. This is the fourfold Varṇa system. A person incapable of doing good deeds on one's own initiative, who is dull-headed, who is always immersed in sadness is called a Sudra. He does not have the capacity to follow the rules of Karma. So a Sudra is not an authority for Vedic Karma. This is not based on birth. This is not to nurture the sectarian divide. This is the mere acceptance of the difference in spiritual and mental capacity of individuals. In whatever clan one is born, a person can acquire all divine godly characters and can become verily an Avataric human. Kṛṣṇa Himself was in the clan of shepherds and Ṛṣis hail Him

> as God Himself. So birth can never be an obstacle for a Hindu in acquiring spiritual knowledge.... So when Brahma Sutra says that the Shudra is not eligible for Vēdāntic knowledge, there is meaning. A person who is not enriched in one's Guṇa and Karma, can never be a spiritual authority. But Guna and Karma are not decided by birth. His/her character and work alone can decide his/her the stage of spiritual evolution. Classification of Varṇas as per birth is completely incompatible with (Vēdāntic) philosophy. If one looks at the world then one will understand this. Birth based arrogation of spiritual knowledge has no place in the Upanishads.[121]

Then he goes on to explain how the commentators of Brahma Śūtra are wrong and disproves their logic with their own sacred texts:

> When the commentator (of *Brahma Sūtra*) wrote that because (Satyakāmā) spoke the truth, he should be a Brahmin, without realising the commentator had conceded that character and not birth was the basis of Brahminhood, though he tries to prove it to the contrary. In the 38th Sūtra it is said that because Smṛti objects to the access of *Vēdātyayana* (ceremonial recital of Vēdās), *Vēdic Karma* (*Vēdic* ritual – here this means authority to conduct *Vēdic* ritual) and *Brahma Jñāna* (Gnosis of Brahman) are denied to the *Śūdras*. Here by *Smṛti* the commentator does not mean *Śrīmad Bhagavat Gīta* but mostly *Manu Smṛti*. Such *Smṛtis* state that molten tin or lac should be poured into the ears of the Śūdra who hears the *Vēdās*. They state that as *Śūdra* is a bipedal crematorium (as he by himself is a defiled space), *Vēdātyayana* should not be performed by his side. They also say if a *Śūdra* recites the Vēdā, his tongue shall be cut off; if he commits it to memory, his body shall be split asunder etc. Then how did Vidura and Dharmavyada attained Vēdāntic liberation? The commentators explain that away by stating that it was the *Puṇya* of good Karma of past lives. But *Smṛtis* also say that all are *Śūdra* by birth and that it was only through *Samskāras* (can ambiguously mean rituals or good deeds) that one becomes

> twice-born (*Dwija*). Perhaps the commentator has forgotten this. Similarly the *Smṛti* considers Śūdra as cremation ground (*Śmaśāna*) and hence disallows *Vēdātyayana* to him. But is cremation ground really defiled as *Smṛti* and commentators lead us to believe? It is *Rudra Bhūmi*. It is a sacred space. In fact, one can consider it a more sacred space than the world where worldly bonded people live. *Śmaśāna* is indeed where Śiva dwells. So to say that there *Vēdātyayana* should not be performed is similar to saying that it cannot recited in the presence of Śiva.... In fact, entire *Kāsi Kshetra* is called *Mahā Śmaśāna*. There dead bodies are burnt all the time. *Yatī*s consider it as the most suitable place for their *Sādhana*. Now to claim that *Kāsi* is *Mahā Śmaśāna* and hence *Vēdātyayana* should not be conducted there is obviously nonsense. On the other hand, *Kāsi Kshetra* has been the traditional seat of *Vēdic* and *Vēdāntic* learning. If one looks deeply then the *Yatī*s and not *Śūdras* who should be considered as *Śmaśāna* because the monks offer themselves *binḍā* – food offered to the dead people – and declare their own death. Thus to all wordly thinks a *Yatī* is considered a dead body. Hence there are traditions where, he is not even allowed in worldly auspicious events like marriages. Then by *Smṛti* injunction *Vēda* recital cannot happen near a *Yatī*. Such a rule is explicitly meaningless.[122]

Charged with the mission of spreading Śrī Rāmakrishna-Vivēkānanda Vēdānta throughout South India during a time of clashes between Dravidianist racial pseudo-rationalism and casteism as pseudo-spirituality, Śwāmi Chithbavānanda took on the challenge. He established Gurukul-style educational institutions offering education from pre-school to PhD level, with 64 schools and seven colleges providing quality and affordable education for all. In the residential schools he founded, Śwāmi Chithbavānanda developed a system to overcome the occupation-based notions of superiority, which was one of the cornerstones of casteism. To this day, the residential students take turns doing tasks such as cleaning toilets, serving food in dining halls, and participating in temple services attached to the schools. This was designed to eliminate any notions of superiority or inferiority based on occupation, thus combatting caste-based notions of superiority. Another innovative concept he introduced was 'Anthar Yōgam', where families could come together for day-long spiritual discourses and Bhajans at various locations, providing a cost-effective form of spiritual retreat. It was a cost-effective spiritual resort, even before the term 'resort', etc., was in currency. They helped ordinary men and women to get the highest spiritual inputs, and this democratized spirituality to a great extent.

A life in *Advaita* lived and hailed by people of Tamil Nadu as *Mahā Śwāmi, Brahma Jñāni* and true Paramācharyendra of Śrī Rāmakṛṣṇa-Vivēkānanda Vēdānta, Śwāmi Chithbavānanda attained Mahā Samādhi on 16 November 1985. He was the greatest living phenomenon of an all-inclusive humanistic Advaita in 20th-century Tamil Nadu.

CHAPTER 15

Kārmic Fatalism versus Dhārmic Entrepreneurial Activism

One of the consistent and most powerful imprints of colonialism in the collective psyche of Indians is the attribution of fatalism to Hinduism and the altruism to colonial religious institutions. Even after independence, this image is strong in the minds of Indians. While at the academic levels, there has been critique of the fatalistic character of Indian society, it has not percolated into the common mind of the powerful English-speaking elite sections which control the media, Indian academia, and polity. So, it is common to see praise for the educational and medical services of the proselytizing religions, often contrasting this to an assumed Hindu indifference. From economic growth to philanthropic work, Hinduism is seen as a civilizational obstacle to human emancipation. This chapter studies the continued depiction of Karmic fatalism characterization and also how even during the colonial times, this stereotyping was challenged by the deeds of typically Hindu entrepreneurs with characteristically Hindu approaches to serving humanity, and how they have far-reaching consequences for human emancipation, often taken for granted, ignored or even distorted in the narrative building. The instances given are from South India. But it is an indicator that it should have been an all-Indian phenomenon.

Karma and Humanitarianism

In Western and Westernized social science worldviews, the concept of karma is more often seen as a fatalistic principle of Hinduism. Although there have been significant academic challenges to this view, the prevailing perspective is that Hindu social values, through karma, hinder the progress of society by promoting fatalism and social inertia. The influence of German sociologist Max Weber (1864-1920), who wrote critically about the impact of Indian religion on its society, is still evident in the media and academia despite academic criticisms and empirical rejections of the negative impact thesis on Hinduism.

Weber's legacy continued well into the post-colonial period through the work of Swiss economist Gunnar Myrdal (1898-1987), who stated that he knew 'of no instance of present-day South Asia where religion has induced social change'.[1]

These views, both colonial as well as post-colonial, have faced significant criticism from a significant number of scholars who are yet a minority in terms of numbers and influence in the academia. So, these views have remained as the dominant view both in academia and media. This is also true in the case of the influential and growing English-speaking elite in India. The persistent nature of the memetic complex which can be called 'India's civilizational deficiency of religion's fatalism' is indeed quite powerful even as these lines are written.

In recent times, particularly after globalization, this view has been contested strongly in the public sphere. For example, Gurcharan Das critiqued such theories of colonial vintage still lingering as almost received wisdom in his book *India Unbound*:

> In my experience, successful Hindu entrepreneurs can be both extremely religious and aggressive in business. The Indian farmer responds quickly to market-based incentives, as the green revolution demonstrates. Brahmins will plow their own land in traditional Uttar Pradesh if they have to,

> and conservative Rajput Thakurs in Rajasthan will shed their feudal ways for the sake of a commercial opportunity. Moreover, there are substantial non-Hindus in India and these communities have also been stuck in the same rut of stagnation. Other Asian countries such as China and Indonesia were equally backward, but they had no 'Hindu equilibrium' to explain away their stagnation. I cannot help but conclude that these cultural stereotypes, and the dirigiste prescriptions that flow from them, stem from a paternalism bordering on contempt for the masses of the Third World. How could these wretched and ignorant peasants behave like rational consumers and producers of classical economics? But they do behave in that way, as empirical evidence has shown beyond doubt. The 1982 Development Report of the World Bank points out, 'All farmers – small, medium, and large – respond to economic incentives. Far from being "tradition-bound peasants," farmers have shown that they share a rationality that far outweighs differences in their social and ecological conditions.'[2]

Economist Surendra Kaushik (1944-2014) gives a visionary yet robust cultural explanation for the much-maligned so-called Hindu rate of growth (HRG), pointing it to be a value-driven 'sustainable growth rate for the world economy':

> The HRG, made famous by Indian economist Raj Krishna, is true just in the first fifty years of independent India following the previous ninety years, the British Raj (1858-1947) but for the Indian economy in the long run. The belittling expression HRG refers to the low annual growth rate of the socialist economy of India before 1991, which was around 3.5 percent from the 1950s to the 1980s, while per capita income growth averaged 1.3 percent. We are not advocating low rates for India, the United States, or the world. Rather, our focus is on reality and not empty dreams, not to mention externalities (destructive results of high growth rates) on the environment, quality of life, and indeed the sustainability of life on earth,

because of carbon dioxide (CO2) and other threats to the planet.

He then outlines ten salient features of Hindu civilization. He suggests that these features if positively influenced by the global economy in an inclusive manner rather than through competition, would lead to a sustained growth rate and usher in holistic wealth for all. These ten Hindu values for sustainable economic growth are as follows:

> (1) a global perspective in thinking; (2) open and welcoming migratory culture; (3) a long view of time-space; (4) an inquisitive and open mind and knowledge-based enterprises; (5) an accepting, assimilating, and tolerant society; (6) reciprocity and exchange based on specialization; (7) an expanding view of self; (8) acceptance of controlled aggression; (9) greater importance placed on knowledge-based enterprises; and (10) satisfaction from balance between the spiritual, mental, and physical lives.... The evidence is clear, in applying the above analysis to India, that nearly all its progress is in knowledge-based activities and industries.... Building up human capital and operation of market forces support from social, political, and business institutions is to economic progress in India in its long and sustainable journey as part of the global family.[3]

Computer scientist and author Kentaro Toyama pointed out the intrinsic individual Hindu capacity for self-emancipation that he witnessed in Indian cab drivers. He suggested that if Max Weber were born a hundred years later and 6,000 kilometres southeast, he might have overlooked Protestant worldly asceticism as the cause of the rational industry. Instead, Weber might have pointed to a Hindu ethic emphasizing uncomplainingly working at the task at hand.[4]

When Weber's argument is expanded to encompass ethics and humanistic values, which manifest in social life as 'charity' and philanthropy, the criticism takes the following form: indifference because karma makes Hindus indifferent to the suffering of people. This view is not superficial and is deeply ingrained even in modern academics who reject Christianity. Ray Billington (1930-2012), a self-declared 'Christian heretic', served as a Methodist minister for nineteen years before embracing existential philosophy and rejecting core Christian beliefs. He wrote the following passage in 1997 in his introduction to Eastern philosophy:

> At a purely practical level, any observer of the Indian scene may, not unfairly, point out that one is more likely to find missions for the down-and-outs run by Christians than by Hindus. The Christian explanation is simple: their religion lays more emphasis on caring for others than does Hinduism, whether in their sacred writings or through their traditions. Like it or not, the apologia concludes, Christianity is at heart both more altruistic and less fatalistic than Hinduism.... The nub of the argument is that if a philosophy of life or a religion has as its outcome a cool indifference to others' needs, it thereby loses points in the benevolence league table, which downgrades it as a religion.... So far as the above suggestion is concerned, that the eradication of poverty in India is, like the removal of the caste system, stalemated by the doctrine of karma there may well be a case.[5]

In the *Encyclopedia of World Poverty*, there is an entry on 'Hinduism and Poverty'. The entry, authored by two Hindu scholars, Rashmi Gupta and Vijayan K Pillay, from the University of Texas, is substantial and authentic:

> Within the Hindu tradition how much wealth a person possesses is subject to three principles of sustainability: *Yajna*, *Dhana*, and *Tapas*, meaning 'sacrifice,' 'giving,' and 'penance'. In sum, Hinduism is a philosophy of life.... Second is *Dhana*, giving. This is replenishment of society.... *Dhana* is not only the little gift

> one gives to the poor. We need to contribute to society through giving money, labor, intelligence, time—any resources a person has. This maintains the ecology of society. If society is based on *Dhana*, there will never be poverty, exploitation, or deprivation. Individuals are free to pursue wealth and sensual pleasure so long as they behave morally and ethically. Hinduism does not advocate a life of poverty. According to the Mahabharatha, 'there is no poverty for the industrious' and 'poverty is a state of sinfulness'. Therefore Hinduism promotes moderation and good *Karma* (deeds).[6]

Three hundred and odd pages later, in the same encyclopaedia, under a more neutral entry, 'Normative Standards' we find the following:

> In Hinduism poverty is viewed as the just deserts or the working-out of the law of karma. The person who is poor is suffering from the effects of past deeds. It is therefore not the duty of a Hindu or other adherents to Eastern religions to reduce the suffering of the poor by charity.... In Christianity, which preaches salvation by the grace of God through the atoning death of Jesus Christ, good works have no saving merit. However, they are considered a sign of the faith of the true believer. Some of the gravest condemnation for false belief in the New Testament is reserved for those who professed faith but ignored the needs of the thirsty, the hungry, the naked, children, orphans, widows or others in need. Social justice and charity are thus considered in Christianity to be good works, and are expected because they are a sign of a grateful heart thanking the Savior for the gift of salvation.[7]

It is evident that colonial stereotypes still persist in academia, which is dominantly influenced by the worldview of theo-colonialism. Indigenous religions, particularly Hinduism (being the only pagan-like family of indigenous religions), are often perceived as spiritually and humanistically inferior to Christianity and Islam.

This perception has its roots in colonial-evangelical stereotypes of Hindus as carriers of fatalistic and uncaring beliefs for more than three millennia. However, at least some rare observations refute such stereotypes. One example is John Howison (1797–1859), an assistant surgeon with the East India Company's military service, who extensively travelled in both India and Canada.

> While we condemn the ostentatious extravagance of the Hindoos on their marriages and at public festivals, and their general improvidence in the management and disposal of their fortunes, we must at the same time view with admiration the noble use to which they often apply their riches. In every part of India are to be found monuments of the munificence and charity of private individuals, in the shape of reservoirs for water, pagodas, wells, or caravanseras; but, of whatever description these may be, they are invariably intended for the benefit of mankind. He who expends thousands in the formation of a tank which shall supply with water thousands of his fellow-creatures, who would otherwise be liable to suffer the greatest extremities from drought, surely deserves the name of a benefactor of the human race; as also does he that builds a house for the shelter and convenience of travellers in some desolate spot where no other accommodation is to be found. Works of public charity are so much esteemed by the Hindoos, that those who cannot accomplish them on a large scale, will sometimes hire a person to sit under a tree by the roadside, with vessels of cool water for the supply of thirsty passengers; or will monthly, on a particular day, give a quantity of grain to every mendicant who may present himself at their doors. Yet the detractors of the Hindoos do not hesitate to assert that all their acts of this kind proceed from ostentation. I will reply to this only by remarking, that it would be well if a similar spirit of ostentation could be introduced into Europe, since it is attended with such happy effects in Hindostan. But a man may travel from the southern extremity of the continent to the polar regions without observing one monument of charity or utility

which has been devised or erected by private munificence. What European nobleman or wealthy citizen ever thinks of expending his money in the construction of any work of art which shall benefit a whole town or village, or call forth the blessings and admiration of the passing traveller?[8]

He contrasts the way an average 'Hindoo' spends a higher proportion of his wealth on public institutional charities than an average rich European. However, as shall be seen, the entrepreneurial success and related philanthropy of Hindus, which could have had an effect on social emancipation, were suppressed in their institutional evolution due to their adaptation to changing modernity and unique colonial circumstances. Author and inter-religious studies scholar Edmund Weber explains how this mindset was created:

It is indeed a horrible falsification of history what happened to the Hindu traditional charity. The propaganda of the colonial missionaries and churches didn't want to admit the vast charitable activities, customs and institutions of Hindu seva. They wanted to show that only their Christianity was able to do charitable work, following the rule of nara seva while the Hindus had in mind only narayana seva, serving God. This propaganda was very successful so that even Hindus educated in Christian schools and coming from less poor background believed that prejudice. They didn't realise that the missionaries were coming from a rich country, rich because it exploited the crown jewel of the empire, Hindustan. The Western research has shown that the wealth of the British was coming from the subcontinent. Therefore, it is indeed very cynical to impoverish a country and to keep down a people by force and then complaining poor conditions of the Hindu society and its alleged lack of interest to help the needy ones. Although the traditional system of charity was under permanent pressure of the system of colonial exploitation it still worked.[9]

Here instances are presented of how Hindu entrepreneurship did not remain passive but struggled under colonialism. Given the stifling circumstances, they achieved considerable and even extraordinary success and, through a characteristically Hindu way, substantially contributed to social emancipation.

Gazulu Lakshminarasu Chetty

The Governor of Madras, George Hay, Eighth Marquess of Tweeddale, was agitated and turning red with anger. 'How is this even possible?' The dark-skinned 'Hindoo heathens of Madras' had made the great British administration a laughingstock. A secret agent working for the 'Hindoos' was working secretly right within the premises of the fort of St George! Governor Tweeddale, as he was called by the 'natives', wrung his hands. The plan was confidential. The British East India Company (EIC), only a facade for the Crown itself, would benefit immensely from it. It would strengthen their emotional and institutional hold on the natives thoroughly. More important than all this – it was the moral and spiritual obligation of the very presence of the British in the infidel land of Hindoostan. But the plan got exposed to the public because of this secret agent inside. All the Governor's men still could not find out the agent working for the 'Hindoos' inside Governor's fort.

The year 1847 was not going exactly right for Hay.

The process of promoting evangelism in Madras went smoothly at first, but now it had turned into a major scandal. He knew who was responsible for this. A confidential document, which proposed including the Bible as a mandatory part of the curriculum at Madras University, was leaked by a 'native' tri-lingual newspaper *Crescent*. This newspaper was run by a 'Hindoo' who had no formal education, at least not education in the British sense.

Gazulu Lakshminarasu Chetty (1806-1868) was a name that struck fear into every EIC administrator in India. Born in 1806, his exact date of birth is not known. as he was not the kind to celebrate his birthday. As a Gomati (also Komati) Chetty born to a Hindu merchant-class family, he received traditional education for his trade. At that time, British rule had already been established in South India, particularly around Madras. Chetty taught himself English and then entered the cotton trade by taking advantage of the trade feuds between America and Britain. He believed that creating wealth (artha) was his duty (dharma) and spending it for betterment of the society was his dharmic way to liberation (moksha).

In colonial Madras, two powerful emerging British institutions were targeting Hindus for proselytizing. Access to governmental services led many families to admit their children to missionary-run schools instead of traditional educational systems like the 'thinnai schools'. In the missionary-run schools, children were made targets of proselytising by the missionaries. The situation was even worse in the courtrooms, where magistrate enquiries sometimes turned into evangelical gatherings attended by powerful individuals of the colonial administration. If at all any judge opposed these unethical acts of promoting evangelical beliefs, they would face repercussions from the authorities.

And it was with such men of power that this peaceful-looking man, wearing a turban and a prominent Vaishnavaitemark on his forehead, had decided to confront, pouring in all his hard-earned wealth into the battle he had taken up. The people he clashed with were the most influential individuals in the Madras of colonial times.

- Sir William Burton, judge of the Madras Sadr Court, who made clear his missionary bias by occasionally delivering evangelical lectures from his seat in the courtroom to the Hindus on trial.

- J.F. Thomas, the chief secretary to the government at the time, who almost made it an unwritten policy that government appointments would be made to those Hindus who converted to Christianity.
- E.B. Thomas, a close relative of J.F. Thomas, who as the collector of Thirunelvelly (Tirunelveli), favoured a policy of rampant Christian conversion.
- William A. Morehead, district judge of Chengalpattu, who would even suspend the court proceedings to have an open-house evangelical preaching
- Finally, as we saw at the beginning of this section, the governor himself.[10]

On 2 October 1844, forty-one years before the formation of the Indian National Congress, Chetty published the first issue of the *Crescent* (*Matiyam*), aiming 'the amelioration of the condition of the Hindus'.[11] Chetty's trusted friend, Edward Harley, a former naval officer and a Hinduphile, became the editor of *Crescent*. This remarkable achievement took place in the prevailing colonial atmosphere. The magazine was published three times a month in Tamil, English, and Telugu and had a wide network of reporters, even within the government premises, including British sympathizers of Hindus.

Reporters and planted informers often obtained confidential plans made by colonial administrators aimed at subverting Hinduism and Hindu society. These plans were published under various noms de plume such as 'Vindex' and 'Plain Speaking Man'. In one issue, *Crescent* published a confidential government document outlining plans to use surplus revenue from Hindu temples for government expenditures. The magazine also published the minutes of the meeting of the Governor, which detailed plans to introduce the Bible as a class book in provincial schools and the Madras University. This was the incident mentioned at the beginning of this section.[12]

It was made clear by the colonial administration that only through English education could a government job be obtained. Then it was made clear again that those in the government who had access to state power were vastly superior to their non-English educated counterparts. This led to a strong demand for English education in the Madras province, particularly in the urban centres. Madras University had been established to further this cause. Missionaries and their facilitators had absolute access to the inner workings of the university, including framing exam questions with a clear Christian theological bias. Those who could not answer them were denied government appointments.

When a high number of native students failed to qualify for government jobs despite their education, it was suggested to introduce the Bible as a solution to this problem. Chetty not only exposed the designs of the governor but also convened a public meeting on 7 October 1846 at the Pachaiyappa institution. He presided over the meeting himself. Following the meeting, a memorandum was created to describe how the actions of the governor betrayed religious neutrality and included 'unscrupulous violations of these sacred pledges during the regime of the Marquis of Tweeddale'. The memorandum also documented how missionaries prevented unconverted 'natives' from passing competitive examinations, the 'active co-operation of government officials with missionaries', and the conversion policy of the missionaries. This expose, along with the public meeting and memorandum. shocked the government. One gentleman, Henry Chamier, a senior member of the governor's council, stated that the acts of the government had been perceived 'as serious blows aimed at the religion of the people and as the breaches of faith on the part of the government'.[13]

It was a warning, he cautioned the company-proxy-British government, that it should not incite popular movements by its own neglect. An investigation was conducted regarding the leaked documents, and a few were suspended. To catch all the informers, the office of *Crescent* was put under heavy police surveillance. The government attempted to suppress the magazine by denying it 'the smallest privileges' that were given to missionary publications. When the magazine's manager submitted an advertisement for insertion in the *Fort St George Gazette*, it was returned as inadmissible, with the chief secretary to the government saying that it was 'of a character not usually inserted'. The colonial authorities alleged that Chetty's speech at the Pachaiyappa institution and the subsequent proceedings that followed 'were calculated to foster a rebellious spirit in the audience and to wean the allegiance of the Hindus away from their British Rulers'. The sheriff of Madras, who was present at the gathering, tried his level best to dissuade the people from signing the memorandum but failed.[14]

In the 1840s, in the Tirunelvēli district of southern Tamil Nadu, Hindu resistance to missionary proselytizing erupted in the form of a '*Vibūti* protest'. This protest involved smearing the Hindu holy ash on the foreheads of transgressing evangelists by Hindus. Soon, a 'Vibhuti Society' was also formed by the Hindus in Tirunelveli. While the British colonialists supported the missionaries, local Hindus in the state formed their own support base. A society called Chatur-Veda Siddhanta Society was established, with its own printing press, the Kalvi Kalanchiam Press (located at 14 Salay Street, near the Ganesha temple, Madras). It was started by Umāpati Muthaliyār. These organizations supported the Hindus who resisted proselytizing and were arrested by EIC government. In a majority verdict of two judges, one of whom was Malcolm Lewin, it was ordered that the arrested Hindus be released. However, one Judge, G.J.

Waters, a fanatical Christian, upheld the arrest of Hindu prisoners. Subsequently, the governor, who was 'far away in Ootacamund ... then took a step without precedent even in the chequered history of Fort St George'. He dismissed the judges and overturned the judgement of the acquittal of Tirunelveli Hindus.[15] Chetty joined hands with Umāpati Muthaliyār and organized protests and collected signatures in a memorandum.

The unique feature of the protests led by Chetty was the natural and easy demonstration of the mastery of secular democratic values and methodology by Chetty. An eminent Malaysian historian, who specialized in the Indian freedom struggle in South India, explains the peculiarity of the movement that Chetty started:

> Here was a Hindu meeting of a new kind. In contrast to caste gatherings, which had traditionally regulated the Internal workings of the Hindus, this was an overtly political demonstration attended by Hindus of different caste and sectarian affiliations in which the wider Implications of an act of public policy were debated. Moreover, this was the first known Hindu gathering In Madras which had all the trappings of a modern political protest meeting: the permission of the sheriff of Madras was secured; a chairman was elected to conduct the meeting; a number of resolutions were passed; and a memorial was approved and signed for submission to the government. The credit for all this belonged to Lakshmanarasu Chetty, a new kind of Hindu leader who was perhaps the first to adopt the Western forms of political protest in South India.[16]

Finally, the tireless toils of Chetty secured a victory for the Hindus. The *Narrative of the Celebration of the Jubilee of Queen Victoria in the Presidency of Madras* (compiled by Sir Charles Lawson) informs that in 1847 'a minute by the Marquis of Tweddale, advocating the introduction of the Bible as a class book, excited much discussion in India' and that by February 'the Marquis resigned'. A few lines later, it also informs that the appointment of Malcolm Lewin, the Unitarian judge who was sympathetic to the Hindu cause, as the provisional member of the council at Madras was cancelled by the Court of Directors.[17] Nevertheless, Malcolm Lewin continued to advocate for the Indian agrarian cause in the famous Torture commission, a result of the efforts of Chetty.

To augment his journalistic work on the ground, Chetty also started the 'Madras Mahājana Sabha' (Madras Native Association) in 1849 after his unsuccessful attempt to revive the defunct 'Madras Hindu Literary Society' (MHLS) with his friend Srinivasa Pillay. At this point, it is important to understand the history of MHLS and Srinivasa Pillay.

MHLS was initially led by Cavelly Venkata Lutchmiah, who was also a member of the Royal Asiatic Society in London.[18] It was supported mainly by Srinivasa Pillay who would later join hands with Chetty in his fight for Hindu rights. Despite its highly respected members, MHLS found that the colonial government only upheld its principles on paper, particularly regarding Hindu self-efforts. The government was unsympathetic towards the Hindu community's attempts at self-organization.

In all these endeavours, Srinivasa Pillay was an important collaborator. He was a wealthy businessman belonging to the Yādava community. He was a reformer in education and recognized the necessity of incorporating Western knowledge into Indian education while maintaining a secular approach without imposing Christian beliefs. The Hindus of Madras at that time were clear in their demands, which was quite surprising, given the negative stereotypes about them then. Towards this end, the society, despite facing financial challenges, started a school that offered education in English, as well as in Tamil, Telugu, and Sanskrit.[19] When the school faced complete financial collapse, it sought help from the government, but its repeated requests went unanswered. Surprisingly advanced for its time, the petitioner, who was the president of the society, highlighted the importance of spreading 'scientific knowledge in English and Oriental language to our youths' in Madras. With only 235 rupees left, the letter pleaded for assistance from the government. Despite their desperation and financial difficulties, the letter maintained the society's self-respect and subtly emphasized the government's responsibility and the need to foster goodwill for the future:

> Many of the respectable Natives are watching a favourable opportunity to observer to what extent the government will bestow their aid towards the Support of this Society and unless the government are graciously pleased to forward its interest with their Patronising care, I feel confident that the exertions of the Natives would be lukewarm.

Despite the petitioners having attached letters of support from the Royal Asiatic Society in London, the government did not even grant them an exemption from postal charges. As a result, by the end of the 1840s, the society had ceased to function.

Hindu schools, despite being started and run against all odds, suffered due to a lack of government support and were starved to death by colonial system. Instead, the government covertly handed over the educational system to evangelicals. The highly uneven situation in 1852 is explained in detail in the multi-volume *Cambridge History of the British Empire*:

> In 1839 Lord Elphinstone, governor of Madras, advocated the establishment of a university open to students who possessed some knowledge of English. The institution came into existence as a school which in 1852 bore the title of the 'Madras University High school'. It was then the only state or state controlled school or college in the presidency. But the gap left by the government had been filled by missionaries of various denominations, Jesuit fathers, Wesleyans and the English, Scottish and American

Churches. The number of missionary schools in Madras exceeded those in all other presidencies put together.[20]

In order to establish and run multiple educational institutions that could match the ways in which transcontinental evangelical institutions were doing so, Hindus required capital. However, as George Norton, the Advocate General of Madras, pointed out in the 1830s, this was a challenging context.: 'The Ryotwar system of tenure and revenue has totally extirpated capital from the Provinces; and litigation in the Supreme Court has entirely swallowed up the Native wealth once exhibited in Madras itself.'[21]

Nevertheless, what the Hindu organizations of Madras achieved definitely changed the way education was given to India for the better, even if it was in a diluted form, from what the Hindu activists of Madras desired. It started on 11 November 1839 with the submission of a petition signed by 70,000 people, organized and drafted by Lakshminarasu Chetty and Srinivasa Pillay of MNA. It was also the same year when a completely 'native' educational charity, Pachaiyappa's Trust Board, was established with considerable intervention from well-meaning British official and Hinduphile George Norton.

Though the petition comes five years after the infamous '*Minute on Indian Education*' by Thomas Babington Macaulay (1800-1859), it did not suffer from the prejudices against Indian culture which was exhibited by the hate rhetoric of Macaulay. Here, the present-day student of Hindu history needs to be vigilant to distinguish the vision and values of Macaulay from the vision and values of the Madras School of Hindu activists. Macaulay had nothing but hatred and contempt for the Hindu religion in every aspect. With years, his hatred for Hindus seemed to have increased. Here is an excerpt from his speech made in 1843, that is eight years after the *Minutes*. It could only be categorized as nothing but hate speech:

> The great majority of the population of India consists of idolaters, blindly attached to doctrines and rites which, considered merely with reference to the temporal interests of mankind, are in the highest degree pernicious. In no part of the world has a religion ever existed more unfavourable to the moral and intellectual health of our race. The Brahminical mythology is so absurd that it necessarily debases every mind which receives it as truth; and with this absurd mythology is bound up an absurd system of physics, an absurd geography, an absurd astronomy. Nor is this form of Paganism more favourable to art than to science. Through the whole Hindoo Pantheon you will look in vain for anything resembling those beautiful and majestic forms which stood in the shrines of ancient Greece. All is hideous, and grotesque, and ignoble. As this superstition is of all superstitions the most irrational, and of all superstitions the most inelegant, so is it of all superstitions the most immoral. Emblems of vice are objects of public worship. Acts of vice are acts of public worship.[22]

Unlike Macaulay, who had nothing but derision for anything 'Hindoo', the Hindu activists of Madras took a more holistic, inclusive, and universal view on civilizational discrimination. They insisted that the curriculum should be more scientific and secular. Led by Chetty and C. Srinivasa Pillay, the Hindu activists of Madras drafted a memorandum on education. They clearly understood the need to obtain knowledge of modern science and other domains from the West, while being clear that there should not be an imposition of religion through education. Their petition reads:

> We, my Lord, who can sensibly feel the infinite benefits which attend the diffusion of useful knowledge, anxiously look that the rising generation may attain instruction in European Literature, Science and Philosophy, as well as in our Native learning and languages; and that they may study the liberal arts of life, and the laws of their country. We believe that they will thereby

> raise themselves in every relation, both civil and social, and we believe that they will at the same time advance the prosperity of this country, and the attachment of the people to the British Government. But we can never be persuaded that no instruction whatever for these objects can be imparted, except through an interference with our religion. We pray that your Lordship will not impose as a condition for any measure of national education that the people should act as if they renounced the religious faith in which they have been brought up.[23]

What is more important is that contrary to the popular perception of the British providing better scientific education and giving Indians the benefits of European enlightenment, it was the Indians, in this case, the Hindu activists of Madras, who demanded that they be provided the best of Western secular education rather than the religious and civilizational prejudices in the name of education. In this, they were ably assisted by secular-minded or Unitarian British officials like George Norton. Officials like Norton and Malcolm Lewin were exceptions and a minority. Yet the Hindus of Madras seized these advantages. They leveraged these advantages for the welfare of Hindus and also in the Hindu resistance against the civilizational onslaught and economic drainage of India, in a way definitely much higher in proportion to the numerical strength. It is unfortunate that even in the post-independent history curriculum, the importance given to the Viceroys is not given to these genuine lovers of Hindu people and culture despite the handicaps of their dominant colonial environment.

Norton himself explains clearly how a strong section of British (not just EIC but those in power in the British governmental ruling class itself) desire that India's education standards be kept low. After forcefully putting forth an argument from his own experience in India, he states:

> I see no reason, but have observed much to the contrary, why a Hindoo may not become as good a lawyer, as any who are in the habit of addressing the bench or jury of the presidencies in which I have passed my time, and attain as high and deserved professional distinction as the best of those whose eminence at the local bar of India I have witnessed. I see no reason why, for extent of legal attainments, for sound and ready sagacity, for perspicuous and expressive reasoning, and for the appropriate aid of general information, a Hindoo might not gain as high a judicial reputation on the bench itself, as the majority of those who have occupied that seat without discredit.... In the science of medicine, not a mere competency, but distinguished merit, has already characterised the Hindoo students who have engaged in that department of professional life. I think it needless to exemplify further.[24]

After making this statement, he pointed out how this would provoke scornful smiles from the majority of the ruling class of Britain. He did not concern himself with those in British society 'who undervalue the effects of education, in the abstract', as they were a small minority. However, there was a majority in the powerful ruling elite who wanted to keep low the quality of education given to India through modern educational institutions, which were increasingly falling under British control. It was these men Norton and Hindu activists from Madras were fighting against. Norton writes of them thus:

> But a larger class of those who undervalue the effects of a superior education, purely secular, although they do not deny the capacity of Natives to acquire it, build on the assumption of the comparatively low standard of the moral character of Natives-and they then proceed to assert, rather than argue upon, the utter inefficiency of mere secular, or (as they more usually term it) profane, instruction to improve it. They maintain the position that mere secular instruction is absolutely pernicious. They maintain that no education short of Bible instruction can

> tend to purify the morals or ameliorate the heart; and they are prone to descant on that love of falsehood inherent in the Native disposition, which they consider Christianity (according to their views of it) can alone expel. Any increase of intellectual powers, therefore, they argue, will only augment these powers for vice and mischief-for they either will not allow that such powers can be checked by any moral virtues—or they will not allow that mere moral virtues, uninspired by the Christian faith, are of any worth or benefit.[25]

The British, of course, succeeded in using history and social sciences to devalue Hinduism and suggest that Hindu culture was racially biased against Dravidians. Prof. Kamil Zvelebil (1927-2009), a Czech Indologist, who was himself given to the Aryan-Dravidian binary, had pointed out how the colonial education system distorted Hindu religious culture with racial innuendos especially those related to Aryan-Dravidian:

> It must be openly admitted: As early as in the eighties of the 19th century, British administrators in India misused the term and the notion of 'Dravidian' in a shameful way. The antagonistic feeling particularly among non-Brahmin landholding castes that ranked just below the Brahmins, was deliberately fostered by the British who used it to stifle political awakening and the growing discontent among the Indians. In 1886, the governor of Madras, Mountstuart Elphinstone Grant-Duff, addressed the graduates of Madras University with these words: 'You are pure Dravidian race.... You have less to do with Sanskrit than we English have.' Ruffianly Europeans have sometimes been known to speak of natives of India as 'Niggers', but they did not, like the proud speakers or writers of Sanskrit, speak of the people of South as legions of monkeys. It was these Sanskrit speakers, not Europeans, who lumped up the Southern race as Rakshasas – demons. It was they who deliberately grounded all social distinctions on Varna, colour.[26]

Again, it is important to highlight the educational reform initiatives made by Hindu activists in Madras. These efforts were pioneering in providing a secular and sound education that was on par with the education available in the West, within the context of colonial prejudices and vested interests. The Madras Hindu movement of the mid-19th century envisioned a scientific, secular education free from religious biases, while also emphasizing the teaching of the mother tongue and its literature. Despite facing significant challenges posed by the colonial government and the support it provided to trans-continental evangelical institutions, funded by the surplus of the Empire, these individuals made valiant efforts that had a lasting impact. They should be considered as the pioneers of scientific and secular education in India.

Lakshminarasu Chetty's *Madras Mahājana Sabha* MNA not only focused on resistance to missionary activities but also observed the changes in the way land-people relations had transformed under British rule. In its very first petition in December 1852, the MNA documented the cruel conditions of torture under which the peasantry in South India suffered. In this submission, drafted by Chetty, he pointed out,

> [G]rievances of your petitioners arise principally from the excessive taxation and the vexations which accompany its collections, and the insufficiency, delays and expense of the Company's Courts of Law; that their chief wants are the construction of roads, bridges and works for the supply of irrigation and a better provision for the education of the people; they also desire a reduction of public expenditure and a form of local Government more generally conducive to the happiness of the subjects and the prosperity of the country.

He also demanded that the rule be transferred directly to the British parliament rather than being carried out through the EIC. In conclusion, he predicted the future government of India might not be under the EIC and that 'the new system, whatever it may be, shall be open to alterations and improvements from time to time, as the well-being of the country may require' and this should come through 'if practicable triennially, but quinquennially at the latest' discussions by representatives in Parliament.[27] One should actually credit Gazulu Lakshminarasu Chetty and his compatriots of Madras for forcefully putting forward a thoroughly democratic self-rule of India aiming at the welfare of all communities.

The same year (1852), Danby Seymour, a member of the British parliament sympathetic to Hindus, visited India. Lakshminarasu Chetty made Seymour his guest and used the opportunity 'of conveying to Mr Seymour information regarding the high-handed manner in which the local authorities curtailed the civil and religious rights of the Hindu community'. Later, Chetty took Seymour on 'a tour through Southern India visiting Cuddalore, Kumbakonam, Coimbatore, and other places' and made him witness first-hand 'how the landholder was assessed at prohibitive rates and how defaulters in the payment of government revenue were subjected to excruciating torture and otherwise inhumanly treated'. During this tour, Seymour observed 'unhappy men standing in the sun fully exposed to its scorching rays and with large stones resting on their backs performing under compulsion the penance and self-immolation which their forefathers voluntarily did in obedience to the regulations of the *Sastras*; some thumb-screwed and others tied down to adjacent trees and posts with their heads holding communion with their toes-and all this in front of the Taluq Cutcherry and within sight of the august tahsildar and magistrate who was holding his office and doing his work without wasting a thought on the unfortunate victims groaning inaudibly within a few yards of the Courthouse!'[28]

Along with showing a respectable British Parliamentarian the plight of Indian farmers under Company rule, Chetty, through MNA, also submitted petitions. This created quite an uproar. The Director of the Board of EIC tried to dismiss the petitions as a collection of exaggerations and misrepresentations.

In the signed memorandum dated 24 January 1853 to the British government, Chetty demanded an inquiry commission:

> If a Commission could be obtained to take information in this country, all the more glaring complaints could be fully substantiated. We have tried to avoid exaggeration in our statements, but the evils alluded to are so great that nothing will convince people in Europe of their truth except the establishment of such Commission.[29]

In July of 1854, Seymour addressed the issue in the House of Commons and provided a firsthand account of the mistreatment of peasants during revenue collection. This led to the creation of the 'Torture Commission' in September to investigate these abuses. Meanwhile, Chetty took action by submitting a petition with numerous signatures to the British parliament. On 14 April 1856, the Earl of Albemarle presented it in the House of Lords. The 'Torture Commission' also presented all the evidence it had gathered to the Home government. The House of Lords was left with no choice but to condemn strongly the use of torture in colonial revenue collection. But even then, the British attempted to shift blame to Indian officials, claiming that torture was a governance custom of corrupt Indian officials and that British officers should control the natives. What *The Economist* wrote scathingly could be considered as the impression created by the 'Torture Commission', when the crimes of EIC in India were brought before the face of England by MNA:

> Do they mean that the Indian Government, though not participating itself in evil practices, has, with almost equal guilt, for-borne to hinder them in others? The acts of Government, the decisions of the law courts, the records of every district prove the contrary. Do they mean that the efforts of the Government have not always and in all cases been successful; that India is not yet wholly civilised; that those Asiatics, to whom these reformers would confide the highest offices of State, are not to be entrusted with the lowest, without incurring some risk of malpractice or corruption; that the heart and nature of a people are not changed in a day; that in spite of all English efforts to the contrary, the Indian people have not yet completely acquired the humanity which adorns our own more complete and matured civilisation? If this is meant, we admit the charge.[30]

In its fifth petition submitted in 1856, MNA emphasized 'that the infliction of torture seeming thus to be a consequence and not a cause' and that 'a more prolonged and more searching inquiry would have endeavoured to trace the evil to its source'. The memorandum also highlighted how the EIC's non-native top administration, already pointed out in their 1852 petition, disregarded the complaint of torture, thus encouraging the practice:

> The complaint was first made to the Collector of the District, next to the Commissioner of the Northern Circars, within which the district is situated; then to the Board of Revenue, and finally to the Governor in Council, who transferred the petition addressed to himself to the Collector; when this officer applied for two years leave of absence; and neither was redress given nor even an enquiry obtained.[31]

In this particular complaint, the petitioners pointed out that the 'complaint thus passed over by the entire round of the Covenanted Service, in regular succession' and that it was not a trivial petition as it involved 'six divisions which contain a population of upwards of two hundred and sixty-four thousand ryots'. The petition charged the 'Covenanted Collector' in the first instance and his subordinate officials in the second. A new assessment of the land was conducted, and previous tax reductions by the old zamindars on account of the 'unfruitfulness of the soil' were withheld. The new assessment now included taxation 'of gardens, tanks, and groves devoted to the purposes of charity; of lands set apart for the burning of the dead; of low tracts, swampy lands, barren grounds, channels, dams, etc., which were before free from taxation'. When the ryots refused to sign this new assessment, it was 'the collector through the instrumentality of his tahsildars, who resorted to cruel acts of corporal punishment, compelled some of the ryots to affix their signatures; and when others of them ran away to escape the same consequences, the collector caused the names of the absentees to be signed by the village *Curnums*; and thus the settlement was declared acknowledged by the ryots.'[32]

The British officers claimed to be ethical as against the 'incompletely civilized' Indians. However, the petitioners provided an entire chain of communication from the British collector to the 'Tasildar of Pariapollium'. 'Streenevassa Row', the tahsildar, 'had left the whole of the loom tax amounting to Rupees 212-8-0 due in the Rallapady village of his Talook uncollected.' Not only that, 'the village Moonsiff and Puttamaneyagar named Gooroovappah Chetty, not only causes the debtors (weavers) not to pay the amount due by them, but has not paid the sum which he owes himself' and 'the amount of 15 Rupees, which was alleged to have collected, was not paid into the Treasury but returned by him to the parties who gave it.' Then the collector ordered,

> As soon as you receive this takeed you must go in person to the said village, and collect the whole of the loom tax without leaving any part whatever unrealized and report the same. If you do not collect it as directed above, a severe order will be issued against you.[33]

The reports of the police superintendent of Madras on the meetings organized by Chetty indicate that his gatherings appealed to all sections of the society. They particularly 'did not fail to alarm the minds of the people from the lower orders as well as ignorant sections of the society'.[34] This was not restricted to the elitist or confined to the 'educated classes'. These meetings led to the torture and collection of the aforesaid money from the weavers. The 'Asiatic' Moonsiff returned the collected money to the weavers after seeing their condition, but the British collector insisted that the tax should be collected, threatening severe action. This resulted in physical punishment for the weavers. This event that was documented in the petition led to an enquiry leading to the dismissal of the tahsildar but only the censure of the collector.[35] However, the MNA had clearly refuted with evidence the racist and civilizational supremacist charges from Imperial quarters related to the torture, arguing that it was not due to the racial nature or/and the ethical deficiency of the nature of Indians.

Simultaneously, Chetty and MNA, under his guidance, were also resisting the missionary onslaught. In 1853, the governor attempted to reintroduce the Bible into the education curriculum, but this too was thwarted by the ever-vigilant Chetty. In 1859, MNA submitted a complaint to Edward Stanley, the secretary of state for India. The complaint addressed the loss of temple lands, criticized the government's support for Bible instruction in educational institutions, and its apathy towards Hindus in general. It also strongly opposed the appointment of a Hindu-hating missionary, Peter Percival, as a professor at Presidency College for 'Sanskrit and Vernacular Languages'. The submission highlighted that Percival had 'merely a smattering of the Tamil ... just commencing study of Telugu, and ... altogether incompetent' to teach Sanskrit. His appointment was an insult to Hindus. It was further pointed out that Percival had fraudulently altered the verses of *Avvaiyar* in his book. It is worth noting that a significant number of Muslims also signed this petition.

Chetty was also a staunch advocate of women education. He founded and funded several schools for girls and advocated for widow remarriage, which was quite progressive for his time. Chetty had a prophetic vision that had the interest of South Indian Hindus at its heart. During the Mysore wars between the British and Tipu Sultan, the Nizam of Hyderabad greatly assisted the British. The British and the Nizam reached an agreement that Mysore would not be restored to the Raja of Mysore; instead, it would be divided between the British company and the Nizam.

After the last Anglo-Mysore war, Chetty observed that the British were still vacillating in returning Mysore to Raja Krishna Raja Udayar [Wodeyar]. So, he went to Mysore and advised the king to adopt a son for the perpetuation of the royal line. Additionally, he went to Sir Salar Jung, the famous minister of Hyderabad, for his support in pressuring the British to return to Mysore's core region. Both actions, the decision to adopt a son by Raja Udayar [Wodeyar] and the pressure from Hyderabad, led to the EIC returning the core of the Mysore region to the Hindu raja and reinstating him.

The British initially considered Chetty a seditious person and closely monitored his writings and lectures as well as his movements. However, after 1857, there was a change. The British decided to mend fences with him. He was awarded the Companion Order of the Star of India in 1861. In 1863 he was made a member of the Madras Legislative Council. However, by this time, Chetty had lost all his wealth. The circulation of his magazine *Crescent* had dropped from 10,809 copies in 1846 to 4794 in 1853 and eventually to 150 in subsequent years. Without the financial means to continue, Chetty had to cease publication of the magazine. In 1868, Chetty passed away in financial poverty but with a rich patriotic spirit.

Kalavala Cuṇṇan Chetty: Forerunner of Midday Meal Scheme

Today, if Tamil Nadu and Kerala stand high in human resources indices, midday meal schemes in the schools have played and continue to play a major role in this achievement. Various political parties, including the Justice Party, Indian National Congress, and AIADMK (All India Anna Dravida Munnetra Kazakam), have claimed credit for implementing this scheme.

Pioneering visionary and humanistic attempts were made in Madras in corporate schools to introduce the midday meals scheme in 1920 by Sundararao Naidu of the Justice Party. Unfortunately, this had to be discontinued due to paucity of funds. Two years earlier, in 1918, a midday meal scheme had been introduced for poor children in the Hindu theological school of Madras by Kurichi Rangaswamy Iyengar.[36] But the pioneer in all of them in the modern period was a Vaishṇavite businessman and philanthropist, Kalavala Cuṇṇan (Kaṇṇan) Chetty (1869-1920). He created a series of institutions that served the poorest sections of the society, particularly in education. His educational institutions served the poor girls to get educated. At this time, he launched an ingenious 'Shera Dhana' (milk-giving service). This was giving milk to poor students every day. A house was dedicated to give milk to the children. There was also feeding of children.[37] Lady Willingdon, the first lady of Madras (wife of the then British Governor, a controversial figure), was so impressed by this innovative service that Kalavala Cuṇṇan (Kaṇṇan) Chetty offered the students. If one goes through the services that Kalavala Cuṇṇan and his brother Kalavala Rāmānujan provided[38] one can see clearly their spiritual basis for the service that stemmed from their Vaishṇava background. They established a library for the benefit of the students of Madras, built a choultry (rest house) near Egmore station 'for the benefit of the passengers alighting at Egmore and struggling for want of accommodation', and founded

Āyurvedic medical centres which provided medical care for the poor in different parts of colonial Madras and even outside – Thiruvallikeṇi, Nellūr and Nuṅgambākkam.[39]

In the 1940s, C.P. Rāmaswamy Iyer, Diwan of Thiruvithāṅcūr princely state introduced the midday meals scheme in all the primary schools of Thiruvithāṅcūr. This was one of the reasons for the state's high literacy rate, which had a positive impact in post-Independent India. This was the first sustained large-scale midday meal scheme launched successfully over a long period of time. Nagercoil Parliamentary Constituency of the Kanyakumari district was originally with Thiruvithāṅcūr princely state, and during the reorganization of states after independence it became part of Tamil Nadu. K. Kamaraj (1903-1975), who was the Chief Minister of Tamil Nadu, was well accustomed to Nagercoil and its developmental history. On 17 July 1956, Kamaraj introduced a midday meals scheme in Ettayapuram of the Thirunelveli district adjacent to Kanyakumari district. Within the next six years, it was scaled up to 27,256 of the 28,005 state government schools as well as state-aided schools. Later, in 1982, Dr M.G. Ramachandran, the then chief minister of Tamil Nadu, covered 56.9 lakh rural school children with a meal of 400 calories per student per day. Soon, with 52,000 centres for 'nutritional meals'covering 31,000 schools, it not only provided meals for 65.7 lakh students and employment for 1.80 lakh people, of which 1.58 lakh were destitute women. The attendance in primary schools went up by 96 per cent and middle school by 66 per cent.[40]

One can very clearly see the dhārmic roots of the scheme coming from the Kalavala Chetty humanitarian service of providing daily milk and possible food to poor students. This practice can be traced back to the great Śrī Rāmānuja Vaiṣṇava tradition. The Chetty brothers belonged to Thenkalai Sri Vaiṣṇava tradition and they would not eat their food unless the daily ceremonial worship to Mahā Viṣṇu was complete. The influence of Sri Vaiṣṇava Sampradāya in the worldview and values of the Kalavala Chetty brothers can be inferred from the numerous Vaiṣṇava temple functions that their charity institutions manage and sponsor to this day:

- Gurupushyam Utsavam at Sri Adikesava Perumal and Bashyakaraswamy Temple, Sriperumbudur.
- Ponna Vahanam Utsavam at Sri Chenna Kesava Perumal Temple, Chennai
- Thiru Adipooram Utsavam at Sri Chenna Kesava Perumal Temple, Chennai
- Brahmotsavam Utsavam at Sri Chenna Kesava Perumal Temple, Chennai
- Mandagapadi Utsavam at Sri Kalyana Varadaraja Perumal Temple, Kaladipet, Chennai
- Kodai Utsavam at Sri Kalyana Varadaraja Perumal Temple, Kaladipet, Chennai
- Yalivahanam Utsavam at Sri Devarajaswamy Temple, Kancheepuram

There is also a community value system here at work. In the Arya-Vaysa or Chetty communities, it was believed that if a couple was unable to have children, it was a sign to serve humanity in order to counteract negative karma. Based on the study of anthropologist Mattison Mines, anthropologist Henrike Donner, and economist Geert De Neve, the charity work carried out by these Hindu trading communities in colonial Madras was connected to their place in Purāṇo-historic spatial memory in the society and the philosophy of Karma Yōga:

> Mines demonstrates how the Beeri Chettiars and the Komatis, two leading merchant castes of Madras City, constructed their neighbourhoods in quite different manners, reflecting their contrasting integration into south Indian society as

> well as their respective relationships with the English East India Company. While the Beeri Chettiars (a left-hand caste) portrayed themselves as a kingly caste and as trustees of major temples, the Komatis (a right-hand caste) followed the style of karmayoga, correct action expressed as piety and charity, and presented themselves as patrons of charity and education.[41]

Though being a successful businessman respected by colonial authorities and a prominent citizen of Madras honoured with 'Rao Bahadur', a title that the British government gave to eminent persons, Kalavala Chetty openly associated his humanitarian services with the national independence movement. He was hailed by nationalist poet Subramanya Bharati and Annie Besant honoured him posthumously as 'Dharma Murthi.' In his final year, he spent a princely sum of 50,000 rupees per annum on his humanitarian works. In his will, he wrote:

> I make this Last Will and Testament because I am anxious that the bulk of my properties should be utilised for charities and that my name should be perpetuated not by descendants but by schemes of public benefaction which I am anxious to organise and provide for.

The Hindu philanthropy of Kalavala Chetty is characteristically rooted in the Hindu vision of karma and dharma, both of which are pro-actively humanistic. Mattison Mines citing the will of Cunnan Chetty states that anthropologist Anastasia Piliavsky suggested that 'one cannot find a clearer description of ... a paternalistic figure, who cares for his society as he might do for his own children.'[42]

P.M. Madurai Piḷḷai[43]

Mārkandamūrthi Piḷḷai, who lived in the 19th-century colonial Madras, belonged to the famous Vaḷḷuvar clan, which was a priestly and scholarly branch of the Paṟaiyar community. He was revered as 'the one who had been living from the very early past in Chennai Vepperi which is Vediyapuri (where Vedic Brahmins live), and also in Purasaipakkam which was once called Raghnatha Puram, and who worked for the welfare of all, who was the light of Ādi Vaḷḷuva Kulam (clan) and Saiva Vaḷḷuva Kulam, the one who came in the lineage of Thiru Vaḷḷuvar'.[44] This indicates that the community held itself in high regard in the non-colonized sociocultural context and that its community members were respected citizens of the society and economically prosperous. His son was named Madurai Piḷḷai (1858-1913).

His hard work and astute business sense soon made him a wealthy businessman, and he went on to become an important Hindu philanthropist. The Tamil community had a long presence in Burma. When Madurai Piḷḷai was growing up, the educational institutions in colonial Madras were mostly under Christian control, and a few Hindu institutions were struggling with social stagnation. As a result, he received his education entirely in Christian institutions, attending the SPG school and completing his higher education at Madras Christian college. But his inspiration for public service and charitable work came from *Periya Purāṇam*. A musical drama and poetic recitation of the life history of one of the Nayanmārs, Thirukuṟippu Thoṇdar was performed during the memorial ritual for Madurai Piḷḷai's father.

After graduating, he worked as a writer for the Duke of Buckingham, who was then the Governor of Madras. Through his exemplary character and hard work, he eventually became a contractor for a steel company and relocated to Burma (today's Myanmar).

On 23 December 1881, he organized the festival of sixty-three Nayanmārs in a grand manner on the streets Madras. In 1882, he built a temple in Burma for all Indians to gather for spiritual and cultural events. In 1896, he established a 'Hindu Youth Drama Club' in Rangoon (today's Yangon) to stage dramas based on Hindu epics and Puranas for the Indian community in Burma. He served as the head of 'Hindu Math Paripalana Sabha' (association for the nurture of Hindu religion) at Rangoon for many years.

He also sponsored Hindu educational and humanistic programmes back home in Tamil Nadu. He started publishing Saivite religious literature, particularly the lives of the Nāyanmars. Additionally, he established a publishing company in his father's name for publishing religious literature, which also helped Tamil poets to publish their works. He offered these services mostly free of charge and gained recognition as an eminent philanthropist. In 1886, he founded an association called 'Sat Vishaya Dhana Sangham' in Vepperi, Madras, to promote Saiva-Vaishnava unity. He also served as a trustee in various Hindu charities. In Nagapattinam, Tamil Nadu, he was instrumental in the formation of 'Hindu Manithabimana Sangham' (Hindu Humanist Association). He also financially assisted the local Hindus in building a 'Hindu Bodhana school' at Nagapattinam. He was the principal financial support for Śiva Jñāna Prakāsa Sabha, which published hymns and books on Nayanmars, Azhvars, and Siddhas.

In 1912, one year before his death, he bought a ship and named it 'Meenakshi'. This was an important milestone in India's maritime history. His chosen personal deity for daily worship was Ganesa. He converted one floor of his Rangoon house into a Ganesa temple. Later, he and his son-in-law built and managed a Ganesa temple at Yangon, which is still operational to date. His son-in-law, Vasudeo Govindaraju Pillai, who married his daughter, Meenakshi, came from a staunch Vaishnava family. His father, Poet Govinda Raja Dasar, had composed a poetic work on Chakkubāi, one of the great women devotees found in

Mahā Bhakta Vijayam. Additionally, he had also published a Vaishnava Bhajan manual. Vasudeo Pillai also founded a school for the education of Indians in Rangoon, named after his father-in-law, Madurai Pillai – Madurai Pillai High School, where students could study and pass Matriculation.

M.C. Madurai Piḷḷai

If he had lived in previous centuries, M.C. Madurai Piḷḷai (1880-1935) would have been hailed as an Āzhwār. He was known as a shrewd businessman with a strong social and ethical conscience. Born in the Paṟaiar community, he worked as a contractor in the gold mines of Kolar, Kolar Gold Field (KGF) which was expanding and evolving into the centre of gold mining in colonial India. Most of the workers in the mines came from disadvantaged backgrounds, the working conditions were bad, and the social milieu was degraded and strife-filled. Exploiting the poverty and difficult working conditions, anti-social elements exacerbated the plight of the workers. The colonial government often covertly relied on missionaries to work towards uplifting the social conditions.

It was under such a condition that Madurai became a contractor at Kolar Gold Field (KGF) contractor and became a wealthy personality. He wanted to improve the condition of the people. In the book *Thiru Avadhāra Vaibhavam*', written by an eminent religious preacher with the title 'Harikathā Prasaṅga Vēdhāntha Rathnāgaram', Sri V.M. Vaduga Nambidhāsar , we can find the following information:

> Sri M.C. Pillai was so devotional and wanted his community people to live in dignity. He chose the path of religion and tried to draw the scheduled caste/tribe people into spirituality which was not allowed in those days by caste Hindus. Once, Sri Pillai visited the Sri Rangam temple and listened to the discourses of Sri Ubhaya Vedhaantha Pravarthaga Srimath

> Arulmaari Thiruvengada Varayogi Swamigal. Pillai attended his programmes daily during the auspicious Maargazhi month in the year 1899 after bathing in the holy cauvery. On enquiry by the disciples of the Swamigal, Pillai disclosed who he was; he also expressed his desire to have the holy pancha samskaara rituals through the Swamigal. On knowing that Pillai belonged to scheduled caste, the disciples refused to allow him near their guru. Pillai was so stubborn and started to observe fast till his demands were fulfilled. Finally Sri Swamigal obliged and accepted Pillai as his disciple; he also named him 'Madhurakavi Ramanujadhaasar'. At the request of Sri. Pillai, the Swamigal visited K.G.F and stayed at the 'Udayavar Sabhai' at Andersonpet. Here he met all the vaishnavite leaders of K.G.F and devotees belonged to scheduled caste and performed Panchasamskaara rituals on hundreds of them. He also consecrated the newly built temple with the holy name Sri Numperumal Sannadhi.[45]

He was given the title 'Vaiṣṇava Śrī'. He built a temple for Mahā Viṣṇu in the Kolār Gold mines region and named the deity Śrī Namperumāḷ. In 1919, he started Śrī Namperumāḷ Primary Schools in both Robertsonpet and Andersonpet. By 1926, they became middle schools. He constantly worked for the welfare of the downtrodden and helped many social reform movements. He coined the name Ādi Drāvidar for the Scheduled Caste communities and founded the Ādi Drāvida Mahā Jana Sabha. He also published a magazine called *Dravidan*. While Aruḷmāri Thiruveṅgada Varayogi Śwāmigal was in KGF, he conferred Pancha Samskara upon a devoted boy Veraiyan from the Scheduled Castes community and initiated him as 'Vaduganmbi Dāsar'. He was both a scholar and devotee of Vaiṣṇava Sampradāya. His expertise was so great that he was given the title 'Śrī Hari Kathā Prasaṅga Vēdantha Rathnākara'. Madurai Piḷḷai made him the editor of *Drāvidan*.[46] Dr S. Srikumar writes:

> This Vaishnavite based paper highlighted to the world, the plight of not only the scheduled caste people of K.G.F, but also of the entire south India. It also worked for the upliftment of other suppressed communities like Buddhists, Saivites, Vaishnavites, Aadhi-Karnatakas, Aadhi-Andhras and even atheists.[47]

The magazine served as a platform for advocating the social and human rights of marginalized communities while being rooted in the philosophy of Śrī Vaiṣṇavaism. Madurai Piḷḷai, through his organizational skills, inclusiveness, and networking with egalitarian terms with other Vaiṣṇavaite communities established a practical and sustainable model for holistic social emancipation. Despite the term 'Drāvida' carrying racial-ethnic connotations in the colonial discourse of Indian history, for the Vaishnava staunch-minded social activists and entrepreneurs like Madurai Piḷḷai , it held a different connotation. They saw it as the basis of Śrī Vaiṣṇavaism itself, rooted in the hymns of Āazhwārs – *Divya Prabantham,* which is referred to as 'Drāvida Vēda Saram' (essence of Vedic wisdom in Drāvida*)*.

Many of the Vaiṣṇavaites from KGF were also supporters and followers of Dr Ambedkar even though at KGF, they had considerably stopped the spread of Buddhism in their community, and they mostly remained strong Vaiṣṇavaites. Madurai Piḷḷai inspired quite a lot of similar philanthropic souls from the Scheduled Community who were in KGF. In this, he was ably guided and also assisted by another towering personality, Sri K. PūSwāmy whose Śrī Vaiṣṇava Dīkṣā name was Bhūmināyagam Rāmānujadhāsar.

Sri K. PūSwāmy – Bhūmināyagam Rāmānujadhāsar – Swadēsi Gold Mine Owner

Sri K. PūSwāmy was a member of the Mysore Representative Assembly (MRA), had expertise in engineering science, and was a successful contractor in KGF. He had a deep devotion for the female Āzhwar *Āṇḍāḷ*, who was worshiped as the incarnation of Mother Earth, the consort of Maha Vishnu. He built a temple for her in Marikoopam village of KGF, using the best tiles imported from Europe, along with sacred images consecrated at Śrī Raṅgam and traditional artisan-made paintings. His commercial ventures were named after her, such as 'Sri Aandaal Motor Works and Sri Aandaal Bus Services'. Additionally, he established the Sri Aandal Primary and Middle School to benefit the children of workers and the economically weak. Furthermore, he constructed the Śrī Rāmānuja Kōtam at the sacred pilgrimage centre of Melkot in the Mandya district of Karnataka, providing accommodation and food for all pilgrims without discrimination.[48]

In those days, cinema halls were only available for Europeans in Mysore. However, Sri PūSwāmy insisted on hiring halls and screening movies for the workers, most of whom were from Scheduled Castes communities in Tamil Nadu. He arranged for the first Tamil movie *Vaḷḷi Thirumaṇam* to be shown in a theatre hall for all Indians in KGF and nearby regions. This was organized under his distributor firm Āṇḍāḷ Cinemas.[49] The movie portrayed the love between God Subrahamaṇya and a tribal girl Vaḷḷi, which was culturally significant as a symbol of inter-caste marriage. Indians have the habit of chewing beetle leaves and then spitting out the reddish spittle. Citing the dirtying of the floors and walls because of this habit, the British authorities highly restricted the hall screening of movies for Indians. So, in 1936, Sri PūSwāmy built a hall for screening movies for Indians.

He worked tirelessly to uplift the downtrodden in society and met Montaq Chemsford, the Viceroy, during his visit to Chennai. At that time, terms like Panchama-Pariah were used in the censuses of Mysore Princely State and Madras Presidency. Sri Pūswamy opposed this and strongly recommended the term Ādi Drāvidar, achieving a significant victory in its implementation.[50]

When a British officer insulted him, Sri Pūswāmy decided he would never work under the British again. Furthermore, he resolved to become an owner of his own gold mine. Challenging the British gold mine owners, he acquired land and established the Bisanattam Goldmines in Andhra Pradesh. Till the end of his life, he worked as the Chief Engineer profitably right in front of his previous employers, John Taylor & sons.[51] Even his death was spiritual. While traveling, a snake appeared in front of his car and displayed its hood. Sri PūSwāmy calmly got out of the car and serenely bowed before the hooded cobra. In the life of Śrī Rāmānuja, one of his disciples, Govinda put his hand into a snake's mouth, removed a thorn and nursed it out of pain. That is the Vaishnava compassion and respect for all life.[52] Right in modern times, Sri PūSwāmy displayed the very same *Vaiṣṇava* compassion before the snake. He could have simply driven the car. He did not. The snake left, and with that bow to all life forms, the great soul, as they say in Vaiṣṇava tradition, 'reached the sacred feet of the Ācharyan'.[53]

R. Āḷavandhārdās

One of the great personalities who carried forward the work done by Madurai Pillai was Āḷavandhārdās (1906-1959), popularly known as R.A. Dās). He was a talented contractor who amassed his wealth through his intelligence and hard work. He utilized his wealth for the betterment of KGF workers and the economically weaker and socially marginalized sections of society. Every Pongal (a Tamil harvest festival similar to Makar-Saṅkrānti), he arranged new clothes and other festival necessities for every family. In 1943, he established the Adi-Dravidar Mahajana Sabhai Hostel for Scheduled Castes students in Robertsonpet near King George Hall. Additionally, R.A. Das was the member of the Mysore Representative Assembly. In this capacity, he got schemes approved for the marginalized communities.

He organized free education and food for underprivileged children. In Vellore, Tamil Nadu, he built another hostel for Scheduled Castes students, naming it 'Rāmadās' after a Vaishnavaite humanist from KGF who was associated with Vellore's Śrī Maṇavāḷa Māmunikaḷ Sabha and Melkote's 'Aruḷmāri Śwāmi Sabha'. A constant factor in all these formidable entrepreneurs who worked in a society under siege by a colonial power and besieged with social stagnation is their spiritual rootedness and value nourishment from Vaishnava tradition, as exemplified by R.A. Das:

> R.A. Das patronized the Melkote Mutt along with Sri K. Pooswamy, where free food and accommodation are provided to the devotees during the Vairamudi Sevai feast. These two leaders also started a mutt in Sriperambudur and maintained it with the aim of promoting spirituality among the downtrodden people. R.A. Das also invited religious teachers (Jeers) from Srirangam to K.G.F for preaching the morals of Vaishnavism.[54]

Madurai Pillai worked in close proximity with Dr Ambedkar to uplift the downtrodden, all the while remaining rooted in his Vedic Śrī Vaiṣṇava bhakti. He 'reached the sacred feet of the acharyan' in 1935. The movement he started in KGF remained strong, providing a practical, pragmatic model for social emancipation without compromising the social values with Indic spirituality as its corc. Iyyā Kaṇṇu, a Buddhist evangelist from the Scheduled Castes community and a scholarly poet confessed the role Śrī Vaiṣṇavaism played in social emancipation in KGF, surpassing both neo-Buddhist and Christian in KGF.[55] Unfortunately, this model has not received the attention and celebration it deserves in Hindu society and Hindu studies.

V.O. Chidambaram Piḷḷai

Vaḷḷināyagam Olaganāthan Chidambaram Piḷḷai (1872-1936), also known as VOC, was a lawyer from the Tirunelveli district of

Southern Tamil Nadu. After being a very active youth involved in rural rough sports and martial arts, he became interested in spirituality. He belonged to the traditional Śaivaite family, and his inclination was towards Advaita. His wife, Valliammaḷ, had a strong influence on him spiritually. She was well-versed in Tamil classics such as *Thirukuraḷ*. VOC mentioned that they used to study the commentaries on this work and discuss them.

He also studied two important Advaitic works: *Kaivalyam* and *Vichāra-Sāgaram*. In this, he was helped by Śwāmi Vaḷḷināyagam. He also studied Jñāna Vasishtam, an advanced Advaitic text, under Śōmasundara *Śwāmi* of Brahmānantha Śwamigal Math.[56]

VOC used to support mendicants and spiritual sages. One such person who came to his place was a blind sage, Virudunagar Śrī Rāmaiah Dēsikar, who belonged to the so-called low caste. Vaḷḷiammāḷ used to serve food herself to this blind sage. This created a lot of anger in the town. VOC himself was irritated, and when he came to ask his wife, she countered him, asking how an Advaitin could see such differences as caste, etc., and that too with a realized soul like Desikar. Her words transformed VOC with respect to the false nature of caste divisions, etc.[57] Unfortunately, a tragedy happened and Vaḷḷiammāḷ died. At this time, VOC was running a magazine in Tamil to propagate traditional Advaita. By 1905, VOC had established, at a relatively young age, proficiency in Tamil literature. He was asked to become a member of the revived Tamil Sangham at Madurai. That was also the year of the Bengal Partition. The call for Swadēsi (national self-dependence) was reverberating throughout India. Tamil Nadu was no different. But VOC was disinterested.

In 1897, Śrī Rāmakrishna Math was established in Madras, and its head was Swāmi Rāmakrishnānanda (the famous 'Sasi' Maharaj), a direct disciple of Sri Ramakrishna. When VOC met him in 1906, the Advaitic monk inquired about the mission and spirit of Swadēsi and Swadēsi industries in Southern Tamil Nadu. VOC found it amusing why a spiritually mature monk of Advaita bothered himself about Swadēsi and Vidēshi, which belong to the realm of Maya. VOC expressed his indifference to such worldly matters. However, the monk emphatically stated that worldly and spiritual Swadēsi alone could be the way forward in the current situation.

By October 1906, VOC was so committed to the Swadēsi spirit that he had launched the 'Swadesi Steam Navigation Company' (SSNC). At a time when India and many parts of Asia, Africa, and South America were suffering under colonialism, and the resulting resource drain and human suffering, VOC envisioned a maritime pan-Asian economic network. In launching SSNC, he aimed to challenge the colonial government-facilitated monopoly of the British India Steam Navigation Company (BISNC) on the trade route between Tuticorin and Sri Lanka.

Paṇdithurai Thēvar (1867–1911) sold a village of his Zamin and used the proceeds to buy shares worth 2 lakhs rupees. The contributors to SSNC represented a diverse cross-section of society. Paṇdithurai Thēvar was the head of the company, Salem Vijayraghavacharyar served as the legal consultant, and Janab Muhammad Fakir Sait provided 2 lakh rupees of the initial investment of 10 lakh rupees. These men, cutting across communities and religion, who were prominent in the colonial society, took a lifetime risk by antagonizing the British, thereby placing themselves in the line of fire for state intimidation. For close to five years, SSNC contested the colonial monopoly in the shallow sea route between Tuticorin and Sri Lanka. But what is astonishing is the futuristic vision that was incorporated in the stated aims of SSNC, among which we find the following:

- Train Indians, Sri Lankans, and people of other Asian continental nations in maritime industries and make them reap the benefits from such endeavours

- Train Indians, Sri Lankans, and people of other Asian continental nations in commanding and building ships
- Establish colleges for students from India, Sri Lanka, and other nations to train them in navigation and shipbuilding
- Create unity and achieve development for the people of India, Sri Lanka, and other Asian countries through maritime trade
- Install Indians, Sri Lankans, and other Asian nationals as agents in various commercial institutions so that they can familiarize and train themselves in (transnational) commercial operations[58]

It is clear that VOC's vision went beyond running a mere commercial swadēsi company; it involved creating a transformational network and challenging the civilizational and economic dominance of the colonial world order that existed.

In 1907, the company bought two ships *S.S. Gallia* and *S.S. Lawoe* and started carrying passengers and goods between Tuticorin and Sri Lanka. Soviet historian A.I. Levkovsky, who specialized in the Indian freedom struggle and trade unions, based on reports from *The Times of India* dated 25 August 1908, 10 November 1908, and 28 March 1908, wrote:

> According to the directors of the new company, the British India Steam Navigation Co. for many years had the sole monopoly of the Tuticorin-Colombo line. 'The British ship owners met their Indian competitors with undisguised hostility. They lowered passenger and freight rates: in order to drive the new company out of business. But here this old, well-tested method was ineffective. Competition between the Swadeshi Steam Navigation Co.-and the British India Steam Navigation Co. rapidly developed from a purely economic issue into an important political one in that part of India.[59, 60]

He also started two sanghas: one for the weavers and another a dharma sangha. In this endeavour, he was supported by two great souls—Śwāmi Abhēdananda and Bhāi Paramānand.[61] Swāmi Abhēdānanda belonged to the Śri Rāmakrishna Vēdānta tradition. Bhai Paramanand came from the Ārya Samāj tradition. In terms of creed, they belonged to different traditions, but in terms of nationalism, they worked unitedly.

The British wanted to sabotage this work, and the other dimension of VOC provided them with exactly that opportunity. That opportunity came in the form of the famous 'Coral mill workers' strike' organized by VOC in 1908. The same year, another great personality joined him, Subramaṇia Śivam.

A British entrepreneur, Frank Harvey, established in 1885 a cotton mill with 10,000 spindles in the Tirunelveli district, producing hydroelectricity from the waterfalls in the region. By 1888, it had become a mill with a capacity of 16,000 spindles. He expanded this as 'Coral Mill' to the harbour town of Tuticorin. British firms like 'Coral Mill' in India were considered good investment destinations because of the cheap labour available, no rules even for minimum labour rights or minimum hours of work, and no trade unions. In 1905, British Parliament one 'Lord' Reoy exhorted British investors to invest in such British firms citing the very above reasons as favourable and profitable investment conditions.[62] The conditions of Indian workers were inhuman. The workers in the mill included children aged ten and twelve. There were no weekly holidays. Leaves were rejected even for loss of pay. A leave taken meant the loss of work. From morning till evening, the workers had to work under the condition called 'Palm line work-run' that is they had to work till their palm line could not be seen with the sunset. The workers were beaten with a cane. The tar-coated mill floor used to melt during mid-day sun and yet the workers had to work standing on it.[63]

Pained by the plight of the workers, VOC started organizing them. Meetings were held. Subramaṇia Śivam, with his extraordinary oratorial skills, explained to the workers how they were the cause of the profit the British firms enjoyed. British police reports state how he explained that three days of strike would considerably affect British profits. He cited the Russian revolution that had happened in 1905 (not the Bolshevik, which would happen only in 1917). That was from the secret police report sent about the meeting on 23 February 1908. On 26 February, Śivam told the workers that there were two ways to fight: one was to destroy the mill equipment, and the other was to provide passive resistance by refusing to work, and he favoured the second method. VOC opined that if needed, it should be a mixture of both types. The point is the duo was able to communicate the idea of a workers' union and strike to the mill workers. Part of the British police (CID) report of these meetings contains a very important announcement made by Pillai. It was that they would start a new Swadēsi mill:

> Pillai got up and said that he had spoken to the Divisional Magistrate and the District Magistrate. The latter asked him not to deliver speeches which were even likely to do mischief and he had replied that he was a lawyer and knew what was seditious and what loyalty was. He told the District Magistrate that Coral Mills strike was not due to his interference but to the mill-owners starving the coolies. The coolies were children of this land and it was his duty to safeguard their interests. He then made the coolies understand that he had influence and friends all over India and that he had appealed to them for help on their behalf to subscribe money for opening Swadeshi Mill within six months' time.[64]

On 27 February, a strike began with VOC and Śivam became the de facto workers' leader. They had three demands: higher wages, a weekly day off, and recognition of leaves. Five hundred workers stopped working. Initially, the British administration and mill owners did not take the strike seriously, assuming the workers would return to work soon. However, Venkatarama Iyer, a staunch supporter of VOC, organized food supplies for the striking workers through a relief fund, boosting their morale. As the strike continued for over a week, the management started to become concerned. On 5 March 1908, *The Hindu* reported:

> The strike at the mills shows no sign of ending. Yesterday morning, the mill Agent with the Videshi Steamer Company's employees went round the town and begged the people to induce the strikers to resume work. The people refused all help. The agent took six maistries by force to the mill premises, confined them there for three hours, and exhorted the others to resume work, misinterpreting that the confined hands had done so. But the strikers refused to return unless and until their grievances were redressed. The confined men scaled over the back wall and escaped home. Then the Agent sent his broker to negotiate and bring the strikers round. The strikers declined. They were paid one week's provision from the Relief Fund raised by Mr. Vakil Venkatarama Aiyar.[65]

This arrangement of providing food to the striking workers attracted the Consul of Tsarist Russia. In the Tsarist Russian Foreign Policy Archive (TRFPA), the communication from Chirkin dated 04 March 1908 this aspect of the strike was particularly highlighted, noting that the 'leaders took care to issue food to the strikers'.[66] Resentment against the British, in general, started increasing. Local merchants refused to sell meat to the Europeans. Whenever people saw Britishers, they surrounded them and shouted 'Vandē Mātaram'. A band of boys shouted 'Vandē Mātaram when a British police official was going. An Indian policeman was suspended for ten days because he did not stop the boys. A barber stopped in the middle of his services when one Rangaswamy Iyengar, a pro-British official, expressed anti-Swadēsi sentiments. When he approached other barbers in the town, they also refused to oblige him. The washerman returned his clothes unwashed the very next day. Such was the Swadēsi spirit in the town during the strike.[67] Perhaps it was Śri Aurobindo who understood the immense importance of this movement and its nature. In his '*Bande Mataram*,'he noted salient features in the movement in his essay dated 5 March 1908:

> The struggle going on at Tuticorin exemplifies this remarkable diversity and intermingling of numerous tendencies each of which would in ordinary times be a separate movement.... Great issues of economics wear the guise of a political conflict; immense political aspirations become mixed up with a purely industrial struggle between indigenous labour and foreign capital.... So long the educated men of the upper castes debated among themselves about the better ordering of society, and outside Bengal and the Punjab it was no better than an academic dispute on the Social Conference platform or between the reforming and orthodox Press. Even in Bengal and the Punjab, the movement was sectional, a revolt of a small minority of the educated few, and did not touch the heart of the people.... The change was from outside and therefore injurious rather than beneficial, for an organism is doomed which, incapable of changing from within, answers only to the pressure of environment. But this immobile state of Hindu society has now begun to pass away and we see the beginning of a profound and incalculable life in the heart of the great organism.... That is a sign of coming social revolution in which neither the conservative forces of society nor the liberal sympathies of the educated few will have much voice. The forces that are being unprisoned, will upheave the whole of our society with a volcanic force and the shape it will take after the eruption is over, does not depend on the wishes or the wisdom of men.... The question of the Namasudras in Bengal has become a political as well as a social problem and in other parts of the country also the line between politics and social questions is threatened with obliteration.... One thing only we are sure of, and one thing we wear as a life-belt which will buoy us up on the waves of the chaos that is coming on the land. This is the fixed and unalterable faith in an overruling purpose

> which is raising India once more from the dead, the fixed and unalterable intention to fight for the renovation of her ancient life and glory. Swaraj is the lifebelt, Swaraj the pilot, Swaraj the star of guidance. If a great social revolution is necessary, it is because the ideal of Swaraj cannot be accomplished by a nation bound to forms which are no longer expressive of the ancient and immutable Self of India.[68]

Aurobindo, who was not yet on his spiritual path, nevertheless saw the movement in a larger canvas of history, both past and future and the uniquely Indian idea of Swarajya as the basis of an organic movement that harmonizes the political, social, economic, and cultural. Contrasting this, more than five decades subsequent to the Coral Mill strike, Soviet-endorsed historians, despite having access to an extensive archive and conducting a thorough examination of the same events, interpreted these occurrences through the lens of Marxist doctrine, confining them within a specific theoretical framework as below:

> In the streets the British were surrounded by hostile crowds who made them pin in the common cry; 'Bande Mataram.'. Thus, in its struggle for market, the national bourgeoisie appealed to the masses and drew them into the movement. On the other hand the actions of the proletariat powerfully furthered the national liberation struggle.[69]

This approach, having a semblance of academic rigour, was more a partial and even distorted view preventing a holistic and more realistic understanding of historical events in a very Indian context.

Finally, on 6 March, the management finally conceded to the demands of the workers after having a discussion with VOC.[70] Around the same time, a relatively unknown lawyer from Gujarat was becoming famous in Indian circles for organizing South African Indians against the discriminatory pass laws. Mohandas

Karamchand Gandhi was asked to leave South Africa, but he refused, resulting in a two-month imprisonment. Śri Aurobindo observed these two movements and, under the heading 'The Tuticorin Victory' wrote about the brilliance of the complete victory in Tuticorin in *Bande Mataram* on 13 March 1908:

> For passive resistance to succeed unity, perseverance and thoroughness are the first requisites. Because this unity, perseverance and thoroughness existed in Tuticorin, the great battle fought over the Coral Mill has ended in a great and indeed absolutely sweeping victory for the people. Every claim made by the strikers has been conceded and British capital has had to submit to the humiliation of an unconditional surrender.... There has been only one other instance of a victory as complete for passive resistance against the might of a great Government. We refer to the struggle in the Transvaal which was carried on with equal unity, perseverance and thoroughness to a success less absolutely unconditional but even more striking from the strength and stubbornness of the enemy it had to overcome.... The Tuticorin leaders must be given the whole credit for the unequalled skill and courage with which the fight was conducted and still more for the complete realization of the true inwardness of the Nationalist gospel which made them identify the interests of the whole Indian nation with the wrongs and grievances of the labourers in the Coral Mill.[71]

On 10 March, there was a rally to condemn the arrest of Bipin Chandra Pal. Again, workers from different institutions entered into a single-day spontaneous strike when denied permission to attend the rally. The inhumane sentencing of a British magistrate, Cox, to flog a 15-year-old boy created widespread resentment.[72] VOC and Śivam were arrested on 12 March 1908. The next day, there was general hartal and shops were closed. People came out in the streets demanding the release of their leaders. Deputy Collector Ash (who would be later assassinated by a revolutionary youth, Vanchi Nathan, belonging to the Brahmin community, on 17 June 1911, 10.40 am at Maniyachi Junction, Tirunelveli district) opened fire indiscriminately, killing four—three Hindus and one Muslim. Of the Hindus killed, one was of the Scheduled Castes community.[73]

Sri Aurobindo wrote on 27 March 1908 about the arrest of VOC:

> Nationalism is or ought to be not merely a political creed but a religious aspiration and a moral attitude. Its business is to build up Indian character by educating it to heroic self-sacrifice and magnificent ambitions, to restore the tone of nobility which it has lost and bring back the ideals of the ancient Aryan gentleman. The qualities of courage, frankness, love and justice are the stuff of which a Nationalist should be made. All honour to Chidambaram Pillai for having shown us the first complete example of an Aryan reborn, and all honour to Madras which has produced such a man.[74]

Aurobindo delivered a talk in Calcutta on 3 April 1908 condemning the arrest. He ended the talk by saying that it was 'no longer time for speaking or writing for the Motherland, but now was the time when the brain had to be prepared for devising plans, the body for working hard and the hand for fighting out the country's cause'.[75] Police notes of this speech would later be produced as evidence in the Alipore bomb case.

The case was conducted for two months in the sessions court, during which lawyers Sadagopachari, Narasimhachari, and Venkarachari argued for VOC. Sessions Judge A.F. Pinhey delivered his judgement on 7 July 1908, in which he observed:

> Chidambaram Pillai under the presumed air of working for industrial development has only been creating a racial enmity between the Englishmen and the Indians. This accusation cannot be denied as false. Pillai is a traitor. Even his skeleton

> has the qualities of a traitor. Siva has been a tool in his hands. These two are responsible for the confusion in Tirunelveli.[76]

VOC was sentenced to two life imprisonment of forty years in the Andamans, while Śivam was sentenced to ten years of rigorous imprisonment in the Andamans. VOC appealed to the High Court. Chief Justice Arnold Wright quoted the following part of the speech by VOC:

> As soon as the English people set foot in India, poverty also made its appearance in the country. So long as the foreign government exists we shall not prosper. So long as we continue to be the servants and slaves of foreigners we shall have to endure hardships. Three-fourths of the Englishmen now in India are traders. If we all unite and make up our minds not to purchase their goods what business will they have here? They must all run back to their country.... Besides, if we avoid going to these accursed Civil Criminal and Police Courts, the remaining one-fourth of the English will have no work to do. Thus all the white men will run away from our country. Being 33 crores of people how astonishing it is that we are slaves to 3 crores. The cause of our growing poorer day by day is that 180 crores of rupees are carried away each year in steam ships to a country 6,000 miles away. What country can stand such treatment as this?

Then the judge remarked, pointing out that what VOC aimed for was not just self-rule under a colonial government but radical complete riddance of foreigners:

> He advocates the boycott of foreign goods not as a means for helping Indian industries, but as a means for getting rid of the English. The dominant note of this portion of the speech is to get rid of the English, the governing class.... What is to be aimed at is the retirement of all foreigners necessarily including in this, the non-trading one-fourth persons authorised by law to administer executive Government.

He reduced the life imprisonment to rigorous imprisonment of six years and four years, which were served concurrently. An appeal to the Privy Council changed to six years rigorous imprisonment on the Andaman Islands to six years of rigorous imprisonment on the Indian mainland. This time he spent in Coimbatore and Cannanore. While in jail, the British threatened and tried to corrupt the shareholders. VOC himself was jailed and tortured by being yoked to an oil press. Ultimately, SSNC was liquidated in 1911.

Even after coming from imprisonment, he did not keep aloof from politics. But the political situation had changed. Gandhian movement had started. He found the Gandhian approach unacceptable. He also had to struggle for his living doing odd jobs—from selling groceries to working in a printing press. Still, on 11 October 1921, he inaugurated the Madras Agricultural Handicrafts Association Ltd in Madras. The aims of this association were as follows:

- To uplift the standard of living of the farmers and labourers.
- To develop agriculture and handicrafts by following modern methods.
- To start factories to manufacture candles and buttons.
- To establish a polytechnic college to teach Swadeshi handicrafts to students.
- To buy the extra cultivable land from the different districts of Tamil Nadu and train farmers to use modern techniques in farming.

At the rate of 10 rupees per share, he planned to collect a sum of ten thousand rupees. This could be paid in 10 monthly instalments. The concession was given to make poor labourers and farmers the shareholders of the association.[77] The concept of owning the shares by workers and farmers was quite a brilliant vision. V.O. Chidambaram Piḷḷai had in him both a trade union activist and also an entrepreneurial visionary. This is perhaps an independent forerunner to the concept of the Employee Stock/ Share Ownership Programme (ESOP). It was economist and political analyst Louis Kelso (1913–1991) who developed the concept of ESOP in 1956. This was more due to the impact of both the Great Depression and the labour unrest in the West. In the case of VOC working under all the disabilities of colonial repression, even a more vibrant and more empowering vision was thought out.

Throughout his life, a strong spiritual stream of Advaita non-dual was a constant source of value system throughout his struggles. There was a unifying vision. Under some of the most unforgiving circumstances, VOC showed how a soul rooted in the Indic vision of Advaitic unity could envision a system where workers' rights and dignity were upheld in a system that would also usher in profit and induce industrial innovation.

Subramaṇia Śivam

Subramaṇia Śivam (1884-1925) was a modest figure in the Indian freedom struggle. He was born in a small village called Vathalakundu near Madurai into a Brahmin family. While in Thiruvananthapuram, Kerala, he was initiated into the spiritual path by Śwāmi Sadānantha of Brahma Nishta Matam, who also inspired Iyyan Kāḷi to join the social reform movement. A strong Vēdāntin, Subramaṇia Śivam, used to deliver impassioned speeches against the British. He was arrested and sentenced alongside VOC, spending rigorous imprisonment from 07 July 1908 to 02 November 1912. In prison, due to poor hygiene and denial of proper medical care, he contracted leprosy. After his release, he attended the Calcutta Congress Session, but he did not align comfortably with the Gandhian form of politics. He continued writing and initiated a project to build a Bhārat Māta temple at Papārapatti., all while under constant police surveillance and occasional intimidation. When his mother died at Kāsi, the British government denied him train travel citing his leprosy. Throughout his writings, one can recognize his strong Vedantic humanism.

> To evolve a civic society, we need an education that makes us realise that all Indians are born in one womb and that the sufferings that one undergoes is a suffering for all of us. The experts in education should aim to usher in such an educational system.[78]
>
> While in reality creating all kinds of high-low binaries in social life, and telling 'all is one' in just words, is of no use. Unity is strength and disunity is weakness.... Considering the infinite variety of creation as the manifestation of the Divine and serving them always alone is the optimal way to attain eternal bliss.[79]
>
> The superiority one attains through caste, wealth, and position lacks inherent vitality. Inner development alone can give the true greatness.... That there is greatness in one occupation and not so in another is simply falsehood. Those who have achieved greatness in any work, they all belong to one category (*Jāti*) of great people.... An important aspect of greatness is self-renouncement.... Between greatness and lowliness there is only a difference of hair strand. A great person self-renounces to help others. One who does not is a lowly person.[80]

Today, there are many social reformers who are working to uplift the so-called depressed classes. In their efforts to uplift those they consider depressed, they often maintain an attitude that they are God-sent messengers to uplift the people. Śrī Rāmakṛṣṇa used to get in the night into the house of the 'untouchable' and clean his toilet.

Śrī Ṣaṇmuga Meijñāna Śivācharya Śwāmigal

Śrī Ṣaṇmuga Meijñāna Śivācharya Śwāmigal (1873-1942) was the fifth head of the Thirukōvilūr Ādhīnam, Thirupāthiripuliyūr Jñāniyār Maṭālayā in Tamil Nadu. He was born in the Vīra Śaiva tradition and was coronated as the Peetathipathi when he was 16 years old. Originally, he was taught Telugu and later mastered Tamil from Deivasigamani Iyer and Śwāminātha Iyer. He also mastered Sanskrit from Sri Rāmanatha Śāstri and studied English. It is noteworthy that he did not simply learn how to read and write in these languages but gained in-depth knowledge of each of them. It is estimated that he spent fifteen years mastering Tamil and Sanskrit, imbibing a complete understanding of all major literary and spiritual works in both languages.

Also known as Jñāniyār Śwāmigal, he was concerned about the rampant cultural and spiritual illiteracy that the British mode of education was spreading. He was equally pained to see how social stagnation was creating its own malaise in society. To address these issues, he embarked on extensive tours, delivering enlightening discourses that showcased the richness of the Tamil language and Saiva spirituality. Additionally, he made efforts to promote harmony between Saiva and Vaishnava traditions. Even E.V. Ramaswamy ('Periyar' to his followers) invited Swamigal to inaugurate the publishing house of the new magazine, *Kudi Arasu*. Incidentally, the masthead of the magazine featured a portrait of Bhārat Māta with the national flag hoisted on the Trishul she holds.

Śwāmigal established several educational institutions with the goal of providing quality and holistic education and cultural literacy to all sections of society. One such institution was '*Śrī Pādalēśwara Dharma Pādasālai*' school, named after *Śrī Pādalēśwara*, the *Ś*iva of *Thirupāthiripuliyūr*.[81] This school, founded in 1917 with the support of philanthropist Nagappa Chettiar, aimed to be inclusive by not mandating a uniform and allowing children from all backgrounds to attend. The first tutor for the school was Rudraswamy Iyer. However, the children had to wear either the Saivite or Sri Vaishnavite marks on their foreheads and those who had no marks would be provided with one.

Students were provided with free textbooks. The school's timings were from 9:00 am to 12:00 and then from 2:00 pm to 5:00 pm, with classes only in the forenoon on Saturdays. There was no holiday on Sundays. Holidays were on full-moon days, new moon days, Pratima days, and all dharmic sacred days, and there was a one-month vacation during the festival of Śrī Pādalēšwara. Initially, classes were held in any available space in the Madālaya, then in rented buildings before the school eventually had its own buildings. The curriculum included secular subjects and also sacred literature in Tamil, and children were taught which hymns to recite before which deity in which way and when in a temple. According to the people of the region, the school was at that time the 'Vidyā Kāmadēnu' for all those who wanted their children to be dharmic. Thus, the children of affluent families sat together with children clad only in their loin clothes and studied. Despite its inclusive approach, the school encountered challenges, including the lack of government recognition.

A Christian educational school in the area objected to the government granting recognition to this school. The colonial administration, hands in gloves with the evangelical institutions, delayed granting recognition. This had the potential to affect the future of many children and lead to a Christian monopoly in education. This incident, buried in the history books, illustrates how Christian dominance in education was achieved in colonial India. It does not reflect a portrayal of selfless missionary workers driven by the so-called Christian love, bringing education to those who were denied knowledge by a vile priestly caste.

The existing educational systems were systematically destroyed by the government, which created bureaucratic obstacles to hinder Hindu efforts to revitalize their own institutions using limited resources. Here is an instance of a celebrated seer-scholar of Tamil Nadu faced opposition from a Christian school when trying to gain government recognition for his efforts to educate the underprivileged. Fortunately, at that time, Sri S. Krishnamurthy Iyer, son of the famous judge T. Sadasiva Iyer (1861-1927), became the District Educational Officer (DEO) in the region. He recognized the school, supporting Jnaaniyar Swamigal's educational efforts. Unfortunately, due to disunity among Swamigal's followers, the school closed despite this victory. Reopening the school with the collective effort of all the Adheenams of Tamil Nadu would be a fitting tribute to the memory of this great scholar-seer.

Here is a historical example of a Hindu seer's attempt to establish a self-reliant education system rooted in local resources and traditions. This effort was stifled in colonial India by the combined strategies of evangelical competitors and colonial bureaucracy. However, the fact that such an attempt was made and achieved considerable success, even for a limited period against all odds, is a testimony to the resilient spirit of the dharmic tradition.

CHAPTER 16

Recapitulation and Conclusion

Indian Exceptionalism: Genuine and Constructed

Are the Jāthi and Varṇa systems of India unique to the country? Birth-based social stratification is common in almost all premodern human societies. Such hierarchies have the unavoidable tendency to create birth-based social aristocracies and social exclusions. This is also a common phenomenon. Both the radical advocates for the eradication of the Jāthi system and the staunch traditionalists who support it perceive the birth-based hierarchy, termed as 'graded inequality' by Dr. Ambedkar, as a distinctive and integral aspect of Indian culture and spirituality. But how much of this is true is what is explored in the first chapter. From the hereditary guilds and inherited concept of pollution in pre-modern Europe to the quasi-hereditary Hukou system made more rigid and institutionalized in post-revolutionary modern China, birth-based stratification and discrimination, with religious and ideological sanction or support, are present in many civilizations and, hence, not a unique development in India.

The thesis of the book, as it explores the diverse streams coursing through five millennia of Hindu history and tradition, is the distinctiveness of Hindu dharma, particularly in terms of its social values. These values are not rooted in establishing or preserving a birth-based social system. Instead, they lie in the relentless pursuit of human liberation through diverse and interconnected spiritual traditions. This naturally leads to questioning of both social stratification and exclusion, underscoring the dynamic nature of the social discourse that Hindu dharma puts forth.

Need for a Hindu Social Science to Study Jāthi and Varṇa

The prevailing interpretations of the Jāthi and Varṇa systems predominantly stem from either a Western viewpoint or a perspective arising from indigenous social stagnation, mainly over the last three centuries. This framework, regardless of its alignment with self-styled traditionalist or contemporary ideologies, is profoundly shaped by a colonial understanding and/or a distorted view of Indian society that has been internalized over time. Hence, there is an urgent need for the development of a Hindu Social Science.

In this context, the transformative journey of the evolutionary biologist and polymath John Burdon Sanderson Haldane (1892-1964) is highly relevant. His encounters with Indian culture, which initially stemmed from a position of colonial disdain, evolved into a condescending Marxist perspective. However, this journey ultimately led him to a profound realization. He discerned that within Indian tradition, a more robust and holistic framework exists for conducting social science research, one that does not suffer from some of the cardinal limitations of both Western social science and Marxism, which are deeply entrenched in colonial biases.

Haldane underscored the urgency for an innovative yet authentic Indian framework to address contemporary issues. In his quest for such a paradigm, he found resonance in the integral framework of Puruṣārtha, as eloquently articulated by Professor Nirmal Kumar Bose in his seminal work, *Cultural Anthropology* (1961). From the work of Prof. Bose, it becomes evident that Hindu anthropology can be seen to contain two important, distinct yet interrelated components: the fundamental and the temporal. The temporal facet is characterized by social stratification. In contrast, the fundamental facet is rooted in a spiritual yearning of the individual and the comprehension of unity in diversity and the emanating from unity. This fundamental aspect has consistently exerted influence over and instigated course corrections within the temporal aspect. Comprehending this interplay consistently in the social dynamics of Indian history could pave the way for developing a radically new and decentralized framework that better approximates the living reality of Indian culture and society than the currently dominant frameworks. Beyond India, this framework also has the potential to harmonize global cultural, religious, and ethnic disparities. Thus, a study of the social dynamics of Indian history is attempted in this framework—how the core of Indian culture and spirituality dealt with social conservation, stagnation, and emancipation from Harappan to modern times.

Continuity of Harappan Social Values

In the realm of academic discourse, the focus often transcends the conventional debates surrounding the myth of the Aryan invasion, the hypothesized Indo-European migration, conjectures of steppe incursions, and the possibility of an indigenous Vedic origin. Instead, the spotlight is cast on the social structures of Harappan society, which remarkably sustained the civilization in the absence of highly centralized power, a characteristic feature of other Bronze Age civilizations.

Archaeological and anthropological evidence appears to indicate a stratified society, potentially characterized by hereditary occupational groups. Anthropologist S.C. Malik strongly suggested the thesis that a jāti-like structure originated in Harappan society. Almost two decades after Malik's proposal, archaeologist Jonathan Mark Kenoyer, in his study of the possible socio-economic structures that could have been present in Harappan civilization based on archaeological correlates, pointed out that if one were to look for 'hierarchical stratification based on ritual purity' to be present in Harappa 'as it is represented in later societies in South Asia', then 'all of the basic data sets are present'.

Epigraphist Iravatham Mahadevan (1930-2018), who studied the Harappan seals, also suggested what he considered a strong indication of social stratification, which could have been hereditary with symbolic religious reinforcement. However, these are not castes as we understand them today. The Harappan functional categories he identified, namely officers with priestly duties, officers with military duties, farmers-tillers-tenants, and servant-attendant or lower functionary, do have a correspondence with the 'Varṇa' system. Archaeologist and historian Madhukar Keshav Dhavalikar (1930-2018) noted that it was 'quite possible that some sort of fourfold division of society, something approximating the latter-day varna system, was in vogue in Harappan society'.

Beyond the acceptance of the sharp contrast between the Indo-European and Harappan cultures or challenging such a binary in light of emerging research and discoveries that blur these distinctions, the scenario of the jāthi-varṇa system as more an indigenous development rather than a construct imposed by intrusive groups, becomes increasingly persuasive. Archaeological evidence further bolstered this interpretation, lending it a compelling depth and richness. This perspective has the strength of illuminating our understanding of the intricate evolution of our sociocultural matrix.

Harappan Yajña, Vedic Agni, and a Vilified Social System

Had the Harappan society solely based itself on a birth-based hierarchical structure, which was mainly based on ritualistic power and hereditary rights, the stark contrast between the affluent castes and the underprivileged ones would have been visible. However, archaeological evidence does not support the existence of such a societal divide. For a society to thrive over millennia in such a manner, a system of mutual exchange and redistribution should have existed. What was that system of redistribution? Archaeologist Jonathan Kenoyer suggested a mechanism of reciprocity similar to the 'Jajmāni system,' which has continued in most Hindu villages even into modern times. Harappan society could have had a similar system of 'hereditary relationships of reciprocal exchange'.

A missionary-turned-sociologist, William Henricks Wiser (1890-1961), published *The Hindu Jajmāni System* in 1936, which remains the basic text in studying the system. Definitely scholarly and path-breaking for Western anthropology in understanding how rural society works, the book also has at its core evangelical and colonial contempt for anything Hindu. So, for Wiser, 'the Hindu Jajmāni System in its purest form was a corruption of the ancient system of "the custom of communal ownership" directed by the *panchayat*.'

However, the Jajmāni system was not as exploitative and corrupt as it has been portrayed. Today, a significant minority of post-colonial academics with empirical data challenge the antiquated perceptions of Indian peasants and the so-called lower castes leading a life of mere subsistence and servitude in pre-colonial Indian hamlets. In his 1998 work comparing the real earnings of 18th-century South Indian peasants and their British counterparts, historian Prasannan Parthasarathi points out that South Indian agricultural labourers had higher earnings and more financial security than their British counterparts. Interestingly, even agricultural labourers from the so-called outcastes in South India had higher real earnings than English farm labourers.

The word Jajmāni or Yejmān (as known in South India) is derived from Yajña. Six years before Wiser, in 1930, Mahatma Gandhi (1869–1948), then incarcerated in the Yeravda Central Prison, in a series of letters to Satyagraha Ashram, explained with a few examples of strong real-life characters the Yajña spirit of rural society in India, or otherwise the Jajmāni system, without naming it. Yajña, or the Vedic fire ritual, forms an archetypal basis for Indian civilization. It is not just the offering of material things to various deities but also the co-creation of the universe as a continued process. The value system of the Jajmāni system ultimately derives its strength and reinforcement from the Vedic archetype of Yajña. Today, there is a strong case for the very physical Yajña as a significant part of the religious life of Harappan society.

In its evolution as the basic process archetype of Indian society, Yajña has become a substrate-independent functional basis of Indian society. It has a dynamic and ever-expanding hermeneutic space to accommodate the ever-evolving social developments. Vedic Yajña, at its highest vision, is the recreation of the cosmic process of Ṛta. Ṛta manifests in human society and interactions as Dharma. Yajña accomplishes the maintenance of Ṛta as Dharma.

The Yajña archetype underlying the Jajmāni system makes all work sacred, and none defiled. The performer of every occupation becomes a performer of Yajña. This also means that social exclusion and social aristocracy, which are products of various political and economic factors, are constantly challenged by such a value system. Given the fact that Yajña is central to Vedic society, one must understand Yajña in the context of Vedic society and its values.

Vēdic Society: Values and Vision

What is called the standard model of Indian social history posits that fundamental to the Vedic worldview of society was the Puruṣa Sūkta, found in the 10th Maṇḍala of the *Ṛig Veda*. In this hymn, the different parts of Puruṣa become the different Varṇas, with the Śūdras being born from the feet of Puruṣa. When Western Indologists combined the Āryan-Dasyu divide and the speculation of a violent Āryan invasion of the native population with the emergence of the four Varṇas from the different body parts of Puruṣa in a definitively hierarchical way, the conclusion strongly suggested a racial origin and religious imposition of a birth-based pyramidal structure on Indians about three thousand years before present.

One of the most scholarly critical studies on the Puruṣa Sūkta was conducted by Dr Bhimrao Ramji Ambedkar (1891-1956). According to Ambedkar, in creating the four Varṇas, the Puruṣa Sūkta (PS) 'stands in complete contrast ... with the other parts of the Rig Veda'. It is important to remember that Dr Ambedkar was one of the earliest scholars in the secular domain, outside a small group of Vedic scholars of the Sri Aurobindo school, to dispute the racial characterization of the Varṇa system, which he did as early as 1946. He proposed that Vedic society originally had only three Varṇas. The fourth Varṇa as a social space was created because of the political rivalry between the Brahmins and Kṣatriyas. When the latter tyrannized the former, the Brahmins retaliated by denying those Kṣatriyas the ritual of Yajñōpavīta, pushing them into a punitive social space called the Śūdra Varṇa. Thus, to him, the primary impulse in the differentiation of Varṇas in the Puruṣa Sūkta is more political than sacred.

Prof. Arvind Sharma, the Birks Professor of Comparative Religion at McGill University, focuses on the alternative version of Varṇa evolution given in the *Brihadāraṇya Upaniṣad* (I.4.11-15). Initially, there were only Brahmins, and desiring more completion, the Kṣatriyas were created. Then, still not being complete, the Vaiśyas were created, and finally, the Śūdras were created. After the creation of the Śūdras, dharma was established over the rulers so that the weak could get justice against even the powerful. Prof. Sharma calls this 'primal egalitarianism', differentiating it from the 'primal hierarchicalism' of the Puruṣa Sūkta.

From this emerges a crucial question: the values Vedic literature insists upon—whether they favour social discrimination and exclusion or social inclusion and a voice against social exclusion. The episode of Kavaṣa Ailuṣa, as it unfolds in the Aitareya Brāhmaṇa, is a defining one for clearly declaring the directional course of Hindu civilizational flow. It intertwines the sacred and the mundane, where the life-giving waters of ceremony mirror the celestial waters above us, which sustain the individual and society when they descend through agriculture. This narrative is more than just a memory from the past; it is a powerful statement against social exclusion and marginalization.

Colonial Reconstruction of Buddha Interlude

The standard model of Indian social history holds that Buddha was a rebel against Hindu dharma. He was either a reformer or a complete opponent of Vedic religion. This pitting of Buddha against Vedic religion and as an anti-caste crusader emerges more from a colonial reconstruction of the image of Buddha. Initially, such a reconstruction was unintentional but carried inherent Euro-centric biases. It recast the Buddha of ancient India into a Christological and/or Lutheran figure. Soon, this colonial reconstruction of Buddha assumed a darker side. It synchronized itself with the negative and vitriolic vilifying of Hindu dharma by evangelicals. Buddhism, as shaped by colonial constructs, positions Hindus as an ignorant populace subjugated by a detestable priesthood. Regrettably, this perspective on Hinduism and Buddhism was internalized by many educated Hindus as well.

The Theosophical movement also fed into this stream. Bodh Gaya emerged as a symbol of Buddhist 'othering' of Hinduism, painting the latter not only as inferior but also malevolent. Catalysed by the work of Edwin Arnold (1832–1904), a born-again Buddhist monk Anagarika Dharmapala (1864–1933), took up the cause of Bodh Gaya. This also marked the starting point of Buddhist-Sinhalese nationalism as a religion-fuelled movement and the notion of 'Aryan racial superiority'.

But the sacredness of the site predates Buddha. Robert DeCaroli, a historian of early Buddhism, argues for continuity in the Buddhist narrative with the pre-Buddhist 'Brahmanical' traditions, which used the site for śrāddha. Another scholar of Buddhist tradition, Matthew Sayers, while questioning the pre-Buddhist śrāddha at Gayā, nevertheless points out that its sanctity predates Buddha's arrival or perhaps caused Buddha's arrival there. So, the presence of non-Buddhist Hindu temples was not a sectarian aggressive occupation of the most holy Buddhist site but rather a site of shared sanctity. In fact, during the Islamist invasions, non-Buddhist Hindus went out of their way to protect the site.

The Nehruvian fascination for Buddhism had a subtle pro-Theravādin bias. This also helped in the exclusive Buddhist brand building of Bodh Gayā by the Government of India itself. Overall, the Bodh Gayā confrontation became the symbol of this inferiorized othering of Hinduism. A reinvented Buddhist identity, shaped through colonial Indological frameworks, served as its religious fulcrum in the Sinhalese racial political revival.

The Anti-Brahmin movement in India, particularly in Tamil Nadu and Andhra, under ideologues like E.V. Ramasamy (known as 'Periyar' to Dravidianists) and Kancha Ilaiah, shows the potential to move towards a violent elimination of Brahmins or anyone deemed 'Aryan,' with a doublespeak of 'eradicating Sanātana Dharma.' In both discourses, Hinduism is depicted as appropriating and destroying Buddhism.

How true is the image of Buddha as a social emancipator that colonial Indology created?

Buddha's Dhamma and Its Social Impact

Buddha, the founder of the path to enlightenment, challenged the Brahmins' perceived monopoly and denounced animal sacrifices. He reinterpreted the Vedic Yajñá, diminishing its significance as a social process model. As Buddhism transformed into an institutionalized religion with royal support, it profoundly influenced the Indian social structure. It planted the seeds for viewing occupations as either noble or defiled, inadvertently hastening the institutionalization of untouchability. This influence extended beyond India into Burma, Sri Lanka, and Japan.

Buddhism and Jainism, with their doctrinal upholding of absolute Ahimsa and strict moralism that often demanded the denial of all worldly pleasures, resulted in an ambivalent attitude towards communities involved in hunting, fishing, meat production, and also communities like bards and courtesans. The flexibility of the quasi-hierarchical Varṇa system, which was more a social space than a birth-based order with the Yajñá societal model of role allocation and redistribution processes, was highly reduced because of the impact of Buddhism and Jainism. It is highly improbable that Buddha or Mahaveera aimed at such a result. Nevertheless, this was an unintentional societal consequence. The artisan and working communities got divided into upper and lower communities. In Aṅguttara Nikāya, Buddha is shown as speaking of 'the family of a scavenger or a hunter or a basket-weaver or a wheelwright or a sweeper' as a low family and corresponds their characteristics to those monks who have no aspiration. There was a proliferation of communities whose works got labelled as defiled. For the first time in the course of India's socio-cultural evolution, the terms Hīna Jāthi (low Jāthi) and Ukkāṭa Jāthi (Higher Jāthi) clearly surface in the Buddhist literature as in Vinaya Piṭaka. At the elite level, philosophical debates were happening with respect to the nature of Brahman or its absence, the nature of Sunya, etc. Definitely, the Vedic, Buddhist, and Jain religions competed for royal patronage, and more often than not, the rulers patronized all the systems. But society at large was becoming socially stagnant.

Bhakti the Phenomenon, Process and Its Social Impact

Bhakti, a religio-psychological phenomenon, has always been an important core of India's social and spiritual life, clearly implicit in the Vedic literature itself. Hence, as a spiritual practice and phenomenon, it could be proto-Vedic. Bhakti seamlessly integrated the practice of Yajña, transforming it into an internal and societal ritual. It re-emerged as a remarkable civilizational endeavour aimed at rectifying any doctrinal corruption.

While social emancipation was not the primary objective of Bhakti, it inevitably brought about societal liberation as a natural consequence, with minimal or almost no violence and sustained community elevation. Bhakti starts with an individual's quest to realize a state of consciousness that embraces all existence. It brings an individual an experience of either non-dual oneness or complete submission to an all-pervasive Oneness, and sometimes both. From this realization and experience, the individual becomes a phenomenon, gathering around him or her many more individuals seeking to share the experience through the outpourings of the individual.

The experience becomes the highest expression of the Divine. The followers become a community, and the community obliterates all societal hierarchies.

Vedic dharma became quite a conducive substratum in which individual expression of bhakti received both structural catalysis and functional freedom. Here, the Bhagavad Gitā played an important role by harmonizing the dynamics of bhakti into the archetypal process of Yajña. This highly democratized spirituality. A spiritual seeking need not happen with a person going to the forest or joining the body of monks divorced from society. Anyone in any profession can become spiritually awakened and an authority. This became one of the most remarkable achievements of the post-Buddhist Bhakti movement, counteracting the influence of Buddhism and Jainism and also influencing both these religions.

Bhakti laid the foundation for future social movements in India, ranging from Khalsa to Gandhi.

Bhakti and Social Emancipation: Pre-Modern Period

The standard model of Indian social history constructs bhakti as a reaction to Buddhism and/or a rebellion against the caste system. Bhakti is a universal phenomenon found in all religious cultures. In Indian culture, from its very beginning, this phenomenon was understood in a very analytical manner and was integrated into Yōga. Parallel to the ascendancy and expansion of Buddhism and the churning made by Jain Sampradāyas, bhakti had a co-evolution in which it integrated Yajña with Bhakti and Yōga. This naturally counteracted the unintentional but institutional defilement of many hereditary occupational groups.

The Śaiva bhakti movement, with its mystic schools, made it clear that asking about or discriminating based on birth-based Jāthi and Varṇa was strictly taboo. Śiva, in His fierce form as

Bhairava, declares to the Goddess that Brahmins, Kṣatriyas, Vaiśyas, Śūdras, and others, all without discrimination, have been enjoined in the Dharma of Śiva: 'Sarve te samadharmāṇaḥ śivadharme niyojitāḥ.' Should a man mention the prior Jāti of a Putraka, Sādhaka, or a Samayin, he would require expiation; otherwise, he would be temporarily in hell. So, Śiva says that one must not discriminate.

Another important tool that Indian culture has evolved in democratizing spirituality is Dīkṣā. In Śaiva Dharma, a person, regardless of caste, enters the Bhairava jāthi once he receives Dīkṣā. In this tradition, an important evolute is the school of Saṁsiddha gurus, who were also called Mahāmunis. Their spiritual egalitarian values impacted society and challenged social stratification and exclusion, empowering society. Bhakti made the sacred feet of the Divine the highest source of grace, as seen in the emergence of the term 'Bhagavat-pāda' in places where Śaivism flourished. This paved the way for the Śūdra Varṇā to elevate their origin into a noble one.

With these developments, the Śaiva tradition became powerful in North India, with its spiritual centre of gravity in Kashmir and an institutional network in Central India. Then, with strong bhakti elements, it further evolved vibrantly in South India. All these developments fed into each other. Bhakti highlighted the saints from fishermen and hunter communities, potter and musician communities, priests, and landless labourers, without any of them having to relinquish their occupational identity, recognizing their spiritual authority as they were.

Reinforcing this through centuries was a compendium of sacralized biographies of the bhaktas of Śiva, derived from different walks of life—from potters to Brahmins to fishermen to kings—sharing the same sacred space. This 12th-century epic work, *Periya Purāṇam* by Chēkkizhār, who was the principal minister in the court of Emperor Anabāya Chōzha (Kulōthuṅga Chōzha-II), became a forerunner for later compendia of bhaktas, cutting across caste lines, ignoring social status, and hierarchies, and rejecting social exclusions.

In this context, this book does not deal with one important spiritual movement that tremendously impacted the Karnataka region and Tamil Nadu. It is the movement of Basavarājā, also belovedly called Basavēśvara or Basavaṇṇa. In the colonial context, more often than not, this 12th-century Vīra Śaiva tradition is compared with Protestant reformism. A tendency to separate itself from the mainstream Hindu body is also present in such views. This has taken a political form of its own, though the inner content of the spiritual tradition stresses the spiritual equality of all humanity. A critique of social stratification and exclusion, based on the spiritual equality of all humans, is a hallmark of Hindu spirituality in all its diverse manifestations.

As with the Śaiva tradition, the Vaiṣṇava tradition has ancient roots. Even during the time of the Mauryan Empire, its Bhāgavata or bhakti tradition was so strong and systematized that it could transform an Indo-Greek ambassador to the Indian mainland. From the Vedic times through the Sangham period and then through the time of the Āzhwārs, Bhakti became a multi-dimensional pathway phenomenon leading to a profoundly transforming mystic experience. With its consolidation in the form of the Śrī Vaiṣṇava tradition of Śrī Rāmānuja, the Śrī Rāmānuja tradition spread and diversified. With all its diverse traditions that branched and evolved from the Śrī Vaiṣṇava tradition, it is arguably the single largest spiritual-social emancipation movement that achieved the empowerment of common humanity in the most non-violent manner for the longest period with sustained vitality. It gave the world the power of passive resistance, which became visibly manifest in

Mahatma Gandhi and was, in turn, adapted by Martin Luther King Jr. in the racial circumstances of the United States.

In the Deccan, bhakti merged with the non-dual monist high Vedanta of the 7th-century CE philosopher-saint, Ādi Śaṅkara. From this fertilization evolved the Dāttātrēya tradition. This became a strong spiritual movement that naturally blunted the structures of social stagnation. From being seen by Smriti-creators as 'moving crematoria,' Advaitic Bhakti made the fourth Varṇa arise from the Divine Feet of Viṣṇu along with the sacred River Gaṅgā. This transformation was, to say the least, revolutionary but nevertheless was radically affected in a very natural manner. It was not gradual either. Thus, a model was created for social emancipation without hatred and conflict. The entire bhakti movement, animating through the movements of Chaitanya and Thukārām, derived its essence from seemingly diverse pan-Indian Hindu traditions. For instance, in the spiritual movement led by Saṅkara Dēva, known as Eka-Hari-nāma-saraṇa-Dharma, the Gnostic Sattra movement of the Bhāgavata Mahāpurāṇa or the Brahma Sattra gets integrated with the Atithi-oriented Sattra, revitalizing it as an institutional network in Assam. Vaiṣṇava equivalents like Periya Purāṇam, namely Bhaktamālā, were composed in the 16th century by Śrī Nābhādās Gōśwāmi, who belonged to the basket weaver community. Then, Śrī Mahā Bhakta Vijayam was composed by Mahipathi in the 18th century. These literatures served as books of divine integration of society, cutting through the walls of social stratification, aristocracy, and social exclusion. They served as sustained catalysts for the transformation of the individual and increased the strands of social emancipation throughout society.

As history moved towards the last centuries of the pre-modern period, bhakti also ushered in bhakti-peasant movements with militant characteristics, as seen in the Satnāmī movement, which stood against the Mughal empire and later resisted colonial proselytizing. As the most malignant manifestation of social stagnation started solidifying the walls of the inhuman social space of untouchability, these movements became the strongest indigenous challenges to break those walls.

Modern Period: Colonial and Anti-Colonial

With colonization came the era of aggressive narrative wars on Indian culture and society. Caste became fossilized. Impoverishment accelerated social stagnation, and its ill effects were used to essentialize Hindu civilization. It was a civilization plagued by the priestcraft of 'Aryan' Brahmins while the autochthonous subjugated races of India were getting empowered by British rule. Through centralized educational institutions and zealous missionary proselytization, the narrative war colonized the educated Indian psyche. The result was that an average educated Indian believed in the inferiority and deficiency of Indian civilization and strongly believed in the British Empire's historical role in humanizing Indian society. This was crucially reinforced by the vested interests that had become enshrined in the dominant classes, which had developed vested interests from their privileged status acquired during the colonial period. Thus, both the dominant sections of Indian society, docile to the British Empire, and the British colonial 'masters' agreed upon the specific form of birth-based social stratification and social exclusion as seen in Indian society, essentializing Indian culture and religion.

This strong narrative, which was superficially supported by the behaviour of educated Indians for and against caste, was challenged by Hindu spirituality. In South India, the Iyyā Vazhi movement critiqued colonialism in Purāṇic language. Śwāmi Vivekānanda and the Śri Rāmakṛṣṇa tradition of Vedantic humanism formulated a strong critique of social stagnation based on Advaita. Emanating from the mystic experiences of Śri Rāmakṛṣṇa, the movement became the most important stream inspiring India's anti-colonial movement while at the same time fighting against social stagnation. Ārya Samāj of Śwāmi Dayānanda Saraswatī, also anchored in the deep spiritual resources of India, became a very strong national movement against social stagnation and untouchability. Nationalist turned mystic Śri Aurobindo became a strong influence in the social outlook of the Baroda king, who in turn became the crucial supporter of Dr Ambedkar. There is a shared value system in Sri Aurobindo and Dr Ambedkar. Both Śri Aurobindo and Dr Ambedkar emphasized liberty, fraternity, and equality derived from Indian sources and stressed that the birth-based system of social discrimination, as well as graded inequality, is against democracy. The Gandhian movement took up the challenge of removing the apartheid-like discrimination against the marginalized sections of society. This movement was energized by the Vaiṣṇava spiritual tradition of Mahatma Gandhi and the uncompromising Advaita of Śrī Nārayana Guru and his spiritual comrade Chattampi Śwāmi. Temple entry for all Hindus through legislation was a great accomplishment achieved by the National movement, in which the moving force was Indian spirituality.

Even with the stranglehold of colonialism, Indian spirituality was able to inspire philanthropic activities through both Śaiva and Vaiṣṇava traditions, which had a great impact on human resource development as well as social emancipation. Indic entrepreneurs worked hard against colonial resistance to create institutions for educational service, humanitarian welfare, etc. This again goes against the stereotyped view of Hindu fatalism and Hindu selfishness promulgated by colonial and colonized perceptions of Indian society.

Of particular interest is the uniquely Indian conception of feeding the student and associating educational institutions with student food security. This can be seen as an adapted extension of the Hindu concept of students in Gurukulas obtaining food through alms. The food security of the student is taken care of by the society/community, which makes the student obligated to the society. Again, Hindu philanthropy is deeply related to the concept of Yajña.

In all these diverse phenomena of Indian social emancipation in varied historical phases, there are certain strong common strands. To understand these common strands and to consciously harness their capacity for social emancipation, an indigenous framework rooted in Indian values and ways of knowledge is needed.

Conclusion: A Hindu Model of Social Evolution and Emancipation

In 1990, thirty-four years after J.B.S. Haldane advocated for Hindu Anthropology, anthropologist McKim Marriott (1924-2024) edited and published a seminal collection of papers on Indian society titled *India through Hindu Categories* (Sage Publications). In his contribution to the volume, Marriott developed a distinctly Hindu model for studying society. Despite facing criticisms, this model challenged the prevailing paradigm in Indian sociology, which was established by anthropologist Louis Dumont (1911-1998). Although Marriott had already engaged in intellectual debates with Dumont in the 1970s, it was in this volume that he transcended mere criticism and formulated a comprehensive framework for studying Indian society based on what he termed 'Hindu categories'.

In many ways, Louis Dumont can be seen as a deep precursor to Samuel Huntington. He posited a profound dichotomy between Hindu and Western societies, particularly regarding their spiritual and social values. Dumont characterized Hindu society by its hierarchical nature, which he argued stemmed from spiritual texts and was reinforced by religion. According to Dumont, this hierarchy was based on the concept of bodily and ritualistic pollution. Thus, he coined the term '*Homo Hierarchicus*' to describe the Hindu individual. In stark contrast, he described Western societies as embodying '*Homo Aequalis*', characterized by notions of individual freedom and equality.

This dichotomy became popular among scholars who had harboured a deep colonial mindset in the post-colonial world. The view provided a post-colonial academic justification to view Indian civilization as inherently deficient and ethically and spiritually inferior to the West. As recently as 2019, the influential Nehruvian historian Ramachandra Guha, in his convocation address at the National Academy of Legal Studies and Research (NALSAR) University, invoked Dumont to essentialize Hindu civilization and society as hierarchical. He then positioned Indian democracy as an unfinished project in opposition to Indian civilization.

In its more extreme forms, such as those espoused by anti-Hindu ideologue Kancha Ilaiah, this conceptualization has morphed into hate literature targeting groups like Brahmins, stereotyping them as monolithic and inherently deficient parasites. Dumont's clever association of Indian religion and society with biological nomenclature inadvertently created a space for the development of such hate rhetoric. This dark transformation has since permeated much of academia and influential sections of the polity in subsequent decades.

Although Dumont claims that the association of religious status and secular power through texts like *Smṛti* and *Dharmaśāstra* uniquely imposed the caste system in Indian religion, evidence from colonial times shows that Western thought also reflected a similar divinely sanctioned social stratification.

Readers should pause and reflect on Dumont's thesis. It is a cleverly crafted socio-historical illusion and not an Indian reality. The core argument is that traditional Hindu civilization cannot conceive individual equality due to its religious framework. In contrast, the post-Enlightenment West is portrayed as strongly upholding individual liberty and equality.

Is this really true?

Giuseppe Maria Bernini (1709-1761), a dedicated Franciscan missionary, founded one of the earliest communities of Hindu converts to Christianity. He also authored some of the first evangelistic tracts. One notable tract features a dialogue between a Christian evangelist and his Hindu target, where the evangelist adeptly addresses all the Hindu's questions, demonstrating the perceived superiority of his faith. Among the topics discussed, the Hindu questions the caste system. The Hindu target states:

> You know that the supreme God is no one's enemy and does not do any injustice to anyone. Therefore I ask you. Why does the supreme God give one person a birth as a wretch or a Candala while he gives another person a birth as someone who is wealthy or is a kshatriya or a brahmin? The cause of this cannot be anything other than what he earned in his past birth. one person was righteous in his past birth. For this reason he got a good rebirth. Another was unrighteous. For this reason he got a bad rebirth.[1]

Indologist David Lorenzen says: 'One would like to think that the Christian would have to reply attacking these two ideas (transmigration and Karma) and insist that all men have an equal right to salvation.'[2]

In reality, Giuseppe Maria makes the Christian answer thus:

> you do not understand things correctly if you believe that people get good births and bad births because of what they earned in their past life, since the real cause of people's separate fates is nothing other than the welfare of this world. This is because it is necessary for the welfare of this world that [our] portions (aṃsa) in this world not be equal. Rather

> one must be greater than another, and one person must be subject to the command of another. This is because if all men were kings, then who would be the kings' peasants? If all were wealthy, then who would do the work of the wealthy persons' servants? If all were brahmins, who would do the work of the artisans? If all were artisans, then who would give work to the artisans? If all were equal, then no one would serve another? No one would accept another's command, and everyone would do what he like and do bad work without fear, because no one would be chief and no one would have enough divine authority (kudrata) to punish the evil-doers. For this reason, if all people were equal, then there would be a great confusion (ajaguta) in the world.[3]

Here, we see that the post-enlightenment Christian theology positing humans as created with inherent inequalities, thereby providing theological support for social stratification. In contrast, the Hindu worldview asserts that the essence of all beings is fundamentally the same. When this essence manifests in humans, all external factors, including social stratification and gender, become subordinate to this essence. Historically, the West has perpetuated the notion of 'deficient human individuals'. Although the Enlightenment era introduced ideas of individuality and equality, these concepts emerged despite Christian theological views. They were further complicated by colonialism, which deprived countless individuals across four continents of their potential over at least five generations. Consequently, Dumont's perspective also contributes to the notion of an 'outsider' humanity as deficient.

When Marriott introduced his scholarly critique—both empirical and conceptual—against the highly unidimensional characterization of Hindu society by Dumont, his vision was both deeply rooted and refreshing. Regrettably, much of Indian academia, driven more by a blend of intellectual lethargy and ideological biases than a genuine quest for truth, favoured Dumont over Marriott.

Marriott's meticulously crafted critique and the alternative he proposed through various well-researched papers did not dismiss analytic universality. Instead, he offered a complementary perspective that enriched the discourse:

> [This perspective, however, was not] a negation of all Western distinctions, and of value only as negation of all Western distinctions, and of value only as refutations of the Western ethnosoical sciences' claims to analytic universality?... The authors of this volume think otherwise; they find that Indian joinings of what the West would split often point to alternative, especially transactional concepts of integrative value.[4]

He set out 'to synthesize a theoretical general system accommodating the realities known to Hindus, using both India's multiple textual sources and the evidence of its highly varied social life'.[5] The following passage from his 1990 paper can provide the depth and holistic effort with which Marriott approached the problem:

> As a people who are etymologically 'riverine', it is serendipitous that Hindus should have a set of sciences that respond so well to hydraulic metaphors.... Unlike points in a Euclidean geometric space, imperfectly bounded fluid entities can never be presumed to be fixed, discrete or absolutely measurable. Modelling Hindu phenomena thus seem to require algorithms more like those used in the sciences of oceanography or meteorology.... Hindu sciences also generally postulate one nonelement and antiaim – the omnipresent, reflexive, nonmaterial, constant process(es) commonly glossed over as 'self' or 'soul' (brahman, atman) or consciousness (purusa). Its function of total, passive consciousness is normally available to humans only on released consciousness, conceivable as the empty and static complement of the universal set (of the

> foregoing particulars), does a sense of wholeness ordinarily arise. By conceptually aggregating all points of view (those of all differently situated, embodied souls) on a fluid world, however this Hindu notion of a ubiquitous consciousness seems to point to the multiperspectival and multidimensional kind of thought about relationships and processes which a Hindu ethnosociology, too, may well attempt. Such consciousness is, of course, the subject of a vast speculative literature, but has only begun to be a focus of ethnography.[6]

Though not without justified criticisms, Marriott's model still offers a refreshing and bold approach for social scientists, historians, and activists. It encourages them to observe society—its history and evolution—and to build models that closely approximate socio-cultural realities, aiming to transform society into one characterized by greater justice and harmony.

Unlike Dumont, Marriott approached Hindu society and civilization with respect and a learner's mindset. In 1974, when Marriott and his colleague Ronald Inden wrote the entry on the caste system for the *Encyclopaedia Britannica*, some academic reviewers criticized the essay, claiming it threatened to overshadow Louis Dumont's contributions. Marriott not only gave a detailed reply in a paper and at the end of it stated thus:

> In the course of our work, we have developed an increasing respect for the indigenous social sciences and other conceptual systems of South Asia, which are predominantly monistic. Most of the Western natural sciences have passed successfully from dualism to monism, and we expect that Western social scientists will also be able to do so. One way for them to try is to stretch their minds around those conceptual systems of South Asia that already have some of the features that the Western social sciences require. We do not pretend that such a *mokṣa* like objective is easily attained, but we think it would not be a bad objective for them to make themselves – the knowers – somewhat like those South Asian objects that they would make known.[7]

Here is a call to enrich social science by integrating elements from the Indian knowledge system, not as an ethnically distinct approach, but as a complementary one. This integration aims to create a more holistic understanding and eliminate distortions and prejudices. The most profound insight in his work is the non-dualist conceptualization of Indian society. He viewed each caste as a dynamic structure whose position within Hindu society is determined not by dualities such as power-status or purity-impurity but through transactions.

According to Marriott, in the Hindu social view, the human being is not an individual 'that is indivisible, bounded units, as they are in much of Western social and psychological theory'[8] but 'are divisible persons made up of particulate substances that can flow across boundaries and thus be shared, exchanged, and transferred'.[9]

Here again, there is a problem. Prem Saran, an IAS officer turned Indic social scientist, finds fault with Marriott because his conceptualization of the Hindu human as a 'dividual' makes the same error as Dumont in finding the Indian human being somehow deficiently different from the Western 'individual'. Based on the fieldwork of other ethnographers, Saran comes to a very important conclusion:

> The supposedly exclusive and peculiar Western type of individuality is an integral part of the South Asian cultural reality. Contrarily modern Western cultural concept of atomistic individualism acts as an ideological blinker that militates against the apprehensions of other types of individuality, especially the non-modern ones like the Indic one.[10]

To him, both Dumont and Marriott are like the proverbial blind men feeling the parts of an elephant. At the same time, 'perhaps it is only the elephant itself that is better placed to reveal its own idiosyncratic nature'.

This critique serves as a caution when employing Marriott's ethno-social science. Marriott's concept of the 'dividual' allows for substituting the Hindu individual with the existential core of their cultural identity. By integrating this individuality with the transactional-exchange perspective of Hindu society, we can offer a compelling vision for both academics and activists.

Another important criticism of Marriott's model is his reliance on Dharmaśāstra literature, in addition to empirical field data—a critique he himself directed at Dumont. Had Marriott incorporated bhakti literature and related narratives, he could have demonstrated how transactional exchanges across community boundaries foster more harmonious and egalitarian bonds. These bonds paradoxically possess the potential to liberate the individual from the web of relationships, leading to 'Moksha', or non-dual liberation.

The lines in the hymn of *Thoṇdaradipodi Āzhwār*, one of the twelve *Āzhwārs*, make the bhakti-catalysed, boundary-independent exchange of tangible and intangible sacred transactions the hallmark of Dharma:

> Oh the Divine who is enshrined in the walled auspicious grand city of Araṅgam, You decreed upon the scholarly masters of the four Vedas, the Brahmins of faultless character and noble lineage, that they should venerate on par with Yourself those devotees who are from (what the society considers as) inferior clans, venerate them and also give and take with them.[11]

This verse highlights the dynamic and emancipatory potential within the transactional understanding of Hindu social stratification. It is essential to delve into this perspective. Rather than viewing Hindu society as an oppressive, anti-democratic, and rigid structure of stratification and exclusion, this approach reveals it as a network of dynamic, stochastic exchanges across semi-permeable boundaries. When energized by the greater vehicle of *dharma* with the aim of *Moksha*, this web transforms into a powerful and sustained force for social emancipation.

Here we need to also take into consideration the views of Pandurang Vaman Kane (1880–1972), who did the Bhagīrathic work on Smṛti and Dharmaśāstra literature. While rejecting mindless criticisms of the social system of ancient India, he bemoaned that 'the great disparity between the high metaphysical teaching of the whole world being one and the treatment meted out to lower classes and untouchables, owing to ideas of exclusiveness, of purity and pollution by touch etc'. He also pointed out that Tilak, four months before his death, had written in *Kesari* (16 March 1920) that 'anyone who spent his life in Indian freedom struggle must be treated as a brahmana to whatever caste or sub-caste he might have belonged by birth, that caste should not be treated as a matter of birth but ... as dependent on qualities and actions'. Tilak had quoted a Pali verse from Suttanipata to fortify his argument. Kane himself, the greatest scholar of his time on Dharmaśāstra literature, sided with the 'reformist' interpretation of the Bhagavad Gīta. According to him, 'words of Gita cannot be used for supporting the present scheme of thousands of castes and sub-castes of water-tight character'. According to him, in verse 4.13 the purport is unambiguous. Varṇa was not based on birth. Otherwise, Kṛṣṇa would have clearly stated as 'Jāthi-karma-vibhāgaśaḥ' or 'Janma-karma-vibhāgaśaḥ'. Kane also pointed out that in the nine kārmaṇi prescribed to Brahmins, the emphasis has been on moral and spiritual values and not on birth. Kane goes on to give a real-life phenomenon involving himself. Under the guidance of Śwāmi Kēvalānanda Saraswati of the Satara district, who knew no English but only Dharmic and Bhakti literature, an organisation called Dharmanirṇaya Maṇdala was formed. Kane was one of its founder-members. This organization advocated congregational prayers without caste differences and the abolition of untouchability. It also took the stand that 'including untouchables' all Hindus as being 'entitled to study the Veda and have upanayana performed with Vedic mantras and priests conversant with the upanayana procedure should be ready to do so, if invited'.[12]

Needless to say, such a movement should have been celebrated by Hindu society. Today many neo-traditionalists use the monumental work of Kane. However, as important as his work is, the understanding that this was the view and value system of the life-long scholar of the Dharmaśāstras, because he knew that this is how the Dharmaśāstra themselves would have evolved indigenously through Indic spirituality had there been no social stagnation, is also equally important.

In effecting this emancipatory transformation, an important role is played by a phenomenon that the Hindu civilization identified as the ṛṣi. The historical role that ṛṣi phenomenon played in the social evolution of India is brought out by Sri Aurobindo:

> [T]he man of a higher spiritual experience and knowledge, born in any of the classes, but exercising an authority by his spiritual personality over all, revered and consulted by the king of whom he was sometimes the religious preceptor and in the then fluid state of social evolution able alone to exercise an important role in evolving new basic ideas and effecting direct and immediate changes of the socio-religious ideas and customs of the people. It was a marked feature of the Indian mind that it sought to attach a spiritual meaning and a religious sanction to all, even to the most external social and political circumstances of its life, imposing on all classes and functions an ideal, not except incidentally of rights and powers, but of duties, a rule of their action and an ideal way and temperament, character, spirit in the action, a dharma

> with a spiritual significance. It was the work of the Rishi to put this stamp enduringly on the national mind, to prolong and perpetuate it, to discover and interpret the ideal law and its practical meaning, to cast the life of the people into the well-shaped ideals and significant forms of a civilisation founded on the spiritual and religious sense.[13]

Sri Aurobindo situates the rṣi within a specific historical context. Yet, the essence of the Ṛṣi transcends time, weaving itself into the very fabric of India's sociocultural and psychological-spiritual evolution. This book endeavours to illuminate this timeless essence through the lives of various spiritual luminaries who have championed sustained liberation. Their profound contributions offer the modern world a blueprint for achieving global peace and harmony. They teach us to embrace and celebrate our natural diversities while dissolving artificial barriers with the transformative power of love and wisdom.

Notes

Foreword

1. Thirumoolar, Thirumanthiram (51st verse), Thiruvaduthurai Adhinam, Thiruvaduthurai, 1954.
2. Vidvan Shrimad Iramalingath thambiran Swamigal, Naangam Thirumurai (Padigam 75, Podu, verse 726), Aram Thirumurai (Padigam 50, verse 4), Jnana sambandham publication, Dharumai Adhinam, Mailadudurai, 1997.
3. Shivakavi Mani C.K. Subramania Mudaliyar, Periya Puranam (12.1), Kovai Tamizhch changam, Coimbatore, 1954.
4. M.A. Venkatakrishnan, Thiruvaimozhi (1.1.7.), (4.6.8.) (Chennai: Gitacharya, 1999).
5. Shrimad Vara vara Munindra Granthamalai (Kanchipuram: Prativadi Bhayankaram Annangaracharyar Publication, 1966).
6. Prof. S.K. Ramachandra Rao, Purandara Sahitya Darshana, Vol. 3 (Bengaluru: The Directorate of Kannada and Culture, Govt. of Karnataka, 1985), 50.
7. Shri Kanaka Dasara Virachita Shri Hari Bhakti Sara (7th verse) (Hubli: Shri Vaibhava Lakshmi Prakashan).
8. Shri Jnaneshwari, Parayana prath, 10th chapter, 25th Shloka, 230th verse (Gorakhpur: Gita press).
9. Jagadguru Shri Tukobarayanchi Vedavani, Abhanga Gatha, Verse no 3153, 525, Dondopanth Dada Shirvalkar, Sant Vang maya prasarak Mandal, Karad, 1997.
10. Molla, Shri Molla Ramayana (6.1.117) (Lucknow: Bhuvana Vani Trust, 1977).
11. Krishnadeva Kaviraja, Chaitanya Charitamruta, Bhaktivedanta Book Trust (Adi Lila, 11.9), 2007.

Chapter 1: Indian Exceptionalism of Birth-based Stratification: Genuine and the Constructed

1 Ramachandra Guha, 'Ramachandra Guha reflects on India at 70', PAN MacMillan. 07 August 2017. https://www.panmacmillan.com/blogs/history/ramachandra-guha-reflects-on-india-at-70

2 Oprah Winfrey (@Oprah) My next @oprahsbookclub pick. Twitter. 4 August 2020. https://twitter.com/Oprah/status/1290634524594929664
3 Isabel Wilkerson, *Caste: The Origins of Our Discontent* (New York: Random House, 2020), 17.
4 Ibid., 363-4.
5 Kathy Stuart, *Defiled Trades and Social Outcasts* (Cambridge: Cambridge University Press, 2000), 2-3.
6 Paul Freedman, *Images of the Medieval Peasant* (Redwood City, CA: Stanford University Press, 1999), 31-2.
7 Ibid.
8 Ibid., 93.
9 Sumit K. Mandal, *Becoming Arab, Creole Histories and Modern Identity in the Malay World* (Cambridge: Cambridge University Press, 2018), 29.
10 Ibid., 163.
11 J.G. Kennedy, *The Flower of Paradise* (New York: Springer Science, 2012), 49.
12 John Flower, *Peasant Consciousness,* in *Post-Socialist Peasant? Rural and Urban Constructions of Identity in Eastern Europe, East Africa and the Former Soviet Union,* ed. D. Kaneff (New York: Springer, 2001), 44-5.
13 Wenfang Tang and Qing Yang, 'The Chinese Urban Caste System in Transition', *The China Quarterly,* 196 (December 2008): 759-9.
14 Tiejun Cheng, *Dialectics of Control the Household Registration (Hukou) System in Contemporary China*, Cambridge University Press, 1991, 81.
15 Glen Peterson, *The Power of Words: Literacy and Revolution in South China, 1949-95* (Vancouver: University of British Columbia, 1997), 121-2.
16 Ibid., 123.
17 Fei-ling Wang, *Organizing through Division and Exclusion: China's Hukou System* (Redwood City, CA: Stanford University Press, 2005), 39.
18 Sulamith Potter and Jack Potter, *China's Peasants: The Anthropology of a Revolution* (Cambridge: Cambridge University Press, 1991), 97.
19 Fei-ling Wang, *Organizing through Division and Exclusion: China's Hukou System* (Redwood City, CA: Stanford University Press, 2005), 9.
20 Eileen Yuk-ha Tsang, *China's Commercial Sexscapes: Rethinking Intimacy, Masculinity, and Criminal Justice* (Toronto: University of Toronto Press, 2019), 36.
21 Dexter Roberts, *Myth of Chinese Capitalism* (New York: St. Martin's Press, 2020), 5.
22 Carol Mason, Martin Harry Greenberg and Patricia Warrick, eds., 'Isaac Asimov notes to *Strikebreaker*', in *Anthropology through Science Fiction* (New York: St. Martin's Press, 1974), 137-49.

23 Barton Scott, *Spiritual Despots: Modern Hinduism and the Genealogies of Self-Rule* (Chicago: University of Chicago Press, 2016), 36-7.

24 Jayantanuja Bandyopadhyaya, *Class and Religion in Ancient India* (New Delhi: Anthem Press, 2007), 87-8.

25 Anya Bernstein, *Religious Bodies Politic Rituals of Sovereignty in Buryat Buddhism* (Chicago: University of Chicago Press, 2013), 38.

26 Borin Van Loon and Vinay Lal, *Introducing Hinduism (Graphic Guides)* (London: Icon Books), 106.

27 Rozino Visram, *Ayahs, Lascars and Princes: The Story of Indians in Britain 1700-1947* (New York: Routledge, 1986), 9.

Chapter 2: Need for a Hindu Social Science and a Fresh View of Varṇa and Jāthi

1 Ronald Clark, *J.B.S: The Life and Work of J.B.S Haldane* (Oxford: Oxford University Press, 1984), 49.

2 Ibid., 50.

3 Diane B. Paul, 'A War on Two Fronts: J.B.S. Haldane and the Response to Lysenkoism in Britain', *Journal of the History of Biology*, 16, no. 1 (1983): 36.

4 J.B.S. Haldane, 'A Rationalist with a Halo, (1954)', in *Science and Life: Essays of a Rationalist* (London: Pemberton, 1968), 89.

5 J.B.S. Haldane, 'A Passage to India', in *Science and Life* (London: Pemberton, 1968), 84.

6 Ibid., 127.

7 Sita Ram Goel, *Hindu Society under Siege* (New Delhi: Voice of India, 1981), 24.

8 J.B.S. Haldane, 'The Argument from Animals to Men: an Examination of Its Validity for Anthropology', *The Journal of the Royal Anthropological Institute of Great Britain and Ireland*, 86, no. 2 (Jul-Dec., 1956): 8.

9 Ibid.

10 Ibid.

11 Nirmal Kumar Bose, *Cultural Anthropology* (New Delhi: Asia Publishing House, 1961), 20-1.

12 Ibid.

13 Ibid.

14 Ibid., 24-5.

15 Nirmal Kumar Bose, *Culture and Society in India* (New Delhi: Asia Publishing House, 1957), 214.

16 Nirmal Kumar Bose, *Cultural History of Arts and Crafts in India* (Imphal: Atombapu Research Centre, 1970), 9.

17 Nirmal Kumar Bose, 'Caste in India', *Man in India* 31, no. 3-4 (July-December, 1951): 107-23.

18 M.S. Golwalkar, *Spotlights* (Bangalore: Sahitya Sindhu, 1974), 110.

19 Suraj Chandra Sinha, *The Heritage of Nirmal Kumar Bose* (New Delhi: IGNCA, 1997), 11-2.

Chapter 3: Harappan 'Caste' Mystery

1 Robert Eric Mortimer Wheeler, *Harappa 1946: The Defences and Cemetery R37* (New Delhi: Archaeological Survey of India, 1947), 74.

2 Ibid., 76.

3 Stuart Piggott, *Prehistoric India to 1000 B.C* (London: Penguin Books, 1950), 200.

4 Ibid., 201.

5 Ibid, 151.

6 R.E. Mortimer Wheeler, *The Cambridge History of India – Supplementary Volume, Indus Civilization* (Cambridge: Cambridge University Press, 1953), 82-3.

7 Robert Caldwell, *Lectures on the Tinnevelly Missions: Descriptive of the Field, the Work, and the Results: With an Introductory Lecture on the Progress of Christianity in India* (London: Bell & Daldy, 1857), 42.

8 Tony Joseph, 'How Genetics is Settling the Aryan Migration Debate', *The Hindu*, 16 June 2017.

9 The next paragraphs are based on Steffan Arvidsson, *Aryan Idols: Indo-European Mythology as Ideology and Science,* trans. Sonia Wichmann (Chicago: The University of Chicago Press, 2006).

10 Ibid., 271-2.

11 Ajay Pathak, Anurag Kadian, Alena Kushniarevich, et al., 'The Genetic Ancestry of Modern Indus Valley Populations from Northwest India', *The American Journal of Human Genetics*, 103, no. 6 (December 2018): 918-29.

12 Maanasa Raghavan, Hannes Schroeder, and Anna-Sapfo Malaspinas, 'An ancient genome from the Indus Valley Civilization', *Cell* 179 (October 2019): 586-8.

13 Jonathan Mark Kenoyer quoted in Stephanie Pappas. 'Mysterious Indus Valley People Gave Rise to Modern-day South Asians', *LiveScience*, 05 September 2019. Details available at https://www.livescience.com/south-asians-descend-from-harappan-civilization.html

14 V.M. Narasimhan, N. Patterson, P. Moorjani, et al., 'The Formation of Human Populations in South and Central Asia', *Science*, 365, no. 6457 (September 2019): eaat7487.

15 J.M. Kenoyer, 'Introduction' in *The People of the Indus and the Birth of Civilization in South Asia* (New Delhi: Penguin, 2022).

16 R.D. Gray and Q.D. Atkinson, 'Language-tree Divergence Times Support the Anatolian Theory of Indo-European Origin', *Nature* 426, no. 6965(2003): 435-39.

17 Will Chang, Chundra Cathcart, David Hall, and Andrew Garrett, 'Ancestry-Constrained Phylogenetic Analysis Supports the Indo-European Steppe Hypothesis', *Language* 91, no. 1 (2015): 194–244.

18 W. Haak, I. Lazaridis, and N. Patterson. 'Massive migration from the steppe was a source for Indo-European languages in Europe', *Nature* 522 (2015): 207–211.

19 Vishnupriya Kolipakam, Fiona M. Jordan, Michael Dunn, et al. 'A Bayesian Phylogenetic Study of the Dravidian Language Family', *Royal Society Open Science* 2018. https://doi.org/10.1098/rsos.171504

20 Paul Heggarty et al. 'Language Trees with Sampled Ancestors Support a Hybrid Model for the Origin of Indo-European Languages', *Science*, 381 (2023): eabg0818. DOI: 10.1126/science.abg0818

21 *Atharva Veda*: XII.I.45

22 Vasudeva S Agrawala, *Ancient Indian Folk Cults* (New Delhi: Prithivi Prakashan, 1970), 3.

23 Irawati Karve, *Hindu Society: An Interpretation* (Poona: Deccan College Press, 1961), 58.

24 Ibid.

25 S.C. Malik, *Indian Civilization: The Formative Period: A Study of Archaeology as Anthropology.* (Shimla: Indian Institute of Advanced Study, 1968), 94.

26 Ibid., 100.

27 Ibid., 101.

28 Ibid., 103.

29 Ibid., 105.

30 Ibid., 106-8.

31 Jonathan Mark Kenoyer, 'Socio-economic Structures of the Indus Civilization as Reflected in Specialized Crafts and the Question of Ritual Segregation, Old Problems and New Perspectives in the Archaeology of South Asia', *Wisconsin Archaeological Reports*, 2 (1989): 188.

32 Iravatham Mahadevan, 'Dravidian Models of Decipherment of the Indus Script: A Case Study', *Tamil Civilization,* 4 (1986): 133-143.

33 Iravatham Mahadevan interviewed by Omar Khan: url: https://www.harappa.com/content/iravatham-mahadevan-complete-interview (accessed on 10 March 2023).

34 Madhukar Keshav Dhavalikar, *Cultural Imperialism Indus Civilization in Western India* (New Delhi: South Asia Books, 1995), 162-7.

35 Lamberg-Karlovsky's theory explained by Edwin Byrant, *The Quest for the Origins of Vedic Culture* (Oxford: Oxford University Press, 2001), 164-5.

Chapter 4: Harappan Yajña and Vedic Agni: Roots of a Social System

1 J.M. Kenoyer, Old Problems and New Perspectives in the Archaeology of South Asia (Ed. Kenpoyer), Department of Anthropology, University of Wisconsin,1989, 189.

2 Ibid.

3 Gerald Berreman, *The Evolutionary Status of Caste in Peasant India, Social Anthropology of Peasantry,* ed. Joan P. Mencher (1983), 237–250.

4 Jane R. McIntosh, *The Ancient Indus Valley: New Perspectives* (California: ABC-Clio, 2008), 270-1.

5 William, Henricks Wiser, *The Hindu Jajmāni System: A Socio-Economic System Interrelating Members of a Hindu Village Community in Service* (Lucknow: Lucknow Publishing House, 1936), 11.

6 Ibid., 138.

7 Ibid., 173-4.

8 Anthony John Ballantyne, *Orientalism and Race: Aryanism in the British Empire* (London: Palgrave, 2002), 52.

9 William Adam, *Law and Custom of Slavery in British India in a Series of Letters to Thomas Fowell Buxton* (Virginia: Weeks-Jordan & Company, 1840), 17.

10 Prasannan Parthasarathi, 'Rethinking wages and competitiveness in eighteenth-century Britain and South India', *Past and Present* 158 (February 1998): 79-109.

11 Bernhard Kölver, 'On the origins of the Jajmānī system', *Journal of the Economic and Social History of the Orient*. 31, no. 3 (1988): 265-85.

12 Mohandas Karamchand Gandhi, *From Yervada Mandir (Ashram Observances),* trans. Valji Govindji Desai, (Ahmedabad: Navajivan Mudranalaya, 1932), 34 and 35-6.

13 Stella Kramrisch, *The Presence of Siva* (Princeton: Princeton University Press, 1981), 6.

14 Ibid., 268-9.

15 Jagat Pati Joshi and B.B. Lal, *Excavations at Kalibangan the Harappans (1960-1969) Part-I* (Archaeological Survey of India, 2015), 133.

16 Shereen Ratnagar, *Enquiries into the Political Organisation of Harappan Society* (Wanawadi: Ravish Publishers, 1991), 119.

17 Jane R. McIntosh, 2008, 278.

18 Swami Vivekananda, *The Complete Works of Swami Vivekananda*, vol 4 (Kolkata: Advaita Ashrama, 1948), 357.
19 Gregory Louis Possehl, *The Indus Civilization: A Contemporary Perspective* (Lanham: Altamira Press, 2002), 57.
20 Petr Andreevich Eltsov, 'From Harappa to Hastinapura: A Study of the Earliest South Asian City and Civilization from the Point of View of Archaeology and Ancient Indian Literature'. PhD Thesis (Boston: Department of Anthropology, Harvard University, 2004), 351.
21 Ibid., 354.
22 Ibid.
23 Ibid., 355.
24 Ibid., 356.
25 Pankaj Jain, 'Reinterpreting Yajna as Vedic sacrifice', *Brahmavidya: Adyar Library Bulletin* (2011): 169.

Chapter 5: Revisiting Vedic Society, Its Values, and Vision

1 Julius Lipner, *Hindus Their Religious Beliefs and Practices* (London: Routledge, 1994), 72.
2 Romila Thapar, *Indian Cultures as Heritage: Contemporary Pasts* (New Delhi: Aleph Book Company, 2018), 105.
3 Ibid., 106.
4 Wendy Doniger, *The Hindus: An Alternative History* (New York: Penguin Press, 2010), 118.
5 Kancha Ilaiah, *Post-Hindu India: A Discourse on Dalit–Bahujan, Socio-Spiritual and Scientific Revolution* (New Delhi: Sage Publications, 2009), 26-7.
6 Ibid., 205.
7 Ibid., 208.
8 Ibid., 188.
9 Bhimrao Ramji Ambedkar, *Who Were the Shudras* (Bombay: Thacker & Co. Ltd., 1946), 2-4.
10 Ibid., 10.
11 *Vishnu Purāṇa*, Book 4. Chapter 8. Verse 1. (Trans. With notes: Horace Hayman Wilson, Vol. IV, 1868, 31.
12 B.R. Ambedkar, *Who were the Shudras* (Thacker & Co. Ltd., 1946), 98-9.
13 Ibid., 147.
14 Ibid., 71.
15 Thomas R. Trautmann, *Aryans and British India* (California: University of California Press, 1997), 197-8 and 203-4.
16 B.R. Ambedkar, *Who Were the Shudras* (Thacker & Co. Ltd., 1946), 239-40.

17 Arvind Sharma, 'The Brihadaranyaka Upanishad and Modernity: New Perspectives', in *Vedanta Concepts and Application* (The Ramakrishna Mission Institute of Culture, 2000), 336-359 (all quotes of Prof. Sharma and the Upanishad, in this section unless otherwise stated, are taken from this paper.

18 *Bṛhadāraṇyaka Upaniṣad*: 1.4.11-15.

19 *Śatapatha Brāhmaṇa*: xiv. 4-2-23.

20 *Śatapatha Brāhmaṇa*: v.5-4-9.

21 *Sukla Yajur Veda*: 26:2.

22 This subsection mainly uses material from Tukaram Tatya, trans., *Aitareya Brahmana* of *Rig Veda* (Theosophical Society of India, 1890), 76-7 and Catherine Ludvik, *Sarasvati Riverine Goddess of Knowledge from the Manuscript-carrying Vina-player to the Weapon-wielding Defender of the Dharma* (Leiden: Brill, 2007), 85-6.

23 Laurie L. Patton, *Bringing the Gods to Mind: Mantra and Ritual in Early Indian Sacrifice* (California: University of California Press, 2005), 109.

24 Sri Aurobindo, *The Life Divine* (Pondicherry: Sri Aurobindo Ashram Trust, 1914), 210.

Chapter 6: Lutheran Buddha and Buddhist Jerusalem

1 This section is mostly based on Philip C. Almond, *The British Discovery of Buddhism* (Cambridge: Cambridge University Press, 1988).

2 Karl Friedrich Neumann, *The Catechism of the Shamans, or, The Laws and Regulations of the Priesthood of Buddha in China*, The Oriental Translation Fund (London, 1831), xxvi-xxvii.

3 Eugene Burnouf cited in Col. James Low, 'General Observations on the Contending Claims to Antiquity of Brahmans and Buddhists', *Journal of the Asiatic Society of Bengal*, 18 (1849): 111.

4 John Whitchurch Bennett, *Ceylon and its Capabilities* (Trumpet Publishers, 1843:1984), 272.

5 William Knighton, *Forest Life in Ceylon*, vol. II (London: Hurst & Blackett, 1854), 10-11.

6 Philip C. Almond, *The British Discovery of Buddhism* (Cambridge: Cambridge University Press, 1988), 72.

7 Alexander Cunningham, *Archaeological Survey of India Reports 1862-1884*, vol. III (Calcutta: Office of the Superintendent of Government Printing, 1873), 100.

8 Max Müller, *Buddhism and Buddhist Pilgrims* (Williams and Norgate, 1857), 7-8.

9 Ibid., 5.

10 Ibid., 5 and 22.

11 Ibid., 14.

12 Philip C. Almond, *The British Discovery of Buddhism* (Cambridge: Cambridge University Press, 1988),3

13 Nile Green, *How Asia Found Herself* (Yale University Press, 2022), 59.

14 Jacob N. Kinnard, *Places in Motion: The Fluid Identities of Temples, Images, and Pilgrims* (Oxford: Oxford University Press, 2014), 97.

15 Edwin Arnold, in Trübner's American and Oriental Literary Record, Vol. IV (January to December, 1883). Trübner & Co., London, 1884, 84.

16 Communication of Sir Edwin Arnold cited by Anagarika Dharmapala, *Buddha Gaya and Its Surroundings, The Buddhist*, 1891 and again in *Maha-Bodhi*, 34 (Aug. 1926), Ananda W.P. Guruge, ed., *Return to Righteousness: A Collection of Speeches, Essays, and Letters of the Anagarika Dharmapala* (Ceylon: Ministry of Education and Cultural Affairs, 1965), 589-90.

17 K.T.S. Sarao, *The History of Mahabodhi Temple at Bodh Gaya* (Berlin: Springer, 2020), 157.

18 Jacob N. Kinnard, *Places in Motion: The Fluid Identities of Temples, Images, and Pilgrims* (Oxford: Oxford University Press, 2014), 89.

19 Joseph Cheah, *Race and Religion in American Buddhism: White Supremacy and Immigrant Adaptation* (Oxford: Oxford University Press, 2011), 33.

20 Anagarika Dharmapala, *The History of Maha Bodhi Temple at Buddha Gaya*, ed. Ananda W.P. Guruge (1965), 603.

21 Exhibit D 22., in *Jaipal Gir and Ors. vs H. Dharmapala* on 22 August 1895, Indian Kanoon. URL: http://indiankanoon.org/doc/1821486/, 5.

22 Justice Macpherson and Justice Banerjee, Jaipal Gir and others (Petitioners) vs. H. Dharmapala (Opposite Party), 1895 August 22 in Indian Law Report, Calcutta Series, Vol.XXIII, January to December, 1896, The Bengal Secretariat Financial Department, 1897, 64.

23 Chronological order of events of Anagarika Dharmapala from *Anagārika Dharmapala's Services to the Cause of the Buddha Sasana from 1882 to 1933, Maha Bodhi Journal*, June 1933, from *The Maha Bodhi Centenary, volume1891-1991* (Calcutta: Maha Bodhi Society of India, 1991), 95-108.

24 Roger Griffin, *Terrorist's Creed: Fanatical Violence and the Human Need for Meaning* (Palgrave Macmillan, 2012), 120.

25 Based on *Amrita Bazar Patrika* report in *The Maha-Bodhi and the United Buddhist World*, XXXI, no.9 (Sep.1923), (Collected Volume-31), 354.

26 K.T.S. Sarao, *The History of Mahabodhi Temple at Bodh Gaya* (Berlin: Springer, 2020), 123.

27 Sameer Chandra Mookerjee, *The Need for Coalition between Hindus and Buddhists*, Maha Bodhi Journal, June 1923, CV-31, 211-2.

28 Mrs. Mary Mikahala Foster of Honolulu, *The Maha-Bodhi and the United Buddhist World,* vol. XXXI, no.10 (October, 1923): 370-3.

29 Jawaharlal Nehru, *The Discovery of India* (Oxford: Oxford University Press, 1946: 1995), 130-1.

30 Ibid., 211.

31 Robert DeCaroli, *Haunting the Buddha: Indian Popular Religions and the Formation of Buddhism* (Oxford: Oxford University Press, 2004), 106-7.

32 Abhishek Singh Amar paraphrasing Matthew Sayers in *Sacred Bodh Gaya: The Buddhaksetra of Gotama Buddha, Cross-disciplinary Perspectives on a Contested Buddhist Site*, ed. David Geary, Matthew Sayers, and Abhishek Singh Amar (London: Routledge, 2012), 33.

33 Gunapala Piyasena Malalasekera, ed., *Encyclopaedia of Buddhism*, vol. 3, no. 3 (Ceylon: Buddhist Council of Ceylon, Ministry of Cultural Affairs, 1973), 399.

34 Upinder Singh, *A History of Ancient and Early Medieval India* (New Delhi: Pearson, 2016), 478.

35 Xuanzang, *Si-Yu-Ki, Buddhist Records of the Western World*, vol. II, trans. Samuel Beal (Trubner & Co, 1884), 119-120.

36 Quoted in Koenraad Elst, *Ayodhya: The Case against the Temple* (Voice of India, New Delhi, 2002), 36.

37 K.T.S. Sarao, *The History of Mahabodhi Temple at Bodh Gaya* (Berlin: Springer, 2020), 121.

38 Jacob N. Kinnard, *Places in Motion: The Fluid Identities of Temples, Images, and Pilgrims* (Oxford: Oxford University Press, 2014), 81 and 88.

Chapter 7: Bhagavān Buddha, His Dhammā, and Its Impact

1 T.W. Rhys Davis, *Early Buddhism* (Edinburg: Archibald Constable & Co., 1908), 10-2.

2 I.B. Horner, trans., *The Book of the Discipline* (*Vinaya Piṭaka*), vol. II (*Sutta Vibhaṅga)* (Oxford: The Pali Text Society, 1940:2004), 187.

3 Rajendralala Mitra, trans., *The Lalita-Vistara or Memoirs of the Ealy Life of Sakya Singha* (Calcutta: Baptist Mission Pres, 1881), 40, 42, 51.

4 All quotes of Gautam Buddha taken from: 'Ambaṭṭha Sutta: Sutta 3' in *The Long Discourses of the Buddha: A Translation of the Dīg Nikāya* , Trans, from Pali: Maurie Walshe (Somerville: Wisdom Publications, 1987), 117-9.

5 *Shukla Yajur Veda*: 26:2 (Trans. Ralph T.H.Griffith (Benares,Lazarus & Co., 1899), 231) The same verse is translated by Arya Samaj scholar Devi Chand in this way: 'I do hereby address this salutary speech for the benefit of humanity, for the Brahmanas, the Kshatriyas, the Shudras, the

Vaishas, the kinsfolk and the men of lowest position in society.' One can see the hermeneutical space in the verse, which has been made specific to social liberation in the context of social stagnation catalyzed by colonial impoverishment. (*The Yajur Veda* translation by Devi Chand, All India Dayanand Salvation Mission, 1959, 270).

6 Swami Vivekananda, *The Religion We are Born In, Complete Works of Swami Vivekananda*, Vol. III (Mayawati: Advaita Ashrama, 1958), 457.

7 *Aitareya Brāhmaṇa*, 2:19.

8 *Chāndogya Upaniṣad*, 4.1.1 -4.3.4.

9 Gaudam Buddha in 'Aṅguttara Nikāya: Tika-nipāta 13' in *The Book of the Gradual Sayings: Anguttara-Nikaya*, vol I (The Pali Text Society, 1932). Translation: F.L. Woodward, 92.

10 Uma Chakravarti, *The Social Dimensions of Early Buddhism* (New Delhi: Munshiram Manoharlal Publishers Pvt. Ltd, 1996), 101

11 Bhikkhu Nanamoli and Bhikku Bodhi, trans., *Madhurā Sutta: The Middle Length Discourses of the Buddha: A New Translation of the Majjihima Nikāya* (Ceylon: Buddhist Publications Society, 1995), 701.

12 Ibid., 102, 109.

13 Vivekanand Jha, 'Caste, untouchability and social justice: early north Indian perspective', *Social Scientist*. 25, no. 11 (November-December, 1997): 25.

14 Uma Chakravarti, *The Social Dimensions of Early Buddhism* (New Delhi: Munshiram Manoharlal Publishers Pvt. Ltd, 1996), 101.

15 Ibid., 109.

16 Donald M. Seekins, *Historical Dictionary of Burma (Myanmar)* (Lanham: Rowman & Littlefield Publishers, 2017), 422.

17 Gwendolen Trench Gascoigne, *Among Pagodas and Fair Ladies: An Account of a Tour through Burma* (A.D. Innes & Co., 1896), 73.

18 Buddhologist Gregory Schopen uses this name to what is usually called '*Pali Vinaya*' or 'Therevāda Vinaya' or simply 'Vinaya Text'. [Gregory Schopen, '*The monastic ownership of servants or slaves: local and legal factors in the redactional history of two vinayas*'. *Journal of the International Association of Buddhist Studies* 17, no. 2 (1994): 149.

19 Ibid., 150.

20 Ibid., 155.

21 Mūlasarvāstivādin Vinaya-vibaṅga cited in Gregory Schopen, 1994, 156.

22 Gwendolen Trench Gascoigne, *Among Pagodas and Fair Ladies: An Account of a Tour through Burma* (A.D. Innes & Co., 1896), 71.

23 Henry Park Cohrane, *Among the Burmans* (Philadelphia: The Judson Press, 1906), 148

24 S.G. Grantham., *Census of India 1921, Burma-Part-I,* vol. X (Rangoon: Office of the Superintendent, Government Printing, 1923), 228.

25 Henry Park Cohrane, *Among the Burmans* (Philadelphia: The Judson Press, 1906), 150-1.

26 S.G. Grantham, *Census of India 1921, Burma-Part-I,* vol. X (Rangoon: Office of the Superintendent, Government Printing, 1923), 228.

27 Edmund Ronald Leach. *Political Systems of Highland Burma: A Study of Kachin Social Structure* (London: The Athlone Press, University of London, 1970), 215.

28 Kitsiri Malalgoda. *Buddhism in Sinhalese Society 1750-1900: A Study of Religious Revival and Change* (California: University of California Press, 1976), 88.

29 Ananda Abeysekara, *Politics of Higher Ordination, Buddhist Monastic Identity, and Leadership in Sri Lanka, Journal of the International Association of Buddhist Studies*, Vol.22, No.2, 1999, 255-280.

30 For example: Bruce Caldwell, 'Marriage in Sri Lanka: a century of change', PhD Thesis submitted to the Department of Demography and Sociology, National University of Australia, 1992, 106.

31 *The Rodiya Commission and its work: who are lower in race: The Kinnaraya or Rodiya? Literary Register Supplement: 'Notes and Queries', Supplement to Tropical Agriculture*, August 1904.

32 Faxian. *A Record of Buddhistic Kingdoms: Being an Account by the Chinese Monk Fa-hsien of Travels in India and Ceylon (AD 399-414) in Search of the Buddhist Books of Discipline*, trans. James Legge (Oxford: Oxford Clarendon Press, 1886), 43.

33 Akepogu Jammanna and Pasala Sudhakar, *Dalits' Struggle for Social Justice in Andhra Pradesh (1956-2008)* (Cambridge: Cambridge Scholars Publishing, 2016), 67-8.

34 Reginald Edward Enthoven, *The Tribes and Castes of Bombay*, vol. I (Bombay: Government Central Press, 1920), 261-2.

35 Bhimarao Ramji Ambedkar, *The Times of India,* 7 February 1951, quoted in Dhananjay Kheer, *Dr. Ambedkar Life and Mission* (Mumbai: Popular Prakashan, 1954), 427.

Chapter 8: Bhakti, Bhagavad Gītā, and the Beginning of the Movement

1 *Rig Veda* 1.127.5.

2 *Rig Veda* 1.156.3.

3 *Aitareya Brāhmaṇa* 1.1.2.13.

4 *Rig Veda* 1.156.3.

5 Max Muller and Moriz Winternitz quoted in Jeanine Miller, 'Bhakti and the Ṛig Veda: Did It Appear There or Not?', in *Love Divine: Studies*

in *Bhakti and Devotional Mysticism*, ed. Karel Werner (New York: Routledge, 1993), 7.

6 George Abraham Grierson, 'Entry for Bhakti-Marga'in *Encyclopaedia of Religion and Ethics*, vol. 2, ed. James Hastings, John Alexander Selbie, and Louis Herbert Gray (T. &T. Clark, 1921), 539 and George A. Grieson, 'Modern Hinduism and its Debt to the Nestorians', *Journal of the Royal Asiatic Society* (April, 1907): 311-35.

7 Jeanine Miller, 'Bhakti and the Ṛg Veda: Did It Appear There or Not?', in *Love Divine: Studies in Bhakti and Devotional Mysticism*, ed. Karel Werner (New York: Routledge, 1993), 1.

8 Ibid., 6.

9 Ibid.

10 Ibid., 8.

11 Jeanine Miller, *The Vision of Cosmic Order in the Vedas* (New York: Routledge & Kegan Paul, 1985), 11

12 Vivekanand Jha, 'Caste, Untouchability and Social Justice: Early North Indian Perspective', *Social Scientist* 25, no.11/12 (1997): 28.

13 Bhimrao Ramji Ambedkar, *Dr. Baba Saheb Ambedkar Writings and Speeches*, vol 3, compiled by Vasant Moon and Hari Narake, (Mumbai: Education Department, Govt. of Maharashtra, 1987), 361-2, 364.

14 Ibid., 240.

15 Hans T. Bakker, *The World of the Skandapurṇa: Northern India in the Sixth and Seventh Centuries* (London: Brill, 2014), 37.

16 Upinder Singh, *Political Violence in Ancient India* (Boston: Harvard University Press, 2017), 174.

17 Ibid., 468.

18 Bhimrao Ramji Ambedkar, *Dr. Baba Saheb Ambedkar Writings and Speeches*, vol 3, compiled by Vasant Moon and Hari Narake (Mumbai: Education Department, Govt. of Maharashtra, 1987), 276.

19 All Māhabhārata quotes taken from *Śānti Parva: Mokṣa Dharma Parva (181)*

20 *Dīgha Nikāya* 27.

21 All Māhabhārata quotes taken from *Vana Parva* 3:177.15.

22 All Māhabhārata quotes taken from *Vana Parva* 3:177.16.

23 All Māhabhārata quotes taken from *Vana Parva* 3:177.20-21.

24 All Māhabhārata quotes taken from *Vana Parva* 3: 177.28.

25 K. Balasubramania Iyer, *Yaksha Prasna* (New Delhi: Bharatiya Vidya Bhavan, 1963), 70-1.

26 All Māhabhārata quotes taken from Vana Parva 3: 206.12.

27 Bal Gangadara Tilak, *Śrīmad Bhagavad Gītā Rahasya*, vol II, trans. Bhalchandra Sitaram Suthankar (Mumbai: Lokmanya Tilak Mandir, 1936), 700.

28 Bhimrao Ramji Ambedkar, 'My Philosophy of Life' in *Dr. Baba Saheb Ambedkar Writings and Speeches,* vol 17, part III, ed. Hari Narake, M. L. Kasare, N.G. Kamble, and Ashok Godghate, (New Delhi: Dr. Ambedkar Foundation 2014), 503.

29 M.R. Sampatkumaran, trans., *Gītābhāṣya or Śri Bhāṣya of Śri Rāmānuja* (Mumbai: Ananthacharya Indological Research Institute, 1985), 456.

30 Mohandas Karamchand Gandhi, *The Gospel of Selfless Action or the Gita according to Mahatma Gandhi*, trans. Mahadev Desai (Ahmedabad: Navjivan Publishing House, 1946), 196.

31 Sanjay Paswan and Pramanshi Jaideva, eds., 'Entry for "Demand for Dalit Rights Under Dalit Leadership"', in *Encyclopaedia of Dalits in India*, vol 13 (New Delhi: Kalpaz Publications, 2002), 152-3.

32 Koenraad Elst, 'Response in the thread "*The Gita and Varna-Sankara*"' (From RISA). Details available at http://jagadanandadas.blogspot.com/2007/02/gita-and-varna-sankara-from-risa.html

33 Bhagavad Gītā 1:40-43.

34 Arvind Sharma, 'Response in the thread "*The Gita and Varna-Sankara*"' (From RISA). Details available at http://jagadanandadas.blogspot.com/2007/02/gita-and-varna-sankara-from-risa.html

35 Bhagavad Gītā 16:15.

36 Bhagavad Gītā 16:18.

37 Bhagavad Gītā 6:29.

38 Bhagavad Gītā 6:30.

Chapter 9: Bhakti, the Holistic Yajña Movement: Vedic to Early Medieval Period

1 Ram Swarup, 'On Hinduism: Reviews and Reflections', *Voice of India*, 2009: 60 and 78.

2 Dilip Chakrabarti, 'The Archaeology of Hinduism' in *Archaeology and World Religion* (Ed. Timothy Insoll), (London: Routledge, 2001), 49.

3 Stella Kramrisch, *The Hindu Temple*, Vol. I, (New Delhi: Motilal Banarasidass Publishers, 1976:2015), 146–7 and 253.

4 *Ṛg Veda* X.151.1

5 Bhagapat Kumar Shastri, *The Bhakti Cult in Ancient India* (Oriental Publishers, 1975), 6 (*Vide Mahā Bhārata Sānti Parva* Ch 59).

6 Minoru Hara, 'Note on Two Sanskrit Religious terms: Śraddhā and Bhakti', *Indo-Iranian Journal*, 7, No. 2/3 (1964): 143.

7 Edwin F.Bryant, *Krishna: A Sourcebook* (Oxford: Oxford University Press, 2007), 5.

8 Manohar Laxman Varadpande, *Ancient Indian and Indo Greek Theatre* (Abinav Publishers, 1981), 68–9.

9 Richard Stoneman, *Megasthenes's Indica: A New Translation of the Fragments with Commentary*, (London: Routledge, 2021), 127.

10 J.N. Banerjea, 'Lakulīśa- the Founder or the Systematiser of the Pāśupata Order', *Proceedings of the Indian History Congress* 14 (1951): 32–36.

11 Hemchandra Raychaudhuri, *Political History of Ancient India from the Accession of Parikshit to the Extinction of the Gupta Dynasty*, 1953, 204.

12 J.Ph. Vogel 'The Garuda Pillar of Besnagar', in *Archaeological Survey of India Report: 1908-09*, (Calcutta: Superintendent Government Printing, 1912), 124–9. Since then, the translation has been made better with the contextual understanding of the Hindu terms.

13 Nayanjot Lahiri, *Finding Forgotten Cities: How the Indus Civilization Was Discovered* (2015), 362–3.

14 Satya Shrava, *The Kushana Numismatics* (Pranava Prakashan,1985), 88.

15 B.N. Mukherjee, *The Great Kushana Testament* (Calcutta: Indian Museum Bulletin, 1995), 11–4.

16 Upinder Singh, *Political Violence in Ancient India* (Boston: Harvard University Press, 2017), 166.

17 Pankaj Jain, 'Reinterpreting Yajña as Vedic sacrifice', *The Adayar Library Bulletin*, 2010–11, 175.

18 *Paripāṭaal* 2:60-68.

19 *Paripāṭaal 3*:63-68.

20 *Paripāṭaal 13*:2-4.

21 *Paripāṭaal 4*:25-32.

22 *Paripāṭaal 4*:10-21.

23 *Paripāṭaal 4*:60-63.

24 Vasudev Vishnu Mirashi (Ed), *Corpus Inscriptionum Indicarum* Vol. IV: *Inscriptions of the Kalachuri-Chedi Era-Part.I* (Ootacamund: Government Epigraphist for India,1955), xlii.

25 Natasja Bosma, 'The Bāleśvara Temple Complex of Śivagupta: Epigraphical Evidence for the Śaiva-Siddhānta and Soma Siddhānta Traditions in Dakṣiṇa Kosala', *Indo-Iranian Journal*, 56, No. 3/4 (2013): 245–61.

26 *Paripāṭaal 4*:67–73.

27 Ṛgveda 1.164.46.

28 *Paripāṭaal 4*:53–57.

29 *Paripāṭaal 3*:73–76; *Puranānūru* 57:2-3; *Pathitruppathu* 15:39–40.

30 *Nakkīraṉār's Tirumurukāṟṟuppaṭai*: 182–186.

31 *Tirumurukāṟṟuppaṭai*: 230–234.

32 *Tirumurukāṟṟuppaṭai*: 178.

33 Govind Chandra Pande, 'Introduction' to Vishwambhar Sharan Pathak, in *History of Saiva Cults in Northern India* (Allahabad: Abinash Prakashan for University of Allahabad, 1980), xi.

34 Vishwa Nath Drabu, *Śaivāgamas: A Study in the Socio-economic Ideas and Institutions of Kashmir (200 BC to AD 700)* (Indus Publishing Company, 1990), 10.

35 Subhash Kak, 'The Poplar and the Chinar: Kashmir in a Historical Outline', *International Journal of Indian Studies*, 3(1993): 33–61.

36 *Sri Svacchanda Tantra*: 4.540–545.

37 Sannyasi Gyanshruti and Sannyasi Srividyananda, *Yajna: A Comprehensive Survey* (Bihar: Yoga Publications Trust, 2006), 330.

38 *Atharvaṇa Veda (AV)* 12.1.1.

39 *Atharvaṇa Veda (AV)* 11.5.3.

40 *Ṛig Veda* 10.136, verses 1-7 (also called *Muni Sūkta*).

41 Edward Fitzpatrick Crangle, *The Origin and Development of Early Indian Contemplative Practices*, (Harrassowitz Verlag, 1994), 28.

42 Vishwa Nath Drabu, *Śaivāgamas: A Study in the Socio-economic Ideas and Institutions of Kashmir (200 BC to AD 700)* (Indus Publishing Company, 1990), 140.

43 The paragraphs on Munis and Monasteries with their powers etc., are based on: R.N. Misra, *Ascetics, Piety and Power*: *Śaivā Siddhānta Monastic Art in the Woodlands of Central India* (Aryan Books International, 2018), 55–75.

44 *Brahma Sutra: Śankara Bhāsya 1.3.38, 233–234:* cited in Anantanand Rambachan, *The Advaita Worldview: God, World, and Humanity* (New York: State University of New York Press, 2006), 28.

45 Stella Kramrisch, *The Presence of Śiva* (Princeton: Princeton University Press, 1981), 299.

46 *Thirumurai*:11: *Kāraikāl Ammaiyār*, 4. *Arputha Thiruvanthāthi*: verse 20.

47 *Thirumurai*:11: *Kāraikāl Ammaiyār*, 4. *Arputha Thiruvanthāthi*: verse 25.

48 *Thirumurai*:11: *Kāraikāl Ammaiyār*, 2. *Tiruvālaṅkāṭu Mūtha Thirupathigam*: verse 2.

49 Elaine Craddock, *Śiva's Demon Devotee: Kāraikāl Ammaiyār* (SUNY, 2010), 71.

50 Verse 2751.

51 *Thirumurai*:3: Thirujñāna Saṃbanthar. 282. Thirukazhumalam: verse 1.

52 *Thirumurai*:1: Thirujñāna Saṃbanthar.. 72. Thirukudanthaikaronam: verse 9.

53 Song-15: Sung by 'Grandpa' Ci. Rajamānickam: '*Nāttu Pādalkal*' (*Folk Songs*, Tamizh) Vol. I, Ku. Mohanarāsu Star Publications, 1988, 136–7

[*As per *Śaivā* tradition, Mangaiyarkarasi was the Pāndya queen who was the staunch supporter of Jñāna Saṃbanthar. Her motherly protection played an important role in the mission of the child prodigy seer.]

54 *Sēkkilār, Periya Purāṇam,* verse 3977.

55 Ibid., verse 4008–4009.

56 Ibid., verse 4011.

57 Prof. Tho.Po.Meenakshi Sundaranar, *Samanarum Saṃbantharum* (Jains and Saṃbanthar, Tamizh) (Rudra Publications, 1957), 137.

58 Richard Gombrich and Gananath Obeyeskere, *Buddhism Transformed: Religious Change in Sri Lanka* (Princeton: Princeton University Press, 1988), 390 and 415–6.

59 Gnanambikai Kulendran, *Karaikkal Ammaiyar Mother of South Indian Music*, Department of Tami Development-Culture, Government of Tamil Nadu, 1996, 51.

60 *Thirumurai* 1: *Thirujñāna Saṃbanthar*:132 *Veezhimizhalai*, verse 10.

61 *Sēkkilār*, *Periya Purāṇam*, verses 4217 and 4220.

62 *Sēkkilār*, *Periya Purāṇam*, verse 4222.

63 *Sēkkilār*, *Periya Purāṇam*, verse 2030.

64 *Sēkkilār*, *Periya Purāṇam*, verse 1858.

65 R. Nagaswamy in 'Foreword' to Dr S.S. Janaki, *Gadyakarṇāmṛita* (Kuppuswami Sastry Research Institute, 1981), ix–x.

66 Thē Ā.Śrīnivasān, *Thiruvunthiyār:Theḷivu Katurai* (Thiruvunthiyār an explanatory paper, Thiruvāvaduthurai Āthīnam, 1954, ii.

67 Don Handelman and David Shulman, *Śiva in the Forest of Pines* (Oxford: Oxford University Press, 2004), 40–1.

68 *Thiruvunthiyār and Thirukaḻṟruppaṭiyār*, with meaning and explanation: Prof. Veḷḷai Vāranan, *Thirupaṉanthāḷ Āthīnam*, 1982, iii.

69 Umāpathi Śivam, *Koṭi-Kavi*. Both the verses of thirteenth century poem as well as the spiritual symbolism of flag and flag-mast taken from Posai Aruna Vasanthan, 'Thirukovil Kodimaram', Sivamanjari, 2014.

70 Dr Na Subbu Reddiyar, *'Śaiva-Siddhāntam or Arimugam'* (Śaiva-Siddhānta: Introduction: Tamizh) (South Indian Śaiva-Siddhānta Publishing House, 2001), 29.

Chapter 10: Bhakti, the Holistic Yajña Movement: Pre-Modern Vaishnavaism in South India

1 Bhāgavata Mahātmāyām, 1:47.

2 Chilapathikāram 1.10.143-47.

3 Bhagavad Gītā 3:14.

4 Chilapathikāram 2.11.46-7.

5 Mahā Bhārata: Ādi Parva: Chapters 233-46.

6 Chilapathikāram 2.11.54-5.
7 Chilapathikāram 2.12.111-2.
8 Chilapathikāram 2.7. 83-8.
9 Chilapathikāram 2.7.133-44.
10 Lavanya Vemsani, *Krishna in History, Thought, and Culture: An Encyclopedia of the Hindu Lord of Many Names* (ABC-CLIO, 2016), 289 [The Vedic reference to cosmic pillar could be associated with the *Viṣṇu's Kūrma Avatar*. Even in later pillar is depicted as both the cosmic *Axis Mundi* – the *Mēru* and also as the turtle simultaneously]
11 Mu.Aruṇācalam, *Nammāzhwār Varalārum Nulāraichiyum*, (*Nammāzhwār, history & literary inquiry, Tamizh*) 1990.
12 Ibid., 101-2
13 P. Sri Acharya, *Sri Ramanujar* (Tamizh) (Sakunthala Nilayam, 2007), 181.
14 Anantanand Rambachan, *The Advaita Worldview: God, World, and Humanity* (SUNY Press, 2006), 28 and 29.
15 *Gautama Dharmasūtra* XII. 4-7.
16 Śrī Kāñchi Prathivāthi Bayangaram Aṇṇañkarāchārya Swāmi, *Guru Paramparā Prabhāvam: Commentary* (Tamizh) (Kāñchipuram: Grantha Māla Office, 1975), 6-14.
17 The entire section on *Nampāṭuvān* is based on '*Kaiśika Purāṇa with Parāśara Bhaṭṭa commentary*' (Tamizh), published by Śrī Kāñchi Prathivāthi Bayangaram Aṇṇañkarāchārya Swāmi (Kāñchipuram: Grantha Māla Office, 1955).
18 Śrīmad Bhāgavata Purāṇa: 7:9.10.
19 Śrīmad Bhāgavata Purāṇa: 9:21.6-18.
20 Śrīmad Bhāgavata Purāṇa: 11:5.32.
21 Thoṇṭaraṭipoṭi Āzhwār, Thirumālai: verse 41.
22 Thoṇṭaraṭipoṭi Āzhwār, Thirumālai: verse 43.
23 Na.Subbu Reddiar, *Āzhwārkaḷin ārāamuthu* (*The never ending-ever flowing nectar of Āzhwārs*, Tamizh), (Inthiṇai Publications, 1987), 221.
24 *Adi Śaṅkara Bhagavatpāda, Manīṣā Pañcakam,* verse 1.
25 C.R. Srinivasa Aiyengar, *The Life and Teachings of Sri Ramanujacharya* (Madras: R. Venkateshwar & Co., 1908), 172.
26 *Kōilozhuku* (Tamizh), Ed. *Śrī Vaiṣṇava Śrī Kṛṣṇamāchāryar,* Vol. VII, Part-I, 2011, 10-6.
27 *Kōilozhuku* (Tamizh), Tirumalai-Tirupati Devasthanam, 1954, 52.
28 Muhammad Habib (Trans.) *The Campaigns of Alauddun Khilji being the Khazainul Futuh (Treasures of Victory) of Hazrat Amir Khusrau*) (Vepery, Chennai: D.B/Taraporewala, Sons & Co., Diocesan Press, 1931), xvi.

29 Job Thomas, *Tiruvengadu Bronzes* (Cre-A, 1986), 19.

30 *Kōilozhuku* (Tamizh) (*Śrī Vaiṣṇava Grantha Prakāsana Samiti*, 1976, pp.72-4).

31 V.N. Hari Rao, *The Srirangam Temple: Art and Architecture* (Tirupati: The Sri Venkateswara University, 1967), 5.

32 Sudalaimuthu Palaniappan, 'On the Unintended Influence of Jainism on the Development of Caste in Post-Classical Tamil Society', *International Journal of Jaina Studies* (Online) 4, No. 2 (2008): 1-65.

33 Viḷāñchōlai Piḷḷai: taken from Pi.Sri Ācārya, *Anbu Valartha Arivu Payir* (The crop of Wisdom nourished by Love: Āzhwārs and Ācharyas, Tamizh) (Kalaimakal Karyalayam, 1959), 90-4.

34 S. Krishnaswami Iyengar, *South India and Her Muhammadan Invaders* (Oxford: Oxford University Press, 1921), 166.

35 Ibid., 166.

36 Sri Vaishnava Sudarshanam (Editor), *Kōilozhuku* (Tamizh) (Sri Krishnaswamy Iyengar, 1976), 29-30.

37 Hari Saravanan, *Gods, Heros and Their Story Tellers: Intangible cultural heritage of South India* (Notion Press, 2016), 247.

38 Ranjeeta Dutta, 'Temple, Urban Landscape, and Production of Space: Śrirangam in Early Modern Tamil Period', in '*Religion and the City in India*' (Ed. Supriya Chaudhuri) (London: Routledge, 2022), 36.

39 Roma Bose (Trans., and annotated) 'Vēdānta-pārijāta-saurabha' in *Nimbārka* and *Vēdānta Kaustubha* of *Śrīnivasa,* Vol. I (Royal Asiatic Society of Bengal, 1940), 195-6.

40 Roma Bose (Trans., and Expounded) 'Vēdānta-pārijāta-saurabha' *in Nimbārka* and *Vēdānta Kaustubha* of *Śrīnivasa* with *Doctrines of Nimbārka and his Followers:* Vol.III (Royal Asiatic Society of Bengal, 1940), 50

41 Ibid., 256.

42 Ibid., 249.

43 Chimanlal M. Vaidya, *Vallabhacharya and His Teachings* (Vallabha Publications, 1984), 41.

44 A.P. Karamkar and N.B. Kalamdani, *Mystic Teachings of the Haridasas of Karnatak* (Karnataka Vidhyavardhak Sangh, 1939), 65.

45 M. Venkatesa Iyengar, 'Haridasas', in *Devotional Poets and Mystics: Vol-II* (Ed. V. Raghavan) (Publications Division, Govt. of India, 1978), 47-8.

46 Ramachandra Dattatreya Ranade, *Pathway to God in Kannada Literature* (Gen. Ed. K.M. Munshi and R.R. Diwakar) (Bharatiya Vidya Bhavan, 1960), 249.

47 William J. Jackson, *Vijayanagara Voices Exploring South Indian History and Hindu Literature* (London: Routledge, 2005), 166-7.

48 A.P. Karamkar and N.B. Kalamdani, *Mystic Teachings of The Haridasas of Karnatak* (Karnataka Vidhyavardhak Sangh, 1939),13-14.

49 E. Hultzsch, *Pithapuram Pillar Inscription of Prithviswara; Saka-Samvat 1108*, verses:1, 2 and 5, *Epigraphia India and Record of the Archaeological Survey of India*, Vol. IV, 1896-97, pp.47-48

50 ibid., Verses 54,55 & 56, p.52

51 Śrīmad Bhāgavata Mahāpurāṇa: 1.8.18-43

52 R.Narasimhachar, *The Kesava Temple At Somanathapur* (Mysore: Mysore Archeological Series, Mysore Government Press, 1917), 3

53 ibid., 10

54 K. Rama Sastri, *Akkalapundi Grant of Singaya-Nayaka: Saka-Samvat 1290*, verses 5-8, *Epigraphia Indica and Record of the Archaeological Survey of India*, Vol.XIII (Ed. Sten Konow & F.W.Thomas), 1915-16: reprint 1982, pp.270

55 ibid., 260-1

56 H.K. Narasimhaswami, *Koduri Grant of Ana-Vota Reddi: Saka 1280*: Epigraphia India, Vol.XXV, 1939, pp.137-8

57 Śrīnātha's Bhimēśvara Purāṇa 1.31 (cited in: Velcheru Narayana Rao et al., 1992)

58 Velcheru Narayana Rao, David Shulman and Sanjay Subramaniam, *Symbols of Substance: Court and State in Nāyaka Period Tamil Nadu* (Delhi: Oxford University Press, 1992), 74-75

Chapter 11: Social Emancipation through Bhakti from Mahārāshtra to the Hindi Heartland

1 Justin E. Abbott and Pandit Narhar R. Godbole, *Stories of Indian Saints* (Trans. of Mahipati's Marathi *Bhaktavijaya*, Vol. I) (New Delhi: Motilal Banarsidas, 1933:1988), 144-46.

2 Guhapriyai, *Śrī Mahā Bhakta Vijayam* (Chennai: The Little Flower Company, 1958), 88-90.

3 Prabhakar Machwe, 'Hindustani Padas: No.2142 "Heen deen meri jati"', in *Namdev: Life and Philosophy*, (Patiala: Publications Bureau, Punjabi University, 1990), 92.

4 Prabhakar Machwe, 'Marathi Abangs: No.1074 "*Ata ahe nahi*", in *Namdev: Life and Philosophy*, (Patiala: Publications Bureau, Punjabi University, 1990), 84.

5 Prabhakar Machwe, 'Hindi Padavali: '*Hari Nam Hira*'", in *Namdev: Life and Philosophy*, (Patiala: Publications Bureau, Punjabi University, 1990), 88.

6 Ibid., 70.

7 Justin E. Abbott and Pandit Narhar R. Godbole, *Stories of Indian Saints* (Trans. of Mahipati's Marathi *Bhaktavijaya*, Vol. I) (New Delhi: Motilal Banarsidas, 1933:1988), 378.

8 Ibid., 380-1.

9 Ibid., 383.

10 Hiroshi Fukazawa, 'State and Caste (Jāti) in the Eighteenth Century Maratha Kingdom', *Hitotsubashi Journal of Economics*, 9 (1) (June 1968), 42.

11 C.B. Agarwal quoted in Eleanor Mae Zelliot, 'Dr. Ambedkar and the Mahar Movement', PhD Thesis (Pennsylvania: University of Pennsylvania, 1969), 54.

12 Report of the Indian Central Committee, 1928-29: Presented by the Secretary of State for India to Parliament, Published: H.M. Stationery Office, 1929, 144.

13 *Lokamānya Ṭiḷaka āṇi Ḍô. Velakara Lokamānyāñcyā rājakīya caḷavaḷītīla Mumbaīcā sahabhāga*, Śrīvidyā Prakāśana, 1996, 115.

14 *Kesari*, 14 Oct. 1932: Trans. Justin.E. Abbott, 1933:1988, xiii.

15 Jayashree B. Gokhale-Turner, 'Bhakti or Vidroha' in *Tradition and Modernity in Bhakti movements*, Jayant Lele (ed.), (BRILL, 1981), 33.

16 Ibid.

17 Bhimrao Ramji Ambedkar, *The Untouchables* (Amrit Books, 1948).

18 Justin E. Abbott (trans), *Eknath: A Translation from the Bhaktililamrita* (Poona: Scottish Mission Industries Co., Ltd, 1927), 202-4

19 Guhapriyai, *Śrī Mahā Bhakta Vijayam* (Chennai: The Little Flower Company, 1958), 202.

20 Bhālacandra Nemāḍe, *Tukārām* (New Delhi: Sahitya Academy, 1980), 8.

21 Ramachandra Dattareya Ranade, *Mysticism in India: The Poet-saints of Maharashtra Vol. 7.* History of Indian Philosophy (ed. Belvalkar and Ranade) (Poona: University of Bombay, Aryabushan Press, 1933), 265.

22 Ibid., 274-5.

23 Ibid.

24 Ibid., 326-7.

25 Guhapriyai, *Śrī Mahā Bhakta Vijayam* (Chennai: The Little Flower Company, 1958), 177-8.

26 Gazetteer of the Bombay Presidency, Vol.18, Pt.2 (Poona: Government Central Press, 1885), 84

27 Vikram M Mehta, *Natural Decadal Climate Variability: societal impacts and predictability* (London: Taylor & Francis, 2017), 61

28 Justin E. Abbott and Narhar R. Godbole, *Stories of Indian Saints* (Trans. of Mahipati's Marathi *Bhaktavijaya)*, Vol. II (New Delhi: Motilal Banarsidas, 1933:1988), 90

29 ibid., 94 5

30 Manmatha Nath Dutt (Trans.) *Markaṇṭēya Purāṇa*, Vol. XVIII: 28 & 29 : (Norwich, VT: Elysium Press, 1896)

31 Ganesh Vasudev Tagare, *Saiva Philosophy* (*Saiva Tattvam*: Trans. From Marātti to Tamizh by Ka. Sri. Srinivasachariyar) (Chennai: Alliance Publication, 1998), 38-9

32 *Ṛig Vēdā* 10.146.1-6.

33 Sudarshana Bhaumik, *The Changing World of Caste and Hierarchy in Bengal; Depiction from the Mangalkavyas c.1700-1931* (New York: Routledge,2023), 128. (Through the typical standard model lens of Indian sociology, Bhaumik sees this as 'a tendency for social uplift not only among the ordinary masses but also among the local deities', though it could well mean also the assertion of Vedic forest goddess resurfacing among the coastal communities.)

34 Dinesh Chandra Sen, *Chaitanya and His Age* (Calcutta: University of Calcutta, 1922), 47.

35 Sukumar Sen, *Chandidas, Makers of Indian Literature Series* (New Delhi: Sahitya Akademi, 1971), 20.

36 Ibid., 21.

37 Dinesh Chandra Sen, *Chaitanya and His Age* (Calcutta: University of Calcutta, 1922), 25-6.

38 Dennis Hudson, *Tantric rites in Antal's Poetry*, in *Tantra in Practice* (Ed. David Gordon White) (Princeton: Princeton University Press, 2000), 207.

39 Sukumar Sen, *Chandidas, Makers of Indian Literature Series* (New Delhi: Sahitya Akademi, 1971), 7.

40 Valya-Līla Śūtra of Kṛṣṇa Dhās quoted in Dinesh Chandra Sen, *Chaitanya and His Age* (Calcutta: University of Calcutta, 1922), 47.

41 Dinesh Chandra Sen, *Chaitanya and His Age* (Calcutta: University of Calcutta, 1922), 145.

42 Ibid., 171.

43 Swami Vivekananda, *The Complete Works of Swami Vivekananda*: Vol.6 (Kolkata: Advaita Ashrama, 1956), 265-7.

44 Kiyakozu Okita, *Hindu Theology in Early Modern South Asia: The Rise of Devotionalism and the Politics of Geneology* (Oxford: Oxford University Press, 2014), 38.

45 Dinesh Chandra Sen, *Chaitanya and His Age* (Calcutta: University of Calcutta, 1922), 278-82.

46 Kiyakozu Okita, *Hindu Theology in Early Modern South Asia: The Rise of Devotionalism and the Politics of Geneology* (Oxford: Oxford University Press, 2014), 38.

47 Dinesh Chandra Sen, *Chaitanya and His Age* (Calcutta: University of Calcutta, 1922), 282.

48 Melville Kennedy, *The Chaitanya Movement: A Study of the Vaishnavism of Bengal* (Oxford: Oxford University Press, 1925), 58-9 and 62.
49 Ibid., 70.
50 Kshiti Mohan Sen, *Hinduism* (New York: Penguin, 1961:1976), 105.
51 Carol Saloman, *City of Mirrors: Songs of Lālan Sãi* (Oxford: Oxford University Press, 2017), 227.
52 Kshiti Mohan Sen, *The Baül Singers of Bengal* (as Appendix in, Rabindranath Tagore, *The Religion of Man*, (George Allen & Unwin, 1922), 218-9.
53 Romila Thapar and Percival Spear, *A History of India*, Vol. I (New Delhi: Penguin Books, 1965), 305.
54 Hara Mohan Das, *Sankara Deva- A Study* (Sri Gauranga Press, 1945), 19 (Most biographical material on Saṅkara Dēva is based on this book.)
55 Ibid., 21.
56 Ibid., 23.
57 Rustom Bharucha, *Thinking the Ramayana Tradition through Performance* in *Performing the Ramayana Tradition: Enactments, Interpretations, and Arguments,* (Ed. Paula Richman and Rustom Bharucha) (Oxford: Oxford University Press, 2021), 47.
58 Michael D. Willis, *The Archaeology of Hindu Ritual: Temples and the Establishment of the Gods* (Cambridge: Cambridge University Press, 2009), 102.
59 Ibid., 104-5.
60 Ibid., 105.
61 Ibid., 106-7.
62 Śrīmad Bhāgavata Mahāpurāṇa: 1.1.4.
63 Pradip Jyoti Mahanta, 'The Sattra Institution of Assam: An Enduring Heritage', in *Glimpses of the Sattra Institution of Assam* (Vivekananda Kendra Institute of Culture, 2006), 7.
64 Kamal Chandra Gōswāmi, 'Egalitarian Elements in the Sattra Institution', in *Glimpses of the Sattra Institution of Assam* (Vivekananda Kendra Institute of Culture, 2006), 65-7.
65 Saṅkara Dēva in *Kīrtana Ghōśa*, verse 1821.
66 Ibid., verse 1822.
67 Ajit Patowary, 'Women Used to Set up Sattras in State: Study', *The Assam Tribune*, 15 September 2010.
68 Chandan Sharma, 'Saṅkara Dēva's Bhakti Movement and Its Impact on the Rural Economy of Assam with reference to Nagaon and Morigaon Districts', Thesis submitted to Mahapurusha Srimanta Sankaradeva Viswavidyalaya, 2018, 117-8.

69 Sagar Barua PhD, *Role of Sattras in Indian Freedom Movement*, in *Glimpses of the Sattra Institution of Asom* (Vivekananda Kendra Institute of Culture, Guwahati, 2006), 78.

70 Ibid., 79.

71 Richard Burghart, 'The Founding of the Ramanandi Sect', *Ethnohistory*, 25 (2) (1978): 121-139.

72 Purushottam Agrawal, *In Search of Ramanand: The Guru of Kabir and Others*.

73 Ibid.

74 Daniela Bevilacqua, 'Do Not Ask about Caste', in *The RāmānandĪ Sampradāya and Its Relationship with Caste: A Historical and Anthropological Overview* in *Cross-cutting South Asian Studies: An Interdisciplinary Approach*, 10 July 2016.

75 Āchārya Hrudayam of Śrī Azhakiya Maṇavāḷa Perumāḷ with Commentary by Śrī Maṇavāḷa Māmunikaḷ, Prakaraṇam 1: Sūrṇikai 37, 38 and 75, 76, Published by Pushparatha Chetty & Co. Madras, 1905, 36-38 and 92-96.

76 Ibid., Prakaraṇam 1: Sūrṇikai 85 and 86. 103 and 111.

77 Daniela Bevilacqua, *Modern Hindu Traditionalism in Contemporary India: The Sri Math and the Jagadguru Ramanandacarya in the Evolution of the Ramanandi Sampradaya* (London: Routledge, 2018), 10.4324/9781315209128.

78 Darshan Singh, *A Study of Bhakta Ravidās* (Chandigarh: Publication Bureau, Punjabi University, 1996), 16

79 *Śvapāca Vālmīkī* based on *Bhaktarasa Bōdhini* of *Śrī Priyadās Gōśwāmi*: verses 71-78

80 Taittirīya Upaniṣad: Bhrigu Valli: 3.7

81 *Sukhsagar* composed by Garib Dās, Skanda-I, Chapter-8: as in the translation at url: https://kabirsahib.jagatgururampalji.org/en/index/the-story-of-supach-sudarshan/ (accessed on 10-12-2022)

82 Awadesh Kumar, 'A Comparative Study of Kabirpanth and Satnami Movements in Chhattisgarh, Madhya Pradesh and their Impact on Scheduled Castes', PhD Thesis, Department of Sociology, Panjab University, 1986, 25.

83 Ravi Dās, 'Pác Vāṇi' in *The Life and Works of Raidās* (Trans. in Winand M. Callewaert and Peter G. Friedlander) (Manohar, 1992), 130.

84 Darshan Singh, *Sant Ravidas and His Times* (Kalyani Publishers, 1977), 8.

85 *Bhaktmālā* cited in Darshan Singh, *Sant Ravidas and His Times* (Kalyani Publishers, 1977), 8.

86 Ravi Dās: Sakhi 134,135,138,140,& 142

87 Sāqi Must'ad Khan, *Maāsir-i-'Ālamgiri: A History of the Emperor Aurangzib-'Ālamgir (reign 1658-1707 AD)* (Trans. Sir. Jadu-nath Sarkar) (Royal Asiatic Society of Bengal, 1947), 71.

88 Irfan Habib, 'Forms of Class Struggle in Mughal India' in *Essays in Indian History towards a Marxist Perception with the Economic History of Medieval India: A Survey* (Anthem Press, 2002), 245.

89 Sāqi Must'ad Khan, *Maāsir-i-'Ālamgiri: A History of the Emperor Aurangzib-'Ālamgir (reign 1658-1707 AD)* (Trans. Sir. Jadu-nath Sarkar) (Royal Asiatic Society of Bengal, 1947), 72.

90 Irfan Habib, *Forms of Class Struggle in Mughal India* in *Essays in Indian History towards a Marxist Perception with the Economic History of Medieval India: A Survey* (Anthem Press, 2002), 245.

91 Śrīmadbhagavadgītā 5:18.

92 Abu'l Fazl Ma'muri quoted by Khafi Khan in Irfan Habib, *The Agrarian System of Mughal India (1556-1707)* (New York: Asia Publishing House for Aligarh Muslim University, 1963), 343.

93 W.L. Allison, *The Sadhs* (Oxford: Oxford University Press, 1935), 11-2.

94 Jadu Nath Sarkar's personal communication to Allison cited in W.L. Allison, *The Sadhs* (Oxford: Oxford University Press, 1935), 12.

95 Jadu Nath Sarkar, 1947, 297.

96 W.L. Allison, *The Sadhs* (Oxford: Oxford University Press, 1935), 112-3.

97 Geo. W. Briggs, *The Chamārs* (Oxford: Oxford University Press, 1920), 220.

98 N. Hanif, *Biographical Encyclopaedia of Sufis of South Asia* (Sarup & Sons, 2000), 70.

99 Ibid., 71.

100 *Census of India, 1901*. Vol. XIII, Prepared by R.V. Russell, I.C.S., Superintendent of Census Operations, Secretariat Press, 1902, 86.

101 W.L. Allison, *The Sadhs* (Oxford: Oxford University Press, 1935), 104-5.

102 K.C. Yadav, *The Revolt of 1857 in Haryana* (ICHR: Manohar Publishers, 1977), 32-33.

103 C.B. Patel., 'Associates of Veer Surendra Sai', *Orissa Review* (August, 2007): 68-9.

104 Saurabh Dube, *Untouchable Pasts Religion, Identity, and Power Among a Central Indian Community, 1780-1950* (New York: State University of New York Press, 1998), 72-3.

105 Ibid., 77.

106 Chad M. Bauman, *Christian Identity and Dalit Religion in Hindu India, 1868-1947* (Eerdmans Publishing Company, 2008), 60-61.

107 Saurabh Dube, *Untouchable Pasts Religion, Identity, and Power among a Central Indian Community, 1780-1950* (New York: State University of New York Press, 1998), 71.

108 Chad M. Bauman, *Christian Identity and Dalit Religion in Hindu India, 1868-1947* (Eerdmans Publishing Company, 2008), 62. Here he cites the following report: H.A. Feierabend's 'Annual Report, 1935-36', AES 82-13a Pr91, Annual Reports, no. 20, 1935.

109 Here Allison equates Mahadeo and Parwati to Adam and Eve, a typical instance of downgrading Hindu spirituality to fit into Christian narrative. W.L. Allison, *The Sadhs* (Oxford: Oxford University Press, 1935), 6-7.

110 Ibid., 52.

111 Ibid., 54-9.

112 Ibid., 96.

113 Geo. W. Briggs, *The Chamārs* (Oxford: Oxford University Press, 1920), 221.

114 *Second Quarterly Report 1938*, AES 82-14 Qu2, Baur, Wm., Quarterly Reports, Articles, Newsletters, 1927-58 cited in Chad M Bauman, *Christian Identity and Dalit Religion in Hindu India, 1868-1947* (Eerdmans Publishing Company, 2008), 56.

115 William R. Pinch, *Peasants and Monks in British India* (London: University of California Press, 1996), 12.

116 *Report Of The Christian Missionary Activities Enquiry Committee Vol. I*, Govt. Printing Press, Madhya Pradesh, 1956, 112.

117 Ibid., 120.

118 Baji Rao Niru, Member of Legislative Assembly (No. 24) in *Report of The Christian Missionary Activities Enquiry Committee* Vol. II Part B, (Govt. Printing Press, Madhya Pradesh, 1956), 78-9.

119 William Henry Sleeman, *Rambles and Recollections of an Indian Official*, Vol. II, (ed. Vincent Arthur Smith) (Archibald Constable & Company, 1893), 262.

120 William Henry Sleeman, *A Report on the System of Megpunnaism* (The Serampore Press, 1839), 11.

121 Daniela Bevilacqua, *Modern Hindu Traditionalism in Contemporary India: The Sri Math and the Jagadguru Ramanandacarya in the Evolution of the Ramanandi Sampradaya* (London: Routledge, 2018), 10. 4324/9781315209128.

Chapter 12: Dharmic Social Emancipation from 19th Century to the Present

1 P. Shungoony Menon, *A History of Travancore from the Earliest Times* (Higginbotham & Co., 1878), 313-17.

2 S. Ramachandran and A. Ganesan, *TholCiilaik Kalakam: Therintha Poikal, Theriyaatha Unmaikal*, (*Shoulder Cloth Riots: Known Falsehoods*

and Unknown Truths in Tamil) (South Indian Social History Research Institute, 2011), 84.

3 Robinson Jose. K, *Human Rights Violations in Post-independent India: Kēraḷa Scenario* (2019), 37-8

4 Ibid., 38.

5 All subsequent narrative unless otherwise mentioned taken from: *Ahila Thiraṭu Ammānai* (Tamizh), Published by Thangayā Nādar, Doss Press, 1963.

6 *Kathōpaniṣad*: 2.3.5

7 Robert Caldwell, *Mission of Edeyenkoody, in the District of Tinnevelly and Diocese of Madras* (London, SPG, 1844:47), 20-2.

8 George Pettitt, *The Tinnevelly Mission of the Church Missionary Society* (London: Seelyes, 1851) 265-8.

9 Report of the Santhapuram District for the year 1858: [ARTDC for the year 1858: Nagercoil: London Missionary Press, 1859, 4-5.

10 Patrick G., *Religion and Subaltern Agency: A Case-study of Ayyā Vaḻi: A Subaltern Religious Phenomenon in South Tiruvitāṅkūr,* Department of Christian Studies, University of Madras (2003), 4.

11 Samuel Mateer, *The Land of Charity: A Descriptive Account of Travancore and Its People, with Especial Reference to Missionary Labour* (Snow & Co., 1871), 222-3.

12 LMS Report: Nagercoil Mission District, Kottaram Division, 24-5.

13 S. Ramachandran and A. Ganesan, 2011, 118-9.

14 Sarfoji letter from 'Proceedings of Board of Revenue', 2.2.1801, Vol. 271C, quoted in Jitendra Bajaj and Mandayam Doddamane Srinivas, *Annam Bahu Kurvita*, Centre for Policy Studies, Madras, 1996, 182.

15 Jitendra Bajaj and Mandayam Doddamane Srinivas, 1996, 181.

16 Mike Davis, *Late Victorian Holocausts El Nino Famines and the Making of the Third World* (Verso, 2002), 336.

17 'Vidyaratnam' Kuppurasu Sarojini, Mallar aka Devendra Kula Vellalar clans and community relations (*Mallar enum Dēvēndrakula Veḷḷaḷār Kulamum Kootamuraikalum*, Tamizh), Tamil Panpattu Samooga Aayvu Mayam, 2001, 18.

18 Vasant Kaiwar quoted in Mike Davis, 2002, 341 (emphasis not in the original).

19 Rāmaliṅga Vaḷḷalār, in *Vaḷḷalār* prose work collection (*Vaḷḷalār Urainadai Nuul, Tamizh*), Vardhamanan Publishing, 1997, 513.

20 Suddhananda Bharati, *Dayananda Jothi* (Tamizh) (Madras: Arya Śamaj M., 1948), 34.

21 Har Bilas Sarda, *Life of Dayanand Saruswati* (Ajmer: Vedic Yantralaya, 1946), 107.

22 Ibid.
23 Ibid., 147.
24 Suddhananda Bharati, *Dayananda Jothi* (Tamizh) (Madras: Arya Samaj M., 1948), 115.
25 *Biradar-i-Hind* or Brahma Samachar Patra dated 1-July-1877: quoted in Har Bilas Sarda, 1946, 181.
26 Yuval Noah Harari, *Homo Deus: A Brief History of Tomorrow* (Random House, 2016), 270.
27 Ruth Harris, *Guru to the World: The Life and Legacy of Vivekananda* (Harvard University Press, 2022), 172.
28 Colin Wilson, *The Occult. A History* (Random House, 1971), 380-1.
29 Helena Blavatsky, *The Theosophist*, Vol. V, No 3 (51), December 1883, 105.
30 Lajpat Rai, *The Arya Samaj: an Account of Its Origin, Doctrines, and Activities, with a Biographical Sketch of the Founder* (Longmans, Green & Co., 1915), 230-1.
31 Velayutha Arya, *Untouchability Sin against Vedas* (in Tamil) (Chennai: Chennai Central Arya Samaj, 1986), 9. Also R.K. Ghai, *Shuddhi Movement in India: A Study of Its Socio-political Dimensions* (Commonwealth Publishers, 1990), 123.
32 Sidney Webb, 'Preface' (1914), in Lajpat Rai, *The Arya Samaj: an Account of Its Origin, Doctrines, and Activities, with a Biographical Sketch of the Founder* (Longmans, Green & Co., 1915), xvii.
33 Herbert Butler quoted in Sir James Robert Dunlop Smith, *Servant of India: A Study of Imperial Rule from 1905 to 1910 as Told through the Correspondence and Diaries of Sir James Dunlop Smith* (Longman, 1966), 97.
34 The chief reference, unless otherwise stated, is mainly based on: Shantan Singh Negi, 'The Dola-Palki Movement: Dalit Struggle for Social Justice in Uttarakhan during 20th Century', *Proceedings of the Indian History Congress*, Vol. 72, PART-I, (2011), 781-92.
35 Mohandas Karamchand Gandhi quoted in P.C. Joshi, 'In the lap of the Himalaya: Gandhi's visit to Uttarakhand', *Economic and Political Weekly*, Vol. 36, No. 34, 25-31 August 2001, 3300-10.
36 Mohandas Karamchand Gandhi, *Harijan*, 10 Oct. 1929 (P.C. Joshi, 2001).
37 Sri Aurobindo, Dayananda and the Veda, *Vedic Magazine*, 1916, in *Bankim-Tilak-Dayananada* (Sri Aurobindo Ashram, 1940:1955), 60.
38 Sri Aurobindo, Dayananda, *Vedic Magazine*, 1915: Ibid., 42 and 44.
39 Swami Saradananda, *Sri Ramakrishna: The Great Master* (Bengali 5 volumes biography), Trans. Swami Jagadananda (Sri Ramakrishna

Math, 1952), 54-55. All incidents in the life of Sri Ramakrishna, unless otherwise referenced, are taken from this biography.

40 Ibid., 115.

41 Ibid., 122.

42 Ibid., 123.

43 Ibid., 127-8.

44 Ibid., 137.

45 Ibid., 167.

46 Ibid., 208.

47 Ibid., 617-8.

48 Swami Premānanda in *Ramakrishna as We Saw Him* (Edited and Translated by Swami Chetananda), (Vēdanta Society of St Louis, 1990), 122.

49 Ibid., 111.

50 Śwāmi Raṅganāthananda, Shankaracharya and an Untouchable, *Prabuddha Bharata*, Vol.113, No.12, Dec. 2008, 25.

51 Colin Wilson, *The Outsider* (Victor Gollanz Ltd, 1956), 251.

52 Swami Gambhirananda, *The Apostles of Shri Ramakrishna* (compiled and edited) (*Advaita Ashrama*, 1972), 5.

53 Ibid., 158.

54 Swami Tapasyananda, *Sri Sarada Devi-Holy Mother: Her Life and Conversations* (Sri Ramakrishna Math, 1958), 6.

55 Ibid., 70-1.

56 Ibid., 264.

57 Ibid., 492-3.

58 Ibid., 206.

59 Jyotirmaya Sharma, *A Restatement of Religion: Swami Vivekananda and the Making of Hindu Nationalism*, (Yale University Press, 2013).

60 Ibid., 178.

61 Śwāmi Vivēkānanda, *Complete Works of Swami Vivekananda*, Vol. IV (Advaita Ashrama, 1958), 372-3 (emphasis not in the original).

62 Ibid., Vol. VIII, 184.

63 Ibid., Vol. VII, 145.

64 Ibid., Vol. I, 22.

65 Ibid., 423.

66 Ibid., Vol. VII, 431-35.

67 Ibid., 308.

68 Ibid., Vol. III, 221-22.

69 Sangharakshita, *Ambedkar and Buddhism* (Motilal Banarsidass Publishers, 1986:2006), 101.

70 Bhimrao Ramji Ambedkar, *The Buddha and the Future of His Religion*, Dr Babasaheb Ambedkar Writings and Speeches, Vol.17, Part 2, 107.

71 M.O. Mathai, *Reminiscences of Nehru* (New Delhi: Vikas Publishing House, 1978), 25.

72 Śwāmi Vivēkānanda, *Complete Works of Swami Vivekananda*, Vol. III, (Advaita Ashrama, 1958), 295.

73 K.P.K. Menon, *Chattambi Swamigal: The Great Scholar-Saint of Kēraḷa* (Trivandrum: Educational Art Press, 1967), 2.

74 Ibid., 9-10.

75 K. Bhaskara Pillai, *Chattampi Swamikal* (Sri Vidhyadiraja Sabha, 1978), 20.

76 S.N. Sadasivan, *A Social History of India* (A.P.H Publishing Corporation, 2000), 91.

77 S. Jagathsimhan Nair. *Selected Works of Sri Chattambi Swamikal* (Trans. S.J. Nair) (Notion Press, 2022), 41.

78 Ibid., 53.

79 Ibid., 58.

80 Swami Jyotirmayananda (ed.), *Vivekananda a Comprehensive Study* (All India Press, 1993:2000), 461.

81 R. Raman Nair and L. Sulochana Devi, *Chattampi Swami: An Intellectual Biography* (Centre for South Indian Studies, 2010), 126-7.

82 Śwāmi Chinmayānanda. 'Secret Initiation: Message', in K.P.K. Menon, *Chattambi Swamigal: The Great Scholar-Saint of Kēraḷa* (Trivandrum: Educational Art Press, 1967), x.

83 Murkot Kunhappa, *Sree Narayana Guru* (New Delhi: National Book Trust, 1982), 2.

84 Nitya Chaitanya Yati, *Narayana Guru* (Indian Council of Philosophical Research, 2005), xiii.

85 Murkot Kunhappa, *Sree Narayana Guru* (New Delhi: National Book Trust, 1982), 19.

86 Nitya Chaitanya Yati, *Narayana Guru* (Indian Council of Philosophical Research, 2005), xiii.

87 Nataraja Guru, *The Word of Guru* (Paico Publishing House, 1952:1968), 24-25.

88 Bhimrao Ramji Ambedkar, 'Annihilation of Caste', in *Writings and Speeches*, Vol. 4, Education Department, Govt. of Maharashtra, 1979, 47 and 72.

89 Murkot Kunhappa, *Sree Narayana Guru* (New Delhi: National Book Trust, 1982), 23.

90 Bhimrao Ramji Ambedkar, *Writings and Speeches*, Vol.4, Education Department, Govt. of Maharashtra, 1987, 285-6.

91 *Isāvasya Upaniashad*, verses 12 and 14.
92 S.N. Sadasivan, *A Social History of India* (A.P.H Publishing Corporation, 2000), 495.
93 Ibid., 495-6.
94 K.M. George, *Kumaran Asan: Makers of Indian Literature Series* (New Delhi: Sahitya Academy, 1972), 48.
95 K. Vinod Chandran, *The Counter Narratives of Power and Identity in Colonial Keralam* (JEC Publication, 2023), 108.
96 Ibid., 109.
97 M.K. Sanu, *Sree Narayana Guru: Life and Times*, trans. Mukundan P.R. (Opendoor Media, 1976), 264-5.
98 Ibid., 165.
99 Ibid., 189.
100 Ibid., 255.
101 K.R. Achyuthan, 'The Social Spectrum in Kerala', *Journal of Kerala Studies*, Vol. X, 1983, 22.
102 S.N. Sadasivan, *A Social History of India* (A.P.H Publishing Corporation, 2000), 365.
103 Translations of *Jāthi Nirṇayam* and *Jāthi Lakshaṇam* composed by *Śrī Nārayana Guru* is by Muni *Nārayana* Prasād, *Narayana Guru Complete Works* (New Delhi: National Book Trust, 2006), 331-35. To denote the socially excluded, the term 'Pariah' has been used, and it has been modified into a generic name in order to avoid a distorted view.
104 M.K. Gandhi, 'Vykom Satyagraha', in *Non-Violent Resistance* (Schocken Books, 1961), 183.
105 Ibid., 185-6.
106 Lakshmi Raghunandan, *At the Turn of the Tide: The Life and Times of Maharani Setu Lakshmi Bayi, the Last Queen of Travancore* (Maharani Sethulakshmibai Memorial Trust, 1995), 125.
107 All information on the dialogue between Guru and Gandhi taken from M.K. Sanu, *Sree Narayana Guru: Life and Times* (Opendoor Media, 1976), 241-3.
108 M.K. Gandhi, *The Collected Works of Mahatma Gandhi*, Vol. 31 (Electronic Book-Publications Division, Government of India, 1999), 53-4.
109 Ibid., 55.
110 Ibid., 56.
111 M.K. Gandhi, *The Collected Works of Mahatma Gandhi*, Vol. 40, (Electronic Book-Publications Division, Government of India, 1999), 2 and 459.
112 Nataraja Guru, *The Word of Guru* (Paico Publishing House, 1952:1968), 186.

113 All biographical details of Iyyankāḷi used in this section, unless otherwise mentioned, is mainly from 'Kēraḷathin Muthal Dalit Pōrali Iyyankāḷi' (Kerala's First Dalit Liberator Iyyankāḷi), a biography originally written in Malayalam by C. Abimanyu and translated into Tamizh by 'Nirmālya' (Tamilini, 2001).

114 *Ayyan-Kali: A brief biography*: http://ambedkar.nspire.in/Ayyan%20 kali.html (accessed 10 Dec. 2022).

115 'Nirmālya', 2001, 117-8.

116 Adoor K.K. Ramachandran Nair (ed), Kerala State Gazetteer, Vol. 2, Part 2, Government of Kerala, 1999, 496.

117 *Ayyan-Kali: A brief biography*: http://ambedkar.nspire.in/Ayyan%20 kali.html (accessed 10 Dec. 2022).

118 Sri Sambamurthy Sastrigal, Sri Kuppuswamy Iyer, Sri 'Sollin Selvan' P.N. Parasuraman, *Pujyasri Mahaswamigal Varalaru* (Tamil) [Alliance Publication (original Tamil version 1957), 85. Also available in English at: https://mahaperiyavaa.files.wordpress.com/2010/05/sri-mahaswamy-charitram-1.pdf

119 Padmanabha Iyer (ed.), *Souvenir of the Sashtiabdapurthi of Sachivothama Sir C.P. Ramaswamy Aiyer*, (A.R.V Press, 1940), 154.

120 H.V. Sheshadri, *RSS: A Vision in Action* (Sahitya Sindhu, 1988:1998), 137.

Chapter 13: Dharmic Emancipation through Bhakti and Advaita in Modern Age: Tradition, Individuals, and Lineages

1 Natṟriṇai, poem no 22.

2 Kasivasi Sri Yatiindra Swami, *Śrī Karapāthria Śivaprakāsa Śwāmigaḷ Sarithram* (in Tamil) (Thiruvotriyuran Veda-Mozhipeyarpu Karyalaya, 1934), 21.

3 Ibid., 95.

4 Śrī Karapāthria Śivaprakāsa Śwāmigaḷ [compiled] *Vēdānta Manana Sinthāmaṇi* (Tamizh), Tāṇdavarāya Mudaliyār, 1911, 398.

5 Ibid., 501.

6 Ibid., 628.

7 Kasivasi Sri Yatiindra Swami, *Śrī Karapāthria Śivaprakāsa Śwāmigaḷ Sarithram* (in Tamil) (Thiruvotriyuran Veda-Mozhipeyarpu Karyalaya, 1934), 96-7.

8 Ibid., 103.

9 Ibid., 104.

10 G.M. Pawar, *The Life and Works of Maharshi Vitthal Ramji Shinde* (1992) (Trans. Sudhakar Marathe) (New Delhi: Sahitya Academy, 2013), 11.

11 Ibid., 13.

12 Ibid., 27-8.
13 Ibid., 128.
14 Ibid., 178.
15 Ibid., 180.
16 Ibid., 311.
17 Ibid., 332.
18 Ibid., 370.
19 Ibid., 390.
20 Annie Besant quoted in Dr Babasaheb Ambedkar, *Writings and Speeches*, Vol. 9, Education Department, Govt. of Maharashtra, 26 January 1991: Dr Ambedkar Foundation, January 2014, 3-6.
21 All quotes from the lecture 'Untouchability' that Sayajirao Gaekwad delivered in 1918 from Anthony X. Soares, *Speeches and addresses: Addresaji Rao III Maharaja Gaekwar of Baroda* (Diocesan Press for Oxford University Press, 1933), 232-244.
22 G.M. Pawar, *The Life and Works of Maharshi Vitthal Ramji Shinde* (1992) (Trans. Sudhakar Marathe) (New Delhi: Sahitya Academy, 2013), 664-5.
23 Unless otherwise specified, the section is mainly based on *The Life and Works of Maharshi Vitthal Ramji Shinde* (1992) (Trans. Sudhakar Marathe) (New Delhi: Sahitya Academy, 2013), 402-5.
24 V.O. Chidambaram Pillai, *Reminiscences and Anecdotes of Lokmanya Tilak*, Vol. III (Kesari Press, 1928), 160.
25 Ibid., 162.
26 Ibid., 163.
27 Govind Sakharam Sardesai, *New History of The Marathas*, Vol. III (Phoenix Publications, 1948), 463.
28 Gazetteer of the Bombay Presidency, Vol. xviii, Pt. ii (Bombay: Government Central Press, 1885), 295-6.
29 Dattatary Bhandalkar, *The Nomadic Tribe in India Understanding Their Struggle and Politics of Exclusion*, in *Education as Development: Deprivation, Poverty, Dispossession* (Ed. Ramdas Rupavath) (London: Routledge, 2023), 169.
30 Gazetteers Department, Maharashtra, Land and Its People, Gazetteers Department, Government of Maharashtra, 2009, 186.
31 Gazetteer of the Bombay Presidency, Vol. xviii, Pt. ii, Government Central Press, Bombay, 1885, 307.
32 ibid., 307-8
33 Richard Temple quoted in Ravinder Kumar, *Western India and the Nineteenth Century* (Australian National University Press, 1968), 283-4.
34 Bal Ram Nanda, *Gokhale: Indian Moderates and the British Raj* (Princeton University Press, 1977), 13

35 Gordon Johnson, *Provincial Politics and Indian Nationalism* (Cambridge: Cambridge University Press, 1973), 104 and 107.

36 Jai Narain Sharma, *The Political Thought of Lokmanya Bal Gangadhar Tilak, Encyclopaedia of Eminent Thinkers Series:* Vol.24 (Concept Publishing Company, 2009), 106.

37 Ibid., 107.

38 Tilak quoted in Jai Narain Sharma, *The Political Thought of Lokmanya Bal Gangadhar Tilak*, Encyclopaedia of Eminent Thinkers Series: Vol. 24 (Concept Publishing Company, 2009), 105.

39 Balagangadhar Tilak, *Śrīmad Bhagavdgītā Rahasya* (Trans. Balchandra Sitaram Sukthankar), Vol. I (Tilak Mandir, 1936), 90-1.

40 Ibid., 464.

41 Bālagaṅgādhar Tilak, *Śrīmad Bhagavdgītā Rahasya* (Trans. Balchandra Sitaram Sukthankar), Vol. II (Tilak Mandir, 1936), 697.

42 Bālagaṅgādhar Tilak, *Śrīmad Bhagavdgītā Rahasya*, (Trans. Balchandra Sitaram Sukthankar), Vol. I (Tilak Mandir, 1936), 615-6.

43 Jai Narain Sharma, *The Political Thought of Lokmanya Bal Gangadhar Tilak*, Encyclopaedia of Eminent Thinkers Series, Vol. 24 (Concept Publishing Company, 2009), 104.

44 *Ṛg Vēdā* IX.112.3.

45 Vālmiki Rāmāyaṇa: 2.63.53 and 2.64.33.

46 Gordhanbhai Ishwarbhai Patel, *Vithalbhai Patel: Life and Times-Book:1* (Shree Laxmi Narayan Press, 1951), 3.

47 Ibid., 304.

48 Manoj Mitta, *Caste Pride: Battles for Equality in Hindu India* (New Delhi: Westland, 2023), 27.

49 Ibid., 247.

50 Sri Aurobindo, 'A letter of Sri Aurobindo', in *Sri Aurobindo: Archives and Research*, Vol. 8, No. 2, December 1984, 190 (highlight not in the original).

51 Gordhanbhai Ishwarbhai Patel, *Vithalbhai Patel: Life and Times Book 1* (Shree Laxmi Narayan Press, 1951), 301.

52 Balakrishna Shivram Moonje, 'Forcible Conversions in Malabar', Dr Moonje's Report, Nagpur, 4 Aug. 1923, Moonje papers, Sub File 12 (1922-3), 16.

53 Christophe Jaffrelot, *The Hindu Nationalist Movement in India* (Columbia University Press, 1996), 21.

54 Manoj Mitta, *Caste Pride: Battles for Equality in Hindu India* (New Delhi: Westland, 2023), 251.

55 Charles Herman Heimsath, *Indian Nationalism and Hindu Social Reform* (Bombay: Princeton University Press: Oxford University Press, 1964), 250.

56 Fatesinghrao Gaekwad, *Sayajirao of Baroda: The Prince and the Man* (Popular Prakashan, 1989), x.

57 Ibid., 258.

58 Ian Copland, *Sayaji Rao Gaekwar and 'Sedition': The Dilemmas of an Indian Prince* in *Rule, Protest and Identity: Aspects of Modern South Asia* (eds. Peter Robb and David Taylor) (Curzon Press, 1978), 28-48.

59 Charles Herman Heimsath, *Indian Nationalism and Hindu Social Reform* (Bombay: Princeton University Press: Oxford University Press, 1964), 250.

60 Shāhu Maharāj quoted by S.M. Fraser in his preface to A.B. Latthe, *Memoirs of Shri Shahu Chhatrapati Maharaja of Kolhapur,* Vol. I (Bombay: The Times Press, 1924), viii.

61 A.B. Latthe, *Memoirs of Shri Shahu Chhatrapati Maharaja of Kolhapur*, Vol. II (Bombay: The Times Press, 1924), 485.

62 Sayajirao Gaekwad, 'Aspects of Social Reform in India', in *Speeches and Addresses of Sayaji Rao III Maharaja Gaekwar of Baroda* (Oxford University Press, 1933), 84-5.

63 Manu Bhagwan, 'Demystifying the "Ideal Progressive": Resistance through Mimicked Modernity in Princely Baroda, 1900-1913', *Modern Asian Studies*, 35, No. 2; 2001: 385-409. The discussion at House of Commons on Baroda Reforms also taken from this paper.

64 Mukund Ramrao Jayakar, *The Story of My Life*, Vol. I (Asia Publishing House, 1958), 129.

65 C.L. Chandavarkar, *Dhondo Keshav Karve* (Publications Division, Govt. of India, 1970), 85.

66 Rahul Sarwate, 'Reimagining the Modern Hindu Self: Caste, Untouchability and Hindu Theology', in 'Colonial South Asia', 1899-1948, PhD Thesis submitted to Columbia University, 2020, 38.

67 Ibid, 41.

68 A.B. Latthe, *Memoirs of Shri Shahu Chhatrapati Maharaja of Kolhapur*, Vol. II (Bombay: The Times Press, 1924), 525.

69 Ibid, 526.

70 Rahul Sarwate, 'Reimagining the Modern Hindu Self: Caste, Untouchability and Hindu Theology', in 'Colonial South Asia, 1899-1948', PhD Thesis submitted to Columbia University, 2020, 45-7

71 *CWMG,* Vol. 30., 371.

72 Lakshmi Raghunandan, *At the Turn of the Tide: The Life and Times of Maharani Setu Lakshmi Bayi: The Last Queen of Travancore*, Maharani Setu Lakshmi Bayi Memorial Charitable Trust, 1995, 131.

73 Gunturu Lakshmikantam, *Nāyana Kavyakantha Vasistha Ganapati Muni* (Telugu, English. Trans. Dr G. Krishna) (Secundrabad, 1978), 151.

74 Ibid, 158.

75 A.V. Ramana, *Mahatapasvi: Biography of Ganapati Muni* (Telugu, Trans. Smt. Sonti Anasuyalnma), Sri Ramanasramam, 2005, 247-8.

76 ibid., 248-9

77 Gunturu Lakshmikantam, *Nāyana Kavyakantha Vasistha Ganapati Muni* (Telugu, English. Trans. Dr G. Krishna) (Secundrabad, 1978), 159.

78 S.R. Leela, *Glory of Vāsiṣṭha Gaṇapathi: Biography*, Sri Aurobindo Kapali Sastry Institute of Vedic Culture, 1999, 218-9. In this account, the author accuses the secretary of mischief and that the assembled Pandits did not want Muni to talk because a Tapasvi like him should not enter debates. However, Lakshmikantam's narration suggests that Muni was informed of their discomfort and that he and Māḷaviā were quitting is not plausible.

79 Gunturu Lakshmikantam, *Nāyana Kavyakantha Vasistha Ganapati Muni* (Telugu, English. Trans. Dr G. Krishna) (Secundrabad, 1978), viii.

80 C. Subramaṇya Bhārati, 'Papā Pattu' in Srini.Viswanathan, *Bhārati Pādalkal: Āyuvu Pathipu* (Bhārati Songs: Researched Publication, Tamizh), Tamil University, 1987, 409.

81 C. Subramaṇya Bhārati, Bhārati Kathaikaḷ (Stories by Bhārati, Tamizh), (Poompuhar Publications, 1977), 438.

82 C. Subramaṇya, Bhārati essay in the collection '*Bhāratiyum Samūgamum*' ('Bhārati and Society', Tamil, compiled by Pe. Thūran) (Vanathi Publications, 1980), 173-183.

83 C. Subramaṇya Bhārati, Bhārati Tamizh Vasana Thirattu (Compilation of Tamizh prose of Bhārati, Tamizh: compiled by Pe. Thūran) (New Delhi: National Book Trust, 1978), 109-113.

84 R. Kanakalingam, *My Revered Guru, Bharatiyar* (Trans. R.Ganapathy) (Central Institute of Indian Languages, 2006), 48-50 (Tamizh original: 1947).

85 Ibid., 530.

86 Ibid., 610.

87 Ibid., 62.

88 A brief biography of Śrī Satchithānanda Śwāmigaḷ by Muthukrishna Reddy included in Śrī Satchithānanda Śwāmigaḷ, translation with commentary on *Dṛg-Dṛśya-Vivekam*, 1899 (second edition), 7-8.

89 Mylai Chinna Thambi Pillai Rajah, *The Oppressed Hindus* (Madras: Huxley Press, 1925), 18-19.

90 Śwāmi Sahajānanda, Madras Legislative Assembly Debates (MLAD), Vol. 2 (20 July 1957), 31.

91 Śwāmi Sahajānanda, Madras Legislative Assembly Debates (MLAD), Vol. 8 (2 Dec. 1938), 432-4.

92 Śwāmi Sahajānanda, Madras Legislative Assembly Debates (MLAD), Vol. 11 (24 March 1939), 632.

93 Ibid., 633-4.

94 Śwāmi Sahajānanda, Madras Legislative Assembly Debates (MLAD), Vol. 11, No. 1-12 (Sep. 1951) (23 July 1952), 62-63.

95 Śwāmi Sahajānanda, Madras Legislative Assembly Debates (MLAD), Vol. 2 (20 July 1957), 32.

Chapter 14: Dharma as Liberator: From a Neo-Buddhist Bodhisattva to an Advaitic Paramacharya

1 Bhimrao Ramji Ambedkar, *Writings and Speeches*, Vol. 4., Dr Ambedkar Foundation Ministry of Social Justice and Empowerment, Govt. of India, 1987:2014, 284.

2 Ibid.

3 Edward Washburn Hopkins, *The Great Epic of India: Character and Origin of the Mahabharata* (1902), Motilal Banarsidass, 1993, 101.

4 Data in this section taken mainly from Fatesinhrao Gaekwad, *Sayajirao of Baroda, the Prince and the Man*, 1989.

5 Ruma Bhattacharya, *Maharaja Sayajirao-III's Ideas and Works on Caste System and Untouchability*, Humanities and Social Sciences Online, 28 October 2008.

6 Sri Aurobindo, *Caste and Democracy*, *Bande Mataram*, 21 Sept. 1907, *Bande Mataram: Political Writings and Speeches* 1890-1908: *The Complete Works of Sri Aurobindo* (CWSA), Vol. 6 and 7, Sri Aurobindo Ashram Trust, 2003, 683.

7 Sri Aurobindo, Conversation dated 12-Aug-1926 in Anilbaran Roy, *Interviews and Conversations with Sri Aurobindo and the Mother*, e-book, 2014.

8 Dr Soumitra Basu, *The Caste System of India: An Aurobindonian Perspective,* Sri Aurobindo Mandir Annual No. 54, 1995.

9 Bhimrao Ramji Ambedkar PhD., *Revolution and Counter Revolution in Ancient India*, Dr. Babasaheb Ambedkar: Writings and Speeches, Vol. 3, Education Department, Govt. of Maharashtra, 1987: Dr. Ambedkar Foundation, 2014, 286-288.

10 Sri Aurobindo, '*The Un-Hindu Spirit of Caste Rigidity*', 20-Sep-1907, *Bande Mataram* in CWSA Vol. 6 & 7, 2002, 680.

11 Bhimrao Ramji Ambedkar PhD, Writings and Speeches (Compiled by Vasant Moon), Vol.13, (Dr. Ambedkar Foundation Ministry of Social Justice & Empowerment, Govt. of India, 1987:2014), 1216.

12 Sri Aurobindo, *Historical Impressions: The French Revolution*, 1910, CWSA, Vol-I (Sri Aurobindo Ashram Trust, 2003), 512.

13 Sri Aurobindo, '*Fraternity*', in *Dharma*, No. 23, February 1910: (Bengali), CWSA Vol.9 (Sri Aurobindo Ashram Trust 2017), 138.

14 Bhimrao Ramji Ambedkar PhD, Writings and Speeches (Compiled by Vasant Moon), Vol.8, Dr. Ambedkar Foundation Ministry of Social Justice & Empowerment, Govt. of India, 1987:2014, *Pakistan or the Partition of India*, 66.

15 Sri Aurobindo, *The Ideal of Human Unity*, CWSA, Vol-X, Sri Aurobindo Ashram Trust, 1997, 570.

16 Bhimrao Ramji Ambedkar, 'What Way Emancipation?', in *Writings and Speeches*, Vol. 17 Pt. 3, (ed. Narake, Kamble, Kasare and Godchate) (Dr Ambedkar Foundation Ministry of Social Justice & Empowerment, Govt. of India, 1979:2019), 122-3.

17 Brihadāraṇya Upaniṣad IV.5.6-7.

18 Bhimrao Ramji Ambedkar, 'Riddles of Hinduism', in *Writings and Speeches*, Vol. IV, (Compiled by Vasant Moon) (Dr Ambedkar Foundation Ministry of Social Justice and Empowerment, Govt. of India, 1987:2014), 283-4.

19 Ibid., 284.

20 Jane Gonda, *Postscript on Mitra, Annals of the Bhandarkar Oriental Research Institute*, 1977-1978, Vol. 58/59, 149-50.

21 Jane Gonda, 'Vedic Mitra and Epic Dharma', *The Journal of the Royal Asiatic Society of Great Britain and Ireland*, No. 2 (1971), 121.

22 Martin G Wiltshire, *Ascetic Figures Before and in Early Buddhism: The Emergence of Gautama as the Buddha* (Mouton de Gruyter, 1990), 266.

23 This sub section is mainly based on: Devendra Swarup and Meenakshi Jain, *The Rajah-Moonje Pact: Documents on a Forgotten Chapter of Indian History* (Books for All Publisher, 2007).

24 Bas van Gool and Frank de Zwart, 'Politics of Representative Bureaucracy in India', in *Representative Bureaucracy in Action: Country Profiles from the Americas, Europe, Africa and Asia* (eds. B. Guy Peters, Eckhard Schröter, Patrick von Maravić) (Edward Elgar Publishing Inc., 2013), 191-92.

25 Bhimrao Ramji Ambedkar, 'Constituent Assembly Debates Official Report', Vol. 7, Lok Sabha Secretariat, Govt. of India, 1999, 39.

26 M.C. Rajah's speech reported in *The Hindu* dated 11 November 1935 in V. Alex, 'M.C. Rajah Sinthanaikaḷ', in *Thoughts of M.C. Rajah*, Vol. I), *Ezhhuthu*, 2007, 217-222.

27 M.C. Rajah statement as reported in the Bombay Depressed Classes' Conference, *The Indian Annual Register*, Vol. II, Jul.-Dec. 1935, The Annual Register Office, 316-318.

28 Rohit Wanchoo, 'The Question of Dalit Conversions in the 1930s', *Studies in History* 36(2), Jawaharlal Nehru University, 2020, 207.
29 M.C. Rajah to Moonje, 20 July 1936.
30 Rajmohan Gandhi, *Rajaji: A Life* (New Delhi: Penguin Books, 1996), 203.
31 M.C. Rajah and Ranganayaki Ammal, *Kindergarten Room* (Indian Publishing House, 1930), available online at: https://www.tamilheritage.org/old/text/ebook/THF_KindergardenRoombyMCRajaJG.pdf
32 M.C. Rajah. 1925, 3-4
33 Ibid., 31-5.
34 Ibid., 38.
35 Ibid., 39.
36 Ibid., 37-8.
37 Ibid., 41.
38 Ibid., 42-3.
39 Gail Omvedt, *Seeking Begumpura: The Social Vision of Anticaste Intellectuals* (Navyana, 2008), 167.
40 As seen in M.C. Rajah, 1925, 46-7, he claims that the Aryans introduced to nature worshipping Adi-Dravidas idol worship.
41 Based on Ambedkarpriyan, *Manithapunithar Kakkan: Saintly Human* (Kakkan, Tamizh), International Institute of Tamil Studies, 2010.
42 Interview with President Award winner Rajeshwari IPS, Behindwoods Air, Published 4 Feb. 2020, https://www.youtube.com/watch?v=FVrgtE8NtLE at 5:05
43 V.I. Muniswamy Pillay, Constituent Assembly Debates Official Report, Vol. XI, No. 4, Lok Sabha Secretariat, 1949, 608.
44 Ibid., 608-9.
45 Ibid., 609.
46 Ibid., 610.
47 Bhimrao Ramji Ambedkar, Constituent Assembly Debates Official Report, Vol. 7, Lok Sabha Secretariat, Govt. of India, 1999, 39.
48 Indrani Jagjivan Ram, *Milestones: A Memoir* (New Delhi: Penguin Books, 2010), 26.
49 Ibid., 28.
50 Ibid., 35.
51 Appendix IV, in *Dr. Babasaheb Ambedkar: Writings and Speeches Vol. 17* (Part 2), Education Department, Govt. of Maharashtra, 2003: Dr Ambedkar Foundation, 2014, 505.
52 Indrani Jagjivan Ram, *Milestones: A Memoir* (New Delhi: Penguin Books, 2010), 53-4.

53 Jagjivan Ram quoted in Appendix VIII in *Dr. Babasaheb Ambedkar: Writings and Speeches Vol. 17* (Part 2), Education Department, Govt. of Maharashtra, 2003: Dr Ambedkar Foundation, 2014, 529-30.

54 Jagjivan Ram, 'Foreword', in *Who Were the Shudras?* (Thackers, 1970), ix-x.

55 Jagjivan Ram, 'Why I am a Hindu?' *Illustrated Weekly of India*, 24 Nov. 1974, 22-3.

56 Dr. T.S.S. Rajan, Madras Legislative Council Debates., Vol. 4, No. 1 (Aug. 1938), 46.

57 Simla Record 2. Confidential File No. 50/16/33-Poll.1933. Government of India Home Department: Policy of Government in respect of the Temple Entry Bill by Mr. C.S. Ranga Iyer, 23.

58 Ibid.

59 Serial No. 14: Telegram to Secretary of State, No. 1604, 24-July-1934 in File No. 50/16/33-Poll.1933, 983.

60 Serial No. 16: Telegram from Secretary of State, No. 1906, 31-July-1934, File No. 50/16/33-Poll.1933, 987.

61 D.O. Letter to E. C. Mieville, Esq., C.S.I., C.M.G., P.S.V., No. D.1581 A/34-POLL., 22-March-1934, File No. 50/16/33-Poll.1933, 13

62 Demi-Official Letter to the Private Secretary to His Holiness Shree Shankaracharya, No.D.-2780/34-POLL. 19-May-1934, File No. 50/16/33-Poll.1933, 15.

63 File No. 50/16/33-Poll.1933, 711.

64 Ibid., 712-3.

65 Ibid., 718.

66 Ibid., 719.

67 Ibid., 380.

68 Ibid.

69 Ibid.

70 Ibid., 382.

71 Ibid., 348-9.

72 Ibid., 447-8.

73 Ibid., 18.

74 Ibid., 20.

75 Ibid., 551.

76 Ibid., 573.

77 Ibid., 577.

78 Jawaharlal Nehru, *An Autobiography* (New Delhi: Oxford University Press, 1936:1942/1982), 381-2.

79 M.C. Rajah in Madras Legislative Assembly debates, Vol. 7, Iss. 1-5, August 19, 1938, 184.

80 C. Rajagopalachariyar, in Madras Legislative Assembly debates, Vol. XIII, No.1-5, 188-9.
81 Śwāmi Sahajānanda, (in Tamizh), Ibid. 194.
82 V.I. Munuswāmy Piḷḷai, in Madras Legislative Assembly debates, Vol. XIII, No. 1-5, 195-6.
83 M.C. Rajah in Madras Legislative Assembly debates, Vol. 7, Iss. 1-5, August 19, 1938, 203-4.
84 M.C. Rajah in Madras Legislative Assembly debates, Vol. 8, Iss. 1-9, 12 Dec. 1938, 680-1.
85 C. Rajagopalachariyar, in Madras Legislative Assembly debates, Vol. XIII No. 1-5, 689
86 C. Rajagopalachariyar, in Madras Legislative Assembly debates, Vol. XIII, No. 1-5, 689-90 & 691.
87 Manoj Mitta, 2023, 512 (Kindle Edition).
88 Rameshwari Nehru, *Gandhi Is My Star* (Acharya Ramlochan Sharan for Pustak Bhandar, 1950), 109.
89 V.I. Munuswāmy Piḷḷai, in Madras Legislative Assembly debates, Vol. XIII No. 1-5, 75.
90 Ibid., 110-111.
91 C. Rajagopalachariyar, in Madras Legislative Assembly debates, Vol. XIII, No. 1-5, 38.
92 C. Rāmachandran, *Valaṅkai Mālaiyum Chāntṟōr Samūka Cheppēṭukaḷum* (*Valaṅkai Mālai and Chāntṟōr Community Copper Inscriptions* in Tamil) (International Institute of Tamil Studies, 2004).
93 R.T.P. Subramaṇian, *Jāthibēthathai Thakartha Rājāji* (*Rājāji Who Shattered Jāthi Differences*), Lok Sevak, 1968: Committee for Republication of Rajaji Works, 2021, 42.
94 R.T.P. Subramaṇian, 1968:2021, 40-50.
95 Mohandas Karamchand Gandhi, *The Collected Works of Mahatma Gandhi*, Vol.76 (Publications Division, Government of India, 1999), 112-3.
96 C. Rajagopalachariyar, in Madras Legislative Assembly debates, Vol. XIII, No. 1-5, 29.
97 C. Rajagopalachariyar, in Madras Legislative Assembly debates, Vol. XIII, No. 1-5, 116-7.
98 Śwāmi Vipulānanda, *Ancient Thoughts for Modern Man*, Sri Ramakrishna Math, 1992, 30-1.
99 Ibid., 92.
100 Ibid., 4.
101 Biographical data of Śwāmi Vipulānanda from the biography written by Sri Ganapathi Pillai, compiled by Sri Thirunavukkarasu, and published by Sri Gopalakrishna Kon, 1951.

102 Śwāmi Agamānanda, *Vīravāṇi*, Vol. III (Kalady, Advaita Āśrama, 1993), 298.
103 Śwāmi Agamānanda, *Vīravāṇi*, Vol. IV (Kalady, Advaita Āśrama, 1993), 471-3.
104 Ibid., 480.
105 Śwāmi Agamānanda, *Vīravāṇi*, Vol. II (Kalady, Advaita Āśrama, 1993), 319.
106 M.V. Nadeshan, *Agamānanda Śwāmikal Kēraḷa Navōdhanathinde Mārgadharsi* (*Agamānanda Śwāmikal: The Visionary Pathfinder of the New Dawn of Kēraḷa*) (Sathsanga Sukrudham, July 2021), 77.
107 Gupthan Nair and Chandrasekharan Nair, *Śwāmi Agamānanda Smāraka Prabhasanaṅṅaḷ* (Kalady, Advaita Āśrama, 1997), 24.
108 Śwāmi Agamānanda, *Vīravāṇi,* Vol. II (Kālady, Advaita Āśrama, 1993), 430.
109 Gupthan Nair and Chandrasekharan Nair, *Śwāmi Agamānanda Smāraka Prabhasanaṅṅaḷ*, (Kalady, Advaita Āśrama, 1997), 44.
110 K.L. Padmas, 'Swami Agamananda: The Concept of Dharma: Theory and Praxis', PhD Thesis submitted to Sri Sankaracharya Sanskrit University, 2007, 96. (Most of the biographical details of the Swami are taken from this thesis.)
111 Śwāmi Chithbavānanda quoted in *The Mountain Path*, Vol. 31, No. 3 & 4, December 1994, 169-70.
112 Śwāmi Chithbavānanda, *Śannyāsi* (*The Monk*), Śrī Rāmakrishna Tapōvanam, 1962, 47.
113 Śwāmi Chithbavānanda, 'Nān Kaṇda Gāndhi' (Gandhi I saw), in *Dharma Chakram* Vol. 20, No. 5, 1971, 175-178.
114 Biographical information based on Saṅghu Siddha Sivaliṅga Nāyanār, Pūraṇānanthōthayam (with biographical sketch, Tamizh edn., V. Ramakrishnan), Adithala Makkal Panpaatu Maiyam (Cultural Centre for Subaltern People), 2009.
115 Śrī Ōm Prakāsa Śwāmigaḷ, *Śrī Satsambāshiṇi* (Tamizh), Asala pītha ulōkōpakāra Vidyādhāna Sabhā, 1939.
116 Śrī Jñāna Yōgi Ratna Śatguru, *Satha-Prakarana* (Tamizh), Advaita Jñāna Mantram, 1990, 40.
117 N. Nagendran, *Swami Chidbhavananda: His Life and Work: A Biographical Study*, PhD Thesis, Madurai Kamaraj University, 2013, 61-2.
118 Ibid., 120.
119 Śwāmi Chithbavānanda, Gayatri, *Śrī Rāmakrishna Tapōvanam*, 1973, 2-8.
120 Śwāmi Chithbavānanda, 1962, 46-8.

121 Śwāmi Chithbavānanda, *Santheham Thelithal* (Removal of Doubts) Vol. I, Śrī Rāmakrishna Tapōvanam, 1958, 100-102.

122 Ibid., 107-9.

Chapter 15: Kārmic Fatalism versus Dhārmic Entrepreneurial Activism

1 Gunnar Myrdal, *Asian Drama: An Inquiry into the Poverty of Nations* (New York: Penguin Press,1972), 40.

2 Gurcharan Das, *India Unbound* (New Delhi: Viking, 2000), 73-4.

3 Surendra Kaushik, 'Culture Sustains the Hindu Rate of Growth in India', *Challenge*, 57, No. 1, (Jan-Feb 2014): 82-108.

4 Kentaro Toyama, *Geek Heresy: Rescuing Social Change from the Cult of Technology* (Public Affairs: Perseus Books, 2015), 176.

5 Ray Billington, *Understanding Eastern Philosophy* (London: Routledge, 1997), 156.

6 Rashmi Gupta and Vijayan K.Pillai, 'Hinduism and Poverty', in *Encyclopaedia of World Poverty* (Sage Publications, 2006), 481.

7 Andrew J. Waskey, 'Normative Standards', in *Encyclopaedia of World Poverty* (Sage Publications, 2006), 481785.

8 John Howison, *European Colonies in Various Parts of the World Viewed in Their Social, Moral and Physical Conditions*, Vol. II (Richard Bentley, 1834), 62-3.

9 Edmund Weber, 'Charity in Inter-religious Perspective'. *Journal of Religious Culture* 46 (2001): 6-7.

10 G. Paramaswaran Pillai, *Representative Indians* (London: George Routledge & Sons, 1897), 195.

11 Ibid., 196.

12 V. Ramakrishna and K.H.S.S. Sundar, 'Reassessing the Madras Native Association (1852-67): Some Formulations', *Proceedings of the Indian History Congress*, 51 (1990): 412-419.

13 G. Paramaswaran Pillai, *Representative Indians* (London: George Routledge & Sons, 1897), 152-3.

14 G. Paramaswaran Pillai, *Representative Indians* (London: George Routledge & Sons, 1897), 198.

15 Robert Eric Frykenberg, 'Modern Education in South India, 1784-1854: Its Roots and Its Role as a Vehicle of Integration under Company Raj', *The American Historical Review*, 91, No. 1 (February 1986): 37-65.

16 R. Suntharalingam, *Politics and Nationalist Awakening in South India, 1852-1891* (Rawat Publications, 1958), 41.

17 Charles Lawson, *Narrative of the Celebration of the Jubilee of Her Most Gracious Majesty Queen Victoria Empress of India in the Presidency of Madras* (Macmillan & Co., 1887), 329.

18 The passage regarding Madras Hindu Literary Association, including the pleading letter, is based on Stuart H. Blackburn, *Print, Folklore, and Nationalism in Colonial South India* (Orient Blackswan, 2006), 109-113.

19 R. Suntharalingam, *Politics and Nationalist Awakening in South India*, 1852-1891 (Rawat Publications, 1958).

20 Henry Dodwell, *The Cambridge History of the British Empire*, Vol. IV (Macmillan, 1929), 117.

21 George Norton, *Native Education in India: Comprising a Review of Its State and Progress within the Presidency of Madras* (Madras: Pharaoh & Co., 1848), 25.

22 Thomas Babington Macaulay, *Macaulay's Speeches by Lord Macaulay with His Minutes on Indian Education*, (Oxford: Oxford University Press, 1935), 202-3.

23 'Petition from the native inhabitants of Madras' (11 Nov. 1839) quoted extensively in George Norton, *Native Education in India: Comprising a Review of Its State and Progress within the Presidency of Madras* (Madras: Pharaoh & Co., 1848), 33-4.

24 George Norton, *Native Education in India: Comprising a Review of Its State and Progress within the Presidency of Madras* (Madras: Pharaoh & Co., 1848), 15-16.

25 Ibid., 17.

26 Kamil Zvelebil, *Companion Studies to the History of Tamil Literature* (Brill, 1992), 256-7117.

27 G. Paramaswaran Pillai, *Representative Indians* (London: George Routledge & Sons, 1897), 200-201.

28 G. Paramaswaran Pillai, *Representative Indians* (London: George Routledge & Sons, 1896), 154.

29 Ibid., 201-2.

30 'Torture in India', *The Economist*, 18 Aug. 1855, 897.

31 *Fifth Petition to the Imperial Parliament from the Members of the Madras Native Association*, The Hindu Press, 1856, 4.

32 Ibid., 5.

33 Communication of C.J. Shubrick Collector dated 5 July 1855 quoted Ibid., 1856, 6.

34 Secret Department, Consultation No.1, Dated: 17 Aug. 1847 cited in V. Ramakrishna and K.H.S.S. Sundar, 1990, 416.

35 R. Suntharalingam, *Politics and Nationalist Awakening in South India*, 1852-1891 (Rawat Publications, 1958), 54.

36 P. Kannan, *MGR: A Life* (New York: Penguin Books, 2017), 290.

37 Randorguy, 'Eminent personalities of Yester Madras'(Tamizh), Dinamani Kathir, 5 January 1992.

38 Centenary Celebration Souvenir, Dharmamurthi Rao Bahadur Calavala Cunnan Chetty Charities Hindu Higher Secondary School, Thiruvallur, 1993.

39 Mattison Mines, 'Temples and Charity: The Neighbourhood Styles of the Komati and Beeri Chettiar Merchants of Madras City', in *The Meaning of the Local: Politics of Place in Urban India* (eds. Geert De Neve and Henrike Donner) (London: Routledge, 2006), 110.

40 P. Kannan, *MGR: A Life* (New York: Penguin Books, 2017), 289-290.

41 Geert De Neve and Henrike Donner, 'Space, Place and Globalisation: Revisiting the Urban Neighbourhood in India', in Geert De Neve and Henrike Donner, 2006, 14.

42 Mattison Mines, 'The Political Economy of Patronage, Pre-eminence and the State in Chennai', in *Patronage as Politics in South Asia* (ed. Anastasia Piliavsky) (Cambridge: Cambridge University Press, 2014), 64.

43 The biography of P.M. Madurai Pillai taken from Anbu Ponnōviam, *Kappalotiya Adi Tamilan* (Chennai: Siddhartha Publications, 2000).

44 As mentioned in *Samara Kavi Panchakam*, an obituary poetry written for those who have high social standing.

45 Quoted in S. Srikumar, *Kolar Gold Field: Unfolding the Untold* (Partridge Publishing India., 2014), 802.

46 K.S. Cītārāmaṉ, *Kōlār Taṅkavayal varalāṟu 1956 Varaiyil* (History of KGF till 1956, Tamizh) (Illusion Electronics Publication, 1989), 67 & 321.

47 S. Srikumar, 2014, 399.

48 K.S. Cītārāmaṉ, *Kōlār Taṅkavayal varalāṟu 1956 Varaiyil* (History of KGF till 1956, Tamizh) (Illusion Electronics Publication, 1989), 322.

49 S. Srikumar, 2014, 799.

50 K.S. Cītārāmaṉ, *Kōlār Taṅkavayal varalāṟu 1956 Varaiyil* (History of KGF till 1956, Tamizh) (Illusion Electronics Publication, 1989), 185.

51 S. Srikumar, 2014, 800.

52 Swami Ramakrishnananda, *Life of Sri Ramanuja* (Sri Ramakrishna Math, 1965), 178.

53 S. Srikumar, 2014, 800.

54 Ibid., 803.

55 A.P. Valli Nayagam, 'Thanga Vayalin Thaniperum Thalaivar Ka.PūSwāmy' (Highly Distinguished Leader of Gold Field-Ka.PūSwāmy) *Dalit Murasu* (Tamil magazine), November 2005.

56 R.N. Sampath and Pe.Su.Mani, *V.O.Chidambaram Pillai* (Publications Division, Govt. of India, 1992), 24.

57 V.O. Chidambaram, *Suyasarithai* (autobiography in poetic form, Tamizh) (Mullai Publishers, 1946), 30. (Published by his son V.O.C. Subramaniam.)

58 Ma. Po. Sivagnanam, 'Kappalootiya Tamizhan (Tamizh Who Steered the Ship, Tamil)', *Inbanilayam*, 1944:49, 33.

59 A.I. Levkovsky, 'The Labour Movement and the Development of the Freedom Struggle (1905-08)', in *Tilak and the Struggle for Indian Freedom* (eds. L.M. Reisner and N.M. Goldberg) (People's Publishing House, 1966), 456.

60 Ibid., 803.

61 V.O. Chidambaram, 1946, 43.

62 A. Sivasubramanian, '*Va.U.Siyum Muthal Thozhilar Velainiruthamum 1908*' ('VOC and the First Workers' Strike 1908', Tamizh), Makkal Veliyiidu, 1986, 20. The references regarding Tuticorin strike, are taken from this book and going to the original sources that A. Sivasubramanian has used as reference in his book.

63 Ibid., 21-22.

64 R.N. Sampath and Pe. Su. Mani, 1992, 57.

65 Ibid., 28.

66 TRFPA, Ibid., Report from Chirkin, 4 March (Old Style), 1908, quoted in I.M. Reisner, *Social and Political Contribution of Bal Gangadhar Tilak*, in L.M. Reisner and N.M. Goldberg, 1966, 645-6.

67 A. Sivasubramanian, 1986, 33-4.

68 Aurobindo Ghosh, 'Swaraj and the Coming Anarchy', *Bande Mataram*, 05 March 1908 in *Bande Mataram: Political Speeches and Writings* (Sri Aurobindo Ashram Publication Department, 2002), 903-6.

69 I.M. Reisner, *Social and Political Contribution of Bal Gangadhar Tilak*, in L.M. Reisner and N.M. Goldberg, 1966, 646.

70 'The Hindu' dated 07 March 1908 and 09 March 1908 in A. Sivasubramanian, 1986, 35-6.

71 Aurobindo Ghosh, 1908 (Sri Aurobindo Ashram Publication Department, 2002), 924-26.

72 I.M. Reisner, *Social and Political Contribution of Bal Gangadhar Tilak*, in L.M. Reisner and N.M. Goldberg, 1966, 646.

73 M.P. Sivagnanam, *The Great Patriot: V.O. Chidambaram Pillai* (Inbha Nilayam, 1972), 39.

74 Aurobindo Ghosh, *Well Done Chidambaram*, *Bande Mataram* (Sri Aurobindo Ashram Publication Department, 2002), 975-6.

75 Aurobindo Ghosh, *Speech at Panti's Math* (Sri Aurobindo Ashram Publication Department, 2002), 1001.

76 M.P. Sivagnanam, *The Great Patriot: V.O. Chidambaram Pillai* (Inbha Nilayam, 1972), 42.

77 Ibid., 24.

78 Subramaṇia Śivam, *Jñāna Bānu*, November 1914.

79 *Jñāna Bānu*, May 1915.

80 *Jñāna Bānu*, September 1915.

81 Ka.Pā.Vēl Murugan, *Siva Thiru Jñāniār Adigal Varalāru* (*Life of Siva Sri Jñāniār Adigal*, Tamizh) in *Tamizh valartha Jñāniār Adigal* (ed. Vallikannan), 1988, 130-140. The history of school as presented here is based on this section of the book.

Chapter 16: Recapitulation and Conclusion

1 David N. Lorenzen, 'Europeans in Late Mughal Asia: The Perceptions of Italian Missionaries', in *Who Invented Hinduism: Essays on Religion in History* (Hauz Khas: Yoda Press, 2006), 208.

2 Ibid.

3 Ibid.

4 McKim Marriott, 'Constructing an Indian Ethnosociology in India through Hindu Categories', *Constructing an Indian Ethnosociology* in *India through Hindu Categories* 23, No. 1 (1989): 1–40.

5 Ibid.

6 Ibid.

7 McKim Marriott and Ronald B. Inden, 'Interpreting Indian Society: A Monistic Alternative to Dumont's Dualism', *Journal of Asian Studies* XXXVI, No. I (1976): 195.

8 McKim Marriott, 'Hindu Transactions: Diversity without Dualism', in *Transactions and Meaning: Directions in Anthropology of Exchange and Symbolic Behaviour*, ed. Bruce Kapferer (Philadelphia: Institute of Study of Human Issues), 111.

9 Diane P. Mines, *Exchange* in *Studying Hinduism Key Concepts and Methods*, eds. Sushil Mittal and Gene Thursby, (London: Routledge, 2008), 148.

10 Prem Saran, *Yoga, Bhoga and Ardhanariswara* (London: Routledge, 2018), 73–5.

11 Thoṇdaradipodi Āzhwār, *Nāllāyira Divya Prabandam*, verse 913.

12 Pandurang Vaman Kane, *History of Dharmaśāstras*, Vol. V, Part II (Poona: Bhandarkar Oriental Research Institute, 1962), 1622, 1635-36, 1706.

13 Sri Aurobindo, *The Foundations of Indian Culture* (New York: Sri Aurobindo Library, 1953), 369.

Index

About the Author

Aravindan Neelakandan is a contributing editor at *Swarajya*. He has worked for more than a decade with the Natural Resources Development Project, Vivekananda Kendra (VK-NARDEP). He has published books on sustainable agricultural technologies and traditional knowledge systems in Tamizh. He is the co-author of the bestseller *Breaking India: Western Interventions in Dravidian and Dalit Faultlines* (BluOne Ink, 2011) and the author of *Hindutva: Origin, Evolution and Future* (BluOne Ink, 2022).

About the Editor